PENGUIN BOOKS

THE PORTABLE THOMAS HARDY

Julian Moynahan is professor of English at Rutgers University and author of several volumes of criticism as well as of three novels: *Sisters and Brothers*, *Pairing Off*, and *Garden State*.

THOMAS HARDY'S WESSEX

Names used by Hardy are in brackets
beneath names of places
Hardy seems to have had in mind.

County Boundaries ·······
Roads --------

- Ilchester
(Ivelchester)

- Sherborne
(Sherton Abbas)

SOMERSET

Yeovil
(Ivell)

East Coker
(Norrobourne)

Crewkerne

BLACKMOOR
(Vale of the Littl

Melbury Osmond
(Little Hintock)
Melbury Sampford
(King's Hintock)

Melbury Park
(King's Hintock Court)

Middlemars
(Marshwood

Minterne Magna
(Great Hintock)

Eversho
(Evershead)

- Pilsdon Pen
909'

Beaminster
(Emminster)

DORSET

NORTH

Cerne Abbas
(Abbot's Cernal)

Piddletrenthide
(Upper Longpudd
Piddlehinto
(Lower Longbu

DEVON

Maiden Newton
(Chalk Newton)

(Yalb
Woo

Eggardon Hill 828
(Haggardon Hill)
(Norcombe)

Poundbur

Stinsfo
(West Myll

Lyme Regis

Bridport
(Port Bredy)

DORCHESTER
(CASTERBRIDGE)

ford
lia

West Bay

RIDGEWAY

Abbotsbury

Portesham
(Po'sham)

Sutton Poyn
(Overcom

N

WEST BAY

Jo
Cle

WEY
BUD

(Deadman's Bay)

Sandsf
(Henry Vill

Portlar
Harbou

Miles
0   2   4   6   8

Fortuneswell
(The Street of Wells)

Church Hope
(Hope Church)

Eas
(East C

Portland
(Isle of Slingers)

Penmoylvac
Cast
(Sylvania

Portland Bill
(The Beal)

The Portable

THOMAS
HARDY

Edited with an introduction by
JULIAN MOYNAHAN

Penguin Books

The Portable

THOMAS
HARDY

‹‹‹‹‹‹‹‹‹‹‹‹‹‹‹‹‹‹‹‹‹‹‹‹‹‹‹‹‹

Selected and with an Introduction by
JULIAN MOYNAHAN

Penguin Books

Penguin Books Ltd, Harmondsworth,
Middlesex, England
Penguin Books, 625 Madison Avenue,
New York, New York 10022, U.S.A.
Penguin Books Australia Ltd, Ringwood
Victoria, Australia
Penguin Books Canada Ltd, 2801 John Street
Markham, Ontario, Canada L3R 1B4
Penguin Books (N.Z.) Ltd, 182–190 Wairau Road,
Auckland 10, New Zealand

First published in the United States of America
in simultaneous hardbound and paperbound editions
by The Viking Press and Penguin Books 1977

Copyright © Viking Penguin Inc., 1977
All rights reserved

LIBRARY OF CONGRESS CATALOGING IN PUBLICATION DATA
Hardy, Thomas, 1840-1928.
The portable Thomas Hardy.
(Viking portable library; 82)
Bibliography: p.
I. Moynahan, Julian, 1925– II. Title.
PR4742.M6   823'.8 [B]   76-11789
ISBN 0-670-70340-0
ISBN 0- 14 015.082 x

Printed in the United States of America by
Offset Paperback Mfrs., Inc., Dallas, Pennsylvania
Set in Linotype Times Roman

ACKNOWLEDGMENTS

THE THOMAS HARDY SOCIETY LTD:
the map of Wessex from the 1968 Thomas Hardy Society Festival.
Copyright © The Thomas Hardy Society Ltd, 1968.
MACMILLAN PUBLISHING CO., INC.:
From Collected Poems of Thomas Hardy.
Copyright 1925 by Macmillan Publishing Co., Inc., renewed 1953
by Lloyds Bank Ltd., Copyright 1928 by Florence E. Hardy and
Sydney Cockerell, renewed 1956 by Lloyds Bank Ltd.

The editor is very grateful to The Birmingham City Museum and
Art Gallery for permission to reproduce the original drawings by Hardy
for Wessex Poems and Other Verses,
which appear on pages 520, 523, 527, 540, 626;
and to the Trustees of the Thomas Hardy Memorial Collection,
Dorset County Museum, Dorchester, for their permission to reproduce
the illustrations from Hardy's architectural notebook which appear on
pages 173, 507, 511, 753. He also wishes to thank Barbara Burn,
Martina D'Alton, and Sherida Yoder for their help in the
preparation of this volume.

Contents

Contents

PART FIVE: FROM THE NON-FICTIONAL PROSE

Editor's Introduction

I

For a long time—and it seems that everything connected with this writer whose full creative career extended over a period of sixty-four years, from the mid-1860s to early 1928, entails daunting amounts of time—Hardy's greatness as a novelist and a poet was not so much secure as secured. The poetry, which was often dismissed by critics as artless and clumsy, was mainly secured by the steady admiration of Hardy's fellow poets, among others Frost, Pound, Ransom, Auden, Dylan Thomas, and Philip Larkin. And the fiction, which was somewhat patronizingly praised by the London reviewers during the 1870s for its rendering of rural and pastoral subjects; which was frequently deplored or denounced by the same or similar reviewers during the 1880s and 1890s on the ground that Hardy's investigations of such topics as unhappy marriage, the abjection of women, and the tribulations of the rural poor were unduly pessimistic; which was deprecated at the turn of the century by such artists in prose fiction as James, Conrad, and Ford on the ground of its lack of formal artistry—also had to be secured and defended by a younger generation of writers, extending from H. G. Wells through D. H. Lawrence to William Faulkner, who paid Hardy's fiction either the tribute of unpatronizing admiration or of emulation. Wells said of Hardy in *Boon* (1915), a work remembered for its all-out attack on Henry James, that he was a first-class writer who preferred for reasons best known to himself to travel on a second-class ticket. Lawrence, in his *Study of Thomas Hardy* (1914), treated him as the starting point of his own major phase of fiction that runs from *Sons and Lovers* through *Women in Love*. Faulkner, so far as I know, said nothing at all about Hardy, but shaped his Southern agrarian mythic world of Yoknapatawpha County along lines and to a scale that surely owe a good deal to Hardy's mapping of the mythic kingdom of Wessex.

The standard nineteenth-century account of Hardy's fiction passed through two stages. In the first stage it was said of him that he was very good at nature painting and rural life, except that his heroines, especially Bathsheba Everdene in *Far From the Madding Crowd*, were troublesome, vain, and capricious creatures, and that his rustics were much too shrewd and humorous to be realistic versions of the dull clods that every townsman had encountered during day excursions into the English countryside. In the second stage, it was discovered that Hardy should have gone on writing simple, beautiful country novels like *Far From the Madding Crowd* and should never have bothered his head about the sorts of dilemmas and mischances undergone by unfortunate provincial persons like Michael Henchard, Tess Durbeyfield, and the tortured, striving, scrupled lovers Jude Fawley and Sue Bridehead. This assessment of Hardy is not shared by all nineteenth-century critics, but there are few exceptions. Havelock Ellis, in two impressive essays written fourteen years apart in 1882 and 1896, discovered that Hardy's subject was passion and the hearts of women and suggested a link between this subject and the preoccupation with nature in so far as "the loving student of the elemental in Nature . . . becomes the loving student of woman, the sensitive historian of her conflicts with 'sin' and with 'repentance,' the creations of man." This was part of an emphatic defence of *Jude the Obscure* as the first English novel of the century to treat in an adult and modern way problems of adult experience, especially sexuality, in and out of marriage.

Hardy's poetry, which came later than the fiction, was reviewed by the critics with the same initial misunderstanding, followed by the same reversal of opinion when one attentive reader, operating against the grain of lingering Victorian biases, really saw and understood a great part of what Hardy was doing. In 1898, some reviewers of *Wessex Poems* thought it faintly ridiculous that an established novelist should bother to trifle with composition in verse. In 1914, Lytton Strachey found something far more interesting to say about what happens when a great novelist, who has been writing poetry all his adult life, makes verse writing his principal activity:

> The originality of his poetry lies in the fact that it bears everywhere upon it the impress of a master of prose fiction. . . . What gives Mr. Hardy's poems their unique flavor is precisely their lack of romanticism, their common, undecorated presentments of things. They are, in fact, modern as no other poems are. The author of *Jude the Obscure* speaks in them, but with the concentration, the intensity, the subtle disturbing force of poetry. And he speaks, he does not sing. Or rather he talks—in the quiet voice of a modern man or woman, who finds it difficult as modern men and women do, to put into words exactly what is in his mind. He is incorrect; but then how unreal and artificial a thing is correctness! He fumbles; but it is that very fumbling that brings him so near ourselves.
>
> (*Literary Essays,* New York, 1949, p. 222).

So much for the nineteenth century and its immediate aftermath. Hardy's reputation is now secure, and the evidence is everywhere: in Raymond Williams's recent work, *The Country and The City* (1973), which treats Hardy's fiction as the essential link in the development of the English novel from George Eliot to Lawrence; in Donald Davie's book on *Thomas Hardy and British Poetry* (1972), which treats him as the virtual begetter and guarantor of everything that is vital and viable in modern English poetry; in Philip Larkin's recent compilation of *The Oxford Book of Twentieth-Century English Verse*, which puts Hardy at the center and Yeats, Pound, and Eliot upon the fringes of the modern tradition so far as

English people are, or ought to be, concerned. Hardy has arrived. "Compassionate," "massive," "sincere," "simple" Thomas Hardy has arrived across the finish line of secure literary pre-eminence, and if it took him a century to get there, we must stress that his preferred means of locomotion were primarily shanks-mare and secondarily the bicycle, and that the fable of the tortoise and the hare makes a lot of sense however and wherever one wishes to apply it. What more is there to say?

For a start, I should say that Hardy is an extraordinarily subtle and complicated writer whose first level of subtlety entails a series of maneuvers by which his reader is tricked into using words like "massive" and "sincere" about him instead of words like "subtle" and "complicated." There is a hint of this in Wells's remark. No Englishman with the means to travel first class travels second unless he is hiding out. Hardy's authorized biography in two volumes, by his second wife, Florence Emily Dugdale Hardy, is mostly an autobiography ghostwritten by Hardy himself and tells, by means of a third-person narrator alternating with carefully culled "notebook entries," a good deal less about him than meets the eye of the thoughtful student of his fiction and verse. Yet it reveals much to anyone who is less than satisfied with words like "massive" as adequate labels for what Hardy accomplished. For instance it tells us in a defence of his verse technique that he approves of an art which conceals art; that the best way to achieve an effect of realism in fiction is through a deliberate distortion of reality; that from childhood onward he never liked to be touched; that he was so shy in society that he mastered the trick of fantasying himself to be a ghost or spirit when entering a room full of people. This meant he could move about, taking in what was being said and done, with no worry that the people he was spying on were also spying on him.

There is a vast amount of spying in Hardy's novels and in his poetry, too. Indeed, the habit is so pronounced in *The Return of the Native*, with Eustacia Vye spying on the mummers' rehearsals through a knothole and on

Clym Yeobright through the vizor of her Turkish knight costume, and Diggory Venn constantly spying on Eustacia and Wildeve, and the birds, rabbits, and ponies of Egdon Heath spying on the human creatures with whom they share Egdon's wilderness habitat, that it operates somewhat as a central structural device or formula in that novel. Turning the formula back upon the biography, we may surmise that Hardy, by becoming the ghost writer of his own life, was able to spy on himself without being spied on in return, and hence to remain untouched. When he was thirty-six or -seven he spied "from the back window of our bedroom" upon the servant girl Jane, who was meeting her lover by moonlight. The girl left the Hardys' employment that very night and two months later "we hear that Jane, our late servant, is soon to have a baby. Yet never a sign of one is there for us." In these notebook entries Hardy is showing us that he longed for children and he is also, I suspect, hinting that the blight upon his first marriage was a sexual one. But he chiefly does it by making us look the other way, away from the iced-in master bedroom shared by religious Emma Lavinia and doubting Thomas to Jane, "who appeared to have only her nightgown on and something round her shoulders," and whose lover "had evidently often stayed in the house," because Hardy that very same night "found that the bolts of the back-door had been oiled."

All art is exhibitionistic, a kindergarten affair of show and tell in its psychological origins, and a man so tongue-in-cheek about his personal frustrations and problems will also operate by extreme indirection in his artistic productions. The first thing that such a writer will want to conceal is his own artistic subtlety and complexity, under the guise of simplicity and straightforwardness; and if he is ever tempted to hint at what he is really up to in his art, he will probably pretend, as Hardy did in the matter of the servant Jane, that he is talking about anything but his own purposes and standards. Shortly after finishing *The Mayor of Casterbridge*, Hardy set down the following comments in his notebook:

Easter Sunday [1885]. Evidences of art in Bible narratives. They are written with a watchful attention (though disguised) as to their effect on their reader. Their so-called simplicity is, in fact, the simplicity of the highest cunning. And one is led to inquire, when even in these latter days artistic development and arrangement are the qualities least appreciated by readers, who was there likely to appreciate the art in these chronicles at that day? . . .

But in these Bible lives and adventures there is the spherical completeness of perfect art. And our first, and second, feeling that they must be true because they are so impressive, becomes, as a third feeling, modified to, "Are they so very true after all? Is not the fact of their being so convincing an argument, not for their actuality, but for the actuality of a consummate artist who was no more content with what Nature offered than Sophocles and Pheidias were content?"

These comments *may* be true of the Bible narratives. They are *certainly* true of Hardy's art at its most consummate. In fact they constitute the nearest thing to an aesthetic manifesto ("though disguised") that Hardy ever wrote.

II

Reporting on *Jude the Obscure* in my Hardy Seminar at Rutgers during April 1974, Ms. Sherida Yoder began by discriminating six "traditions" or strands of thought which contribute to the design of that novel. These were Medievalism, to which she would return for fuller consideration later; Hellenism, in its late Victorian, defeatist and Swinburnian form, as represented, for example, by Sue Bridehead's pitiful collection of classical reproductions and her habit of quoting the tag line of Swinburne's "Hymn to Proserpine" ("Thou hast conquered, O pale Galilean"); Hebraism, that is to say the force of the Old Testament ethic, which may seem muted or suspended for much of the novel until it returns with a vengeance in Sue's final surrender to a self-punishing retributive morality and in

Jude's deathbed scenes; Naturalism, as an ethic and as a way of describing reality, especially the reality of a robust immoralist such as Arabella; Romanticism, which is the source for Sue's and Jude's idea that their love gives them a common identity and an inescapable identification with each other; and Modernism, which would be the novel's representation of its principal characters as victims and instances of a new or accelerated social and personal uprooting and "restlessness." Modernism would also include the attending physician's appalling metapsychological analysis of Little Father Time's hanging himself and the other children in the Christminster lodging house as "the beginning of the coming universal wish not to live."

Turning back to the medieval theme, Ms. Yoder treated Jude's quest for learning and culture at Christminster as an ironic inversion of the quest motif of medieval romance. Christminster, on Jude's first view of it, is a veritable Camelot of glittering pinnacles and cloud-capped towers. But up close it is a Victorian city of wealth and privilege. It is tricked out to be sure in the dead-letter medievalism of its collegiate architecture, academic festivals, and Latin orations, and dominated by the quaint mock-feudalism of its academic hierarchies; yet it spells nothing but defeat and death for an idealist born into the wrong class at the wrong time. The time depicted is the decade from 1860 to 1870, the very height of the neo-medievalism of the Oxford Movement, of Ruskin, and of the pre-Raphaelite Movement, and the city of course is a close likeness of mid-nineteenth century Oxford.

This was only a preliminary to her principal insight, which was to show us in detail how Hardy had developed the passional themes of the novel, centering upon the vicissitudes in love of Jude, Sue, Arabella and Phillotson with constant, secretive reference to the medieval legend of Tristan, the two Iseults, and King Mark. There are substantial changes, naturally, in Hardy's modern treatment of this romance: Jude and Sue are not undone by potions, accidents, and external sanctions like the tradi-

tional one against adultery. Forms of fate have been
internalized, reappearing as moral scruple, nervous strain,
and perhaps a general failure of nerve in Jude and Sue
which testifies to the diminished prospects for passionate
fulfillment in the era of Little Father Time.

If *Jude the Obscure* looks richly back to a medieval
love story, it also looks ahead to Ford's *The Good Soldier,*
that "saddest" tale of passion set at the brink of World
War I, whose quartet of desperately nervous lovers take
the road to madness and suicide because they will neither
violate the outward decorums of civilized intercourse nor
heed the promptings of what the frantic narrator calls
in so many words the "unconscious self." I should think
also that *Jude* looks forward to Proust, although this connection may take some curious explaining. In July 1926—
at the age of eighty-six!—Hardy was reading in French
the middle volumes of *Remembrance of Things Past.*
There Proust demonstrated that fulfillment in love was
impossible because the lover seeks a virtual identification
with the beloved in an eternal moment which time will
not allow. Hardy felt he had anticipated this idea in
his late short novel, *The Well-Beloved* (1897). In fact
he had anticipated it in his much greater book *Jude,*
wherein he had secretively conflated a medieval tale of
profane passion with a romantic and Proustian conception
of love as the impossible quest for identity between two
lovers, Jude Fawley and Sue Bridehead, who belong fully
and concretely to a recognizable, workaday nineteenth-
century world of social exclusion and economic hardship,
yet who have no place in that world because, like Tristan
and Iseult before them, they love very unwisely and much
too well.

III

Ms. Yoder's rich report gets at Hardy's subtlety and
originality by showing that he scrutinized human reality
through multiple temporal and historical perspectives. In
other words, Hardy took a very long view and a layered
view of things. Archaic, classical, medieval, romantic, and

modern aspects all persist in the life of civilization and underlie one another, not only in old cities and in ongoing culture, but also in continuing habits of feeling and knowing. Analogies with archaeological sites, with geological strata, and with the used and reused papyrus manuscripts called palimpsests suggest themselves and must be extended to Hardy's treatment of character and behavior. The natives of Egdon Heath light their Guy Fawkes bonfire upon the ashes of thousands of years of similar fires at the same place and season and proceed to perform a saturnalian dance much like the dance of their remote ancestors. Eustacia Vye is a troubled young woman of the nineteenth century whose deepest instincts and feelings, it is suggested, link her with the infernal goddess Persephone and to other underworld forces in ancient myth. And Michael Henchard, the corn-factor of *The Mayor of Casterbridge*, in his dealings with the melodious young Scot, Donald Farfrae, who supplants him as the town's leading citizen, re-enacts without knowing it the desperate struggle of the Biblical King Saul against his once-beloved protegé, David.

There is a poem called "Her Dilemma" in *Wessex Poems* which Hardy illustrated with a drawing that architects call a cross-section. The drawing shows two former lovers standing in the aisle of a church having final words because he is soon to die. Underneath the church floor are shown the dead in their crypts and deeper down the scattered bones of the more ancient dead. It is of course, as Hardy knew, only a section of a section. Still farther down lie the remains of the Roman colonists of Wessex, and deeper still the dust of the pre-Roman Britons, and under them the sedimentary geologic layers of earth crammed with fossil remnants of still-living and extinct forms, and under them the bedrock of earth. In another poem, "Aquae Sulis," the goddess of a Roman temple at Bath, upon whose shrine a Christian church was later erected, holds midnight parle with "the God overhead," then abandons her complaint of having been evicted with the wry recognition that they are mere "images both" whose heyday is over—"a Jumping-jack you, and myself but a

poor Jumping-jill." And there is that extraordinary apparitional moment in *The Mayor of Casterbridge* when, we
are told, certain persons, who had repaired to the ancient
grassed-over Roman amphitheatre outside Casterbridge in
order to meet in total privacy, saw in the full light of day,
for a split second, the amphitheatre filled row upon row
with staring Roman legionaries. In Hardy's layered world
there are spies everywhere, including ghosts from the
remote, yet ever-living past gazing in upon the troubled
present. And this haunting of the present by the past
is not incidental or merely picturesque; rather, it is substantial and real. In the poem called "The Two Houses"
the old house expresses contempt for the new house, saying

> "You have not known
> Men's lives, deaths, toils, and teens;
> You are but a heap of stick and stone:
> A new house has no sense of the have-beens."

So much for the value of a brand-new house in Hardy's
view of real estate and the human estate. But what are we
to make of his persistent and lively "sense of the have-
beens," which I have been calling a layered view of human
reality, as it works itself out in his fictional and poetic
art? Certainly it is nothing so simple as a preference for
the past over the present, or so two-dimensional as a mere
technique of ironical juxtaposition by which grand figures
out of old histories or legends are used to point up the
shortcomings and diminished stature of their modern
equivalents. Michael Henchard, the Casterbridge corn-
factor, is less than a king out of Biblical times, yet the
tragic ordeal of his decline and lonely dying are as impressive as the fate of King Saul. The same claim can be
made about Eustacia Vye in her link with Persephone
and about Jude in his link to Tristan. If we argue the
other way round and claim that Henchard's haunting, or
possession, by the spirit of Saul enhances his role as a
tragic protagonist in nineteenth-century times, we are still
left with a one-to-one correspondence that fails to encom-
pass the richest implications of our chosen metaphor of
multiple layering. The goddess in "Aquae Sulis" is told

by the pale Galilean that they are *both* back numbers, and this is established by the fact that the Christian church above is being tunnelled into by archaeologists, as could never have happened when Christianity was still at full tide. Nevertheless, the goddess goes on talking in her pert and joky fashion, and the Galilean is there to hear her and presumably to respond to her concluding, winsome invitation, "Let us kiss and be friends." To effect this reconciliation between two phases of past religious faith from a vantage point in time lying beyond both of them is to do something rather complicated with time and with history, suggesting as it does that such phases thrust up into the fully modern and skeptical consciousness of the poet even while he remains fully aware of the erosions that all phases of human illusion endure as time goes on.

Sigmund Freud employed the paradigm of layering in his exploration of the archaic stratum of psychic functioning he named the Id, and in his descriptions of the sedimentary layers of thwarted instinct that are laid down under the repressive forces of civilization. Sir James Frazer's investigation of ancient classical religious cults in *The Golden Bough*, centering upon vegetation rites and the myth of the dying god, assumed the persistence or thrusting up of such magical thinking into modern times under the guise of superstition and folk custom. And C. G. Jung purported to discover a racial unconscious underlying the individual consciousness to the extent that a modern citizen of Zürich might exhibit in the imagery of his dreams or in his free associations traces of the mental functioning of a primitive European lake dweller. It might be interesting to trace affinities and hidden relationships between Hardy's use of the paradigm of layering in his art and these social scientists' use of it in their psychological and anthropological researches undertaken mainly within the span of Hardy's lifetime. However, an even more interesting relationship lies between Hardy and Charles Darwin, the greatest of all the nineteenth-century life scientists, whose *On the Origin of Species* established the essential paradigm of scientific thought that made possible the researches and discoveries of Freud, Frazer, and

Jung. I am convinced that Hardy is unique among the writers of late Victorianism and early Modernism for the creative and imaginative response he made to Darwin's epochal theses about the origin and evolution of species through natural selection and the struggle for existence. It is not altogether easy to make the relationship and the response clear, but perhaps a beginning can be attempted.

IV

Hardy and Darwin

The first edition of *On the Origin of Species* was published in 1859 although Darwin had published a substantial sketch of his evolutionary theory as early as 1844. In the longer work he argued that "each species had not been independently created, but had descended, like varieties, from other species" over vast aeons of time. The mechanism of this unbroken descent he called "Natural Selection," which is the rule that some species will win out over other species in an unremitting struggle for existence that continues everywhere in nature because of the high rate at which all organic beings tend to increase and consequently to crowd each other out or eat each other up in a given habitat. Certain species which are more favored than others because of superior vigor or because of accidentally acquired modifications of structure or habit which help their adaptation to a particular environment will flourish and proliferate for a time. However, since the more successful species will tend to produce a greater range of varieties, and since, according to the laws of variation, these offspring will proliferate into numerous further sub-varieties, there is an excellent chance, amounting to a statistical certainty, that some of these variations will survive to render the parent-species extinct in the constant battle of life which is Nature's *modus vivendi*. In the long Darwinian view a biological race, which would include numerous interrelated species descended from a common parent, may be favored in the struggle for life, but no single species can be thus favored. In fact, a species is nothing but a well-marked, populous, and flourishing variety which in its turn will be supplanted by further variation as time continues.

Darwin's representation of these evolutionary developments is what we call nowadays "value free." While he often exclaims over the beauty and wonder of the intricate co-adaptations of biological species in nature, and while he speaks admiringly of the superior vitality of some species to others, he never suggests that evolution is good or desirable, nor does he speculate about the cosmic necessities and conditions that originally set the evolutionary machinery in motion, nor about the endpoint or goal to which this tremendous motion or commotion in nature tends. From the vantage point of modern times we might claim that Darwin's greatest discovery or emphasis was the idea of nature in ceaseless movement of change or the idea of nature energized. As the late distinguished British historian of science and Blake scholar Jacob Bronowski recently put it:

> When all the foolish wind and wit that [the theory of evolution by natural selection] raised had blown away, the living world was different because it was seen to be a world in movement. The creation is not static, but changes in time in a way that physical processes do not. The physical world ten million years ago was the same as it is today, and its laws were the same. But the living world is not the same: for example, ten million years ago there were no human beings to discuss it. Unlike physics, every generalization about biology is a slice in time, and it is evolution which is the real creator of novelty in the universe.
>
> (*The Ascent of Man*. Boston, 1974, pp. 308–9)

This tremendous spectacle of nature in movement, of nature maximally and relentlessly energized, appalled the Victorians. It appalled Tennyson, who recorded his distress in sundry verses of *In Memoriam*. It frightened the pre-Raphaelite poets and painters, whose glassy, dreamy, prettified, and falsely naïve art seems essentially to have been an attempt to play hide-and-seek with the realities of Darwinian nature. And it saddened Arnold, who cried out in the melancholy strains of "Dover Beach" against the amoral, meaningless clashing to-and-fro of "ignorant" agencies and powers. If the needed task was to reconstruct the image of man in light of what Darwin had shown, then these writers were still too close to the watershed of Darwinian thought to attempt it. If nature was movement and ferment and a furious upwelling of chaotic energies, as Tennyson seemed to be saying it was in a late poem like his "Lucretius," then he—Tennyson— would really rather be dead and let the motion proceed without him.

Hardy's first exposure to Darwin came in the mid-1860s, which was also the period when he began writing poetry and gave up, because of increasing religious doubts, a cherished ambition to become a clergyman. From this point onward he was concerned to come to terms with the implications of the evolutionary paradigm, and this concern is reflected in his artistic work and his general thinking both naïvely and in a profound, creative way. There is a charming naïveté, for example, in his notebook comment, set down as late as 1909, that "the discovery of the law of evolution, which revealed that all organic creatures are of one family, shifted the centre of altruism to the whole conscious world collectively." What he means is that we should be kind to dogs and horses because they are our close relatives. Erected into a global scheme called "evolutionary meliorism," the same appealing but unwarranted inference from the laws of evolution informs the ending of his play, The Dynasts, when the Spirit of Pity expresses the fond hope that the Immanent Will, which is nothing less than an abstraction from Darwin's deified principle of Natural Selection, might itself evolve toward consciousness and an attitude of loving-kindness to earth and its creatures. Perhaps the best comment here is Hardy's own, in a letter of February 20, 1908 to Edward Clodd, where he remarks that The Dynasts, like Milton's Paradise Lost, proves nothing.

Much less naïvely, but still not yet profoundly, Hardy plays with Darwinian themes in various poems and narratives. One thinks of the excellent poem called "Heredity," which confers a kind of biologic immortality on "the family face" that turns up in generation after generation, though each generation of the family goes down to oblivion; and of the playful treatment of the "family foot" of the Days in *Under the Greenwood Tree*. Diggory Venn in *The Return of the Native* gets characterized with respect to his trade of reddleman as a "living fossil," and a character in *A Pair of Blue Eyes* is shown clinging to the side of a towering Cornish cliff and steadying his nerves until his rescue by inspecting the forms of the extinct organisms called trilobites in the exposed strata of the cliff he clings to. Questions of biological heredity and lineage are raised in *Tess of the d'Urbervilles* about Tess herself and in *Jude the Obscure* about both Jude and Sue. These have evident Darwinian associations, but their handling is perhaps too ambiguous and tentative to shed much light on the characters' fate. And there is that beautiful and strange descriptive passage in *The Return* showing Clym at work cutting furze on the heath, with bees, butterflies, grasshoppers, "huge flies," snakes, and "litters of young rabbits" crowding and flourishing about him in the blazing light and heat of a July day, the source of which is surely Darwin's famous representation of the natural economy in its aspect of burgeoning growth and procreative vigor under the image of "an entangled bank."

If Darwin showed Hardy how to take a close view of nature as incessant movement and change in a local habitat, he also and simultaneously showed him how to take the opposite, though perfectly compatible, view of nature as a grand panorama in space and time that continues and endures. Hardy alone among the major Victorians works to a scale of effect in space and time that appropriates the true Darwinian measure: the vast reaches of chronology over which evolutionary developments occur; the vertical representation of natural history as a record of unbroken ascent from the deepest, oldest sedimentary layers of extinguished life to the life that moves and struggles on the surface of earth in the now and hereafter; the wide, embracing view of the whole earth as the setting in which all created beings contest their destinies. Working with this vastly augmented scale Hardy was able to suggest a permanence that goes hand in hand with the idea of a world in movement, and an enduring strength and significant mystery in human kind that owe nothing to the illusion that man is a separately created and privileged species or that the brief chronicle comprised by all human history and civilization has added very much to the long evolutionary history of organisms.

Thus, Egdon Heath, in the great meditation on waste nature with which *The Return of the Native* opens, appears under the vanishing light of a November afternoon as "a vast tract of unenclosed wild" that seems "to stretch out to the distant rims of the world and the firmament." Changeless "ever since the beginning of vegetation," yet it wakes at night to a "watchful intentness" and changes countenance and hue according to the cycle of the seasons and according to the growth and decay of its populations of plants and animals. "Civilization was its enemy," and yet it steadies the mind "adrift on Change and harrassed by the irrepressible New" of modern civilization by show- ing that mind how "everything around and underneath had been from prehistoric times as unaltered as the stars overhead." Finally, it is not at all inimical to man in his essential character for it is:

> a place perfectly accordant with man's nature— neither ghastly, hateful, nor ugly; neither common- place, unmeaning, nor tame; but, like man, slighted and enduring; and withal singularly colossal and mysterious.

It may be objected that I am primitivising as well as Darwinizing Hardy with this emphasis on the colossal and mysterious and untamed in nature and in man, and it may be argued that his greatest novels are about social and cultural change and that his characters are actually defeated by their inability to meet societal standards and challenges. Granted, but only with the proviso that in Hardy generally the drama of society is set closely within —though out of phase with—what Darwin called "the slowly changing drama" of natural history and that Hardy's most fully realized, or most richly layered, characters are those with too much heath nature in them to become great social successes. D. H. Lawrence saw tragedy generated in Hardy's world by the conflict between the "passional purposes," the powerful impulse to flower into "fullness of being" of his singularly unconventional characters—Tess, Eustacia, Clym, and the like—and those civilized standards and values which the characters mistakenly assume to be important. He felt that Hardy could neither quite believe in society nor in the feasibility of cutting his characters free from civilization so that they might survive—or fail with a grander effect of tragedy—in the midst of nature's colossal drama. Hardy showed Lawrence that civilization is only "the little fold of law and order" men construct in the face of nature's fathomless mystery and powers, and that Egdon Heath underlies Paris, London, and New York in as much as any civilized construction of man must fall back in time into the arms of mother earth. Here Lawrence may be taking more out of Hardy than Hardy put in. Mainly, however, he is carrying forward the project of reconstructing the image of man in himself, and in his relations to nature and society, that was required after Darwin set the created world in movement. This is the project which Hardy took up and carried far forward while so many of his contemporaries wrung their hands and muttered about nature "red in tooth and claw."

There is a final point to be made about Hardy's relationship to Darwin. Hardy never violates the integrity and mystery of his fictional characters by presenting them, after the fashion of the nineteenth-century literary naturalists and the social Darwinists, as mere victims of environmental conditions and/or of hereditary defects. Let us consider in this connection his most victimized heroine, Tess Durbeyfield. On the one hand, she is a poor agricultural worker from a declining and sickly family of rural laborers who suffers rape, the death of her illegitimate child, and desertion by her husband, and who ends on the gallows after murdering the man who kept her at the cheap expense of maintaining her mother and younger siblings. On the other hand, Hardy's subtitle to the novel defines her with respect and love as "a pure woman faithfully presented," and just about every reader, with the notable exception of Henry James, has agreed with this assessment. She is vivid, vigorous, even dominating, also deeply charitable and faithful, as she struggles against appalling circumstances to get control of her own fate. One thinks of how she stands up like a prophetess of old to baptize her dying baby according to a rite of her own devising when the parson is prevented from coming to her parents' cottage; of the power of her presentation in the Dairy-lands episode when she strolls in the rank, untended garden, appearing like some goddess of the vegetation, while the orphic strains of Angel Clare's harp playing are wafted from a high window nearby; of the mysterious impressiveness of her attitude at the end, when she lies down on the sun-warmed stones at Stonehenge and gives herself up as a blood sacrifice, not only to the social forces of law and order closing in upon her, but also to the hidden powers that rule the universe and for whose propitiation the builders of Stonehenge had thousands of years before designed their temple of the winds and sun.

Tess's magnificent vitality does her no good, just as the species vitality over which Darwin so often exclaims does that species no good in the long running on of evolutionary destinies. Yet it is a good in Hardy's presentation of her living and dying and confers on her a true dimension of purity and tragedy. It seems that Hardy's great creative accomplishment here has been to keep alive, even to enhance, all those values in human existence that had seemed to dissolve into sheer illusion after Darwin had made known his thoughts about the origin and evolution of species to the world.

V

If I have neglected to emphasize Hardy's notorious pessimism and determinism, it is because, given his place in

cultural history and in the development of modern attitudes, he does not seem to me to be particularly faint-
hearted or gloomy about human prospects. Hardy himself
liked to emphasize the tentative and provisional nature of
his insights, remarking in the preface to one of his col-
lections of verse, for example, that he was conducting
"questionings in the exploration of reality." According to
a passage from the biography by Florence Hardy that
deals with his state of mind during the period of the
First World War:

> (Hardy) said once—perhaps oftener—that although
> invidious critics had cast slurs upon him as Non-
> conformist, Agnostic, Atheist, Infidel, Immoralist,
> Heretic, Pessimist . . . they had never thought of
> calling him what they might have called him much
> more plausibly—churchy; not in an intellectual sense,
> but in so far as instincts and emotions ruled.*

By "churchy" I suppose he meant that he would have
remained a devout church member if the religious explanation of things had remained convincing to him for
the time he lived through. Perhaps he was also hinting
that he was the same man he had been before the world
beat a path to his door at Max Gate and that it had
better take him on his own terms if it wanted to take
his meaning at all.

This is not to deny that there is a strain of unappeasable
sadness in Hardy's work that seems to well up from deep
recesses in his temperament where instinct and emotion
do indeed hold sway. There is a recurring theme, running
through his fiction and poetry like an underground river,
which might be called the tragedy of non-arrival. The child
Jude, crushed by his inability to make much sense of the
ragged copies of the classical grammars he holds in his
hands, longs for someone to come and teach him, but
"Nobody did come, because nobody does." Mrs. Yeobright, dying of exhaustion and heartbreak on Egdon

* Florence Hardy, *The Life of Thomas Hardy* London: 1930,
p. 376.

Heath, is asked by little Johnny Nunsuch, "Does your
father come home at six too?" and replies, "No; he never
comes; nor my son either, nor anybody." There are all
those poems and stories about missed appointments, postponed marriages, belated recognitions, reconciliations that
failed to come off because somebody did turn up but
only when it was too late. There is the poem entitled
"Nobody Comes," written in Hardy's eighty-fifth year,
in the era of arrival by motor car, which ends

> And mute by the gate I stand again alone,
> And nobody pulls up there.

Also, there is the poem of opulent negativity which we
can form for ourselves out of the first lines of his poems
that begin with "No-" in the index of his collected verses:

> No more summer for Molly and me
> No; No
> "No smoke spreads out of this chimney pot
> No use hoping, or feeling vext
> Nobody says: Ah, that is the place
> Nobody took any notice of her as she stood
>   on the causey kerb
> Not a line of her writing have I
> "Nothing matters much," he said
> Now I am dead you sing to me
> Now that my page is exiled, doomed, maybe
> "Now shall I sing

I have transposed the last two lines to end the series
on an upbeat, to emphasize that he did, despite Lytton
Strachey's claim that he was no singer, sing a song
which will go on echoing through our literature for many
living, and dying, generations. Perhaps it is the song
of a disappointed lover of the God who disappeared from
view during the nineteenth century, or even the song
of a man who secretively loved a female cousin who
moved away, and married somebody else, and died too
soon. In any event it is the song of a man who was so
deeply touched by the life he spied upon that he never
liked to be touched by anyone his long life through.

Thomas Hardy—A Chronology

1840: Born June 2, at Higher Bockhampton in Dorset, his father a master mason and small builder, his mother of peasant stock.

1844: Learns violin playing from father. Will play at country social gatherings during boyhood.

1845: Already reading, he receives the educational rudiments from Lady Julia Augusta Martin, at Kingston Maurward House.

1847: The London railroad is extended from Southampton to Dorchester, Dorset's county seat.

1848: Enters the new village school at Lower Bockhampton.

1849: Changes to a school in Dorchester.

1850–55: Learns Latin, receives prize book for diligence in studies, begins Sunday School teaching at Stinsford Parish Church.

1856: Is apprenticed to the Dorchester architect, John Hicks. Continues studying Latin and begins Greek on his own.

1857: Begins friendship with Horace Moule of Fordington, Dorset, and Queen's College, Cambridge, who encourages his persistence in private study.

1859–60: Through Moule becomes acquainted with new developments in theological, scientific, and philosophic thought of the mid-Victorian era.

1862: Proposes marriage to Mary Waight of Dorchester, is rejected. Moves to London and starts work in the architectural offices of Arthur Blomfield. Calls on Lady Julia Martin, now resident in London.

1863: Wins prize medal for an essay on the uses of glazed brick and terra cotta in modern architecture. Much reading of the English poets in this period.

1864–66: Publishes first fiction, a sketch entitled "How I

Built Myself a House," in *Chambers's Journal*. Studies French at King's College, London. Reads contemporary authors of unorthodox tendency, including Darwin, Mill, T. H. Huxley, and Herbert Spencer. Considers becoming a clergyman and matriculating at Cambridge but abandons these plans because of increasing religious doubts. Develops lifelong admiration for Swinburne after reading *Poems and Ballads*. Begins writing poetry.

1867: In ill health, returns to Dorset and to his former Dorchester employer, William Hicks. Falls in love with a cousin, Tryphena Sparks of Puddletown (born 1850), to whom he later becomes secretly engaged.

1868–69: Seeks publisher for first novel, *The Poor Man and the Lady*. Advised to try again by both Alexander Macmillan and Chapman & Hall's chief reader, George Meredith, starts *Desperate Remedies*. Moves to Weymouth on Dorset coast, continues working at architecture.

1870: Further work on *Desperate Remedies*. Meets Emma Lavinia Gifford at St. Joliot in Cornwall while supervising the repair of a church.

1871: *Desperate Remedies* published. Several visits to Emma Gifford in Cornwall. Begins writing *Under the Greenwood Tree*.

1872: *Under the Greenwood Tree* published. Works in London designing schools. Tryphena Sparks, now qualified as a teacher, enters the public school system at Plymouth. About this time the engagement to Tryphena is broken, Hardy becomes engaged to Emma.

1873: *A Pair of Blue Eyes* published. Horace Moule, Hardy's Cambridge mentor, commits suicide. Work begun on *Far from the Madding Crowd*.

1874: *Far from the Madding Crowd* published. Marries Emma Gifford in London. A honeymoon in France.

1875–76: Brief residences in London, Swanage, and Yeovil, a longer one in Sturminster Newton. The Hardys tour the Lowlands in May, 1876, and *The Hand of Ethelberta* is completed and published this year also.

1877: Begins *The Return of the Native*, takes first notes for a drama of the Napoleonic Wars.

1878: *The Return of the Native* published. Moves from Sturminster Newton to London, is elected a member of the Savile Club.

1879: Florence Emily Dugdale, later to become Hardy's second wife, is born. Hardy begins writing *The Trumpet Major,* is elected to the Rabelais Club, the membership of which is restricted to "virile" authors.

1880: *The Trumpet Major* published. A holiday trip to France. Residence at Upper Tooting, London, where Hardy is seriously ill but dictates *A Laodicean* to meet contractual obligations for serial publication.

1881: *A Laodicean* published in book form. His health improved, Hardy moves to Wimborne Minster, travels to Edinburgh, begins writing *Two on a Tower.*

1882: *Two on a Tower* published. Starts work on *The Romantic Adventures of a Milkmaid.*

1883: *The Romantic Adventures of a Milkmaid* published. Hardy moves to Dorchester; designs and begins building his final home, Max Gate, on the outskirts of Dorchester.

1884–85: *The Mayor of Casterbridge* begun. The move into Max Gate, June, 1885.

1886: *The Mayor of Casterbridge* published. *The Woodlanders* begun. In this year Hardy does research for his Napoleonic epic at the British Museum, and the Dorset poet, William Barnes, dies.

1887: *The Woodlanders* published. A trip to Italy and a long visit to London.

1888: Publication of *Wessex Tales,* and a visit to Paris.

1889: *Tess of the d'Urbervilles* begun.

1890: Death of Tryphena Sparks (Mrs. Charles Gale since 1877). Visit to the grave site near Exeter with brother Henry, whom he also accompanies to Paris in the same year.

1891: Publication of *Tess of the d'Urbervilles* and *A Group of Noble Dames.*

1892: Death of Hardy's father. Serial publication of *The Well-Beloved.*

1893: Spring in London followed by a visit to Dublin, where he meets Mrs. Arthur Henniker. Later that year in London helps Mrs. Henniker revise her story, "The Spectre of the Real."

1894: *Life's Little Ironies* published. *Jude the Obscure* is begun. Hardy in London, April to August.

1895: *Jude the Obscure* published as volume VIII of The

Wessex Novels, "first uniform and complete edition" of Hardy's novels and tales, 1895–96.

1896: Spring in London. September trip to Brussels and Waterloo field with plans for his Napoleonic drama, *The Dynasts,* in Hardy's mind. Volumes IX–XVI of The Wessex Novels issued.

1897: *The Well-Beloved* is published in book form, bringing to an end Hardy's career as a novelist. The Hardys visit Switzerland and are in Lausanne on the anniversary of Gibbon's completing *The Decline and Fall* in that city.

1898: *Wessex Poems,* Hardy's first volume of verse, is published.

1901: Publication of *Poems of the Past and Present* (dated 1902).

1904: *The Dynasts,* Part First, published. Hardy's mother dies. Florence Emily Dugdale accompanies Mrs. Henniker on a visit to Max Gate.

1905: Goes to Aberdeen, receives LL.D. (*hon.*) from Aberdeen University.

1906: *The Dynasts,* Part Second, published.

1907: Mrs. Hardy visits London alone in February to march in suffragette parade. Both Hardys in London for the Season and to attend King Edward's Garden Party at Windsor.

1908: *The Dynasts,* Part Third, published; also Hardy's edition of *The Select Poems of William Barnes.*

1909–10: Becomes President of The Society of Authors, is awarded the Order of Merit, and receives "the freedom of Dorchester."

1912: Receives the gold medal of the Royal Society of Literature. Mrs. Hardy dies at Max Gate. The Wessex Edition of Hardy's works, incorporating the author's prefaces, editorial notes, and minor textual revisions, is published. Further volumes will be added to this edition until 1931.

1913: Litt. D. (*hon.*) and honorary fellowship from Cambridge University. Hardy revisits scenes of his courtship of Emma Gifford in Cornwall.

1914: *Satires of Circumstance* published. *A Changed Man*

and Other Tales published. Marries Florence Emily Dugdale.

1916: *Selected Poems* published. Visits a military hospital and a prisoner of war camp in Dorchester area.

1917: *Moments of Vision* published.

1920: Litt. D. (*hon.*) from Oxford University. Attends performance of scenes from *The Dynasts* staged by the Oxford University Dramatic Society. Makes last visit to London.

1922: *Late Lyrics and Earlier* published. LL. D. (*hon.*) from St. Andrew's University.

1923: *The Famous Tragedy of the Queen of Cornwall* published. Visits Oxford for the last time and is visited at Max Gate by the Prince of Wales.

1925: *Human Shows* published. Litt. D. (*hon.*) from Bristol University.

1926: Last visit to birthplace at Higher Bockhampton.

1928: Dies January 11. Heart is buried in Stinsford churchyard, his ashes in the Poet's Corner, Westminster Abbey. *Winter Words* published October 2; *The Early Life of Thomas Hardy,* by Florence Emily Hardy, on November 2.

1930: *The Later Years of Thomas Hardy,* also by Florence Hardy, published.

1931: The Wessex Edition (XXIV Volumes) is completed with inclusion of *Human Shows, Winter Words*.

1965: *An Indiscretion in the Life of an Heiress* first published in book form. [This story appeared in a magazine in 1878 but was omitted from the Wessex Edition. Its importance is that it is based upon some scenes in Hardy's rejected first novel, *The Poor Man and the Lady,* and tells us something of the mood and manner of Hardy's writing at the very beginning of his career.]

1

SEVEN TALES

Editor's Note

Hardy wrote more than forty short narratives before giving up fiction altogether in the late 1890s; he collected the bulk of them into four volumes of the Wessex Edition. "The Three Strangers" first appeared in *Longman's Magazine* in 1883 and was reprinted in *Wessex Tales* (1888, 1912). "Interlopers at the Knap" was first published in the *English Illustrated Magazine* in 1884 and was also collected into *Wessex Tales*. "A Tryst at an Ancient Earthwork" first appeared in the *Detroit Post* in 1885 and was collected into *A Changed Man* (1913). "The Withered Arm" first appeared in 1888 in *Blackwood's Magazine* and in *Wessex Tales*. "A Few Crusted Characters," of which "The Winters and the Palmleys" constitutes a self-contained episode, appeared as "Wessex Folk" in *Harper's Magazine* in 1891 and was retitled and collected into *Life's Little Ironies* (1894, 1912). "Barbara of the House of Grebe" first appeared in *A Group of Noble Dames* (1891). "The Fiddler of the Reels" was first published in *Scribner's Magazine* in 1893 and was reprinted in *Life's Little Ironies*.

The mainstream of the modern short story issues from Flaubert and Chekhov and leads to the masterpieces of Hemingway and Faulkner by way of James, Conrad, and Joyce. In this tradition emphasis is overwhelmingly upon "showing, not telling," upon "rendering" and "presentation," upon a unity of imaginative effect achieved through carefully controlled technical means including a dramatized or objectified point of view, scrupulous tonal consistency, employment of what Ford Maddox Ford called "telling details," key symbols, the avoidance of overt moralizing, circumstantiality, or ampleness in narrating.

It is an admirable tradition, despite Lawrence's complaint that it makes for a disabling self-consciousness and manipulativeness in all but the best writers who have followed it. Yet it is a tradition from which Hardy is largely isolated.

In his short fiction Hardy is content to *tell* stories in an ample, leisurely manner, either *in propria persona* or by means of a substitute narrator whose relation to events usually remains that of a storyteller. Dramatic conflicts and resolutions, tragic or ironic patterns in the lives of his characters, are allowed to come into view at their own pace and rarely lead to those emphasized moments of epiphany or tense self-recognition with which stories in the Flaubertian mold are often concerned. One might say that Hardy's characters do not see themselves as fictional characters at all, nor are they viewed in that light by their creator. Paying them the tribute of a deep sympathetic interest, the author refuses to violate the privacy and integrity of private lives by subordinating the purposes of the characters to the artful intentions of the story itself. If this begins to sound like a defence of artlessness, perhaps it can be maintained that artlessness is itself an art. In the age of the nonfiction novel and of a new journalism claiming to exploit the devices of modern fiction in making "exposés" of contemporary personalities, there is something refreshing and revivifying in an art that draws very little from a formal vocabulary so codified and standardized by now that it offers a set of handy clichés to journalists.

"Interlopers at the Knap" is a story about the baffling of good intentions by circumstances that were only avoidable in part. The farmer should not have temporized over his proposal to Sally Hall after the problem of her widowed sister-in-law was cleared up. However, his hesitation is consonant with his deliberate, robust character, and besides, she does live out of the way of day-to-day encounter and contact. The story comes to a point upon her determined, final refusal to marry at all. For her it has become intuitively a point of honor. Only Hardy, among the male writers of his period, was capable of grasping that honor has meaning for women as well as men, for ordinary people as well as the gentry. Sally's decision to remain a spinster must be seen as wholehearted as well as thoughtful and moral under the circumstances.

In "A Tryst at an Ancient Earthwork" the narrator's tryst is with the stirring ghosts of the early Celtic hordes and the later Roman militia who teem around the great hill fortress, whereas the tryst of the amateur archaeologist is merely with portable property. The narrator need take nothing away because the remote past for him is ever-living, if apparitional, through the remarkable resources of an "acoustic" imagination which was Hardy's own. The conflict, which remains unspoken in the discreet dealings of the two men with each other, is between contrasted ways of appropriating a past that for neither man can or should remain buried. To the many impressive nocturnal episodes or night pieces in Hardy's fiction and poetry this one adds something essential and unforgettable.

"The Winters and the Palmleys"—a native returning from a long absence abroad rides toward the village of Longpuddle aboard a country omnibus and hears a series of tales about his home village from his fellow-passengers. This brief and terrible story, told by the groceress, is number eight in the sequence entitled "A Few Crusted Characters," and shows Hardy employing a framing narrative device that was already hoary in the time of Chaucer. Jack Winter would not have died on the gallows had he not feared so intensely the shame of an exposure of his ill-spelt letters by Harriet Palmley. But public shaming is a social sanction of country life far more ancient than the system of written and proscriptive laws which attempts to displace it. Jack becomes the victim of a conflict which at bottom is between ancient and modern. After listening to all the stories, the returned native decides to go abroad again. That is all the moral "A Few Crusted Characters" cares to offer.

"The Fiddler of the Reels," which is perhaps Hardy's greatest brief tale, begins with a crucial metaphor concerning a "geological fault" in time and proceeds to bring "ancient and modern into absolute contact" through its account of Car'line Aspent's "hysterical" sensitivity to the fiddle playing of Wat Ollamoor. Wat of course is the god Orpheus reconstituted as a lounging and greasy village Paganini, and the ancient buried strata of feeling in Car'line to which his music reaches are incontestably sexual. Hardy's choice of a temporal setting, the era of the Great Exhibition of 1851, which featured that unprecedented "modern" structure, the Crystal Palace, along with the opening of a rail link between Waterloo Station and South Wessex, was an inspired one. It only remains to mention that Hardy himself experienced hysterical seizures while listening to violin music in early childhood and that several major characters in his novels are undone through their responses to the orphic power of music.

I have included these brief commentaries on several but not all of the stories here as a way of suggesting that Hardy's "old-fashioned" storytelling art has a richness and subtlety all its own. The "gothic" of "Barbara and the House of Grebe," the insight into folk psychology and superstition in "The Withered Arm," and the symmetrical ironies of the ballad-like "The Three Strangers" deserve our admiration as well, but it is likely that these tales are so well-known as to need little or no introduction to most readers.

ᗰᗰᗰᗰᗰᗰᗰᗰᗰᗰᗰᗰᗰᗰᗰᗰᗰᗰᗰᗰ

THE THREE STRANGERS

Among the few features of agricultural England which retain an appearance but little modified by the lapse of centuries, may be reckoned the long, grassy and furzy downs, coombs, or ewe-leases, as they are called according to their kind, that fill a large area of certain counties in the south and south-west. If any mark of human occupation is met with hereon, it usually takes the form of the solitary cottage of some shepherd.

Fifty years ago such a lonely cottage stood on such a down, and may possibly be standing there now. In spite of its loneliness, however, the spot, by actual measurement, was not three miles from a country-town. Yet that affected it little. Three miles of irregular upland, during the long inimical seasons, with their sleets, snows, rains, and mists, afford withdrawing space enough to isolate a Timon or a Nebuchadnezzar; much less, in fair weather, to please that less repellent tribe, the poets, philosophers, artists, and others who "conceive and meditate of pleasant things."

Some old earthen camp or barrow, some clump of trees, at least some starved fragment of ancient hedge is usually taken advantage of in the erection of these forlorn dwellings. But, in the present case, such a kind of shelter had been disregarded. Higher Crowstairs, as the house was called, stood quite detached and undefended. The only reason for its precise situation seemed to be the crossing of two footpaths at right angles hard by, which may have crossed there and thus for a good five hundred years. Hence the house was exposed to the elements on all sides. But, though the wind up here blew unmistakably when it did blow, and the rain hit hard whenever it fell, the various weathers of the winter season were not quite so formidable on the down as they were imagined to be by dwellers on low ground. The raw rimes were not so pernicious as in the hollows, and the frosts were scarcely so severe. When the shepherd and his family who tenanted the house were pitied for their sufferings from the exposure, they said that upon the whole they were less inconvenienced by 'wuzzes and flames' (hoarses and phlegms) than when they had lived by the stream of a snug neighbouring valley.

The night of March 28, 182–, was precisely one of the nights that were wont to call forth these expressions of commiseration. The level rainstorm smote walls, slopes, and hedges like the clothyard shafts of Senlac and Crecy. Such sheep and outdoor animals as had no shelter stood with their buttocks to the winds; while the tails of little birds trying to roost on some scraggy thorn were blown inside-out like umbrellas. The gable-end of the cottage was stained with wet, and the eavesdroppings flapped against the wall. Yet never was commiseration for the shepherd more misplaced. For that cheerful rustic was entertaining a large party in glorification of the christening of his second girl.

The guests had arrived before the rain began to fall, and they were all now assembled in the chief or living room of the dwelling. A glance into the apartment at eight o'clock on this eventful evening would have resulted in the opinion that it was as cosy and comfortable a nook as could be wished for in boisterous weather. The calling of its inhabitant was proclaimed by a number of highly-polished sheep-crooks without stems that were hung ornamentally over the fireplace, the curl of each shining crook varying from the antiquated type engraved in the patriarchal pictures of old family Bibles to the most approved fashion of the last local sheep-fair. The room was lighted by half-a-dozen candles, having wicks only a trifle smaller than the grease which enveloped them, in candlesticks that were never used but at high-days, holy-days, and family feasts. The lights were scattered about the room, two of them standing on the chimney-piece. This position of candles was in itself significant. Candles on the chimney-piece always meant a party.

On the hearth, in front of a back-brand to give substance, blazed a fire of thorns, that crackled "like the laughter of the fool."

Nineteen persons were gathered here. Of these, five women, wearing gowns of various bright hues, sat in chairs along the wall; girls shy and not shy filled the window-bench; four men, including Charley Jake the hedge-carpenter, Elijah New the parish-clerk, and John Pitcher, a neighbouring dairyman, the shepherd's father-in-law, lolled in the settle; a young man and maid, who were blushing over tentative *pourparlers* on a life-companionship, sat beneath the corner-cupboard; and an elderly engaged man of fifty or upward moved restlessly about from spots where his betrothed was not to the spot where she was. Enjoyment was pretty general, and so much the more prevailed in being unhampered by conventional restrictions. Absolute confidence in each other's good opinion begat perfect ease, while the finishing stroke of manner, amounting to a truly princely serenity, was lent to the majority by the absence of any expression or trait denoting that they wished to get on in the world, enlarge their minds, or do any eclipsing thing whatever—which nowadays so generally nips the bloom and *bonhomie* of all except the two extremes of the social scale.

Shepherd Fennel had married well, his wife being a dairyman's daughter from a vale at a distance, who brought fifty guineas in her pocket—and kept them there, till they should be required for ministering to the needs of a coming family. This frugal woman had been somewhat exercised as to the character that should be given to the gathering. A sit-still party had its advantages; but an undisturbed position of ease in chairs and settles was apt to lead on the men to such an unconscionable deal of toping that they would sometimes fairly drink the house dry. A dancing-party was the alternative; but this, while avoiding the foregoing objection on the score of good drink, had a counterbalancing disadvantage in the matter of good victuals, the ravenous appetites engendered by the exercise causing immense havoc in the buttery. Shepherdess Fennel fell back upon the intermediate plan of mingling short dances with short periods of talk and singing, so as to hinder any ungovernable rage in either. But this scheme was entirely confined to her own gentle mind: the shepherd himself was in the mood to exhibit the most reckless phases of hospitality.

The fiddler was a boy of those parts, about twelve years of age, who had a wonderful dexterity in jigs and reels, though his fingers were so small and short as to necessitate a constant shifting for the high notes, from which he scrambled back to the first position with sounds not of unmixed purity of tone. At seven the shrill tweedle-dee of this youngster had begun, accompanied by a booming ground-bass from Elijah New, the parish-clerk, who had thoughtfully brought with him his favourite musical instrument, the serpent. Dancing was instantaneous, Mrs. Fennel privately enjoining the players on no account to let the dance exceed the length of a quarter of an hour.

But Elijah and the boy in the excitement of their position quite forgot the injunction. Moreover, Oliver Giles, a man of seventeen, one of the dancers, who was enamoured of his partner, a fair girl of thirty-three rolling years, had recklessly handed a new crown-piece to the musicians, as a bribe to keep going as long as they had muscle and wind. Mrs. Fennel seeing the steam begin to generate on the countenances of her guests, crossed over and touched the fiddler's elbow and put her hand on the serpent's mouth. But they took no notice, and fearing she might lose her character of genial hostess if she were to interfere too markedly, she retired and sat down helpless. And so the dance whizzed on with cumulative fury, the performers moving in their planet-like courses, direct and retrograde, from apogee to perigee, till the hand of the well-kicked clock at the bottom of the room had travelled over the circumference of an hour.

While these cheerful events were in course of enactment within Fennel's pastoral dwelling an incident having considerable bearing on the party had occurred in the gloomy night without. Mrs. Fennel's concern about the growing fierceness of the dance corresponded in point of time with the ascent of a human figure to the solitary hill of Higher Crowstairs from the direction of the distant town. This personage strode on through the rain without a pause, following the little-worn path which, further on in its course, skirted the shepherd's cottage.

It was nearly the time of full moon, and on this account, though the sky was lined with a uniform sheet of dripping cloud, ordinary objects out of doors were readily visible. The sad wan light revealed the lonely pedestrian to be a man of supple frame; his gait suggested that he had somewhat passed the period of perfect and instinctive agility, though not so far as to be otherwise than rapid of motion when occasion required. At a rough guess, he might have been about forty years of age. He appeared tall, but a recruiting sergeant, or other person accustomed to the judging of men's heights by the eye, would have discerned that this was chiefly owing to his gauntness, and that he was not more than five-feet-eight or -nine.

Notwithstanding the regularity of his tread there was caution in it, as in that of one who mentally feels his way; and despite the fact that it was not a black coat nor a dark garment of any sort that he wore, there was something about him which suggested that he naturally belonged to the black-coated tribes of men. His clothes were of fustian, and his boots hobnailed, yet in his progress he showed not the mud-accustomed bearing of hobnailed and fustianed peasantry.

By the time that he had arrived abreast of the shepherd's premises the rain came down, or rather came along, with yet more determined violence. The outskirts of the little settlement partially broke the force of wind and rain, and this induced him to stand still. The most salient of the shepherd's domestic erections was an empty sty at the forward corner of his hedgeless garden, for in these latitudes the principle of masking the homelier features of your establishment by a conventional frontage was unknown. The traveller's eye was attracted to this small building by the pallid shine of the wet slates that covered it. He turned aside, and, finding it empty, stood under the pent-roof for shelter.

While he stood the boom of the serpent within the adjacent house, and the lesser strains of the fiddler, reached the spot as an accompaniment to the surging hiss of the flying rain on the sod, its louder beating on the cabbage-leaves of the garden, on the straw hackles of eight or ten beehives just discernible by the path, and its dripping from the eaves into a row of buckets and pans that had been placed under the walls of the cottage. For at Higher Crowstairs, as at all such elevated domiciles, the grand difficulty of housekeeping was an insufficiency of water; and a casual rainfall was utilized by turning out, as catchers, every utensil that the house contained. Some queer stories might be told of the contrivances for economy in suds and dishwaters that are absolutely necessitated in upland habitations during the droughts of summer. But at this season there were no such exigencies; a mere acceptance of what the skies bestowed was sufficient for an abundant store.

At last the notes of the serpent ceased and the house was silent. This cessation of activity aroused the solitary pedestrian from the reverie into which he had lapsed, and, emerging from the shed, with an apparently new intention, he walked up the path to the house-door. Arrived here, his first act was to kneel down on a large stone beside the row of vessels, and to drink a copious draught from one of them. Having quenched his thirst he rose and lifted his hand to knock, but paused with his eye upon the panel. Since the dark surface of the wood revealed absolutely nothing, it was evident that he must be mentally looking through the door, as if he wished to measure thereby all the possibilities that a house of this sort might include, and how they might bear upon the question of his entry.

In his indecision he turned and surveyed the scene around. Not a soul was anywhere visible. The garden-path stretched downward from his feet, gleaming like the track of a snail; the roof of the little well (mostly dry), the wellcover, the top rail of the garden-gate, were varnished with the same dull liquid glaze; while, far away in the vale, a faint whiteness of more than usual extent showed that the rivers were high in the meads. Beyond all this winked a few bleared lamplights through the beating drops—lights that denoted the situation of the county-town from which he had appeared to come. The absence of all notes of life in that direction seemed to clinch his intentions, and he knocked at the door.

Within, a desultory chat had taken the place of movement and musical sound. The hedge-carpenter was suggesting a song to the company, which nobody just then was inclined to undertake, so that the knock afforded a not unwelcome diversion.

"Walk in!" said the shepherd promptly.

The latch clicked upward, and out of the night our

pedestrian appeared upon the door-mat. The shepherd
arose, snuffed two of the nearest candles, and turned to
look at him.

Their light disclosed that the stranger was dark in complexion and not unprepossessing as to feature. His hat,
which for a moment he did not remove, hung low over his
eyes, without concealing that they were large, open, and
determined, moving with a flash rather than a glance
round the room. He seemed pleased with his survey, and,
baring his shaggy head, said, in a rich deep voice, "The
rain is so heavy, friends, that I ask leave to come in and
rest awhile."

"To be sure, stranger," said the shepherd. "And faith,
you've been lucky in choosing your time, for we are
having a bit of a fling for a glad cause—though, to be
sure, a man could hardly wish that glad cause to happen
more than once a year."

"Nor less," spoke up a woman. "For 'tis best to get
your family over and done with, as soon as you can, so
as to be all the earlier out of the fag o't."

"And what may be this glad cause?" asked the stranger.

"A birth and christening," said the shepherd.

The stranger hoped his host might not be made unhappy
either by too many or too few of such episodes, and being
invited by a gesture to a pull at the mug, he readily
acquiesced. His manner, which, before entering, had been
so dubious, was now altogether that of a careless and
candid man.

"Late to be traipsing athwart this coomb—hey?" said
the engaged man of fifty.

"Late it is, master, as you say. —I'll take a seat in the
chimney-corner, if you have nothing to urge against it,
ma'am; for I am a little moist on the side that was
next the rain."

Mrs. Shepherd Fennel assented, and made room for the
self-invited comer, who, having got completely inside the
chimney-corner, stretched out his legs and his arms with
the expansiveness of a person quite at home.

"Yes, I am rather cracked in the vamp," he said freely,

seeing that the eyes of the shepherd's wife fell upon his boots, "and I am not well fitted either. I have had some rough times lately, and have been forced to pick up what I can get in the way of wearing, but I must find a suit better fit for working-days when I reach home."

"One of hereabouts?" she inquired.

"Not quite that—further up the country."

"I thought so. And so be I; and by your tongue you come from my neighbourhood."

"But you would hardly have heard of me," he said quickly. "My time would be long before yours, ma'am, you see."

This testimony to the youthfulness of his hostess had the effect of stopping her cross-examination.

"There is only one thing more wanted to make me happy," continued the new-comer. "And that is a little baccy, which I am sorry to say I am out of."

"I'll fill your pipe," said the shepherd.

"I must ask you to lend me a pipe likewise."

"A smoker, and no pipe about 'ee?"

"I have dropped it somewhere on the road."

The shepherd filled and handed him a new clay pipe, saying, as he did so, "Hand me your baccy-box—I'll fill that too, now I am about it."

The man went through the movement of searching his pockets.

"Lost that too?" said his entertainer, with some surprise.

"I am afraid so," said the man with some confusion. "Give it to me in a screw of paper." Lighting his pipe at the candle with a suction that drew the whole flame into the bowl, he resettled himself in the corner and bent his looks upon the faint steam from his damp legs, as if he wished to say no more.

Meanwhile the general body of guests had been taking little notice of this visitor by reason of an absorbing discussion in which they were engaged with the band about a tune for the next dance. The matter being settled, they were about to stand up when an interruption came in the shape of another knock at the door.

At sound of the same the man in the chimney-corner took up the poker and began stirring the brands as if doing it thoroughly were the one aim of his existence; and a second time the shepherd said, "Walk in!" In a moment another man stood upon the straw-woven door-mat. He too was a stranger.

This individual was one of a type radically different from the first. There was more of the commonplace in his manner, and a certain jovial cosmopolitanism sat upon his features. He was several years older than the first arrival, his hair being slightly frosted, his eyebrows bristly, and his whiskers cut back from his cheeks. His face was rather full and flabby, and yet it was not altogether a face without power. A few grog-blossoms marked the neighbour-hood of his nose. He flung back his long drab greatcoat, revealing that beneath it he wore a suit of cinder-grey shade throughout, large heavy seals, of some metal or other that would take a polish, dangling from his fob as his only personal ornament. Shaking the water-drops from his low-crowned glazed hat, he said, "I must ask for a few minutes' shelter, comrades, or I shall be wetted to my skin before I get to Casterbridge."

"Make yourself at home, master," said the shepherd, perhaps a trifle less heartily than on the first occasion. Not that Fennel had the least tinge of niggardliness in his composition; but the room was far from large, spare chairs were not numerous, and damp companions were not altogether desirable at close quarters for the women and girls in their bright-coloured gowns.

However, the second comer, after taking off his great-coat, and hanging his hat on a nail in one of the ceiling-beams as if he had been specially invited to put it there, advanced and sat down at the table. This had been pushed so closely into the chimney-corner, to give all available room to the dancers, that its inner edge grazed the elbow of the man who had ensconced himself by the fire; and thus the two strangers were brought into close companion-ship. They nodded to each other by way of breaking the ice of unacquaintance, and the first stranger handed his neighbour the family mug—a huge vessel of brown ware, having its upper edge worn away like a threshold by the rub of whole generations of thirsty lips that had gone the way of all flesh, and bearing the following inscription burnt upon its rotund side in yellow letters:—

THERE IS NO FUN
UNTILL *i* CUM.

The other man, nothing loth, raised the mug to his lips, and drank on, and on, and on—till a curious blueness overspread the countenance of the shepherd's wife, who had regarded with no little surprise the first stranger's free offer to the second of what did not belong to him to dispense.

"I knew it!" said the toper to the shepherd with much satisfaction. "When I walked up your garden before coming in, and saw the hives all of a row, I said to myself, 'Where there's bees there's honey, and where there's honey there's mead.' But mead of such a truly comfortable sort as this I really didn't expect to meet in my older days." He took yet another pull at the mug, till it assumed an ominous elevation.

"Glad you enjoy it!" said the shepherd warmly.

"It is goodish mead," assented Mrs. Fennel, with an absence of enthusiasm which seemed to say that it was possible to buy praise for one's cellar at too heavy a price. "It is trouble enough to make—and really I hardly think we shall make any more. For honey sells well, and we ourselves can make shift with a drop o' small mead and metheglin for common use from the comb-washings."

"O, but you'll never have the heart!" reproachfully cried the stranger in cinder-grey, after taking up the mug a third time and setting it down empty." I love mead, when 'tis old like this, as I love to go to church o' Sundays, or to relieve the needy any day of the week."

"Ha, ha, ha!" said the man in the chimney-corner, who, in spite of the taciturnity induced by the pipe of tobacco, could not or would not refrain from this slight testimony to his comrade's humour.

Now the old mead of those days, brewed of the purest first-year or maiden honey, four pounds to the gallon—with its due complement of white of eggs, cinnamon, ginger, cloves, mace, rosemary, yeast, and processes of working, bottling, and cellaring—tasted remarkably strong; but it did not taste so strong as it actually was. Hence, presently, the stranger in cinder-grey at the table, moved by its creeping influence, unbuttoned his waistcoat, threw himself back in his chair, spread his legs, and made his presence felt in various ways.

"Well, well, as I say," he resumed, "I am going to Casterbridge, and to Casterbridge I must go. I should have been almost there by this time; but the rain drove me into your dwelling, and I'm not sorry for it."

"You don't live in Casterbridge?" said the shepherd.

"Not as yet; though I shortly mean to move there."

"Going to set up in trade, perhaps?"

"No, no," said the shepherd's wife. "It is easy to see that the gentleman is rich, and don't want to work at anything."

The cinder-grey stranger paused, as if to consider whether he would accept that definition of himself. He presently rejected it by answering, "Rich is not quite the word for me, dame. I do work, and I must work. And even if I only get to Casterbridge by midnight I must begin work there at eight to-morrow morning. Yes, het or wet, blow or snow, famine or sword, my day's work to-morrow must be done."

"Poor man! Then, in spite o' seeming, you be worse off than we?" replied the shepherd's wife.

" 'Tis the nature of my trade, men and maidens. 'Tis the nature of my trade more than my poverty. . . . But really and truly I must up and off, or I shan't get a lodging in the town." However, the speaker did not move, and directly added, "There's time for one more draught of friendship before I go; and I'd perform it at once if the mug were not dry."

"Here's a mug o' small," said Mrs. Fennel. "Small, we call it, though to be sure 'tis only the first wash o' the combs."

"No," said the stranger disdainfully. "I won't spoil your first kindness by partaking o' your second.'

"Certainly not," broke in Fennel. "We don't increase and multiply every day, and I'll fill the mug again." He went away to the dark place under the stairs where the barrel stood. The shepherdess followed him.

"Why should you do this?" she said reproachfully, as soon as they were alone. "He's emptied it once, though it held enough for ten people; and now he's not contented wi' the small, but must needs call for more o' the strong! And a stranger unbeknown to any of us. For my part, I don't like the look o' the man at all."

"But he's in the house, my honey; and 'tis a wet night, and a christening. Daze it, what's a cup of mead more or less? There'll be plenty more next bee-burning."

"Very well—this time, then," she answered, looking wistfully at the barrel. "But what is the man's calling, and where is he one of, that he should come in and join us like this?"

"I don't know. I'll ask him again."

The catastrophe of having the mug drained dry at one pull by the stranger in cinder-grey was effectually guarded against this time by Mrs. Fennel. She poured out his allowance in a small cup, keeping the large one at a discreet distance from him. When he had tossed off his portion the shepherd renewed his inquiry about the stranger's occupation.

The latter did not immediately reply, and the man in the chimney-corner, with sudden demonstrativeness, said, "Anybody may know my trade—I'm a wheelwright."

"A very good trade for these parts," said the shepherd.

"And anybody may know mine—if they've the sense to find it out," said the stranger in cinder-grey.

"You may generally tell what a man is by his claws," observed the hedge-carpenter, looking at his own hands, "My fingers be as full of thorns as an old pin-cushion is of pins."

The hands of the man in the chimney-corner instinctively sought the shade, and he gazed into the fire as he resumed his pipe. The man at the table took up the hedge-carpenter's remark, and added smartly, "True; but the oddity of my trade is that, instead of setting a mark upon me, it sets a mark upon my customers."

No observation being offered by anybody in elucidation of this enigma the shepherd's wife once more called for a song. The same obstacles presented themselves as at the former time—one had no voice, another had forgotten the first verse. The stranger at the table, whose soul had now risen to a good working temperature, relieved the difficulty by exclaiming that, to start the company, he would sing himself. Thrusting one thumb into the arm-hole of his waistcoat, he waved the other hand in the air, and, with an extemporizing gaze at the shining sheep-crooks above the mantelpiece, began:—

> "O my trade it is the rarest one,
> > Simple shepherds all—
> My trade is a sight to see;
> For my customers I tie, and take them up on high
> And waft 'em to a far countree!"

The room was silent when he had finished the verse—with one exception, that of the man in the chimney-corner, who, at the singer's word, "Chorus!" joined him in a deep bass voice of musical relish—

> "And waft 'em to a far countree!"

Oliver Giles, John Pitcher the dairyman, the parish-clerk, the engaged man of fifty, the row of young women against the wall, seemed lost in thought not of the gayest kind. The shepherd looked meditatively on the ground, the shepherdess gazed keenly at the singer, and with some suspicion; she was doubting whether this stranger were merely singing an old song from recollection, or was composing one there and then for the occasion. All were as perplexed at the obscure revelation as the guests at Belshazzar's Feast, except the man in the chimney-corner, who quietly said, "Second verse, stranger," and smoked on.

The singer thoroughly moistened himself from his lips inwards, and went on with the next stanza as requested:—

> "My tools are but common ones,
>   Simple shepherds all—
> A little hempen string, and a post whereon to swing,
>   Are implements enough for me!"

Shepherd Fennel glanced round. There was no longer any doubt that the stranger was answering his question rhythmically. The guests one and all started back with suppressed exclamations. The young woman engaged to the man of fifty fainted half-way, and would have proceeded, but finding him wanting in alacrity for catching her she sat down trembling.

"O, he's the ——!" whispered the people in the background, mentioning the name of an ominous public officer. "He's come to do it! 'Tis to be at Casterbridge jail to-morrow—the man for sheep-stealing—the poor clockmaker we heard of, who used to live away at Shottsford and had no work to do—Timothy Summers, whose family were a-starving, and so he went out of Shottsford by the high-road, and took a sheep in open daylight, defying the farmer and the farmer's wife and the farmer's lad, and every man jack among 'em. He" (and they nodded towards the stranger of the deadly trade) "is come from up the country to do it because there's not enough to do in his own county-town, and he's got the place here now our own county man's dead; he's going to live in the same cottage under the prison wall."

The stranger in cinder-grey took no notice of this whispered string of observations, but again wetted his lips. Seeing that his friend in the chimney-corner was the only one who reciprocated his joviality in any way, he held out his cup towards that appreciative comrade, who also held out his own. They clinked together, the eyes of the rest of the room hanging upon the singer's actions. He parted his lips for the third verse; but at that moment another knock was audible upon the door. This time the knock was faint and hesitating.

The company seemed scared; the shepherd looked with consternation towards the entrance, and it was with some effort that he resisted his alarmed wife's deprecatory glance, and uttered for the third time the welcoming words, "Walk in!"

The door was gently opened, and another man stood upon the mat. He, like those who had preceded him, was a stranger. This time it was a short, small personage, of fair complexion, and dressed in a decent suit of dark clothes.

"Can you tell me the way to——?" he began: when, gazing round the room to observe the nature of the company amongst whom he had fallen, his eyes lighted on the stranger in the cinder-grey. It was just at the instant when the latter, who had thrown his mind into his song with such a will that he scarcely heeded the interruption, silenced all whispers and inquiries by bursting into his third verse:—

> "To-morrow is my working day,
> > Simple shepherds all—
> To-morrow is a working day for me:
> For the farmer's sheep is slain, and the lad who did it ta'en,
> > And on his soul may God ha' merc-y!"

The stranger in the chimney-corner, waving cups with the singer so heartily that his mead splashed over on the hearth, repeated in his bass voice as before:—

> "And on his soul may God ha' merc-y!"

All this time the third stranger had been standing in the doorway. Finding now that he did not come forward or go on speaking, the guests particularly regarded him. They noticed to their surprise that he stood before them the picture of abject terror—his knees trembling, his hand shaking so violently that the door-latch by which he supported himself rattled audibly: his white lips were parted, and his eyes fixed on the merry officer of justice in the middle of the room. A moment more and he had turned, closed the door, and fled.

"What a man can it be?" said the shepherd.

The rest, between the awfulness of their late discovery and the odd conduct of this third visitor, looked as if they knew not what to think, and said nothing. Instinctively they withdrew further and further from the grim gentleman in their midst, whom some of them seemed to take for the Prince of Darkness himself, till they formed a remote circle, an empty space of floor being left between them and him—

". . . circulus, cujus centrum diabolus."

The room was so silent—though there were more than twenty people in it—that nothing could be heard but the patter of the rain against the window-shutters, accompanied by the occasional hiss of a stray drop that fell down the chimney into the fire, and the steady puffing of the man in the corner, who had now resumed his pipe of long clay.

The stillness was unexpectedly broken. The distant sound of a gun reverberated through the air—apparently from the direction of the county-town.

"Be jiggered!" cried the stranger who had sung the song, jumping up.

"What does that mean?" asked several.

"A prisoner escaped from the jail—that's what it means.

All listened. The sound was repeated, and none of them spoke but the man in the chimney-corner, who said quietly, "I've often been told that in this county they fire a gun at such times; but I never heard it till now."

"I wonder if it is *my* man?" murmured the personage in cinder-grey.

"Surely it is!" said the shepherd involuntarily. "And surely we've zeed him! That little man who looked in at the door by now, and quivered like a leaf when he zeed ye and heard your song!"

"His teeth chattered, and the breath went out of his body," said the dairyman.

"And his heart seemed to sink within him like a stone," said Oliver Giles.

"And he bolted as if he'd been shot at," said the hedge-carpenter.

"True—his teeth chattered, and his heart seemed to sing; and he bolted as if he'd been shot at," slowly summed up the man in the chimney-corner.

"I didn't notice it," remarked the hangman.

"We were all a-wondering what made him run off in such a fright," faltered one of the women against the wall, "and now 'tis explained!"

The firing of the alarm-gun went on at intervals, low and sullenly, and their suspicions became a certainty. The sinister gentleman in cinder-grey roused himself. "Is there a constable here?" he asked, in thick tones. "If so, let him step forward."

The engaged man of fifty stepped quavering out from the wall, his betrothed beginning to sob on the back of the chair.

"You are a sworn constable?"

"I be, sir."

"Then pursue the criminal at once, with assistance, and bring him back here. He can't have gone far."

"I will, sir, I will—when I've got my staff. I'll go home and get it, and come sharp here, and start in a body."

"Staff! —never mind your staff; the man'll be gone!"

"But I can't do nothing without my staff—can I, William, and John, and Charles Jake? No; for there's the king's royal crown a painted on en in yaller and gold, and the lion and the unicorn, so as when I raise en up and hit my prisoner, 'tis made a lawful blow thereby. I wouldn't 'tempt to take up a man without my staff—no, not I. If I hadn't the law to gie me courage, why, instead o' my taking up him he might take up me!"

"Now, I'm a king's man myself, and can give you authority enough for this," said the formidable officer in grey. "Now then, all of ye, be ready. Have ye any lanterns?"

"Yes—have ye any lanterns? —I demand it!" said the constable.

"And the rest of you able-bodied——"

"Able-bodied men—yes—the rest of ye!" said the constable.

"Have you some good stout staves and pitchforks——"

"Staves and pitchforks—in the name o' the law! And take 'em in yer hands and go in quest, and do as we in authority tell ye!"

Thus aroused, the men prepared to give chase. The evidence was, indeed, though circumstantial, so convincing, that but little argument was needed to show the shepherd's guests that after what they had seen it would look very much like connivance if they did not instantly pursue the unhappy third stranger, who could not as yet have gone more than a few hundred yards over such uneven country.

A shepherd is always well provided with lanterns; and, lighting these hastily, and with hurdle-staves in their hands, they poured out of the door, taking a direction along the crest of the hill, away from the town, the rain having fortunately a little abated.

Disturbed by the noise, or possibly by unpleasant dreams of her baptism, the child who had been christened began to cry heart-brokenly in the room overhead. These notes of grief came down through the chinks of the floor to the ears of the women below, who jumped up one by one, and seemed glad of the excuse to ascend and comfort the baby, for the incidents of the last half-hour greatly oppressed them. Thus in the space of two or three minutes the room on the ground-floor was deserted quite.

But it was not for long. Hardly had the sound of footsteps died away when a man returned round the corner of the house from the direction the pursuers had taken. Peeping in at the door, and seeing nobody there, he entered leisurely. It was the stranger of the chimney-corner, who had gone out with the rest. The motive of his return was shown by his helping himself to a cut piece of skimmercake that lay on a ledge beside where he had sat, and which he had apparently forgotten to take with him. He also poured out half a cup more mead from the quantity that remained, ravenously eating and drinking these as he stood. He had not finished when another figure came in just as quietly—his friend in cinder-grey.

"O—you here?" said the latter, smiling. "I thought you had gone to help in the capture." And this speaker also revealed the object of his return by looking solicitously round for the fascinating mug of old mead.

"And I thought you had gone," said the other, continuing his skimmer-cake with some effort.

"Well, on second thoughts, I felt there were enough without me," said the first confidentially, "and such a night as it is, too. Besides, 'tis the business o' the Government to take care of its criminals—not mine."

"True; so it is. And I felt as you did, that there were enough without me."

"I don't want to break my limbs running over the humps and hollows of this wild country."

"Nor I neither, between you and me."

"These shepherd-people are used to it—simple-minded souls, you know, stirred up to anything in a moment. They'll have him ready for me before the morning, and no trouble to me at all."

"They'll have him, and we shall have saved ourselves all labour in the matter."

"True, true. Well, my way is to Casterbridge; and 'tis as much as my legs will do to take me that far. Going the same way?"

"No, I am sorry to say! I have to get home over there" (he nodded indefinitely to the right), "and I feel as you do, that it is quite enough for my legs to do before bedtime."

The other had by this time finished the mead in the mug, after which, shaking hands heartily at the door, and wishing each other well, they went their several ways.

In the meantime the company of pursuers had reached the end of the hog's-back elevation which dominated this part of the down. They had decided on no particular plan of action; and, finding that the man of the baleful trade was no longer in their company, they seemed quite unable to form any such plan now. They descended in all directions down the hill, and straightway several of the party fell into the snare set by Nature for all misguided midnight ramblers over this part of the cretaceous formation. The "lanchets," or flint slopes, which belted the escarpment at intervals of a dozen yards, took the less cautious ones unawares, and losing their footing on the rubbly steep they slid sharply downwards, the lanterns rolling from their hands to the bottom, and there lying on their sides till the horn was scorched through.

When they had again gathered themselves together the shepherd, as the man who knew the country best, took the lead, and guided them round these treacherous inclines. The lanterns, which seemed rather to dazzle their eyes and warn the fugitive than to assist them in the exploration, were extinguished, due silence was observed; and in this more rational order they plunged into the vale. It was a grassy, briery, moist defile, affording some shelter to any person who had sought it; but the party perambulated it in vain, and ascended on the other side. Here they wandered apart, and after an interval closed together again to report progress. At the second time of closing in they found themselves near a lonely ash, the single tree on this part of the coomb, probably sown there by a passing bird some fifty years before. And here, standing a little to one side of the trunk, as motionless as the trunk itself, appeared the man they were in quest of, his outline being well defined against the sky beyond. The band noiselessly drew up and faced him.

"Your money or your life!" said the constable sternly to the still figure.

"No, no," whispered John Pitcher. " 'Tisn't our side ought to say that. That's the doctrine of vagabonds like him, and we be on the side of the law."

"Well, well," replied the constable impatiently; "I must say something, mustn't I? and if you had all the weight o' this undertaking upon your mind, perhaps you'd say the wrong thing too! —Prisoner at the bar, surrender, in the name of the Father—the Crown, I mane!"

The man under the tree seemed now to notice them for the first time, and, giving them no opportunity whatever for exhibiting their courage, he strolled slowly towards them. He was, indeed, the little man, the third stranger; but his trepidation had in a great measure gone.

"Well, travellers,' he said, 'did I hear ye speak to me?"

"You did: you've got to come and be our prisoner at once!" said the constable. "We arrest 'ee on the charge of not biding in Casterbridge jail in a decent proper manner to be hung to-morrow morning. Neighbours, do your duty, and seize the culpet!"

On hearing the charge the man seemed enlightened, and, saying not another word, resigned himself with preternatural civility to the search-party, who, with their staves in their hands, surrounded him on all sides, and marched him back towards the shepherd's cottage.

It was eleven o'clock by the time they arrived. The light shining from the open door, a sound of men's voices within, proclaimed to them as they approached the house that some new events had arisen in their absence. On entering they discovered the shepherd's living room to be invaded by two officers from Casterbridge jail, and a well-known magistrate who lived at the nearest country-seat, intelligence of the escape having become generally circulated.

"Gentlemen," said the constable, "I have brought back your man—not without risk and danger; but every one must do his duty! He is inside this circle of able-bodied persons, who have lent me useful aid, considering their ignorance of Crown work. Men, bring forward your prisoner!" And the third stranger was let to the light.

"Who is this?" said one of the officials.

"The man," said the constable.

"Certainly not," said the turnkey; and the first corroborated his statement.

"But how can it be otherwise?" asked the constable. "Or why was he so terrified at sight o' the singing instrument of the law who sat there?" Here he related the strange behaviour of the third stranger on entering the house during the hangman's song.

"Can't understand it," said the officer coolly. "All I know is that it is not the condemned man. He's quite a different character from this one; a gauntish fellow, with dark hair and eyes, rather good-looking, and with a musical bass voice that if you heard it once you'd never mistake as long as you lived."

"Why, souls—'twas the man in the chimney-corner!"

"Hey—what?" said the magistrate, coming forward after inquiring particulars from the shepherd in the background. "Haven't you got the man after all?"

"Well, sir," said the constable, "he's the man we were in search of, that's true; and yet he's not the man we were in search of. For the man we were in search of was not the man we wanted, sir, if you understand my every-day way; for 'twas the man in the chimney-corner!"

"A pretty kettle of fish altogether!" said the magistrate. "You had better start for the other man at once."

The prisoner now spoke for the first time. The mention of the man in the chimney-corner seemed to have moved him as nothing else could do. "Sir," he said, stepping forward to the magistrate, "take no more trouble about me. The time is come when I may as well speak. I have done nothing; my crime is that the condemned man is my brother. Early this afternoon I left home at Shottsford to tramp it all the way to Casterbridge jail to bid him farewell. I was benighted, and called here to rest and ask the way. When I opened the door I saw before me the very man, my brother, that I thought to see in the condemned cell at Casterbridge. He was in this chimney-corner; and jammed close to him, so that he could not have got out if he had tried, was the executioner who'd come to take his life, singing a song about it and not knowing that it was his victim who was close by, joining in to save appearances. My brother threw a glance of agony at me, and I knew he meant, 'Don't reveal what you see; my life depends on it.' I was so terror-struck that I could hardly stand, and, not knowing what I did, I turned and hurried away."

The narrator's manner and tone had the stamp of truth and his story made a great impression on all around. "And do you know where your brother is at the present time?" asked the magistrate.

"I do not. I have never seen him since I closed this door."

"I can testify to that, for we've been between ye ever since," said the constable.

"Where does he think to fly to? —what is his occupation?"

"He's a watch-and-clock-maker, sir."

"'A said 'a was a wheelwright—a wicked rouge," said the constable.

"The wheels of clocks and watches he meant, no doubt," said Shepherd Fennel. "I thought his hands were palish for's trade."

"Well, it appears to me that nothing can be gained by retaining this poor man in custody," said the magistrate: "your business lies with the other, unquestionably."

And so the little man was released off-hand; but he looked nothing the less sad on that account, it being beyond the power of magistrate or constable to raze out the written troubles in his brain, for they concerned another whom he regarded with more solicitude than himself. When this was done, and the man had gone his way, the night was found to be so far advanced that it was deemed useless to renew the search before the next morning.

Next day, accordingly, the quest for the clever sheep-stealer became general and keen, to all appearance at least. But the intended punishment was cruelly disproportioned to the transgression, and the sympathy of a great many country-folk in that district was strongly on the side of the fugitive. Moreover, his marvellous coolness and daring in hob-and-nobbing with the hangman, under the unprecedented circumstances of the shepherd's party, won their admiration. So that it may be questioned if all those who ostensibly made themselves so busy in exploring woods and fields and lanes were quite so thorough when it came to the private examination of their own lofts and out-houses. Stories were afloat of a mysterious figure being occasionally seen in some old overgrown trackway or other, remote from turnpike roads; but when a search was instituted in any of these suspected quarters nobody was found. Thus the days and weeks passed without tidings.

In brief, the bass-voiced man of the chimney-corner was never recaptured. Some said that he went across the sea, others that he did not, but buried himself in the depths of a populous city. At any rate, the gentleman in cinder-grey never did his morning's work at Casterbridge, nor met any where at all, for business purposes, the genial comrade with whom he had passed an hour of relaxation in the lonely house on the slope of the coomb.

The grass has long been green on the graves of Shepherd Fennel and his frugal wife; the guests who made up the christening party have mainly followed their entertainers to the tomb; the baby in whose honour they all had met is a matron in the sere and yellow leaf. But the arrival of the three strangers at the shepherd's that night, and the details connected therewith, is a story as well known as ever in the country about Higher Crowstairs.

ᵡᵉᵡᵉᵡᵉᵡᵉᵡᵉᵡᵉᵡᵉᵡᵉᵡᵉᵡᵉᵡᵉᵡᵉᵡᵉᵡᵉᵡᵉᵡᵉᵡᵉᵡᵉ

INTERLOPERS AT THE KNAP

I

The north road from Casterbridge is tedious and lonely, especially in winter-time. Along a part of its course it connects with Long-Ash Lane, a monotonous track without a village or hamlet for many miles, and with very seldom a turning. Unapprized wayfarers who are too old, or too young, or in other respects too weak for the distance to be traversed, but who, nevertheless, have to walk it, say, as they look wistfully ahead, "Once at the top of that hill, and I must·surely see the end of Long-Ash Lane!" But they reach the hilltop, and Long-Ash Lane stretches in front as mercilessly as before.

Some few years ago a certain farmer was riding through this lane in the gloom of a winter evening. The farmer's friend, a dairyman, was riding beside him. A few paces in the rear rode the farmer's man. All three were well horsed on strong, round-barrelled cobs; and to be well

horsed was to be in better spirits about Long-Ash Lane
than poor pedestrians could attain to during its passage.

But the farmer did not talk much to his friend as
he rode along. The enterprise which had brought him
there filled his mind; for in truth it was important. Not
altogether so important was it, perhaps, when estimated
by its value to society at large; but if the true measure of
a deed be proportionate to the space it occupies in the
heart of him who undertakes it, Farmer Charles Darton's
business to-night could hold its own with the business of
kings.

He was a large farmer. His turnover, as it is called,
was probably thirty thousand pounds a year. He had a
great many draught horses, a great many milch cows, and
of sheep a multitude. This comfortable position was, however, none of his own making. It had been created by his
father, a man of a very different stamp from the present
representative of the line.

Darton, the father, had been a one-idea'd character, with
a buttoned-up pocket and a chink-like eye brimming with
commercial subtlety. In Darton the son, this trade subtlety
had become transmuted into emotional, and the harshness had disappeared; he would have been called a sad
man but for his constant care not to divide himself from
lively friends by piping notes out of harmony with theirs.
Contemplative, he allowed his mind to be a quiet meeting-
place for memories and hopes. So that, naturally enough,
since succeeding to the agricultural calling, and up to his
present age of thirty-two, he had neither advanced nor
receded as a capitalist—a stationary result which did not
agitate one of his unambitious, unstrategic nature, since he
had all that he desired. The motive of his expedition
to-night showed the same absence of anxious regard for
Number One.

The party rode on in the slow, safe trot proper to
night-time and bad roads, Farmer Darton's head jigging
rather unromantically up and down against the sky, and
his motions being repeated with bolder emphasis by his
friend Japheth Johns; while those of the latter were

travestied in jerks still less softened by art in the person
of the lad who attended them. A pair of whitish objects
hung one on each side of the latter, bumping against him
at each step, and still further spoiling the grace of his
seat. On close inspection they might have been perceived
to be open rush baskets—one containing a turkey, and
the other some bottles of wine.

"D'ye feel ye can meet your fate like a man, neighbour
Darton?" asked Johns, breaking a silence which had lasted
while five-and-twenty hedgerow trees had glided by.

Mr. Darton with a half-laugh murmured, "Ay—call
it my fate! Hanging and wiving go by destiny." And then
they were silent again.

The darkness thickened rapidly, at intervals shutting
down on the land in a perceptible flap, like the wave of
a wing. The customary close of day was accelerated by
a simultaneous blurring of the air. With the fall of night
had come a mist just damp enough to incommode, but
not sufficient to saturate them. Countrymen as they were—
born, as may be said, with only an open door between them
and the four seasons—they regarded the mist but as an
added obscuration, and ignored its humid quality.

They were travelling in a direction that was enlivened
by no modern current of traffic, the place of Darton's
pilgrimage being an old-fashioned village—one of the
Hintocks (several villages of that name, with a distinctive
prefix or affix, lying thereabout)—where the people make
the best cider and cider-wine in all Wessex, and where
the dunghills smell of pomace instead of stable refuse
as elsewhere. The lane was sometimes so narrow that the
brambles of the hedge, which hung forward like anglers'
rods over a stream, scratched their hats and hooked their
whiskers as they passed. Yet this neglected lane had been
a highway to Queen Elizabeth's subjects and the cavalcades
of the past. Its day was over now, and its history as a
national artery done for ever.

"Why I have decided to marry her," resumed Darton
(in a measured musical voice of confidence which revealed
a good deal of his composition), as he glanced round to

see that the lad was not too near, "is not only that I like her, but that I can do no better, even from a fairly practical point of view. That I might ha' looked higher is possibly true, though it is really all nonsense. I have had experience enough in looking above me. 'No more superior women for me,' said I—you know when. Sally is a comely, independent, simple character, with no make-up about her, who'll think me as much a superior to her as I used to think—you know who I mean—was to me."

"Ay," said Johns. "However, I shouldn't call Sally Hall simple. Primary, because no Sally is; secondary, because if some could be, this one wouldn't. 'Tis a wrong denomination to apply to a woman, Charles, and affects me, as your best man, like cold water. 'Tis like recommending a stage play by saying there's neither murder, villainy, nor harm of any sort in it, when that's what you've paid your half-crown to see."

"Well; may your opinion do you good. Mine's a different one." And turning the conversation from the philosophical to the practical, Darton expressed a hope that the said Sally had received what he'd sent on by the carrier that day.

Johns wanted to know what that was.

"It is a dress," said Darton. "Not exactly a wedding-dress; though she may use it as one if she likes. It is rather serviceable than showy—suitable for the winter weather."

"Good," said Johns. "Serviceable is a wise word in a bridgegroom. I commend 'ee, Charles."

"For," said Darton, "why should a woman dress up like a rope-dancer because she's going to do the most solemn deed of her life except dying?"

"Faith, why? But she will, because she will, I suppose," said Dairyman Johns.

"H'm," said Darton.

The lane they followed had been nearly straight for several miles, but they now left it for a smaller one which after winding uncertainly for some distance forked into two. By night country roads are apt to reveal ungainly qualities which pass without observation during day; and though Darton had travelled this way before, he had not done so frequently, Sally having been wooed at the house of a relative near his own. He never remembered seeing at this spot a pair of alternative ways looking so equally probable as these two did now. Johns rode on a few steps.

"Don't be out of heart, sonny," he cried. "Here's a hand-post. Ezra—come and climb this post, and tell us the way."

The lad dismounted, and jumped into the hedge where the post stood under a tree.

"Unstrap the baskets, or you'll smash up that wine!" cried Darton, as the young man began spasmodically to climb the post, baskets and all.

"Was there ever less head in a brainless world?" said Johns. "Here, simple Ezzy, I'll do it." He leapt off, and with much puffing climbed the post, striking a match when he reached the top, and moving the light along the arm, the lad standing and gazing at the spectacle.

"I have faced tantalization these twenty years with a temper as mild as milk!" said Japheth; "but such things as this don't come short of devilry!" And flinging the match away, he slipped down to the ground.

"What's the matter?" asked Darton.

"Not a letter, sacred or heathen—not so much as would tell us the way to the town of Smokeyhole—ever I should sin to say it! Either the moss and mildew have eat away the words, or we have arrived in a land where the natyves have lost the art o' writing, and should ha' brought our compass like Christopher Columbus."

"Let us take the straightest road," said Darton placidly; "I shan't be sorry to get there—'tis a tiresome ride. I would have driven if I had known."

"Nor I neither, sir," said Ezra. "These straps plough my shoulder like a zull. If 'tis much further to your lady's home, Maister Darton, I shall ask to be let carry half of these good things in my innerds—hee, hee!"

"Don't you be such a reforming radical, Ezra," said Johns sternly. "Here, I'll take the turkey."

This being done, they went forward by the right-hand lane, which ascended a hill, the left winding away under a plantation. The pit-a-pat of their horses' hoofs lessened up the slope; and the ironical directing-post stood in solitude as before, holding out its blank arms to the raw breeze, which brought a snore from the wood as if Skrymir the Giant were sleeping there.

II

Three miles to the left of the travellers, along the road they had not followed, rose an old house with mullioned windows of Ham-hill stone, and chimneys of lavish solidity. It stood at the top of a slope beside King's-Hintock village-street, only a mile or two from King's-Hintock Court, yet quite shut away from that mansion and its precincts. Immediately in front of it grew a large sycamore tree, whose bared roots formed a convenient staircase from the road below to the front door of the dwelling. Its situation gave the house what little distinctive name it possessed, namely, "The Knap." Some forty yards off a brook dribbled past, which, for its size, made a great deal of noise. At the back was a dairy barton, accessible for vehicles and live-stock by a side "drong." Thus much only of the character of the homestead could be divined out of doors at this shady evening-time.

But within there was plenty of light to see by, as plenty was construed at Hintock. Beside a Tudor fireplace, whose moulded four-centred arch was nearly hidden by a figured blue-cloth blower, were seated two women—mother and daughter—Mrs. Hall, and Sarah, or Sally; for this was a part of the world where the latter modification had not as yet been effaced as a vulgarity by the march of intellect. The owner of the name was the young woman by whose means Mr. Darton proposed to put an end to his bachelor condition on the approaching day.

The mother's bereavement had been so long ago as not to leave much mark of its occurrence upon her now, either in face or clothes. She had resumed the mob-cap of her early married life, enlivening its whiteness by a few rose-du-Barry ribbons. Sally required no such aids to pinkness. Roseate good-nature lit up her gaze; her features showed curves of decision and judgment; and she might have been regarded without much mistake as a warm-hearted, quick-spirited, handsome girl.

She did most of the talking, her mother listening with a half-absent air, as she picked up fragments of red-hot wood ember with the tongs, and piled them upon the brands. But the number of speeches that passed was very small in proportion to the meanings exchanged. Long experience together often enabled them to see the course of thought in each other's minds without a word being spoken. Behind them, in the centre of the room, the table was spread for supper, certain whiffs of air laden with fat vapours, which ever and anon entered from the kitchen, denoting its preparation there.

"The new gown he was going to send you stays about on the way like himself," Sally's mother was saying.

"Yes, not finished, I daresay," cried Sally independently. "Lord, I shouldn't be amazed if it didn't come at all! Young men make such kind promises when they are near you, and forget 'em when they go away. But he doesn't intend it as a wedding-gown—he gives it to me merely as a gown to wear when I like—a travelling-dress is what it would be called by some. Come rathe or come late it don't much matter, as I have a dress of my own to fall back upon. But what time is it?"

She went to the family clock and opened the glass, for the hour was not otherwise discernible by night, and indeed at all times was rather a thing to be investigated than beheld, so much more wall than window was there in the apartment. "It is nearly eight," said she.

"Eight o'clock, and neither dress nor man," said Mrs. Hall.

"Mother, if you think to tantalize me by talking like that, you are much mistaken! Let him be as late as he will —or stay away altogether—I don't care," said Sally. But a tender, minute quaver in the negation showed that there was something forced in that statement.

Mrs. Hall perceived it, and drily observed that she was not so sure about Sally not caring. "But perhaps you don't care so much as I do, after all," she said. "For I see what

you don't, that it is a good and flourishing match for you;
a very honourable offer in Mr. Darton. And I think I see a
kind husband in him. So pray God 'twill go smooth, and
wind up well."

Sally would not listen to misgivings. Of course it would
go smoothly, she asserted. "How you are up and down,
mother!" she went on. "At this moment, whatever hinders
him, we are not so anxious to see him as he is to be
here, and his thought runs on before him, and settles
down upon us like the star in the east. Hark!" she exclaimed, with a breath of relief, her eyes sparkling. "I
heard something. Yes—here they are!"

The next moment her mother's slower ear also distinguished the familiar reverberation occasioned by footsteps
clambering up the roots of the sycamore.

"Yes it sounds like them at last," she said. "Well, it is
not so very late after all, considering the distance."

The footfall ceased, and they arose, expecting a knock.
They began to think it might have been, after all, some
neighbouring villager under Bacchic influence, giving the
centre of the road a wide berth, when their doubts were
dispelled by the new-comer's entry into the passage. The
door of the room was gently opened, and there appeared,
not the pair of travellers with whom we have already
made acquaintance, but a pale-faced man in the garb of
extreme poverty—almost in rags.

"O, it's a tramp—gracious me!" said Sally, starting back.

His cheeks and eye-orbits were deep concaves—rather,
it might be, from natural weakness of constitution than
irregular living, though there were indications that he had
led no careful life. He gazed at the two women fixedly for
a moment: then with an abashed, humiliated demeanour,
dropped his glance to the floor, and sank into a chair
without uttering a word.

Sally was in advance of her mother, who had remained
standing by the fire. She now tried to discern the visitor
across the candles.

"Why—mother," said Sally faintly, turning back to Mrs.
Hall. "It is Phil, from Australia!"

Mrs. Hall started, and grew pale, and a fit of coughing

seized the man with the ragged clothes. "To come home like this!" she said. "O, Philip—are you ill?"

"No, no, mother," replied he impatiently, as soon as he could speak.

"But for God's sake how do you come here—and just now too?"

"Well, I am here," said the man. "How it is I hardly know. I've come home, mother, because I was driven to it. Things were against me out there, and went from bad to worse."

"Then why didn't you let us know?—you've not writ a line for the last two or three years."

The son admitted sadly that he had not. He said that he had hoped and thought he might fetch up again, and be able to send good news. Then he had been obliged to abandon that hope, and had finally come home from sheer necessity—previously to making a new start. "Yes, things are very bad with me," he repeated, perceiving their commiserating glances at his clothes.

They brought him nearer the fire, took his hat from his thin hand, which was so small and smooth as to show that his attempts to fetch up again had not been in a manual direction. His mother resumed her inquiries, and dubiously asked if he had chosen to come that particular night for any special reason.

For no reason, he told her. His arrival had been quite at random. Then Philip Hall looked round the room, and saw for the first time that the table was laid somewhat luxuriously, and for a larger number than themselves; and that an air of festivity pervaded their dress. He asked quickly what was going on.

"Sally is going to be married in a day or two," replied the mother; and she explained how Mr. Darton, Sally's intended husband, was coming there that night with the groomsman, Mr. Johns, and other details. "We thought it must be their step when we heard you," said Mrs. Hall.

The needy wanderer looked again on the floor. "I see— I see," he murmured. "Why, indeed, should I have come to-night? Such folk as I are not wanted here at these times, naturally. And I have no business here—spoiling other people's happiness."

"Phil," said his mother, with a tear in her eye, but with a thinness of lip and severity of manner which were presumably not more than past events justified; "since you speak like that to me, I'll speak honestly to you. For these three years you have taken no thought for us. You left home with a good supply of money, and strength and education, and you ought to have made good use of it all. But you come back like a beggar; and that you come in a very awkward time for us cannot be denied. Your return to-night may do us much harm. But mind— you are welcome to this home as long as it is mine. I don't wish to turn you adrift. We will make the best of a bad job; and I hope you are not seriously ill?"

"O no. I have only this infernal cough."

She looked at him anxiously. "I think you had better go to bed at once," she said.

"Well—I shall be out of the way there," said the son wearily. "Having ruined myself, don't let me ruin you by being seen in these togs, for Heaven's sake. Who do you say Sally is going to be married to—a Farmer Darton?"

"Yes—a gentleman-farmer—quite a wealthy man. Far better in station than she could have expected. It is a good thing, altogether."

"Well done, little Sal!" said her brother, brightening and looking up at her with a smile. "I ought to have written; but perhaps I have thought of you all the more. But let me get out of sight. I would rather go and jump into the river than be seen here. But have you anything I can drink? I am confoundedly thirsty with my long tramp."

"Yes, yes, we will bring something upstairs to you," said Sally, with grief in her face.

"Ay, that will do nicely. But, Sally and mother—" He stopped, and they waited. "Mother, I have not told you all," he resumed slowly, still looking on the floor between his knees. "Sad as what you see of me is, there's worse behind."

His mother gazed upon him in grieved suspense, and Sally went and leant upon the bureau, listening for every sound, and sighing. Suddenly she turned round, saying, "Let them come, I don't care! Philip, tell the worst, and take your time."

"Well, then," said the unhappy Phil, "I am not the only one in this mess. Would do Heaven I were! But——"

"O, Phil!"

"I have a wife as destitute as I."

"A wife?" said his mother.

"Unhappily!"

"A wife! Yes, that is the way with sons!"

"And besides——" said he.

"Besides! O, Philip, surely——"

"I have two little children."

"Wife and children!" whispered Mrs. Hall, sinking down confounded.

"Poor little things!" said Sally involuntarily.

His mother turned again to him. "I suppose these helpless beings are left in Australia?"

"No. They are in England."

"Well, I can only hope you've left them in a respectable place."

"I have not left them at all. They are here—within a few yards of us. In short, they are in the stable."

"Where?"

"In the stable. I did not like to bring them indoors till I had seen you, mother, and broken the bad news a bit to you. They were very tired, and are resting out there on some straw."

Mrs. Hall's fortitude visibly broken down. She had been brought up not without refinement, and was even more moved by such a collapse of genteel aims as this than a substantial dairyman's widow would in ordinary have been moved. "Well, it must be borne," she said, in a low voice, with her hands tightly joined. "A starving son, a starving wife, starving children! Let it be. But why is this come to us now, to-day, to-night? Could no other misfortune happen to helpless women than this, which will quite upset my poor girl's chance of a happy life? Why have you done us this wrong, Philip? What respectable man will come here, and marry open-eyed into a family of vagabonds?"

"Nonsense, mother!" said Sally vehemently, while her face flushed. ""Charley isn't the man to desert me. But if he should be, and won't marry me because Phil's come, let him go and marry elsewhere. I won't be ashamed of my own flesh and blood for any man in England—not I!" And then Sally turned away and burst into tears.

"Wait till you are twenty years older and you will tell a different tale," replied her mother.

The son stood up. "Mother," he said bitterly, "as I have come, so I will go. All I ask of you is that you will allow me and mine to lie in your stable to-night. I give you my word that we'll be gone by break of day, and trouble you no further!"

Mrs. Hall, the mother, changed at that. "O no," she answered hastily; "never shall it be said that I sent any of my own family from my door. Bring 'em in, Philip, or take me out to them."

"We will put 'em all into the large bedroom," said Sally, brightening, "and make up a large fire. Let's go and help them in, and call Rebekah." (Rebekah was the woman who assisted at the dairy and housework; she lived in a cottage hard by with her husband, who attended to the cows.)

Sally went to fetch a lantern from the back-kitchen, but her brother said, "You won't want a light. I lit the lantern that was hanging there."

"What must we call your wife?" asked Mrs. Hall.

"Helena," said Philip.

With shawls over their heads they proceeded towards the back door.

"One minute before you go," interrupted Philip. "I— I haven't confessed all."

"Then Heaven help us!" said Mrs. Hall, pushing to the door and clasping her hands in calm despair.

"We passed through Evershead as we came," he con-

tinued, "and I just looked in at the 'Sow-and-Acorn' to
see if old Mike still kept on there as usual. The carrier had
come in from Sherton Abbas at that moment, and guessing that I was bound for this place—for I think he knew
me—he asked me to bring on a dressmaker's parcel for
Sally that was marked 'immediate.' My wife had walked
on with the children. 'Twas a flimsy parcel, and the paper
was torn, and I found on looking at it that it was a
thick warm gown. I didn't wish you to see poor Helena
in a shabby state. I was ashamed that you should—'twas
not what she was born to. I untied the parcel in the road,
took it on to her where she was waiting in the Lower Barn,
and told her I had managed to get it for her, and that
she was to ask no question. She, poor thing, must have
supposed I obtained it on trust, through having reached
a place where I was known, for she put it on gladly enough.
She has it on now. Sally has other gowns, I daresay."

Sally looked at her mother, speechless.

"You have others, I daresay!" repeated Phil, with a
sick man's impatience. "I thought to myself, 'Better Sally
cry than Helena freeze.' Well, is the dress of great consequence? 'Twas nothing very ornamental, as far as I
could see."

"No—no; not of consequence," returned Sally sadly,
adding in a gentle voice, "You will not mind if I lend
her another instead of that one, will you?"

Philip's agitation at the confession had brought on
another attack of the cough, which seemed to shake him
to pieces. He was so obviously unfit to sit in a chair that
they helped him upstairs at once; and having hastily given
him a cordial and kindled the bedroom fire, they descended
to fetch their unhappy new relations.

III

It was with strange feelings that the girl and her mother,
lately so cheerful, passed out of the back door into the
open air of the barton, laden with hay scents and the
herby breath of cows. A fine sleet had begun to fall, and

they trotted across the yard quickly. The stable-door was open; a light shone from it—from the lantern which always hung there, and which Philip had lighted, as he said. Softly nearing the door, Mrs. Hall pronounced the name "Helena!"

There was no answer for the moment. Looking in she was taken by surprise. Two people appeared before her. For one, instead of the drabbish woman she had expected, Mrs. Hall saw a pale, dark-eyed, ladylike creature, whose personality ruled her attire rather than was ruled by it. She was in a new and handsome gown, Sally's own, and an old bonnet. She was standing up, agitated; her hand was held by her companion—none else than Sally's affianced, Farmer Charles Darton, upon whose fine figure the pale stranger's eyes were fixed, as his were fixed upon her. His other hand held the rein of his horse, which was standing saddled as if just led in.

At sight of Mrs. Hall they both turned, looking at her in a way neither quite conscious nor unconscious, and without seeming to recollect that words were necessary as a solution to the scene. In another moment Sally entered also, when Mr. Darton dropped his companion's hand, led the horse aside, and came to greet his betrothed and Mrs. Hall.

"Ah!" he said, smiling—with something like forced composure—"this is a roundabout way of arriving, you will say, my dear Mrs. Hall. But we lost our way, which made us late. I saw a light here, and led in my horse at once— my friend Johns and my man have gone onward to the little inn with theirs, not to crowd you too much. No sooner had I entered than I saw that this lady had taken temporary shelter here—and found I was intruding."

"She is my daughter-in-law," said Mrs. Hall calmly. "My son, too, is in the house, but he has gone to bed unwell."

Sally had stood staring wonderingly at the scene until this moment, hardly recognizing Darton's shake of the hand. The spell that bound her was broken by her perceiving the two little children seated on a heap of hay.

She suddenly went forward, spoke to them, and took one on her arm and the other in her hand.

"And two children?" said Mr. Darton, showing thus that he had not been there long enough as yet to understand the situation.

"My grandchildren," said Mrs. Hall, with as much affected ease as before.

Philip Hall's wife, in spite of this interruption to her first rencounter, seemed scarcely so much affected by it as to feel any one's presence in addition to Mr. Darton's. However, arousing herself by a quick reflection, she threw a sudden critical glance of her sad eyes upon Mrs. Hall; and, apparently finding her satisfactory, advanced to her in a meek initiative. Then Sally and the stranger spoke some friendly words to each other, and Sally went on with the children into the house. Mrs. Hall and Helena followed, and Mr. Darton followed these, looking at Helena's dress and outline, and listening to her voice like a man in a dream.

By the time the others reached the house Sally had already gone upstairs with the tired children. She rapped against the wall for Rebekah to come in and help to attend to them, Rebekah's house being a little "spit-and-daub" cabin leaning against the substantial stonework of Mrs. Hall's taller erection. When she came a bed was made up for the little ones, and some supper given to them. On descending the stairs after seeing this done Sally went to the sitting-room. Young Mrs. Hall entered it just in advance of her, having in the interim retired with her mother-in-law to take off her bonnet, and otherwise make herself presentable. Hence it was evident that no further communication could have passed between her and Mr. Darton since their brief interview in the stable.

Mr. Japheth Johns now opportunely arrived, and broke up the restraint of the company, after a few orthodox meteorological commentaries had passed between him and Mrs. Hall by way of introduction. They at once sat down to supper, the present of wine and turkey not being produced for consumption tonight, lest the premature display of those gifts should seem to throw doubt on Mrs. Hall's capacities as a provider.

"Drink hearty, Mr. Johns—drink hearty," said that matron magnanimously. "Such as it is there's plenty of. But perhaps cider-wine is not to your taste?—though there's body in it."

"Quite the contrairy, ma'am—quite the contrairy," said the dairyman. "For though I inherit the malt-liquor principle from my father, I am a cider-drinker on my mother's side. She came from these parts, you know. And there's this to be said for't—'tis a more peaceful liquor, and don't lie about a man like your hotter drinks. With care, one may live on it a twelve month without knocking down a neighbour, or getting a black eye from an old acquaintance."

The general conversation thus begun was continued briskly, though it was in the main restricted to Mrs. Hall and Japheth, who in truth required but little help from anybody. There being slight call upon Sally's tongue, she had ample leisure to do what her heart most desired, namely, watch her intended husband and her sister-in-law with a view of elucidating the strange momentary scene in which her mother and herself had surprised them in the stable. If that scene meant anything, it meant, at least, that they had met before. That there had been no time for explanations Sally could see, for their manner was still one of suppressed amazement at each other's presence there. Darton's eyes, too, fell continually on the gown worn by Helena as if this were an added riddle to his perplexity; though to Sally it was the one feature in the case which was no mystery. He seemed to feel that fate had impishly changed his *vis-à-vis* in the lover's jig he was about to foot; that while the gown had been expected to enclose a Sally, a Helena's face looked out from the bodice; that some long-lost hand met his own from the sleeves.

Sally could see that whatever Helena might know of Darton, she knew nothing of how the dress entered into his embarrassment. And at moments the young girl would have persuaded herself that Darton's looks at her sister-in-law were entirely the fruit of the clothes query. But surely at other times a more extensive range of speculation and sentiment was expressed by her lover's eye than that which the changed dress would account for.

Sally's independence made her one of the least jealous of women. But there was something in the relations of these two visitors which ought to be explained.

Japheth Johns continued to converse in his well-known style, interspersing his talk with some private reflections on the position of Darton and Sally, which, though the sparkle in his eye showed them to be highly entertaining to himself, were apparently not quite communicable to the company. At last he withdrew for the night, going off to the roadside inn half-a-mile ahead, whither Darton promised to follow him in a few minutes.

Half-an-hour passed, and then Mr. Darton also rose to leave, Sally and her sister-in-law simultaneously wishing him good-night as they retired upstairs to their rooms. But on his arriving at the front door with Mrs. Hall a sharp shower of rain began to come down, when the widow suggested that he should return to the fireside till the storm ceased.

Darton accepted her proposal, but insisted that, as it was getting late, and she was obviously tired, she should not sit up on his account, since he could let himself out of the house, and would quite enjoy smoking a pipe by the hearth alone. Mrs. Hall assented; and Darton was left by himself. He spread his knees to the brands, lit up his tobacco as he had said, and sat gazing into the fire, and at the notches of the chimney-crook which hung above.

An occasional drop of rain rolled down the chimney with a hiss, and still he smoked on; but not like a man whose mind was at rest. In the long run, however, despite his meditations, early hours afield and a long ride in the open air produced their natural result. He began to doze.

How long he remained in this half-unconscious state he did not know. He suddenly opened his eyes. The back-brand had burnt itself in two, and ceased to flame; the light which he had placed on the mantelpiece had nearly gone out. But in spite of these deficiencies there was a light in the apartment, and it came from elsewhere. Turning his head he saw Philip Hall's wife standing at the entrance of the room with a bed-candle in one hand, a small brass tea-kettle in the other, and *his* gown, as it certainly seemed, still upon her.

"Helena!" said Darton, starting up.

Her countenance expressed dismay, and her first words were an apology. "I—did not know you were here, Mr. Darton," she said, while a blush flashed to her cheek. "I thought every one had retired—I was coming to make a little water boil; my husband seems to be worse. But perhaps the kitchen fire can be lighted up again."

"Don't go on my account. By all means put it on here as you intended," said Darton. "Allow me to help you." He went forward to take the kettle from her hand, but she did not allow him, and placed it on the fire herself.

They stood some way apart, one on each side of the fireplace, waiting till the water should boil, the candle on the mantel between them, and Helena with her eyes on the kettle. Darton was the first to break the silence. "Shall I call Sally?" he said.

"O no," she quickly returned. "We have given trouble enough already. We have no right here. But we are the sport of fate, and were obliged to come."

"No right here!" said he in surprise.

"None. I can't explain it now," answered Helena. "This kettle is very slow."

There was another pause; the proverbial dilatoriness of watched pots was never more clearly exemplified.

Helena's face was of that sort which seems to ask for assistance without the owner's knowledge—the very antipodes of Sally's, which was self-reliance expressed. Darton's eyes travelled from the kettle to Helena's face, then back to the kettle, then to the face for rather a longer time. "So I am not to know anything of the mystery that has distracted me all the evening?" he said. "How is it that a woman, who refused me because (as I supposed) my

position was not good enough for her taste, is found to
be the wife of a man who certainly seems to be worse
off than I?"

"He had the prior claim," said she.

"What! you knew him at that time?"

"Yes, yes! And he went to Australia, and sent for me,
and I joined him out there!"

"Ah—that was the mystery!"

"Please say no more," she implored. "Whatever my
errors, I have paid for them during the last five years!"

The heart of Darton was subject to sudden overflowings.
He was kind to a fault. "I am sorry from my soul," he
said, involuntarily approaching her. Helena withdrew a
step or two, at which he became conscious of his movement, and quickly took his former place. Here he stood
without speaking, and the little kettle began to sing.

"Well, you might have been my wife if you had chosen,"
he said at last. "But that's all past and gone. However, if
you are in any trouble or poverty I shall be glad to be
of service, and as your relation by marriage I shall have
a right to be. Does your uncle know of your distress?"

"My uncle is dead. He left me without a farthing. And
now we have two children to maintain."

"What, left you nothing? How could he be so cruel
as that?"

"I disgraced myself in his eyes."

"Now," said Darton earnestly, "let me take care of
the children, at least while you are so unsettled. *You* belong
to another, so I cannot take care of you."

"Yes you can," said a voice; and suddenly a third figure
stood beside them. It was Sally. "You can, since you
seem to wish to?" she repeated. "She no longer belongs
to another. . . . My poor brother is dead!"

Her face was red, her eyes sparkled, and all the woman
came to the front. "I have heard it!" she went on to him
passionately. "You can protect her now as well as the
children!" She turned then to her agitated sister-in-law.
"I heard something," said Sally (in a gentle murmur, differing much from her previous passionate words), "and

I went into his room. It must have been the moment you left. He went off so quickly, and weakly, and it was so unexpected, that I couldn't leave even to call you."

Darton was just able to gather from the confused discourse which followed that, during his sleep by the fire, Sally's brother whom he had never seen had become worse; and that during Helena's absence for water the end had unexpectedly come. The two young women hastened upstairs, and he was again left alone.

After standing there a short time he went to the front door and looked out; till, softly closing it behind him, he advanced and stood under the large sycamore-tree. The stars were flickering coldly, and the dampness which had just descended upon the earth in rain now sent up a chill from it. Darton was in a strange position, and he felt it. The unexpected appearance, in deep poverty, of Helena— a young lady, daughter of a deceased naval officer, who had been brought up by her uncle, a solicitor, and had refused Darton in marriage years ago—the passionate, almost angry demeanour of Sally at discovering them, the abrupt announcement that Helena was a widow; all this coming together was a conjuncture difficult to cope with in a moment, and made him question whether he ought to leave the house or offer assistance. But for Sally's manner he would unhesitatingly have done the latter.

He was still standing under the tree when the door in front of him opened, and Mrs. Hall came out. She went round to the garden-gate at the side without seeing him. Darton followed her, intending to speak. Pausing outside, as if in thought, she proceeded to a spot where the sun came earliest in spring-time, and where the north wind never blew; it was where the row of beehives stood under the wall. Discerning her object, he waited till she had accomplished it.

It was the universal custom thereabout to wake the bees by tapping at their hives whenever a death occurred in the household, under the belief that if this were not done the bees themselves would pine away and perish during

the ensuing year. As soon as an interior buzzing responded
to her tap at the first hive Mrs. Hall went on to the
second, and thus passed down the row. As soon as she
came back he met her.

"What can I do in this trouble, Mrs. Hall?" he said.

"O—nothing, thank you, nothing," she said in a tearful
voice, now just perceiving him. "We have called Rebekah
and her husband, and they will do everything necessary."
She told him in a few words the particulars of her son's
arrival, broken in health—indeed, at death's very door,
though they did not suspect it—and suggested, as the result
of a conversation between her and her daughter, that the
wedding should be postponed.

"Yes, of course," said Darton. "I think now to go
straight to the inn and tell Johns what has happened." It
was not till after he had shaken hands with her that he
turned hesitatingly and added, "Will you tell the mother
of his children that, as they are now left fatherless, I shall
be glad to take the eldest of them, if it would be any
convenience to her and to you?"

Mrs. Hall promised that her son's widow should be
told of the offer, and they parted. He retired down the
rooty slope and disappeared in the direction of the inn,
where he informed Johns of the circumstances. Meanwhile
Mrs. Hall had entered the house. Sally was downstairs in
the sitting-room alone, and her mother explained to her
that Darton had readily assented to the postponement.

"No doubt he has," said Sally, with sad emphasis. "It
is not put off for a week, or a month, or a year. I shall
never marry him, and she will!"

IV

Time passed, and the household on the Knap became again
serene under the composing influences of daily routine. A
desultory, very desultory correspondence, dragged on
between Sally Hall and Darton, who, not quite knowing
how to take her petulant words on the night of her
brother's death, had continued passive thus long. Helena

and her children remained at the dairy-house, almost of
necessity, and Darton therefore deemed it advisable to
stay away.

One day, seven months later on, when Mr. Darton was
as usual at his farm, twenty miles from King's-Hintock, a
note reached him from Helena. She thanked him for his
kind offer about her children, which her mother-in-law
had duly communicated, and stated that she would be
glad to accept it as regarded the eldest, the boy. Helena
had, in truth, good need to do so, for her uncle had left
her penniless, and all application to some relatives in the
north had failed. There was, besides, as she said, no good
school near Hintock to which she could send the child.

On a fine summer day the boy came. He was accompanied half-way by Sally and his mother—to the "White
Horse," the fine old Elizabethan inn at Chalk Newton,*
where he was handed over to Darton's bailiff in a shining
spring-cart, who met them there.

He was entered as a day-scholar at a popular school at
Casterbridge, three or four miles from Darton's, having
first been taught by Darton to ride a forest-pony, on which
he cantered to and from the aforesaid fount of knowledge,
and (as Darton hoped) brought away a promising headful
of the same at each diurnal expedition. The thoughtful
taciturnity into which Darton had latterly fallen was quite
dissipated by the presence of this boy.

When the Christmas holidays came it was arranged that
he should spend them with his mother. The journey was,
for some reason or other, performed in two stages, as
at his coming, except that Darton in person took the
place of the bailiff, and that the boy and himself rode on
horseback.

Reaching the renowned "White Horse," Darton inquired
if Miss and young Mrs. Hall were there to meet little
Philip (as they had agreed to be). He was answered by
the appearance of Helena alone at the door.

    * It is now pulled down, and its site occupied by a modern one
in red brick (1912).—T.H.

"At the last moment Sally would not come," she faltered.

That meeting practically settled the point towards which these long-severed persons were converging. But nothing was broached about it for some time yet. Sally Hall had, in fact, imparted the first decisive motion to events by refusing to accompany Helena. She soon gave them a second move by writing the following note:—

[*Private.*]

DEAR CHARLES,—Living here so long and intimately with Helena, I have naturally learnt her history, especially that of it which refers to you. I am sure she would accept you as a husband at the proper time, and I think you ought to give her the opportunity. You inquire in an old note if I am sorry that I showed temper (which it *wasn't*) that night when I heard you talking to her. No, Charles, I am not sorry at all for what I said then.—Yours sincerely,

SALLY HALL.

Thus set in train, the transfer of Darton's heart back to its original quarters proceeded by mere lapse of time. In the following July, Darton went to his friend Japheth to ask him at last to fulfil the bridal office which had been in abeyance since the previous January twelvemonths.

"With all my heart, man o' constancy!" said Dairyman Johns warmly. "I've lost most of my genteel fair complexion haymaking this hot weather, 'tis true, but I'll do your business as well as them that look better. There be scents and good hair-oil in the world yet, thank God, and they'll take off the roughest o' my edge. I'll compliment her. 'Better late than never, Sally Hall,' I'll say."

"It is not Sally," said Darton hurriedly. "It is young Mrs. Hall."

Japheth's face, as soon as he really comprehended, became a picture of reproachful dismay. "Not Sally?" he said. "Why not Sally? I can't believe it! Young Mrs. Hall! Well, well—where's your wisdom?"

Darton shortly explained particulars; but Johns would not be reconciled. "She was a woman worth having if ever woman was," he cried. "And now to let her go!"

"But I suppose I can marry where I like," said Darton.

"H'm," replied the dairyman, lifting his eyebrows expressively. "This don't become you, Charles—it really do not. If I had done such a thing you would have sworn I was a curst no'thern fool to be drawn off the scent by such a red-herring doll-oll-oll."

Farmer Darton responded in such sharp terms to this laconic opinion that the two friends finally parted in a way they had never parted before. Johns was to be no groomsman to Darton after all. He had flatly declined. Darton went off sorry, and even unhappy, particularly as Japheth was about to leave that side of the county, so that the words which had divided them were not likely to be explained away or softened down.

A short time after the interview Darton was united to Helena at a simple matter-of-fact wedding; and she and her little girl joined the boy who had already grown to look on Darton's house as home.

For some months the farmer experienced an unprecedented happiness and satisfaction. There had been a flaw in his life, and it was as neatly mended as was humanly possible. But after a season the stream of events followed less clearly, and there were shades in his reveries. Helena was a fragile woman, of little staying power, physically or morally, and since the time that he had originally known her—eight or ten years before—she had been severely tried. She had loved herself out, in short, and was now occasionally given to moping. Sometimes she spoke regretfully of the gentilities of her early life, and instead of comparing her present state with her condition as the wife of the unlucky Hall, she mused rather on what it had been before she took the first fatal step of clandestinely marrying him. She did not care to please such people as those with whom she was thrown as a thriving farmer's wife. She allowed the pretty trifles of agricultural domesticity to glide by her as sorry details, and had it not been for the children Darton's house would have seemed but little brighter than it had been before.

This led to occasional unpleasantness, until Darton sometimes declared to himself that such endeavours as his to rectify early deviations of the heart by harking back to the old point mostly failed of success. "Perhaps Johns was right," he would say. "I should have gone on with Sally. Better go with the tide and make the best of its course than stem it at the risk of a capsize." But he kept these unmelodious thoughts to himself, and was outwardly considerate and kind.

This somewhat barren tract of his life had extended to less than a year and half when his ponderings were cut short by the loss of the woman they concerned. When she was in her grave he thought better of her than when she had been alive; the farm was a worse place without her than with her, after all. No woman short of divine could have gone through such an experience as hers with her first husband without becoming a little soured. Her stagnant sympathies, her sometimes unreasonable manner, had covered a heart frank and well meaning, and originally hopeful and warm. She left him a tiny red infant in white wrappings. To make life as easy as possible to this touching object became at once his care.

As this child learnt to walk and talk Darton learnt to see feasibility in a scheme which pleased him. Revolving the experiment which he had hitherto made upon life, he fancied he had gained wisdom from his mistakes and caution from his miscarriages.

What the scheme was needs no penetration to discover. Once more he had opportunity to recast and rectify his ill-wrought situations by returning to Sally Hall, who still lived quietly on under her mother's roof at Hintock. Helena had been a woman to lend pathos and refinement to a home; Sally was the woman to brighten it. She would not, as Helena did, despise the rural simplicities of a farmer's fireside. Moreover, she had a pre-eminent qualification for Darton's household; no other woman could make so desirable a mother to her brother's two children and Darton's one as Sally—while Darton, now that Helena had gone, was a more promising husband for Sally than he had ever been when liable to reminders from an uncured sentimental wound.

Darton was not a man to act rapidly, and the working out of his reparative designs might have been delayed for some time. But there came a winter evening precisely like the one which had darkened over that former ride to Hintock, and he asked himself why he should postpone longer, when the very landscape called for a repetition of that attempt.

He told his man to saddle the mare, booted and spurred himself with a younger horseman's nicety, kissed the two youngest children, and rode off. To make the journey a complete parallel to the first, he would fain have had his old acquaintance Japheth Johns with him. But Johns, alas! was missing. His removal to the other side of the county had left unrepaired the breach which had arisen between him and Darton; and though Darton had forgiven him a hundred times, as Johns had probably forgiven Darton, the effort of reunion in present circumstances was one not likely to be made.

He screwed himself up to as cheerful a pitch as he could without his former crony, and became content with his own thoughts as he rode, instead of the words of a companion. The sun went down; the boughs appeared scratched in like an etching against the sky; old crooked men with faggots at their backs said "Good-night, sir," and Darton replied "Good-night" right heartily.

By the time he reached the forking roads it was getting as dark as it had been on the occasion when Johns climbed the directing-post. Darton made no mistake this time. "Nor murmured. It gave him peculiar satisfaction to think that shall I be able to mistake, thank Heaven, when I arrive," he the proposed marriage, like his first, was of the nature of setting in order things long awry, and not a momentary freak of fancy.

Nothing hindered the smoothness of his journey, which seemed not half its former length. Though dark, it was only between five and six o'clock when the bulky chimneys of Mrs. Hall's residence appeared in view behind the sycamore-tree. On second thoughts he retreated and put up at the ale-house as in former time; and when he had plumed himself before the inn mirror, called for something to drink, and smoothed out the incipient wrinkles of care, he walked on to the Knap with a quick step.

V

That evening Sally was making "pinners" for the milkers,
who were now increased by two, for her mother and
herself no longer joined in milking the cows themselves.
But upon the whole there was little change in the household economy, and not much in its appearance, beyond
such minor particulars as that the crack over the window,
which had been a hundred years coming, was a trifle wider;
that the beams were a shade blacker; that the influence of
modernism had supplanted the open chimney corner by
a grate; that Rebekah, who had worn a cap when she had
plenty of hair, had left it off now she had scarce any,
because it was reported that caps were not fashionable;
and that Sally's face had naturally assumed a more
womanly and experienced cast.

Mrs. Hall was actually lifting coals with the tongs, as
she had used to do.

"Five years ago this very night, if I am not mistaken——" she said, laying on an ember.

"Not this very night—though t'was one night this week,"
said the correct Sally.

"Well, 'tis near enough. Five years ago Mr. Darton
came to marry you, and my poor boy Phil came home to
die." She sighed. "Ah, Sally," she presently said, "if you
had managed well Mr. Darton would have had you, Helena
or none."

"Don't be sentimental about that, mother," begged Sally.
"I didn't care to manage well in such a case. Though I
liked him, I wasn't so anxious. I would never have married
the man in the midst of such a hitch as that was," she
added with decision; "and I don't think I would if he
were to ask me now."

"I am not sure about that, unless you have another in
your eye."

"I wouldn't; and I'll tell you why. I could hardly marry
him for love at this time o' day. And as we've quite enough
to live on if we give up the dairy to-morrow, I should
have no need to marry for any meaner reason. . . . I am
quite happy enough as I am, and there's an end of it."

Now it was not long after this dialogue that there came a mild rap at the door, and in a moment there entered Rebekah, looking as though a ghost had arrived. The fact was that that accomplished skimmer and churner (now a resident in the house) had overheard the desultory observations between mother and daughter, and on opening the door to Mr. Darton thought the coincidence must have a grisly meaning in it. Mrs. Hall welcomed the farmer with warm surprise, as did Sally, and for a moment they rather wanted words.

"Can you push up the chimney-crook for me, Mr. Darton? the notches hitch," said the matron. He did it, and the homely little act bridged over the awkward consciousness that he had been a stranger for four years.

Mrs. Hall soon saw what he had come for, and left the principals together while she went to prepare him a late tea, smiling at Sally's recent hasty assertions of indifference, when she saw how civil Sally was. When tea was ready she joined them. She fancied that Darton did not look so confident as when he had arrived; but Sally was quite light-hearted, and the meal passed pleasantly.

About seven he took his leave of them. Mrs. Hall went as far as the door to light him down the slope. On the doorstep he said frankly—

"I came to ask your daughter to marry me; chose the night and everything, with an eye to a favourable answer. But she won't."

"Then she's a very ungrateful girl!" emphatically said Mrs. Hall.

Darton paused to shape his sentence, and asked, "I—I suppose there's nobody else more favoured?"

"I can't say that there is, or that there isn't," answered Mrs. Hall. "She's private in some things. I'm on your side, however, Mr. Darton, and I'll talk to her."

"Thank 'ee, thank 'ee!" said the farmer in a gayer accent; and with this assurance the not very satisfactory visit came to an end. Darton descended the roots of the sycamore, the light was withdrawn, and the door closed. At the bottom of the slope he nearly ran against a man about to ascend.

"Can a jack-o'-lent believe his few senses on such a dark night, or can't he?" exclaimed one whose utterance Darton recognized in a moment, despite its unexpectedness. "I dare not swear he can, though I fain would!" The speaker was Johns.

Darton said he was glad of this opportunity, bad as it was, of putting an end to the silence of years, and asked the dairyman what he was travelling that way for.

Japheth showed the old jovial confidence in a moment. "I'm going to see your—relations—as they always seem to me," he said—"Mrs. Hall and Sally. Well, Charles, the fact is I find the natural barbarousness of man is much increased by a bachelor life, and, as your leavings were always good enough for me, I'm trying civilisation here." He nodded towards the house.

"Not with Sally—to marry her?" said Darton, feeling something like a rill of ice water between his shoulders.

"Yes, by the help of Providence and my personal charms. And I think I shall get her. I am this road every week— my present dairy is only four miles off, you know, and I see her through the window. 'Tis rather odd that I was going to speak practical to-night to her for the first time. You've just called?"

"Yes, for a short while. But she didn't say a word about you."

"A good sign, a good sign. Now that decides me. I'll swing the mallet and get her answer this very night as I planned."

A few more remarks, and Darton, wishing his friend joy of Sally in a slightly hollow tone of jocularity, bade him good-bye. Johns promised to write particulars, and ascended, and was lost in the shade of the house and tree. A rectangle of light appeared when Johns was admitted, and all was dark again.

"Happy Japheth!" said Darton. "This then is the explanation!"

He determined to return home that night. In a quarter of an hour he passed out of the village, and the next day went about his swede-lifting and storing as if nothing had occurred.

He waited and waited to hear from Johns whether the wedding-day was fixed: but no letter came. He learnt not a single particular till, meeting Johns one day at a horse-auction, Darton exclaimed genially—rather more genially than he felt—"When is the joyful day to be?"

To his great surprise a reciprocity of gladness was not conspicuous in Johns. "Not at all," he said, in a very sub-dued tone. " 'Tis a bad job; she won't have me."

Darton held his breath till he said with treacherous solicitude, "Try again—'tis coyness."

"O no," said Johns decisively. "There's been none of that. We talked it over dozens of times in the most fair and square way. She tells me plainly, I don't suit her. 'Twould be simply annoying her to ask her again. Ah, Charles, you threw a prize away when you let her slip five years ago."

"I did—I did," said Darton.

He returned from that auction with a new set of feelings in play. He had certainly made a surprising mistake in thinking Johns his successful rival. It really seemed as if he might hope for Sally after all.

This time, being rather pressed by business, Darton had recourse to pen-and-ink, and wrote her as manly and straightforward a proposal as any woman could wish to receive. The reply came promptly:—

DEAR MR. DARTON,—I am as sensible as any woman can be of the goodness that leads you to make me this offer a second time. Better women than I would be proud of the honour, for when I read your nice long speeches on mangold-wurzel, and such like topics, at the Casterbridge Farmers' Club, I do feel it an honour, I assure you. But my answer is just the same as before. I will not try to explain what, in truth, I cannot explain—my reasons; I will simply say that I must decline to be married to you. With good wishes as in former times, I am, your faithful friend, SALLY HALL.

Darton dropped the letter hopelessly. Beyond the nega-tive, there was just a possibility of sarcasm in it—"nice long speeches on mangold-wurzel" had a suspicious sound.

However, sarcasm or none, there was the answer, and he had to be content.

He proceeded to seek relief in a business which at this time engrossed much of his attention—that of clearing up a curious mistake just current in the county, that he had been nearly ruined by the recent failure of a local bank. A farmer named Darton had lost heavily, and the similarity of name had probably led to the error. Belief in it was so persistent that it demanded several days of letter-writing to set matters straight, and persuade the world that he was as solvent as ever he had been in his life. He had hardly concluded this worrying task when, to his delight, another letter arrived in the handwriting of Sally.

Darton tore it open; it was very short.

> DEAR MR. DARTON,—We have been so alarmed these last few days by the report that you were ruined by the stoppage of ——'s Bank, that, now it is contradicted, I hasten, by my mother's wish, to say how truly glad we are to find there is no foundation for the report. After your kindness to my poor brother's children. I can do no less than write at such a moment. We had a letter from each of them a few days ago.—Your faithful friend,
>
> SALLY HALL.

"Mercenary little woman!" said Darton to himself with a smile. "Then that was the secret of her refusal this time—she thought I was ruined."

Now, such was Darton, that as hours went on he could not help feeling too generously towards Sally to condemn her in this. What did he want in a wife? he asked himself. Love and integrity. What next? Worldly wisdom. And was there really more than worldly wisdom in her refusal to go aboard a sinking ship? She now knew it was otherwise. "Begad," he said, "I'll try her again."

The fact was he had so set his heart upon Sally, and Sally alone, that nothing was to be allowed to baulk him; and his reasoning was purely formal.

Anniversaries having been unpropitious, he waited on

till a bright day late in May—a day when all animate nature was fancying, in its trusting, foolish way, that it was going to bask under blue sky for evermore. As he rode through Long-Ash Lane it was scarce recognizable as the track of his two winter journeys. No mistake could be made now, even with his eyes shut. The cuckoo's note was at its best, between April tentativeness and midsummer decrepitude, and the reptiles in the sun behaved as winningly as kittens on a hearth. Though afternoon, and about the same time as on the last occasion, it was broad day and sunshine when he entered Hintock, and the details of the Knap dairy-house were visible far up the road. He saw Sally in the garden, and was set vibrating. He had first intended to go on to the inn; but "No," he said; "I'll tie my horse to the garden-gate. If all goes well it can soon be taken round: if not, I mount and ride away."

The tall shade of the horseman darkened the room in which Mrs. Hall sat, and made her start, for he had ridden by a side path to the top of the slope, where riders seldom came. In a few seconds he was in the garden with Sally.

Five—ay, three minutes—did the business at the back of that row of bees. Though spring had come, and heavenly blue consecrated the scene, Darton succeeded not. "*No*," said Sally firmly. "I will never, never marry you, Mr. Darton. I would have done it once; but now I never can."

"But!"—implored Mr. Darton. And with a burst of real eloquence he went on to declare all sorts of things that he would do for her. He would drive her to see her mother every week—take her to London—settle so much money upon her—Heaven knows what he did not promise, suggest, and tempt her with. But it availed nothing. She interposed with a stout negative which closed the course of his argument like an iron gate across a highway. Darton paused.

"Then," said he simply, "you hadn't heard of my supposed failure when you declined last time?"

"I had not," she said. "That you believed me capable of refusing you for such a reason does not help your cause."

"And 'tis not because of any soreness from my slighting you years ago?"

"No. That soreness is long past."

"Ah—then you despise me, Sally!"

"No," she slowly answered. "I don't altogether despise you. I don't think you quite such a hero as I once did—that's all. The truth is, I am happy enough as I am; and I don't mean to marry at all. Now, may *I* ask a favour, sir?" She spoke with an ineffable charm, which, whenever he thought of it, made him curse his loss of her as long as he lived.

"To any extent."

"Please do not put this question to me any more. Friends as long as you like, but lovers and married never."

"I never will," said Darton. "Not if I live a hundred years."

And he never did. That he had worn out his welcome in her heart was only too plain.

When his step-children had grown up and were placed out in life all communication between Darton and the Hall family ceased. It was only by chance that, years after, he learnt that Sally, notwithstanding the solicitations her attractions drew down upon her, had refused several offers of marriage, and steadily adhered to her purpose of leading a single life.

A TRYST AT AN ANCIENT EARTHWORK

At one's every step forward it rises higher against the south sky, with an obtrusive personality that compels the senses to regard it and consider. The eyes may bend in another direction, but never without the consciousness of its heavy, high-shouldered presence at its point of vantage. Across the intervening levels the gale races in a straight line from the fort, as if breathed out of it hitherward. With the shifting of the clouds the faces of the steeps vary in colour and in shade, broad lights appearing where mist and vagueness had prevailed, dissolving in their turn into melancholy grey, which spreads over and eclipses the luminous bluffs. In this so-thought immutable spectacle all is change.

Out of the invisible marine region on the other side birds soar suddenly into the air, and hang over the summits of the heights with the indifference of long familiarity. Their forms are white against the tawny concave of cloud, and the curves they exhibit in their floating signify that they are sea-gulls which have journeyed inland from expected stress of weather. As the birds rise behind the fort, so do the clouds rise behind the birds, almost, as it seems, stroking with their bagging bosoms the uppermost flyers.

The profile of the whole stupendous ruin, as seen at a distance of a mile eastward, is cleanly cut as that of a marble inlay. It is varied with protuberances, which from hereabouts have the animal aspect of warts, wens, knuckles, and hips. It may indeed be likened to an enormous many-limbed organism of an antediluvian time—partaking of the cephalopod in shape—lying lifeless, and covered with a thin green cloth, which hides its substance, while revealing its contour. This dull green mantle of herbage stretches down towards the levels, where the ploughs have essayed for centuries to creep up near and yet nearer to the base of the castle, but have always stopped short before reaching it. The furrows of these environing attempts show themselves distinctly, bending to the incline as they trench upon it; mounting in steeper curves, till the steepness baffles them, and their parallel threads show like the striae of waves pausing on the curl. The peculiar place of which these are some of the features is "Mai-Dun," "The Castle of the Great Hill," said to be the Dunium of Ptolemy, the capital of the Durotriges, which eventually came into Roman occupation, and was finally deserted on their withdrawal from the island.

The evening is followed by a night on which an invisible moon bestows a subdued, yet pervasive light—without radiance, as without blackness. From the spot whereon I am ensconced in a cottage, a mile away, the fort has now ceased to be visible; yet, as by day, to anybody whose thoughts have been engaged with it and its barbarous grandeurs of past time the form asserts its existence behind the night gauzes as persistently as if it had a voice. Moreover, the southwest wind continues to feed the intervening arable flats with vapours brought directly from its sides.

The midnight hour for which there has been occasion to wait at length arrives, and I journey towards the stronghold in obedience to a request urged earlier in the day. It concerns an appointment, which I rather regret my decision to keep now that night is come. The route thither is hedgeless and treeless—I need not add deserted. The moonlight is sufficient to disclose the pale riband-like surface of the way as it trails along between the expanses of darker fallow. Though the road passes near the fortress it does not conduct directly to its fronts. As the place is without an inhabitant, so it is without a trackway. So presently leaving the macadamized road to pursue its course elsewhither, I step off upon the fallow, and plod stumblingly across it. The castle looms out off the shade by degrees, like a thing waking up and asking what I want there. It is now so enlarged by nearness that its whole shape cannot be taken in at one view. The ploughed ground ends as the rise sharpens, the sloping basement of grass begins, and I climb upward to invade Mai-Dun.

Impressive by day as this largest Ancient-British work in the kingdom undoubtedly is, its impressiveness is increased now. After standing still and spending a few minutes in adding its age to its size, and its size to its solitude, it becomes appallingly mournful in its growing closeness. A squally wind blows in the face with an impact which proclaims that the vapours of the air sail low to-night. The slope that I so laboriously clamber up the wind skips sportively down. Its track can be discerned even in this light by the undulations of the withered grass-bents—the only produce of this upland summit except moss. Four minutes of ascent, and a vantage-ground of some sort is gained. It is only the crest of the outer rampart. Immediately within this a chasm gapes; its bottom is imperceptible, but the counterscarp slopes not too steeply to admit of a sliding descent if cautiously performed. The shady bottom, dank and chilly, is thus gained, and reveals itself as a kind of winding lane, wide enough for a waggon to pass along, floored with rank herbage, and trending away, right and left, into obscurity, between the concentric walls of earth. The towering closeness of these on each hand, their impenetrability, and their ponderousness, are felt as a physical pressure. The way is now up the second of them, which stands steeper and higher than the first. To turn aside, as did Christian's companion, from such a Hill Difficulty, is the more natural tendency; but the way to the interior is upward. There is, of course, an entrance to the fortress; but that lies far off on the other side. It might possibly have been the wiser course to seek for easier ingress there.

However, being here, I ascend the second acclivity. The grass stems—the grey beard of the hill—sway in a mass close to my stooping face. The dead heads of these various grasses—fescues, fox-tails, and ryes—bob and twitch as if pulled by a string underground. From a few thistles a whistling proceeds; and even the moss speaks, in its humble way, under the stress of the blast.

That the summit of the second line of defence has been gained is suddenly made known by a contrasting wind from a new quarter, coming over with the curve of a cascade. These novel gusts raise a sound from the whole camp or castle, playing upon it bodily as upon a harp. It is with some difficulty that a foothold can be preserved under their sweep. Looking aloft for a moment I perceive that the sky is much more overcast than it has been hitherto, and in a few instants a dead lull in what is now a gale ensues with almost preternatural abruptness. I take advantage of this to sidle down the second counterscarp, but by the time the ditch is reached the lull reveals itself to be but the precursor of a storm. It begins with a heave of the whole atmosphere, like the sigh of a weary strong man on turning to recommence unusual exertion, just as I stand here in the second fosse. That which now radiates from the sky upon the scene is not so much light as vaporous phosphorescence.

The wind, quickening, abandons the natural direction it has pursued on the open upland, and takes the course of the gorge's length, rushing along therein helter-skelter, and carrying thick rain upon its back. The rain is followed by hailstones which fly through the defile in battalions—rolling, hopping, ricochetting, snapping, clattering down the shelving banks in an undefinable haze of confusion. The earthen sides of the fosse seem to quiver under the drenching onset, though it is practically no more to them than the blows of Thor upon the giant of Jotun-land. It is impossible to proceed further till the storm somewhat abates, and I draw up behind a spur of the inner scarp, where possibly a barricade stood two thousand years ago; and thus await events.

The roar of the storm can be heard travelling the complete circuit of the castle—a measured mile—coming round at intervals like a circumambulating column of infantry. Doubtless such a column has passed this way in its time, but the only columns which enter in these latter days are the columns of sheep and oxen that are sometimes seen here now; while the only semblance of heroic voices heard are the utterances of such, and of the many winds which make their passage through the ravines.

The expected lightning radiates round, and a rumbling as from its subterranean vaults—if there are any—fills the castle. The lightning repeats itself, and, coming after the aforesaid thoughts of martial men, it bears a fanciful resemblance to swords moving in combat. It has the very brassy hue of the ancient weapons that here were used. The so sudden entry upon the scene of this metallic flame is as the entry of a presiding exhibitor who unrolls the maps, uncurtains the pictures, unlocks the cabinets, and effects a transformation by merely exposing the materials of his science, unintelligibly cloaked till then. The abrupt configuration of the bluffs and mounds is now for the first time clearly revealed—mounds whereon, doubtless, spears and shields have frequently lain while their owners loosened their sandals and yawned and stretched their arms in the sun. For the first time, too, a glimpse is obtainable of the true entrance used by its occupants of old, some way ahead.

There, where all passage has seemed to be inviolably barred by an almost vertical façade, the ramparts are found to overlap each other like loosely clasped fingers, between which a zigzag path may be followed—a cunning construction that puzzles the uninformed eye. But its cunning, even where not obscured by dilapidation, is now wasted on the solitary forms of a few wild badgers, rabbits, and hares. Men must have often gone out by those gates in the morning to battle with the Roman legions under Vespasian; some to return no more, others to come back at evening, bringing with them the noise of their heroic deeds. But not a page, not a stone, has preserved their fame.

Acoustic perceptions multiply to-night. We can almost hear the stream of years that have borne those deeds away from us. Strange articulations seem to float on the air from that point, the gateway, where the animation in past times must frequently have concentrated itself at hours of coming and going, and general excitement. There arises an ineradicable fancy that they are human voices; if so, they must be the lingering air-borne vibrations of conversations uttered at least fifteen hundred years ago. The attention is attracted from mere nebulous imaginings about yonder spot by a real moving of something close at hand.

I recognize by the now moderate flashes of lightning, which are sheet-like and nearly continuous, that it is the gradual elevation of a small mound of earth. At first no larger than a man's fist it reaches the dimensions of a hat, then sinks a little and is still. It is but the heaving of a mole who chooses such weather as this to work in from some instinct that there will be nobody abroad to molest him. As the fine earth lifts and lifts and falls loosely aside fragments of burnt clay roll out of it—clay that once formed part of cups or other vessels used by the inhabitants of the fortress.

The violence of the storm has been counterbalanced by

its transitoriness. From being immersed in well-nigh solid
media of cloud and hail shot with lightning, I find myself
uncovered of the humid investiture and left bare to the
mild gaze of the moon, which sparkles now on every wet
grass-blade and frond of moss.

But I am not yet inside the fort, and the delayed ascent
of the third and last escarpment is now made. It is steeper
than either. The first was a surface to walk up, the second
to stagger up, the third can only be ascended on the hands
and toes. On the summit obtrudes the first evidence which
has been met with in these precincts that the time is
really the nineteenth century; it is in the form of a white
notice-board on a post, and the wording can just be
discerned by the rays of the setting moon:

> CAUTION.—Any Person found removing Relics,
> Skeletons, Stones, Pottery, Tiles, or other Material
> from this Earthwork, or cutting up the Ground, will
> be Prosecuted as the Law directs.

Here one observes a difference underfoot from what
has gone before: scraps of Roman tile and stone chippings
protrude through the grass in meagre quantity, but sufficient to suggest that masonry stood on the spot. Before
the eye stretches under the moonlight the interior of the
fort. So open and so large is it as to be practically an upland
plateau, and yet its area lies wholly within the walls of what
may be designated as one building. It is a long-violated
retreat; all its corner-stones, plinths, and architraves were
carried away to build neighbouring villages even before
mediæval or modern history began. Many a block which
once may have helped to form a bastion here rests now in
broken and diminished shape as part of the chimney-
corner of some shepherd's cottage within the distant horizon, and the corner-stones of this heathen altar may form
the base-course of some adjoining village church.

Yet the very bareness of these inner courts and wards,
their condition of mere pasturage, protects what remains
of them as no defences could do. Nothing is left visible
that the hands can seize on or the weather overturn, and

a permanence of general outline at least results, which no
other condition could ensure.

The position of the castle on this isolated hill bespeaks
deliberate and strategic choice exercised by some remote
mind capable of prospective reasoning to a far extent. The
natural configuration of the surrounding country and its
bearing upon such a stronghold were obviously long considered and viewed mentally before its extensive design
was carried into execution. Who was the man that said,
"Let it be built here!"—not on that hill yonder, or on
that ridge behind, but on this best spot of all? Whether he
were some great one of the Belgae, or of the Durotriges,
or the travelling engineer of Britain's united tribes, must
for ever remain time's secret; his form cannot be realized,
nor his countenance, nor the tongue that he spoke, when
he set down his foot with a thud and said, "Let it be here!"

Within the innermost enclosure, though it is so wide that
at a superficial glance the beholder has only a sense of
standing on a breezy down, the solitude is rendered yet
more solitary by the knowledge that between the benighted
sojourner herein and all kindred humanity are those three
concentric walls of earth which no being would think of
scaling on such a night as this, even were he to hear the
most pathetic cries issuing hence that could be uttered by
a spectre-chased soul. I reach a central mound or platform—the crown and axis of the whole structure. The
view from here by day must be of almost limitless extent.
On this raised floor, daïs, or rostrum, harps have probably
twanged more or less tuneful notes in celebration of daring,
strength, or cruelty; of worship, superstition, love, birth,
and death; of simple loving-kindness perhaps never. Many
a time must the king or leader have directed his keen
eyes hence across the open lands towards the ancient road,
the Icening Way, still visible in the distance, on the watch
for armed companies approaching either to succour or
to attack.

I am startled by a voice pronouncing my name. Past and
present have become so confusedly mingled under the
associations of the spot that for a time it has escaped my

memory that this mound was the place agreed on for the aforesaid appointment. I turn and behold my friend. He stands with a dark lantern in his hand and a spade and light pickaxe over his shoulder. He expresses both delight and surprise that I have come. I tell him I had set out before the bad weather began.

He, to whom neither weather, darkness, nor difficulty seems to have any relation or significance, so entirely is his soul wrapt up in his own deep intentions, asks me to take the lantern and accompany him. I take it and walk by his side. He is a man about sixty, small in figure, with grey old-fashioned whiskers cut to the shape of a pair of crumb-brushes. He is entirely in black broadcloth—or rather, at present, black and brown, for he is bespattered with mud from his heels to the crown of his low hat. He has no consciousness of this—no sense of anything but his purpose, his ardour for which causes his eyes to shine like those of a lynx, and gives his motions all the elasticity of an athlete's.

"Nobody to interrupt us at this time of night!" he chuckles with fierce enjoyment.

We retreat a little way and find a sort of angle, an elevation in the sod, a suggested squareness amid the mass of irregularities around. Here, he tells me, if anywhere, the king's house stood. Three months of measurement and calculation have confirmed him in this conclusion.

He requests me now to open the lantern, which I do, and the light streams out upon the wet sod. At last divining his proceedings I say that I had no idea, in keeping the tryst, that he was going to do more at such an unusual time than meet me for a meditative ramble through the stronghold. I ask him why, having a practicable object, he should have minded interruptions and not have chosen the day? He informs me, quietly pointing to his spade, that it was because his purpose is to dig, then signifying with a grim nod the gaunt notice-post against the sky beyond. I inquire why, as a professed and well-known antiquary with capital letters at the tail of his name, he did not obtain the necessary authority, considering the stringent penalties for this sort of thing; and he chuckles fiercely again with suppressed delight, and says, "Because they wouldn't have given it!"

He at once begins cutting up the sod, and, as he takes the pickaxe to follow on with, assures me that, penalty or no penalty, honest men or marauders, he is sure of one thing, that we shall not be disturbed at our work till after dawn.

I remember to have heard of men who, in their enthusiasm for some special science, art, or hobby, have quite lost the moral sense which would restrain them from indulging it illegitimately; and I conjecture that here, at last, is an instance of such an one. He probably guesses the way my thoughts travel, for he stands up and solemnly asserts that he has a distinctly justifiable intention in this matter; namely, to uncover, to search, to verify a theory or displace it, and to cover up again. He means to take away nothing—not a grain of sand. In this he says he sees no such monstrous sin. I inquire if this is really a promise to me? He repeats that it is a promise, and resumes digging. My contribution to the labour is that of directing the light constantly upon the hole. When he has reached something more than a foot deep he digs more cautiously, saying that, be it much or little there, it will not lie far below the surface; such things never are deep. A few minutes later the point of the pickaxe clicks upon a stony substance. He draws the implement out as feelingly as if it had entered a man's body. Taking up the spade he shovels with care, and a surface, level as an altar, is presently disclosed. His eyes flash anew; he pulls handfuls of grass and mops the surface clean, finally rubbing it with his handkerchief. Grasping the lantern from my hand he holds it close to the ground, when the rays reveal a complete mosaic—a pavement of minute tesserae of many colours, of intricate pattern, a work of much art, of much time, and of much industry. He exclaims in a shout that he knew it always— that it is not a Celtic stronghold exclusively, but also a Roman; the former people having probably contributed little more than the original framework which the latter took and adapted till it became the present imposing structure.

I ask, What if it is Roman?

A great deal, according to him. That it proves all the world to be wrong in this great argument, and himself alone to be right! Can I wait while he digs further?

I agree—reluctantly; but he does not notice my reluctance. At an adjoining spot he begins flourishing the tools anew with the skill of a navvy, this venerable scholar with letters after his name. Sometimes he falls on his knees, burrowing with his hands in the manner of a hare, and where his old-fashioned broadcloth touches the sides of the hole it gets plastered with the damp earth. He continually murmurs to himself how important, how very important, this discovery is! He draws out an object; we wash it in the same primitive way by rubbing it with the wet grass, and it proves to be a semi-transparent bottle of iridescent beauty, the sight of which draws groans of luxurious sensibility from the digger. Further and further search brings out a piece of a weapon. It is strange indeed that by merely peeling off a wrapper of modern accumulations we have lowered ourselves into an ancient world. Finally a skeleton is uncovered, fairly perfect. He lays it out on the grass, bone to its bone.

My friend says the man must have fallen fighting here, as this is no place of burial. He turns again to the trench, scrapes, feels, till from a corner he draws out a heavy lump—a small image four or five inches high. We clean it as before. It is a statuette, apparently of gold, or, more probably, of bronze-gilt—a figure of Mercury, obviously, its head being surmounted with the petasus or winged hat, the usual accessory of that deity. Further inspection reveals the workmanship to be of good finish and detail, and, preserved by the limy earth, to be as fresh in every line as on the day it left the hands of its artificer.

We seem to be standing in the Roman Forum and not on a hill in Wessex. Intent upon this truly valuable relic of the old empire of which even this remote spot was a component part, we do not notice what is going on in the present world till reminded of it by the sudden renewal of the storm. Looking up I perceive that the wide extinguisher of cloud has again settled down upon the fortress-town, as if resting upon the edge of the inner rampart, and shutting out the moon. I turn my back to the tempest, still directing the light across the hole. My companion digs on unconcernedly; he is living two thousand years ago, and despises things of the moment as dreams. But at last he is fairly beaten, and standing up beside me looks round on what he has done. The rays of the lantern pass over the trench to the tall skeleton stretched upon the grass on the other side. The beating rain has washed the bones clean and smooth, and the forehead, cheek-bones, and two-and-thirty teeth of the skull glisten in the candle-shine as they lie.

This storm, like the first, is of the nature of a squall, and it ends as abruptly as the other. We dig no further. My friend says that it is enough—he has proved his point. He turns to replace the bones in the trench and covers them. But they fall to pieces under his touch: the air has disintegrated them, and he can only sweep in the fragments. The next act of his plan is more than difficult, but is carried out. The treasures are inhumed again in their respective holes: they are not ours. Each deposition seems to cost him a twinge; and at one moment I fancied I saw him slip his hand into his coat pocket.

"We must re-bury them *all*," say I.

"O yes," he answers with integrity. "I was wiping my hand."

The beauties of the tesselated floor of the governor's house are once again consigned to darkness; the trench is filled up; the sod laid smoothly down; he wipes the perspiration from his forehead with the same handkerchief he had used to mop the skeleton and tesserae clean; and we make for the eastern gate of the fortress.

Dawn bursts upon us suddenly as we reach the opening. It comes by the lifting and thinning of the clouds that way till we are bathed in a pink light. The direction of his homeward journey is not the same as mine, and we part under the outer slope.

Walking along quickly to restore warmth I muse upon my eccentric friend, and cannot help asking myself this question: Did he really replace the gilded image of the god Mercurius with the rest of the treasures? He seemed to do so; and yet I could not testify to the fact. Probably, however, he was as good as his word.

It was thus I spoke to myself, and so the adventure ended. But one thing remains to be told, and that is concerned with seven years after. Among the effects of my friend, at that time just deceased, was found, carefully preserved, a gilt statuette representing Mercury, labelled "Debased Roman." No record was attached to explain how it came into his possession. The figure was bequeathed to the Casterbridge Museum.

ᘓᘓᘓᘓᘓᘓᘓᘓᘓᘓᘓᘓᘓᘓᘓᘓᘓᘓᘓᘓᘓᘓᘓ

THE WITHERED ARM

A LORN MILKMAID

I

It was an eighty-cow dairy, and the troop of milkers, regular and supernumerary, were all at work; for, though the time of year was as yet but early April, the feed lay entirely in water-meadows, and the cows were "in full pail." The hour was about six in the evening, and three-fourths of the large, red, rectangular animals having been finished off, there was opportunity for a little conversation.

"He do bring home his bride to-morrow, I hear. They've come as far as Anglebury to-day."

The voice seemed to proceed from the belly of the cow called Cherry, but the speaker was a milking-woman, whose face was buried in the flank of that motionless beast.

"Hav' anybody seen her?" said another.

There was a negative response from the first. 'Though they say she's a rosy-cheeked, tisty-tosty little body enough, she added; and as the milkmaid spoke she turned her face so that she could glance past her cow's tail to the other side of the barton, where a thin, fading woman of thirty milked somewhat apart from the rest.

"Years younger than he, they say," continued the second with also a glance of reflectiveness in the same direction.

"How old do you call him, then?"

"Thirty or so."

"More like forty," broke in an old milkman near, in a long white pinafore or "wropper," and with the brim of his hat tied down, so that he looked like a woman. " 'A was born before our Great Weir was builded, and I hadn't man's wages when I laved water there.'

The discussion waxed so warm that the purr of the milk streams became jerky, till a voice from another cow's belly cried with authority, "Now then, what the Turk do it matter to us about Farmer Lodge's age, or Farmer Lodge's new mis'ess? I shall have to pay him nine pound a year for the rent of every one of these milchers, whatever his age or hers. Get on with your work, or 'twill be dark afore we have done. The evening is pinking in a'ready." This speaker was the dairyman himself, by whom the milkmaids and men were employed.

Nothing more was said publicly about Farmer Lodge's wedding, but the first woman murmured under her cow to her next neighbour, " 'Tis hard for *she*," signifying the thin worn milkmaid aforesaid.

"O no," said the second. "He ha'n't spoke to Rhoda Brook for years."

When the milking was done they washed their pails and hung them on a many-forked stand made as usual of the peeled limb of an oak-tree, set upright in the earth, and resembling a colossal antlered horn. The majority then dispersed in various directions homeward. The thin woman who had not spoken was joined by a boy of twelve or thereabout, and the twain went away up the field also.

Their course lay apart from that of the others, to a lonely spot high above the water-meads, and not far from the border of Egdon Heath, whose dark countenance was visible in the distance as they drew nigh to their home.

"They've just been saying down in barton that your

father brings his young wife home from Anglebury
to-morrow," the woman observed. "I shall want to send
you for a few things to market, and you'll be pretty sure
to meet 'em."

"Yes, mother," said the boy. "Is father married then?"

"Yes. . . . You can give her a look, and tell me what
she's like, if you do see her."

"Yes, mother."

"If she's dark or fair, and if she's tall—as tall as I. And
if she seems like a woman who has ever worked for a living
or one that has been always well off, and has never done
anything, and shows marks of the lady on her, as I
expect she do."

"Yes."

They crept up the hill in the twilight and entered the
cottage. It was built of mud-walls, the surface of which had
been washed by many rains into channels and depressions
that left none of the original flat face visible; while here
and there in the thatch above a rafter showed like a bone
protruding through the skin.

She was kneeling down in the chimney-corner, before
two pieces of turf laid together with the heather inwards,
blowing at the red-hot ashes with her breath till the turves
flamed. The radiance lit her pale cheek, and made her dark
eyes, that had once been handsome, seem handsome anew.
"Yes," she resumed, "see if she is dark or fair, and if you
can, notice if her hands white; if not, see if they look as
though she had ever done housework, or are milker's
hands like mine."

The boy again promised, inattentively this time, his
mother not observing that he was cutting a notch with
his pocket-knife in the beech-backed chair.

THE YOUNG WIFE

II

The road from Anglebury to Holmstoke is in general level;
but there is one place where a sharp ascent breaks its
monotony. Farmers homeward-bound from the former

market-town, who trot all the rest of the way, walk their
horses up this short incline.

The next evening while the sun was yet bright a handsome new gig, with a lemon-coloured body and red wheels,
was spinning westward along the level highway at the heels
of a powerful mare. The driver was a yeoman in the prime
of life, cleanly shaven like an actor, his face being toned to
that bluish-vermillion hue which so often graces a thriving
farmer's features when returning home after successful
dealings in the town. Beside him sat a woman, many years
his junior—almost, indeed, a girl. Her face too was fresh
in colour, but it was of a totally different quality—soft
and evanescent, like the light under a heap of rose-petals.

Few people travelled this way, for it was not a main
road; and the long white riband of gravel that stretched
before them was empty, save of one small scarce-moving
speck, which presently resolved itself into the figure of
a boy, who was creeping on at a snail's pace, and continually looking behind him—the heavy bundle he carried
being some excuse for, if not the reason of, his dilatoriness. When the bouncing gig-party slowed at the bottom
of the incline above mentioned, the pedestrian was only a
few yards in front. Supporting the large bundle by putting
one hand on his hip, he turned and looked straight at the
farmer's wife as though he would read her through and
through, pacing along abreast of the horse.

The low sun was full in her face, rendering every feature, shade, and contour distinct, from the curve of her
little nostril to the colour of her eyes. The farmer, though
he seemed annoyed at the boy's persistent presence, did
not order him to get out of the way; and thus the lad
preceded them, his hard gaze never leaving her, till they
reached the top of the ascent, when the farmer trotted on
with relief in his lineaments—having taken no outward
notice of the boy whatever.

"How that poor lad stared at me!" said the young wife.

"Yes, dear; I saw that he did."

"He is one of the village, I suppose?"

"One of the neighbourhood. I think he lives with his
mother a mile or two off."

"He knows who we are, no doubt?"

"O yes. You must expect to be stared at just at first, my pretty Gertrude."

"I do,—though I think the poor boy may have looked at us in the hope we might relieve him of his heavy load, rather than from curiosity."

"O no," said her husband off-handedly. "These country lads will carry a hundredweight once they get it on their backs; besides his pack had more size than weight in it. Now, then, another mile and I shall be able to show you our house in the distance—if it is not too dark before we get there." The wheels spun round, and particles flew from their periphery as before, till a white house of ample dimensions revealed itself, with farm-buildings and ricks at the back.

Meanwhile the boy had quickened his pace, and turning up a by-lane some mile and a half short of the white farmstead, ascended towards the leaner pastures, and so on to the cottage of his mother.

She had reached home after her day's milking at the outlying dairy, and was washing cabbage at the doorway in the declining light. "Hold up the net a moment," she said, without preface, as the boy came up.

He flung down his bundle, held the edge of the cabbage-net, and as she filled its meshes with the dripping leaves she went on, "Well, did you see her?"

"Yes; quite plain."

"Is she ladylike?"

"Yes; and more. A lady complete."

"Is she young?"

"Well, she's growed up, and her ways be quite a woman's."

"Of course. What colour is her hair and face?"

"Her hair is lightish, and her face as comely as a live doll's."

"Her eyes, then, are not dark like mine?"

"No—of a bluish turn, and her mouth is very nice and red; and when she smiles, her teeth show white."

"Is she tall?" said the woman sharply.

"I couldn't see. She was sitting down."

"Then do you go to Holmstoke church to-morrow morning: she's sure to be there. Go early and notice her walking in, and come home and tell me if she's taller than I."

"Very well, mother. But why don't you go and see for yourself?"

"*I* go to see her! I wouldn't look up at her if she were to pass my window this instant. She was with Mr. Lodge, of course. What did he say or do?"

"Just the same as usual."

"Took no notice of you?"

"None."

Next day the mother put a clean shirt on the boy, and started him off for Holmstoke church. He reached the ancient little pile when the door was just being opened, and he was the first to enter. Taking his seat by the font, he watched all the parishioners file in. The well-to-do Farmer Lodge came nearly last; and his young wife, who accompanied him, walked up the aisle with the shyness natural to a modest woman who had appeared thus for the first time. As all other eyes were fixed upon her, the youth's stare was not noticed now.

When he reached home his mother said, "Well?" before he had entered the room.

"She is not tall. She is rather short," he replied.

"Ah!" said his mother, with satisfaction.

"But she's very pretty—very. In fact, she's lovely." The youthful freshness of the yeoman's wife had evidently made an impression even on the somewhat hard nature of the boy.

"That's all I want to hear," said his mother quickly. "Now, spread the table-cloth. The hare you wired is very tender; but mind that nobody catches you. —You've never told me what sort of hands she had."

"I have never seen 'em. She never took off her gloves."

"What did she wear this morning?"

"A white bonnet and a silver-coloured gownd. It whewed and whistled so loud when it rubbed against the pews that the lady coloured up more than ever for very shame at the noise, and pulled it in to keep it from touching; but when she pushed into her seat, it whewed more than ever. Mr. Lodge, he seemed pleased, and his waistcoat stuck out, and his great golden seals hung like a lord's; but she seemed to wish her noisy gownd anywhere but on her."

"Not she! However, that will do now."

These descriptions of the newly-married couple were continued from time to time by the boy at his mother's request, after any chance encounter he had had with them. But Rhoda Brook, though she might easily have seen young Mrs. Lodge for herself by walking a couple of miles, would never attempt an excursion towards the quarter where the farmhouse lay. Neither did she, at the daily milking in the dairyman's yard on Lodge's outlying second farm, ever speak on the subject of the recent marriage. The dairyman, who rented the cows of Lodge, and knew perfectly the tall milkmaid's history, with manly kindliness always kept the gossip in the cow-barton from annoying Rhoda. But the atmosphere thereabout was full of the subject during the first days of Mrs. Lodge's arrival; and from her boy's description and the casual words of the other milkers, Rhoda Brook could raise a mental image of the unconscious Mrs. Lodge that was realistic as a photograph.

A VISION

III

One night, two or three weeks after the bridal return, when the boy was gone to bed, Rhoda sat a long time over the turf ashes that she had raked out in front of her to extinguish them. She contemplated so intently the new wife, as presented to her in her mind's eye over the embers, that she forgot the lapse of time. At last, wearied with her day's work, she too retired.

But the figure which had occupied her so much during

this and the previous days was not to be banished at night. For the first time Gertrude Lodge visited the supplanted woman in her dreams. Rhoda Brook dreamed—since her assertion that she really saw, before falling asleep, was not to be believed—that the young wife, in the pale silk dress and white bonnet, but with features shockingly distorted, and wrinkled as by age, was sitting upon her chest as she lay. The pressure of Mrs. Lodge's person grew heavier; the blue eyes peered cruelly into her face; and then the figure thrust forward its left hand mockingly, so as to make the wedding-ring it wore glitter in Rhoda's eyes. Maddened mentally, and nearly suffocated by pressure, the sleeper struggled; the incubus, still regarding her, withdrew to the foot of the bed, only, however, to come forward by degrees, resume her seat, and flash her left hand as before.

Gasping for breath, Rhoda, in a last desperate effort, swung out her right hand, seized the confronting spectre by its obtrusive left arm, and whirled it backward to the floor, starting up herself as she did so with a low cry.

"O, merciful heaven!" she cried, sitting on the edge of the bed in a cold sweat; "that was not a dream—she was here!"

She could feel her antagonist's arm within her grasp even now—the very flesh and bone of it, as it seemed. She looked on the floor whither she had whirled the spectre, but there was nothing to be seen.

Rhoda Brook slept no more that night, and when she went milking at the next dawn they noticed how pale and haggard she looked. The milk that she drew quivered into the pail; her hand had not calmed even yet, and still retained the feel of the arm. She came home to breakfast as wearily as if it had been supper-time.

"What was that noise in your chimmer, mother, last night?" said her son. "You fell off the bed, surely?"

"Did you hear anything fall? At what time?"

"Just when the clock struck two."

She could not explain, and when the meal was done went silently about her household work, the boy assisting

her, for he hated going afield on the farms, and she indulged his reluctance. Between eleven and twelve the
garden-gate clicked, and she lifted her eyes to the window.
At the bottom of the garden, within the gate, stood the
woman of her vision. Rhoda seemed transfixed.

"Ah, she said she would come!" exclaimed the boy,
also observing her.

"Said so—when? How does she know us?"

"I have seen and spoken to her. I talked to her yesterday."

"I told you," said the mother, flushing indignantly,
"never to speak to anybody in that house, or go near the
place."

"I did not speak to her till she spoke to me. And I
did not go near the place. I met her in the road."

"What did you tell her?"

"Nothing. She said, 'Are you the poor boy who had
to bring the heavy load from market? And she looked at
my boots, and said they would not keep my feet dry if
it came on wet, because they were so cracked. I told her
I lived with my mother, and we had enough to do to
keep ourselves, and that's how it was; and she said then,
'I'll come and bring you some better boots, and see your
mother.' She gives away things to other folks in the
meads besides us."

Mrs. Lodge was by this time close to the door—not in
her silk, as Rhoda had dreamt of in the bed-chamber,
but in a morning hat, and gown of common light material,
which became her better than silk. On her arm she
carried a basket.

The impression remaining from the night's experience
was still strong. Brook had almost expected to see the
wrinkles, the scorn, and the cruelty on her visitor's face.
She would have escaped an interview, had escape been
possible. There was, however, no backdoor to the cottage, and in an instant the boy had lifted the latch to
Mrs. Lodge's gentle knock.

"I see I have come to the right house," said she,
glancing at the lad, and smiling. "But I was not sure till
you opened the door."

The figure and action were those of the phantom; but her voice was so indescribably sweet, her glance so winning, her smile so tender, so unlike that of Rhoda's midnight visitant, that the latter could hardly believe the evidence of her senses. She was truly glad that she had not hidden away in sheer aversion, as she had been inclined to do. In her basket Mrs. Lodge brought the pair of boots that she had promised to the boy, and other useful articles.

At these proofs of a kindly feeling towards her and hers Rhoda's heart reproached her bitterly. This innocent young thing should have her blessing and not her curse. When she left them a light seemed gone from the dwelling. Two days later she came again to know if the boots fitted; and less than a fortnight after that paid Rhoda another call. On this occasion the boy was absent.

"I walk a good deal," said Mrs. Lodge, "and your house is the nearest outside our own parish. I hope you are well. You don't look quite well."

Rhoda said she was well enough; and, indeed, though the paler of the two, there was more of the strength that endures in her well-defined features and large frame than in the soft-cheeked young woman before her. The conversation became quite confidential as regarded their powers and weaknesses; and when Mrs. Lodge was leaving, Rhoda said, "I hope you will find this air agree with you, ma'am, and not suffer from the damp of the water meads."

The younger one replied that there was not much doubt of it, her general health being usually good. "Though, now you remind me," she added, "I have one little ailment which puzzles me. It is nothing serious, but I cannot make it out."

She uncovered her left hand and arm; and their outline confronted Rhoda's gaze as the exact original of the limb she had beheld and seized in her dream. Upon the pink round surface of the arm were faint marks of an unhealthy colour, as if produced by a rough grasp. Rhoda's eyes became riveted on the discolorations; she fancied that she discerned in them the shape of her own four fingers.

"How did it happen?" she said mechanically.

"I cannot tell," replied Mrs. Lodge, shaking her head.

"One night when I was sound asleep, dreaming I was away in some strange place, a pain suddenly shot into my arm there, and was so keen as to awaken me. I must have struck it in the daytime, I suppose, though I don't remember doing so." She added, laughing, "I tell my dear husband that it looks just as if he had flown into a rage and struck me there. O, I daresay it will soon disappear."

"Ha, ha! Yes. . . . On what night did it come?"

Mrs. Lodge considered, and said it would be a fortnight ago on the morrow. "When I awoke I could not remember where I was," she added, "till the clock striking two reminded me."

She had named the night and the hour of Rhoda's spectral encounter, and Brook felt like a guilty thing. The artless disclosure startled her; she did not reason on the freaks of coincidence; and all the scenery of that ghastly night returned with double vividness to her mind.

"O, can it be," she said to herself, when her visitor had departed, "that I exercise a malignant power over people against my own will?" She knew that she had been slily called a witch since her fall; but never having understood why that particular stigma had been attached to her, it had passed disregarded. Could this be the explanation, and had such things as this ever happened before?

A SUGGESTION

IV

The summer drew on, and Rhoda Brook almost dreaded to meet Mrs. Lodge again, notwithstanding that her feeling for the young wife amounted well-nigh to affection. Something in her own individuality seemed to convict Rhoda of crime. Yet a fatality sometimes would direct the steps of the latter to the outskirts of Holmstoke whenever she left her house for any other purpose than her daily work; and hence it happened that their next encounter was out of doors. Rhoda could not avoid the subject which had so mystified her, and after the first few words she stammered, "I hope your—arm is well again, ma'am?" She had perceived with consternation that Gertrude Lodge carried her left arm stiffly.

"No, it is not quite well. Indeed it is no better at all; it is rather worse. It pains me dreadfully sometimes."

"Perhaps you had better go to a doctor, ma'am."

She replied that she had already seen a doctor. Her husband had insisted upon her going to one. But the surgeon had not seemed to understand the afflicted limb at all; he had told her to bathe it in hot water, and she had bathed it, but the treatment had done no good.

"Will you let me see it?" said the milkwoman.

Mrs. Lodge pushed up her sleeve and disclosed the place, which was a few inches above the wrist. As soon as Rhoda Brook saw it, she could hardly preserve her composure. There was nothing of the nature of a wound, but the arm at that point had a shrivelled look, and the outline of the four fingers appeared more distinct than at the former time. Moreover, she fancied that they were imprinted in precisely the relative position of her clutch upon the arm in the trance; the first finger towards Gertrude's wrist, and the fourth towards her elbow.

What the impress resembled seemed to have struck Gertrude herself since their last meeting. "It looks almost like finger-marks," she said; adding with a faint laugh, "my husband says it is as if some witch, or the devil himself, had taken hold of me there, and blasted the flesh."

Rhoda shivered. "That's fancy," she said hurriedly. "I wouldn't mind it, if I were you."

"I shouldn't so much mind it," said the younger, with hesitation, "if—if I hadn't a notion that it makes my husband—dislike me—no, love me less. Men think so much of personal appearance."

"Some do—he for one."

"Yes; and he was very proud of mine, at first."

"Keep your arm covered from his sight."

"Ah—he knows the disfigurement is there!" She tried to hide the tears that filled her eyes.

"Well, ma'am, I earnestly hope it will go away soon."

And so the milkwoman's mind was chained anew to

the subject by a horrid sort of spell as she returned home.
The sense of having been guilty of an act of malignity
increased, affect as she might to ridicule her superstition.
In her secret heart Rhoda did not altogether object to a
slight diminution of her successor's beauty, by whatever
means it had come about; but she did not wish to inflict
upon her physical pain. For though this pretty young
woman had rendered impossible any reparation which
Lodge might have made Rhoda for his past conduct,
everything like resentment at the unconscious usurpation
had quite passed away from the elder's mind.

If the sweet and kindly Gertrude Lodge only knew of
the dream-scene in the bed-chamber, what would she think?
Not to inform her of it seemed treachery in the presence
of her friendliness; but tell she could not of her own accord
—neither could she devise a remedy.

She mused upon the matter the greater part of the night;
and the next day, after the morning milking, set out to
obtain another glimpse of Gertrude Lodge if she could,
being held to her by a gruesome fascination. By watching
the house from a distance the milkmaid was presently
able to discern the farmer's wife in a ride she was taking
alone—probably to join her husband in some distant
field. Mrs. Lodge perceived her, and cantered in her direction.

"Good morning, Rhoda!" Gertrude said, when she had
come up. "I was going to call."

Rhoda noticed that Mrs. Lodge held the reins with some
difficulty.

"I hope—the bad arm," said Rhoda.

"They tell me there is possibly one way by which I
might be able to find out the cause, and so perhaps the
cure, of it," replied the other anxiously. "It is by going to
some clever man over in Egdon Heath. They did not
know if he was still alive—and I cannot remember his
name at this moment; but they said that you knew more
of his movements than anybody else hereabout, and could
tell me if he were still to be consulted. Dear me—what
was his name? But you know."

"Not Conjuror Trendle?" said her thin companion, turning pale.

"Trendle—yes. Is he alive?"

"I believe so," said Rhoda, with reluctance.

"Why do you call him conjuror?"

"Well—they say—they used to say he was a—he had powers other folks have not."

"O, how could my people be so superstitious as to recommend a man of that sort! I thought they meant some medical man. I shall think no more of him."

Rhoda looked relieved, and Mrs. Lodge rode on. The milkwoman had inwardly seen, from the moment she heard of her having been mentioned as a reference for this man, but there must exist a sarcastic feeling among the work-folk that a sorceress would know the whereabouts of the exorcist. They suspected her, then. A short time ago this would have given no concern to a woman of her comman-sense. But she had a haunting reason to be superstitious now; and she had been seized with sudden dread that this Conjuror Trendle might name her as the malignant influence which was blasting the fair person of Gertrude, and so lead her friend to hate her for ever, and to treat her as some fiend in human shape.

But all was not over. Two days after, a shadow intruded into the window-pattern thrown on Rhoda Brook's floor by the afternoon sun. The woman opened the door at once, almost breathlessly.

"Are you alone?" said Gertrude. She seemed to be no less harassed and anxious than Brook herself.

"Yes," said Rhoda.

"The place on my arm seems worse, and troubles me!" the young farmer's wife went on. "It is so mysterious! I do hope it will not be an incurable wound. I have again been thinking of what they said about Conjuror Trendle. I don't really believe in such men, but I should not mind just visiting him, from curiosity—though on no account must my husband know. Is it far to where he lives?"

"Yes—five miles," said Rhoda backwardly. "In the heart of Egdon."

"Well, I should have to walk. Could not you go with me to show me the way—say to-morrow afternoon?"

"O, not I; that is——," the milkwoman murmured, with a start of dismay. Again the dread seized her that something to do with her fierce act in the dream might be revealed, and her character in the eyes of the most useful friend she had ever had be ruined irretrievably.

Mrs. Lodge urged, and Rhoda finally assented, though with much misgiving. Sad as the journey would be to her, she could not conscientiously stand in the way of a possible remedy for her patron's strange affliction. It was agreed that, to escape suspicion of their mystic intent, they should meet at the edge of the heath at the corner of a plantation which was visible from the spot where they now stood.

CONJUROR TRENDLE

V

By the next afternoon Rhoda would have done anything to escape this inquiry. But she had promised to go. Moreover, there was a horrid fascination at times in becoming instrumental in throwing such possible light on her own character as would reveal her to be something greater in the occult world than she had ever herself suspected.

She started just before the time of day mentioned between them, and half-an-hour's brisk walking brought her to the south-eastern extension of the Egdon tract of country, where the fir plantation was. A slight figure, cloaked and veiled, was already there. Rhoda recognized, almost with a shudder, that Mrs. Lodge bore her left arm in a sling.

They hardly spoke to each other, and immediately set out on their climb into the interior of this solemn country, which stood high above the rich alluvial soil they had left half-an-hour before. It was a long walk; thick clouds made the atmosphere dark, though it was as yet only early afternoon; and the wind howled dismally over the slopes of

the heath—not improbably the same heath which had
witnessed the agony of the Wessex King Ina, presented to
after-ages as Lear. Gertrude Lodge talked most, Rhoda
replying with monosyllabic preoccupation. She had a
strange dislike to walking on the side of her companion
where hung the afflicted arm, moving round to the other
when inadvertently near it. Much heather had been brushed
by their feet when they descended upon a cart-track,
beside which stood the house of the man they sought.

He did not profess his remedial practices openly, or
care anything about their continuance, his direct interests
being those of a dealer in furze, turf, "sharp sand," and
other local products. Indeed, he affected not to believe
largely in his own powers, and when warts that had been
shown him for cure miraculously disappeared—which it
must be owned they infallibly did—he would say lightly,
"O, I only drink a glass of grog upon 'em at your expense—
perhaps it's all chance," and immediately turn the subject.

He was at home when they arrived, having in fact seen
them descending into his valley. He was a grey-bearded
man, with a reddish face, and he looked singularly at
Rhoda the first moment he beheld her. Mrs. Lodge told
him her errand; and then with words of self-disparagement
he examined her arm.

"Medicine can't cure it," he said promptly. " 'Tis the
work of an enemy."

Rhoda shrank into herself, and drew back.

"An enemy? What enemy?" asked Mrs. Lodge.

He shook his head. "That's best known to yourself," he
said. "If you like, I can show the person to you, though I
shall not myself know who it is. I can do no more; and
don't wish to do that."

She pressed him; on which he told Rhoda to wait outside where she stood, and took Mrs. Lodge into the room.
It opened immediately from the door; and, as the latter
remained ajar, Rhoda Brook could see the proceedings
without taking part in them. He brought a tumbler from
the dresser, nearly filled it with water, and fetching an
egg, prepared it in some private way; after which he

broke it on the edge of the glass, so that the white went
in and the yolk remained. As it was getting gloomy, he
took the glass and its contents to the window, and told
Gertrude to watch the mixture closely. They leant over
the table together, and the milkwoman could see the
opaline hue of the egg-fluid changing form as it sank in
the water, but she was not near enough to define the
shape that it assumed.

"Do you catch the likeness of any face or figure as you
look?" demanded the conjuror of the young woman.

She murmured a reply, in tones so low as to be inaudible
to Rhoda, and continued to gaze intently into the glass.
Rhoda turned, and walked a few steps away.

When Mrs. Lodge came out, and her face was met by
the light, it appeared exceedingly pale—as pale as Rhoda's
—against the sad dun shades of the upland's garniture.
Trendle shut the door behind her, and they at once started
homeward together. But Rhoda perceived that her companion had quite changed.

"Did he charge much?" she asked tentatively.

"O no—nothing. He would not take a farthing," said
Gertrude.

"And what did you see?" inquired Rhoda.

"Nothing I—care to speak of." The constraint in her
manner was remarkable; her face was so rigid as to wear
an oldened aspect, faintly suggestive of the face in Rhoda's
bedchamber.

"Was it you who first proposed coming here?" Mrs.
Lodge suddenly inquired, after a long pause. "How very
odd, if you did!"

"No. But I am not sorry we have come, all things considered," she replied. For the first time a sense of triumph
possessed her, and she did not altogether deplore that
the young thing at her side should learn that their lives
had been antagonized by other influences than their own.

The subject was no more alluded to during the long and
dreary walk home. But in some way or other a story was
whispered about the many-dairied lowland that winter that
Mrs. Lodge's gradual loss of the use of her left arm was
owing to her being "overlooked" by Rhoda Brook. The

latter kept her own counsel about the incubus, but her face grew sadder and thinner; and in the spring she and her boy disappeared from the neighborhood of Holmstoke.

VI

Half a dozen years passed away, and Mr. and Mrs. Lodge's married experience sank into prosiness, and worse. The farmer was usually gloomy and silent: the woman whom he had wooed for her grace and beauty was contorted and disfigured in the left limb; moreover, she had brought him no child, which rendered it likely that he would be the last of a family who had occupied the valley for some two hundred years. He thought of Rhoda Brook and her son; and feared this might be a judgment from heaven upon him.

The once blithe-hearted and enlightened Gertrude was changing into an irritable, superstitious woman, whose whole time was given to experimenting upon her ailment with every quack remedy she came across. She was honestly attached to her husband, and was ever secretly hoping against hope to win back his heart again by regaining some at least of her personal beauty. Hence it arose that her closet was lined with bottles, packets, and ointment-pots of every description—nay, bunches of mystic herbs, charms, and books of necromancy, which in her schoolgirl time she would have ridiculed as folly.

"Damned if you won't poison yourself with these apothecary messes and witch mixtures some time or other," said her husband, when his eye chanced to fall upon the multitudinous array.

She did not reply, but turned her sad, soft glance upon him in such heart-swollen reproach that he looked sorry for his words, and added, "I only meant it for your good, you know, Gertrude."

"I'll clear out the whole lot, and destroy them," said she huskily, "and try such remedies no more!"

"You want somebody to cheer you," he observed. "I once thought of adopting a boy; but he is too old now. And he is gone away I don't know where."

She guessed to whom he alluded; for Rhoda Brook's story had in the course of years become known to her; though not a word had ever passed between her husband and herself on the subject. Neither had she ever spoken to him of her visit to Conjuror Trendle, and of what was revealed to her, or she thought was revealed to her, by that solitary heathman.

She was now five-and-twenty; but she seemed older. "Six years of marriage, and only a few months of love," she sometimes whispered to herself. And then she thought of the apparent cause, and said, with a tragic glance at her withering limb, "If I could only again be as I was when he first saw me!"

She obediently destroyed her nostrums and charms; but there remained a hankering wish to try something else— some other sort of cure altogether. She had never revisited Trendle since she had been conducted to the house of the solitary by Rhoda against her will; but it now suddenly occurred to Gertrude that she would, in a last desperate effort at deliverance from this seeming curse, again seek out the man, if he yet lived. He was entitled to a certain credence, for the indistinct form he had raised in the glass had undoubtedly resembled the only woman in the world who—as she now knew, though not then—could have a reason for bearing her ill-will. The visit should be paid.

This time she went alone, though she nearly got lost on the heath, and roamed a considerable distance out of her way. Trendle's house was reached at last, however: he was not indoors, and instead of waiting at the cottage, she went to where his bent figure was pointed out to her at work a long way off. Trendle remembered her, and laying down the handful of furze-roots which he was gathering and throwing into a heap, he offered to accompany her in her homeward direction, as the distance was considerable and the days were short. So they walked together, his head bowed nearly to the earth, and his form of a colour with it.

"You can send away warts and other excrescences, I know," she said; "why can't you send away this?" And the arm was uncovered.

"You think too much of my powers!" said Trendle; and I am old and weak now, too. No, no; it is too much for me to attempt in my own person. What have ye tried?"

She named to him some of the hundred medicaments and counterspells which she had adopted from time to time. He shook his head.

"Some were good enough," he said approvingly; "but not many of them for such as this. This is of the nature of a blight, not of the nature of a wound; and if you ever do throw it off, it will be all at once."

"If I only could!"

"There is only one chance of doing it known to me. It has never failed in kindred afflictions,—that I can declare. But it is hard to carry out, and especially for a woman."

"Tell me!" said she.

"You must touch with the limb the neck of a man who's been hanged."

She started a little at the image he had raised.

"Before he's cold—just after he's cut down," continued the conjuror impassively.

"How can that do good?"

"It will turn the blood and change the constitution. But, as I say, to do it is hard. You must go to the jail when there's a hanging, and wait for him when he's brought off the gallows. Lots have done it, though perhaps not such pretty women as you. I used to send dozens for skin complaints. But that was in former times. The last I sent was in '13—near twelve years ago."

He had no more to tell her; and, when he had put her into a straight track homeward, turned and left her, refusing all money as at first.

A RIDE

VII

The communication sank deep into Gertrude's mind. Her nature was rather a timid one; and probably of all remedies that the white wizard could have suggested there was not one which would have filled her with so much aversion as this, not to speak of the immense obstacles in the way of its adoption.

Casterbridge, the county-town, was a dozen or fifteen miles off; and though in those days, when men were executed for horse-stealing, arson, and burglary, an assize seldom passed without a hanging, it was not likely that she could get access to the body of the criminal unaided. And the fear of her husband's anger made her reluctant to breathe a word of Trendle's suggestion to him or to anybody about him.

She did nothing for months, and patiently bore her disfigurement as before. But her woman's nature, craving for renewed love, through the medium of renewed beauty (she was but twenty-five), was ever stimulating her to try what, at any rate, could hardy do her any harm. "What came by a spell will go by a spell surely," she would say. Whenever her imagination pictured the act she shrank in terror from the possibility of it: then the words of the conjuror, "It will turn your blood," were seen to be capable of a scientific no less than a ghastly interpretation; the mastering desire returned, and urged her on again.

There was at this time but one county paper, and that her husband only occasionally borrowed. But old-fashioned days had old-fashioned means, and news was extensively conveyed by word of mouth from market to market, or from fair to fair, so that, whenever such an event as an execution was about to take place, few within a radius of twenty miles were ignorant of the coming site; and, so far as Holmstoke was concerned, some enthusiasts had been known to walk all the way to Casterbridge and back in one day, solely to witness the spectacle. The next assizes were in March; and when Gertrude Lodge heard that they had been held, she inquired stealthily at the inn as to the result, as soon as she could find opportunity.

She was, however, too late. The time at which the sentences were to be carried out had arrived, and to make the journey and obtain admission at such short notice required at least her husband's assistance. She dared not tell him, for she had found by delicate experiment that these smouldering village beliefs made him furious if mentioned, partly because he half entertained them himself. It was therefore necessary to wait for another opportunity.

Her determination received a fillip from learning that two epileptic children had attended from this very village of Holmstoke many years before with beneficial results, though the experiment had been strongly condemned by the neighbouring clergy. April, May, June, passed; and it is no overstatement to say that by the end of the last-named month Gertrude well-nigh longed for the death of a fellow-creature. Instead of her formal prayers each night, her unconscious prayer was, "O Lord, hang some guilty or innocent person soon!"

This time she made earlier inquiries, and was altogether more systematic in her proceedings. Moreover, the season was summer, between the haymaking and the harvest, and in the leisure thus afforded him her husband had been holiday-taking away from home.

The assizes were in July, and she went to the inn as before. There was to be one execution—only one—for arson.

Her greatest problem was not how to get to Casterbridge, but what means she should adopt for obtaining admission to the jail. Though access for such purposes had formerly never been denied, the custom had fallen into desuetude; and in contemplating her possible difficulties, she was again almost driven to fall back upon her husband. But, on sounding him about the assizes, he was so uncommunicative, so more than usually cold, that she did not proceed, and decided that whatever she did she would do alone.

Fortune, obdurate hitherto, showed her unexpected favour. On the Thursday before the Saturday fixed for the execution, Lodge remarked to her that he was going away from home for another day or two on business at a fair, and that he was sorry he could not take her with him.

She exhibited on this occasion so much readiness to

stay at home that he looked at her in surprise. Time had been when she would have shown deep disappointment at the loss of such a jaunt. However, he lapsed into his usual taciturnity, and on the day named left Holmstoke.

It was now her turn. She at first had thought of driving, but on reflection held that driving would not do, since it would necessitate her keeping to the turnpike-road, and so increase by tenfold the risk of her ghastly errand being found out. She decided to ride, and avoid the beaten track, notwithstanding that in her husband's stables there was no animal just at present which by any stretch of imagination could be considered a lady's mount, in spite of his promise before marriage to always keep a mare for her. He had, however, many cart-horses, fine ones of their kind; and among the rest was a serviceable creature, an equine Amazon, with a back as broad as a sofa, on which Gertrude had occasionally taken an airing when unwell. This horse she chose.

On Friday afternoon one of the men brought it round. She was dressed, and before going down looked at her shrivelled arm. "Ah!" she said to it, "if it had not been for you this terrible ordeal would have been saved me!"

When strapping up the bundle in which she carried a few articles of clothing, she took occasion to say to the servant, "I take these in case I should not get back to-night from the person I am going to visit. Don't be alarmed if I am not in by ten, and close up the house as usual. I shall be at home to-morrow for certain." She meant then to tell her husband privately: the deed accomplished was not like the deed projected. He would almost certainly forgive her.

And then the pretty palpitating Gertrude Lodge went from her husband's homestead; but though her goal was Casterbridge she did not take the direct route thither through Stickleford. Her cunning course at first was in precisely the opposite direction. As soon as she was out of sight, however, she turned to the left, by a road which led into Egdon, and on entering the heath wheeled round, and set out in the true course, due westerly. A more private way down the county could not be imagined; and as to direction, she had merely to keep her horse's head to a point a little to the right of the sun. She knew that she would light upon a furze-cutter or cottager of some sort from time to time, from whom she might correct her bearing.

Though the date was comparatively recent, Egdon was much less fragmentary in character than now. The attempts —successful and otherwise—at cultivation on the lower slopes, which intrude and break up the original heath into small detached heaths, had not been carried far; Enclosure Acts had not taken effect, and the banks and fences which now exclude the cattle of those villagers who formerly enjoyed rights of commonage thereon, and the carts of those who had turbary privileges which kept them in firing all the year round, were not erected. Gertrude, therefore, rode along with no other obstacles than the prickly furze-bushes, the mats of heather, the white water-courses, and the natural steeps and declivities of the ground.

Her horse was sure, if heavy-footed and slow, and though a draught animal, was easy-paced; had it been otherwise, she was not a woman who could have ventured to ride over such a bit of country with a half-dead arm. It was therefore nearly eight o'clock when she drew rein to breathe her bearer on the last outlying high point of heath-land towards Casterbridge, previous to leaving Egdon for the cultivated valleys.

She halted before a pool called Rushy-pond, flanked by the ends of two hedges; a railing ran through the centre of the pond, dividing it in half. Over the railing she saw the low green country; over the green trees the roots of the town; over the roofs a white flat façade, denoting the entrance to the county jail. On the roof of this front specks were moving about; they seemed to be workmen erecting something. Her flesh crept. She descended slowly, and was soon amid corn-fields and pastures. In another half-hour, when it was almost dusk, Gertrude reached the White Hart, the first inn of the town on that side.

Little surprise was excited by her arrival; farmer's wives rode on horseback then more than they do now; though, for that matter, Mrs. Lodge was not imagined to be a wife at all; the innkeeper supposed her some harum-skarum young woman who had come to attend "hang-fair" next day. Neither her husband nor herself ever dealt in Caster-bridge market, so that she was unknown. While dis-mounting she beheld a crowd of boys standing at the door of a harnessmaker's shop just above the inn, looking inside it with deep interest.

"What is going on there?" she asked of the ostler.

"Making the rope for to-morrow."

She throbbed responsively, and contracted her arm.

" 'Tis sold by the inch afterwards," the man continued. "I could get you a bit, miss, for nothing, if you'd like?"

She hastily repudiated any such wish, all the more from a curious creeping feeling that the condemned wretch's destiny was becoming interwoven with her own; and having engaged a room for the night, sat down to think.

Up to this time she had formed but the vaguest notions about her means of obtaining access to the prison. The words of the cunning-man returned to her mind. He had implied that she should use her beauty, impaired though it was, as a pass-key. In her inexperience she knew little about jail functionaries; she had heard of a high-sheriff and an under-sheriff, but dimly only. She knew, however, that there must be a hangman, and to the hangman she determined to apply.

A WATER-SIDE HERMIT

VIII

At this date, and for several years after, there was a hangman to almost every jail. Gertrude found, on inquiry, that the Casterbridge official dwelt in a lonely cottage by a deep slow river flowing under the cliff on which the prison buildings were situate—the stream being the self-same one, though she did not know it, which watered the Stickleford and Holmstoke meads lower down in its course.

Having changed her dress, and before she had eaten or drunk—for she could not take her ease till she had ascertained some particulars—Gertrude pursued her way by a path along the water-side to the cottage indicated. Passing thus the outskirts of the jail, she discerned on the level roof over the gateway three rectangular lines against the sky, where the specks had been moving in her distant view; she recognized what the erection was, and passed quickly on. Another hundred yards brought her to the executioner's house, which a boy pointed out. It stood close to the same stream, and was hard by a weir, the water of which emitted a steady roar.

While she stood hesitating the door opened, and an old man come forth shading a candle with one hand. Locking the door on the outside, he turned to a flight of wooden steps fixed against the end of the cottage, and began to ascend them, this being evidently the staircase to his bedroom. Gertrude hastened forward, but by the time she reached the foot of the ladder he was at the top. She called to him loudly enough to be heard above the roar of the weir; he looked down and said, "What d'ye want here?"

"To speak to you a minute."

The candle-light, such as it was, fell upon her imploring, pale, upturned face, and Davies (as the hangman was called) backed down the ladder. "I was just going to bed," he said: " 'Early to bed and early to rise,' but I don't mind stopping a minute for such a one as you. Come into house." He reopened the door, and preceded her to the room within.

The implements of his daily work, which was that of a jobbing gardener, stood in a corner, and seeing probably that she looked rural, he said, "If you want me to undertake country work I can't come, for I never leave Casterbridge for gentle nor simple—not I. My real calling is officer of justice," he added formally.

"Yes, yes! That's it. To-morrow!"

"Ah! I thought so. Well, what's the matter about that? 'Tis no use to come here about the knot—folks do come continually, but I tell 'em one knot is as merciful as another if ye keep it under the ear. Is the unfortunate man a relation; or, I should say, perhaps" (looking at her dress) "a person who's been in your employ?"

"No. What time is the execution?"

"The same as usual—twelve o'clock, or as soon after as the London mail-coach gets in. We always wait for that, in case of 'a reprieve."

"O—a reprieve—I hope not!" she said involuntarily.

"Well,—hee, hee!—as a matter of business, so do I! But still, if ever a young fellow deserved to be let off, this one does; only just turned eighteen, and only present by chance when the rick was fired. Howsomever, there's not much risk of it, as they are obliged to make an example of him, there having been so much destruction of property that way lately."

"I mean," she explained, "that I want to touch him for a charm, a cure of an affliction, by the advice of a man who has proved the virtue of the remedy."

"O yes, miss! Now I understand. I've had such people come in past years. But it didn't strike me that you looked of a sort to require blood-turning. What's the complaint? The wrong kind for this, I'll be bound."

"My arm." She reluctantly showed the withered skin.

"Ah!—'tis all a-scram!" said the hangman, examining it.

"Yes," said she.

"Well," he continued, with interest, "that *is* the class o' subject, I'm bound to admit! I like the look of the wownd; it is truly as suitable for the cure as any I ever saw. 'Twas a knowing-man that sent 'ee, whoever he was."

"You can contrive for me all that's necessary?" she said breathlessly.

"You should really have gone to the governor of the jail, and your doctor with 'ee, and given your name and address—that's how it used to be done, if I recollect. Still, perhaps, I can manage it for a trifling fee."

"O, thank you! I would rather do it this way, as I should like it kept private."

"Lover not to know, eh?"

"No—husband."

"Aha! Very well. I'll get 'ee a touch of the corpse."

"Where is it now?" she said, shuddering.

"It?—he, you mean; he's living yet. Just inside that little small winder up there in the glum." He signified the jail on the cliff above.

She thought of her husband and her friends. "Yes, of course," she said; "and how am I to proceed?"

He took her to the door. "Now, do you be waiting at the little wicket in the wall, that you'll find up there in the lane, not later than one o'clock. I will open it from the inside, as I shan't come home to dinner till he's cut down. Good-night. Be punctual; and if you don't want anybody to know 'ee, wear a veil. Ah—once I had such a daughter as you!"

She went away, and climbed the path above, to assure herself that she would be able to find the wicket next day. Its outline was soon visible to her—a narrow opening in the outer wall of the prison precincts. The steep was so great that, having reached the wicket, she stopped a moment to breathe; and, looking back upon the waterside cot, saw the hangman again ascending his outdoor staircase. He entered the loft or chamber to which it led, and in a few minutes extinguished his light.

The town clock struck ten, and she returned to the White Hart as she had come.

A RENCOUNTER

IX

It was one o'clock on Saturday. Gertrude Lodge, having been admitted to the jail as above described, was sitting in a waiting-room within the second gate, which stood under a classic archway of ashlar, then comparatively modern, and bearing the inscription, "COVNTY JAIL: 1793." This had been the façade she saw from the heath the day before. Near at hand was a passage to the roof on which the gallows stood.

The town was thronged, and the market suspended; but Gertrude had seen scarcely a soul. Having kept her room till the hour of the appointment, she had proceeded to the spot by a way which avoided the open space below the cliff where the spectators had gathered; but she could, even now, hear the multitudinous babble of their voices, out of which rose at intervals the hoarse croak of a single voice uttering the words, "Last dying speech and confession!" There had been no reprieve, and the execution was over; but the crowd still waited to see the body taken down.

Soon the persistent woman heard a trampling overhead, then a hand beckoned to her, and, following directions, she went out and crossed the inner paved court beyond the gatehouse, her knees trembling so that she could scarcely walk. One of her arms was out of its sleeve, and only covered by her shawl.

On the spot at which she had now arrived were two trestles, and before she could think of their purpose she heard heavy feet descending stairs somewhere at her back. Turn her head she would not, or could not, and, rigid in this position, she was conscious of a rough coffin passing her shoulder, borne by four men. It was open, and in it lay the body of a young man, wearing the smockfrock of a rustic, and fustian breeches. The corpse had been thrown into the coffin so hastily that the skirt of the smockfrock was hanging over. The burden was temporarily deposited on the trestles.

By this time the young woman's state was such that a grey mist seemed to float before her eyes, on account of which, and the veil she wore, she could scarcely discern anything: it was as though she had nearly died, but was·held up by a sort of galvanism.

"Now!" said a voice close at hand, and she was just conscious that the word had been addressed to her.

By a last strenuous effort she advanced, at the same time hearing persons approaching behind her. She bared her poor curst arm; and Davies, uncovering the face of the corpse, took Gertrude's hand, and held it so that her arm lay across the dead man's neck, upon a line the colour of an unripe blackberry, which surrounded it.

Gertrude shrieked: "the turn o' the blood," predicted by the conjuror, had taken place. But at that moment a second shriek rent the air of the enclosure: it was not Gertrude's, and its effect upon her was to make her start round.

Immediately behind her stood Rhoda Brook, her face drawn, and her eyes red with weeping. Behind Rhoda stood Gertrude's own husband; his countenance lined, his eyes dim, but without a tear.

"D——n you! what are you doing here?" he said hoarsely.

"Hussy—to come between us and our child now!" cried Rhoda. "This is the meaning of what Satan showed me in the vision! You are like her at last!" And clutching the bare arm of the younger woman, she pulled her unresistingly back against the wall. Immediately Brook had loosened her hold the fragile young Gertrude slid down against the feet of her husband. When he lifted her up she was unconscious.

The mere sight of the twain had been enough to suggest to her that the dead young man was Rhoda's son. At that time the relatives of an executed convict had the privilege of claiming the body for burial, if they chose to do so; and it was for this purpose that Lodge was awaiting the inquest with Rhoda. He had been summoned by her as soon as the young man was taken in the crime, and at different times since; and he had attended in court during the trial. This was the "holiday" he had been indulging in of late. The two wretched parents had wished to avoid exposure; and hence had come themselves for the body, a waggon and sheet for its conveyance and covering being in waiting outside.

Gertrude's case was so serious that it was deemed advisable to call to her the surgeon who was at hand. She was taken out of the jail into the town; but she never reached home alive. Her delicate vitality, sapped perhaps by the paralyzed arm, collapsed under the double shock that followed the severe strain, physical and mental, to which she had subjected herself during the previous twenty-four hours. Her blood had been "turned" indeed—too far. Her death took place in the town three days after.

Her husband was never seen in Casterbridge again; once only in the old market-place at Anglebury, which he had so much frequented, and very seldom in public anywhere. Burdened at first with moodiness and remorse, he eventually changed for the better, and appeared as a chastened and thoughtful man. Soon after attending the funeral of his poor young wife he took steps towards giving up the farms in Holmstoke and the adjoining parish, and, having sold every head of his stock, he went away to Port-Bredy, at the other end of the county, living there in solitary lodgings till his death two years later of a painless decline. It was then found that he had bequeathed the whole of his not inconsiderable property to a reformatory for boys, subject to the payment of a small annuity to Rhoda Brook, if she could be found to claim it.

For some time she could not be found; but eventually she reappeared in her old parish,—absolutely refusing, however, to have anything to do with the provision made for her. Her monotonous milking at the dairy was resumed, and followed for many long years, till her form became bent, and her once abundant dark hair white and worn away at the forehead—perhaps by long pressure against the cows. Here, sometimes, those who knew her experiences would stand and observe her, and wonder what sombre thoughts were beating inside that impassive, wrinkled brow, to the rhythm of the alternating milk-streams.

THE WINTERS AND THE PALMLEYS

"And, of course, my old acquaintance, the annuitant, Mrs. Winter, who always seemed to have something on her mind, is dead and gone?" said the home-comer, after a long silence.

Nobody in the van seemed to recollect the name.

"O yes, she must be dead long since: she was seventy when I as a child knew her," he added.

"I can recollect Mrs. Winter very well, if nobody else can," said the aged groceress. "Yes, she's been dead these five-and-twenty year at least. You knew what it was upon her mind, sir, that gave her that hollow-eyed look, I suppose?"

"It had something to do with a son of hers, I think I once was told. But I was too young to know particulars."

The groceress sighed as she conjured up a vision of days long past. "Yes," she murmured, "it had all to do with a son." Finding that the van was still in a listening mood, she spoke on:—

"To go back to the beginning—if one must—there were two women in the parish when I was a child, who were to a certain extent rivals in good looks. Never mind particulars, but in consequence of this they were at daggers-drawn, and they did not love each other any better when one of them tempted the other's lover away from her and married him. He was a young man of the name of Winter, and in due time they had a son.

"The other woman did not marry for many years: but when she was about thirty a quiet man named Palmley asked her to be his wife, and she accepted him. You don't mind when the Palmleys were Longpuddle folk, but I do well. She had a son also, who was, of course, nine or ten years younger than the son of the first. The child proved to be of rather weak intellect, though his mother loved him as the apple of her eye.

"This woman's husband died when the child was eight years old, and left his widow and boy in poverty. Her former rival, also a widow now, but fairly well provided for, offered for pity's sake to take the child as errand-boy, small as he was, her own son, Jack, being hard upon seventeen. Her poor neighbour could do no better than let the child go there. And to the richer woman's house little Palmley straightway went.

"Well, in some way or other—how, it was never exactly known—the thriving woman, Mrs. Winter, sent the little boy with a message to the next village one December

day, much against his will. It was getting dark, and
the child prayed to be allowed not to go, because he
would be afraid coming home. But the mistress insisted,
more out of thoughtlessness than cruelty, and the child
went. On his way back he had to pass through Yalbury
Wood, and something came out from behind a tree and
frightened him into fits. The child was quite ruined by
it; he became quite a drivelling idiot, and soon afterward died.

"Then the other woman had nothing left to live for,
and vowed vengeance against that rival who had first
won away her lover, and now had been the cause of her
bereavement. This last affliction was certainly not intended
by her thriving acquaintance, though it must be owned
that when it was done she seemed but little concerned.
Whatever vengeance poor Mrs. Palmley felt, she had no
opportunity of carrying it out, and time might have
softened her feelings into forgetfulness of her supposed
wrongs as she dragged on her lonely life. So matters
stood when, a year after the death of the child, Mrs.
Palmley's niece, who had been born and bred in the
city of Exonbury, came to live with her.

"This young woman—Miss Harriet Palmley—was a
proud and handsome girl, very well brought up, and
more stylish and genteel than the people of our village,
as was natural, considering where she came from. She
regarded herself as much above Mrs. Winter and her
son in position as Mrs. Winter and her son considered
themselves above poor Mrs. Palmley. But love is an
unceremonious thing, and what in the world should happen
but that young Jack Winter must fall wofully and wildly
in love with Harriet Palmley almost as soon as he saw her.

"She being better educated than he, and caring nothing
for the village notion of his mother's superiority to her
aunt, did not give him much encouragement. But Longpuddle being no very large world, the two could not help
seeing a good deal of each other while she was staying
there, and, disdainful young woman as she was, she did
seem to take a little pleasure in his attentions and advances.

"One day when they were picking apples together, he asked her to marry him. She had not expected anything so practical as that at so early a time, and was led by her surprise into a half-promise; at any rate she did not absolutely refuse him, and accepted some little presents that he made her.

"But he saw that her view of him was rather as a simple village lad than as a young man to look up to, and he felt that he must do something bold to secure her. So he said one day, 'I am going away, to try to get into a better position than I can get here.' In two or three weeks he wished her good-bye, and went away to Monksbury, to superintend a farm, with a view to start as a farmer himself; and from there he wrote regularly to her, as if their marriage were an understood thing.

"Now Harriet liked the young man's presents and the admiration of his eyes; but on paper he was less attractive to her. Her mother had been a schoolmistress, and Harriet had besides a natural aptitude for pen-and-ink work, in days when to be a ready writer was not such a common thing as it is now, and when actual handwriting was valued as an accomplishment in itself. Jack Winter's performances in the shape of love-letters quite jarred her city nerves and her finer taste, and when she answered one of them, in the lovely running hand that she took such pride in, she very strictly and loftily bade him to practise with a pen and spelling-book if he wished to please her. Whether he listened to her request or not nobody knows, but his letters did not improve. He ventured to tell her in his clumsy way that if her heart were more warm towards him she would not be so nice about his handwriting and spelling; which indeed was true enough.

"Well, in Jack's absence the weak flame that had been set alight in Harriet's heart soon sank low, and at last went out altogether. He wrote and wrote, and begged and prayed her to give a reason for her coldness; and then she told him plainly that she was town born, and he was not sufficiently well educated to please her.

"Jack Winter's want of pen-and-ink training did not

make him less thin-skinned than others; in fact, he was terribly tender and touchy about anything. This reason that she gave for finally throwing him over grieved him, shamed him, and mortified him more than can be told in these times; the pride of that day in being able to write with beautiful flourishes, and the sorrow at not being able to do so, raging so high. Jack replied to her with an angry note, and then she hit back with smart little stings, telling him how many words he had misspelt in his last letter, and declaring again that this alone was sufficient justification for any woman to put an end to an understanding with him. Her husband must be a better scholar.

"He bore her rejection of him in silence, but his suffering was sharp—all the sharper in being untold. She communicated with Jack no more; and as his reason for going out into the world had been only to provide a home worthy of her, he had no further object in planning such a home now that she was lost to him. He therefore gave up the farming occupation by which he had hoped to make himself a master-farmer, and left the spot to return to his mother.

"As soon as he got back to Longpuddle he found that Harriet had already looked wi' favour upon another lover. He was a young road-contractor, and Jack could not but admit that his rival was both in manners and scholarship much ahead of him. Indeed, a more sensible match for the beauty who had been dropped into the village by fate could hardly have been found than this man, who could offer her so much better a chance than Jack could have done, with his uncertain future and narrow abilities for grappling with the world. The fact was so clear to him that he could hardly blame her.

"One day by accident Jack saw on a scrap of paper the handwriting of Harriet's new beloved. It was flowing like a stream, well spelt, the work of a man accustomed to the ink-bottle and the dictionary, of a man already called in the parish a good scholar. And then it struck all of a sudden into Jack's mind what a constrast the letters of this young man must make to his own miserable old

letters, and how ridiculous they must make his lines
appear. He groaned and wished he had never written to
her, and wondered if she had ever kept his poor performances. Possibly she had kept them, for women are in the
habit of doing that, he thought, and whilst they were in
her hands there was always a chance of his honest, stupid
love-assurances to her being joked over by Harriet with
her present lover, or by anybody who should accidentally
uncover them.

"The nervous, moody young man could not bear the
thought of it, and at length decided to ask her to return
them, as was proper when engagements were broken off.
He was some hours in framing, copying, and recopying
the short note in which he made his request, and having
finished it he sent it to her house. His messenger came
back with the answer, by word of mouth, that Miss Palmley bade him say she should not part with what was hers,
and wondered at his boldness in troubling her.

"Jack was much affronted at this, and determined to
go for his letters himself. He chose a time when he knew
she was at home, and knocked and went in without much
ceremony; for though Harriet was so high and mighty,
Jack had small respect for her aunt, Mrs. Palmley, whose
little child had been his boot-cleaner in earlier days.
Harriet was in the room, this being the first time they
had met since she had jilted him. He asked for his letters
with a stern and bitter look at her.

"At first she said he might have them for all that she
cared, and took them out of the bureau where she kept
them. Then she glanced over the outside one of the
packet, and suddenly altering her mind, she told him
shortly that his request was a silly one, and slipped the
letters into her aunt's work-box, which stood open on
the table, locking it, and saying with a bantering laugh
that of course she thought it best to keep 'em, since they
might be useful to produce as evidence that she had good
cause for declining to marry him.

"He blazed up hot. 'Give me those letters!' he said.
'They are mine!'

" 'No, they are not,' she replied; 'they are mine.'

" 'Whos'ever they are I want them back,' says he. 'I don't want to be made sport of for my penmanship: you've another young man now! He has your confidence, and you pour all your tales into his ear. You'll be showing them to him!'

" 'Perhaps,' said my lady Harriet, with calm coolness, like the heartless woman that she was.

"Her manner so maddened him that he made a step towards the work-box, but she snatched it up, locked it in the bureau, and turned upon him triumphant. For a moment he seemed to be going to wrench the key of the bureau out of her hand; but he stopped himself, and swung round upon his heel and went away.

"When he was out-of-doors alone, and it got night, he walked about restless, and stinging with the sense of being beaten at all points by her. He could not help fancying her telling her new lover or her acquaintances of this scene with himself, and laughing with them over those poor blotted, crooked lines of his that he had been so anxious to obtain. As the evening passed on he worked himself into a dogged resolution to have them back at any price, come what might.

"At the dead of night he came out of his mother's house by the back door, and creeping through the garden hedge went along the field adjoining till he reached the back of her aunt's dwelling. The moon struck bright and flat upon the walls, 'twas said, and every shiny leaf of the creepers was like a little looking-glass in the rays. From long acquaintance Jack knew the arrangement and position of everything in Mrs. Palmley's house as well as in his own mother's. The back window close to him was a casement with little leaded squares, as it is to this day, and was, as now, one of two lighting the sitting-room. The other, being in front, was closed up with shutters, but this back one had not even a blind, and the moonlight as it streamed in showed every article of the furniture to him outside. To the right of the room is the fireplace, as you may remember; to the left was the bureau at that time; inside the bureau was Harriet's work-box, as he supposed (though it was really her aunt's), and inside the work-box were his letters. Well, he took out his pocket-knife, and without noise lifted the leading of one of the panes, so that he could take out the glass, and putting his hand through the hole he unfastened the casement, and climbed in through the opening. All the household—that is to say, Mrs. Palmley, Harriet, and the little maidservant—were asleep. Jack went straight to the bureau, so he said, hoping it might have been unfastened again—it not being kept locked in ordinary—but Harriet had never unfastened it since she secured her letters there the day before. Jack told afterward how he thought of her sleep upstairs, caring nothing for him, and of the way she had made sport of him and of his letters; and having advanced so far, he was not to be hindered now. By forcing the large blade of his knife under the flap of the bureau, he burst the weak lock; within was the rosewood work-box just as she had placed it in her hurry to keep it from him. There being no time to spare for getting the letters out of it then, he took it under his arm, shut the bureau, and made the best of his way out of the house, latching the casement behind him, and refixing the pane of glass in its place.

"Winter found his way back to his mother's as he had come, and being dog-tired, crept upstairs to bed, hiding the box till he could destroy its contents. The next morning early he set about doing this, and carried it to the linhay at the back of his mother's dwelling. Here by the hearth he opened the box, and began burning one by one the letters that had cost him so much labour to write and shame to think of, meaning to return the box to Harriet, after repairing the slight damage he had caused it by opening it without a key, with a note—the last she would ever receive from him—telling her triumphantly that in refusing to return what he had asked for she had calculated too surely upon his submission to her whims.

"But on removing the last letter from the box he received a shock; for underneath it, at the very bottom, lay money—several golden guineas—"Doubtless Harriet's pocket-money," he said to himself; though it was not, but Mrs. Palmley's. Before he had got over his qualms at this discovery he heard footsteps coming through the house-passage to where he was. In haste he pushed the box and what was in it under some brushwood which lay in the linhay; but Jack had been already seen. Two constables entered the out-house, and seized him as he knelt before the fireplace, securing the work-box and all it contained at the same moment. They had come to apprehend him on a charge of breaking into the dwelling-house of Mrs. Palmley on the night preceding; and almost before the lad knew what had happened to him they were leading him along the lane that connects that end of the village with this turnpike-road, and along they marched him between 'em all the way to Casterbridge jail.

"Jack's act amounted to night burglary—though he had never thought of it—and burglary was felony, and a capital offense in those days. His figure had been seen by some one against the bright wall as he came away from Mrs. Palmley's back window, and the box and money were found in his possession, while the evidence of the broken bureau-lock and tinkered window-pane was more than enough for circumstantial detail. Whether his protestation that he went only for his letters, which he believed to be wrongfully kept from him, would have availed him anything if supported by other evidence I do not know; but the one person who could have borne it out was Harriet, and she acted entirely under the sway of her aunt. That aunt was deadly towards Jack Winter. Mrs. Palmley's time had come. Here was her revenge upon the woman who had first won away her lover, and next ruined and deprived her of her heart's treasure—her little son. When the assize week drew on, and Jack had to stand his trial, Harriet did not appear in the case at all, which was allowed to take its course, Mrs. Palmley testifying to the general facts of the burglary. Whether Harriet would have come forward if Jack had appealed to her is not known; possibly she would have done it for pity's sake; but Jack was too proud to ask a single favour of a girl who had jilted him; and he let her alone.

The trial was a short one, and the death sentence was passed.

"The day o' young Jack's execution was a cold dusty Saturday in March. He was so boyish and slim that they were obliged in mercy to hang him in the heaviest fetters kept in the jail, lest his heft should not break his neck, and they weighed so upon him that he could hardly drag himself up to the drop. At that time the gover'ment was not strict about burying the body of an executed person within the precincts of the prison, and at the earnest prayer of his poor mother his body was allowed to be brought home. All the parish waited at their cottage doors in the evening for its arrival: I remember how, as a very little girl, I stood by my mother's side. About eight o'clock, as we hearkened on our door-stones in the cold bright starlight, we could hear the faint crackle of a waggon from the direction of the turnpike-road. The noise was lost as the waggon dropped into a hollow, then it was plain again as it lumbered down the next long incline, and presently it entered Longpuddle. The coffin was laid in the belfry for the night, and the next day, Sunday, between the services, we buried him. A funeral sermon was preached the same afternoon, the text chosen being, 'He was the only son of his mother, and she was a widow.' . . . Yes, they were cruel times!

"As for Harriet, she and her lover were married in due time; but by all account her life was no jocund one. She and her good-man found that they could not live comfortably at Longpuddle, by reason of her connection with Jack's misfortunes, and they settled in a distant town, and were no more heard of by us; Mrs. Palmley, too, found it advisable to join 'em shortly after. The dark-eyed, gaunt old Mrs. Winter, remembered by the emigrant gentleman here, was, as you will have foreseen, the Mrs. Winter of this story; and I can well call to mind how lonely she was, how afraid the children were of her, and how she kept herself as a stranger among us, though she lived so long."

BARBARA OF THE HOUSE OF GREBE

It was apparently an idea, rather than a passion, that inspired Lord Uplandtowers' resolve to win her. Nobody ever knew when he formed it, or whence he got his assurance of success in the face of her manifest dislike of him. Possibly not until after that first important act of her life which I shall presently mention. His matured and cynical doggedness at the age of nineteen, when impulse mostly rules calculation, was remarkable, and might have owed its existence as much to his succession to the earldom and its accompanying local honours in childhood, as to the family character; an elevation which jerked him into maturity, so to speak, without his having known adolescence. He had only reached his twelfth year when his father, the fourth Earl, died, after a course of the Bath waters.

Nevertheless, the family character had a great deal to do with it. Determination was hereditary in the bearers of that escutcheon; sometimes for good, sometimes for evil.

The seats of the two families were about ten miles apart, the way between them lying along the now old, then new, turnpike-road connecting Havenpool and Warborne with the city of Melchester; a road which, though only a branch from what was known as the Great Western Highway, is probably, even at present, as it has been for the last hundred years, one of the finest examples of a macadamized turnpike-track that can be found in England.

The mansion of the Earl, as well as that of his neighbour, Barbara's father, stood back about a mile from the highway, with which each was connected by an ordinary drive and lodge. It was along this particular highway that the young Earl drove on a certain evening at Christmastide some twenty years before the end of the last century, to attend a ball at Chene Manor, the home of Barbara and her parents Sir John and Lady Grebe. Sir John's was a baronetcy created a few years before the breaking out of the Civil War, and his lands were even more extensive than those of Lord Uplandtowers himself, comprising this Manor of Chene, another on the coast near, half the Hundred of Cockdene, and well-enclosed lands in several other parishes, notably Warborne and those contiguous. At this time Barbara was barely seventeen, and the ball is the first occasion on which we have any tradition of Lord Uplandtowers attempting tender relations with her; it was early enough, God knows.

An intimate friend—one of the Drenkhards—is said to have dined with him that day, and Lord Uplandtowers had, for a wonder, communicated to his guest the secret design of his heart.

"You'll never get her—sure; you'll never get her!" this friend had said at parting. "She's not drawn to your lordship by love: and as for thought of a good match, why, there's no more calculation in her than in a bird."

"We'll see," said Lord Uplandtowers impassively.

He no doubt thought of his friend's forecast as he travelled along the highway in his chariot; but the sculptural repose of his profile against the vanishing daylight on his right hand would have shown his friend that the Earl's equanimity was undisturbed. He reached the solitary wayside tavern called Lornton Inn—the rendezvous of many a daring poacher for operations in the adjoining forest; and he might have observed, if he had taken the trouble, a strange post-chaise standing in the halting-space before the inn. He duly sped past it, and half-an-hour after through the little town of Warborne. Onward, a mile further, was the house of his entertainer.

At this date it was an imposing edifice—or, rather, congeries of edifices—as extensive as the residence of the Earl himself, though far less regular. One wing showed extreme antiquity, having huge chimneys, whose substructures projected from the external walls like towers; and a kitchen of vast dimensions, in which (it was said) breakfasts had been cooked for John of Gaunt. Whilst he was yet in the forecourt he could hear the rhythm of French horns and clarionets, the favourite instruments of those days at such entertainments.

Entering the long parlour, in which the dance had just

been opened by Lady Grebe with a minuet—it being now
seven o'clock, according to the tradition—he was received
with a welcome befitting his rank, and looked round for
Barbara. She was not dancing, and seemed to be pre-
occupied—almost, indeed, as though she had been waiting
for him. Barbara at this time was a good and pretty girl,
who never spoke ill of any one, and hated other pretty
women the very least possible. She did not refuse him
for the country-dance which followed, and soon after was
his partner in a second.

The evening wore on, and the horns and clarionets
tootled merrily. Barbara evinced towards her lover neither
distinct preference nor aversion; but old eyes would have
seen that she pondered something. However, after supper
she pleaded a headache, and disappeared. To pass the
time of her absence, Lord Uplandtowers went into a little
room adjoining the long gallery, where some elderly ones
were sitting by the fire—for he had a phlegmatic dislike
of dancing for its own sake,—and, lifting the window-
curtains, he looked out of the window into the park and
wood, dark now as a cavern. Some of the guests appeared
to be leaving even so soon as this, two lights showing
themselves as turning away from the door and sinking
to nothing in the distance.

His hostess put her head into the room to look for
partners for the ladies, and Lord Uplandtowers came out.
Lady Grebe informed him that Barbara had not returned
to the ballroom: she had gone to bed in sheer necessity.

"She has been so excited over the ball all day," her
mother continued, "that I feared she would be worn out
early. . . . But sure, Lord Uplandtowers, you won't be
leaving yet?"

He said that it was near twelve o'clock, and that some
had already left.

"I protest nobody has gone yet," said Lady Grebe.

To humour her he stayed till midnight, and then set
out. He had made no progress in his suit; but he had
assured himself that Barbara gave no other guest the
preference, and nearly everybody in the neighborhood
was there.

" 'Tis only a matter of time," said the calm young philosopher.

The next morning he lay till near ten o'clock, and he had only just come out upon the head of the staircase when he heard hoofs upon the gravel without; in a few moments the door had been opened, and Sir John Grebe met him in the hall, as he set foot on the lowest stair.

"My lord—where's Barbara—my daughter?"

Even the Earl of Uplandtowers could not repress amazement. "What's the matter, my dear Sir John," says he.

The news was startling, indeed. From the Baronet's disjointed explanation Lord Uplandtowers gathered that after his own and the other guests' departure Sir John and Lady Grebe had gone to rest without seeing any more of Barbara; it being understood by them that she had retired to bed when she sent word to say that she could not join the dancers again. Before then she had told her maid that she would dispense with her services for this night; and there was evidence to show that the young lady had never lain down at all, the bed remaining unpressed. Circumstances seemed to prove that the deceitful girl had feigned indisposition to get an excuse for leaving the ball-room, and that she had left the house within ten minutes, presumably during the first dance after supper.

"I saw her go," said Lord Uplandtowers.

"The devil you did!" says Sir John.

"Yes." And he mentioned the retreating carriage-lights, and how he was assured by Lady Grebe that no guest had departed.

"Surely that was it!" said the father. "But she's not gone alone, d'ye know!"

"Ah—who is the young man?"

"I can on'y guess. My worst fear is my most likely guess. I'll say no more. I thought—yet I would not believe—it possible that you was the sinner. Would that you had been! But 'tis t'other, by Heaven! I must e'en up and after 'em!"

"Whom do you suspect?"

Sir John would not give a name, and, stultified rather than agitated, Lord Uplandtowers accompanied him back to Chene. He again asked upon whom were the Baronet's suspicions directed; and the impulsive Sir John was no match for the insistence of Uplandtowers.

He said at length, "I fear 'tis Edmond Willowes."

"Who's he?"

"A young fellow of Shottsford-Forum—a widow-woman's son," the other told him, and explained that Willowes's father, or grandfather, was the last of the old glass-painters in that place, where (as you may know) the art lingered on when it had died out in every other part of England.

"By God that's bad—mighty bad!" said Lord Upland-towers, throwing himself back in the chaise in frigid despair.

They despatched emissaries in all directions; one by the Melchester Road, another by Shottsford-Forum, another coastwards.

But the lovers had a ten-hours' start; and it was apparent that sound judgment had been exercised in choosing as their time of flight the particular night when the movements of a strange carriage would not be noticed, either in the park or on the neighbouring highway, owing to the general press of vehicles. The chaise which had been seen waiting at Lornton Inn was, no doubt, the one they had escaped in; and the pair of heads which had planned so cleverly thus far had probably contrived marriage ere now.

The fears of her parents were realized. A letter sent by special messenger from Barbara, on the evening of that day, briefly informed them that her lover and herself were on the way to London, and before this communication reached her home they would be united as husband and wife. She had taken this extreme step because she loved her dear Edmond as she could love no other man, and because she had seen closing round her the doom of marriage with Lord Uplandtowers, unless she put that threatened fate out of possibility by doing as she had done. She had well considered the step beforehead, and was prepared to live like any other country-townsman's wife if her father repudiated her for her action.

"Damn her!" said Lord Uplandtowers, as he drove homeward that night. "Damn her for a fool!"—which shows the kind of love he bore her.

Well; Sir John had already started in pursuit of them as a matter of duty, driving like a wild man to Melchester, and thence by the direct highway to the capital. But he soon saw that he was acting to no purpose; and by and by, discovering that the marriage had actually taken place, he forebore all attempts to unearth them in the City, and returned and sat down with his lady to digest the event as best they could.

To proceed against this Willowes for the abduction of our heiress was, possibly, in their power; yet, when they considered the now unalterable facts, they refrained from violent retribution. Some six weeks passed, during which time Barbara's parents, though they keenly felt her loss, held no communication with the truant, either for reproach or condonation. They continued to think of the disgrace she had brought upon herself; for, though the young man was an honest fellow, and the son of an honest father, the latter had died so early, and his widow had had such struggles to maintain herself, that the son was very imperfectly educated. Moreover, his blood was, as far as they knew, of no distinction whatever, whilst hers, through her mother, was compounded of the best juices of ancient baronial distillation, containing tinctures of Maundeville, and Mohun, and Syward, and Peverell, and Culliford, and Talbot, and Plantagenet, and York, and Lancaster, and God knows what besides, which it was a thousand pities to throw away.

The father and mother sat by the fireplace that was spanned by the four-centred arch bearing the family shields on its haunches, and groaned aloud—the lady more than Sir John.

"To think this should have come upon us in our old age!" said he.

"Speak for yourself!" she snapped through her sobs, "I am only one-and-forty! . . . Why didn't ye ride faster and overtake 'em!"

In the meantime the young married lovers, caring no more about their blood than about ditch-water, were intensely happy—happy, that is, in the descending scale which, as we all know, Heaven in its wisdom has ordained for such rash cases; that is to say, the first week they were in the seventh heaven, the second in the sixth, the third week temperate, the fourth reflective, and so on; a lover's heart after possession being comparable to the earth in its geologic stages, as described to us sometimes by our worthy President; first a hot coal, then a warm one, then a cooling cinder, then chilly—the simile shall be pursued no further. The long and the short of it was that one day a letter, sealed with their daughter's own little seal, came into Sir John and Lady Grebe's hands; and, on opening it, they found it to contain an appeal from the young couple to Sir John to forgive them for what they had done, and they would fall on their naked knees and be most dutiful children for evermore.

Then Sir John and his lady sat down again by the fireplace with the four-centred arch, and consulted, and re-read the letter. Sir John Grebe, if the truth must be told, loved his daughter's happiness far more, poor man, than he loved his name and lineage; he recalled to his mind all her little ways, gave vent to a sigh; and, by this time acclimatized to the idea of the marriage, said that what was done could not be undone, and that he supposed they must not be too harsh with her. Perhaps Barbara and her husband were in actual need; and how could they let their only child starve?

A slight consolation had come to them in an unexpected manner. They had been credibly informed that an ancestor of plebeian Willowes was once honoured with intermarriage with a scion of the aristocracy who had gone to the dogs. In short, such is the foolishness of distinguished parents, and sometimes of others also, that they wrote that very day to the address Barbara had given them, informing her that she might return home and bring her husband with her; they would not object to see him, would not reproach her, and would endeavour to welcome both, and to discuss with them what could best be arranged for their future.

In three or four days a rather shabby post-chaise drew up at the door of Chene Manor-house, at sound of which the tender-hearted baronet and his wife ran out as if to welcome a prince and princess of the blood. They were overjoyed to see their spoilt child return safe and sound—though she was only Mrs. Willowes, wife of Edmond Willowes of nowhere. Barbara burst into penitential tears, and both husband and wife were contrite enough, as well they might be, considering that they had not a guinea to call their own.

When the four had calmed themselves, and not a word of chiding had been uttered to the pair, they discussed the position soberly, young Willowes sitting in the background with great modesty till invited forward by Lady Grebe in no frigid tone.

"How handsome he is!" she said to herself. "I don't wonder at Barbara's craze for him."

He was, indeed, one of the handsomest men who ever set his lips on a maid's. A blue coat, murrey waistcoat, and breeches of drab set off a figure that could scarcely be surpassed. He had large dark eyes, anxious now, as they glanced from Barbara to her parents and tenderly back again to her; observing whom, even now in her trepidation, one could see why the *sang froid* of Lord Uplandtowers had been raised to more than lukewarmness. Her fair young face (according to the tale handed down by old women) looked out from under a grey conical hat, trimmed with white ostrich-feathers, and her little toes peeped from a buff petticoat worn under a puce gown. Her features were not regular: they were almost infantine, as you may see from miniatures in possession of the family, her mouth showing much sensitiveness, and one could be sure that her faults would not lie on the side of bad temper unless for urgent reasons.

Well, they discussed their state as became them, and the desire of the young couple to gain the goodwill of those upon whom they were literally dependent for everything induced them to agree to any temporizing measure that was not too irksome. Therefore, having been nearly two months united, they did not oppose Sir John's proposal that he should furnish Edmond Willowes with funds sufficient for him to travel a year on the Continent in the company of a tutor, the young man undertaking to lend himself with the utmost diligence to the tutor's instructions, till he became polished outwardly and inwardly to the degree required in the husband of such a lady as Barbara. He was to apply himself to the study of languages, manners, history, society, ruins, and everything else that came under his eyes, till he should return to take his place without blushing by Barbara's side.

"And by that time," said worthy Sir John, "I'll get my little place out at Yewsholt ready for you and Barbara to occupy on your return. The house is small and out of the way; but it will do for a young couple for a while."

"If 'twere no bigger than a summer-house it would do!" says Barbara.

"If 'twere no bigger than a sedan-chair!" says Willowes. "And the more lonely the better."

"We can put up with the loneliness," said Barbara, with less zest. "Some friends will come, no doubt."

All this being laid down, a travelled tutor was called in —a man of many gifts and great experience,—and on a fine morning away tutor and pupil went. A great reason urged against Barbara accompanying her youthful husband was that his attentions to her would naturally be such as to prevent his zealously applying every hour of his time to learning and seeing—an argument of wise prescience, and unanswerable. Regular days for letter-writing were fixed, Barbara and her Edmond exchanged their last kisses at the door, and the chaise swept under the archway into the drive.

He wrote to her from Le Havre, as soon as he reached that port, which was not for seven days, on account of adverse winds; he wrote from Rouen, and from Paris; described to her his sight of the King and Court at Versailles, and the wonderful marble-work and mirrors in that palace; wrote next from Lyons; then, after a comparatively long interval, from Turin, narrating his fearful adventures in crossing Mont Cenis on mules, and how he was overtaken with a terrific snowstorm, which had wellnigh been the end of him, and his tutor, and his guides. Then he wrote glowingly of Italy; and Barbara could see the development of her husband's mind reflected in his letters month by month; and she much admired the forethought of her father in suggesting this education for Edmond. Yet she sighed sometimes—her husband being no longer in evidence to fortify her in her choice of him —and timidly dreaded what mortifications might be in store for her by reason of this *mésalliance*. She went out very little; for on the one or two occasions on which she had shown herself to former friends she noticed a distinct difference in their manner, as though they should say, "Ah, my happy swain's wife; you're caught!"

Edmond's letters were as affectionate as ever; even more affectionate, after a while, than hers were to him. Barbara observed this growing coolness in herself; and like a good and honest lady was horrified and grieved, since her only wish was to act faithfully and uprightly. It troubled her so much that she prayed for a warmer heart, and at last wrote to her husband to beg him, now that he was in the land of Art, to send her his portrait, ever so small, that she might look at it all day and every day, and never for a moment forget his features.

Willowes was nothing loth, and replied that he would do more than she wished: he had made friends with a sculptor in Pisa, who was much interested in him and his history; and he had commissioned this artist to make a bust of himself in marble, which when finished he would send her. What Barbara had wanted was something immediate; but she expressed no objection to the delay; and in his next communication Edmond told her that the sculptor, of his own choice, had decided to extend the bust to a full-length statue, so anxious was he to get a specimen of his skill introduced to the notice of the English aristocracy. It was progressing well, and rapidly,

Meanwhile, Barbara's attention began to be occupied at home with Yewsholt Lodge, the house that her kind-hearted father was preparing for her residence when her husband returned. It was a small place on the plan of a large one—a cottage built in the form of a mansion, having a central hall with a wooden gallery running round it, and rooms no bigger than closets to support this introduction. It stood on a slope so solitary, and sur-rounded by trees so dense, that the birds who inhabited the boughs sang at strange hours, as if they hardly could distinguish night from day.

During the progress of repairs at this bower Barbara frequently visited it. Though so secluded by the dense growth, it was near the high road, and one day while looking over the fence she saw Lord Uplandtowers riding past. He saluted her courteously, yet with mechanical stiffness, and did not halt. Barbara went home, and con-tinued to pray that she might never cease to love her husband. After that she sickened, and did not come out of doors again for a long time.

The year of education had extended to fourteen months, and the house was in order for Edmond's return to take up his abode there with Barbara, when, instead of the accustomed letter for her, came one to Sir John Grebe in the handwriting of the said tutor, informing him of a terrible catastrophe that had occurred to them at Venice. Mr. Willowes and himself had attended the theatre one night during the Carnival of the preceding week, to witness the Italian comedy, when, owing to the carelessness of one of the candle-snuffers, the theatre had caught fire, and been burnt to the ground. Few persons had lost their lives, owing to the superhuman exertions of some of the audience in getting out the senseless sufferers; and, among them all, he who had risked his own life the most heroically was Mr. Willowes. In re-entering for the fifth time to save his fellow-creatures some fiery beams had fallen upon him, and he had been given up for lost. He was, however, by the blessing of Providence, recov-ered, with the life still in him, though he was fearfully burnt; and by almost a miracle he seemed likely to survive, his constitution being wondrously sound. He was, of course, unable to write, but he was receiving the attention of several skilful surgeons. Further report would be made by the next mail or by private hand.

The tutor said nothing in detail of poor Willowes's sufferings, but as soon as the news was broken to Barbara she realized how intense they must have been, and her immediate instinct was to rush to his side, though, on consideration, the journey seemed impossible to her. Her health was by no means what it had been, and to post across Europe at that season of the year, or to traverse the Bay of Biscay in a sailing-craft, was an undertaking that would hardly be justified by the result. But she was anxious to go till, on reading to the end of the letter, her husband's tutor was found to hint very strongly against such a step if it should be contemplated, this being also the opinion of the surgeons. And though Willowes's comrade refrained from giving his reasons, they disclosed themselves plainly enough in the sequel.

The truth was that the worst of the wounds resulting from the fire had occurred to his head and face—that handsome face which had won her heart from her,—and both the tutor and the surgeons knew that for a sensitive young woman to see him before his wounds had healed would cause more misery to her by the shock than happiness to him by her ministrations.

Lady Grebe blurted out what Sir John and Barbara had thought, but had had too much delicacy to express.

"Sure, 'tis mighty hard for you, poor Barbara, that the one little gift he had to justify your rash choice of him—his wonderful good looks—should be taken away like this, to leave 'ee no excuse at all for your conduct in the world's eyes. . . . Well, I wish you'd married t'other—that do I!" And the lady sighed.

"He'll soon get right again," said her father soothingly.

Such remarks as the above were not often made; but they were frequent enough to cause Barbara an uneasy sense of self-stultification. She determined to hear them no longer; and the house at Yewsholt being ready and furnished, she withdrew thither with her maids, where for the first time she could feel mistress of a home that would be hers and her husband's exclusively, when he came.

After long weeks Willowes had recovered sufficiently to be able to write himself, and slowly and tenderly he enlightened her upon the full extent of his injuries. It was a mercy, he said, that he had not lost his sight entirely; but he was thankful to say that he still retained full vision in one eye, though the other was dark for ever. The sparing manner in which he meted out particulars of his condition told Barbara how appalling had been his experience. He was grateful for her assurance that nothing could change her; but feared she did not fully realize that he was so sadly disfigured as to make it doubtful if she would recognize him. However, in spite of all, his heart was as true to her as it ever had been.

Barbara saw from his anxiety how much lay behind. She replied that she submitted to the decrees of Fate, and would welcome him in any shape as soon as he could come. She told him of the pretty retreat in which she had taken up her abode, pending their joint occupation of it, and did not reveal how much she had sighed over the information that all his good looks were gone. Still less did she say that she felt a certain strangeness in awaiting him, the weeks they had lived together having been so short by comparison with the length of his absence.

Slowly drew on the time when Willowes found himself well enough to come home. He landed at Southampton, and posted thence towards Yewsholt. Barbara arranged to go out to meet him as far as Lornton Inn—the spot between the Forest and the Chase at which he had waited for night on the evening of their elopement. Thither she drove at the appointed hour in a little ponychaise, presented by her father on her birthday for her especial use in her new house; which vehicle she sent back on arriving at the inn, the plan agreed upon being that she should perform the return journey with her husband in his hired coach.

There was not much accommodation for a lady at

this wayside tavern; but, as it was a fine evening in early summer, she did not mind—walking about outside, and straining her eyes along the highway for the expected one. But each cloud of dust that enlarged in the distance and drew near was found to disclose a conveyance other than his post-chaise. Barbara remained till the appointment was two hours passed, and then began to fear that owing to some adverse wind in the Channel he was not coming that night.

While waiting she was conscious of a curious trepidation that was not entirely solicitude, and did not amount to dread; her tense state of incertitude bordered both on disappointment and on relief. She had lived six or seven weeks with an imperfectly educated yet handsome husband whom now she had not seen for seventeen months, and who was so changed physically by an accident that she was assured she would hardly know him. Can we wonder at her compound state of mind?

But her immediate difficulty was to get away from Lornton Inn, for her situation was becoming embarrassing. Like too many of Barbara's actions, this drive had been undertaken without much reflection. Expecting to wait no more than a few minutes for her husband in his post-chaise, and to enter it with him, she had not hesitated to isolate herself by sending back her own little vehicle. She now found that, being so well known in this neighbourhood, her excursion to meet her long-absent husband was exciting great interest. She was conscious that more eyes were watching her from the inn-windows than met her own gaze. Barbara had decided to get home by hiring whatever kind of conveyance the tavern afforded, when, straining her eyes for the last time over the now darkening highway, she perceived yet another dust-cloud drawing near. She paused; a chariot ascended to the inn, and would have passed had not its occupant caught sight of her standing expectantly. The horses were checked on the instant.

"You here—and alone, my dear Mrs. Willowes?" said Lord Uplandtowers, whose carriage it was.

She explained what had brought her into this lonely

situation; and, as he was going in the direction of her own home, she accepted his offer of a seat beside him. Their conversation was embarrassed and fragmentary at first; but when they had driven a mile or two she was surprised to find herself talking earnestly and warmly to him: her impulsiveness was in truth but the natural consequence of her late existence—a somewhat desolate one by reason of the strange marriage she had made; and there is no more indiscreet mood than that of a woman surprised into talk who has long been imposing upon herself a policy of reserve. Therefore her ingenuous heart rose with a bound into her throat when, in response to his leading questions, or rather hints, she allowed her troubles to leak out of her. Lord Uplandtowers took her quite to her own door, although he had driven three miles out of his way to do so; and in handing her down she heard from him a whisper of stern reproach: "It need not have been thus if you had listened to me!'

She made no reply, and went indoors. There, as the evening wore away, she regretted more and more that she had been so friendly with Lord Uplandtowers. But he had launched himself upon her so unexpectedly: if she had only foreseen the meeting with him, what a careful line of conduct she would have marked out! Barbara broke into a perspiration of disquiet when she thought of her unreserve, and, in self-chastisement, resolved to sit up till midnight on the bare chance of Edmond's return; directing that supper should be laid for him, improbable as his arrival till the morrow was.

The hours went past, and there was dead silence in and around about Yewsholt Lodge, except for the soughing of the trees; till, when it was near upon midnight, she heard the noise of hoofs and wheels approaching the door. Knowing that it could only be her husband, Barbara instantly went into the hall to meet him. Yet she stood there not without a sensation of faintness, so many were the changes since their parting! And, owing to her casual encounter with Lord Uplandtowers, his voice and image still remained with her, excluding Edmond, her husband, from the inner circle of her impressions.

But she went to the door, and the next moment a figure stepped inside, of which she knew the outline, but little besides. Her husband was attired in a flapping black cloak and slouched hat, appearing altogether as a foreigner, and not as the young English burgess who had left her side. When he came forward into the light of the lamp, she perceived with surprise, and almost with fright, that he wore a mask. At first she had not noticed this—there being nothing in its colour which would lead a casual observer to think he was looking on anything but a real countenance.

He must have seen her start of dismay at the unexpectedness of his appearance, for he said hastily: "I did not mean to come in to you like this—I thought you would have been in bed. How good you are, dear Barbara!" He put his arm round her, but he did not attempt to kiss her.

"O Edmond—it *is* you?—it must be?" she said, with clasped hands, for though his figure and movement were almost enough to prove it, and the tones were not unlike the old tones, the enunciation was so altered as to seem that of a stranger.

"I am covered like this to hide myself from the curious eyes of the inn-servants and others," he said, in a low voice. "I will send back the carriage and join you in a moment."

"You are quite alone?"

"Quite. My companion stopped at Southampton."

The wheels of the post-chaise rolled away as she entered the dining-room, where the supper was spread; and presently he rejoined her there. He had removed his cloak and hat, but the mask was still retained; and she could now see that it was of special make, of some flexible material like silk, coloured so as to represent flesh; it joined naturally to the front hair, and was otherwise cleverly executed.

"Barbara—you look ill," he said, removing his glove, and taking her hand.

"Yes—I have been ill," said she.

"Is this pretty little house ours?"

"O—yes." She was hardly conscious of her words, for

the hand he had ungloved in order to take hers was contorted, and had one or two of its fingers missing; while through the mask she discerned the twinkle of one eye only.

"I would give anything to kiss you, dearest, now at this moment!" he continued, with mournful passionateness. "But I cannot—in this guise. The servants are abed, I suppose?"

"Yes," said she. "But I can call them? You will have some supper?"

He said he would have some, but that it was not necessary to call anybody at that hour. Thereupon they approached the table, and sat down, facing each other.

Despite Barbara's scared state of mind, it was forced upon her notice that her husband trembled, as if he feared the impression he was producing, or was about to produce, as much as, or more than, she. He drew nearer, and took her hand again.

"I had this mask made at Venice," he began, in evident embarrassment. "My darling Barbara—my dearest wife— do you think you—will mind when I take it off? You will not dislike me—will you?"

"O Edmond, of course I shall not mind," said she. "What has happened to you is our misfortune; but I am prepared for it."

"Are you sure you are prepared?"

"O yes! You are my husband."

"You really feel quite confident that nothing external can affect you?" he said again, in a voice rendered uncertain by his agitation.

"I think I am—quite," she answered faintly.

He bent his head. "I hope, I hope you are," he whispered.

In the pause which followed, the ticking of the clock in the hall seemed to grow loud; and he turned a little aside to remove the mask. She breathlessly awaited the operation, which was one of some tediousness, watching him one moment, averting her face the next; and when it was done she shut her eyes at the dreadful spectacle that was revealed. A quick spasm of horror had passed

through her; but though she quailed she forced herself
to regard him anew, repressing the cry that would naturally
have escaped from her ashy lips. Unable to look at him
longer, Barbara sank down on the floor beside her
chair, covering her eyes.

"You cannot look at me!" he groaned in a hopeless
way. "I am too terrible an object even for you to bear!
I knew it; yet I hoped against it. O, this is a bitter fate—
curse the skill of those Venetian surgeons who saved
me alive! . . . Look up, Barbara," he continued beseech-
ingly; "view me completely; say you loathe me, if you
do loathe me, and settle the case between us for ever!"

His unhappy wife pulled herself together for a desperate
strain. He was her Edmond; he had done her no wrong;
he had suffered. A momentary devotion to him helped
her, and lifting her eyes as bidden she regarded this
human remnant, this *écorché*, a second time. But the sight
was too much. She again involuntarily looked aside and
shuddered.

"Do you think you can get used to this?" he said.
"Yes or no! Can you bear such a thing of the charnel-
house near you? Judge for yourself, Barbara. Your Adonis,
your matchless man, has come to this!"

The poor lady stood beside him motionless, save for
the restlessness of her eyes. All her natural sentiments
of affection and pity were driven clean out of her by
a sort of panic; she had just the same sense of dismay
and fearfulness that she would have had in the presence
of an apparition. She could nohow fancy this to be her
chosen one—the man she had loved; he was metamor-
phosed to a specimen of another species. "I do not loathe
you," she said with trembling. "But I am so horrified—
so overcome! Let me recover myself. Will you sup now?
And while you do so may I go to my room to—regain
my old feeling for you? I will try, if I may leave you
awhile? Yes, I will try!"

Without waiting for an answer from him, and keeping
her gaze carefully averted, the frightened woman crept
to the door and out of the room. She heard him sit down

to the table, as if to begin supper; though, Heaven knows,
his appetite was slight enough after a reception which
had confirmed his worst surmises. When Barbara had
ascended the stairs and arrived in her chamber she sank
down, and buried her face in the coverlet of the bed.

Thus she remained for some time. The bed-chamber
was over the dining-room, and presently as she knelt
Barbara heard Willowes thrust back his chair, and rise
to go into the hall. In five minutes that figure would
probably come up the stairs and confront her again; it,—
this new and terrible form, that was not her husband's.
In the loneliness of this night, with neither maid nor
friend beside her, she lost all self-control, and at the first
sound of his footstep on the stairs, without so much as
flinging a cloak round her, she flew from the room, ran
along the gallery to the back staircase, which she
descended, and, unlocking the back door, let herself out.
She scarcely was aware what she had done till she found
herself in the greenhouse, crouching on a flower-stand.

Here she remained, her great timid eyes strained
through the glass upon the garden without, and her skirts
gathered up, in fear of the field-mice which sometimes
came there. Every moment she dreaded to hear footsteps
which she ought by law to have longed for, and a voice
that should have been as music to her soul. But Edmond
Willowes came not that way. The nights were getting
short at this season, and soon the dawn appeared, and
the first rays of the sun. By daylight she had less fear than
in the dark. She thought she could meet him, and accustom
herself to the spectacle.

So the much-tried young woman unfastened the door
of the hot-house, and went back by the way she had
emerged a few hours ago. Her poor husband was probably
in bed and asleep, his journey having been long; and she
made as little noise as possible in her entry. The house
was just as she had left it, and she looked about in the
hall for his cloak and hat, but she could not see them;
nor did she perceive the small trunk which had been all
that he brought with him, his heavier baggage having

been left at Southampton for the road-waggon. She summoned courage to mount the stairs; the bedroom-door was open as she had left it. She fearfully peeped round; the bed had not been pressed. Perhaps he had lain down on the dining-room sofa. She descended and entered; he was not there. On the table beside his unsoiled plate lay a note, hastily written on the leaf of a pocketbook. It was something like this:

> MY EVER-BELOVED WIFE.—The effect that my forbidding appearance has produced upon you was one which I foresaw as quite possible. I hoped against it, but foolishly so. I was aware that no *human* love could survive such a catastrophe. I confess I thought yours divine; but, after so long an absence, there could not be left sufficient warmth to overcome the too natural first aversion. It was an experiment, and it has failed. I do not blame you; perhaps, even, it is better so. Good-bye. I leave England for one year. You will see me again at the expiration of that time, if I live. Then I will ascertain your true feeling; and, if it be against me, go away for ever.
>
> E.W.

On recovering from her surprise, Barbara's remorse was such that she felt herself absolutely unforgivable. She should have regarded him as an afflicted being, and not have been this slave to mere eyesight, like a child. To follow him and entreat him to return was her first thought. But on making inquiries she found that nobody had seen him: he had silently disappeared.

More than this, to undo the scene of last night was impossible. Her terror had been too plain, and he was a man unlikely to be coaxed back by her efforts to do her duty. She went and confessed to her parents all that had occurred; which, indeed, soon became known to more persons than those of her own family.

The year passed, and he did not return; and it was doubted if he were alive. Barbara's contrition for her unconquerable repugnance was now such that she longed to build a church-aisle, or erect a monument, and devote herself to deeds of charity for the remainder of her days. To that end she made inquiry of the excellent parson under whom she sat on Sundays, at a vertical distance of a dozen feet. But he could only adjust his wig and tap his snuff-box; for such was the lukewarm state of religion in those days, that not an aisle, steeple, porch, east window, Ten-Commandment board, lion-and-unicorn, or brass candlestick, was required anywhere at all in the neighborhood as a votive offering from a distracted soul —the last century contrasting greatly in this respect with the happy times in which we live, when urgent appeals for contributions to such objects pour in by every morning's post, and nearly all churches have been made to look like new pennies. As the poor lady could not ease her conscience this way, she determined at least to be charitable, and soon had the satisfaction of finding her porch thronged every morning by the raggedest, vilest, most drunken, hypocritical, and worthless tramps in Christendom.

But human hearts are as prone to change as the leaves of the creeper on the wall, and in the course of time, hearing nothing of her husband, Barbara could sit unmoved whilst her mother and friends said in her hearing, "Well, what has happened is for the best." She began to think so herself, for even now she could not summon up that lopped and mutilated form without a shiver, though whenever her mind flew back to her early wedded days, and the man who had stood beside her then, a thrill of tenderness moved her, which if quickened by his living presence might have become strong. She was young and inexperienced, and had hardly on his late return grown out of the capricious fancies of girlhood.

But he did not come again, and when she thought of his word that he would return once more, if living, and how unlikely he was to break his word, she gave him up for dead. So did her parents; so also did another person— that man of silence, of irresistible incisiveness, of still countenance, who was as awake as seven sentinels when he seemed to be as sound asleep as the figures on his family monument. Lord Uplandtowers, though not yet thirty, had chuckled like a caustic fogey of threescore when he heard of Barbara's terror and flight at her husband's return, and of the latter's prompt departure. He felt pretty sure, however, that Willowes, despite his hurt feelings, would have reappeared to claim his bright-eyed property if he had been alive at the end of the twelve months.

As there was no husband to live with her, Barbara had relinquished the house prepared for them by her father, and taken up her abode anew at Chene Manor, as in the days of her girlhood. By degrees the episode with Edmond Willowes seemed but a fevered dream, and as the months grew to years Lord Uplandtowers' friendship with the people at Chene—which had somewhat cooled after Barbara's elopement—revived considerably, and he again became a frequent visitor there. He could not make the most trivial alteration or improvement at Knolling-wood Hall, where he lived, without riding off to consult with his friend Sir John at Chene; and thus putting himself frequently under her eyes, Barbara grew accustomed to him, and talked to him as freely as to a brother. She even began to look up to him as a person of authority, judgment, and prudence; and though his severity on the bench towards poachers, smugglers, and turnip-stealers was matter of common notoriety, she trusted that much of what was said might be misrepresentation.

Thus they lived on till her husband's absence had stretched to years, and there could be no longer any doubt of his death. A passionless manner of renewing his addresses seemed no longer out of place in Lord Upland-towers. Barbara did not love him, but hers was essentially one of those sweet-pea or with-wind natures which require a twig of stouter fibre than its own to hang upon and bloom. Now, too, she was older, and admitted to herself that a man whose ancestor had run scores of Saracens through and through in fighting for the site of the Holy Sepulchre was a more desirable husband, socially considered, than one who could only claim with certainty to know that his father and grandfather were respectable burgesses.

Sir John took occasion to inform her that she might legally consider herself a widow; and, in brief, Lord Uplandtowers carried his point with her, and she married him, though he could never get her to own that she loved him as she had loved Willowes. In my childhood I knew an old lady whose mother saw the wedding, and she said that when Lord and Lady Uplandtowers drove away from her father's house in the evening it was in a coach-and-four, and that my lady was dressed in green and silver, and wore the gayest hat and feather that ever were seen; though whether it was that the green did not suit her complexion, or otherwise, the Countess looked pale, and the reverse of blooming. After their marriage her husband took her to London, and she saw the gaieties of a season there; then they returned to Knollingwood Hall, and thus a year passed away.

Before their marriage her husband had seemed to care but little about her inability to love him passionately. "Only let me win you," he had said, "and I will submit to all that." But now her lack of warmth seemed to irritate him, and he conducted himself towards her with a resentfulness which led her to passing many hours with him in painful silence. The heir-presumptive to the title was a remote relative, whom Lord Uplandtowers did not exclude from the dislike he entertained towards many persons and things besides, and he had set his mind upon a lineal successor. He blamed her much that there was no promise of this, and asked her what she was good for.

On a particular day in her gloomy life a letter, addressed to her as Mrs. Willowes, reached Lady Uplandtowers from an unexpected quarter. A sculptor in Pisa, knowing nothing of her second marriage, informed her that the long-delayed life-sized statue of Mr. Willowes, which, when her husband left that city, he had been directed to retain till it was sent for, was still in his studio. As his commission had not wholly been paid, and the statue was taking up room he could ill spare, he should be glad to have the debt cleared off, and directions where to forward the figure. Arriving at a time when the Countess was beginning to have little secrets (of a harmless kind, it is true) from her husband, by reason of their growing estrangement, she replied to this letter without saying a word to Lord Uplandtowers, sending off the balance that was owing to the sculptor, and telling him to despatch the statue to her without delay.

It was some weeks before it arrived at Knollingwood Hall, and, by a singular coincidence, during the interval she received the first absolutely conclusive tidings of her Edmond's death. It had taken place years before, in a foreign land, about six months after their parting, and had been induced by the sufferings he had already undergone, coupled with much depression of spirit, which had caused him to succumb to a slight ailment. The news was sent her in a brief and formal letter from some relative of Willowes's in another part of England.

Her grief took the form of passionate pity for his misfortunes, and of reproach to herself for never having been able to conquer her aversion to his latter image by recollection of what Nature had originally made him. The sad spectacle that had gone from earth had never been her Edmond at all to her. O that she could have met him as he was at first! Thus Barbara thought. It was only a few days later that a waggon with two horses, containing an immense packing-case, was seen at breakfast-time both by Barbara and her husband to drive round to the back of the house, and by-and-by they were informed that a case labelled "Sculpture" had arrived for her ladyship.

"What can that be?" said Lord Uplandtowers.

"It is the statue of poor Edmond, which belongs to me, but has never been sent till now," she answered.

"Where are you going to put it?" asked he.

"I have not decided," said the Countess. "Anywhere, so that it will not annoy you."

"Oh, it won't annoy me," says he.

When it had been unpacked in a back room of the house, they went to examine it. The statue was a full-length figure, in the purest Carrara marble, representing Edmond Willowes in all his original beauty, as he had stood at parting from her when about to set out on his travels; a specimen of manhood almost perfect in every line and contour. The work had been carried out with absolute fidelity.

"Phœbus-Apollo, sure," said the Earl of Uplandtowers, who had never seen Willowes, real or represented, till now.

Barbara did not hear him. She was standing in a sort of trance before the first husband, as if she had no consciousness of the other husband at her side. The mutilated features of Willowes had disappeared from her mind's eye; this perfect being was really the man she had loved, and not that later pitiable figure; in whom tenderness and truth should have seen this image always, but had not done so.

It was not till Lord Uplandtowers said roughly, "Are you going to stay here all the morning worshipping him?" that she roused herself.

Her husband had not till now the least suspicion that Edmond Willowes originally looked thus, and he thought how deep would have been his jealousy years ago if Willowes had been known to him. Returning to the Hall in the afternoon he found his wife in the gallery, whither the statue had been brought.

She was lost in reverie before it, just as in the morning.

"What are you doing?" he asked.

She started and turned. "I am looking at my husb— my statue, to see if it is well done," she stammered. "Why should I not?"

"There's no reason why," he said. "What are you going to do with the monstrous thing? It can't stand here for ever."

"I don't wish it," she said. "I'll find a place."

In her boudoir there was a deep recess, and while the Earl was absent from home for a few days in the following week, she hired joiners from the village, who under her directions enclosed the recess with a panelled door. Into the tabernacle thus formed she had the statue placed, fastening the door with a lock, the key of which she kept in her pocket.

When her husband returned he missed the statue from the gallery, and, concluding that it had been put away out of deference to his feelings, made no remark. Yet at moments he noticed something on his lady's face which he had never noticed there before. He could not construe it; it was a sort of silent ecstasy, a reserved beatification. What had become of the statue he could not divine, and growing more and more curious, looked about here and there for it till, thinking of her private room, he went towards that spot. After knocking he heard the shutting of a door, and the click of a key; but when he entered his wife was sitting at work, on what was in those days called knotting. Lord Uplandtowers' eye fell upon the newly-painted door where the recess had formerly been.

"You have been carpentering in my absence then, Barbara," he said carelessly.

"Yes, Uplandtowers."

"Why did you go putting up such a tasteless enclosure as that—spoiling the handsome arch of the alcove?"

"I wanted more closet-room; and I thought that as this was my own apartment——"

"Of course," he returned. Lord Uplandtowers knew now where the statue of young Willowes was.

One night, or rather in the smallest hours of the morning, he missed the Countess from his side. Not being a man of nervous imaginings he fell asleep again before he had much considered the matter, and the next morning had forgotten the incident. But a few nights later the same circumstances occurred. This time he fully roused himself; but before he had moved to search for her she returned to the chamber in her dressing-gown, carrying a candle, which she extinguished as she approached, deeming him asleep. He could discover from her breathing that she was strangely moved; but not on this occasion either did he reveal that he had seen her. Presently, when she had lain down, affecting to wake, he asked her some trivial questions, "Yes, *Edmond*," she replied absently.

Lord Uplandtowers became convinced that she was in the habit of leaving the chamber in this queer way more frequently than he had observed, and he determined to watch. The next midnight he feigned deep sleep, and shortly after perceived her stealthily rise and let herself out of the room in the dark. He slipped on some clothing and followed. At the further end of the corridor, where the clash of flint and steel would be out of the hearing of one in the bedchamber, she struck a light. He stepped aside into an empty room till she had lit a taper and had passed on to her boudoir. In a minute or two he followed. Arrived at the door of the boudoir, he beheld the door of the private recess open, and Barbara within it, standing with her arms clasped tightly round the neck of her Edmond, and her mouth on his. The shawl which she had thrown round her nightclothes had slipped from her shoulders, and her long white robe and pale face lent her the balanced appearance of a second statue embracing the first. Between her kisses, she apostrophized it in a low murmur of infantine tenderness:

"My only love—how could I be so cruel to you, my perfect one—so good and true—I am ever faithful to you, despite my seeming infidelity! I always think of you —dream of you—during the long hours of the day, and in the night-watches! O Edmond, I am always yours!" Such words as these, intermingled with sobs, and streaming tears, and dishevelled hair, testified to an intensity of feeling in his wife which Lord Uplandtowers had not dreamed of her possessing.

"Ha, ha!" says he to himself. "This is where we evaporate —this is where my hopes of a successor in the title dissolve—ha! ha! This must be seen to, verily!"

Lord Uplandtowers was a subtle man when once he set himself to strategy; though in the present instance he never thought of the simple stratagem of constant tenderness. Nor did he enter the room and surprise his wife as a blunderer would have done, but went back to his chamber as silently as he had left it. When the Countess returned thither, shaken by spent sobs and sighs, he appeared to be soundly sleeping as usual. The next day he began his countermoves by making inquiries as to the whereabouts of the tutor who had travelled with his wife's first husband; this gentleman, he found, was now master of a grammar-school at no great distance from Knollingwood. At the first convenient moment Lord Uplandtowers went thither and obtained an interview with the said gentleman. The schoolmaster was much gratified by a visit from such an influential neighbour, and was ready to communicate anything that his lordship desired to know.

After some general conversation on the school and its progress, the visitor observed that he believed the schoolmaster had once travelled a good deal with the unfortunate Mr. Willowes, and had been with him on the occasion of his accident. He, Lord Uplandtowers, was interested in knowing what had really happened at that time, and had often thought of inquiring. And then the Earl not only heard by word of mouth as much as he wished to know, but, their chat becoming more intimate, the schoolmaster drew upon paper a sketch of the disfigured head, explaining with bated breath various details in the representation.

"It was very strange and terrible!" said Lord Uplandtowers, taking the sketch in his hand. "Neither nose nor ears, nor lips scarcely!"

A poor man in the town nearest to Knollingwood Hall, who combined the art of sign-painting with ingenious mechanical occupations, was sent for by Lord Uplandtowers to come to the Hall on a day in that week when the Countess had gone on a short visit to her parents. His employer made the man understand that the business in which his assistance was demanded was to be considered private, and money insured the observance of this request. The lock of the cupboard was picked, and the ingenious mechanic and painter, assisted by the schoolmaster's sketch, which Lord Uplandtowers had put in his pocket, set to work upon the god-like countenance of the statue under my lord's direction. What the fire had maimed in the original the chisel maimed in the copy. It was a fiendish disfigurement, ruthlessly carried out, and was rendered still more shocking by being tinted to the hues of life, as life had been after the wreck.

Six hours after, when the workman was gone, Lord Uplandtowers looked upon the result, and smiled grimly, and said:

"A statue should represent a man as he appeared in life, and that's as he appeared. Ha! ha! But 'tis done to good purpose, and not idly."

He locked the door of the closet with a skeleton key, and went his way to fetch the Countess home.

That night she slept, but he kept awake. According to the tale, she murmured soft words in her dream; and he knew that the tender converse of her imaginings was held with one whom he had supplanted but in name. At the end of her dream the Countess of Uplandtowers awoke and arose, and then the enactment of former nights was repeated. Her husband remained still and listened. Two strokes sounded from the clock in the pediment without, when, leaving the chamber-door ajar, she passed along the corridor to the other end, where, as usual, she obtained a light. So deep was the silence that he could even from his bed hear her softly blowing the tinder to a glow after striking the steel. She moved on into the boudoir, and he heard, or fancied he heard, the turning of the key in the closet-door. The next moment there came from that direction a loud and prolonged shriek, which resounded to the furthest corners of the house. It was repeated, and there was the noise of a heavy fall.

Lord Uplandtowers sprang out of bed. He hastened along the dark corridor to the door of the boudoir, which stood ajar, and, by the light of the candle within, saw his poor young Countess lying in a heap in her nightdress on the floor of the closet. When he reached her side he found that she had fainted, much to the relief of his

fears that matters were worse. He quickly shut up and
locked in the hated image which had done the mischief,
and lifted his wife in his arms, where in a few instants
she opened her eyes. Pressing her face to his without
saying a word, he carried her back to her room, endeav-
ouring as he went to disperse her terrors by a laugh
in her ear, oddly compounded of causticity, predilection,
and brutality.

"Ho—ho—ho!" says he. "Frightened, dear one, hey?
What a baby 'tis! Only a joke, sure, Barbara—a splendid
joke! But a baby should not go to closets at midnight
to look for the ghost of the dear departed! If it do it
must expect to be terrified at his aspect—ho—ho—ho!"

When she was in her bed-chamber, and had quite come
to herself, though her nerves were still much shaken, he
spoke to her more sternly. "Now, my lady, answer me:
do you love him—eh?"

"No—no!" she faltered, shuddering, with her expanded
eyes fixed on her husband. "He is too terrible—no, no!"

"You are sure?"

"Quite sure!" replied the poor broken-spirited Countess.

But her natural elasticity asserted itself. Next morning
he again inquired of her: "Do you love him now?" She
quailed under his gaze, but did not reply.

"That means that you do still, by God!" he continued.

"It means that I will not tell an untruth, and do not
wish to incense my lord," she answered, with dignity.

"Then suppose we go and have another look at him?"
As he spoke, he suddenly took her by the wrist, and
turned as if to lead her towards the ghastly closet.

"No—no! O—no!" she cried, and her desperate wriggle
out of his hand revealed that the fright of the night had
left more impression upon her delicate soul than super-
ficially appeared.

"Another dose or two, and she will be cured," he
said to himself.

It was now so generally known that the Earl and
Countess were not in accord, that he took no great
trouble to disguise his deeds in relation to this matter.

During the day he ordered four men with ropes and
rollers to attend him in the boudoir. When they arrived,
the closet was open, and the upper part of the statue tied
up in canvas. He had it taken to the sleeping-chamber.
What followed is more or less matter of conjecture. The
story, as told to me, goes on to say that, when Lady
Uplandtowers retired with him that night, she saw facing
the foot of the heavy oak four-poster, a tall dark wardrobe, which had not stood there before; but she did not
ask what its presence meant.

"I have had a little whim," he explained when they
were in the dark.

"Have you?" says she.

"To erect a little shrine, as it may be called."

"A little shrine?"

"Yes; to one whom we both equally adore—eh? I'll
show you what it contains."

He pulled a cord which hung covered by the bed-
curtains, and the doors of the wardrobe slowly opened,
disclosing that the shelves within had been removed
throughout, and the interior adapted to receive the ghastly
figure, which stood there as it had stood in the boudoir,
but with a wax candle burning on each side of it to
throw the cropped and distorted features into relief. She
clutched him, uttered a low scream, and buried her head
in the bedclothes. "O, take it away—please take it away!"
she implored.

"All in good time; namely, when you love me best,"
he returned calmly. "You don't quite yet—eh?"

"I don't know—I think—O Uplandtowers, have mercy
—I cannot bear it—O, in pity, take it away!"

"Nonsense; one gets accustomed to anything. Take
another gaze."

In short, he allowed the doors to remain unclosed at
the foot of the bed, and the wax-tapers burning; and such
was the strange fascination of the grisly exhibition that
a morbid curiosity took possession of the Countess as she
lay, and, at his repeated request, she did again look out
from the coverlet, shuddered, hid her eyes, and looked

again, all the while begging him to take it away, or it would drive her out of her senses. But he would not do so yet, and the wardrobe was not locked till dawn.

The scene was repeated the next night. Firm in enforcing his ferocious correctives, he continued the treatment till the nerves of the poor lady were quivering in agony under the virtuous tortures inflicted by her lord, to bring her truant heart back to faithfulness.

The third night, when the scene had opened as usual, and she lay staring with immense wild eyes at the horrid fascination, on a sudden she gave an unnatural laugh; she laughed more and more, staring at the image, till she literally shrieked with laughter: then there was silence, and he found her to have become insensible. He thought she had fainted, but soon saw that the event was worse: she was in an epileptic fit. He started up, dismayed by the sense that, like many other subtle personages, he had been too exacting for his own interests. Such love as he was capable of, though rather a selfish gloating than a cherishing solicitude, was fanned into life on the instant. He closed the wardrobe with the pulley, clasped her in his arms, took her gently to the window, and did all he could to restore her.

It was a long time before the Countess came to herself, and when she did so, a considerable change seemed to have taken place in her emotions. She flung her arms around him, and with gasps of fear abjectly kissed him many times, at last bursting into tears. She had never wept in this scene before.

"You'll take it away, dearest—you will!" she begged plaintively.

"If you love me."

"I do—oh, I do!"

"And hate him, and his memory?"

"Yes—yes!"

"Thoroughly?"

"I cannot endure recollection of him!" cried the poor Countess slavishly. "It fills me with shame—how could I ever be so depraved! I'll never behave badly again,

Uplandtowers; and you will never put the hated statue again before my eyes?"

He felt that he could promise with perfect safety. "Never," said he.

"And then I'll love you," she returned eagerly, as if dreading lest the scourge should be applied anew. "And I'll never, never dream of thinking a single thought that seems like faithlessness to my marriage vow."

The strange thing now was that this fictitious love wrung from her by terror took on, through mere habit of enactment, a certain quality of reality. A servile mood of attachment to the Earl became distinctly visible in her contemporaneously with an actual dislike for her late husband's memory. The mood of attachment grew and continued when the statue was removed. A permanent revulsion was operant in her, which intensified as time wore on. How fright could have effected such a change of idiosyncrasy learned physicians alone can say; but I believe such cases of reactionary instinct are not unknown.

The upshot was that the cure became so permanent as to be itself a new disease. She clung to him so tightly that she would not willingly be out of his sight for a moment. She would have no sitting-room apart from his, though she could not help starting when he entered suddenly to her. Her eyes were well-nigh always fixed upon him. If he drove out, she wished to go with him; his slightest civilities to other women made her frantically jealous; till at length her very fidelity became a burden to him, absorbing his time, and curtailing his liberty, and causing him to curse and swear. If he ever spoke sharply to her now, she did not revenge herself by flying off to a mental world of her own; all that affection for another, which had provided her with a resource, was now a cold black cinder.

From that time the life of this scared and enervated lady—whose existence might have been developed to so much higher purpose but for the ignoble ambition of her parents and the conventions of the time—was one of obsequious amativeness towards a perverse and cruel man. Little personal events came to her in quick succession—half a dozen, eight, nine, ten such events—in brief, she bore him no less than eleven children in the nine following years, but half of them came prematurely into the world, or died a few days old; only one, a girl, attained to maturity; she in after years became the wife of the Honourable Mr. Beltonleigh, who was created Lord d'Almaine, as may be remembered.

There was no living son and heir. At length, completely worn out in mind and body, Lady Uplandtowers was taken abroad by her husband, to try the effect of a more genial climate upon her wasted frame. But nothing availed to strengthen her, and she died at Florence, a few months after her arrival in Italy.

Contrary to expectation, the Earl of Uplandtowers did not marry again. Such affection as existed in him—strange, hard, brutal as it was—seemed untransferable, and the title, as is known, passed at his death to his nephew. Perhaps it may not be so generally known that, during the enlargement of the Hall for the sixth Earl, while digging in the grounds for the new foundations, the broken fragments of a marble statue were unearthed. They were submitted to various antiquaries, who said that, so far as the damaged pieces would allow them to form an opinion, the statue seemed to be that of a mutilated Roman satyr; or, if not, an allegorical figure of Death. Only one or two old inhabitants guessed whose statue those fragments had composed.

I should have added that, shortly after the death of the Countess, an excellent sermon was preached by the Dean of Melchester, the subject of which, though names were not mentioned, was unquestionably suggested by the aforesaid events. He dwelt upon the folly of indulgence in sensuous love for a handsome form merely; and showed that the only rational and virtuous growths of that affection were those based upon intrinsic worth. In the case of the tender but somewhat shallow lady whose life I have related, there is no doubt that an infatuation for the person of young Willowes was the chief feeling that induced her to marry him; which was the more deplorable in that his beauty, by all tradition, was the least of his recommendations, every report bearing out the inference that he must have been a man of steadfast nature, bright intelligence, and promising life.

ℋℋℋℋℋℋℋℋℋℋℋℋℋℋℋℋℋℋℋℋℋ

THE FIDDLER OF THE REELS

"Talking of Exhibitions, World's Fairs, and what not," said the old gentleman, "I would not go round the corner to see a dozen of them nowadays. The only exhibition that ever made, or ever will make, any impression upon my imagination was the first of the series, the parent of them all, and now a thing of old times—the Great Exhibition of 1851, in Hyde Park, London. None of the younger generation can realize the sense of novelty it produced in us who were then in our prime. A noun substantive went so far as to become an adjective in honour of the occasion. It was 'exhibition' hat, 'exhibition' razor-strop, 'exhibition' watch; nay, even 'exhibition' weather, 'exhibition' spirits, sweethearts, babies, wives— for the time.

"For South Wessex, the year formed in many ways an extraordinary chronological frontier or transit-line, at which there occurred what one might call a precipice in Time. As in a geological 'fault,' we had presented to us a sudden bringing of ancient and modern into absolute contact, such as probably in no other single year since the Conquest was ever witnessed in this part of the country."

These observations led us onward to talk of the different personages, gentle and simple, who lived and moved within our narrow and peaceful horizon at that time; and of three people in particular, whose queer little history was oddly touched at points by the Exhibition, more concerned with it than that of anybody else who dwelt in those outlying shades of the world, Stickleford, Mellstock, and Egdon. First in prominence among these three came Wat Ollamoor—if that were his real name—whom the seniors in our party had known well.

He was a woman's man, they said,—supremely so —externally little else. To men he was not attractive; perhaps a little repulsive at times. Musician, dandy, and company-man in practice; veterinary surgeon in theory, he lodged awhile in Mellstock village, coming from nobody knew where; though some said his first appearance in this neighborhood had been as fiddle-player in a show at Greenhill Fair.

Many a worthy villager envied him his power over unsophisticated maidenhood—a power which seemed sometimes to have a touch of the weird and wizardly in it. Personally he was not ill-favoured, though rather un-English, his complexion being a rich olive, his rank hair dark and rather clammy—made still clammier by secret ointments, which, when he came fresh to a party, caused him to smell like "boys'-love" (southern-wood) steeped in lamp-oil. On occasion he wore curls—a double row—running almost horizontally around his head. But as these were sometimes noticeably absent, it was concluded that they were not altogether of Nature's making. By girls whose love for him had turned to hatred he had been nicknamed "Mop," from this abundance of hair, which was long enough to rest upon his shoulders; as time passed the name more and more prevailed.

His fiddling possibly had the most to do with the fascination he exercised, for, to speak fairly, it could claim for itself a most peculiar and personal quality, like that in a moving preacher. There were tones in it which bred the immediate conviction that indolence and averseness to systematic application were all that lay between "Mop" and the career of a second Paganini.

While playing he invariably closed his eyes; using no notes, and, as it were, allowing the violin to wander on

at will into the most plaintive passages ever heard by
rustic man. There was a certain lingual character in the
supplicatory expressions he produced, which would well-
nigh have drawn an ache from the heart of a gate-post.
He could make any child in the parish, who was at all
sensitive to music, burst into tears in a few minutes by
simply fiddling one of the old dance-tunes he almost
entirely affected—country jigs, reels, and "Favourite Quick
Steps" of the last century—some mutilated remains of
which even now reappear as nameless phantoms in new
quadrilles and gallops, where they are recognized only
by the curious, or by such old-fashioned and far-between
people as have been thrown with men like Wat Ollamoor
in their early life.

His date was a little later than that of the old Mellstock
quire-band which comprised the Dewys, Mail, and the
rest—in fact, he did not rise above the horizon thereabout
till those well-known musicians were disbanded as ecclesias-
tical functionaries. In their honest love of thoroughness
they despised the new man's style. Theophilus Dewy (Reuben the tranter's younger brother) used to say there was
no "plumness" in it—no bowing, no solidity—it was all
fantastical. And probably this was true. Anyhow, Mop
had, very obviously, never bowed a note of church-music
from his birth; he never once sat in the gallery of Mellstock church where the others had tuned their venerable
psalmody so many hundreds of times; had never, in all
likelihood, entered a church at all. All were devil's tunes
in his repertory. "He could no more play the Wold
Hundredth to his true time than he could play the
brazen serpent," the tranter would say. (The brazen
serpent was supposed in Mellstock to be a musical instrument particularly hard to blow.)

Occasionally Mop could produce the aforesaid moving
effect upon the souls of grown-up persons, especially
young women of fragile and responsive organization. Such
as one was Car'line Aspent. Though she was already
engaged to be married before she met him, Car'line, of
them all, was the most influenced by Mop Ollamoor's

heart-stealing melodies, to her discomfort, nay, positive
pain and ultimate injury. She was a pretty, invocating,
weak-mouthed girl, whose chief defect as a companion
with her sex was a tendency to peevishness now and then.
At this time she was not a resident in Mellstock parish
where Mop lodged, but lived some miles off at Stickleford, further down the river.

How and where she first made acquaintance with him
and his fiddling is not truly known, but the story
was that it either began or was developed on one spring
evening, when, in passing through Lower Mellstock, she
chanced to pause on the bridge near his house to rest
herself, and languidly leaned over the parapet. Mop was
standing on his door-step, as was his custom, spinning
the insidious thread of semi and demi semiquavers from
the E string of his fiddle for the benefit of passers-by,
and laughing as the tears rolled down the cheeks of the
little children hanging around him. Car'line pretended to
be engrossed with the rippling of the stream under the
arches, but in reality she was listening, as he knew.
Presently the aching of the heart seized her simultaneously
with a wild desire to glide airily in the mazes of an
infinite dance. To shake off the fascination she resolved
to go on, although it would be necessary to pass him
as he played. On stealthily glancing ahead at the performer, she found to her relief that his eyes were closed
in abandonment to instrumentation, and she strode on
boldly. But when closer her step grew timid, her tread
convulsed itself more and more accordantly with the time
of the melody, till she very nearly danced along. Gaining
another glance at him when immediately opposite, she
saw that *one* of his eyes was open, quizzing her as he
smiled at her emotional state. Her gait could not divest
itself of its compelled capers till she had gone a long
way past the house; and Car'line was unable to shake off
the strange infatuation for hours.

After that day, whenever there was to be in the neighbourhood a dance to which she could get an invitation,
and where Mop Ollamoor was to be the musician, Car'line

contrived to be present, though it sometimes involved a
walk of several miles; for he did not play so often in
Stickleford as elsewhere.

The next evidences of his influence over her were
singular enough, and it would require a neurologist to
fully explain them. She would be sitting quietly, any evening
after dark, in the house of her father, the parish clerk,
which stood in the middle of Stickleford village street, this
being the high-road between Lower Mellstock and Moreford, five miles eastward. Here, without a moment's warning, and in the midst of a general conversation between
her father, sister, and the young man before alluded to,
who devotedly wooed her in ignorance of her infatuation,
she would start from her seat in the chimney-corner as
if she had received a galvanic shock, and spring convulsively towards the ceiling; then she would burst into tears,
and it was not till some half-hour had passed that she
grew calm as usual. Her father, knowing her hysterical
tendencies, was always excessively anxious about this
trait in his youngest girl, and feared the attack to be a
species of epileptic fit. Not so her sister Julia. Julia had
found out what was the cause. At the moment before
the jumping, only an exceptionally sensitive ear situated
in the chimney-nook could have caught from down the
flue the beat of a man's footstep along the highway without. But it was in that footfall, for which she had been
waiting, that the origin of Car'line's involuntary springing
lay. The pedestrian was Mop Ollamoor, as the girl well
knew; but his business that way was not to visit her;
he sought another woman whom he spoke of as his
Intended, and who lived at Moreford, two miles further
on. On one, and only one, occasion did it happen that
Car'line could not control her utterance; it was when her
sister alone chanced to be present. "O—O—O—!" she
cried. "He's going to *her*, and not coming to *me*!"

To do the fiddler justice he had not at first thought
greatly of, or spoken much to, this girl of impressionable
mould. But he had soon found out her secret, and could
not resist a little by-play with her too easily hurt heart,

as an interlude between his more serious lovemakings at
Moreford. The two became well acquainted, though only
by stealth, hardly a soul in Stickleford except her sister,
and her lover Ned Hipcroft, being aware of the attachment. Her father disapproved of her coldness to Ned;
her sister, too, hoped she might get over this nervous
passion for a man of whom so little was known. The ultimate result was that Car'line's manly and simple wooer
Edward found his suit becoming practically hopeless. He
was a respectable mechanic, in a far sounder position than
Mop the nominal horse-doctor; but when, before leaving
her, Ned put his flat and final question, would she marry
him, then and there, now or never, it was with little
expectation of obtaining more than the negative she gave
him. Though her father ·supported him and her sister
supported him, he could not play the fiddle so as to draw
your soul out of your body like a spider's thread, as Mop
did, till you felt as limp as withywind and yearned for
something to cling to. Indeed, Hipcroft had not the slightest
ear for music; could not sing two notes in tune, much
less play them.

The No he had expected and got from her, in spite
of a preliminary encouragement, gave Ned a new start
in life. It had been uttered in such a tone of sad entreaty
that he resolved to persecute her no more; she should
not even be distressed by a sight of his form in the
distant perspective of the street and lane. He left the
place, and his natural course was to London.

The railway to South Wessex was in process of construction, but it was not as yet opened for traffic; and
Hipcroft reached the capital by a six days' trudge on
foot, as many a better man had done before him. He
was one of the last of the artizan class who used that
now extinct method of travel to the great centres of
labour, so customary then from time immemorial.

In London he lived and worked regularly at his trade.
More fortunate than many, his disinterested willingness
recommended him from the first. During the ensuing
four years he was never out of employment. He neither

advanced nor receded in the modern sense; he improved as a workman, but he did not shift one jot in social position. About his love for Car'line he maintained a rigid silence. No doubt he often thought of her; but being always occupied, and having no relations at Stickleford, he held no communication with that part of the country, and showed no desire to return. In his quiet lodging in Lambeth he moved about after working-hours with the facility of a woman, doing his own cooking, attending to his stocking-heels, and shaping himself by degrees to a lifelong bachelorhood. For this conduct one is bound to advance the canonical reason that time could not efface from his heart the image of little Car'line Aspent—and it may be in part true; but there was also the inference that his was a nature not greatly dependent upon the ministrations of the other sex for its comfort.

The fourth year of his residence as a mechanic in London was the year of the Hyde-Park Exhibition already mentioned, and at the construction of this huge glass house, then unexampled in the world's history, he worked daily. It was an era of great hope and activity among the nations and industries. Though Hipcroft was, in small way, a central man in the movement, he plodded on with his usual outward placidity. Yet for him, too, the year was destined to have its surprises, for when the bustle of getting the building ready for the opening day was past, the ceremonies had been witnessed, and people were flocking thither from all parts of the globe, he received a letter from Car'line. Till that day the silence of four years between himself and Stickleford had never been broken.

She informed her old lover, in an uncertain penmanship which suggested a trembling hand, of the trouble she had been put to in ascertaining his address, and then broached the subject which had prompted her to write. Four years ago, she said with the greatest delicacy of which she was capable, she had been so foolish as to refuse him. Her wilful wrongheadedness had since been a grief to her many times, and of late particularly. As

for Mr. Ollamoor, he had been absent almost as long
as Ned—she did not know where. She would gladly
marry Ned now if he were to ask her again, and be
a tender little wife to him till her life's end.

A tide of warm feeling must have surged through Ned
Hipcroft's frame on receipt of this news, if we may
judge by the issue. Unquestionably he loved her still,
even if not to the exclusion of every other happiness.
This from his Car'line, she who had been dead to him
these many years, alive to him again as of old, was in
itself a pleasant, gratifying thing. Ned had grown so
resigned to, or satisfied with, his lonely lot, that he
probably would not have shown much jubilation at anything. Still, a certain ardour of preoccupation, after his
first surprise, revealed how deeply her confession of faith
in him had stirred him. Measured and methodical in his
ways, he did not answer the letter that day, nor the
next, nor the next. He was having "a good think." When
he did answer it, there was a great deal of sound reasoning mixed in with the unmistakable tenderness of his
reply; but the tenderness itself was sufficient to reveal
that he was pleased with her straightforward frankness;
that the anchorage she had once obtained in his heart
was renewable, if it had not been continuously firm.

He told her—and as he wrote his lips twitched humorously over the few gentle words of raillery he indited
among the rest of his sentences—that it was all very well
for her to come round at this time of day. Why wouldn't
she have him when he wanted her? She had no doubt
learned that he was not married, but suppose his affections had since been fixed on another? She ought to beg
his pardon. Still, he was not the man to forget her. But
considering how he had been used, and what he had
suffered, she could not quite expect him to go down to
Stickleford and fetch her. But if she would come to him,
and say she was sorry, as was only fair; why, yes, he
would marry her, knowing what a good little woman she
was at the core. He added that the request for her to
come to him was a less one to make than it would have

been when he first left Stickleford, or even a few months
ago; for the new railway into South Wessex was now
open, and there had just begun to be run wonderfully
contrived special trains, called excursion-trains, on account
of the Great Exhibition; so that she could come up easily
alone.

She said in her reply how good it was of him to treat
her so generously, after her hot and cold treatment of
him; that though she felt frightened at the magnitude of
the journey, and was never as yet in a railway-train,
having only seen one pass at a distance, she embraced his
offer with all her heart; and would, indeed, own to him
how sorry she was, and beg his pardon, and try to be
a good wife always, and make up for lost time.

The remaining details of when and where were soon
settled, Car'line informing him, for her ready identification in the crowd, that she would be wearing "my new
sprigged-laylock cotton gown," and Ned gaily responding
that, having married her the morning after her arrival, he
would make a day of it by taking her to the Exhibition. One
early summer afternoon, accordingly, he came from his
place of work, and hastened towards Waterloo Station to
meet her. It was as wet and chilly as an English June
day can occasionally be, but as he waited on the platform
in the drizzle he glowed inwardly, and seemed to have
something to live for again.

The "excursion-train"—an absolutely new departure in
the history of travel—was still a novelty on the Wessex
line, and probably everywhere. Crowds of people had
flocked to all the stations on the way up to witness the
unwonted sight of so long a train's passage, even where
they did not take advantage of the opportunity it offered.
The seats for the humbler class of travellers in these early
experiments in steam-locomotion were open trucks, without any protection whatever from the wind and rain; and
damp weather having set in with the afternoon, the unfortunate occupants of these vehicles were, on the train
drawing up at the London terminus, found to be in a pitiable condition from their long journey; blue-faced, stiff-
necked, sneezing, rain-beaten, chilled to the marrow,

many of the men being hatless; in fact, they resembled
people who had been out all night in an open boat on
a rough sea, rather than inland excursionists for pleasure.
The women had in some degree protected themselves by
turning up the skirts of their gowns over their heads,
but as by this arrangement they were additionally exposed
about the hips, they were all more or less in a sorry plight.

In the bustle and crush of alighting forms of both sexes
which followed the entry of the huge concatenation into
the station, Ned Hipcroft soon discerned the slim little
figure his eye was in search of, in the sprigged lilac, as
described. She came up to him with a frightened smile—
still pretty, though so damp, weather-beaten, and shivering
from long exposure to the wind.

"O Ned!" she sputtered, "I—I—" He clasped her in
his arms and kissed her, whereupon she burst into a flood
of tears.

"You are wet, my poor dear! I hope you'll not get
cold," he said. And surveying her and her multifarious
surrounding packages, he noticed that by the hand she
led a toddling child—a little girl of three or so—whose
hood was as clammy and tender face as blue as those
of the other travellers.

"Who is this—somebody you know?" asked Ned curiously.

"Yes, Ned. She's mine."

"Yours?"

"Yes—my own."

"Your own child?"

"Yes!"

"But who's the father?"

"The young man I had after you courted me."

"Well—as God's in——"

"Ned, I didn't name it in my letter, because, you see,
it would have been so hard to explain! I thought that
when we met I could tell you how she happened to be
born, so much better than in writing! I hope you'll excuse
it this once, dear Ned, and not scold me, now I've come
so many, many miles!"

"This means Mr. Mop Ollamoor, I reckon!" said Hip-

croft, gazing palely at them from the distance of the
yard or two to which he had withdrawn with a start.

Car'line gasped. "But he's been gone away for years!"
she supplicated. "And I never had a young man before!
And I was so onlucky to be catched the first time he
took advantage o' me, though some of the girls down
there go on like anything!"

Ned remained in silence, pondering.

"You'll forgive me, dear Ned?" she added, beginning
to sob outright. "I haven't taken 'ee in after all, because
—because you can pack us back again, if you want to;
though 'tis hundreds o' miles, and so wet, and night
a-coming on, and I with no money!"

"What the devil can I do!" Hipcroft groaned.

A more pitiable picture than the pair of helpless creatures presented was never seen on a rainy day, as they
stood on the great, gaunt, puddled platform, a whiff of
drizzle blowing under the roof upon them now and then;
the pretty attire in which they had started from Stickleford
in the early morning bemuddled and sodden, weariness on
their faces, and fear of him in their eyes; for the child
began to look as if she thought she too had done some
wrong, remaining in an appalled silence till the tears
rolled down her chubby cheeks.

"What's the matter, my little maid?" said Ned mechanically.

"I do want to go home!" she let out, in tones that
told of a bursting heart. "And my totties be cold, an' I
shan't have no bread an' butter no more!"

"I don't know what to say to it all!" declared Ned,
his own eyes moist as he turned and walked a few steps
with his head down; then regarded them again point-
blank. From the child escaped troubled breaths and
silently welling tears.

"Want some bread and butter, do 'ee?" he said, with
factitious hardness.

"Ye—e—s!"

"Well, I dare say I can get 'ee a bit! Naturally, you
must want some. And you, too, for that matter, Car'line."

"I do feel a little hungered. But I can keep it off," she murmured.

"Folk shouldn't do that," he said gruffly. . . . "There, come along!" He caught up the child, as he added, "You must bide here to-night, anyhow, I s'pose! What can you do otherwise? I'll get 'ee some tea and victuals; and as for this job, I'm sure I don't know what to say! This is the way out."

They pursued their way, without speaking, to Ned's lodgings, which were not far off. There he dried them and made them comfortable, and prepared tea; they thankfully sat down. The ready-made household of which he suddenly found himself the head imparted a cosy aspect to his room, and a paternal one to himself. Presently he turned to the child and kissed her now blooming cheeks; and, looking wistfully at Car'line, kissed her also.

"I don't see how I can send you back all them miles," he growled, "now you've come all the way o' purpose to join me. But you must trust me, Car'line, and show you've real faith in me. Well, do you feel better now, my little woman?"

The child nodded beamingly, her mouth being otherwise occupied.

"I did trust you, Ned, in coming; and I shall always!"

Thus, without any definite agreement to forgive her, he tacitly acquiesced in the fate that Heaven had sent him; and on the day of their marriage (which was not quite so soon as he had expected it could be, on account of the time necessary for banns) he took her to the Exhibition when they came back from church, as he had promised. While standing near a large mirror in one of the courts devoted to furniture, Car'line started, for in the glass appeared the reflection of a form exactly resembling Mop Ollamoor's—so exactly, that it seemed impossible to believe anybody but that artist in person to be the original. On passing round the objects which hemmed in Ned, her, and the child from a direct view, no Mop was to be seen. Whether he were really in London or not at that time was never known; and Car'line

always stoutly denied that her readiness to go and meet
Ned in town arose from any rumour that Mop had also
gone thither; which denial there was no reasonable ground
for doubting.

And then the year glided away, and the Exhibition
folded itself up and became a thing of the past. The
park trees that had been enclosed for six months were
again exposed to the winds and storms, and the sod grew
green anew. Ned found that Car'line resolved herself
into a very good wife and companion, though she had
made herself what is called cheap to him; but in that she
was like another domestic article, a cheap tea-pot, which
often brews better tea than a dear one. One autumn
Hipcroft found himself with but little work to do, and
a prospect of less for the winter. Both being country born
and bred, they fancied they would like to live again in
their natural atmosphere. It was accordingly decided between them that they should leave the pent-up London
lodging, and that Ned should seek out employment near
his native place, his wife and her daughter staying with
Car'line's father during the search for occupation and
an abode of their own.

Tinglings of pride pervaded Car'line's spasmodic little
frame as she journeyed down with Ned to the place she
had left two or three years before, in silence and under
a cloud. To return to where she had once been despised,
a smiling London wife with a distinct London accent,
was a triumph which the world did not witness every day.

The train did not stop at the petty roadside station that
lay nearest to Stickleford, and the trio went on to Casterbridge. Ned thought it a good opportunity to make a few
preliminary inquiries for employment at workshops in
the borough where he had been known; and feeling cold
from her journey, and it being dry underfoot and only
dusk as yet, with a moon on the point of rising, Car'line
and her little girl walked on toward Stickleford, leaving
Ned to follow at a quicker pace, and pick her up at a
certain half-way house, widely known as an inn.

The woman and child pursued the well-remembered way

comfortably enough, though they were both becoming wearied. In the course of three miles they had passed Heedless William's Pond, the familiar landmark by Bloom's End, and were drawing near the Quiet Woman, a lone roadside hostel on the lower verge of the Egdon Heath, since and for many years abolished. In stepping up towards it Car'line heard more voices within than had formerly been customary at such an hour, and she learned that an auction of fat stock had been held near the spot that afternoon. The child would be the better for a rest as well as herself, she thought, and she entered.

The guests and customers overflowed into the passage, and Car'line had no sooner crossed the threshold than a man whom she remembered by sight came forward with a glass and mug in his hands towards a friend leaning against the wall; but, seeing her, very gallantly offered her a drink of the liquor, which was gin-and-beer hot, pouring her out a tumblerful and saying, in a moment or two: 'Surely, 'tis little Car'line Aspent that was—down at Stickleford?'

She assented, and, though she did not exactly want this beverage, she drank it since it was offered, and her entertainer begged her to come in further and sit down. Once within the room she found that all the persons present were seated close against the walls, and there being a chair vacant she did the same. An explanation of their position occurred the next moment. In the opposite corner stood Mop, rosining his bow and looking just the same as ever. The company had cleared the middle of the room for dancing, and they were about to dance again. As she wore a veil to keep off the wind she did not think he had recognized her, or could possibly guess the identity of the child; and to her satisfied surprise she found that she could confront him quite calmly—mistress of herself in the dignity her London life had given her. Before she had quite emptied her glass the dance was called, the dancers formed in two lines, the music sounded, and the figure began.

Then matters changed for Car'line. A tremor quickened

itself to life in her, and her hand so shook that she could
hardly set down her glass. It was not the dance nor the
dancers, but the notes of that old violin which thrilled
the London wife, these having still all the witchery that
she had so well known of yore, and under which she had
used to lose her power of independent will. How it all
came back! There was the fiddling figure against the wall;
the large, oily, mop-like head of him, and beneath the
mop the face with closed eyes.

After the first moments of paralyzed reverie the familiar
tune in the familiar rendering made her laugh and shed
tears simultaneously. Then a man at the bottom of the
dance, whose partner had dropped away, stretched out
his hand and beckoned to her to take the place. She did
not want to dance; she entreated by signs to be left where
she was, but she was entreating of the tune and its player
rather than of the dancing man. The saltatory tendency
which the fiddler and his cunning instrument had ever
been able to start in her was seizing Car'line just at it
had done in earlier years, possibly assisted by the gin-and-
beer hot. Tired as she was she grasped her little girl by the
hand, and plunging in at the bottom of the figure, whirled
about with the rest. She found that her companions were
mostly people of the neighbouring hamlets and farms—
Bloom's End, Mellstock, Lewgate, and elsewhere; and by
degrees she was recognized as she convulsively danced on,
wishing that Mop would cease and let her heart rest
from the aching he caused, and her feet also.

After long and many minutes the dance ended, when
she was urged to fortify herself with more gin-and-beer;
which she did, feeling very weak and overpowered with
hysteric emotion. She refrained from unveiling, to keep
Mop in ignorance of her presence, if possible. Several
of the guests having left, Car'line hastily wiped her lips
and also turned to go; but, according to the account of
some who remained, at that very moment a five-handed
reel was proposed, in which two or three begged her to join.

She declined on the plea of being tired and having to
walk to Stickleford, when Mop began aggressively twee-

dling "My Fancy-Lad," in D major, as the air to which the
reel was to be footed. He must have recognized her,
though she did not know it, for it was the strain of all
seductive strains which she was least able to resist—the
one he had played when she was leaning over the bridge
at the date of their first acquaintance. Car'line stepped
despairingly into the middle of the room with the other
four.

Reels were resorted to hereabouts at this time by
the more robust spirits, for the reduction of superfluous
energy which the ordinary figure-dancers were not powerful enough to exhaust. As everybody knows or does not
know, the five reelers stood in the form of a cross, the
reel being performed by each line of three alternately,
the persons who successively came to the middle place
dancing in both directions. Car'line soon found herself in
this place, the axis of the whole performance, and could
not get out of it, the tune turning into the first part
without giving her opportunity. And now she began to
suspect that Mop did know her, and was doing this on
purpose, though whenever she stole a glance at him his
closed eyes betokened obliviousness to everything outside
his own brain. She continued to wend her way through the
figure of 8 that was formed by her course, the fiddler
introducing into his notes the wild and agonizing sweet-
ness of a living voice in one too highly wrought; its pathos
running high and running low in endless variation, projecting through her nerves excruciating spasms, a sort of
blissful torture. The room swam, the tune was endless; and
in about a quarter of an hour the only other woman in
the figure dropped out exhausted, and sank panting on a
bench.

The reel instantly resolved itself into a four-handed
one. Car'line would have given anything to leave off; but
she had, or fancied she had, no power, while Mop
played such tunes; and thus another ten minutes slipped
by, a haze of dust now clouding the candles, the floor
being of stone, sanded. Then another dancer fell out—one
of the men—and went into the passage in a frantic search

for liquor. To turn the figure into a three-handed reel was the work of a second, Mop modulating at the same time into "The Fairy Dance," as better suited to the contracted movement, and no less one of those foods of love which, as manufactured by his bow, had always intoxicated her.

In a reel for three there was no rest whatever, and four or five minutes were enough to make her remaining two partners, now thoroughly blown, stamp their last bar, and, like their predecessors, limp off into the next room to get something to drink. Car'line, half-stifled inside her veil, was left dancing alone, the apartment now being empty of everybody save herself, Mop, and their little girl.

She flung up the veil, and cast her eyes upon him, as if imploring him to withdraw himself and his acoustic magnetism from the atmosphere. Mop opened one of his own orbs, as though for the first time, fixed it peeringly upon her, and smiling dreamily, threw into his strains the reserve of expression which he could not afford to waste on a big and noisy dance. Crowds of little chromatic subtleties, capable of drawing tears from a statue, proceeded straightway from the ancient fiddle, as if it were dying of the emotion which had been pent up within it ever since its banishment from some Italian or German city where it first took shape and sound. There was that in the look of Mop's one dark eye which said: "You cannot leave off, dear, whether you would or no!" and it bred in her a paroxysm of desperation that defied him to tire her down.

She thus continued to dance alone, defiantly as she thought, but in truth slavishly and abjectly, subject to every wave of the melody, and probed by the gimletlike gaze of her fascinator's open eye; keeping up at the same time a feeble smile in his face, as a feint to signify it was still her own pleasure which led her on. A terrified embarrassment as to what she could say to him if she were to leave off, had its unrecognized share in keeping her going. The child, who was beginning to be distressed by the strange situation, came up and whimpered: "Stop, mother, stop, and let's go home!" as she seized Car'line's hand.

Suddenly Car'line sank staggering to the floor; and rolling over on her face, prone she remained. Mop's fiddle thereupon emitted an elfin shriek of finality; stepping quickly down from the nine-gallon beer-cask which had formed his rostrum, he went to the little girl, who disconsolately bent over her mother.

The guests who had gone into the back-room for liquor and change of air, hearing something unusual, trooped back hitherward, where they endeavoured to revive poor, weak Car'line by blowing her with the bellows and opening the window. Ned, her husband, who had been detained in Casterbridge, as aforesaid, came along the road at this juncture, and hearing excited voices through the open casement, and to his great surprise, the mention of his wife's name, he entered amid the rest upon the scene. Car'line was now in convulsions, weeping violently, and for a long time nothing could be done with her. While he was sending for a cart to take her onward to Stickleford Hipcroft anxiously inquired how it had all happened; and then the assembly explained that a fiddler formerly known in the locality had lately visited his old haunts, and had taken upon himself without invitation to play that evening at the inn and raise a dance.

Ned demanded the fiddler's name, and they said Ollamoor.

"Ah!" exclaimed Ned, looking round him. "Where is he, and where—where's my little girl?"

Ollamoor had disappeared, and so had the child. Hipcroft was in ordinary a quiet and tractable fellow, but a determination which was to be feared settled in his face now. "Blast him!" he cried. "I'll beat his skull in for'n, if I swing for it to-morrow!"

He had rushed to the poker which lay on the hearth, and hastened down the passage, the people following. Outside the house, on the other side of the highway, a mass of dark heath-land rose sullenly upward to its not easily accessible interior, a ravined plateau, whereon jutted into the sky, at the distance of a couple of miles, the firwoods of Mistover backed by the Yalbury coppices—a place of Dantesque gloom at this hour, which would have afforded secure hiding for a battery of artillery, much less a man and a child.

Some other men plunged thitherward with him, and more went along the road. They were gone about twenty minutes altogether, returning without result to the inn. Ned sat down in the settle, and clasped his forehead with his hands.

"Well—what a fool the man is, and hev been all these years, if he thinks the child his, as a' do seem to!" they whispered. "And everybody else knowing otherwise!"

"No, I don't think 'tis mine!" cried Ned hoarsely, as he looked up from his hands. "But she *is* mine, all the same! Ha'n't I nussed her? Ha'n't I fed her and teached her? Ha'n't I played wi' her? O, little Carry—gone with that rogue—gone!"

"You ha'n't lost your mis'ess, anyhow," they said to console him. "She's throwed up the sperrits, and she is feeling better, and she's more to 'ee than a child that isn't yours."

"She isn't! She's not so particular much to me, especially now she's lost the little maid! But Carry's the whole world to me!"

"Well, ver' like you'll find her to-morrow."

"Ah—but shall I? Yet he *can't* hurt her—surely he can't! Well—how's Car'line now? I am ready. Is the cart here?"

She was lifted into the vehicle, and they sadly lumbered on toward Stickleford. Next day she was calmer; but the fits were still upon her; and her will seemed shattered. For the child she appeared to show singularly little anxiety, though Ned was nearly distracted by his passionate paternal love for a child not his own. It was nevertheless quite expected that the impish Mop would restore the lost one after a freak of a day or two; but time went on, and neither he nor she could be heard of, and Hipcroft murmured that perhaps he was exercising upon her some unholy musical charm, as he had done upon Car'line herself. Weeks passed, and still they could obtain no clue either to the fiddler's whereabouts or to the girl's; and

how he could have induced her to go with him remained
a mystery.

Then Ned, who had obtained only temporary employment in the neighborhood, took a sudden hatred toward
his native district, and a rumour reaching his ears through
the police that a somewhat similar man and child had
been seen at a fair near London, he playing a violin,
she dancing on stilts, a new interest in the capital took
possession of Hipcroft with an intensity which would
scarcely allow him time to pack before returning thither.
He did not, however, find the lost one, though he made
it the entire business of his over-hours to stand about in
by-streets in the hope of discovering her, and would start
up in the night, saying, "That rascal's torturing her to
maintain him!" To which his wife would answer peevishly,
"Don't 'ee raft yourself so, Ned! You prevent my getting
a bit o' rest! He won't hurt her!" and fall asleep again.

That Carry and her father had emigrated to America
was the general opinion; Mop, no doubt, finding the girl
a highly desirable companion when he had trained her
to keep him by her earnings as a dancer. There, for that
matter, they may be performing in some capacity now,
though he must be an old scamp verging on three-score-
and-ten, and she a woman of four-and-forty.

2

THE LIFE AND DEATH
OF THE MAYOR
OF CASTERBRIDGE

A Story of a Man of Character

Editor's Note

In 1911, Hardy prepared a "General Preface" to the comprehensive Wessex Edition of his novels and poems which his principal bibliographer, R. L. Purdy, has called "the definitive edition of Hardy's work and the last authority in questions of text." This important essay, reprinted in full in Part Six, begins with mention of a threefold classification of the "fictitious chronicles"—Novels of Character and Environment, Romances and Fantasies, Novels of Ingenuity—and offers a rather modest rationale for the scheme. In rough paraphrase, Hardy says that the classification reflects in descending order the varying levels of achievement at which he aimed, the aim sometimes missing the intended achievement owing to various exigent circumstances the chief of which were modifications and compromises forced on him by "the necessities of magazine publication," i.e., the serialization and partial bowdlerization of his novels which normally preceded their appearance in book form. He then goes on to discount further this heavily qualified apologia by remarking, "that many of [the novels], if any, stand as they would stand if written *now* is not to be supposed." In 1914, the scheme became fourfold when the volume of shorter narratives entitled *A Changed Man* was issued under the rubric of Mixed Novels. Despite the apparent advantages of hindsight, Hardy's play with classifications, carried on some fifteen years after he had ceased to write fiction, sheds equal amounts of light and darkness. It is clear, however, that the Novels of Character and Environment represented to him, as they do to us, his best—most truthful, least compromised—aim and achievement in fiction.

The classification contains seven novels, of which *The*

Mayor of Casterbridge is the fourth. To read through the sequence chronologically, from the playful village comedy of *Under the Greenwood Tree* (1872) to the tragic misadventures of *Jude the Obscure* (1895), is to get an overview of one of the great mythic creations in English fiction, the myth of nineteenth-century Wessex, constructed by Hardy over several decades of writing, reflecting aspects of permanence and change of a real place and a real people in southwestern England during several generations, reflecting also what was permanent and what was changeable in Hardy's imaginative conceiving of human kind and the human environment as a whole from the years of his early manhood to those of his late maturity. In his preface to the Wessex Edition (1912) of *Far From the Madding Crowd*, Hardy describes his rich creation, its origins, and some of its impact:

. . . It was in the chapters of *Far from the Madding Crowd* [1874], as they appeared month by month in a popular magazine, that I first ventured to adopt the word "Wessex" from the pages of early English history, and give it a fictitious significance as the existing name of the district once included in that extinct kingdom. The series of novels I projected being mainly of the kind called local, they seemed to require a territorial definition of some sort to lend unity to their scene. Finding that the area of a single county did not afford a canvas large enough for this purpose, and that there were objections to an invented name, I disinterred the old one. The region designated was known but vaguely, and I was often asked even by educated people where it lay. However, the press and the public were kind enough to welcome the fanciful plan, and willingly joined me in the anachronism of imagining a Wessex population living under Queen Victoria;—a modern Wessex of railways, the penny post, mowing and reaping machines, union workhouses, lucifer matches, labourers who could read and write, and National school children. But I believe I am correct in stating that, until the existence of this contemporaneous

Wessex in place of the usual counties was announced in the present story, in 1874, it had never been heard of in fiction and current speech, if at all, and that the expression, "a Wessex peasant," or "a Wessex custom," would theretofore have been taken to refer to nothing later in date than the Norman Conquest. . . .

Since then the appellation which I had thought to reserve to the horizons and landscapes of a partly real, partly dream-country, has become more and more popular as a practical provincial definition; and the dream-country has, by degrees, solidified into a utilitarian region which people can go to, take a house in, and write to the papers from. But I ask all good and idealistic readers to forget this, and to refuse steadfastly to believe that there are any inhabitants of a Victorian Wessex outside these volumes in which their lives and conversations are detailed. [1895, 1902]

Hardy's own relation to Wessex is very complicated. He knew and loved it with the intimate knowledge of a

native and a countryman. He recovered the earlier phases of its life with the intense, directed curiosity of a regional historian, understood the processes, both destructive and progressive, of its alteration as the century waned with the insight of a social critic, and described the features of its flora and fauna, its weather and topography, with the verbal resources of a great poet as well as the perspectives of a student of the nineteenth-century evolutionary sciences. Yet for all this intimacy and knowledge, Hardy was separated from Wessex too: separated through the heightened and burdened consciousness intrinsic to literary genius; through the long and ample education in the arts, sciences, and history he achieved without benefit of public school or university attendance; and finally, by the mere fact of his great literary success which gained him access to cultured and urbane circles in London and the great university centers for whom the countryside exists by and large as scenic panorama, playground, and bookish subject matter.

Although the essential integrity of Hardy's relation to Wessex could not be violated, he must also appear to us as a version of that familiar Hardy character-type, the "native" who tries to come home to the solace of the customary and familiar, only to find himself a misfit by virtue of his experiences and sojournings in the greater, more complex world. Hardy designed and built Max Gate outside Dorchester and made his home there from 1885 onwards. Although it became a literary shrine within his lifetime, it must also be said that it is a gloomy house, quite out of keeping with local building traditions, and was the scene of the protracted unhappiness with his first wife which Hardy records in the great poems of elegy and regret he wrote to her memory during 1912–13. It seems that the only home territory to which Hardy could make an unequivocal return was the one he created in his great works of fiction.

In the major Wessex cycle novel presented here, *The Mayor of Casterbridge*, first published in 1866, the central character is a hay-trusser, Michael Henchard, who rises high in the world of Wessex after ridding himself of his domestic encumbrances. By middle age he is a prosperous grain dealer and borough mayor. Yet he can neither escape the consequences of the brutal act with which the book begins, nor come to terms with the mystery of his own inchoate nature which mingles generosity, sensitivity, sullenness, and a suicidal rashness. If Henchard is "man against himself" he is also a character drawn on a grand tragic scale. The arrogance of his overreaching and the pain and loneliness of his end put him in the company of Lear and of the Biblical King Saul. The time of the action, 1831–56, saw important developments in the economy of Wessex, and Henchard must also be viewed to some extent as a victim of the struggle between customary and innovative ways in the evolution of an agrarian society.

THE MAYOR OF CASTERBRIDGE

I

One evening of late summer, before the nineteenth century had reached one-third of its span, a young man and woman, the latter carrying a child, were approaching the large village of Weydon-Priors, in Upper Wessex, on foot. They were plainly but not ill clad, though the thick hoar of dust which had accumulated on their shoes and garments from an obviously long journey lent a disadvantageous shabbiness to their appearance just now.

The man was of fine figure, swarthy, and stern in aspect; and he showed in profile a facial angle so slightly inclined as to be almost perpendicular. He wore a short jacket of brown corduroy, newer than the remainder of his suit, which was a fustian waistcoat with white horn buttons, breeches of the same, tanned leggings, and a straw hat overlaid with black glazed canvas. At his back he carried by a looped strap a rush basket, from which protruded at one end the crutch of a hay-knife, a wimble for hay-bonds being also visible in the aperture. His measured, springless walk was the walk of the skilled countryman as distinct from the desultory shamble of the general laborer; while in the turn and plant of each foot there was, further, a dogged and cynical indifference personal to himself, showing its presence even in the regularly interchanging fustian folds, now in the left leg, now in the right, as he paced along.

What was really peculiar, however, in this couple's progress, and would have attracted the attention of any casual observer otherwise disposed to overlook them, was the perfect silence they preserved. They walked side by side in such a way as to suggest afar off the low, easy, confidential chat of people full of reciprocity; but on closer view it could be discerned that the man was reading, or pretending to read, a ballad sheet which he kept before his eyes with some difficulty by the hand that was passed through the basket strap. Whether this apparent cause were the real cause, or whether it were an assumed one to escape an intercourse that would have been irksome to him, nobody but himself could have said precisely; but his taciturnity was unbroken, and the woman enjoyed no society whatever from his presence. Virtually she walked the highway alone, save for the child she bore. Sometimes the man's bent elbow almost touched her shoulder, for she kept as close to his side as was possible without actual contact; but she seemed to have no idea of taking his arm, nor he of offering it; and far from exhibiting surprise at his ignoring silence she appeared to receive it as a natural thing. If any word at all were uttered by the little group, it was an occasional whisper of the woman to the child—a tiny girl in short clothes and blue boots of knitted yarn—and the murmured babble of the child in reply.

The chief—almost the only—attraction of the young woman's face was its mobility. When she looked down sideways to the girl she became pretty, and even handsome, particularly that in the action her features caught slantwise the rays of the strongly colored sun, which made transparencies of her eyelids and nostrils and set fire on her lips. When she plodded on in the shade of the hedge, silently thinking, she had the hard, half-apathetic expression of one who deems anything possible at the hands of Time and Chance except, perhaps, fair play. The first phase was the work of Nature, the second probably of civilization.

That the man and woman were husband and wife, and the parents of the girl in arms, there could be little doubt. No other than such relationship would have accounted for the atmosphere of stale familiarity which the trio carried along with them like a nimbus as they moved down the road.

The wife mostly kept her eyes fixed ahead, though with little interest—the scene for that matter being one that might have been matched at almost any spot in any county in England at this time of the year; a road neither straight nor crooked, neither level nor hilly, bordered by hedges, trees, and other vegetation, which had entered the blackened-green stage of color that the doomed leaves pass through on their way to dingy, and yellow, and red. The grassy margin of the bank, and the nearest hedgerow boughs, were powdered by the dust that had been stirred over them by hasty vehicles, the same dust as it lay on the road deadening their footfalls like a carpet; and this, with the aforesaid total absence of conversation, allowed every extraneous sound to be heard.

For a long time there was none, beyond the voice of a weak bird singing a trite old evening song that might doubtless have been heard on the hill at the same hour, and with the self-same trills, quavers, and breves, at any sunset of that season for centuries untold. But as they approached the village sundry distant shouts and rattles reached their ears from some elevated spot in that direction, as yet screened from view by foliage. When the out-lying houses of Weydon-Priors could just be described, the family group was met by a turnip-hoer with his hoe on his shoulder, and his dinner-bag suspended from it. The reader promptly glanced up.

"Any trade doing here?" he asked phlegmatically, des-ignating the village in his van by a wave of the broad-sheet. And thinking the laborer did not understand him, he added, "Any thing in the hay-trussing line?"

The turnip-hoer had already begun shaking his head. "Why, save the man, what wisdom's in him that 'a should come to Weydon for a job of that sort this time o' year?"

"Then is there any house to let—a little small new cottage just a builded, or such like?" asked the other.

The pessimist still maintained a negative. "Pulling down is more the nater of Weydon. There were five houses cleared away last year, and three this; and the volk nowhere to go—no, not so much as a thatched hurdle; that's the way o' Weydon-Priors."

The hay-trusser, which he obviously was, nodded with some superciliousness. Looking towards the village, he continued, "There is something going on here, however, is there not?"

"Ay. 'Tis Fair Day. Though what you hear now is little more than the clatter and scurry of getting away the money o' children and fools, for the real business is done earlier than this. I've been working within sound o't all day, but I didn't go up—not I. 'Twas no business of mine."

The trusser and his family proceeded on their way, and soon entered the Fair-field, which showed standing-places and pens where many hundreds of horses and sheep had been exhibited and sold in the forenoon, but were now in great part taken away. At present, as their informant had observed, but little real business remained on hand, the chief being the sale by auction of a few inferior animals, that could not otherwise be disposed of, and had been absolutely refused by the better class of traders, who came and went early. Yet the crowd was denser now than during the morning hours, the frivolous contingent of visitors, including journeymen out for a holiday, a stray soldier or two home on furlough, village shopkeepers, and the like, having latterly flocked in; persons whose activities found a congenial field among the peep-shows, toy-stands, waxworks, inspired monsters, disinterested medical men who travelled for the public good, thimble-riggers, nick-nack vendors, and readers of Fate.

Neither of our pedestrians had much heart for these things, and they looked around for a refreshment tent among the many which dotted the down. Two, which stood nearest to them in the ochreous haze of expiring sunlight, seemed almost equally inviting. One was formed of new, milk-hued canvas, and bore red flags on its summit; it announced "Good Home-brewed Beer, Ale, and Cyder." The other was less new; a little iron stove-pipe came out of it at the back, and in front appeared the placard, "Good Furmity Sold Hear." The man mentally weighed the two inscriptions, and inclined to the former tent.

"No—no—the other one," said the woman. "I always like furmity; and so does Elizabeth-Jane; and so will you. It is nourishing after a long hard day."

"I've never tasted it," said the man. However, he gave way to her representations, and they entered the furmity booth forthwith.

A rather numerous company appeared within, seated at the long narrow tables that ran down the tent on each side. At the upper end stood a stove, containing a charcoal fire, over which hung a large three-legged crock, sufficiently polished round the rim to show that it was made of bell-metal. A haggish creature of about fifty presided, in a white apron, which, as it threw an air of respectability over her as far as it extended, was made so wide as to reach nearly round her waist. She slowly stirred the contents of the pot. The dull scrape of her large spoon was audible throughout the tent as she thus kept from burning the mixture of corn in the grain, flour, milk, raisins, currants, and what not, that composed the antiquated slop in which she dealt. Vessels holding the separate ingredients stood on a white-clothed table of boards and trestles close by.

The young man and woman ordered a basin each of the mixture, steaming hot, and sat down to consume it at leisure. This was very well so far, for furmity, as the woman had said, was nourishing, and as proper a food as could be obtained within the four seas; though, to those not accustomed to it, the grains of wheat swollen as large as lemon-pips, which floated on its surface, might have a deterrent effect at first.

But there was more in that tent than met the cursory glance; and the man, with the instinct of a perverse character, scented it quickly. After a mincing attack on his bowl, he watched the hag's proceedings from the corner of his eye, and saw the game she played. He winked to her, and passed up his basin in reply to her nod; when she took a bottle from under the table, slily measured out a quantity of its contents, and tipped the same into the man's furmity. The liquor poured in was rum. The man as slily sent back money in payment.

He found the concoction, thus strongly laced, much more to his satisfaction than it had been in its natural state. His wife had observed the proceeding with much uneasiness; but he persuaded her to have hers laced also, and she agreed to a milder allowance after some misgiving.

The man finished his basin, and called for another, the rum being signalled for in yet stronger proportion. The effect of it was soon apparent in his manner, and his wife but too sadly perceived that in strenuously steering off the rocks of the licensed liquor-tent she had only got into maelstrom depths here amongst the smugglers.

The child began to prattle impatiently, and the wife more than once said to her husband, "Michael, how about our lodging? You know we may have trouble in getting it if we don't go soon."

But he turned a deaf ear to those bird-like chirpings. He talked loud to the company. The child's black eyes, after slow, round, ruminating gazes at the candles when they were lighted, fell together; then they opened, then shut again, and she slept.

At the end of the first basin the man had risen to serenity; at the second he was jovial; at the third, argumentative; at the fourth, the qualities signified by the shape of his face, the occasional clench of his mouth, and the fiery spark of his dark eye, began to tell in his conduct; he was overbearing—even brilliantly quarrelsome.

The conversation took a high turn, as it often does on such occasions. The ruin of good men by bad wives, and, more particularly, the frustration of many a promising youth's high aims and hopes and the extinction of his energies by an early imprudent marriage, was the theme.

"I did for myself that way thoroughly," said the trusser, with a contemplative bitterness that was well-nigh resentful. "I married at eighteen, like the fool that I was; and this is the consequence o't." He pointed at himself and family with a wave of the hand intended to bring out the penuriousness of the exhibition.

The young woman, his wife, who seemed accustomed to such remarks, acted as if she did not hear them, and continued her intermittent private words on tender trifles to the sleeping and waking child, who was just big enough to be placed for a moment on the bench beside her when she wished to ease her arms. The man continued—

"I haven't more than fifteen shillings in the world, and yet I am a good experienced hand in my line. I'd challenge England to beat me in the fodder business; and if I were a free man again I'd worth a thousand pound before I'd done o't. But a fellow never knows these little things till all chance of acting upon 'em is past."

The auctioneer selling the old horses in the field outside could be heard saying, "Now this is the last lot—now who'll take the last lot for a song? Shall I say forty shillings? 'Tis a very promising brood-mare, a trifle over five years old, and nothing the matter with the hoss at all, except that she's a little holler in the back and had her left eye knocked out by the kick of another, her own sister, coming along the road."

"For my part I don't see why men who have got wives and don't want 'em, shouldn't get rid of 'em as these gipsy fellows do their old horses," said the man in the

tent. "Why shouldn't they put 'em up and sell 'em by
auction to men who are in need of such articles? Hey?
Why, begad, I'd sell mine this minute if anybody would
buy her!"

"There's them that would do that," some of the guests
replied, looking at the woman, who was by no means
ill-favored.

"True," said a smoking gentleman, whose coat had the
fine polish about the collar, elbows, seams, and shoulder-
blades that long-continued friction with grimy surfaces
will produce, and which is usually more desired on furniture than on clothes. From his appearance he had possibly
been in former time groom or coachman to some neighboring county family. "I've had my breedings in as good
circles, I may say, as any man," he added, "and I know
true cultivation, or nobody do; and I can declare she's
got it—in the bone, mind ye, I say—as much as any
female in the fair—though it may want a little bringing
out." Then, crossing his legs, he resumed his pipe with
a nicely-adjusted gaze at a point in the air.

The fuddled young husband stared for a few seconds at
this unexpected praise of his wife, half in doubt of the
wisdom of his own attitude towards the possessor of such
qualities. But he speedily lapsed into his former conviction,
and said harshly—

"Well, then, now is your chance; I am open to an
offer for this gem o' creation."

She turned to her husband and murmured, "Michael,
you have talked this nonsense in public places before. A
joke is a joke, but you may make it once too often, mind!"

"I know I've said it before; I meant it. All I want is
a buyer."

At the moment a swallow, one among the last of the
season, which had by chance found its way through an
opening into the upper part of the tent, flew to and fro
in quick curves above their heads, causing all eyes to
follow it absently. In watching the bird till it made its
escape the assembled company neglected to respond to
the workman's offer, and the subject dropped.

But a quarter of an hour later the man, who had gone on lacing his furmity more and more heavily, though he was either so strong-minded or such an intrepid toper that he still appeared fairly sober, recurred to the old strain, as in a musical fantasy the instrument fetches up the original theme. "Here—I am waiting to know about this offer of mine. The woman is no good to me. Who'll have her?"

The company had by this time decidedly degenerated, and the renewed inquiry was received with a laugh of appreciation. The woman whispered; she was imploring and anxious: "Come, come, it is getting dark, and this nonsense won't do. If you don't come along, I shall go without you. Come!"

She waited and waited; yet he did not move. In ten minutes the man broke in upon the desultory conversation of the furmity drinkers with, "I asked this question, and nobody answered to't. Will any Jack Rag or Tom Straw among ye buy my goods?"

The woman's manner changed, and her face assumed the grim shape and color of which mention has been made. "Mike, Mike," said she; "this is getting serious. Oh!—too serious!"

"Will anybody buy her?" said the man.

"I wish somebody would," said she firmly. "Her present owner is not at all to her liking!"

"Nor you to mine," said he. "So we are agreed about that. Gentlemen, you hear? It's an agreement to part. She shall take the girl if she wants to, and go her ways. I'll take my tools, and go my ways. 'Tis simple as Scripture history. Now then, stand up, Susan, and show yourself."

"Don't, my chiel," whispered a buxom staylace dealer in voluminous petticoats, who sat near the woman: "yer good man don't know what he's saying."

The woman, however, did stand up. "Now, who's auctioneer?" cried the hay-trusser.

"I be," promptly answered a short man, with a nose resembling a copper knob, a damp voice, and eyes like button-holes. "Who'll make an offer for this lady?"

The woman looked on the ground, as if she maintained her position by a supreme effort of will.

"Five shillings," said some one, at which there was a laugh.

"No insults," said the husband. "Who'll say a guinea?"

Nobody answered; and the female dealer in staylaces interposed.

"Behave yerself moral, good man, for Heaven's love! Ah, what a cruelty is the poor soul married to! Bed and board is dear at some figures, 'pon my 'vation 'tis!"

"Set it higher, auctioneer," said the trusser.

"Two guineas!" said the auctioneer; and no one replied.

"If they don't take her for that, in ten seconds they'll have to give more," said the husband. "Very well. Now, auctioneer, add another."

"Three guineas—going for three guineas!" said the rheumy man.

"No bid?" said the husband. "Good Lord, why she's cost me fifty times the money, if a penny. Go on."

"Four guineas!" cried the auctioneer.

"I'll tell ye what—I won't sell her for less than five," said the husband, bringing down his fist so that the basins danced. "I'll sell her for five guineas to any man that will pay me the money, and treat her well; and he shall have her for ever, and never hear aught o' me. But she shan't go for less. Now then—five guineas—and she's yours. Susan, you agree?"

She bowed her head with absolute indifference.

"Five guineas," said the auctioneer, "or she'll be withdrawn. Do anybody give it? The last time. Yes or no?"

"Yes," said a loud voice from the doorway.

All eyes were turned. Standing in the triangular opening which formed the door of the tent was a sailor, who unobserved by the rest, had arrived there within the last two or three minutes. A dead silence followed his affirmation.

"You say you do?" asked the husband, staring at him.

"I say so," replied the sailor.

"Saying is one thing, and paying is another. Where's the money?"

The sailor hesitated a moment, looked anew at the woman, came in, unfolded five crisp pieces of paper, and threw them down upon the table-cloth. They were Bank-of-England notes for five pounds. Upon the face of this he chinked down the shillings severally—one, two, three, four, five.

The sight of real money in full amount, in answer to a challenge for the same till then deemed slightly hypo-thetical, had a great effect upon the spectators. Their eyes became riveted upon the faces of the chief actors, and then upon the notes as they lay, weighted by the shillings, on the table.

Up to this moment it could not positively have been asserted that the man, in spite of his tantalizing declara-tion, was really in earnest. The spectators had indeed taken the proceedings throughout as a piece of mirthful irony carried to extremes; and had assumed that, being out of work, he was, as a consequence, out of temper with the world, and society, and his nearest kin. But with the demand and response of real cash the jovial frivolity of the scene departed. A lurid color seemed to fill the tent, and change the aspect of all therein. The mirth-wrinkles left the listeners' faces, and they waited with parting lips.

"Now," said the woman, breaking the silence, so that her low dry voice sounded quite loud, "before you go further, Michael, listen to me. If you touch that money, I and this girl go with the man. Mind, it is a joke no longer."

"A joke? Of course it is not a joke!" shouted her husband, his resentment rising at her suggestion. "I take the money: the sailor takes you. That's plain enough. It has been done elsewhere—and why not here?"

" 'Tis quite on the understanding that the young woman is willing," said the sailor blandly. "I wouldn't hurt her feelings for the world."

"Faith, nor I," said her husband. "But she is willing, provided she can have the child. She said so only the other day when I talked o't!"

"That you swear?" said the sailor to her.

"I do," said she, after glancing at her husband's face and seeing no repentance there.

"Very well, she shall have the child, and the bargain's complete," said the trusser. He took the sailor's notes and deliberately folded them, and put them with the shillings in a high remote pocket, with an air of finality.

The sailor looked at the woman and smiled. "Come along!" he said kindly. "The little one too—the more the merrier!" She paused for an instant, with a close glance at him. Then dropping her eyes again, and saying nothing, she took up the child and followed him as he made towards the door. On reaching it, she turned, and pulling off her wedding-ring, flung it across the booth in the hay-trusser's face.

"Mike," she said, "I've lived with thee a couple of years, and had nothing but temper! Now I'm no more to 'ee; I'll try my luck elsewhere. 'Twill be better for me and Elizabeth-Jane, both. So good-bye!"

Seizing the sailor's arm with her right hand, and mounting the little girl on her left, she went out of the tent sobbing bitterly.

A stolid look of concern filled the husband's face, as if, after all, he had not quite anticipated this ending; and some of the guests laughed.

"Is she gone?" he said.

"Faith, ay; she gone clane enough," said some rustics near the door.

He rose and walked to the entrance with the careful tread of one conscious of his alcoholic load. Some others followed, and they stood looking into the twilight. The difference between the peacefulness of inferior nature and the wilful hostilities of mankind was very apparent at this place. In contrast with the harshness of the act just ended within the tent was the sight of several horses crossing their necks and rubbing each other lovingly as they waited in patience to be harnessed for the homeward journey. Outside the fair, in the valleys and woods, all was quiet. The sun had recently set, and the west heaven was hung with rosy cloud, which seemed permanent, yet slowly changed. To watch it was like looking at some grand feat of stagery from a darkened auditorium. In presence of this scene after the other there was a natural instinct to abjure man as the blot on an otherwise kindly universe; till it was remembered that all terrestrial conditions were intermittent, and that mankind might some night be innocently sleeping when these quiet objects were raging loud.

"Where do the sailor live?" asked a spectator, when they had vainly gazed around.

"God knows that," replied the man who had seen high life. "He's without doubt a stranger here."

"He came in about five minutes ago," said the furmity woman, joining the rest with her hands on her hips. "And then 'a stepped back, and then 'a looked in again. I'm not a penny the better for him."

"Serves the husband well be-right," said the staylace vendor. "A comely respectable body like her—what can a man want more? I glory in the woman's sperrit. I'd ha' done it myself—od send if I wouldn't, if a husband had behaved so to me! I'd go, and 'a might call, and call, till his keacorn was raw; but I'd never come back—no, not till the great trumpet, would I!"

Well, the woman will be better off," said another of a more deliberative turn. "For seafaring natures be very good shelter for shorn lambs, and the man do seem to have plenty of money, which is what she's not been used to lately, by all showings."

"Mark me—I'll not go after her!" said the trusser, returning doggedly to his seat. "Let her go! If she's up to such vagaries she must suffer for 'em. She'd no business to take the maid—'tis my maid; and if it were the doing again she shouldn't have her!"

Perhaps from some little sense of having countenanced an indefensible proceeding, perhaps because it was late, the customers thinned away from the tent shortly after this episode. The man stretched his elbows forward on the table, leant his face upon his arms, and soon began to snore. The furmity seller decided to close for the night, and after seeing the rum-bottles, milk, corn, raisins, etc., that remained on hand, loaded into the cart, came to where the man reclined. She shook him, but could not wake him. As the tent was not to be struck that night, the fair continuing for two or three days, she decided to let the sleeper, who was obviously no tramp, stay where he was, and his basket with him. Extinguishing the last candle, and lowering the flap of the tent, she left it, and drove away.

II

The morning sun was streaming through the crevices of the canvas when the man awoke. A warm glow pervaded the whole atmosphere of the marquee, and a single big blue fly buzzed musically round and round it. Besides the buzz of the fly there was not a sound. He looked about— at the benches—at the table supported by trestles—at his basket of tools—at the stove where the furmity had been boiled—at the empty basins—at some shed grains of wheat—at the corks which dotted the grassy floor. Among the odds and ends he discerned a little shining object, and picked it up. It was his wife's ring.

A confused picture of the events of the previous evening seemed to come back to him, and he thrust his hand into his breast-pocket. A rustling revealed the sailor's bank-notes thrust carelessly in.

This second verification of his dim memories was enough; he knew now they were not dreams. He remained seated, looking on the ground for some time. "I must get out of this as soon as I can," he said deliberately at last, with the air of one who could not catch his thoughts without pronouncing them. "She's gone—to be sure she is—gone with that sailor who bought her, and little Elizabeth-Jane. We walked here, and I had the furmity, and rum in it— and sold her. Yes, that's what happened, and here am I. Now, what am I to do—am I sober enough to walk, I wonder?" He stood up, found that he was in fairly good condition for progress, unencumbered. Next he shouldered his tool basket, and found he could carry it. Then lifting the tent door he emerged into the open air.

Here the man looked around with gloomy curiosity. The freshness of the September morning inspired and braced him as he stood. He and his family had been weary when they arrived the night before, and they had observed but little of the place; so that he now beheld it as a new thing. It exhibited itself as the top of an open down, bounded on one extreme by a plantation, and approached by a winding road. At the bottom stood the village which lent its name to the upland and the annual fair that was held thereon. The spot stretched downward into valleys, and onward to other uplands, dotted with barrows, and trenched with the remains of prehistoric forts. The whole scene lay under the rays of a newly risen sun, which had not as yet dried a single blade of the heavily dewed grass, whereon the shadows of the yellow and red vans were projected far away, those thrown by the felloe of each wheel being elongated in shape to the orbit of a comet. All the gipsies and showmen who had remained on the ground lay snug within their carts and tents, or wrapped in horse-cloths under them, and were silent and still as death, with the exception of an occasional snore that revealed their presence. But the Seven Sleepers had a dog; and dogs of the mysterious breeds that vagrants own, that are as much like cats as dogs and as much like foxes as cats, also lay about here. A little one started up under one of the carts, barked as a matter of principle, and quickly lay down again. He was the only positive spectator of the hay-trusser's exit from the Weydon Fair-field.

This seemed to accord with his desire. He went on in silent thought, unheeding the yellowhammers which flitted about the hedges with straws in their bills, the crowns of the mushrooms, and the tinkling of local sheep-bells, whose wearers had had the good fortune not to be included in the fair. When he reached a lane, a good mile from the scene of the previous evening, the man pitched his basket and leant upon a gate. A difficult problem or two occupied his mind.

"Did I tell my name to anybody last night, or didn't I tell my name?" he said to himself; and at last concluded that he did not. His general demeanor was enough to show how he was surprised and nettled that his wife had taken him so literally—as much could be seen in his face, and in the way he nibbled a straw which he pulled from the hedge. He knew that she must have been somewhat excited to do this; moreover, she must have believed that there was some sort of binding force in the transaction. On this latter point he felt almost certain, knowing her freedom from levity of character, and the extreme simplicity of her intellect. There may, too, have been enough recklessness and resentment beneath her ordinary placidity to make her stifle any momentary doubts. On a previous occasion when he had declared during a fuddle that he would dispose of her as he had done, she had replied that she would not hear him say that many times more before it happened, in the resigned tones of a fatalist. . . . "Yet she knows I am not in my senses when I do that!" he exclaimed. "Well, I must walk about till I find her. . . . Seize her, why didn't she know better than bring me into this disgrace!" he roared out. "She wasn't queer if I was. 'Tis like Susan to show such idiotic simplicity. Meek—that meekness has done me more harm than the bitterest temper!"

When he was calmer he turned to his original conviction that he must somehow find her and his little Elizabeth-Jane, and put up with the shame as best he could. It was of his own making, and he ought to bear it. But first he resolved to register an oath, a greater oath than he had ever sworn before: and to do it properly he required a fit place and imagery; for there was something fetichistic in this man's beliefs.

He shouldered his basket and moved on, casting his eyes inquisitively round upon the landscape as he walked, and at the distance of three or four miles perceived the roofs of a village and the tower of a church. He instantly made towards the latter object. The village was quite still, it being that motionless hour of rustic daily life which fills the interval between the departure of the field-laborers to their work, and the rising of their wives and daughters to prepare the breakfast for their return. Hence he reached the church without observation, and the door being only latched he entered. The hay-trusser deposited his basket by the font, went up the nave till he reached the altar-rails, and opening the gate entered the sacrarium, where he seemed to feel a sense of the strangeness for a moment; then he knelt upon the foot-pace. Dropping his head upon the clamped book which lay on the Communion-table, he said aloud—

"I, Michael Henchard, on this morning of the sixteenth of September, do take an oath before God here in this solemn place that I will avoid all strong liquors for the space of twenty-one years to come, being a year for every year that I have lived. And this I swear upon the book before me; and may I be strook dumb, blind, and helpless, if I break this my oath!"

When he had said it and kissed the big book, the hay-trusser arose, and seemed relieved at having made a start in a new direction. While standing in the porch a moment he saw a thick jet of wood smoke suddenly start up from the red chimney of a cottage near, and knew that the occupant had just lit her fire. He went round to the door, and the housewife agreed to prepare him some breakfast for a trifling payment, which was done. Then he started on the search for his wife and child.

The perplexing nature of the undertaking became apparent soon enough. Though he examined and inquired, and walked hither and thither day after day, no such characters as those he described had anywhere been seen since the evening of the fair. To add to the difficulty he could gain no sound of the sailor's name. As money was short with him he decided, after some hesitation, to spend the sailor's money in the prosecution of this search; but it was equally in vain. The truth was that a certain shyness of revealing his conduct prevented Michael Henchard from following up the investigation with the loud hue-and-cry such a pursuit demanded to render it effectual; and it was probably for this reason that he obtained no clue, though everything was done by him that did not involve an explanation of the circumstances under which he had lost her.

Weeks counted up to months, and still he searched on, maintaining himself by small jobs of work in the intervals. By this time he had arrived at a seaport, and there he derived intelligence that persons answering somewhat to his description had emigrated a little time before. Then he said he would search no longer, and that he would go and settle in the district which he had had for some time in his mind. Next day he started, journeying south-westward, and did not pause, except for nights' lodgings, till he reached the town of Casterbridge, in a far distant part of Wessex.

III

The highroad into the village of Weydon-Priors was again carpeted with dust. The trees had put on as of yore their aspect of dingy green, and where the Henchard family of three had once walked along, two persons not unconnected with that family walked now.

The scene in its broad aspect had so much of its previous character, even to the voices and rattle from the neighboring village down, that it might for that matter have been the afternoon following the previously recorded episode. Change was only to be observed in details; but here it was obvious that a long procession of years had passed by. One of the two who walked the road was she who had figured as the young wife of Henchard on the previous occasion; now her face had lost much of its rotundity; her skin had undergone a textural change; and though her hair had not lost color it was considerably thinner than heretofore. She was dressed in the mourning clothes of a widow. Her companion, also in black, appeared as a well-formed young woman about eighteen, completely possessed of that ephemeral precious essence youth, which is itself beauty, irrespective of complexion or contour.

A glance was sufficient to inform the eye that this was Susan Henchard's grown-up daughter. While life's middle summer had set its hardening mark on the mother's face, her former spring-like specialities were transferred so dexterously by Time to the second figure, her child, that the absence of certain facts within her mother's knowledge from the girl's mind would have seemed for the moment, to one reflecting on those facts, to be a curious imperfection in Nature's powers of continuity.

They walked with joined hands, and it could be perceived that this was the act of simple affection. The daughter carried in her outer hand a withy basket of old-fashioned make; the mother a blue bundle, which contrasted oddly with her black stuff gown.

Reaching the outskirts of the village they pursued the same track as formerly, and ascended to the fair. Here, too, it was evident that the years had told. Certain mechanical improvements might have been noticed in the roundabouts and highfliers, machines for testing rustic strength and weight, and in the erections devoted to shooting for nuts. But the real business of the fair had considerably dwindled. The new periodical great markets of neighboring towns were beginning to interfere seriously with the trade carried on here for centuries. The pens for sheep, the tie-ropes for horses, were about half as long as they had been. The stalls of tailors, hosiers, coopers, linen-drapers, and other such trades had almost disappeared, and the vehicles were far less numerous. The mother and daughter threaded the crowd for some little distance, and then stood still.

"Why did we hinder our time by coming in here? I thought you wished to get onward?" said the maiden.

"Yes, my dear Elizabeth-Jane," explained the other. "But I had a fancy for looking up here."

"Why?"

"It was here I first met with Newson—on such a day as this."

"First met with father here? Yes, you have told me so before. And now he's drowned and gone from us!" As she spoke the girl drew a card from her pocket and looked at it with a sigh. It was edged with black, and inscribed within a design resembling a mural tablet were the words, "In affectionate memory of Richard Newson, mariner, who was unfortunately lost at sea, in the month of November 184—, aged forty-one years."

"And it was here," continued her mother, with more hesitation, "that I last saw the relation we are going to look for—Mr. Michael Henchard."

"What is his exact kin to us, mother? I have never clearly had it told me."

"He is, or was—for he may be dead—a connection by marriage," said her mother deliberately.

"That's exactly what you have said a score of times before!" replied the young woman, looking about her inattentively. "He's not a near relation, I suppose?"

"Not by any means."

"He was a hay-trusser, wasn't he, when you last heard of him?"

"He was."

"I suppose he never knew me?" the girl innocently continued.

Mrs. Henchard paused for a moment, and answered uneasily, "Of course not, Elizabeth-Jane. But come this way." She moved on to another part of the field.

"It is not much use inquiring here for anybody, I should think," the daughter observed, as she gazed round about. "People at fairs change like the leaves of trees; and I daresay you are the only one here to-day who was here all those years ago."

"I am not so sure of that," said Mrs. Newson, as she now called herself, keenly eyeing something under a green bank a little way off. "See there."

The daughter looked in the direction signified. The object pointed out was a tripod of sticks stuck into the earth, from which hung a three-legged crock, kept hot by a smouldering wood fire beneath. Over the pot stooped an old woman, haggard, wrinkled, and almost in rags. She stirred the contents of the pot with a large spoon, and occasionally croaked in a broken voice, "Good furmity sold here!"

It was indeed the former mistress of the furmity tent—once thriving, cleanly, white-aproned, and chinking with money—now tentless, dirty, owning no tables or benches, and having scarce any customers except two small whitey-brown boys, who came up and asked for "A ha'p'orth, please—good measure," which she served in a couple of chipped yellow basins of commonest clay.

"She was here at that time," resumed Mrs. Newson, making a step as if to draw nearer.

"Don't speak to her—it isn't respectable!" urged the other.

"I will just say a word—you, Elizabeth-Jane, can stay here."

The girl was not loth, and turned to some stalls of colored prints while her mother went forward. The old woman begged for the latter's custom as soon as she saw her, and responded to Mrs. Henchard-Newson's request for a pennyworth with more alacrity than she had shown in selling sixpennyworths in her younger days. When the *soi-disant* widow had taken the basin of thin poor slop that stood for the rich concoction of the former time, the hag opened a little basket behind the fire, and looking up slily, whispered, "Just a thought o'rum in it?—smuggled, you know—say two penn'orth—'twill make it slip down like cordial!"

Her customer smiled bitterly at this survival of the old trick, and shook her head with a meaning the old woman was far from translating. She pretended to eat a little of the furmity with the leaden spoon offered, and as she did so said blandly to the hag, "You've seen better days?"

"Ah, ma'am—well ye may say it!" responded the old woman, opening the sluices of her heart forthwith. "I've stood in this fairground, maid, wife, and widow, these nine-and-thirty year, and in that time have known what it was to do business with the richest stomachs in the land! Ma'am, you'd hardly believe that I was once the owner of a great pavilion-tent that was the attraction of the fair. Nobody could come, nobody could go, without having a dish of Mrs. Goodenough's furmity. I knew the clergy's taste, the dandy gent's taste; I knew the town's taste, the country's taste. I even knowed the taste of the coarse shameless females. But Lord's my life—the world's no memory; straightforward dealings don't bring profit—'tis the sly and the underhand that get on in these times!"

Mrs. Newson glanced round—her daughter was still bending over the distant stalls. "Can you call to mind," she said cautiously to the old woman, "the sale of a wife by her husband in your tent eighteen years ago to-day?"

The hag reflected, and half shook her head. "If it had been a big thing I should have minded it in a moment," she said. "I can mind every serious fight o' married parties, every murder, every manslaughter, even every pocket-picking—leastwise large ones—that 't has been my lot to witness. But a selling? Was it done quiet-like?"

"Well, yes. I think so."

The furmity woman half shook her head again. "And yet," she said, "I do. At any rate, I can mind a man doing something o' the sort—a man in a cord jacket, with a basket of tools; but, Lord bless ye, we don't gi'e it head-room, we don't, such as that. The only reason why I can mind the man is that he came back here to the next year's fair, and told me quite private-like that if a woman ever asked for him I was to say he had gone to—where?—Casterbridge—yes—to Casterbridge, said he. But, Lord's my life, I shouldn't ha' thought of it again!"

Mrs. Newson would have rewarded the old woman as far as her small means afforded, had she not discreetly borne in mind that it was by that unscrupulous person's liquor her husband had been degraded. She briefly thanked her informant, and rejoined Elizabeth, who greeted her with, "Mother, do let's go on—it was hardly respectable for you to buy refreshments there. I see none but the lowest do."

"I have learned what I wanted, however," said her mother quietly. "The last time our relative visited this fair he said he was living at Casterbridge. It is a long, long way from here, and it was many years ago that he said it; but there I think we'll go."

With this they descended out of the fair, and went onward to the village, where they obtained a night's lodging.

IV

Henchard's wife acted for the best, but she had involved herself in difficulties. A hundred times she had been upon the point of telling her daughter Elizabeth-Jane the true story of her life, the tragical crisis of which had been the transaction at Weydon Fair, when she was not much older than the girl now beside her. But she had refrained. An innocent maiden had thus grown up in the belief that the relations between the genial sailor and her mother were the ordinary ones that they had always appeared to be. The risk of endangering a child's strong affection by disturbing ideas which had grown with her growth was to Mrs. Henchard too fearful a thing to contemplate. It had seemed, indeed, folly to think of making Elizabeth-Jane wise.

But Susan Henchard's fear of losing her dearly loved daughter's heart by a revelation had little to do with any sense of wrongdoing on her own part. Her simplicity—the original ground of Henchard's contempt for her—had allowed her to live on in the conviction that Newson had acquired a morally real and justifiable right to her by his purchase—though the exact bearings and legal limits of that right were vague. It may seem strange to sophisticated minds that a sane young matron could believe in the seriousness of such a transfer; and were there not numerous other instances of the same belief the thing might scarcely be credited. But she was by no means the first or last peasant woman who had religiously adhered to her purchaser, as too many rural records show.

The history of Susan Henchard's adventures in the interim can be told in two or three sentences. Absolutely helpless she had been taken off to Canada, where they had lived several years without any great worldly success, though she worked as hard as any woman could to keep their cottage cheerful and well-provided. When Elizabeth-Jane was about twelve years old the three returned to England, and settled at Falmouth, where Newson made a living for a few years as boatman and general handy shoreman.

He then engaged in the Newfoundland trade, and it was during this period that Susan had an awakening. A friend to whom she confided her history ridiculed her grave acceptance of her position; and all was over with her peace of mind. When Newson came home at the end of one winter he saw that the delusion he had so carefully sustained had vanished for ever.

There was then a time of sadness, in which she told him her doubts if she could live with him longer. Newson left home again on the Newfoundland trade when the season came round. The vague news of his loss at sea a little later on solved a problem which had become torture to her meek conscience. She saw him no more.

Of Henchard they heard nothing. To the liege subjects of Labor, the England of those days was a continent, and a mile a geographical degree.

Elizabeth-Jane developed early into womanliness. One day, a month or so after receiving intelligence of Newson's death off the Bank of Newfoundland, when the girl was about eighteen, she was sitting on a willow chair in the cottage they still occupied, working twine nets for the fishermen. Her mother was in a back corner of the same room, engaged in the same labor; and dropping the heavy wood needle she was filling she surveyed her daughter thoughtfully. The sun shone in at the door upon the young woman's head and hair, which was worn loose, so that the rays streamed into its depths as into a hazel copse. Her face, though somewhat wan and incomplete, possessed the raw materials of beauty in a promising degree. There was an under-handsomeness in it, struggling to reveal itself through the provisional curves of immaturity, and the casual disfigurements that resulted from the straitened circumstances of their lives. She was handsome in the bone, hardly as yet handsome in the flesh. She possibly might never be fully handsome, unless the carking accidents of her daily existence could be evaded before the mobile parts of her countenance had settled to their final mould.

The sight of the girl made her mother sad—not vaguely, but by logical inference. They both were still in that strait-

waistcoat of poverty from which she had tried so many
times to be delivered for the girl's sake. The woman had
long perceived how zealously and constantly the young
mind of her companion was struggling for enlargement;
and yet now, in her eighteenth year, it still remained but
little unfolded. The desire—sober and repressed—of Elizabeth-Jane's heart was indeed to see, to hear, and to understand. How could she become a woman of wider knowledge, higher repute—"better," as she termed it—this was
her constant inquiry of her mother. She sought further
into things than other girls in her position ever did, and
her mother groaned as she felt she could not aid in the
search.

The sailor, drowned or no, was probably now lost to
them; and Susan's staunch, religious adherence to him as
her husband in principle, till her views had been disturbed
by enlightenment, was demanded no more. She asked herself whether the present moment, now that she was a free
woman again, were not as opportune a one as she would
find in a world where everything had been so inopportune,
for making a desperate effort to advance Elizabeth. To
pocket her pride and search for the first husband seemed,
wisely or not, the best initiatory step. He had possibly
drunk himself into his tomb. But he might, on the other
hand, have had too much sense to do so; for in her time
with him he had been given to bouts only, and was not
a habitual drunkard.

At any rate, the propriety of returning to him, if he
lived, was unquestionable. The awkwardness of searching
for him lay in enlightening Elizabeth, a proceeding which
her mother could not endure to contemplate. She finally
resolved to undertake the search without confiding to the
girl her former relations with Henchard, leaving it to him
if they found him to take what steps he might choose to
that end. This will account for their conversation at the
fair and the half-informed state in which Elizabeth was
led onward.

In this attitude they proceeded on their journey, trusting
solely to the dim light afforded of Henchard's whereabouts

by the furmity woman. The strictest economy was indispensable. Sometimes they might have been seen on foot,
sometimes on farmers' wagons, sometimes in carriers' vans;
and thus they drew near to Casterbridge. Elizabeth-Jane
discovered to her alarm that her mother's health was not
what it once had been, and there was ever and anon in
her talk that renunciatory tone which showed that, but
for the girl, she would not be very sorry to quit a life
she was growing thoroughly weary of.

It was on a Friday evening, near the middle of September, and just before dusk, that they reached the summit
of a hill within a mile of the place they sought. There were
high-banked hedges to the coach-road here, and they
mounted upon the green turf within, and sat down. The
spot commanded a full view of the town and its environs.

"What an old-fashioned place it seems to be!" said
Elizabeth-Jane, while her silent mother mused on other
things than topography. "It is huddled all together; and
it is shut in by a square wall of trees, like a plot of
garden ground by a box-edging."

Its squareness was, indeed, the characteristic which most
struck the eye in this antiquated borough, the borough of
Casterbridge—at that time, recent as it was, untouched by
the faintest sprinkle of modernism. It was compact as a
box of dominoes. It had no suburbs—in the ordinary sense.
Country and town met at a mathematical line.

To birds of the more soaring kind Casterbridge must
have appeared on this fine evening as a mosaic-work of
subdued reds, browns, greys, and crystals, held together
by a rectangular frame of deep green. To the level eye of
humanity it stood as an indistinct mass behind a dense
stockade of limes and chestnuts, set in the midst of miles
of rotund down and concave field. The mass became gradually dissected by the vision into towers, gables, chimneys,
and casements, the highest glazings shining bleared and
bloodshot with the coppery fire they caught from the belt
of sunlit cloud in the west.

From the center of each side of this tree-bound square
ran avenues east, west, and south into the wide expanse

of corn-land and coomb to the distance of a mile or so. It was by one of these avenues that the pedestrians were about to enter. Before they had risen to proceed two men passed outside the hedge, engaged in argumentative conversation.

"Why, surely," said Elizabeth, as they receded, "those men mentioned the name of Henchard in their talk—the name of our relative?"

"I thought so too," said Mrs. Newson.

"That seems a hint to us that he is still here."

"Yes."

"Shall I run after them, and ask them about him ——"

"No, no, no! Not for the world just yet. He may be in the workhouse, or in the stocks, for all we know."

"Dear me—why should you think that, mother?"

" 'Twas just something to say—that's all! But we must make private inquiries."

Having sufficiently rested they proceeded on their way at evenfall. The dense trees of the avenue rendered the road dark as a tunnel, though the open land on each side was still under a faint daylight; in other words, they passed down a midnight between two gloamings. The features of the town had a keen interest for Elizabeth's mother, now that the human side came to the fore. As soon as they had wandered about they could see that the stockade of gnarled trees which framed in Casterbridge was itself an avenue, standing on a low green bank or escarpment, with a ditch yet visible without. Within the avenue and bank was a wall more or less discontinuous, and within the wall were packed the abodes of the burghers.

Though the two women did not know it these external features were but the ancient defences of the town, planted as a promenade.

The lamplights now glimmered through the engirdling trees, conveying a sense of great snugness and comfort inside, and rendering at the same time the unlighted country without strangely solitary and vacant in aspect, considering its nearness to life. The difference between burgh and champaign was increased, too, by sounds which now reached them above others—the notes of a brass band. The travellers returned into the High Street, where there were timber houses with overhanging stories, whose small-paned lattices were screened by dimity curtains on a drawing-string, and under whose barge-boards old cobwebs waved in the breeze. There were houses of brick-nogging, which derived their chief support from those adjoining. There were slate roofs patched with titles, and tile roofs patched with slate, with occasionally a roof of thatch.

The agricultural and pastoral character of the people upon whom the town depended for its existence was shown by the class of objects displayed in the shop windows. Scythes, reap-hooks, sheep-shears, bill-hooks, spades, mattocks, and hoes at the ironmonger's; bee-hives, butter-firkins, churns, milking stools and pails, hay-rakes, field-flagons, and seed-lips at the cooper's; cart-ropes and plough-harness at the saddler's; carts, wheel-barrows, and millgear at the wheel-wright's and machinist's; horse-embrocations at the chemist's; at the glover's and leather-cutter's, hedging-gloves, thatchers' knee-caps, ploughmen's leggings, villagers' pattens and clogs.

They came to a grizzled church, whose massive square tower rose unbroken into the darkening sky, the lower parts being illuminated by the nearest lamps sufficiently to show how completely the mortar from the joints of the stone-work had been nibbled out by time and weather, which had planted in the crevices thus made little tufts of stone-crop and grass almost as far up as the very battlements. From this tower the clock struck eight, and thereupon a bell began to toll with a peremptory clang. The curfew was still rung in Casterbridge, and it was utilized by the inhabitants as a signal for shutting their shops. No sooner did the deep notes of the bell throb between the house-fronts than a clatter of shutters arose through the whole length of the High Street. In a few minutes business at Caster-bridge was ended for the day.

Other clocks struck eight from time to time—one gloomily from the gaol, another from the gable of an alms-house, with a preparative creak of machinery, more audible than the note of the bell; a row of tall, varnished case-clocks from the interior of a clockmaster's shop joined in one after another just as the shutters were enclosing them, like a row of actors delivering their final speeches before the fall of the curtain; then chimes were heard stammering out the Sicilian Mariners' Hymn; so that chronologists of the advanced school were appreciably on their way to the next hour before the whole business of the old one was satisfactorily wound up.

In an open space before the church walked a woman with her gown-sleeves rolled up so high that the edge of her under-linen was visible, and her skirt tucked up through her pocket hole. She carried a loaf under her arm from which she was pulling pieces of bread, and handing them to some other women who walked with her; which pieces they nibbled critically. The sight reminded Mrs. Henchard-Newson and her daughter that they had an appetite; and they inquired of the woman for the nearest baker's.

"Ye may as well look for manna-food as good bread in Casterbridge just now," she said, after directing them. "They can blare their trumpets and thump their drums, and have their roaring dinners"—waving her hand towards a point further along the street, where the brass band could be seen standing in front of an illuminated building—"but we must needs be put-to for want of a wholesome crust. There's less good bread than good beer in Casterbridge now."

"And less good beer than swipes," said a man with his hands in his pockets.

"How does it happen there's no good bread?" asked Mrs. Henchard.

"Oh, 'tis the corn-factor—he's the man that our millers and bakers all deal wi', and he has sold 'em growed wheat, which they didn't know was growed, so they *say*, till the dough ran all over the ovens like quicksilver; so that the loaves be as flat as toads, and like suet pudden inside. I've been a wife, and I've been a mother, and I never see such unprincipled bread in Casterbridge as this before.

—But you must be a real stranger here not to know what's made all the poor volks' insides plim like blowed bladders this week?"

"I am," said Elizabeth's mother shyly.

Not wishing to be observed further till she knew more of her future in this place, she withdrew with her daughter from the speaker's side. Getting a couple of biscuits at the shop indicated as a temporary substitute for a meal, they next bent their steps instinctively to where the music was playing.

V

A few score yards brought them to the spot where the town band was now shaking the window-panes with the strains of "The Roast Beef of Old England."

The building before whose doors they had pitched their music-stands was the chief hotel in Casterbridge—namely, the King's Arms. A spacious bow-window projected into the street over the main portico, and from the open sashes came the babble of voices, the jingle of glasses, and the drawing of corks. The blinds, moreover, being left unclosed, the whole interior of this room could be surveyed from the top of a flight of stone steps to the road-wagon office opposite, for which reason a knot of idlers had gathered there.

"We might, perhaps, after all, make a few inquiries about—our relation Mr. Henchard," whispered Mrs. Newson who, since her entry into Casterbridge, had seemed strangely weak and agitated. "And this, I think, would be a good place for trying it—just to ask, you know, how he stands in the town—if he is here, as I think he must be. You, Elizabeth-Jane, had better be the one to do it. I'm too worn out to do anything—pull down your fall first."

She sat down upon the lowest step, and Elizabeth-Jane obeyed her directions and stood among the idlers.

"What's going on to-night?" asked the girl, after singling out an old man and standing by him long enough to acquire a neighborly right of converse.

"Well, ye must be a stranger sure," said the old man, without taking his eyes from the window. "Why, 'tis a great public dinner of the gentle-people and such like leading volk—wi' the Mayor in the chair. As we plainer fellows bain't invited, they leave the winder-shutters open that we may get jist a sense o't out here. If you mount the steps you can see 'em. That's Mr. Henchard, the Mayor, at the end of the table, a facing ye; and that's the council men right and left. . . . Oh, lots of them when they begun life were no more than I be now!"

"Henchard!" said Elizabeth-Jane, surprised, but by no means suspecting the whole force of the revelation. She ascended to the top of the steps.

Her mother, though her head was bowed, had already caught from the inn-window tones that strangely riveted her attention, before the old man's words, "Mr. Henchard, the Mayor," reached her ears. She arose, and stepped up to her daughter's side as soon as she could do so without showing exceptional eagerness.

The interior of the hotel dining-room was spread out before her, with its tables, and glass, and plate, and inmates. Facing the window, in the chair of dignity, sat a man about forty years of age; of heavy frame, large features, and commanding voice; his general build being rather coarse than compact. He had a rich complexion, which verged on swarthiness, a flashing black eye, and dark, bushy brows and hair. When he indulged in an occasional loud laugh at some remark among the guests, his large mouth parted so far back as to show to the rays of the chandelier a full score or more of the two-and-thirty sound white teeth that he obviously still could boast of.

That laugh was not encouraging to strangers; and hence it may have been well that it was rarely heard. Many theories might have been built upon it. It fell in well with conjectures of a temperament which would have no pity for weakness, but would be ready to yield ungrudging admiration to greatness and strength. Its producer's personal goodness, if he had any, would be of a very fitful cast—an occasional almost oppressive generosity rather than a mild and constant kindness.

Susan Henchard's husband—in law, at least—sat before them, matured in shape, stiffened in line, exaggerated in traits; disciplined, thought-marked—in a word, older. Elizabeth, encumbered with no recollections as her mother was, regarded him with nothing more than the keen curiosity and interest which the discovery of such unexpected social standing in the long-sought relative naturally begot. He was dressed in an old-fashioned evening suit, an expanse of frilled shirt showing on his broad breast; jewelled studs, and a heavy gold chain. Three glasses stood at his right hand; but, to his wife's surprise, the two for wine were empty, while the third, a tumbler, was half full of water.

When last she had seen him he was sitting in a corduroy jacket, fustian waistcoat and breeches, and tanned leather leggings, with a basin of hot furmity before him. Time, the magician, had wrought much here. Watching him, and thus thinking of past days, she became so moved that she shrank back against the jamb of the wagon-office doorway to which the steps gave access, the shadow from it conveniently hiding her features. She forgot her daughter till a touch from Elizabeth-Jane aroused her. "Have you seen him, mother?" whispered the girl.

"Yes, yes," answered her companion hastily. "I have seen him, and it is enough for me! Now I only want to go— pass away—die."

"Why—oh what?" She drew closer, and whispered in her mother's ear, "Does he seem to you not likely to befriend us? I thought he looked a generous man. What a gentleman he is, isn't he? and how his diamond studs shine! How strange that you should have said he might be in the stocks, or in the workhouse, or dead! Did ever anything go more by contraries! Why do you feel so afraid of him? I am not at all; I'll call upon him—he can but say he don't own such remote kin."

"I don't know at all—I can't tell what to set about. I feel so down."

"Don't be that, mother, now we have got here and all!

Rest there where you be a little while—I will look on and find out more about him."

"I don't think I can ever meet Mr. Henchard. He is not how I thought he would be—he overpowers me! I don't wish to see him any more."

"But wait a little time and consider."

Elizabeth-Jane had never been so much interested in anything in her life as in their present position, partly from the natural elation she felt at discovering herself akin to a coach; and she gazed again at the scene. The younger guests were talking and eating with animation; their elders were searching for tit-bits, and sniffing and grunting over their plates like sows nuzzling for acorns. Three drinks seemed to be sacred to the company—port, sherry, and rum; outside which old-established trinity few or no palates ranged.

A row of ancient rummers with ground figures on their sides, and each primed with a spoon, was now placed down the table, and these were promptly filled with grog at such high temperatures as to raise serious considerations for the articles exposed to its vapors. But Elizabeth-Jane noticed that, though this filling went on with great promptness up and down the table, nobody filled the Mayor's glass, who still drank large quantities of water from the tumbler behind the clump of crystal vessels intended for wine and spirits.

"They don't fill Mr. Henchard's wine-glasses," she ventured to say to her elbow acquaintance, the old man.

"Ah no; don't ye know him to be the celebrated abstaining worthy of that name? He scorns all tempting liquors; never touches nothing. O yes, he've strong qualities that way. I have heard tell that he sware a gospel oath in bygone times, and has bode by it ever since. So they don't press him, knowing it would be unbecoming in the face of that; for yer gospel oath is a serious thing."

Another elderly man, hearing this discourse, now joined in by inquiring, "How much longer have he got to suffer from it, Solomon Longways?"

"Another two year, they say. I don't know the why and

the wherefore of his fixing such a time, for 'a never has told anybody. But 'tis two calendar years longer, they say. A powerful mind to hold out so long!"

"True. . . . But there's great strength in hope. Knowing that in four-and-twenty months' time ye'll be out of your bondage, and able to make up for all you've suffered, by partaking without stint—why, it keeps a man up, no doubt."

"No doubt, Christopher Coney, no doubt. And 'a must need such reflections—a lonely widow man," said Longways.

"When did he lose his wife?" asked Elizabeth.

"I never knowed her. 'Twas afore he came to Casterbridge," Solomon Longways replied with terminative emphasis, as if the fact of his ignorance of Mrs. Henchard were sufficient to deprive her history of all interest. "But I know that 'a's a banded tee-totaller, and that if any of his men be ever so little overtook by a drop he's down upon 'em as stern as the Lord upon the jovial Jews."

"Has he many men, then?" said Elizabeth-Jane.

"Many! Why, my good maid, he's the powerfullest member of the Town Council, and quite a principal man in the country round besides. Never a big dealing in wheat, barley, oats, hay, roots, and such-like but Henchard's got a hand in it. Ay, and he'll go into other things too; and that's where he makes his mistake. He worked his way up from nothing when 'a came here; and now he's a pillar of the town. Not but what he's been shaken a little to-year about this bad corn he has supplied in his contracts. I've seen the sun rise over Durnover Moor these nine-and-sixty year, and though Mr. Henchard has never cussed me unfairly ever since I've worked for'n, seeing I be but a little small man, I must say that I have never before tasted such rough bread as has been made from Henchard's wheat lately. 'Tis that growed out that ye could a'most call it malt, and there's a list at bottom o' the loaf as thick as the sole of one's shoe."

The band now struck up another melody, and by the time it was ended the dinner was over, and speeches began to be made. The evening being calm, and the windows still open, these orations could be distinctly heard. Henchard's voice arose above the rest; he was telling a story of his hay-dealing experiences, in which he had outwitted a sharper who had been bent upon outwitting him.

"Ha-ha-ha!" responded his audience at the upshot of the story; and hilarity was general till a new voice arose with, "This is all very well; but how about the bad bread?"

It came from the lower end of the table, where there sat a group of minor tradesmen who, although part of the company, appeared to be a little below the social level of the others; and who seemed to nourish a certain independence of opinion and carry on discussions not quite in harmony with those at the head; just as the west end of a church is sometimes persistently found to sing out of time and tune with the leading spirits in the chancel.

This interruption about the bad bread afforded infinite satisfaction to the loungers outside, several of whom were in the mood which finds its pleasure in others' discomfiture; and hence they echoed pretty freely, "Hey! How about the bad bread, Mr. Mayor?" Moreover, feeling none of the restraints of those who shared the feast, they could afford to add, "You rather ought to tell the story o' that, sir."

The interruption was sufficient to compel the Mayor to notice it.

"Well, I admit that the wheat turned out badly," he said. "But I was taken in in buying it as much as the bakers who bought it o' me."

"And the poor folk who had to eat it whether or no," said the inharmonious man outside the window.

Henchard's face darkened. There was temper under the thin bland surface—the temper which, artificially intensified, had banished a wife nearly a score of years before.

"You must make allowances for the accidents of a large business," he said. "You must bear in mind that the weather just at the harvest of that corn was worse than we have known it for years. However, I have mended my arrangements on account o't. Since I have found my business too large to be well looked after by myself alone, I have advertised for a thorough good man as manager of the corn department. When I've got him you will find these mistakes will no longer occur—matters will be better looked into."

"But what are you going to do to repay us for the past?" inquired the man who had before spoken, and who seemed to be a baker or miller. "Will you replace the grown flour we've still got by sound grain?"

Henchard's face had become still more stern at these interruptions, and he drank from his tumbler of water as if to calm himself or gain time. Instead of vouchsafing a direct reply, he stiffly observed—

"If anybody will tell me how to turn grown wheat into wholesome wheat, I'll take it back with pleasure. But it can't be done."

Henchard was not to be drawn again. Having said this, he sat down.

VI

Now the group outside the window had within the last few minutes been reinforced by new arrivals, some of them respectable shopkeepers and their assistants, who had come out for a whiff of air after putting up the shutters for the night; some of them of a lower class. Distinct from either there appeared a stranger—a young man of remarkably pleasant aspect—who carried in his hand a carpet-bag of the smart floral pattern prevalent in such articles at that time.

He was ruddy and of a fair countenance, bright-eyed, and slight in build. He might possibly have passed by without stopping at all, or at most for half a minute to glance in at the scene, had not his advent coincided with the discussion on corn and bread; in which event this history had never been enacted. But the subject seemed to arrest him, and he whispered some inquiries of the other bystanders, and remained listening.

When he heard Henchard's closing words, "It can't be

done," he smiled impulsively, drew out his pocketbook, and wrote down a few words by the aid of the light in the window. He tore out the leaf, folded and directed it, and seemed about to throw it in through the open sash upon the dining-table; but, on second thoughts, edged himself through the loiterers, till he reached the door of the hotel, where one of the waiters who had been serving inside was now idly leaning against the door-post.

"Give this to the Mayor at once," he said, handing in his hasty note.

Elizabeth-Jane had seen his movements and heard the words, which attracted her both by their subject and by their accent—a strange one for those parts. It was quaint and northerly.

The waiter took the note, while the young stranger continued—

"And can ye tell me of a respectable hotel that's a little more moderate than this?"

The waiter glanced indifferently up and down the street.

"They say the Three Mariners, just below here, is a very good place," he languidly answered; "but I have never stayed there myself."

The Scotchman, as he seemed to be, thanked him, and strolled on in the direction of the Three Mariners aforesaid, apparently more concerned about the question of an inn than about the fate of his note, now that the momentary impulse of writing it was over. While he was disappearing slowly down the street the waiter left the door, and Elizabeth-Jane saw with some interest the note brought into the dining-room and handed to the Mayor.

Henchard looked at it carelessly, unfolded it with one hand, and glanced it through. Thereupon it was curious to note an unexpected effect. The nettled, clouded aspect which had held possession of his face since the subject of his corn-dealings had been broached, changed itself into one of arrested attention. He read the note slowly, and fell into thought, not moody, but fitfully intense, as that of a man who has been captured by an idea.

By this time toasts and speeches had given place to

songs, the wheat subject being quite forgotten. Men were putting their heads together in twos and threes, telling good stories, with pantomimic laughter which reached convulsive grimace. Some were beginning to look as if they did not know how they had come there, what they had come for, or how they were going to get home again; and provisionally sat on with a dazed smile. Square-built men showed a tendency to become hunchbacks; men with a dignified presence lost it in a curious obliquity of figure, in which their features grew disarranged and one-sided; whilst the heads of a few who had dined with extreme thoroughness were somehow sinking into their shoulders, the corners of their mouth and eyes being bent upwards by the subsidence. Only Henchard did not conform to these flexuous changes; he remained stately and vertical, silently thinking.

The clock struck nine. Elizabeth-Jane turned to her companion. "The evening is drawing on, mother," she said. "What do you propose to do?"

She was surprised to find how irresolute her mother had become. "We must get a place to lie down in," she murmured. "I have seen—Mr. Henchard; and that's all I wanted to do."

"That's enough for to-night, at any rate," Elizabeth-Jane replied soothingly. "We can think to-morrow what is best to do about him. The question now is—is it not?—how shall we find a lodging?"

As her mother did not reply Elizabeth-Jane's mind reverted to the words of the waiter, that the Three Mariners was an inn of moderate charges. A recommendation good for one person was probably good for another. "Let's go where the young man has gone to," she said. "He is respectable. What do you say?"

Her mother assented, and down the street they went.

In the meantime the Mayor's thoughtfulness, engendered by the note as stated, continued to hold him in abstraction; till, whispering to his neighbor to take his place, he found opportunity to leave the chair. This was just after the departure of his wife and Elizabeth.

Outside the door of the assembly-room he saw the waiter, and beckoning to him asked who brought the note which had been handed in a quarter of an hour before.

"A young man, sir—a sort of traveller. He was a Scotchman seemingly."

"Did he say how he had got it?"

"He wrote it himself, sir, as he stood outside the window."

"Oh—wrote it himself. . . . Is the young man in the hotel?"

"No, sir. He went to the Three Mariners, I believe."

The Mayor walked up and down the vestibule of the hotel with his hands under his coat tails, as if he were merely seeking a cooler atmosphere than that of the room he had quitted. But there could be no doubt that he was in reality still possessed to the full by the new idea, whatever that might be. At length he went back to the door of the dining-room, paused, and found that the songs, toasts, and conversation were proceeding quite satisfactorily without his presence. The Corporation, private residents, and major and minor tradesmen had, in fact, gone in for comforting beverages to such an extent that they had quite forgotten, not only the Mayor, but all those vast political, religious, and social differences which they felt necessary to maintain in the daytime, and which separated them like iron grills. Seeing this the Mayor took his hat, and when the waiter had helped him on with a thin holland overcoat, went out and stood under the portico.

Very few persons were now in the street; and his eyes, by a sort of attraction, turned and dwelt upon a spot about a hundred yards further down. It was the house to which the writer of the note had gone—the Three Mariners— whose two prominent Elizabethan gables, bow-window, and passage-light could be seen from where he stood. Having kept his eyes on it for a while he strolled in that direction.

This ancient house of accommodation for man and beast, now, unfortunately, pulled down, was built of mellow sandstone, with mullioned windows of the same material, markedly out of perpendicular from the settlement of foundations. The bay window projecting into the street, whose interior was so popular among the frequenters of the inn, was closed with shutters, in each which appeared a heart-shaped aperture, somewhat more attenuated in the right and left ventricles than is seen in Nature. Inside these illuminated holes, at a distance of about three inches, were ranged at this hour, as every passer knew, the ruddy polls of Billy Wills the glazier, Smart the shoemaker, Buzzford the general dealer, and others of a secondary set of worthies, of a grade somewhat below that of the diners at the King's Arms, each with his yard of clay.

A four-centered Tudor arch was over the entrance, and over the arch the signboard, now visible in the rays of an opposite lamp. Hereon the Mariners, who had been represented by the artist as persons of two dimensions only —in other words, flat as a shadow—were standing in a row in paralyzed attitudes. Being on the sunny side of the street the three comrades had suffered largely from warping, splitting, fading, and shrinkage, so that they were but a half-visible film upon the reality of the grain, and knots, and nails, which composed the signboard. As a matter of fact, this state of things was not so much owing to Stannidge the landlord's neglect, as from the lack of a painter in Casterbridge who would undertake to reproduce the features of men so traditional.

A long, narrow, dimly-lit passage gave access to the inn, within which passage the horses going to their stalls at the back, and the coming and departing human guests, rubbed shoulders indiscriminately, the latter running no slight risk of having their toes trodden upon by the animals. The good stabling and the good ale of the Mariners, though somewhat difficult to reach on account of there being but this narrow way to both, were nevertheless perseveringly sought out by the sagacious old heads who knew what was what in Casterbridge.

Henchard stood without the inn for a few instants; then lowering the dignity of his presence as much as possible by buttoning the brown holland coat over his shirt-front, and in other ways toning himself down to his ordinary everyday appearance, he entered the inn door.

VII

Elizabeth-Jane and her mother had arrived some twenty minutes earlier. Outside the house they had stood and considered whether even this homely place, though recommended as moderate, might not be too serious in its prices for their light pockets. Finally, however, they had found courage to enter, and duly met Stannidge the landlord; a silent man, who drew and carried frothing measures to this room and to that, shoulder to shoulder with his waiting-maids—a stately slowness, however, entering into his ministrations by contrast with theirs, as became one whose service was somewhat optional. It would have been altogether optional but for the orders of the landlady, a person who sat in the bar, corporeally motionless, but with a flitting eye and quick ear, with which she observed and heard through the open door and hatchway the pressing needs of customers whom her husband overlooked though close at hand. Elizabeth and her mother were passively accepted as sojourners, and shown to a small bedroom under one of the gables, where they sat down.

The principle of the inn seemed to be to compensate for the antique awkwardness, crookedness, and obscurity of the passages, floors, and windows, by quantities of clean linen spread about everywhere, and this had a dazzling effect upon the travellers.

" 'Tis too good for us—we can't meet it!" said the elder woman, looking round the apartment with misgiving as soon as they were left alone.

"I fear it is, too," said Elizabeth. "But we must be respectable."

"We must pay our way even before we must be respectable," replied her mother. "Mr. Henchard is too high for us to make ourselves known to him, I much fear; so we've only our own pockets to depend on."

"I know what I'll do," said Elizabeth-Jane after an interval of waiting, during which their needs seemed quite forgotten under the press of business below. And leaving the room, she descended the stairs and penetrated to the bar.

If there was one good thing more than another which characterized this single-hearted girl it was a willingness to sacrifice her personal comfort and dignity to the common weal.

"As you seem busy here to-night, and mother's not well off, might I take out part of our accommodation by helping?" she asked of the landlady.

The latter, who remained as fixed in the arm-chair as if she had been melted into it when in a liquid state, and could not now be unstuck, looked the girl up and down inquiringly, with her hands on the chair-arms. Such arrangements as the one Elizabeth proposed were not uncommon in country villages; but, though Casterbridge was old-fashioned, the custom was well-nigh obsolete here. The mistress of the house, however, was an easy woman to strangers, and she made no objection. Thereupon Elizabeth, being instructed by nods and motions from the taciturn landlord as to where she could find the different things, trotted up and down stairs with materials for her own and her parent's meal.

While she was doing this the wood partition in the center of the house thrilled to its center with the tugging of a bell-pull upstairs. A bell below tinkled a note that was feebler in sound than the twanging of wires and cranks that had produced it.

" 'Tis the Scotch gentleman," said the landlady omnisciently; and turning her eyes to Elizabeth, "Now then, can you go and see if his supper is on the tray? If it is you can take it up to him. The front room over this."

Elizabeth-Jane, though hungry, willingly postponed serving herself awhile, and applied to the cook in the kitchen, whence she brought forth the tray of supper viands, and proceeded with it upstairs to the apartment indicated. The accommodation of the Three Mariners was far from spacious, despite the fair area of ground it covered. The room demanded by intrusive beams and rafters, partitions, passages, staircases, disused ovens, settles, and four-posters, left comparatively small quarters for human beings. Moreover, this being at a time before home-brewing was abandoned by the smaller victuallers, and a house in which the twelve-bushel strength was still religiously adhered to by the landlord in his ale, the quality of the liquor was the chief attraction of the premises, so that everything had to make way for utensils and operations in connection therewith. Thus Elizabeth found that the Scotsman was located in a room quite close to the small one that had been allotted to herself and her mother.

When she entered nobody was present but the young man himself—the same whom she had seen lingering without the windows of the King's Arms Hotel. He was now idly reading a copy of the local paper, and was hardly conscious of her entry, so that she looked at him quite coolly, and saw how his forehead shone where the light caught it, and how nicely his hair was cut, and the sort of velvet-pile or down that was on the skin at the back of his neck, and how his cheek was so truly curved as to be part of a globe, and how clearly drawn were the lids and lashes which hid his bent eyes.

She set down the tray, spread his supper, and went away without a word. On her arrival below the landlady, who was as kind as she was fat and lazy, saw that Elizabeth-Jane was rather tired, though in her earnestness to be useful she was waiving her own needs altogether. Mrs. Stannidge thereupon said with a considerate peremptoriness that she and her mother had better take their own supper if they meant to have any.

Elizabeth fetched their simple provisions, as she had fetched the Scotchman's, and went up to the little chamber where she had left her mother, noiselessly pushing open the door with the edge of the tray. To her surprise her mother, instead of being reclined on the bed where she had left her, was in an erect position, with lips parted. At Elizabeth's entry she lifted her finger.

The meaning of this was soon apparent. The room allotted to the two women had at one time served as a dressing-room to the Scotchman's chamber, as was evidenced by signs of a door of communication between them—now screwed up and pasted over with the wall

paper. But, as is frequently the case with hotels of far
higher pretensions than the Three Mariners, every word
spoken in either of these rooms was distinctly audible in
the other. Such sounds came through now.

Thus silently conjured Elizabeth deposited the tray, and
her mother whispered as she drew near, " 'Tis he."

"Who?" said the girl.

"The Mayor."

The tremors in Susan Henchard's tone might have led
any person but one so perfectly unsuspicious of the truth
as the girl was, to surmise some closer connection than
the admitted simple kinship as a means of accounting for
them.

Two men were indeed talking in the adjoining chamber,
the young Scotchman and Henchard, who, having entered
the inn while Elizabeth-Jane was in the kitchen waiting for
the supper, had been deferentially conducted upstairs by
host Stannidge himself. The girl noiselessly laid out their
little meal, and beckoned to her mother to join her, which
Mrs. Henchard mechanically did, her attention being fixed
on the conversation through the door.

"I merely strolled in on my way home to ask you a
question about something that has excited my curiosity,"
said the Mayor, with careless geniality. "But I see you
have not finished supper."

"Ay, but I will be done in a little! Ye needn't go, sir.
Take a seat. I've almost done, and it makes no difference
at all."

Henchard seemed to take the seat offered, and in a
moment he resumed: "Well, first I should ask, did you
write this?" A rustling of paper followed.

"Yes, I did," said the Scotchman.

"Then," said Henchard, "I am under the impression
that we have met by accident while waiting for the morning to keep an appointment with each other? My name
is Henchard; ha'n't you replied to an advertisement for
a corn-factor's manager that I put into the paper—ha'n't
you come here to see me about it?"

"No," said the Scotchman, with some surprise.

"Surely you are the man," went on Henchard insisting,

"who arranged to come and see me? Joshua, Joshua, Jipp
—Jopp—what was his name?"

"You're wrong!" said the young man. "My name is
Donald Farfrae. It is true I am in the corren trade—but
I have replied to no advairrtisment, and arranged to see
no one. I am on my way to Bristol—from there to other
side of the warrld, to try my fortune in the great wheat-
growing districts of the West! I have some inventions useful
to the trade, and there is no scope for developing them
heere."

"To America—well, well," said Henchard, in a tone
of disappointment, so strong as to make itself felt like
a damp atmosphere. "And yet I could have sworn you were
the man!"

The Scotchman murmured another negative, and there
was a silence, till Henchard resumed: "Then I am truly
and sincerely obliged to you for the few words you wrote
on that paper."

"It was nothing, sir."

"Well, it has a great importance for me just now. This
row about my grown wheat, which I declare to Heaven I
didn't know to be bad till the people came complaining,
has put me to my wits' end. I've some hundreds of quarters
of it on hand; and if your renovating process will make
it wholesome, why, you can see what a quag 'twould get
me out of. I saw in a moment there might be truth in it.
But I should like to have it proved; and of course you
don't care to tell the steps of the process sufficiently for
me to do that, without my paying ye well for't first."

The young man reflected a moment or two. "I don't
know that I have any objection," he said. "I'm going to
another country, and curing bad corn is not the line I'll
take up there. Yes, I'll tell ye the whole of it—you'll
make more out of it heere than I will in a foreign country.
Just look heere a minute, sir. I can show ye by a sample
in my carpet-bag."

The click of a lock followed, and there was a sifting
and rustling; then a discussion about so many ounces
to the bushel, and drying, and refrigerating, and so on.

"These few grains will be sufficient to show ye with,"

came in the young fellow's voice; and after a pause, during which some operation seemed to be intently watched by them both, he exclaimed, "There, now, do you taste that."

"It's complete!—quite restored, or—well—nearly."

"Quite enough restored to make good seconds out of it," said the Scotchman. "To fetch it back entirely is impossible; Nature won't stand so much as that, but heere you go a great way towards it. Well, sir, that's the process; I don't value it, for it can be but of little use in countries where the weather is more settled than in ours; and I'll be only too glad if it's of service to you."

"But hearken to me," pleaded Henchard. "My business, you know, is in corn and in hay; but I was brought up as a hay-trusser simply, and hay is what I understand best, though I now do more in corn than in the other. If you'll accept the place, you shall manage the corn branch entirely, and receive a commission in addition to salary."

"You're liberal—very liberal; but no, no—I cannet!" the young man still replied, with some distress in his accents.

"So be it!" said Henchard conclusively. "Now—to change the subject—one good turn deserves another; don't stay to finish that miserable supper. Come to my house; I can find something better for 'ee than cold ham and ale."

Donald Farfrae was grateful—said he feared he must decline—that he wished to leave early next day.

"Very well," said Henchard quickly, "please yourself. But I tell you, young man, if this holds good for the bulk, as it has done for the sample, you have saved my credit, stranger though you be. What shall I pay you for this knowledge?"

"Nothing at all, nothing at all. It may not prove necessary to ye to use it often, and I don't value it at all. I thought I might just as well let ye know, as you were in a difficulty, and they were harrd upon ye."

Henchard paused. "I shan't soon forget this," he said. "And from a stranger! . . . I couldn't believe you were not the man I had engaged! Says I to myself, 'He knows who I am, and recommends himself by this stroke.' And yet it turns out, after all, that you are not the man who answered my advertisement, but a stranger!"

"Ay, ay; that's so," said the young man.

Henchard again suspended his words, and then his voice came thoughtfully: "Your forehead, Farfrae, is something like my poor brother's—now dead and gone; and the nose, too, isn't unlike his. You must be, what—five foot nine, I reckon? I am six foot one and a half out of my shoes. But what of that? In my business, 'tis true that strength and bustle build up a firm. But judgment and knowledge are what keep it established. Unluckily, I am bad at science, Farfrae; bad at figures—a rule o'thumb sort of man. You are just the reverse—I can see that. I have been looking for such as you these two years, and yet you are not for me. Well, before I go, let me ask this: Though you are not the young man I thought you were, what's the difference? Can't ye stay just the same? Have you really made up your mind about this American notion? I won't mince matters. I feel you would be invaluable to me—that needn't be said—and if you will bide and be my manager, I will make it worth your while."

"My plans are fixed," said the young man, in negative tones. "I have formed a scheme, and so we need na say any more about it. But will you not drink with me, sir? I find this Casterbridge ale warreming to the stomach."

"No, no; I fain would, but I can't," said Henchard gravely, the scraping of his chair informing the listeners that he was rising to leave. "When I was a young man I went in for that sort of thing too strong—far too strong— and was well-nigh ruined by it! I did a deed on account of it which I shall be ashamed of to my dying day. It made such an impression on me that I swore, there and then, that I'd drink nothing stronger than tea for as many years as I was old that day. I have kept my oath; and though, Farfrae, I am sometimes that dry in the dog days that I could drink a quarter-barrel to the pitching, I think o' my oath, and touch no strong drink at all."

"I'll no' press ye, sir—I'll no' press ye. I respect your vow."

"Well, I shall get a manager somewhere, no doubt," said Henchard, with strong feeling in his tones. "But it will be long before I see one that would suit me so well!"

The young man appeared much moved by Henchard's warm convictions of his value. He was silent till they reached the door. "I wish I could stay—sincerely I would like to," he replied. "But no—it cannet be! it cannet! I want to see the warrld."

VIII

Thus they parted; and Elizabeth-Jane and her mother remained each in her thoughts over their meal, the mother's face being strangely bright since Henchard's avowal of shame for a past action. The quivering of the partition to its core presently denoted that Donald Farfrae had again rung his bell, no doubt to have his supper removed; for humming a tune, and walking up and down, he seemed to be attracted by the lively bursts of conversation and melody from the general company below. He sauntered out upon the landing, and descended the staircase.

When Elizabeth-Jane had carried down his supper tray, and also that used by her mother and herself, she found the bustle of serving to be at its height below, as it always was at this hour. The young woman shrank from having anything to do with the ground-floor serving, and crept silently about observing the scene—so new to her, fresh from the seclusion of a seaside cottage. In the general sitting-room, which was large, she remarked the two or three dozen strong-backed chairs that stood round against the wall, each fitted with its genial occupant; the sanded floor; the black settle which, projecting endwise from the wall within the door, permitted Elizabeth to be a spectator of all that went on without herself being particularly seen.

The young Scotchman had just joined the guests. These, in addition to the respectable master-tradesmen occupying the seats of privilege in the bow-window and its neighborhood, included an inferior set at the unlighted end, whose seats were mere benches against the wall, and who drank from cups instead of from glasses. Among the latter she noticed some of those personages who had stood outside the windows of the King's Arms.

Behind their backs was a small window, with a wheel ventilator in one of the panes, which would suddenly start off spinning with a jingling sound, as suddenly stop, and as suddenly start again.

While thus furtively making her survey the opening words of a song greeted her ears from the front of the settle, in a melody and accent of peculiar charm. There had been some singing before she came down; and now the Scotchman had made himself so soon at home that, at the request of some of the master-tradesmen, he, too, was favoring the room with a ditty.

Elizabeth-Jane was fond of music; she could not help pausing to listen; and the longer she listened the more she was enraptured. She had never heard any singing like this; and it was evident that the majority of the audience had not heard such frequently, for they were attentive to a much greater degree than usual. They neither whispered, nor drank, nor dipped their pipe-stems in their ale to moisten them, nor pushed the mug to their neighbors. The singer himself grew emotional, till she could imagine a tear in his eye as the words went on:—

"It's hame, and it's hame, hame fain would I be,
Oh hame, hame, hame to my ain countree!
There's an eye that ever weeps, and a fair face will
    be fain,
As I pass through Annan Water with my bonnie
    bands again;
When the flower is in the bud, and the leaf upon
    the tree,
The lark shall sing me hame to my ain countree!"

There was a burst of applause, and a deep silence which was even more eloquent than the applause. It was of such a kind that the snapping of a pipe-stem too long for him by old Solomon Longways, who was one of those gathered at the shady end of the room, seemed a harsh and irreverent act. Then the ventilator in the window-pane spasmodically started off for a new spin, and the pathos of Donald's song was temporarily effaced.

" 'Twas not amiss—not at all amiss!" muttered Christopher Coney, who was also present. And removing his pipe a finger's breadth from his lips, he said aloud, "Draw on with the next verse, young gentleman, please."

"Yes. Let's have it again, stranger," said the glazier, a stout, bucket-headed man, with a white apron rolled up round his waist. "Folks don't lift up their hearts like that in this part of the world." And turning aside, he said in undertones, "Who is the young man?—Scotch, d'ye say?"

"Yes, straight from the mountains of Scotland, I believe," replied Coney.

Young Farfrae repeated the last verse. It was plain that nothing so pathetic had been heard at the Three Mariners for a considerable time. The difference of accent, the excitability of the singer, the intense local feeling, and the seriousness with which he worked himself up to a climax, surprised this set of worthies, who were only too prone to shut up their emotions with caustic words.

"Danged if our country down here is worth singing about like that!" continued the glazier, as the Scotchman again melodized with a dying fall, "My ain countree!" "When you take away from among us the fools and the rogues, and the lammigers, and the wanton hussies, and the slatterns, and such like, there's cust few left to ornament a song with in Casterbridge, or the country round."

"True," said Buzzford, the dealer, looking at the grain of the table. "Casterbridge is a old, hoary place o' wickedness, by all account. 'Tis recorded in history that we rebelled against the King one or two hundred years ago, in the time of the Romans, and that lots of us was hanged on Gallows Hill, and quartered, and our different jints sent about the country like butcher's meat; and for my part I can well believe it."

"What did ye come away from yer own country for, young maister, if ye so wownded about it?" inquired Christopher Coney, from the background, with the tone of a man who preferred the original subject. "Faith, it wasn't worth your while on our account, for, as Maister Billy Wills says, we be bruckle folk here—the best o' us hardly honest sometimes, what with hard winters, and so many mouths to fill, and God-a'mighty sending his little taties so terrible small to fill 'em with. We don't think about flowers and fair faces, not we—except in the shape o' cauliflowers and pigs' chaps."

"But, no!" said Donald Farfrae, gazing round into their faces with earnest concern; "the best of ye hardly honest— not that surely? None of ye has been stealing what didn't belong to him?"

"Lord! no, no!" said Solomon Longways, smiling grimly. "That's only his random way o' speaking. 'A was always such a man of under-thoughts." (And reprovingly towards Christopher): "Don't ye be so over-familiar with a gentleman that ye know nothing of—and that's travelled a'most from the North Pole."

Christopher Coney was silenced, and as he could get no public sympathy, he mumbled his feelings to himself: "Be dazed, if I loved my country half as well as the young feller do, I'd live by claning my neighbor's pigsties afore I'd go away! For my part I've no more love for my country than I have for Botany Bay!"

"Come," said Longways; "let the young man draw onward with his ballet, or we shall be here all night."

"That's all of it," said the singer apologetically.

"Soul of my body, then we'll have another!" said the general dealer.

"Can you turn a strain to the ladies, sir?" inquired a fat woman with a figured purple apron, the waist-string of which was overhung so far by her sides as to be invisible.

"Let him breathe—let him breathe, Mother Cuxsom. He hain't got his second wind yet," said the master glazier.

"Oh yes, but I have!" exclaimed the young man; and he at once rendered "O Nannie" with faultless modulations, and another or two of the like sentiment, winding up at their earnest request with "Auld Lang Syne."

By this time he had completely taken possession of the hearts of the Three Mariners' inmates, including even old Coney. Notwithstanding an occasional odd gravity which awoke their sense of the ludicrous for the moment, they began to view him through a golden haze which the tone of his mind seemed to raise around him. Casterbridge had sentiment—Casterbridge had romance; but this stranger's sentiment was of differing quality. Or rather, perhaps, the difference was mainly superficial; he was to them like the poet of a new school who takes his contemporaries by storm; who is not really new, but is the first to articulate what all his listeners have felt, though but dumbly till then.

The silent landlord came and leant over the settle while the young man sang; and even Mrs. Stannidge managed to unstick herself from the framework of her chair in the bar and get as far as the door-post, which movement she accomplished by rolling herself round, as a cask is trundled on the chine by a drayman without losing much of its perpendicular.

"And are you going to bide in Casterbridge, sir?" she asked.

"Ah—no!" said the Scotchman, with melancholy fatality in his voice, "I'm only passing thirrough! I am on my way to Bristol, and on frae there to foreign parts."

"We be truly sorry to hear it," said Solomon Longways. "We can ill afford to lose tuneful wynd-pipes like yours when they fall among us. And verily, to mak' acquaintance with a man a-come from so far, from the land o' perpetual snow, as we may say, where wolves and wild boars and other dangerous animalcules be as common as blackbirds hereabout—why, 'tis a thing we can't do every day; and there's good sound information for bide-at-homes like we when such a man opens his mouth."

"Nay, but ye mistake my country," said the young man, looking round upon them with tragic fixity, till his eye lighted up and his cheek kindled with a sudden enthusiasm to right their errors. "There are not perpetual snow and wolves at all in it!—except snow in winter, and—well— a little in summer just sometimes, and a 'gaberlunzie' or two stalking about here and there, if ye may call them dangerous. Eh, but you should take a summer jarreny to Edinboro', and Arthur's Seat, and all round there, and then go on to the lochs, and all the Highland scenery—

in May and June—and you would never say 'tis the land of wolves and perpetual snow!"

"Of course not—it stands to reason," said Buzzford. " 'Tis barren ignorance that leads to such words. He's a simple home-spun man, that never was fit for good company—think nothing of him, sir."

"And do ye carry your flock bed, and your quilt, and your crock, and your bit of chiney? or do ye go in bare bones, as I may say?" inquired Christopher Coney.

"I've sent on my luggage—though it isn't much; for the voyage is long." Donald's eyes dropped into a remote gaze as he added: "But I said to myself, 'Never a one of the prizes of life will I come by unless I undertake it!' and I decided to go."

A general sense of regret, in which Elizabeth-Jane shared not least, made itself apparent in the company. As she looked at Farfrae from the back of the settle she decided that his statements showed him to be no less thoughtful than his fascinating melodies revealed him to be cordial and impassioned. She admired the serious light in which he looked at serious things. He had seen no jest in ambiguities and roguery, as the Casterbridge toss-pots had done; and rightly not—there was none. She disliked those wretched humors of Christopher Coney and his tribe; and he did not appreciate them. He seemed to feel exactly as she felt about life and its surroundings—that they were a tragical rather than a comical thing; that though one could be gay on occasion, moments of gaiety were interludes, and no part of the actual drama. It was extraordinary how similar their views were.

Though it was still early the young Scotchman expressed his wish to retire, whereupon the landlady whispered to Elizabeth to run upstairs and turn down his bed. She took a candlestick and proceeded on her mission, which was the act of a few moments only. When, candle in hand, she reached the top of the stairs on her way down again, Mr. Farfrae was at the foot coming up. She could not very well retreat; they met and passed in the turn of the staircase.

She must have appeared interesting in some way—notwithstanding her plain dress—or rather, possibly, in consequence of it, for she was a girl characterized by earnestness and soberness of mien, with which simple drapery accorded well. Her face flushed, too, at the slight awkwardness of the meeting, and she passed him with her eyes bent on the candle-flame that she carried just below her nose. Thus it happened that when confronting her he smiled; and then, with the manner of a temporarily lighthearted man, who has started himself on a flight of song whose momentum he cannot readily check, he softly tuned an old ditty that she seemed to suggest—

> "As I come in by my bower door,
>   As day was waxin' wearie,
> Oh wha came tripping down the stair
>   But bonnie Peg my dearie."

Elizabeth-Jane, rather disconcerted, hastened on; and the Scotchman's voice died away, humming more of the same within the closed door of his room.

Here the scene and sentiment ended for the present. When, soon after, the girl rejoined her mother, the latter was still in thought—on quite another matter than a young man's song.

"We've made a mistake," she whispered (that the Scotchman might not overhear). "On no account ought ye to have helped serve here to-night. Not because of ourselves, but for the sake of *him*. If he should befriend us, and take us up, and then find out what you did when staying here, 'twould grieve and wound his natural pride as Mayor of the town."

Elizabeth, who would perhaps have been more alarmed at this than her mother had she known the real relationship, was not much disturbed about it as things stood. Her "he" was another man than her poor mother's. "For myself," she said, "I didn't at all mind waiting a little upon him. He's so respectable, and educated—far above the rest of 'em in the inn. They thought him very simple not to know their grim broad way of talking about themselves here. But of course he didn't know—he was too refined in his mind to know such things!" Thus she earnestly pleaded.

Meanwhile, the "he" of her mother was not so far away as even they thought. After leaving the Three Mariners he had sauntered up and down the empty High Street, passing and repassing the inn in his promenade. When the Scotchman sang his voice had reached Henchard's ears through the heart-shaped holes in the window-shutters, and had led him to pause outside them a long while.

"To be sure, to be sure, how that fellow does draw me!" he had said to himself. "I suppose 'tis because I'm so lonely. I'd have given him a third share in the business to have stayed!"

IX

When Elizabeth-Jane opened the hinged casement next morning the mellow air brought in the feel of imminent autumn almost as distinctly as if she had been in the remotest hamlet. Casterbridge was the complement of the rural life around; not its urban opposite. Bees and butterflies in the cornfields at the top of the town, who desired to get to the meads at the bottom, took no circuitous course, but flew straight down High Street without any apparent consciousness that they were traversing strange latitudes. And in autumn airy spheres of thistledown floated into the same street, lodged upon the shop fronts, blew into drains; and innumerable tawny and yellow leaves skimmed along the pavement, and stole through people's doorways into their passages with a hesitating scratch on the floor, like the skirts of timid visitors.

Hearing voices, one of which was close at hand, she withdrew her head and glanced from behind the window-curtains. Mr. Henchard—now habited no longer as a great personage, but as a thriving man of business—was pausing on his way up the middle of the street, and the Scotchman was looking from the window adjoining her own. Henchard, it appeared, had gone a little way past the inn before he had noticed his acquaintance of the previous evening. He came back a few steps, Donald Farfrae opening the window further.

"And you are off soon, I suppose?" said Henchard upwards.

"Yes—almost this moment, sir," said the other. "Maybe I'll walk on till the coach makes up on me."

"Which way?"

"The way ye are going."

"Then shall we walk together to the top o' town?"

"If ye'll wait a minute," said the Scotchman.

In a few minutes the latter emerged, bag in hand. Henchard looked at the bag as at an enemy. It showed there was no mistake about the young man's departure. "Ah, my lad," he said, "you should have been a wise man, and have stayed with me."

"Yes, yes—it might have been wiser," said Donald, looking microscopically at the houses that were furthest off. "It is only telling ye the truth when I say my plans are vague."

They had by this time passed on from the precincts of the inn, and Elizabeth-Jane heard no more. She saw that they continued in conversation, Henchard turning to the other occasionally, and emphasizing some remark with a gesture. Thus they passed the King's Arms Hotel, the Market House, St. Peter's churchyard wall, ascending to the upper end of the long street till they were small as two grains of corn; when they bent suddenly to the right into the Bristol Road, and were out of view.

"He was a good man—and he's gone," she said to herself. "I was nothing to him, and there was no reason why he should have wished me good-bye."

The simple thought, with its latent sense of slight, had moulded itself out of the following little fact: when the Scotchman came out at the door he had by accident glanced up at her; and then he had looked away again without nodding, or smiling, or saying a word.

"You are still thinking, mother," she said, when she turned inwards.

"Yes; I am thinking of Mr. Henchard's sudden liking

for that young man. He was always so. Now, surely, if he takes so warmly to people who are not related to him at all, may he not take as warmly to his own kin?"

While they debated this question a procession of five large wagons went past, laden with hay up to the bedroom windows. They came in from the country, and the steaming horses had probably been travelling a great part of the night. To the shaft of each hung a little board, on which was painted in white letters, "Henchard, corn-factor and hay-merchant." The spectacle renewed his wife's conviction that, for her daughter's sake, she should strain a point to rejoin him.

The discussion was continued during breakfast, and the end of it was that Mrs. Henchard decided, for good or for ill, to send Elizabeth-Jane with a message to Henchard, to the effect that his relative Susan, a sailor's widow, was in the town; leaving it to him to say whether or not he would recognize her. What had brought her to this determination were chiefly two things. He had been described as a lonely widower; and he had expressed shame for a past transaction of his life. There was promise in both.

"If he says no," she enjoined, as Elizabeth-Jane stood, bonnet on, ready to depart; "if he thinks it does not become the good position he has reached to in the town, to own—to let us call on him as—his distant kinsfolk, say, 'Then, sir, we would rather not intrude; we will leave Casterbridge as quietly as we have come, and go back to our own country.' . . . I almost feel that I would rather he did say so, as I have not seen him for so many years, and we are so—little allied to him!"

"And if he say yes?" inquired the more sanguine one.

"In that case," answered Mrs. Henchard cautiously, "ask him to write me a note, saying when and how he will see us—or *me*."

Elizabeth-Jane went a few steps towards the landing. "And tell him," continued her mother, "that I fully know I have no claim upon him—that I am glad to find he is thriving; that I hope his life may be long and happy— there, go." Thus with a half-hearted willingness, a smothered reluctance, did the poor forgiving woman start her unconscious daughter on this errand.

It was about ten o'clock, and market-day, when Elizabeth paced up the High Street, in no great hurry; for to herself her position was only that of a poor relation deputed to hunt up a rich one. The front doors of the private houses were mostly left open at this warm autumn time, no thought of umbrella stealers disturbing the minds of the placid burgesses. Hence, through the long, straight, entrance passages thus unclosed could be seen, as through tunnels, the mossy gardens at the back, glowing with nasturtiums, fuchsias, scarlet geraniums, "bloody warriors," snapdragons, and dahlias, this floral blaze being backed by crusted grey stone-work remaining from a yet remoter Casterbridge than the venerable one visible in the street. The old-fashioned fronts of these houses, which had older than old-fashioned backs, rose sheer from the pavement, into which the bow-windows protruded like bastions, necessitating a pleasing *chassez-déchassez* movement to the time-pressed pedestrian at every few yards. He was bound also to evolve other Terpsichorean figures in respect of door-steps, scrapers, cellar-hatches, church buttresses, and the overhanging angles of walls which, originally unobtrusive, had become bow-legged and knock-kneed.

In addition to these fixed obstacles which spoke so cheerfully of individual unrestraint as to boundaries, movables occupied the path and roadway to a perplexing extent. First the vans of the carriers in and out of Casterbridge, who hailed from Mellstock, Weatherbury, The Hintocks, Sherton-Abbas, Kingsbere, Overcombe, and many other towns and villages round. Their owners were numerous enough to be regarded as a tribe, and had almost distinctiveness enough to be regarded as a race. Their vans had just arrived, and were drawn up on each side of the street in close file, so as to form at places a wall between the pavement and the roadway. Moreover every shop pitched out half its contents upon trestles and boxes on the curb, extending the display each week a little further and further into the roadway, despite the expostulations of the two feeble old constables, until there remained but a tortuous defile for carriages down the center of the street, which afforded fine opportunities for skill with the reins. Over the pavement on the sunny side of the way hung shopblinds so constructed as to give the passenger's hat a smart buffet off his head, as from the unseen hands of Cranstoun's Goblin Page, celebrated in romantic lore.

Horses for sale were tied in rows, their forelegs on the pavement, their hind legs in the street, in which position they occasionally nipped little boys by the shoulder who were passing to school. And any inviting recess in front of a house that had been modestly kept back from the general line was utilized by pig-dealers as a pen for their stock.

The yeomen, farmers, dairymen, and townsfolk, who came to transact business in these ancient streets, spoke in other ways than by articulation. Not to hear the words of your interlocutor in metropolitan centers is to know nothing of his meaning. Here the face, the arms, the hat, the stick, the body throughout spoke equally with the tongue. To express satisfaction the Casterbridge marketman added to his utterance a broadening of the cheeks, a crevicing of the eyes, a throwing back of the shoulders, which was intelligible from the other end of the street. If he wondered, though all Henchard's carts and wagons were rattling past him, you knew it from perceiving the inside of his crimson mouth, and a target-like circling of his eyes. Deliberation caused sundry attacks on the moss of adjoining walls with the end of his stick, a change of his hat from the horizontal to the less so; a sense of tediousness announced itself in a lowering of the person by spreading the knees to a lozenge-shaped aperture and contorting the arms. Chicanery, subterfuge, had hardly a place in the streets of this honest borough to all appearance; and it was said that the lawyers in the Court House hard by occasionally threw in strong arguments for the other side out of pure generosity (though apparently by mischance) when advancing their own.

Thus Casterbridge was in most respects but the pole, focus, or nerve-knot of the surrounding country life; differing from the many manufacturing towns which are as foreign bodies set down, like boulders on a plain, in a green world with which they have nothing in common. Casterbridge lived by agriculture at one remove further from the fountain-head than the adjoining villages—no more. The townsfolk understood every fluctuation in the rustic's condition, for it affected their receipts as much as the laborer's; they entered into the troubles and joys which moved the aristocratic families ten miles round—for the same reason. And even at the dinner-parties of the professional families the subjects of discussion were corn, cattle-disease, sowing and reaping, fencing and planting; while politics were viewed by them less from their own stand-point of burgesses with rights and privileges than from the standpoint of their country neighbors.

All the venerable contrivances and confusions which delighted the eye by their quaintness, and in a measure reasonableness, in this rare old market-town, were metropolitan novelties to the unpractised eyes of Elizabeth-Jane, fresh from netting fish-seines in a sea-side cottage. Very little inquiry was necessary to guide her footsteps. Henchard's house was one of the best, faced with dull red-and-grey old brick. The front door was open, and, as in other houses, she could see through the passage to the end of the garden—nearly a quarter of a mile off.

Mr. Henchard was not in the house, but in the store-yard. She was conducted into the mossy garden, and through a door in the wall, which was studded with rusty nails speaking of generations of fruit-trees that had been trained there. The door opened upon the yard, and here she was left to find him as she could. It was a place flanked by hay-barns, into which tons of fodder, all in trusses, were being packed from the wagons she had seen pass the inn that morning. On other sides of the yard were wooden granaries on stone staddles, to which access was given by Flemish ladders, and a store-house several floors high. Wherever the doors of these places were open, a closely packed throng of bursting wheat-sacks could be seen standing inside, with the air of awaiting a famine that would not come.

She wandered about this place, uncomfortably conscious of the impending interview, till she was quite weary of searching; she ventured to inquire of a boy in what quarter Mr. Henchard could be found. He directed her to an office which she had not seen before, and knocking at the door she was answered by a cry of "Come in."

Elizabeth turned the handle; and there stood before her, bending over some sample-bags on a table, not the corn-merchant, but the young Scotchman Mr. Farfrae—in the act of pouring some grains of wheat from one hand to the other. His hat hung on a peg behind him, and the roses of his carpet-bag glowed from the corner of the room.

Having toned her feelings and arranged words on her lips for Mr. Henchard, and for him alone, she was for the moment confounded.

"Yes, what is it?" said Scotchman, like a man who permanently ruled there.

She said she wanted to see Mr. Henchard.

"Ah, yes; will you wait a minute? He's engaged just now," said the young man, apparently not recognizing her as the girl at the inn. He handed her a chair, bade her sit down, and turned to his sample-bags again. While Elizabeth-Jane sits waiting in great amaze at the young man's presence we may briefly explain how he came there.

When the two new acquaintances had passed out of sight that morning towards the Bath and Bristol road they went on silently, except for a few commonplaces, till they had gone down an avenue on the town walls called the Chalk Walk, leading to an angle where the North and West escarpments met. From this high corner of the square earthworks a vast extent of country could be seen. A footpath ran steeply down the green slope, conducting from the shady promenade on the walls to a road at the bottom of the scarp. It was by this path the Scotchman had to descend.

"Well, here's success to 'ee," said Henchard, holding out his right hand and leaning with his left upon the wicket which protected the descent. In the act there was the inelegance of one whose feelings are nipped and wishes defeated. "I shall often think of this time, and of how you came at the very moment to throw a light upon my difficulty."

Still holding the young man's hand he paused, and then

added deliberately: "Now I am not the man to let a cause be lost for want of a word. And before ye are gone for ever I'll speak. Once more, will ye stay? There it is, flat and plain. You can see that it isn't all selfishness that makes me press 'ee; for my business is not quite so scientific as to require an intellect entirely out of the common. Others would do for the place without doubt. Some selfishness perhaps there is, but there is more; it isn't for me to repeat what. Come bide with me—and name your own terms. I'll agree to 'em willingly and 'ithout a word of gainsaying; for, hang it, Farfrae, I like thee well!"

The young man's hand remained steady in Henchard's for a moment or two. He looked over the fertile country that stretched beneath them, then backward along the shaded walk reaching to the top of the town. His face flushed.

"I never expected this—I did not!" he said. "It's Providence! Should any one go against it? No; I'll not go to America; I'll stay and be your man!"

His hand, which had lain lifeless in Henchard's, returned the latter's grasp.

"Done," said Henchard.

"Done," said Donald Farfrae.

The face of Mr. Henchard beamed forth a satisfaction that was almost fierce in its strength. "Now you are my friend!" he exclaimed. "Come back to my house; let's clinch it at once by clear terms, so as to be comfortable in our minds." Farfrae caught up his bag and retraced the North-West Avenue in Henchard's company as he had come. Henchard was all confidence now.

"I am the most distant fellow in the world when I don't care for a man," he said. "But when a man takes my fancy he takes it strong. Now I am sure you can eat another breakfast? You couldn't have eaten much so early, even if they had anything at that place to gi'e thee, which they hadn't; so come to my house and we will have a solid, staunch tuck-in, and settle terms in black-and-white if you like; though my word's my bond. I can always make a good meal in the morning. I've got a splendid cold pigeon-pie going just now. You can have some home-brewed if you want to, you know."

"It is too airly in the morning for that," said Farfrae with a smile.

"Well, of course, I didn't know. I don't drink it because of my oath; but I am obliged to brew for my work-people."

Thus talking they returned, and entered Henchard's premises by the back way or traffic entrance. Here the matter was settled over the breakfast, at which Henchard heaped the young Scotchman's plate to a prodigal fulness. He would not rest satisfied till Farfrae had written for his luggage from Bristol, and despatched the letter to the post-office. When it was done this man of strong impulses declared that his new friend should take up his abode in his house—at least till some suitable lodgings could be found.

He then took Farfrae round and showed him the place, and the stores of grain, and other stock; and finally entered the offices where the younger of them had already been discovered by Elizabeth.

X

While she still sat under the Scotchman's eyes a man came up to the door, reaching it as Henchard opened the door of the inner office to admit Elizabeth. The new-comer stepped forward like the quicker cripple at Bethesda, and entered in her stead. She could hear his words to Henchard: "Joshua Jopp, sir—by appointment—the new manager!"

"The new manager!—he's in his office," said Henchard bluntly.

"In his office!" said the man, with a stultified air.

"I mentioned Thursday," said Henchard; "and as you did not keep your appointment, I have engaged another manager. At first I thought he must be you. Do you think I can wait when business is in question?"

"You said Thursday or Saturday, sir," said the new-comer, pulling out a letter.

"Well, you are too late," said the corn-factor. "I can say no more."

"You as good as engaged me," murmured the man.

"Subject to an interview," said Henchard. "I am sorry for you—very sorry indeed. But it can't be helped."

There was no more to be said, and the man came out, encountering Elizabeth-Jane in his passage. She could see that his mouth twitched with anger, and that bitter disappointment was written in his face everywhere.

Elizabeth-Jane now entered, and stood before the master of the premises. His dark pupils—which always seemed to have a red spark of light in them, though this could hardly be a physical fact—turned indifferently round under his dark brows until they rested on her figure. "Now then, what is it, my young woman?" he said blandly.

"Can I speak to you—not on business, sir?" said she.

"Yes—I suppose." He looked at her more thoughtfully.

"I am sent to tell you, sir," she innocently went on, "that a distant relative of yours by marriage, Susan Newson, a sailor's widow, is in the town; and to ask whether you would wish to see her."

The rich *rouge-et-noir* of his countenance underwent a slight change. "Oh—Susan is—still alive?" he asked with difficulty.

"Yes, sir."

"Are you her daughter?"

"Yes, sir—her only daughter."

"What—do you call yourself—your Christian name?"

"Elizabeth-Jane, sir."

"Newson?"

"Elizabeth-Jane Newson."

This at once suggested to Henchard that the transaction of his early married life at Weydon Fair was unrecorded in the family history. It was more than he could have expected. His wife had behaved kindly to him in return for his unkindness, and had never proclaimed her wrong to her child or to the world.

"I am—a good deal interested in your news," he said. "And as this is not a matter of business, but pleasure, suppose we go indoors."

It was with a gentle delicacy of manner, surprising to Elizabeth, that he showed her out of the office, and through the outer room, where Donald Farfrae was overhauling bins and samples with the inquiring inspection of a beginner in charge. Henchard preceded her through the door in the wall to the suddenly changed scene of the garden and flowers, and onward into the house. The dining-room to which he introduced her still exhibited the remnants of the lavish breakfast laid for Farfrae. It was furnished to profusion with heavy mahogany furniture of the deepest red-Spanish hues. Pembroke tables, with leaves hanging so low that they well-nigh touched the floor, stood against the walls on legs and feet shaped like those of an elephant, and on one lay three huge folio volumes—a Family Bible, a "Josephus," and a "Whole Duty of Man." In the chimney corner was a fire-grate with a fluted semi-circular back, having urns and festoons cast in relief thereon; and the chairs were of the kind which, since that day, has cast luster upon the names of Chippendale and Sheraton, though, in point of fact, their patterns may have been such as those illustrious carpenters never saw or heard of.

"Sit down—Elizabeth-Jane—sit down," he said, with a shake in his voice as he uttered her name; and sitting down himself he allowed his hands to hang between his knees, while he looked upon the carpet. "Your mother, then, is quite well?"

"She is rather worn out, sir, with travelling."

"A sailor's widow—when did he die?"

"Father was lost last spring."

Henchard winced at the word "father," thus applied. "Do you and she come from abroad—America or Australia?" he asked.

"No. We have been in England some years. I was twelve when we came here from Canada."

"Ah; exactly." By such conversation he discovered the circumstances which had enveloped his wife and her child in such total obscurity that he had long ago believed them to be in their graves. These things being clear, he returned to the present. "And where is your mother staying?"

"At the Three Mariners."

"And you are her daughter Elizabeth-Jane?" repeated Henchard. He arose, came close to her, and glanced in her face. "I think," he said, suddenly turning away with a wet eye, "you shall take a note from me to your mother. I should like to see her. . . . She is not left very well off by her late husband?" His eye fell on Elizabeth's clothes, which, though a respectable suit of black, and her very best, were decidedly old-fashioned even to Casterbridge eyes.

"Not very well," she said, glad that he had divined this without her being obliged to express it.

He sat down at the table and wrote a few lines; next taking from his pocket-book a five-pound note, which he put in the envelope with the letter, adding to it, as by an after-thought, five shillings. Sealing the whole up carefully, he directed it to "Mrs. Newson, Three Mariners Inn," and handed the packet to Elizabeth.

"Deliver it to her personally, please," said Henchard. "Well, I am glad to see you here, Elizabeth-Jane—very glad. We must have a long talk together—but not just now."

He took her hand at parting, and held it so warmly that she, who had known so little friendship, was much affected, and tears rose to her aerial-grey eyes. The instant that she was gone Henchard's state showed itself more distinctly; having shut the door he sat in his dining-room stiffly erect, gazing at the opposite wall as if he read his history there.

"Begad!" he suddenly exclaimed, jumping up. "I didn't think of that. Perhaps these are impostors—and Susan and the child dead after all!"

However, a something in Elizabeth-Jane soon assured him that, as regarded her, at least, there could be little doubt. And a few hours would settle the question of her mother's identity; for he had arranged in his note to see her that evening.

"It never rains but it pours!" said Henchard. His keenly excited interest in his new friend the Scotchman was now eclipsed by this event; and Donald Farfrae saw so little of him during the rest of the day that he wondered at the suddenness of his employer's moods.

In the meantime Elizabeth had reached the inn. Her mother, instead of taking the note with the curiosity of a poor woman expecting assistance, was much moved at sight of it. She did not read it at once, asking Elizabeth to describe her reception, and the very words Mr. Henchard used. Elizabeth's back was turned when her mother opened the letter. It ran thus:—

> Meet me at eight o'clock this evening, if you can, at the Ring on the Budmouth road. The place is easy to find. I can say no more now. The news upsets me almost. The girl seems to be in ignorance. Keep her so till I have seen you.   M.H.

He said nothing about the enclosure of five guineas. The amount was significant; it may tacitly have said to her that he bought her back again. She waited restlessly for the close of the day, telling Elizabeth-Jane that she was invited to see Mr. Henchard; that she would go alone. But she said nothing to show that the place of meeting was not at his house, nor did she hand the note to Elizabeth.

XI

The Ring at Casterbridge was merely the local name of one of the finest Roman Amphitheaters, if not the very finest, remaining in Britain.

Casterbridge announced old Rome in every street, alley, and precinct. It looked Roman, bespoke the art of Rome, concealed dead men of Rome. It was impossible to dig more than a foot or two deep about the town fields and gardens without coming upon some tall soldier or other of the Empire, who had lain there in his silent unobtrusive rest for a space of fifteen hundred years. He was mostly found lying on his side, in an oval scoop in the chalk, like a chicken in its shell; his knees drawn up to his chest; sometimes with the remains of his spear against his arm;

a fibula or brooch of bronze on his breast or forehead; an urn at his knees, a jar at his throat, a bottle at his mouth; and mystified conjecture pouring down upon him from the eyes of Casterbridge street boys and men, who had turned a moment to gaze at the familiar spectacle as they passed by.

Imaginative inhabitants, who would have felt an unpleasantness at the discovery of a comparatively modern skeleton in their gardens, were quite unmoved by these hoary shapes. They had lived so long ago, their time was so unlike the present, their hopes and motives were so widely removed from ours, that between them and the living there seemed to stretch a gulf too wide for even a spirit to pass.

The Amphitheater was a huge circular enclosure, with a notch at opposite extremities of its diameter north and south. From its sloping internal form it might have been called the spittoon of the Jötuns. It was to Casterbridge what the ruined Coliseum is to modern Rome, and was nearly of the same magnitude. The dusk of evening was the proper hour at which a true impression of this suggestive place could be received. Standing in the middle of the arena at that time there by degrees became apparent its real vastness, which a cursory view from the summit at noon-day was apt to obscure. Melancholy, impressive, lonely, yet accessible from every part of the town, the historic circle was the frequent spot for appointments of a furtive kind. Intrigues were arranged there; tentative meetings were there experimented after divisions and feuds. But one kind of appointment—in itself the most common of any—seldom had place in the Amphitheater: that of happy lovers.

Why, seeing that it was pre-eminently an airy, accessible, and sequestered spot for interviews, the cheerfullest form of those occurrences never took kindly to the soil of the ruin, would be a curious inquiry. Perhaps it was because its associations had about them something sinister. Its history proved that. Apart from the sanguinary nature of the games originally played therein, such incidents attached to its past as these: that for scores of years the town-gallows had stood at one corner; that in 1705 a woman who had murdered her husband was half-strangled and then burnt there in the presence of ten thousand spectators. Tradition reports that at a certain stage of the burning her heart burst and leapt out of her body, to the terror of them all, and that not one of those ten thousand people ever cared particularly for hot roast after that. In addition to these old tragedies, pugilistic encounters almost to the death had come off down to recent dates in that secluded arena, entirely invisible to the outside world save by climbing to the top of the enclosure, which few townspeople in the daily round of their lives ever took the trouble to do. So that, though close to the turnpike-road, crimes might be perpetrated there unseen at mid-day.

Some boys had latterly tried to impart gaiety to the ruin by using the central arena as a cricket-ground. But the game usually languished for the aforesaid reason—the dismal privacy which the earthen circle enforced, shutting out every appreciative passer's vision, every commendatory remark from outsiders—everything, except the sky; and to play at games in such circumstances was like acting to an empty house. Possibly, too, the boys were timid, for some old people said that at certain moments in the summer time, in broad daylight, persons sitting with a book or dozing in the arena had, on lifting their eyes, beheld the slopes lined with a gazing legion of Hadrian's soldiery as if watching the gladiatorial combat; and had heard the roar of their excited voices; that the scene would remain but a moment, like a lightning flash, and then disappear.

It was related that there still remained under the south entrance excavated cells for the reception of the wild animals and athletes who took part in the games. The arena was still smooth and circular, as if used for its original purpose not so very long ago. The sloping pathways by which spectators had ascended to their seats were pathways yet. But the whole was grown over with grass, which now, at the end of summer, was bearded with withered bents that formed waves under the brush of the wind, returning to the attentive ear Æolian modulations, and detaining for moments the flying globes of thistledown.

Henchard had chosen this spot as being the safest from observation which he could think of for meeting his long-lost wife, and at the same time as one easily to be found by a stranger after nightfall. As Mayor of the town, with a reputation to keep up, he could not invite her to come to his house till some definite course had been decided on.

Just before eight he approached the deserted earthwork, and entered by the south path which descended over the *débris* of the former dens. In a few moments he could discern a female figure creeping in by the great north gap, or public gateway. They met in the middle of the arena. Neither spoke just at first—there was no necessity for speech—and the poor woman leant against Henchard, who supported her in his arms.

"I don't drink," he said in a low, halting, apologetic voice. "You hear, Susan?—I don't drink now—I haven't since that night." Those were his first words.

He felt her bow her head in acknowledgment that she understood. After a minute or two he again began:

"If I had known you were living, Susan! But there was every reason to suppose you and the child were dead and gone. I took every possible step to find you—travelled—advertised. My opinion at last was that you had started for some colony with that man, and had been drowned on your voyage out. Why did you keep silent like this?"

"O Michael! because of him—what other reason could there be? I thought I owed him faithfulness to the end of one of our lives—foolishly I believed there was something solemn and binding in the bargain; I thought that even in honor I dared not desert him when he had paid so much for me in good faith. I meet you now only as his widow—I consider myself that, and that I have no claim upon you. Had he not died I should never have come—never! Of that you may be sure."

"Ts-s-s! How could you be so simple?"

"I don't know. Yet it would have been very wicked—
if I had not thought like that!" said Susan, almost crying.

"Yes—yes—so it would. It is only that which makes
me feel 'ee an innocent woman. But—to lead me into this!"

What, Michael?" she asked, alarmed.

"Why, this difficulty about our living together again,
and Elizabeth-Jane. She cannot be told all—she would so
despise us both that—I could not bear it!"

"That was why she was brought up in ignorance of you.
I could not bear it either."

"Well—we must talk of a plan for keeping her in her
present belief, and getting matters straight in spite of it.
You have heard I am in a large way of business here—
that I am Mayor of the town, and churchwarden, and I
don't know what all?"

"Yes," she murmured.

"These things, as well as the dread of the girl discovering
our disgrace, makes it necessary to act with extreme caution. So that I don't see how you two can return openly
to my house as the wife and daughter I once treated badly,
and banished from me; and there's the rub o't."

"We'll go away at once. I only came to see——"

"No, no, Susan; you are not to go—you mistake me!"
he said, with kindly severity. "I have thought of this plan:
that you and Elizabeth take a cottage in the town as the
widow Mrs. Newson and her daughter; that I meet you,
court you, and marry you, Elizabeth-Jane coming to my
house as my step-daughter. The thing is so natural and easy
that it is half done in thinking o't. This would leave my
shady, headstrong, disgraceful life as a young man absolutely unopened; the secret would be yours and mine only;
and I should have the pleasure of seeing my own only
child under my roof, as well as my wife."

"I am quite in your hands, Michael," she said meekly.
"I came here for the sake of Elizabeth; for myself, if you
tell me to leave again to-morrow morning, and never come
near you more, I am content to go."

"Now, now; we don't want to hear that," said Henchard
gently. "Of course you won't leave again. Think over the

plan I have proposed for a few hours; and if you can't hit upon a better one we'll adopt it. I have to be away for a day or two on business, unfortunately; but during that time you can get lodgings—the only ones in the town fit for you are those over the china-shop in High Street—and you can also look for a cottage."

"If the lodgings are in High Street they are dear, I suppose?"

"Never mind—you *must* start genteel if our plan is to be carried out. Look to me for money. Have you enough till I come back?"

"Quite," said she.

"And are you comfortable at the inn?"

"O yes."

"And the girl is quite safe from learning the shame of her case and ours?—that's what makes me most anxious of all."

"You would be surprised to find how unlikely she is to dream of the truth. How could she ever suppose such a thing?"

"True!"

"I like the idea of repeating our marriage," said Mrs. Henchard, after a pause. "It seems the only right course, after all this. Now I think I must go back to Elizabeth-Jane, and tell her that our kinsman, Mr. Henchard, kindly wishes us to stay in the town."

"Very well—arrange that yourself. I'll go some way with you."

"No, no. Don't run any risk!" said his wife anxiously. "I can find my way back—it is not late. Please let me go alone."

"Right," said Henchard. "But just one word. Do you forgive me, Susan?"

She murmured something; but seemed to find it difficult to frame her answer.

"Never mind—all in good time," said he. "Judge me by my future works—good-bye!"

He retreated, and stood at the upper side of the Amphitheater while his wife passed out through the lower way, and descended under the trees to the town. Then Henchard himself went homeward, going so fast that by the time he reached his door he was almost upon the heels of the unconscious woman from whom he had just parted. He watched her up the street, and turned into his house.

XII

On entering his own door after watching his wife out of sight, the Mayor walked on through the tunnel-shaped passage into the garden, and thence by the back door towards the stores and granaries. A light shone from the office-window, and there being no blind to screen the interior Henchard could see Donald Farfrae still seated where he had left him, initiating himself into the managerial work of the house by overhauling the books. Henchard entered, merely observing, "Don't let me interrupt you, if ye will stay so late."

He stood behind Farfrae's chair, watching his dexterity in clearing up the numerical fogs which had been allowed to grow so thick in Henchard's books as almost to baffle even the Scotchman's perspicacity. The corn-factor's mien was half admiring, and yet it was not without a dash of pity for the tastes of any one who could care to give his mind to such finnikin details. Henchard himself was mentally and physically unfit for grubbing subtleties from soiled paper; he had in a modern sense received the education of Achilles, and found penmanship a tantalizing art.

"You shall do no more to-night," he said at length, spreading his great hand over the paper. "There's time enough to-morrow. Come indoors with me and have some supper. Now you shall! I am determined on't." He shut the account-books with friendly force.

Donald had wished to get to his lodgings; but he already saw that his friend and employer was a man who knew no moderation in his requests and impulses, and he yielded gracefully. He liked Henchard's warmth, even if it inconvenienced him; the great difference in their characters adding to the liking.

They locked up the office, and the young man followed his companion through the private little door which, admitting directly into Henchard's garden, permitted a passage from the utilitarian to the beautiful at one step. The garden was silent, dewy, and full of perfume. It extended a long way back from the house, first as lawn and flower-beds, then as fruit-garden, where the long-tied espaliers, as old as the old house itself, had grown so stout, and cramped, and gnarled that they had pulled their stakes out of the ground and stood distorted and writhing in vegetable agony, like leafy Laocoöns. The flowers which smelt so sweetly were not discernible; and they passed through them into the house.

The hospitalities of the morning were repeated, and when they were over Henchard said, "Pull your chair round to the fireplace, my dear fellow, and let's make a blaze— there's nothing I hate like a black grate, even in September." He applied a light to the laid-in fuel, and a cheerful radiance spread around.

"It is odd," said Henchard, "that two men should meet as we have done on a purely business ground, and that at the end of the first day I should wish to speak to 'ee on a family matter. But, damn it all, I am a lonely man, Farfrae: I have nobody else to speak to; and why shouldn't I tell it to 'ee?"

"I'll be glad to hear it, if I can be of any service," said Donald, allowing his eyes to travel over the intricate wood-carvings of the chimney-piece, representing garlanded lyres, shields, and quivers, on either side of a draped ox-skull, and flanked by heads of Apollo and Diana in low relief.

"I've not been always what I am now," continued Henchard, his firm deep voice being ever so little shaken. He was plainly under that strange influence which some-times prompts men to confide to the new-found friend what they will not tell to the old. "I began life as a working hay-trusser, and when I was eighteen I married on the strength o' my calling. Would you think me a married man?"

"I heard in the town that you were a widower."

"Ah, yes—you would naturally have heard that. Well, I lost my wife nineteen years ago or so—by my own fault. . . . This is how it came about. One summer evening I was travelling for employment, and she was walking at my side, carrying the baby, our only child. We came to a booth in a country fair. I was a drinking man at that time."

Henchard paused a moment, threw himself back so that his elbow rested on the table, his forehead being shaded by his hand, which, however, did not hide the marks of introspective inflexibility on his features as he narrated in fullest detail the incidents of the transaction with the sailor. The tinge of indifference which had at first been visible in the Scotchman now disappeared.

Henchard went on to describe his attempts to find his wife; the oath he swore; the solitary life he led during the years which followed. "I have kept my oath for nineteen years," he went on; "I have risen to what you see me now."

"Ay!"

"Well—no wife could I hear of in all that time; and being by nature something of a woman-hater, I have found it no hardship to keep mostly at a distance from the sex. No wife could I hear of, I say, till this very day. And now—she has come back."

"Come back, has she!"

"This morning—this very morning. And what's to be done?"

"Can ye no' take her and live with her, and make some amends?"

"That's what I've planned and proposed. But, Farfrae," said Henchard gloomily, "by doing right with Susan I wrong another innocent woman."

"Ye don't say that?"

"In the nature of things, Farfrae, it is almost impossible that a man of my sort should have the good fortune to tide through twenty years o' life without making more blunders than one. It has been my custom for many years to run across to Jersey in the way of business, particularly in the potato and root season. I do a large trade wi' them in that line. Well, one autumn when stopping there I fell quite ill, and in my illness I sank into one of those gloomy fits I sometimes suffer from, on account o' the loneliness of my domestic life, when the world seems to have the blackness of hell, and, like Job, I curse the day that gave me birth."

"Ah, now, I never feel like it," said Farfrae.

"Then pray to God that you never may, young man. While in this state I was taken pity on by a woman—a young lady I should call her, for she was of good family, well bred, and well educated—the daughter of some harum-scarum military officer who had got into difficulties, and had his pay sequestrated. He was dead now, and her mother too, and she was as lonely as I. This young creature was staying at the boarding-house where I happened to have my lodging; and when I was pulled down she took upon herself to nurse me. From that she got to have a foolish liking for me. Heaven knows why, for I wasn't worth it. But being together in the same house, and her feelings warm, we got naturally intimate. I won't go into particulars of what our relations were. It is enough to say that we honestly meant to marry. There arose a scandal, which did me no harm, but was of course ruin to her. Though, Farfrae, between you and me, as man and man, I solemnly declare that philandering with womankind has neither been my vice nor my virtue. She was terribly careless of appearances, and I was perhaps more, because o' my dreary state; and it was through this that the scandal arose. At last I was well, and came away. When I was gone she suffered much on my account, and didn't forget to tell me so in letters one after another; till, latterly, I felt I owed her something, and thought that, as I had not heard of Susan for so long, I would make this other one the only return I could make, and ask her if she would run the risk of Susan being alive (very slight as I believed) and marry me, such as I was. She jumped for joy, and we should no doubt soon have been married—but, behold, Susan appears!"

Donald showed his deep concern at a complication so far beyond the degree of his simple experiences.

"Now see what injury a man may cause around him! Even after that wrong-doing at the fair when I was young, if I had never been so selfish as to let this giddy girl devote herself to me over at Jersey, to the injury of her name, all might now be well. Yet, as it stands, I must bitterly disappoint one of these women; and it is the second. My first duty is to Susan—there's no doubt about that."

"They are both in a very melancholy position, and that's true!" murmured Donald.

"They are! For myself I don't care—'twill all end one way. But these two." Henchard paused in reverie. "I feel I should like to treat the second, no less than the first, as kindly as a man can in such a case."

"Ah, well, it cannet be helped!" said the other, with philosophic woefulness. "You mun write to the young lady, and in your letter you must put it plain and honest that it turns out she cannet be your wife, the first having come back; that ye cannet see her more; and that—ye wish her weel."

"That won't do. 'Od seize it, I must do a little more than that! I must—though she did always brag about her rich uncle or rich aunt, and her expectations from 'em— I must send a useful sum of money to her, I suppose— just as a little recompense, poor girl. . . . Now, will you help me in this, and draw up an explanation to her of all I've told ye, breaking it as gently as you can? I'm so bad at letters."

"And I will."

"Now, I haven't told you quite all yet. My wife Susan has my daughter with her—the baby that was in her arms at the fair; and this girl knows nothing of me beyond that I am some sort of relation by marriage. She has grown up in the belief that the sailor to whom I made over her mother, and who is now dead, was her father, and her mother's husband. What her mother has always felt, she and I together feel now—that we can't proclaim our disgrace to the girl by letting her know the truth. Now what would you do?—I want your advice."

"I think I'd run the risk, and tell her the truth. She'll forgive ye both."

"Never!" said Henchard. "I am not going to let her know the truth. Her mother and I be going to marry again; and it will not only help us to keep our child's respect, but it will be more proper. Susan looks upon herself as the sailor's widow, and won't think o' living with me as formerly without another religious ceremony—and she's right."

Farfrae thereupon said no more. The letter to the young Jersey woman was carefully framed by him, and the interview ended, Henchard saying, as the Scotchman left, "I feel it a great relief, Farfrae, to tell some friend o' this! You see now that the Mayor of Casterbridge is not so thriving in his mind as it seems he might be from the state of his pocket."

"I do. And I am sorry for ye!" said Farfrae.

When he was gone Henchard copied the letter, and, enclosing a cheque, took it to the post-office, from which he walked back thoughtfully.

"Can it be that it will go off so easily!" he said. "Poor thing—God knows! Now then, to make amends to Susan!"

XIII

The cottage which Michael Henchard hired for his wife Susan, under her name of Newson—in pursuance of their plan—was in the upper or western part of the town, near the Roman wall, and the avenue which overshadowed it. The evening sun seemed to shine more yellowly there than anywhere else this autumn—stretching its rays, as the hours grew later, under the lowest sycamore boughs, and steeping the ground-floor of the dwelling, with its green shutters, in a substratum of radiance which the foliage screened from the upper parts. Beneath these sycamores on the town walls could be seen from the sitting-room the tumuli and earth forts of the distant uplands; making it altogether a pleasant spot, with the usual touch of melancholy that a past-marked prospect lends.

As soon as the mother and daughter were comfortably installed, with a white-aproned servant and all complete, Henchard paid them a visit, and remained to tea. During the entertainment Elizabeth was carefully hoodwinked by the very general tone of the conversation that prevailed—a proceeding which seemed to afford some humor to Henchard, though his wife was not particularly happy in it. The visit was repeated again and again with business-like determination by the Mayor, who seemed to have schooled himself into a course of strict mechanical rightness towards this woman of prior claim, at any expense to the later one and to his own sentiments.

One afternoon the daughter was not indoors when Henchard came, and he said drily, "This is a very good opportunity for me to ask you to name the happy day, Susan."

The poor woman smiled faintly; she did not enjoy pleasantries on a situation into which she had entered solely for the sake of her girl's reputation. She liked them so little, indeed, that there was room for wonder why she had countenanced deception at all, and had not bravely let the girl know her history. But the flesh is weak; and the true explanation came in due course.

"O Michael!" she said, "I am afraid all this is taking up your time and giving trouble—when I did not expect any such thing!" And she looked at him and at his dress as a man of affluence, and at the furniture he had provided for the room—ornate and lavish to her eyes.

"Not at all," said Henchard, in rough benignity. "This is only a cottage—it costs me next to nothing. And as to taking up my time"—here his red and black visage kindled with satisfaction—"I've a splendid fellow to superintend my business now—a man whose like I've never been able to lay hands on before. I shall soon be able to leave everything to him, and have more time to call my own than I've had for these last twenty years."

Henchard's visits here grew so frequent and so regular

that it soon became whispered, and then openly discussed in Casterbridge that the masterful, coercive Mayor of the town was captured and enervated by the genteel widow Mrs. Newson. His well-known haughty indifference to the society of womankind, his silent avoidance of converse with the sex, contributed a piquancy to what would otherwise have been an unromantic matter enough. That such a poor fragile woman should be his choice was inexplicable, except on the ground that the engagement was a family affair in which sentimental passion had no place; for it was known that they were related in some way. Mrs. Henchard was so pale that the boys called her "The Ghost." Sometimes Henchard overheard this epithet when they passed together along the Walks—as the avenues on the walls were named—at which his face would darken with an expression of destructiveness towards the speakers ominous to see; but he said nothing.

He pressed on the preparations for his union, or rather reunion, with this pale creature in a dogged, unflinching spirit which did credit to his conscientiousness. Nobody would have conceived from his outward demeanor that there was no amatory fire or pulse of romance acting as stimulant to the bustle going on in his gaunt, great house; nothing but three large resolves—one, to make amends to his neglected Susan; another, to provide a comfortable home for Elizabeth-Jane under his paternal eye; and a third, to castigate himself with the thorns which these restitutory acts brought in their train; among them the lowering of his dignity in public opinion by marrying so comparatively humble a woman.

Susan Henchard entered a carriage for the first time in her life when she stepped into the plain brougham which drew up at the door on the wedding-day to take her and Elizabeth-Jane to church. It was a windless morning of warm November rain, which floated down like meal, and lay in a powdery form on the nap of hats and coats. Few people had gathered round the church door though they were well packed within. The Scotchman, who assisted as groomsman, was of course the only one present, beyond the chief actors, who knew the true situation of the contracting parties. He, however, was too inexperienced, too thoughtful, too judicial, too strongly conscious of the serious side of the business, to enter into the scene in its dramatic aspect. That required the special genius of Christopher Coney, Solomon Longways, Buzzford, and their fellows. But they knew nothing of the secret; though, as the time for coming out of church drew on, they gathered on the pavement adjoining, and expounded the subject according to their lights.

" 'Tis five-and-forty years since I had my settlement in this here town," said Coney; "but daze me if ever I see a man wait so long before to take so little! There's a chance even for thee after this, Nance Mockridge." The remark was addressed to a woman who stood behind his shoulder —the same who had exhibited Henchard's bad bread in public when Elizabeth and her mother entered Caster-bridge.

"Be cust if I'd marry any such as he, or thee either," replied that lady. "As for thee, Christopher, we know what ye be, and the less said the better. And as for he—well, there—(lowering her voice) 'tis said 'a was a poor parish 'prentice—I wouldn't say it for all the world—but 'a was a poor parish 'prentice, that began life wi' no more belonging to 'en than a carrion crow."

"And now he's worth ever so much a minute," murmured Longways. "When a man is said to be worth so much a minute, he's a man to be considered!"

Turning, he saw a circular disc reticulated with creases, and recognized the smiling countenance of the fat woman who had asked for another song at the Three Mariners. "Well, Mother Cuxsom," he said, "how's this? Here's Mrs. Newson, a mere skellinton, has got another husband to keep her, while a woman of your tonnage have not."

"I have not. Nor another to beat me. . . . Ah, yes, Cuxsom's gone, and so shall leather breeches!"

"Yes; with the blessing of God leather breeches shall go."

" 'Tisn't worth my old while to think of another husband," continued Mrs. Cuxsom. "And yet I'll lay my life I'm as respectable born as she."

"True; your mother was a very good woman—I can

mind her. She were rewarded by the Agricultural Society for having begot the greatest number of healthy children without parish assistance, and other virtuous marvels."

" 'Twas that that kept us so low upon ground—that great hungry family."

"Ay. Where the pigs be many the wash runs thin."

"And dostn't mind how mother would sing, Christopher?" continued Mrs. Cuxsom, kindling at the retrospection; "and how we went with her to the party at Mellstock, do ye mind?—at old Dame Ledlow's, farmer Shinar's aunt, do ye mind?—she we used to call Toad-skin, because her face were so yaller and freckled, do ye mind?"

"I do, hee-hee, I do!" said Christopher Coney.

"And well do I—for I was getting up husband-high at that time—one-half girl, and t'other half woman, as one may say. And canst mind"—she prodded Solomon's shoulder with her finger-tip, while her eyes twinkled between the crevices of their lids—"canst mind the sherry-wine, and the zilver-snuffers, and how Joan Dummett was took bad when we were coming home, and Jack Griggs was forced to carry her through the mud; and how 'a let her fall in Dairyman Sweetapple's cow-barton, and we had to clane her gown wi' grass—never such a mess as 'a were in?"

"Ay—that I do—hee-hee, such doggery as there was in them ancient days, to be sure! Ah, the miles I used to walk then; and now I can hardly step over a furrow!"

Their reminiscences were cut short by the appearance of the reunited pair—Henchard looking round upon the idlers with that ambiguous gaze of his, which at one moment seemed to mean satisfaction, and at another fiery disdain.

"Well—there's a difference between 'em, though he do call himself a teetotaller," said Nance Mockridge. "She'll wish her cake dough afore she's done of him. There's a bluebeardy look about 'en; and 'twill out in time."

"Stuff—he's well enough! Some folk want their luck buttered. If I had a choice as wide as the ocean sea I wouldn't wish for a better man. A poor twanking woman like her—'tis a godsend for her, and hardly a pair of jumps or night-rail to her name."

The plain little brougham drove off in the mist, and the idlers dispersed. "Well, we hardly know how to look at things in these times!" said Solomon. "There was a man dropped down dead yesterday, not so very many miles from here; and what wi' that, and this moist weather, 'tis scarce worth one's while to begin any work o' consequence to-day. I'm in such a low key with drinking nothing but small table ninepenny this last week or two that I shall call and warm up at the Mar'ners as I pass along."

"I don't know but that I may as well go with 'ee, Solomon," said Christopher; "I'm as clammy as a cockle-snail."

XIV

A martinmas summer of Mrs. Henchard's life set in with her entry into her husband's large house and respectable social orbit; and it was as bright as such summers well can be. Lest she should pine for deeper affection than he could give he made a point of showing some semblance of it in external action. Among other things he had the iron railings, that had smiled sadly in dull rust for the last eighty years, painted a bright green, and the heavy-barred, small-paned Georgian sash windows enlivened with three coats of white. He was as kind to her as a man, mayor, and churchwarden could possibly be. The house was large, the rooms lofty, and the landings wide; and the two unassuming women scarcely made a perceptible addition to its contents.

To Elizabeth-Jane the time was a most triumphant one. The freedom she experienced, the indulgence with which she was treated, went beyond her expectations. The reposeful, easy, affluent life to which her mother's marriage had introduced her was, in truth, the beginning of a great change in Elizabeth. She found she could have nice personal possessions and ornaments for the asking, and, as the mediæval saying puts it, "Take, have, and keep, are pleasant words." With peace of mind came development, and with development beauty. Knowledge—the result of great natural insight—she did not lack; learning, accomplishments—those, alas, she had not; but as the winter and spring passed by her thin face and figure filled out in rounder and softer curves; the lines and contractions upon her young brow went away; the muddiness of skin which she had looked upon as her lot by nature departed with a change to abundance of good things, and a bloom came upon her cheek. Perhaps, too, her grey, thoughtful eyes revealed an arch gaiety sometimes; but this was infrequent; the sort of wisdom which looked from their pupils did not readily keep company with these lighter moods. Like all people who have known rough times, light-heartedness seemed to her too irrational and inconsequent to be indulged in except as a reckless dram now and then; for she had been too early habituated to anxious reasoning to drop the habit suddenly. She felt none of those ups and downs of spirit which beset so many people without cause; never—to paraphrase a recent poet—never a gloom in Elizabeth-Jane's soul but she well knew how it came there; and her present cheerfulness was fairly proportionate to her solid guarantees for the same.

It might have been supposed that, given a girl rapidly becoming good-looking, comfortably circumstanced, and for the first time in her life commanding ready money, she would go and make a fool of herself by dress. But no. The reasonableness of almost everything that Elizabeth did was nowhere more conspicuous than in this question of clothes. To keep in the rear of opportunity in matters of indulgence is as valuable a habit as to keep abreast of opportunity in matters of enterprise. This unsophisticated girl did it by an innate perceptiveness that was almost genius. Thus she refrained from bursting out like a water-flower that spring, and clothing herself in puffings and knick-knacks, as most of the Casterbridge girls would have done in her circumstances. Her triumph was tempered by circumspection; she had still that field-mouse fear of the coulter of destiny despite fair promise, which is common among the thoughtful who have suffered early from poverty and oppression.

"I won't be too gay on any account," she would say to herself. "It would be tempting Providence to hurl mother and me down, and afflict us again as He used to do."

We now see her in a black silk bonnet, velvet mantle or silk spencer, dark dress, and carrying a sunshade. In this latter article she drew the line at fringe, and had it plain edged, with a little ivory ring for keeping it closed. It was odd about the necessity for that sunshade. She discovered that with the clarification of her complexion and the birth of pink cheeks her skin had grown more sensitive to the sun's rays. She protected those cheeks forthwith, deeming spotlessness part of womanliness.

Henchard had become very fond of her, and she went out with him more frequently than with her mother now. Her appearance one day was so attractive that he looked at her critically.

"I happened to have the ribbon by me, so I made it up," she faltered, thinking him perhaps dissatisfied with some rather bright trimming she had donned for the first time.

"Ay—of course—to be sure," he replied in his leonine way. "Do as you like—or rather as your mother advises ye. 'Od send—I've nothing to say to't!"

Indoors she appeared with her hair divided by a parting that arched like a white rainbow from ear to ear. All in front of this line was covered with a thick encampment of curls; all behind was dressed smoothly, and drawn to a knob.

The three members of the family were sitting at breakfast one day, and Henchard was looking silently, as he often did, at this head of hair, which in color was brown— rather light than dark. "I thought Elizabeth-Jane's hair— didn't you tell me that Elizabeth-Jane's hair promised to be black when she was a baby?" he said to his wife.

She looked startled, jerked his foot warningly, and murmured, "Did I?"

As soon as Elizabeth was gone to her own room Henchard resumed. "Begad, I nearly forgot myself just now! What I meant was that the girl's hair certainly looked as if it would be darker, when she was a baby."

"It did; but they alter so," replied Susan.

"Their hair gets darker, I know—but I wasn't aware it lightened ever?"

"Oh, yes." And the same uneasy expression came out on her face, to which the future held the key. It passed as Henchard went on:

"Well, so much the better. Now, Susan, I want to have her called Miss Henchard—not Miss Newson. Lot's o' people do it already in carelessness—it is her legal name—so it may as well be made her usual name—I don't like t'other name at all for my own flesh and blood. I'll advertise it in the Casterbridge paper—that's the way they do it. She won't object."

"No. Oh no. But——"

"Well, then, I shall do it," said he, peremptorily. "Surely, if she's willing, you must wish it as much as I?"

"Oh yes—if she agrees let us do it by all means," she replied.

Then Mrs. Henchard acted somewhat inconsistently; it might have been called falsely, but that her manner was emotional and full of the earnestness of one who wishes to do right at great hazard. She went to Elizabeth-Jane, whom she found sewing in her own sitting-room upstairs, and told her what had been proposed about her surname. "Can you agree—is it not a slight upon Newson—now he's dead and gone?"

Elizabeth reflected. "I'll think of it, mother," she answered.

When, later in the day, she saw Henchard, she adverted to the matter at once, in a way which showed that the line of feeling started by her mother had been persevered in. "Do you wish this change so very much, sir?" she asked.

"Wish it? Why, my blessed fathers, what an ado you women make about a trifle! I proposed it—that's all. Now, 'Lizabeth-Jane, just please yourself. Curse me if I care what you do. Now, you understand, don't 'ee go agreeing to it to please me."

Here the subject dropped, and nothing more was said, and nothing was done, and Elizabeth still passed as Miss Newson, and not by her legal name.

Meanwhile the great corn and hay traffic conducted by Henchard throve under the management of Donald Farfrae as it had never thriven before. It had formerly moved in jolts; now it went on oiled castors. The old crude *vivâ voce* system of Henchard, in which everything depended upon his memory, and bargains were made by the tongue alone, was swept away. Letters and ledgers took the place of "I'll do't," and "you shall hae't"; and, as in all such cases of advance, the rugged picturesqueness of the old method disappeared with its inconveniences.

The position of Elizabeth-Jane's room—rather high in the house, so that it commanded a view of the hay-stores and granaries across the garden—afforded her opportunity for accurate observation of what went on there. She saw that Donald and Mr. Henchard were inseparables. When walking together Henchard would lay his arm familiarly on his manager's shoulder, as if Farfrae were a younger brother, bearing so heavily that his slight figure bent under the weight. Occasionally she would hear a perfect cannonade of laughter from Henchard, arising from something Donald had said, the latter looking quite innocent and not laughing at all. In Henchard's somewhat lonely life he evidently found the young man as desirable for comradeship as he was useful for consultations. Donald's brightness of intellect maintained in the corn-factor the admiration it had won at the first hour of their meeting. The poor opinion, and but ill-concealed, that he entertained of the slim Farfrae's physical girth, strength, and dash was more than counterbalanced by the immense respect he had for his brains.

Her quiet eye discerned that Henchard's tigerish affection for the younger man, his constant liking to have Farfrae near him, now and then resulted in a tendency to domineer, which, however, was checked in a moment when Donald exhibited marks of real offence. One day, looking down on their figures from on high, she heard the latter remark, as they stood in the doorway between the garden and yard, that their habit of walking and driving about together rather neutralized Farfrae's value as a second pair of eyes, which should be used in places where the principal was not. "'Od damn it," cried Henchard, "what's all the world! I like a fellow to talk to. Now come along and hae some supper, and don't take too much thought about things, or ye'll drive me crazy."

When she walked with her mother, on the other hand, she often beheld the Scotchman looking at them with a curious interest. The fact that he had met her at the Three Mariners was insufficient to account for it, since on the occasions on which she had entered his room he had never raised his eyes. Besides, it was at her mother more particularly than at herself that he looked, to Elizabeth-Jane's half-conscious, simple-minded, perhaps pardonable, disappointment. Thus she could not account for this interest by her own attractiveness, and she decided that it might be apparent only—a way of turning his eyes that Mr. Farfrae had.

She did not divine the ample explanation of his manner, without personal vanity, that was afforded by the fact of Donald being the depositary of Henchard's confidence in respect of his past treatment of the pale, chastened mother who walked by her side. Her conjectures on that past never went further than faint ones based on things casually heard and seen—mere guesses that Henchard and her mother might have been lovers in their younger days, who had quarrelled and parted.

Casterbridge, as has been hinted, was a place deposited in the block upon a corn-field. There was no suburb in the modern sense, or transitional intermixture of town and down. It stood, with regard to the wide fertile land adjoining, clean-cut and distinct, like a chess-board on a green tablecloth. The farmer's boy could sit under his barley-mow and pitch a stone into the office-window of the town-clerk; reapers at work among the sheaves nodded to acquaintances standing on the pavement-corner; the red-robed judge, when he condemned a sheep-stealer, pronounced sentence to the tune of Baa, that floated in at the window from the remainder of the flock browsing hard by; and at executions the waiting crowd stood in a meadow immediately before the drop, out of which the cows had been temporarily driven to give the spectators room.

The corn grown on the upland side of the borough was garnered by farmers who lived in an eastern purlieu called Durnover. Here wheat-ricks overhung the old Roman street, and thrust their eaves against the church tower; green-thatched barns, with doorways as high as the gates of Solomon's temple, opened directly upon the main thorough-fare. Barns indeed were so numerous as to alternate with every half-dozen houses along the way. Here lived bur-gesses who daily walked the fallow; shepherds in an intramural squeeze. A street of farmers' homesteads—a street ruled by a mayor and corporation, yet echoing with the thump of the flail, the flutter of the winnowing-fan, and the purr of the milk into the pails—a street which had nothing urban in it whatever—this was the Durnover end of Casterbridge.

Henchard, as was natural, dealt largely with this nursery or bed of small farmers close at hand—and his wagons were often down that way. One day, when arrangements were in progress for getting home corn from one of the aforesaid farms, Elizabeth-Jane received a note by hand, asking her to oblige the writer by coming at once to a granary on Durnover Hill. As this was the granary whose contents Henchard was removing, she thought the request had something to do with his business, and proceeded thither as soon as she had put on her bonnet. The granary was just within the farm-yard, and stood on stone stad-dles, high enough for persons to walk under. The gates were open, but nobody was within. However, she entered and waited. Presently she saw a figure approaching the gate—that of Donald Farfrae. He looked up at the church clock, and came in. By some unaccountable shyness, some wish not to meet him there alone, she quickly ascended the step-ladder leading to the granary door, and entered it before he had seen her. Farfrae advanced, imagining him-self in solitude; and a few drops of rain beginning to fall he moved and stood under the shelter where she had just been standing. Here he leant against one of the staddles, and gave himself up to patience. He, too, was plainly expecting some one; could it be herself? if so, why? In a few minutes he looked at his watch, and then pulled out a note, a duplicate of the one she had herself received.

The situation began to be very awkward, and the longer she waited the more awkward it became. To emerge from a door just above his head and descend the ladder, and show she had been in hiding there, would look so very foolish that she still waited on. A winnowing machine stood close beside her, and to relieve her suspense she gently moved the handle; whereupon a cloud of wheat husks flew out into her face, and covered her clothes and bonnet, and stuck into the fur of her victorine. He must have heard the slight movement, for he looked up, and then ascended the steps.

"Ah—it's Miss Newson," he said as soon as he could see into the granary. "I didn't know you were there. I have kept the appointment, and am at your service."

"O Mr. Farfrae," she faltered; "so have I. But I didn't know it was you who wished to see me, otherwise I——"

"I wished to see you? Oh no—at least, that is, I am afraid there may be a mistake."

"Didn't you ask me to come here? Didn't you write this?" Elizabeth held out her note.

"No. Indeed, at no hand would I have thought of it! And for you—didn't you ask me? This is not your writing?" And he held up his.

"By no means."

"And is that really so! Then it's somebody wanting to see us both. Perhaps we would do well to wait a little longer."

Acting on this consideration they lingered, Elizabeth-Jane's face being arranged to an expression of preternatural composure, and the young Scot, at every footstep in the street without, looking from under the granary to see if the passer were about to enter and declare himself their summoner. They watched individual drops of rain creeping down the thatch of the opposite rick—straw after straw—till they reached the bottom; but nobody came, and the granary roof began to drip.

"The person is not likely to be coming," said Farfrae. "It's a trick perhaps, and if so, it's a great pity to waste our time like this, and so much to be done."

" 'Tis a great liberty," said Elizabeth.

"It's true, Miss Newson. We'll hear news of this some day, depend on't, and who it was that did it. I wouldn't stand for it hindering myself; but you, Miss Newson"——

"I don't mind—much," she replied.

"Neither do I."

They lapsed again into silence. "You are anxious to get back to Scotland, I suppose, Mr. Farfrae?" she inquired.

"Oh no, Miss Newson. Why would I be?"

"I only supposed you might be from the song you sang at the Three Mariners—about Scotland and home, I mean —which you seemed to feel so deep down in your heart; so that we all felt for you."

"Ay—and I did sing there—I did—— But, Miss Newson"—and Donald's voice musically undulated between two semitones, as it always did when he became earnest— "it's well you feel a song for a few minutes, and your eyes they get quite tearful; but you finish it, and for all you felt you don't mind it or think of it again for a long while. Oh no, I don't want to go back! Yet I'll sing the song to you wi' pleasure whenever you like. I could sing it now, and not mind at all?"

"Thank you, indeed. But I fear I must go—rain or no."

"Ay! Then, Miss Newson, ye had better say nothing about this hoax, and take no heed of it. And if the person should say anything to you, be civil to him or her, as if you did not mind it—so you'll take the clever person's laugh away." In speaking his eyes became fixed upon her dress, still sown with wheat husks. "There's husks and dust on you. Perhaps you don't know it?" he said, in tones of extreme delicacy. "And it's very bad to let rain come upon clothes when there's chaff on them. It washes in and spoils them. Let me help you—blowing is the best."

As Elizabeth neither assented nor dissented, Donald Farfrae began blowing her back hair, and her side hair, and her neck, and the crown of her bonnet, and the fur of her victorine, Elizabeth saying, "Oh, thank you," at every puff. At last she was fairly clean, though Farfrae, having got over his first concern at the situation, seemed in no manner of hurry to be gone.

"Ah—now I'll go and get ye an umbrella," he said.

She declined the offer, stepped out and was gone. Farfrae walked slowly after, looking thoughtfully at her diminishing figure, and whistling in undertones, "As I came down through Cannobie."

XV

At first Miss Newson's budding beauty was not regarded with much interest by anybody in Casterbridge. Donald Farfrae's gaze, it is true, was now attracted by the Mayor's so-called step-daughter, but he was only one. The truth is that she was but a poor illustrative instance of the prophet Baruch's sly definition: "The virgin that loveth to go gay." When she walked abroad she seemed to be occupied with an inner chamber of ideas, and to have slight need for visible objects. She formed curious resolves on checking gay fancies in the matter of clothes, because it was inconsistent with her past life to blossom gaudily the moment she had become possessed of money. But nothing is more insidious than the evolution of wishes from mere fancies, and of wants from mere wishes. Henchard gave Elizabeth-Jane a box of delicately-tinted gloves one spring day. She wanted to wear them to show her appreciation of his kindness, but she had no bonnet that would harmonize. As an artistic indulgence she thought she would have such a bonnet. When she had a bonnet that would go with the gloves she had no dress that would go with the bonnet. It was now absolutely necessary to finish; she ordered the requisite article, and found that she had no sunshade to go with the dress. In for a penny in for a pound; she bought the sunshade, and the whole structure was at last complete.

Everybody was attracted, and some said that her bygone simplicity was the art that conceals art, the "delicate imposition" of Rochefoucauld; she had produced an effect, a contrast, and it had been done on purpose. As a matter of fact this was not true, but it had its result; for as soon as Casterbridge thought her artful it thought her worth notice. "It is the first time in my life that I have been so much admired," she said to herself; "though perhaps it is by those whose admiration is not worth having."

But Donald Farfrae admired her, too; and altogether the time was an exciting one; sex had never before asserted itself in her so strongly, for in former days she had perhaps been too impersonally human to be distinctly feminine. After an unprecedented success one day she came indoors, went upstairs, and leant upon her bed face downwards, quite forgetting the possible creasing and damage. "Good Heavens," she whispered, "can it be? Here am I setting up as the town beauty!"

When she had thought it over, her usual fear of exaggerating appearances engendered a deep sadness. "There is something wrong in all this," she mused. "If they only knew what an unfinished girl I am—that I can't talk Italian, or use globes, or show any of the accomplishments they learn at boarding-schools, how they would despise me! Better sell all this finery and buy myself grammar-books and dictionaries and a history of all the philosophies!"

She looked from the window and saw Henchard and Farfrae in the hay-yard talking, with that impetuous cordiality on the Mayor's part, and genial modesty on the younger man's, that was now so generally observable in their intercourse. Friendship between and man and man; what a rugged strength there was in it, as evinced by these two. And yet the seed that was to lift the foundation of this friendship was at that moment taking root in a chink of its structure.

It was about six o'clock; the men were dropping off homeward one by one. The last to leave was a round-shouldered, blinking young man of nineteen or twenty, whose mouth fell ajar on the slightest provocation, seemingly because there was no chin to support it. Henchard called aloud to him as he went out of the gate. "Here—Abel Whittle!"

Whittle turned, and ran back a few steps. "Yes, sir," he said, in breathless deprecation, as if he knew what was coming next.

"Once more—be in time to-morrow morning. You see what's to be done, and you hear what I say, and you know I'm not going to be trifled with any longer."

"Yes, sir." Then Abel Whittle left, and Henchard and Farfrae; and Elizabeth saw no more of them.

Now there was good reason for this command on Henchard's part. Poor Abel, as he was called, had an inveterate habit of oversleeping himself and coming late to his work. His anxious will was to be among the earliest; but if his comrades omitted to pull the string that he always tied round his great toe and left hanging out of the window for that purpose, his will was as wind. He did not arrive in time.

As he was often second hand at the hay-weighing, or at the crane which lifted the sacks, or was one of those who had to accompany the wagons into the country to fetch away stacks that had been purchased, this affliction of Abel's was productive of much inconvenience. For two mornings in the present week he had kept the others waiting nearly an hour; hence Henchard's threat. It now remained to be seen what would happen to-morrow.

Six o'clock struck, and there was no Whittle. At half-past six Henchard entered the yard; the wagon was horsed that Abel was to accompany; and the other man had been waiting twenty minutes. Then Henchard swore, and Whittle coming up breathless at that instant, the corn-factor turned on him, and declared with an oath that this was the last time; that if he were behind once more, by God, he would come and drag him out o' bed.

"There is sommit wrong in my make, your worshipful!" said Abel, "especially in the inside, whereas my poor dumb brain gets as dead as a clot afore I've said my few scrags of prayers. Yes—it came on as a stripling, just afore I'd got man's wages, whereas I never enjoy my bed at all, for no sooner do I lie down than I be asleep, and afore I be awake I be up. I've fretted my gizzard green about it, maister, but what can I do? Now last night, afore I went to bed, I only had a scantling o' cheese and"——

"I don't want to hear it!" roared Henchard. "To-morrow the wagons must start at four, and if you're not here, stand clear. I'll mortify thy flesh for thee!"

"But let me clear up my points, your worshipful"——

Henchard turned away.

"He asked me and he questioned me, and then a' wouldn't hear my points!" said Abel, to the yard in general. "Now, I shall twitch like a moment-hand all night to-night for fear o' him!"

The journey to be taken by the wagons next day was a long one into Blackmoor Vale, and at four o'clock lanterns were moving about the yard. But Abel was missing. Before either of the other men could run to Abel's and warn him, Henchard appeared in the garden doorway. "Where's Abel Whittle? Not come after all I've said? Now I'll carry out my word, by my blessed fathers—nothing else will do him any good! I'm going up that way."

Henchard went off, entered Abel's house, a little cottage in Back Street, the door of which was never locked because the inmates had nothing to lose. Reaching Whittle's bedside the corn-factor shouted a bass note so vigorously that Abel started up instantly, and beholding Henchard standing over him, was galvanized into spasmodic movements which had not much relation to getting on his clothes.

"Out of bed, sir, and off to the granary, or you leave my employ to-day! 'Tis to teach ye a lesson. March on; never mind your breeches!"

The unhappy Whittle threw on his sleeve waistcoat, and managed to get into his boots at the bottom of the stairs, while Henchard thrust his hat over his head. Whittle then trotted on down Back Street, Henchard walking sternly behind.

Just at this time Farfrae, who had been to Henchard's house to look for him, came out of the back gate, and saw something white fluttering in the morning gloom, which he soon perceived to be the part of Abel's shirt that showed below his waistcoat.

"For maircy's sake, what object's this?" said Farfrae, following Abel into the yard, Henchard being some way in the rear by this time.

"Ye see, Mr. Farfrae," gibbered Abel with a resigned smile of terror, "he said he'd mortify my flesh if so be I didn't get up sooner, and now he's a-doing on't! Ye see it can't be helped, Mr. Farfrae; things do happen queer sometimes! Yes—I'll go to Blackmoor Vale half naked as I be, since he do command; but I shall kill myself afterwards; I can't outlive the disgrace; for the women-folk will be looking out of their winders at my mortification all the way along, and laughing me to scorn as a man 'ithout breeches! You know how I feel such things, Maister Farfrae, and how forlorn thoughts get hold upon me. Yes —I shall do myself harm—I feel it coming on!"

"Get back home, and slip on your breeches, and come to wark like a man! If ye go not, you'll ha'e your death standing there!"

"I'm afeard I mustn't! Mr. Henchard said"——

"I don't care what Mr. Henchard said, nor anybody else! 'Tis simple foolishness to do this. Go and dress yourself instantly, Whittle."

"Hullo, hullo!" said Henchard, coming up behind. "Who's sending him back?"

All the men looked towards Farfrae.

"I am," said Donald. "I say this joke has been carried far enough."

"And I say it hasn't! Get up in the wagon, Whittle."

"Not if I am manager," said Farfrae. "He either goes home, or I march out of this yard for good."

Henchard looked at him with a face stern and red. But he paused for a moment, and their eyes met. Donald went up to him, for he saw in Henchard's look that he began to regret this.

"Come," said Donald quietly, "a man o' your position should ken better, sir! It is tyrannical and no worthy of you."

" 'Tis not tyrannical!" murmured Henchard, like a sullen boy. "It is to make him remember!" He presently added, in a tone of one bitterly hurt: "Why did you speak to me before them like that, Farfrae? You might have stopped till we were alone. Ah—I know why! I've told ye the secret o' my life—fool that I was to do't—and you take advantage of me!"

"I had forgot it," said Farfrae simply.

Henchard looked on the ground, said nothing more, and turned away. During the day Farfrae learnt from the men that Henchard had kept Abel's old mother in coals and snuff all the previous winter, which made him less antagonistic to the corn-factor. But Henchard continued moody and silent, and when one of the men inquired of him if some oats should be hoisted to an upper floor or not, he said shortly, "Ask Mr. Farfrae. He's master here!"

Morally he was; there could be no doubt of it. Henchard, who had hitherto been the most admired man in his circle, was the most admired no longer. One day the daughters of a deceased farmer in Durnover wanted an opinion on the value of their haystack, and sent a messenger to ask Mr. Farfrae to oblige them with one. The messenger, who was a child, met in the yard not Farfrae, but Henchard.

"Very well," he said. "I'll come."

"But please will Mr. Farfrae come?" said the child.

"I am going that way. . . . Why Mr. Farfrae?" said Henchard, with the fixed look of thought. "Why do people always want Mr. Farfrae?"

"I suppose because they like him so—that's what they say."

"Oh—I see—that's what they say—hey? They like him because he's cleverer than Mr. Henchard, and because he knows more; and, in short, Mr. Henchard can't hold a candle to him—hey?"

"Yes—that's just it, sir—some of it."

"Oh, there's more? Of course there's more! What besides? Come, here's sixpence for a fairing."

" 'And he's better-tempered, and Henchard's a fool to him,' they say. And when some of the women were a-walking home they said, 'He's a diment—he's a chap o' wax—he's the best—he's the horse for my money,' says they. And they said, 'He's the most understanding man o' them two by long chalks. I wish he was the master instead of Henchard,' they said."

"They'll talk any nonsense," Henchard replied with covered gloom. "Well, you can go now. And *I* am coming to value the hay, d'ye hear?—I." The boy departed, and Henchard murmured, "Wish he were master here, do they?"

He went towards Durnover. On his way he overtook Farfrae. They walked on together, Henchard looking mostly on the ground.

"You're no yoursel' the day?" Donald inquired.

"Yes, I am very well," said Henchard.

"But ye are a bit down—surely ye are down? Why, there's nothing to be angry about! 'Tis splendid stuff that we've got from Blackmoor Vale. By the by, the people in Durnover want their hay valued."

"Yes. I am going there."

"I'll go with ye."

As Henchard did not reply, Donald practised a piece of music *sotto voce,* till, getting near the bereaved people's door, he stopped himself with—

"Ah, as their father is dead, I won't go on with such as that. How could I forget?"

"Do you care so very much about hurting folks' feelings?" observed Henchard with a half sneer. "You do, I know—especially mine!"

"I am sorry if I have hurt yours, sir," replied Donald, standing still, with a second expression of the same sentiment in the regretfulness of his face. "Why should you say it—think it?"

The cloud lifted from Henchard's brow, and as Donald finished the corn-merchant turned to him, regarding his breast rather than his face.

"I have been hearing things that vexed me," he said.

" 'Twas that made me short in my manners—made me overlook what you really are. Now, I don't want to go in here about this hay—Farfrae, you can do it better than I. They sent for 'ee, too. I have to attend a meeting of the Town Council at eleven, and 'tis drawing on for't."

They parted thus in renewed friendship, Donald forbearing to ask Henchard for meanings that were not very plain to him. On Henchard's part there was now again repose; and yet, whenever he thought of Farfrae, it was with a dim dread; and he often regretted that he had told the young man his whole heart, and confided to him the secrets of his life.

XVI

On this account Henchard's manner towards Farfrae insensibly became more reserved. He was courteous—too courteous—and Farfrae was quite surprised at the good breeding which now for the first time showed itself among the qualities of a man he had hitherto thought undisciplined, if warm and sincere. The corn-factor seldom or never again put his arm upon the young man's shoulder so as to nearly weigh him down with the pressure of mechanized friendship. He left off coming to Donald's lodgings and shouting into the passage, "Hoy, Farfrae, boy, come and have some dinner with us! Don't sit here in solitary confinement!" But in the daily routine of their business there was little change.

Thus their lives rolled on till a day of public rejoicing was suggested to the country at large in celebration of a national event that had recently taken place.

For some time Casterbridge, by nature slow, made no response. Then one day Donald Farfrae broached the subject to Henchard by asking if he would have any objection to lend some rick-cloths to himself and a few others, who contemplated getting up an entertainment of some sort on the day named, and required a shelter for the same, to which they might charge admission at the rate of so much a head.

"Have as many cloths as you like," Henchard replied.

When his manager had gone about the business Henchard was fired with emulation. It certainly had been very remiss of him, as Mayor, he thought, to call no meeting ere this, to discuss what should be done on this holiday. But Farfrae had been so cursed quick in his movements as to give old-fashioned people in authority no chance of the initiative. However, it was not too late; and on second thoughts he determined to take upon his own shoulders the responsibility of organizing some amusements, if the other Councilmen would leave the matter in his hands. To this they quite readily agreed, the majority being fine old crusted characters who had a decided taste for living without worry.

So Henchard set about his preparations for a really brilliant thing—such as should be worthy of the venerable town. As for Farfrae's little affair, Henchard nearly forgot it; except once now and then when, on it coming into his mind, he said to himself, "Charge admission at so much a head—just like a Scotchman!—who is going to pay anything a head?" The diversions which the Mayor intended to provide were to be entirely free.

He had grown so dependent upon Donald that he could scarcely resist calling him in to consult. But by sheer self-coercion he refrained. No, he thought, Farfrae would be suggesting such improvements in his damned luminous way that in spite of himself he, Henchard, would sink to the position of second fiddle, and only scrape harmonies to his manager's talents.

Everybody applauded the Mayor's proposed entertainment, especially when it became known that he meant to pay for it all himself.

Close to the town was an elevated green spot surrounded by an ancient square earthwork—earthworks square, and not square, were as common as blackberries hereabout—a spot whereon the Casterbridge people usually held any kind of merry-making, meeting, or sheep-fair that required more space than the streets would afford. On one side it sloped to the river Froom, and from any point a view was obtained of the country round for many miles. This pleasant upland was to be the scene of Henchard's exploit.

He advertised about the town, in long posters of a pink color, that games of all sorts would take place here; and set to work a little battalion of men under his own eye. They erected greasy-poles for climbing, with smoked hams and local cheeses at the top. They placed hurdles in rows for jumping over; across the river they laid a slippery pole, with a live pig of the neighborhood tied at the other end, to become the property of the man who could walk over and get it. There were also provided wheelbarrows for racing, donkeys for the same, a stage for boxing, wrestling, and drawing blood generally; sacks for jumping in. Moreover, not forgetting his principles, Henchard provided a mammoth tea, of which everybody who lived in the borough was invited to partake without payment. The tables were laid parallel with the inner slope of the rampart, and awnings were stretched overhead.

Passing to and fro the Mayor beheld the unattractive exterior of Farfrae's erection in the West Walk, rick-cloths of different sizes and colors being hung up to the arching trees without any regard to appearance. He was easy in his mind now, for his own preparations far transcended these.

The morning came. The sky, which had been remarkably clear down to within a day or two, was overcast, and the weather threatening, the wind having an unmistakable hint of water in it. Henchard wished he had not been quite so sure about the continuance of a fair season. But it was too late to modify or postpone, and the proceedings went on. At twelve o'clock the rain began to fall, small and steady, commencing and increasing so insensibly that it was difficult to state exactly when dry weather ended or wet established itself. In an hour the slight moisture resolved itself into a monotonous smiting of earth by heaven, in torrents to which no end could be prognosticated.

A number of people had heroically gathered in the field, but by three o'clock Henchard discerned that his project was doomed to end in failure. The hams at the top of the poles dripped watered smoke in the form of a brown liquor, the pig shivered in the wind, the grain of the deal tables showed through the sticking tablecloths, for the awning allowed the rain to drift under at its will, and to enclose the sides at this hour seemed a useless undertaking. The landscape over the river disappeared; the wind played on the tent-cords in Æolian improvisations; and at length rose to such a pitch that the whole erection slanted to the ground, those who had taken shelter within it having to crawl out on their hands and knees.

But towards six the storm abated, and a drier breeze shook the moisture from the grass bents. It seemed possible to carry out the program after all. The awning was set up again; the band was called out from its shelter, and ordered to begin, and where the tables had stood a place was cleared for dancing.

"But where are the folk?" said Henchard, after the lapse of half-an-hour, during which time only two men and a woman had stood up to dance. "The shops are all shut. Why don't they come?"

"They are at Farfrae's affair in the West Walk," answered a Councilman who stood in the field with the Mayor.

"A few, I suppose. But where are the body o' 'em?"

"All out of doors are there."

"Then the more fools they!"

Henchard walked away moodily. One or two young fellows gallantly came to climb the poles, to save the hams from being wasted; but as there were no spectators, and the whole scene presented the most melancholy appearance, Henchard gave orders that the proceedings were to be suspended, and the entertainment closed, the food to be distributed among the poor people of the town. In a short time nothing was left in the field but a few hurdles, the tents, and the poles.

Henchard returned to his house, had tea with his wife and daughter, and then walked out. It was now dusk. He soon saw that the tendency of all promenaders was towards a particular spot in the Walks, and eventually proceeded

thither himself. The notes of a stringed band came from
the enclosure that Farfrae had erected—the pavilion as
he called it—and when the Mayor reached it he perceived that a gigantic tent had been ingeniously constructed without poles or ropes. The densest point of the
avenue of sycamores had been selected, where the boughs
made a closely interlaced vault overhead; to these boughs
the canvas had been hung, and a barrel roof was the
result. The end towards the wind was enclosed, the other
end was open. Henchard went round and saw the interior.

In form it was like the nave of a cathedral with one
gable removed, but the scene within was anything but
devotional. A reel or fling of some sort was in progress;
and the usually sedate Farfrae was in the midst of the
other dancers in the costume of a wild Highlander, flinging himself about and spinning to the tune. For a moment
Henchard could not help laughing. Then he perceived the
immense admiration for the Scotchman that revealed
itself in the women's faces; and when this exhibition was
over, and a new dance proposed, and Donald had disappeared for a time to return in his natural garments, he
had an unlimited choice of partners, every girl being in
a coming-on disposition towards one who so thoroughly
understood the poetry of motion as he.

All the town crowded to the Walk, such a delightful idea
of a ball room never having occurred to the inhabitants
before. Among the rest of the onlookers were Elizabeth
and her mother—the former thoughtful yet much interested, her eyes beaming with a longing lingering light, as
if Nature had been advised by Correggio in their creation.
The dancing progressed with unabated spirit, and Henchard
walked and waited till his wife should be disposed to go
home. He did not care to keep in the light, and when
he went into the dark it was worse, for there he heard
remarks of a kind which were becoming too frequent:

"Mr. Henchard's rejoicings couldn't say good morning
to this," said one. "A man must be a headstrong stunpoll
to think folk would go up to that bleak place to-day."

The other answered that people said it was not only in

such things as those that the Mayor was wanting. "Where would his business be if it were not for this young fellow? 'Twas verily Fortune sent him to Henchard. His accounts were like a bramble-wood when Mr. Farfrae came. He used to reckon his sacks by chalk strokes all in a row like garden-palings, measure his ricks by stretching with his arms, weigh his trusses by a lift, judge his hay by a chaw, and settle the price with a curse. But now this accomplished young man does it all by ciphering and mensuration. Then the wheat—that sometimes used to taste so strong o' mice when made into bread that people could fairly tell the breed—Farfrae has a plan for purifying, so that nobody would dream the smallest four-legged beast had walked over it once. Oh yes, everybody is full of him, and the care Mr. Henchard has to keep him, to be sure!" concluded this gentleman.

"But he won't do it for long, good-now," said the other.

"No!" said Henchard to himself behind the tree. "Or if he do, he'll be honeycombed clean out of all the character and standing that he's built up in these eighteen year!"

He went back to the dancing pavilion. Farfrae was footing a quaint little dance with Elizabeth-Jane—an old country thing, the only one she knew, and though he considerately toned down his movements to suit her demurer gait, the pattern of the shining little nails in the soles of his boots became familiar to the eyes of every bystander. The tune had enticed her into it; being a tune of a busy, vaulting, leaping sort—some low notes on the silver string of each fiddle, then a skipping on the small, like running up and down ladders—"Miss M'Leod of Ayr" was its name, so Mr. Farfrae had said, and that it was very popular in his own country.

It was soon over, and the girl looked at Henchard for approval; but he did not give it. He seemed not to see her. "Look here, Farfrae," he said, like one whose mind was elsewhere, "I'll go to Port-Bredy Great Market to-morrow myself. You can stay and put things right in your clothes-box, and recover strength to your knees after your vagaries." He planted on Donald an antagonistic glare that had begun as a smile.

Some other townsmen came up, and Donald drew aside. "What's this, Henchard," said Alderman Tubber, applying his thumb to the corn-factor like a cheese-taster. "An opposition randy to yours, eh? Jack's as good as his master, eh? Cut ye out quite, hasn't he?"

"You see, Mr. Henchard," said the lawyer, another good-natured friend, "where you made the mistake was in going so far afield. You should have taken a leaf out of his book, and have had your sports in a sheltered place like this. But you didn't think of it, you see; and he did, and that's where he's beat you."

"He'll be top-sawyer soon of you two, and carry all afore him," added jocular Mr. Tubber.

"No," said Henchard gloomily. "He won't be that, because he's shortly going to leave me." He looked towards Donald, who had again come near. "Mr. Farfrae's time as my manager is drawing to a close—isn't it, Farfrae?"

The young man, who could now read the lines and folds of Henchard's strongly-traced face as if they were clear verbal inscriptions, quietly assented; and when people deplored the fact, and asked why it was, he simply replied that Mr. Henchard no longer required his help.

Henchard went home, apparently satisfied. But in the morning, when his jealous temper had passed away, his heart sank within him at what he had said and done. He was the more disturbed when he found that this time Farfrae was determined to take him at his word.

XVII

Elizabeth-Jane had perceived from Henchard's manner that in assenting to dance she had made a mistake of some kind. In her simplicity she did not know what it was till a hint from a nodding acquaintance enlightened her. As the Mayor's step-daughter, she learnt, she had not been quite in her place in treading a measure amid such a mixed throng as filled the dancing pavilion.

Thereupon her ears, cheeks, and chin glowed like live coals at the dawning of the idea that her tastes were not good enough for her position, and would bring her into disgrace.

This made her very miserable, and she looked about for her mother; but Mrs. Henchard, who had less idea of conventionality than Elizabeth herself, had gone away, leaving her daughter to return at her own pleasure. The latter moved on into the dark dense old avenues, or rather vaults of living woodwork, which ran along the town boundary, and stood reflecting.

A man followed in a few minutes, and her face being towards the shine from the tent he recognized her. It was Farfrae—just come from the dialogue with Henchard which had signified his dismissal.

"And it's you, Miss Newson?—and I've been looking for ye everywhere!" he said, overcoming a sadness imparted by the estrangement with the corn-merchant. "May I walk on with you as far as your street-corner?"

She thought there might be something wrong in this, but did not utter any objection. So together they went on, first down the West Walk, and then into the Bowling Walk, till Farfrae said, "It's like that I'm going to leave you soon."

She faltered "Why?"

"Oh—as a mere matter of business—nothing more. But we'll not concern ourselves about it—it is for the best. I hoped to have another dance with you."

She said she could not dance—in any proper way.

"Nay, but you do! It's the feeling for it rather than the learning of steps that makes pleasant dancers. . . . I fear I offended your father by getting up this! And now, perhaps, I'll have to go to another part o' the warrld altogether!"

This seemed such a melancholy prospect that Elizabeth-Jane breathed a sigh—letting it off in fragments that he might not hear her. But darkness makes people truthful, and the Scotchman went on impulsively—perhaps he had heard her after all:

"I wish I was richer, Miss Newson; and your step-father had not been offended; I would ask you something in a short time—yes, I would ask you to-night. But that's not for me!"

What he would have asked her he did not say, and instead of encouraging him she remained incompetently silent. Thus afraid one of another, they continued their promenade along the walls till they got near the bottom of the Bowling Walk; twenty steps further and the trees would end, and the street-corner and lamps appear. In consciousness of this they stopped.

"I never found out who it was that sent us to Durnover granary on a fool's errand that day," said Donald, in his undulating tones. "Did ye ever know yourself, Miss Newson?"

"Never," said she.

"I wonder why they did it!"

"For fun, perhaps."

"Perhaps it was not for fun. It might have been that they thought they would like us to stay waiting there, talking to one another? Ay, well! I hope you Casterbridge folk will not forget me if I go."

"That I'm sure we won't!" she said earnestly. "I—wish you wouldn't go at all."

They had got into the lamplight. "Now, I'll think over that," said Donald Farfrae. "And I'll not come up to your door; but part from you here; lest it make your father more angry still."

They parted, Farfrae returning into the dark Bowling Walk, and Elizabeth-Jane going up the street. Without any consciousness of what she was doing she started running with all her might till she reached her father's door. "Oh dear me—what am I at?" she thought, as she pulled up breathless.

Indoors she fell to conjecturing the meaning of Farfrae's enigmatic words about not daring to ask her what he fain would. Elizabeth, that silent observing woman, had long noted how he was rising in favor among the townspeople; and knowing Henchard's nature now she had feared that Farfrae's days as manager were numbered; so that the announcement gave her little surprise. Would Mr. Farfrae stay in Casterbridge despite his words and her father's dismissal? His occult breathings to her might be solvable by his course in that respect.

The next day was windy—so windy that walking in the garden she picked up a portion of the draft of a letter on business in Donald Farfrae's writing, which had flown over the wall from the office. The useless scrap she took indoors, and began to copy the calligraphy, which she much admired. The letter began "Dear Sir," and presently writing on a loose slip "Elizabeth-Jane," she laid the latter over "Sir," making the phrase "Dear Elizabeth-Jane." When she saw the effect a quick red ran up her face and warmed her through, though nobody was there to see what she had done. She quickly tore up the slip, and threw it away. After this she grew cool and laughed at herself, walked about the room, and laughed again; not joyfully, but distressfully rather.

It was quickly known in Casterbridge that Farfrae and Henchard had decided to dispense with each other. Elizabeth-Jane's anxiety to know if Farfrae were going away from the town reached a pitch that disturbed her, for she could no longer conceal from herself the cause. At length the news reached her that he was not going to leave the place. A man following the same trade as Henchard, but on a very small scale, had sold his business to Farfrae, who was forthwith about to start as corn and hay merchant on his own account.

Her heart fluttered when she heard of this step of Donald's proving that he meant to remain; and yet, would a man who cared one little bit for her have endangered his suit by setting up a business in opposition to Mr. Henchard's? Surely not; and it must have been a passing impulse only which had led him to address her so softly.

To solve the problem whether her appearance on the evening of the dance were such as to inspire a fleeting love at first sight, she dressed herself up exactly as she had dressed then—the muslin, the spencer, the sandals, the parasol—and looked in the mirror. The picture glassed back was, in her opinion, precisely of such a kind as to inspire that fleeting regard, and no more—"just enough to make him silly, and not enough to keep him so," she said luminously; and Elizabeth thought, in a much lower key, that by this time he had discovered how plain and homely was the informing spirit of that pretty outside.

Hence, when she felt her heart going out to him, she would say to herself with a mock pleasantry that carried an ache with it, "No, no, Elizabeth-Jane—such dreams are not for you!" She tried to prevent herself from seeing him, and thinking of him; succeeding fairly well in the former attempt, in the latter not so completely.

Henchard, who had been hurt at finding that Farfrae did not mean to put up with his temper any longer, was incensed beyond measure when he learnt what the young man had done as an alternative. It was in the town-hall, after a council meeting, that he first became aware of Farfrae's coup for establishing himself independently in the town; and his voice might have been heard as far as the town-pump expressing his feelings to his fellow councilmen. Those tones showed that, though under a long reign of self-control he had become Mayor and churchwarden and what not, there was still the same unruly volcanic stuff beneath the rind of Michael Henchard as when he had sold his wife at Weydon Fair.

"Well, he's a friend of mine, and I'm a friend of his— or if we are not, what are we? 'Od send, if I've not been his friend, who has, I should like to know? Didn't he come here without a sound shoe to his voot? Didn't I keep him here—help him to a living? Didn't I help him to money, or whatever he wanted? I stuck out for no terms— I said 'Name your own price.' I'd have shared my last crust with that young fellow at one time, I liked him so well. And now he's defied me! But damn him, I'll have a tussle with him now—at fair buying and selling, mind— at fair buying and selling! And if I can't overbid such a stripling as he, then I'm not wo'th a varden! We'll show that we know our business as well as one here and there!"

His friends of the Corporation did not specially respond. Henchard was less popular now than he had been when, nearly two years before, they had voted him to the chief magistracy on account of his amazing energy. While they had collectively profited by this quality of the corn-factor's they had been made to wince individually on more than one occasion. So he went out of the hall and down the street alone.

Reaching home he seemed to recollect something with a sour satisfaction. He called Elizabeth-Jane. Seeing how he looked when she entered she appeared alarmed.

"Nothing to find fault with," he said, observing her concern. "Only I want to caution you, my dear. That man, Farfrae—it is about him. I've seen him talking to you two or three times—he danced with 'ee at the rejoicings, and came home with 'ee. Now, now, no blame to you. But just hearken: Have you made him any foolish promise? Gone the least bit beyond sniff and snaff at all?"

"No. I have promised him nothing."

"Good. All's well that ends well. I particularly wish you not to see him again."

"Very well, sir."

"You promise?"

She hesitated for a moment, and then said—

"Yes, if you much wish it."

"I do. He's an enemy to our house!"

When she had gone he sat down, and wrote in a heavy hand to Farfrae thus:—

> Sir,—I make request that henceforth you and my step-daughter be as strangers to each other. She on her part has promised to welcome no more addresses from you; and I trust, therefore, you will not attempt to force them upon her.   M. HENCHARD.

One would almost have supposed Henchard to have had policy to see that no better *modus vivendi* could be arrived at with Farfrae than by encouraging him to become his son-in-law. But such a scheme for buying over a rival had nothing to recommend it to the Mayor's headstrong faculties. With all domestic *finesse* of that kind he was hopelessly at variance. Loving a man or hating him, his diplomacy was as wrongheaded as a buffalo's; and his wife had not ventured to suggest the course which she, for many reasons, would have welcomed gladly.

Meanwhile Donald Farfrae had opened the gates of

commerce on his own account at a spot on Durnover Hill
—as far as possible from Henchard's stores, and with
every intention of keeping clear of his former friend and
employer's customers. There was, it seemed to the younger
man, room for both of them and to spare. The town was
small, but the corn- and hay-trade was proportionately
large, and with his native sagacity he saw opportunity
for a share of it.

So determined was he to do nothing which should
seem like trade-antagonism to the Mayor that he refused
his first customer—a large farmer of good repute—
because Henchard and this man had dealt together within
the preceding three months.

"He was once my friend," said Farfrae, "and it's not
for me to take business from him. I am sorry to disappoint
you, but I cannot hurt the trade of a man who's been
so kind to me."

In spite of this praiseworthy course the Scotchman's
trade increased. Whether it were that his northern energy
was an over-mastering force among the easy-going Wessex
worthies, or whether it was sheer luck, the fact remained
that whatever he touched he prospered in. Like Jacob
in Padan-Aram, he would no sooner humbly limit himself
to the ringstraked-and-spotted exceptions of trade than
the ringstraked-and-spotted would multiply and prevail.

But most probably luck had little do with it. Character
is Fate, said Novalis, and Farfrae's character was just
the reverse of Henchard's who might not inaptly be
described as Faust has been described—as a vehement
gloomy being who had quitted the ways of vulgar men
without light to guide him on a better way.

Farfrae duly received the request to discontinue attentions to Elizabeth-Jane. His acts of that kind had been so
slight that the request was almost superfluous. Yet he
had felt a considerable interest in her, and after some
cogitation he decided that it would be as well to enact
no Romeo part just then—for the young girl's sake no
less than his own. Thus the incipient attachment was
stifled down.

A time came when, avoid collision with his former

friend as he might, Farfrae was compelled, in sheer self-defense, to close with Henchard in mortal commercial combat. He could no longer parry the fierce attacks of the latter by simple avoidance. As soon as their war of prices began everybody was interested, and some few guessed the end. It was, in some degree, Northern insight matched against Southron doggedness—the dirk against the cudgel—and Henchard's weapon was one which, if it did not deal ruin at the first or second stroke, left him afterwards well-nigh at his antagonist's mercy.

Almost every Saturday they encountered each other amid the crowd of farmers which thronged about the market-place in the weekly course of their business. Donald was always ready, and even anxious, to say a few friendly words; but the Mayor invariably gazed stormfully past him, like one who had endured and lost on his account, and could in no sense forgive the wrong; nor did Farfrae's snubbed manner of perplexity at all appease him. The large farmers, corn-merchants, millers, auctioneers, and others had each an official stall in the corn-market room, with their names painted thereon; and when to the familiar series of "Henchard," "Everdene," "Shiner," Darton," and so on, was added one inscribed "Farfrae," in staring new letters, Henchard was stung into bitterness; like Bellerophon, he wandered away from the crowd, cankered in soul.

From that day Donald Farfrae's name was seldom mentioned in Henchard's house. If at breakfast or dinner Elizabeth-Jane's mother inadvertently alluded to her favorite's movements, the girl would implore her by a look to be silent; and her husband would say, "What—are you, too, my enemy?"

XVIII

There came a shock which had been foreseen for some time by Elizabeth, as the box passenger foresees the approaching jerk from some channel across the highway. Her mother was ill—too unwell to leave her room.

Henchard, who treated her kindly, except in moments of irritation, sent at once for the richest, busiest doctor, whom he supposed to be the best. Bedtime came, and they burnt a light all night. In a day or two she rallied.

Elizabeth, who had been staying up, did not appear at breakfast on the second morning, and Henchard sat down alone. He was startled to see a letter for him from Jersey in a writing he knew too well, and had expected least to behold again. He took it up in his hands and looked at it as at a picture, a vision, a vista of past enactments; and then he read it as an unimportant finale to conjecture.

The writer said that she at length perceived how impossible it would be for any further communications to proceed between them now that his re-marriage had taken place. That such reunion had been the only straightforward course open to him she was bound to admit.

On calm reflection, therefore (she went on), I quite forgive you for landing me in such a dilemma, remembering that you concealed nothing before our ill-advised acquaintance; and that you really did set before me in your grim way the fact of there being a certain risk in intimacy with you, slight as it seemed to be after fifteen or sixteen years of silence on your wife's part. I thus look upon the whole as a misfortune of mine, and not a fault of yours.

So that, Michael, I must ask you to overlook those letters with which I pestered you day after day in the heat of my feelings. They were written whilst I thought your conduct to me cruel; but now I know more particulars of the position you were in I see how inconsiderate my reproaches were.

Now you will, I am sure, perceive that the one condition which will make any future happiness possible for me is that the past connection between our lives be kept secret outside this isle. Speak of it I know you will not; and I can trust you not to write of it. One safeguard more remains to be mentioned—that no writings of mine, or trifling articles belonging to me, should be left in your possession through neglect or forgetfulness. To this end may I request you to return to me any such you may have, particularly the letters written in the first abandonment of feeling.

For the handsome sum you forwarded to me as a plaster to the wound I heartily thank you.

I am now on my way to Bristol, to see my only relative. She is rich, and I hope will do something for me. I shall return through Casterbridge and Budmouth, where I shall take the packet-boat. Can you meet me with the letters and other trifles? I shall be in the coach which changes horses at the Antelope Hotel at half-past five Wednesday evening; I shall be wearing a Paisley shawl with a red center, and thus may easily be found. I should prefer this plan of receiving them to having them sent. — I remain still, yours ever, LUCETTA.

Henchard breathed heavily. "Poor thing—better you had not known me! Upon my heart and soul, if ever I should be left in a position to carry out that marriage with thee, I *ought* to do it—I ought to do it, indeed!"

The contingency that he had in his mind was, of course, the death of Mrs. Henchard.

As requested, he sealed up Lucetta's letters, and put the parcel aside till the day she had appointed; this plan of returning them by hand being apparently a little *ruse* of the young lady for exchanging a word or two with him on past times. He would have preferred not to see her; but deeming that there could be no great harm in acquiescing thus far, he went at dusk and stood opposite the coach-office.

The evening was chilly, and the coach was late. Henchard crossed over to it while the horses were being changed; but there was no Lucetta inside or out. Concluding that something had happened to modify her arrangements he gave the matter up and went home, not without a sense of relief.

Meanwhile Mrs. Henchard was weakening visibly. She could not go out of doors any more. One day, after much thinking which seemed to distress her, she said she wanted to write something. A desk was put upon her bed with pen and paper, and at her request she was left alone. She remained writing for a short time, folded her paper carefully, called Elizabeth-Jane to bring a taper and wax, and then, still refusing assistance, sealed up the sheet, directed it, and locked it in her desk. She had directed it in these words:—

"Mr. Michael Henchard. Not to be opened till Elizabeth-Jane's wedding-day."

The latter sat up with her mother to the utmost of her strength night after night. To learn to take the universe seriously there is no quicker way than to watch—to be a "waker" as the country-people call it. Between the hours at which the last toss-pot went by and the first sparrow shook himself, the silence in Casterbridge—barring the rare sound of the watchman—was broken in Elizabeth's ear only by the time-piece in the bedroom ticking frantically against the clock on the stairs; ticking harder and harder till it seemed to clang like a gong; and all this while the subtle-souled girl asking herself why she was born, why sitting in a room, and blinking at the candle; why things around her had taken the shape they wore in preference to every other possible shape. Why they stared at her so helplessly, as if waiting for the touch of some wand that should release them from terrestrial constraint; what that chaos called consciousness, which spun in her at this moment like a top, tended to, and began in. Her eyes fell together; she was awake, yet she was asleep.

A word from her mother roused her. Without preface, and as the continuation of a scene already progressing in her mind, Mrs. Henchard said: "You remember the note sent to you and Mr. Farfrae—asking you to meet some one in Durnover Barton—and that you thought it was a trick to make fools of you?"

"Yes."

"It was not to make fools of you—it was done to bring you together. 'Twas I did it."

"Why?" said Elizabeth, with a start.

"I—wanted you to marry Mr. Farfrae."

"O mother!" Elizabeth-Jane bent down her head so

much that she looked quite into her own lap. But as her mother did not go on, she said, "What reason?"

"Well, I had a reason. 'Twill out one day. I wish it could have been in my time! But there—nothing is as you wish it! Henchard hates him."

"Perhaps they'll be friends again," murmured the girl.

"I don't know—I don't know." After this her mother was silent, and dozed; and she spoke on the subject no more.

Some little time later on Farfrae was passing Henchard's house on a Sunday morning, when he observed that the blinds were all down. He rang the bell so softly that it only sounded a single full note and a small one; and then he was informed that Mrs. Henchard was dead— just dead—that very hour.

At the town-pump there were gathered when he passed a few old inhabitants, who came there for water whenever they had, as at present, spare time to fetch it, because it was purer from that original fount than from their own wells. Mrs. Cuxsom, who had been standing there for an indefinite time with her pitcher, was describing the incidents of Mrs. Henchard's death, as she had learnt them from the nurse.

"And she was as white as marble-stone," said Mrs. Cuxsom. "And likewise such a thoughtful woman, too— ah, poor soul—that a' minded every little thing that wanted tending. 'Yes,' says she, 'when I'm gone, and my last breath's blowed, look in the top drawer o' the chest in the back room by the window, and you'll find all my coffin clothes; a piece of flannel—that's to put under me, and the little piece is to put under my head; and my new stockings for my feet—they are folded alongside, and all my other things. And there's four ounce pennies, the heaviest I could find, a-tied up in bits of linen, for weights —two for my right eye and two for my left,' she said. 'And when you've used 'em, and my eyes don't open no more, bury the pennies, good souls, and don't ye go spending 'em, for I shouldn't like it. And open the windows as soon as I am carried out, and make it as cheerful as you can for Elizabeth-Jane.' "

"Ah, poor heart!"

"Well, and Martha did it, and buried the ounce pennies in the garden. But if ye'll believe words, that man, Christopher Coney, went and dug 'em up, and spent 'em at the Three Mariners. 'Faith,' he said, 'why should death rob life o' fourpence? Death's not of such good report that we should respect 'en to that extent,' says he."

" 'Twas a cannibal deed!" deprecated her listeners.

"Gad, then, I won't quite ha'e it," said Solomon long-ways. "I say it to-day, and 'tis a Sunday morning, and I wouldn't speak wrongfully for a zilver zixpence at such a time. I don't see noo harm in it. To respect the dead is sound doxology; and I wouldn't sell skellintons—least-wise respectable skellintons—to be varnished for 'natomies, except I were out o' work. But money is scarce, and throats get dry. Why *should* death rob life o' fourpence? I say there was no treason in it."

"Well, poor soul; she's helpless to hinder that or any-thing now," answered Mother Cuxsom. "And all her shin-ing keys will be took from her, and her cupboards opened; and little things a' didn't wish seen, anybody will see; and her wishes and ways will all be as nothing!"

XIX

Henchard and Elizabeth sat conversing by the fire. It was three weeks after Mrs. Henchard's funeral; the candles were not lighted, and a restless, acrobatic flame, poised on a coal, called from the shady walls the smiles of all shapes that could respond—the old pier-glass, with gilt columns and huge entablature, the picture-frames, sundry knobs and handles, and the grass rosette at the bottom of each riband bell-pull on either side of the chimney-piece.

"Elizabeth, do you think much of old times?" said Henchard.

"Yes, sir; often," said she.

"Who do you put in your pictures of 'em?"

"Mother and father—nobody else hardly."

Henchard always looked like one bent on resisting pain when Elizabeth-Jane spoke of Richard Newson as "father." "Ah! I am out of all that, am I not?" he said. . . . "Was Newson a kind father?"

"Yes, sir; very."

Henchard's face settled into an expression of stolid loneliness which gradually modulated into something softer. "Suppose I had been your real father?" he said. "Would you have cared for me as much as you cared for Richard Newson?"

"I can't think it," she said quickly. "I can think of no other as my father, except my father."

Henchard's wife was dissevered from him by death; his friend and helper Farfrae by estrangement; Elizabeth-Jane by ignorance. It seemed to him that only one of them could possibly be recalled, and that was the girl. His mind began vibrating between the wish to reveal himself to her and the policy of leaving well alone, till he could no longer sit still. He walked up and down, and then he came and stood behind her chair, looking down upon the top of her head. He could no longer restrain his impulse. "What did your mother tell you about me—my history?" he asked.

"That you were related by marriage."

"She should have told more—before you knew me! Then my task would not have been such a hard one. . . . Elizabeth, it is I who am your father, and not Richard Newson. Shame alone prevented your wretched parents from owning this to you while both of 'em were alive."

The back of Elizabeth's head remained still, and her shoulders did not denote even the movements of breathing. Henchard went on: "I'd rather have your scorn, your fear, anything than your ignorance; 'tis that I hate! Your mother and I were man and wife when we were young. What you saw was our second marriage. Your mother was too honest. We had thought each other dead—and—Newson became her husband."

This was the nearest approach Henchard could make to the full truth. As far as he personally was concerned he would have screened nothing; but he showed a respect for the young girl's sex and years worthy of a better man.

When he had gone on to give details which a whole series of slight and unregarded incidents in her past life strangely corroborated; when, in short, she believed his story to be true, she became greatly agitated, and turning round to the table flung her face upon it weeping.

"Don't cry—don't cry!" said Henchard, with vehement pathos, "I can't bear it, I won't bear it. I am your father; why should you cry? Am I so dreadful, so hateful to 'ee? Don't take against me, Elizabeth-Jane!" he cried, grasping her wet hand. "Don't take against me—though I was a drinking man once, and used your mother roughly—I'll be kinder to you than *he* was! I'll do anything, if you will only look upon me as your father!"

She tried to stand up and confront him trustfully; but she could not; she was troubled at his presence, like the brethren at the avowal of Joseph.

"I don't want you to come to me all of a sudden," said Henchard in jerks, and moving like a great tree in a wind. "No, Elizabeth, I don't. I'll go away and not see you till to-morrow, or when you like; and then I'll show 'ee papers to prove my words. There, I am gone, and won't disturb you any more. . . . 'Twas I that chose your name, my daughter; your mother wanted it Susan. There, don't forget 'twas I gave you your name!" He went out at the door and shut her softly in, and she heard him go away into the garden. But he had not done. Before she had moved, or in any way recovered from the effect of his disclosure, he reappeared.

"One word more, Elizabeth," he said. "You'll take my surname now—hey? Your mother was against it; but it will be much more pleasant to me. 'Tis legally yours, you know. But nobody need know that. You shall take it as if by choice. I'll talk to my lawyer—I don't know the law of it exactly; but will you do this—let me put a few lines into the newspaper that such is to be your name?"

"If it is my name I must have it, mustn't I?" she asked.

"Well, well; usage is everything in these matters."

"I wonder why mother didn't wish it?"

"Oh, some whim of the poor soul's. Now get a bit of paper and draw up a paragraph as I shall tell you. But let's have a light."

"I can see by the firelight," she answered. "Yes—I'd rather."

"Very well."

She got a piece of paper, and bending over the fender wrote at his dictation words which he had evidently got by heart from some advertisement or other—words to the effect that she, the writer, hitherto known as Elizabeth-Jane Newson, was going to call herself Elizabeth-Jane Henchard forthwith. It was done, and fastened up, and directed to the office of the *Casterbridge Chronicle*.

"Now," said Henchard, with the blaze of satisfaction that he always emitted when he had carried his point— though tenderness softened it this time—"I'll go upstairs and hunt for some documents that will prove it all to you. But I won't trouble you with them till to-morrow. Good night, my Elizabeth-Jane!"

He was gone before the bewildered girl could realize what it all meant, or adjust her filial sense to the new center of gravity. She was thankful that he had left her to herself for the evening, and sat down over the fire. Here she remained in silence, and wept—not for her mother now, but for the genial sailor Richard Newson, to whom she seemed doing a wrong.

Henchard in the meantime had gone upstairs. Papers of a domestic nature he kept in a drawer in his bedroom, and this he unlocked. Before turning them over he leant back and indulged in reposeful thought. Elizabeth was his at last, and she was a girl of such good sense and kind heart that she would be sure to like him. He was the kind of man to whom some human object for pouring out his heat upon—were it emotive or were it choleric—was almost a necessity. The craving of his heart for the reestablishment of this tenderest human tie had been great during his wife's lifetime, and now he had submitted to its mastery without reluctance and without fear. He bent over the drawer again, and proceeded in his search.

Among the other papers had been placed the contents of his wife's little desk, the keys of which had been handed to him at her request. Here was the letter addressed to him with the restriction, *"Not to be opened till Elizabeth-Jane's wedding-day."*

Mrs. Henchard, though more patient than her husband, had been no practical hand at anything. In sealing up the sheet, which was folded and tucked in without an envelope, in the old-fashioned way, she had overlaid the junction with a large mass of wax without the requisite under-touch of the same. The seal had cracked, and the letter was open. Henchard had no reason to suppose the restriction one of serious weight, and his feelings for his late wife had not been of the nature of deep respect. "Some trifling fancy or other of poor Susan's, I suppose," he said; and without curiosity he allowed his eyes to scan the letter:—

MY DEAR MICHAEL,—For the good of all three of us I have kept one thing a secret from you till now. I hope you will understand why; I think you will; though perhaps you may not forgive me. But, dear Michael, I have done it for the best. I shall be in my grave when you read this, and Elizabeth-Jane will have a home. Don't curse me, Mike—think of how I was situated. I can hardly write it, but here it is. Elizabeth-Jane is not your Elizabeth-Jane—the child who was in my arms when you sold me. No; she died three months after that, and this living one is my other husband's. I christened her by the same name we had given to the first, and she filled up the ache I felt at the other's loss. Michael, I am dying, and I might have held my tongue; but I could not. Tell her husband of this or not, as you may judge; and forgive, if you can, a woman you once deeply wronged, as she forgives you.   SUSAN HENCHARD.

Her husband regarded the paper as if it were a window-pane through which he saw for miles. His lip twitched, and he seemed to compress his frame, as if to bear better. His usual habit was not to consider whether destiny were hard upon him or not—the shape of his ideas in cases of affliction being simply a moody "I am to suffer, I perceive." "This much scourging, then, is it for me." But now through his passionate head there stormed this thought —that the blasting disclosure was what he had deserved.

His wife's extreme reluctance to have the girl's name altered from Newson to Henchard was now accounted for fully. It furnished another illustration of that honesty in dishonesty which had characterized her in other things.

He remained unnerved and purposeless for near a couple of hours; till he suddenly said, "Ah—I wonder if it is true!"

He jumped up in an impulse, kicked off his slippers, and went with a candle to the door of Elizabeth-Jane's room, where he put his ear to the keyhole and listened. She was breathing profoundly. Henchard softly turned the handle, entered, and shading the light, approached the bedside. Gradually bringing the light from behind a screening curtain he held it in such a manner that it fell slant-wise on her face without shining on her eyes. He steadfastly regarded her features.

They were fair; his were dark. But this was an unimportant preliminary. In sleep there come to the surface buried genealogical facts, ancestral curves, dead men's traits, which the mobility of daytime animation screens and overwhelms. In the present statuesque repose of the young girl's countenance Richard Newson's was unmistakably reflected. He could not endure the sight of her, and hastened away.

Misery taught him nothing more than defiant endurance of it. His wife was dead, and the first impulse for revenge died with the thought that she was beyond him. He looked out at the night as at a fiend. Henchard, like all his kind, was superstitious, and he could not help thinking that the concatenation of events this evening had produced was the scheme of some sinister intelligence bent on punishing him. Yet they had developed naturally. If he had not revealed his past history to Elizabeth he would not have searched the drawer for papers, and so on. The mockery was, that he should have no sooner taught a girl

to claim the shelter of his paternity than he discovered
her to have no kinship with him.

This ironical sequence of things angered him like an
impish trick from a fellow-creature. Like Prester John's,
his table had been spread, and infernal harpies had
snatched up the food. He went out of the house, and
moved sullenly onward down the pavement till he came
to the bridge at the bottom of the High Street. Here he
turned in upon a bypath on the river bank, skirting the
north-eastern limits of the town.

These precincts embodied the mournful phases of Casterbridge life, as the south avenues embodied its cheerful
moods. The whole way along here was sunless, even in
summer time; in spring, white frosts lingered here when
other places were steaming with warmth; while in winter
it was the seed-field of all the aches, rheumatisms, and
torturing cramps of the year. The Casterbridge doctors
must have pined away for want of sufficient nourishment
but for the configuration of the landscape on the north-
eastern side.

The river—slow, noiseless, and dark—the Schwarzwas-
ser of Casterbridge—ran beneath a low cliff, the two
together forming a defence which had rendered walls and
artificial earthworks on this side unnecessary. Here were
ruins of a Franciscan priory, and a mill attached to the
same, the water of which roared down a back-hatch like
the voice of desolation. Above the cliff, and behind the
river, rose a pile of buildings, and in the front of the pile
a square mass cut into the sky. It was like a pedestal lacking its statue. This missing feature, without which the
design remained incomplete, was, in truth, the corpse of
a man; for the square mass formed the base of the gallows, the extensive buildings at the back being the county
gaol. In the meadow where Henchard now walked the
mob were wont to gather whenever an execution took
place, and there to the tune of the roaring weir they
stood and watched the spectacle.

The exaggeration which darkness imparted to the glooms
of this region impressed Henchard more than he had

expected. The lugubrious harmony of the spot with his
domestic situation was too perfect for him, impatient of
effects, scenes, and adumbrations. It reduced his heart-
burning to melancholy, and he exclaimed, "Why the deuce
did I come here!" He went on past the cottage in which
the old local hangman had lived and died, in times before
that calling was monopolized over all England by a single
gentleman; and climbed up by a steep back lane into the
town.

For the sufferings of that night, engendered by his
bitter disappointment, he might well have been pitied. He
was like one who had half fainted, and could neither
recover nor complete the swoon. In words he could blame
his wife, but not in his heart; and had he obeyed the
wise directions outside her letter this pain would have
been spared him for long—possibly for ever, Elizabeth-
Jane seeming to show no ambition to quit her safe and
secluded maiden courses for the speculative path of
matrimony.

The morning came after this night of unrest, and with
it the necessity for a plan. He was far too self-willed to
recede from a position, especially as it would involve
humiliation. His daughter he had asserted her to be, and
his daughter she should always think herself, no matter
what hypocrisy it involved.

But he was ill-prepared for the first step in this new
situation. The moment he came into the breakfast-room
Elizabeth advanced with open confidence to him and took
him by the arm.

"I have thought and thought all night of it," she said
frankly. "And I see that everything must be as you say.
And I am going to look upon you as the father that you
are, and not to call you Mr. Henchard any more. It is
so plain to me now. Indeed, father, it is. For, of course,
you would not have done half the things you have done
for me, and let me have my own way so entirely, and
bought me presents, if I had only been your step-daughter!
He—Mr. Newson—whom my poor mother married by
such a strange mistake" (Henchard was glad that he had

disguised matters here), "was very kind—O so kind!" (she spoke with tears in her eyes); "but that is not the same thing as being one's real father after all. Now, father, breakfast is ready!" said she cheerfully.

Henchard bent and kissed her cheek. The moment and the act he had prefigured for weeks with a thrill of pleasure; yet it was no less than a miserable insipidity to him now that it had come. His reinstation of her mother had been chiefly for the girl's sake, and the fruition of the whole scheme was such dust and ashes as this.

XX

Of all the enigmas which ever confronted a girl there can have been seldom one like that which followed Henchard's announcement of himself to Elizabeth as her father. He had done it in an ardor and an agitation which had half carried the point of affection with her; yet, behold, from the next morning onwards his manner was constrained as she had never seen it before.

The coldness soon broke out into open chiding. One grievous failing of Elizabeth's was her occasional pretty and picturesque use of dialect words—those terrible marks of the beast to the truly genteel.

It was dinner-time—they never met except at meals—and she happened to say when he was rising from table, wishing to show him something, "If you'll bide where you be a minute, father, I'll get it."

" 'Bide where you be,' " he echoed sharply. "Good God, are you only fit to carry wash to a pig-trough, that ye use such words as those?"

She reddened with shame and sadness.

"I meant, 'Stay where you are,' father," she said, in a low, humble voice. "I ought to have been more careful."

He made no reply, and went out of the room.

The sharp reprimand was not lost upon her, and in time it came to pass that for "fay" she said "succeed"; that she no longer spoke of "dumbledores" but of "humble bees"; no longer said of young men and women that they "walked together," but that they were "engaged"; that she grew to talk of "greggles" as "wild hyacinths"; that when she had not slept she did not quaintly tell the servants next morning that she had been "hag-rid," but that she had "suffered from indigestion."

These improvements, however, are somewhat in advance of the story. Henchard, being uncultivated himself, was the bitterest critic the fair girl could possibly have had of her own lapses—really slight now, for she read omnivorously. A gratuitous ordeal was in store for her in the matter of her own handwriting. She was passing the dining-room door one evening, and had occasion to go in for something. It was not till she had opened the door that she knew the Mayor was there in the company of a man with whom he transacted business.

"Here, Elizabeth-Jane," he said, looking round at her, "just write down what I tell you—a few words of an agreement for me and this gentleman to sign. I am a poor tool with a pen."

"Be jowned, and so be I," said the gentleman.

She brought forward blotting-book, paper, and ink, and sat down.

"Now then—'An agreement entered into this sixteenth day of October'—write that first."

She started the pen in an elephantine march across the sheet. It was a splendid round, bold hand of her own conception, a style that would have stamped a woman as Minerva's own in more recent days. But other ideas reigned then: Henchard's creed was that proper young girls wrote ladies'-hand—nay, he believed that bristling characters were as innate and inseparable a part of refined womanhood as sex itself. Hence when, instead of scribbling, like the Princess Ida,—

> "In such a hand as when a field of corn
> Bows all its ears before the roaring East,"

Elizabeth-Jane produced a line of chain-shot and sandbags, he reddened in angry shame for her, and, peremptorily saying, "Never mind—I'll finish it," dismissed her there and then.

Her considerate disposition became a pitfall to her now. She was, it must be admitted, sometimes provokingly and unnecessarily willing to saddle herself with manual labors. She would go to the kitchen instead of ringing, "Not to make Phœbe come up twice." She went down on her knees, shovel in hand, when the cat overturned the coal-scuttle; moreover, she would persistently thank the parlor-maid for everything, till one day, as soon as the girl was gone from the room, Henchard broke out with, "Good God, why dostn't leave off thanking that girl as if she were a goddess-born! Don't I pay her a dozen pound a year to do things for 'ee?" Elizabeth shrank so visibly at the exclamation that he became sorry a few minutes after, and said that he did not mean to be rough.

These domestic exhibitions were the small protruding needle-rocks which suggested rather than revealed what was underneath. But his passion had less terror for her than his coldness. The increasing frequency of the latter mood told her the sad news that he disliked her with a growing dislike. The more interesting that her appearance and manners became under the softening influences which she could now command, and in her wisdom did command, the more she seemed to estrange him. Sometimes she caught him looking at her with a louring invidiousness that she could hardly bear. Not knowing his secret it was a cruel mockery that she should for the first time excite his animosity when she had taken his surname.

But the most terrible ordeal was to come. Elizabeth had latterly been accustomed of an afternoon to present a cup of cider or ale and bread-and-cheese to Nance Mockridge, who worked in the yard wimbling hay-bonds. Nance accepted this offering thankfully at first; afterwards as a matter of course. On a day when Henchard was on the premises he saw his step-daughter enter the hay-barn on this errand; and, as there was no clear spot on which to deposit the provisions, she at once set to work arranging two trusses of hay as a table, Mockridge meanwhile standing with her hands on her hips, easefully looking at the preparations on her behalf.

"Elizabeth, come here!" said Henchard; and she obeyed.

"Why do you lower yourself so confoundedly?" he said with suppressed passion. "Haven't I told you o't fifty times? Hey? Making yourself a drudge for a common workwoman of such a character as hers! Why, ye'll disgrace me to the dust!"

Now these words were uttered loud enough to reach Nance inside the barn door, who fired up immediately at the slur upon her personal character. Coming to the door she cried, regardless of consequences, "Come to that, Mr. Michael Henchard, I can let 'ee know she've waited on worse!"

"Then she must have had more charity than sense," said Henchard.

"Oh no, she hadn't. 'Twere not for charity but for hire; and at a public-house in this town!"

"It is not true!" cried Henchard indignantly.

"Just ask her," said Nance, folding her naked arms in such a manner that she could comfortably scratch her elbows.

Henchard glanced at Elizabeth-Jane, whose complexion, now pink and white from confinement, lost nearly all of the former color. "What does this mean?" he said to her. "Anything or nothing?"

"It is true," said Elizabeth-Jane. "But it was only——"

"Did you do it, or didn't you? Where was it?"

"At the Three Mariners; one evening for a little while, when we were staying there."

Nance glanced triumphantly at Henchard, and sailed into the barn; for assuming that she was to be discharged on the instant she had resolved to make the most of her victory. Henchard, however, said nothing about discharging her. Unduly sensitive on such points by reason of his own past, he had the look of one completely ground down to the last indignity. Elizabeth followed him to the house like a culprit; but when she got inside she could not see him. Nor did she see him again that day.

Convinced of the scathing damage to his local repute and position that must have been caused by such a fact, though it had never before reached his own ears, Henchard showed a positive distaste for the presence of this girl not his own, whenever he encountered her. He mostly dined with the farmers at the market-room of one of the two chief hotels, leaving her in utter solitude. Could he have seen how she made use of those silent hours he might have found reason to reverse his judgment on her quality. She read and took notes incessantly, mastering facts with painful laboriousness, but never flinching from her self-imposed task. She began the study of Latin, incited by the Roman characteristics of the town she lived in. "If I am not well-informed it shall be by no fault of my own," she would say to herself through the tears that would occasionally glide down her peachy cheeks when she was fairly baffled by the portentous obscurity of many of these educational works.

Thus she lived on, a dumb, deep-feeling, great-eyed creature, construed by not a single contiguous being; quenching with patient fortitude her incipient interest in Farfrae, because it seemed to be one-sided, unmaidenly, and unwise. True, that for reasons best known to herself, she had, since Farfrae's dismissal, shifted her quarters from the back room affording a view of the yard (which she had occupied with such zest) to a front chamber overlooking the street; but as for the young man, whenever he passed the house he seldom or never turned his head.

Winter had almost come, and unsettled weather made her still more dependent upon indoor resources. But there were certain early winter days in Casterbridge—days of firmamental exhaustion which followed angry south-westerly tempests—when, if the sun shone, the air was like velvet. She seized on these days for her periodical visits to the spot where her mother lay buried—the still-used burial-ground of the old Roman-British city, whose curious feature was this, its continuity as a place of sepulture. Mrs. Henchard's dust mingled with the dust of women who lay ornamented with glass hair-pins and amber necklaces, and men who held in their mouths coins of Hadrian, Posthumus, and the Constantines.

Half-past ten in the morning was about her hour for

seeking this spot—a time when the town avenues were deserted as the avenues of Karnac. Business had long since passed down them into its daily cells, and Leisure had not arrived there. So Elizabeth-Jane walked and read, or looked over the edge of the book to think, and thus reached the churchyard.

There, approaching her mother's grave, she saw a solitary dark figure in the middle of the gravel-walk. This figure, too, was reading; but not from a book; the words which engrossed it being the inscription on Mrs. Henchard's tombstone. The personage was in mourning like herself, was about her age and size, and might have been her wraith or double, but for the fact that it was a lady much more beautifully dressed than she. Indeed, comparatively indifferent as Elizabeth-Jane was to dress, unless for some temporary whim or purpose, her eyes were arrested by the artistic perfection of the lady's appearance. Her gait, too, had a flexuousness about it, which seemed to avoid angularity of movement less from choice than from predisposition. It was a revelation to Elizabeth that human beings could reach this stage of external development—she had never suspected it. She felt all the freshness and grace to be stolen from herself on the instant by the neighborhood of such a stranger. And this was in face of the fact that Elizabeth could now have been writ handsome, while the young lady was simply pretty.

Had she been envious she might have hated the woman; but she did not do that—she allowed herself the pleasure of feeling fascinated. She wondered where the lady had come from. The stumpy and practical walk of honest homeliness which mostly prevailed there, the two styles of dress thereabout, the simple and the mistaken, equally avouched that this figure was no Casterbridge woman's, even if a book in her hand resembling a guidebook had not also suggested it.

The stranger presently moved from the tombstone of Mrs. Henchard, and vanished behind the corner of the wall. Elizabeth went to the tomb herself; beside it were two footprints distinct in the soil, signifying that the lady had stood there a long time. She returned homeward, musing on what she had seen, as she might have mused on a rainbow or the Northern Lights, a rare butterfly or a cameo.

Interesting as things had been out of doors, at home it turned out to be one of her bad days. Henchard, whose two years' mayoralty was ending, had been made aware that he was not to be chosen to fill a vacancy in the list of aldermen; and that Farfrae was likely to become one of the Council. This caused the unfortunate discovery that she had played the waiting-maid in the town of which he was Mayor to rankle in his mind yet more poisonously. He had learnt by personal inquiry at the time that it was to Donald Farfrae—that treacherous upstart—that she had thus humiliated herself. And though Mrs. Stannidge seemed to attach no great importance to the incident—the cheerful souls at the Three Mariners having exhausted its aspects long ago—such was Henchard's haughty spirit that the simple thrifty deed was regarded as little less than a social catastrophe by him.

Ever since the evening of his wife's arrival with her daughter there had been something in the air which had changed his luck. That dinner at the King's Arms with his friends had been Henchard's Austerlitz: he had had his successes since, but his course had not been upward. He was not to be numbered among the aldermen—that Peerage of burghers—as he had expected to be, and the consciousness of this soured him to-day.

"Well, where have you been?" he said to her with off-hand laconism.

"I've been strolling in the Walks and churchyard, father, till I feel quite leery." She clapped her hand to her mouth, but too late.

This was just enough to incense Henchard after the other crosses of the day. "I *won't* have you talk like that!" he thundered. " 'Leery,' indeed. One would think you worked upon a farm! One day I learn that you lend a hand in public-houses. Then I hear you talk like a clod-hopper. I'm burned, if it goes on, this house can't hold us two."

The only way of getting a single pleasant thought to go

to sleep upon after this was by recalling the lady she had seen that day, and hoping she might see her again.

Meanwhile Henchard was sitting up, thinking over his jealous folly in forbidding Farfrae to pay his addresses to this girl who did not belong to him, when if he had allowed them to go on he might not have been encumbered with her. At last he said to himself with satisfaction as he jumped up and went to the writing-table: "Ah! he'll think it means peace, and a marriage portion—not that I don't want my house to be troubled with her, and no portion at all!" He wrote as follows:—

> SIR,—On consideration, I don't wish to interfere with your courtship of Elizabeth-Jane, if you care for her. I therefore withdraw my objection; excepting in this—that the business be not carried on in my house. — Yours,
>
> M. HENCHARD.

Mr. Farfrae.

The morrow, being fairly fine, found Elizabeth-Jane again in the churchyard; but while looking for the lady she was startled by the apparition of Farfrae, who passed outside the gate. He glanced up for a moment from a pocket-book in which he appeared to be making figures as he went; whether or not he saw her he took no notice, and disappeared.

Unduly depressed by a sense of her own superfluity, she thought he probably scorned her; and quite broken in spirit sat down on a bench. She fell into painful thought on her position, which ended with her saying quite loud, "Oh, I wish I was dead with dear mother!"

Behind the bench was a little promenade under the wall where people sometimes walked instead of on the gravel. The bench seemed to be touched by something; she looked round, and a face was bending over her, veiled, but still distinct, the face of the young woman she had seen yesterday.

Elizabeth-Jane looked confounded for a moment, knowing she had been overheard, though there was pleasure in her confusion. "Yes, I heard you," said the lady, in a vivacious voice, answering her look. "What can have happened?"

"I don't—I can't tell you," said Elizabeth, putting her hand to her face to hide a quick flush that had come.

There was no movement or word for a few seconds; then the girl felt that the young lady was sitting down beside her.

"I guess how it is with you," said the latter. "That was your mother." She waved her hand towards the tombstone. Elizabeth looked up at her as if inquiring of herself whether there should be confidence. The lady's manner was so desirous, so anxious, that the girl decided there should be confidence. "It was my mother," she said, "my only friend."

"But your father, Mr. Henchard. He is living?"

"Yes, he is living," said Elizabeth-Jane.

"Is he not kind to you?"

"I've no wish to complain of him."

"There has been a disagreement?"

"A little."

"Perhaps you were to blame," suggested the stranger.

"I was—in many ways," sighed the meek Elizabeth. "I swept up the coals when the servant ought to have done it; and I said I was leery;—and he was angry with me."

The lady seemed to warm towards her for that reply. "Do you know the impression your words give me?" she said ingenuously. "That he is a hot-tempered man—a little proud—perhaps ambitious; but not a bad man." Her anxiety not to condemn Henchard while siding with Elizabeth was curious.

"Oh no; certainly not *bad*," agreed the honest girl. "And he has not even been unkind to me till lately— since mother died. But it has been very much to bear while it has lasted. All is owing to my defects, I daresay; and my defects are owing to my history."

"What is your history?"

Elizabeth-Jane looked wistfully at her questioner. She found that her questioner was looking at her; turned her eyes down; and then seemed compelled to look back again. "My history is not gay or attractive," she said. "And yet I can tell it, if you really want to know."

The lady assured her that she did want to know; whereupon Elizabeth-Jane told the tale of her life as she understood it, which was in general the true one, except that the sale at the fair had no part therein.

Contrary to the girl's expectation her new friend was not shocked. This cheered her; and it was not till she thought of returning to that home in which she had been treated so roughly of late that her spirits fell.

"I don't know how to return," she murmured. "I think of going away. But what can I do? Where can I go?"

"Perhaps it will be better soon," said her friend gently. "So I would not go far. Now what do you think of this: I shall soon want somebody to live in my house, partly as housekeeper, partly as companion; would you mind coming to me? But perhaps——"

"Oh yes," cried Elizabeth, with tears in her eyes. "I would, indeed—I would do anything to be independent; for then perhaps my father might get to love me. But, ah!"

"What?"

"I am no accomplished person. And a companion to *you* must be that."

"Oh, not necessarily."

"Not? But I can't help using rural words sometimes, when I don't mean to."

"Never mind, I shall like to know them."

"And—O, I know I shan't do!"—she cried with a distressful laugh. "I accidentally learned to write round hand instead of ladies'-hand. And, of course, you want some one who can write that?"

"Well, no."

"What, not necessary to write ladies'-hand?" cried the joyous Elizabeth.

"Not at all."

"But where do you live?"

"In Casterbridge, or rather I shall be living here after twelve o'clock to-day."

Elizabeth expressed her astonishment.

"I have been staying at Budmouth for a few days while my house was getting ready. The house I am going into is that one they call High-Place Hall—the old stone one looking down the lane to the Market. Two or three rooms are fit for occupation, though not all: I sleep there to-night for the first time. Now will you think over my proposal, and meet me here the first fine day next week, and say if you are still in the same mind?"

Elizabeth, her eyes shining at this prospect of a change from an unbearable position, joyfully assented; and the two parted at the gate of the churchyard.

XXI

As a maxim glibly repeated from childhood remains practically unmarked till some mature experience enforces it, so did this High-Place Hall now for the first time really show itself to Elizabeth-Jane, though her ears had heard its name on a hundred occasions.

Her mind dwelt upon nothing else but the stranger, and the house, and her own chance of living there, all the rest of the day. In the afternoon she had occasion to pay a few bills in the town and do a little shopping, when she learnt that what was a new discovery to herself had become a common topic about the streets. High-Place Hall was undergoing repair; a lady was coming there to live shortly; all the shop-people knew it, and had already discounted the chance of her being a customer.

Elizabeth-Jane could, however, add a capping touch to information so new to her in the bulk. The lady, she said, had arrived that day.

When the lamps were lighted, and it was yet not so dark as to render chimneys, attics, and roofs invisible, Elizabeth, almost with a lover's feeling, thought she would like to look at the outside of High-Place Hall. She went up the street in that direction.

The Hall, with its grey *façade* and parapet, was the only residence of its sort so near the center of the town.

It had, in the first place, the characteristics of a country mansion—birds' nests in its chimneys, damp nooks where fungi grew, and irregularities of surface direct from Nature's trowel. At night the forms of passengers were patterned by the lamps in black shadows upon the pale walls.

This evening motes of straw lay around, and other signs of the premises having been in that lawless condition which accompanies the entry of a new tenant. The house was entirely of stone, and formed an example of dignity without great size. It was not altogether aristocratic, still less consequential, yet the old-fashioned stranger instinctively said, "Blood built it, and Wealth enjoys it," however vague his opinions of those accessories might be.

Yet as regards the enjoying it the stranger would have been wrong, for until this very evening, when the new lady had arrived, the house had been empty for a year or two, while before that interval its occupancy had been irregular. The reason of its unpopularity was soon made manifest. Some of its rooms overlooked the market-place; and such a prospect from such a house was not considered desirable or seemly by its would-be occupiers.

Elizabeth's eyes sought the upper rooms, and saw lights there. The lady had obviously arrived. The impression that this woman of comparatively practised manner had made upon the studious girl's mind was so deep that she enjoyed standing under an opposite archway merely to think that the charming lady was inside the confronting walls, and to wonder what she was doing. Her admiration for the architecture of that front was entirely on account of the inmate it screened. Though for that matter the architecture deserved admiration, or at least study, on its own account. It was Palladian, and like most architecture erected since the Gothic age was a compilation rather than a design. But its reasonableness made it impressive. It was not rich, but rich enough. A timely consciousness of the ultimate vanity of human architecture, no less than of other human things, had prevented artistic superfluity.

Men had till quite recently been going in and out with

parcels and packing-cases, rendering the door and hall within like a public thoroughfare. Elizabeth trotted through the open door in the dusk, but becoming alarmed at her own temerity she went quickly out again by another which stood open in the lofty wall of the back court. To her surprise she found herself in one of the little-used alleys of the town. Looking round at the door which had given her egress, by the light of the solitary lamp fixed in the alley, she saw that it was arched and old—older even than the house itself. The door was studded, and the keystone of the arch was a mask. Originally the mask had exhibited a comic leer, as could still be discerned; but generations of Casterbridge boys had thrown stones at the mask, aiming at its open mouth; and the blows thereof had chipped off the lips and jaws as if they had been eaten away by disease. The appearance was so ghastly by the weakly lamp-glimmer that she could not bear to look at it—the first unpleasant feature of her visit.

The position of the queer old door and the odd presence of the leering mask suggested one thing above all others as appertaining to the mansion's past history—intrigue. By the alley it had been possible to come unseen from all sorts of quarters in the town—the old play-house, the old bull-stake, the old cock-pit, the pool wherein nameless infants had been used to disappear. High-Place Hall could boast of its conveniences undoubtedly.

She turned to come away in the nearest direction homeward, which was down the alley, but hearing footsteps approaching in that quarter, and having no great wish to be found in such a place at such a time she quickly retreated. There being no other way out she stood behind a brick pier till the intruder should have gone his ways.

Had she watched she would have been surprised. She would have seen that the pedestrian on coming up made straight for the arched doorway: that as he paused with his hand upon the latch the lamplight fell upon the face of Henchard.

But Elizabeth-Jane clung so closely to her nook that she discerned nothing of this. Henchard passed in, as ignorant of her presence as she was ignorant of his identity, and disappeared in the darkness. Elizabeth came out a second time into the alley, and made the best of her way home.

Henchard's chiding, by begetting in her a nervous fear of doing anything definable as unlady-like, had operated thus curiously in keeping them unknown to each other at a critical moment. Much might have resulted from recognition—at the least a query on either side in one and the self-same form: What could he or she possibly be doing there?

Henchard, whatever his business at the lady's house, reached his own home only a few minutes later than Elizabeth-Jane. Her plan was to broach the question of leaving his roof this evening; the events of the day had urged her to the course. But its execution depended upon his mood, and she anxiously awaited his manner towards her. She found that it had changed. He showed no further tendency to be angry; he showed something worse. Absolute indifference had taken the place of irritability; and his coldness was such that it encouraged her to departure, even more than hot temper could have done.

"Father, have you any objection to my going away?" she asked.

"Going away! No—none whatever. Where are you going?"

She thought it undesirable and unnecessary to say anything at present about her destination to one who took so little interest in her. He would know that soon enough. "I have heard of an opportunity of getting more cultivated and finished, and being less idle," she answered, with hesitation. "A chance of a place in a household where I can have advantages of study, and seeing refined life."

"Then make the best of it, in Heaven's name—if you can't get cultivated where you are."

"You don't object?"

"Object—I? Ho—no! Not at all." After a pause he said, "But you won't have enough money for this lively scheme without help, you know? If you like I should be willing to make you an allowance, so that you be not bound to live upon the starvation wages refined folk are likely to pay 'ee."

She thanked him for this offer.

"It had better be done properly," he added after a pause. "A small annuity is what I should like you to have —so as to be independent of me—and so that I may be independent of you. Would that please ye?"

"Certainly."

"Then I'll see about it this very day." He seemed relieved to get her off his hands by this arrangement, and as far as they were concerned the matter was settled. She now simply waited to see the lady again.

The day and the hour came; but a drizzling rain fell. Elizabeth-Jane, having now changed her orbit from one of gay independence to laborious self-help, thought the weather good enough for such declined glory as hers, if her friend would only face it—a matter of doubt. She went to the boot-room where her pattens had hung ever since her apotheosis; took them down, had their mildewed leathers blacked, and put them on as she had done in old times. Thus mounted, and with cloak and umbrella, she went off to the place of appointment—intending, if the lady were not there, to call at the house.

One side of the churchyard—the side towards the weather—was sheltered by an ancient thatched mud wall whose eaves overhung as much as one or two feet. At the back of the wall was a corn-yard with its granary and barns—the place wherein she had met Farfrae many months earlier. Under the projection of the thatch she saw a figure. The young lady had come.

Her presence so exceptionally substantiated the girl's utmost hopes that she almost feared her good fortune. Fancies find room in the strongest minds. Here, in a churchyard old as civilization, in the worst of weathers, was a strange woman of curious fascinations never seen elsewhere: there might be some devilry about her presence. However, Elizabeth went on to the church tower, on whose summit the rope of a flag-staff rattled in the wind; and thus she came to the wall.

The lady had such a cheerful aspect in the drizzle that

Elizabeth forgot her fancy. "Well," said the lady, a little of the whiteness of her teeth appearing with the word through the black fleece that protected her face, "have you decided?"

"Yes, quite," said the other eagerly.

"Your father is willing?"

"Yes."

"Then come along."

"When?"

"Now—as soon as you like. I had a good mind to send to you to come to my house, thinking you might not venture up here in the wind. But as I like getting out of doors, I thought I would come and see first."

"It was my own thought."

"That shows we shall agree. Then can you come to-day? My house is so hollow and dismal that I want some living thing there."

"I think I might be able to," said the girl, reflecting.

Voices were borne over to them at that instant on the wind and raindrops from the other side of the wall. There came such words as "sacks," "quarters," "threshing," "tailing," "next Saturday's market," each sentence being disorganized by the gusts like a face in a cracked mirror. Both the women listened.

"Who are those?" said the lady.

"One is my father. He rents that yard and barn."

The lady seemed to forget the immediate business in listening to the technicalities of the corn trade. At last she said suddenly, "Did you tell him where you were going to?"

"No."

"Oh—how was that?"

"I thought it safer to get away first—as he is so uncertain in his temper."

"Perhaps you are right. . . . Besides, I have never told you my name. It is Miss Templeman. . . . Are they gone —on the other side?"

"No. They have only gone up into the granary."

"Well, it is getting damp here. I shall expect you to-day —this evening, say, at six."

"Which way shall I come, ma'am?"

"The front way—round by the gate. There is no other that I have noticed."

Elizabeth-Jane had been thinking of the door in the alley.

"Perhaps, as you have not mentioned your destination, you may as well keep silent upon it till you are clear off. Who knows but that he may alter his mind?"

Elizabeth-Jane shook her head. "On consideration I don't fear it," she said sadly. "He has grown quite cold to me."

"Very well. Six o'clock then."

When they had emerged upon the open road and parted, they found enough to do in holding their bowed umbrellas to the wind. Nevertheless the lady looked in at the corn-yard gates as she passed them, and paused on one foot for a moment. But nothing was visible there save the ricks, and the humpbacked barn cushioned with moss, and the granary rising against the church-tower behind, where the smacking of the rope against the flag-staff still went on.

Now Henchard had not the slightest suspicion that Elizabeth-Jane's movement was to be so prompt. Hence when, just before six, he reached home and saw a fly at the door from the King's Arms, and his step-daughter, with all her little bags and boxes, getting into it, he was taken by surprise.

"But you said I might go, father?" she explained through the carriage window.

"Said!—yes. But I thought you meant next month, or next year. 'Od, seize it—you take time by the forelock! This, then, is how you be going to treat me for all my trouble about ye?"

"O father! how can you speak like that? It is unjust of you!" she said with spirit.

"Well, well, have your own way," he replied. He entered the house, and, seeing that all her things had not yet been brought down, went up to her room to look on. He had never been there since she had occupied it. Evidences of her care, of her endeavors for improvement, were visible all around, in the form of books, sketches, maps, and little arrangements for tasteful effects. Henchard had known nothing of these efforts. He gazed at them, turned suddenly about, and came down to the door.

"Look here," he said, in an altered voice—he never called her by name now—"don't 'ee go away from me. It may be I've spoke roughly to you—but I've been grieved beyond everything by you—there's something that caused it."

"By me?" she said, with deep concern. "What have I done?"

"I can't tell you now. But if you'll stop, and go on living as my daughter, I'll tell you all in time."

But the proposal had come ten minutes too late. She was in the fly—was already, in imagination, at the house of the lady whose manner had such charms for her. "Father," she said, as considerately as she could, "I think it best for us that I go on now. I need not stay long; I shall not be far away; and if you want me badly I can soon come back again."

He nodded ever so slightly, as a receipt of her decision, and no more. "You are not going far, you say. What will be your address, in case I wish to write to you? Or am I not to know?"

"Oh yes—certainly. It is only in the town—High-Place Hall."

"Where?" said Henchard, his face stilling.

She repeated the words. He neither moved nor spoke, and waving her hand to him in utmost friendliness she signified to the flyman to drive up the street.

XXII

We go back for a moment to the preceding night, to account for Henchard's attitude.

At the hour when Elizabeth-Jane was contemplating her stealthy reconnoitering excursion to the abode of the lady of her fancy, he had been not a little amazed at receiving a letter by hand in Lucetta's well-known characters. The self-repression, the resignation of her previous communication had vanished from her mood; she wrote with some of the natural lightness which had marked her in their early acquaintance.

HIGH-PLACE HALL.

MY DEAR MR. HENCHARD,—Don't be surprised. It is for your good and mine, as I hope, that I have come to live at Casterbridge—for how long I cannot tell. That depends upon another; and he is a man, and a merchant, and a Mayor, and one who has the first right to my affections.

Seriously, *mon ami,* I am not so light-hearted as I may seem to be from this. I have come here in consequence of hearing of the death of your wife—whom you used to think of as dead so many years before! Poor woman, she seems to have been a sufferer, though uncomplaining, and though weak in intellect not an imbecile. I am glad you acted fairly by her. As soon as I knew she was no more, it was brought home to me very forcibly by my conscience that I ought to endeavor to disperse the shade which my *étourderie* flung over my name, by asking you to carry out your promise to me. I hope you are of the same mind, and that you will take steps to this end. As, however, I did not know how you were situated, or what had happened since our separation, I decided to come and establish myself here before communicating with you.

You probably feel as I do about this. I shall be able to see you in a day or two. Till then, farewell.— Yours,

LUCETTA.

P. S. — I was unable to keep my appointment to meet you for a moment or two in passing through Casterbridge the other day. My plans were altered by a family event, which it will surprise you to hear of.

Henchard had already heard that High-Place Hall was being prepared for a tenant. He said with a puzzled air to the first person he encountered, "Who is coming to live at the Hall?"

"A lady of the name of Templeman, I believe, sir," said his informant.

Henchard thought it over. "Lucetta is related to her, I suppose," he said to himself. "Yes, I must put her in her proper position, undoubtedly."

It was by no means with the oppression that would once have accompanied the thought that he regarded the moral necessity now; it was, indeed, with interest, if not warmth. His bitter disappointment at finding Elizabeth-Jane to be none of his, and himself a childless man, had left an emotional void in Henchard that he unconsciously craved to fill. In this frame of mind, though without strong feeling, he had strolled up the alley and into High-Place Hall by the postern at which Elizabeth had so nearly encountered him. He had gone on thence into the court, and inquired of a man whom he saw unpacking china from a crate if Miss Le Sueur was living there. Miss Le Sueur had been the name under which he had known Lucetta—or "Lucette," as she had called herself at that time.

The man replied in the negative; that Miss Templeman only had come. Henchard went away, concluding that Lucetta had not as yet settled in.

He was in this interested stage of the inquiry when he witnessed Elizabeth-Jane's departure the next day. On hearing her announce the address, there suddenly took possession of him the strange thought that Lucetta and Miss Templeman were one and the same person, for he could recall that in her season of intimacy with him the name of the rich relative whom he had deemed somewhat a mythical personage had been given as Templeman. Though he was not a fortune-hunter, the possibility that Lucetta had been sublimed into a lady of means by some munificent testament on the part of this relative lent a charm to her image which it might not otherwise have acquired. He was getting on towards the dead level of middle age, when material things increasingly possess the mind.

But Henchard was not left long in suspense. Lucetta was rather addicted to scribbling, as had been shown by the torrent of letters after the *fiasco* in their marriage arrangements, and hardly had Elizabeth gone away when another note came to the Mayor's house from High-Place Hall.

> I am in residence [she said] and comfortable, though getting here has been a wearisome undertaking. You probably know what I am going to tell you, or do you not? My good Aunt Templeman, the banker's widow, whose very existence you used to doubt, much more her affluence, has lately died, and bequeathed some of her property to me. I will not enter into details except to say that I have taken her name—as a means of escape from mine, and its wrongs.
>
> I am now my own mistress, and have chosen to reside in Casterbridge—to be tenant of High-Place Hall, that at least you may be put to no trouble if you wish to see me. My first intention was to keep you in ignorance of the changes in my life till you should meet me in the street; but I have thought better of this.
>
> You probably are aware of my arrangement with your daughter, and have doubtless laughed at the—what shall I call it?—practical joke (in all affection) of my getting her to live with me. But my first meeting with her was purely an accident. Do you see, Michael, partly why I have done it?—why, to give you an excuse for coming here as if to visit *her,* and thus to form my acquaintance naturally. She is a dear, good girl, and she thinks you have treated her with undue severity. You may have done so in your haste, but not deliberately, I am sure. As the result has been to bring her to me I am not disposed to upbraid you. — In haste, yours always,
>
> LUCETTA.

The excitement which these announcements produced in Henchard's gloomy soul was to him most pleasurable. He sat over his dining-table long and dreamily, and by an almost mechanical transfer the sentiments which had run to waste since his estrangement from Elizabeth-Jane and Donald Farfrae gathered around Lucetta before they had grown dry. She was plainly in a very coming-on disposition for marriage. But what else could a poor woman be who had given her time and heart to him so thought-lessly, at that former time, as to lose her credit by it? Probably conscience no less than affection had brought her here. On the whole he did not blame her.

"The artful little woman!" he said, smiling (with reference to Lucetta's adroit and pleasant maneuver with Elizabeth-Jane).

To feel that he would like to see Lucetta was with Henchard to start for her house. He put on his hat and went. It was between eight and nine o'clock when he reached her door. The answer brought him was that Miss Templeman was engaged for that evening; but that she would be happy to see him the next day.

"That's rather like giving herself airs!" he thought. "And considering what we——" But after all, she plainly had not expected him, and he took the refusal quietly. Nevertheless he resolved not to go next day. "These cursed women—there's not an inch of straight grain in 'em!" he said.

Let us follow the track of Mr. Henchard's thought as if it were a clue line, and view the interior of High-Place Hall on this particular evening.

On Elizabeth-Jane's arrival she had been phlegmatically asked by an elderly woman to go upstairs and take off her things. She had replied with great earnestness that she would not think of giving that trouble, and on the instant divested herself of her bonnet and cloak in the passage. She was then conducted to the first door on the landing, and left to find her way further alone.

The room disclosed was prettily furnished as a boudoir or small drawing-room, and on a sofa with two cylindrical pillows reclined a dark-haired, large-eyed, pretty woman, of unmistakably French extraction on one side or the other. She was probably some years older than Elizabeth, and had a sparkling light in her eye. In front of the sofa was a small table, with a pack of cards scattered upon it faces upward.

The attitude had been so full of abandonment that she bounded up like a spring on hearing the door open.

Perceiving that it was Elizabeth she lapsed into ease, and came across to her with a reckless skip that innate grace only prevented from being boisterous.

"Why, you are late," she said, taking hold of Elizabeth-Jane's hands.

"There were so many little things to put up."

"And you seem dead-alive and tired. Let me try to enliven you by some wonderful tricks I have learnt, to kill time. Sit there and don't move." She gathered up the pack of cards, pulled the table in front of her, and began to deal them rapidly, telling Elizabeth to choose some.

"Well, have you chosen?" she asked, flinging down the last card.

"No," stammered Elizabeth, arousing herself from a reverie. "I quite forgot, I was thinking of—you, and me —and how strange it is that I am here."

Miss Templeman looked at Elizabeth-Jane with interest, and laid down the cards. "Ah! never mind," she said. "I'll lie here while you sit by me; and we'll talk."

Elizabeth drew up silently to the head of the sofa, but with obvious pleasure. It could be seen that though in years she was younger than her entertainer in manner and general vision she seemed more of the sage. Miss Templeman deposited herself on the sofa in her former flexuous position, and throwing her arm above her brow —somewhat in the pose of a well-known conception of Titian's—talked up at Elizabeth-Jane invertedly across her forehead and arm.

"I must tell you something," she said. "I wonder if you have suspected it. I have only been mistress of a large house and fortune a little while."

"Oh—only a little while?" murmured Elizabeth-Jane, her countenance slightly falling.

"As a girl I lived about in garrison towns and elsewhere with my father, till I was quite flighty and unsettled. He was an officer in the army. I should not have mentioned this had I not thought it best you should know the truth."

"Yes, yes." She looked thoughtfully round the room—

at the little square piano with brass inlayings, at the
window-curtains, at the lamp, at the fair and dark kings
and queens on the card-table, and finally at the inverted
face of Lucetta Templeman, whose large lustrous eyes
had such an odd effect upside down.

Elizabeth's mind ran on acquirements to an almost
morbid degree. "You speak French and Italian fluently,
no doubt," she said. "I have not been able to get beyond
a wretched bit of Latin yet."

"Well, for that matter, in my native isle speaking French
does not go for much. It is rather the other way."

"Where is your native isle?"

It was with rather more reluctance that Miss Templeman said, "Jersey. There they speak French on one side
of the street and English on the other, and a mixed tongue
in the middle of the road. But it is a long time since I
was there. Bath is where my people really belong to,
though my ancestors in Jersey were as good as anybody in
England. They were the Le Sueurs, an old family who
have done great things in their time. I went back and
lived there after my father's death. But I don't value
such past matters, and am quite an English person in my
feelings and tastes."

Lucetta's tongue had for a moment outrun her discre-
tion. She had arrived at Casterbridge as a Bath lady, and
there were obvious reasons why Jersey should drop out
of her life. But Elizabeth had tempted her to make free,
and a deliberately formed resolve had been broken.

It could not, however, have been broken in safer company. Lucetta's words went no further, and after this day
she was so much upon her guard that there appeared no
chance of her identification with the young Jersey woman
who had been Henchard's dear comrade at a critical time.
Not the least amusing of her safeguards was her resolute
avoidance of a French word if one by accident came to
her tongue more readily than its English equivalent. She
shirked it with the suddenness of the weak Apostle at
the accusation, "Thy speech bewrayeth thee!"

Expectancy sat visibly upon Lucetta the next morning.

She dressed herself for Mr. Henchard, and restlessly awaited his call before mid-day; as he did not come she waited on through the afternoon. But she did not tell Elizabeth that the person expected was the girl's stepfather.

They sat in adjoining windows of the same room in Lucetta's great stone mansion, netting, and looking out upon the market, which formed an animated scene. Elizabeth could see the crown of her stepfather's hat among the rest beneath, and was not aware that Lucetta watched the same object with yet intenser interest. He moved about amid the throng, at this point lively as an anthill; elsewhere more reposeful, and broken up by stalls of fruit and vegetables. The farmers as a rule preferred the open *carrefour* for their transactions, despite its inconvenient jostlings and the danger from crossing vehicles, to the gloomy sheltered market-room provided for them. Here they surged on this one day of the week, forming a little world of leggings, switches, and sample-bags; men of extensive stomachs, sloping like mountain sides; men whose heads in walking swayed as the trees in November gales; who in conversing varied their attitudes much, lowering themselves by spreading their knees, and thrusting their hands into the pockets of remote inner jackets. Their faces radiated tropical warmth; for though when at home their countenances varied with the seasons, their market-faces all the year round were glowing little fires.

All over-clothes here were worn as if they were an inconvenience, a hampering necessity. Some men were well-dressed; but the majority were careless in that respect, appearing in suits which were historical records of their wearer's deeds, sun-scorchings, and daily struggles for many years past. Yet many carried ruffled cheque-books in their pockets which regulated at the bank hard by a balance of never less than four figures. In fact, what these gibbous human shapes specially represented was ready money—money insistently ready—not ready next year like a nobleman's—often not merely ready at the bank like a professional man's, but ready in their large plump hands.

It happened that to-day there rose in the midst of them all two or three tall apple-trees standing as if they grew on the spot; till it was perceived that they were held by men from the cider-districts who came here to sell them, bringing the clay of their county on their boots. Elizabeth-Jane, who had often observed them, said, "I wonder if the same trees come every week?"

"What trees?" said Lucetta, absorbed in watching for Henchard.

Elizabeth replied vaguely, for an incident checked her. Behind one of the trees stood Farfrae, briskly discussing a sample-bag with a farmer. Henchard had come up, accidentally encountering the young man, whose face seemed to inquire, "Do we speak to each other?"

She saw her stepfather throw a shine into his eye which answered "No!" Elizabeth-Jane sighed.

"Are you particularly interested in anybody out there?" said Lucetta.

"Oh no," said her companion, a quick red shooting over her face.

Luckily Farfrae's figure was immediately covered by the apple-tree.

Lucetta looked hard at her. "Quite sure?" she said.

"Oh yes," said Elizabeth-Jane.

Again Lucetta looked out. "They are all farmers, I suppose?" she said.

"No. There's Mr. Bulge—he's a wine merchant; there's Benjamin Brownlet—a horse dealer; and Kitson, the pig breeder; and Yopper, the auctioneer; besides malsters, and millers—and so on." Farfrae stood out quite distinctly now; but she did not mention him.

The Saturday afternoon slipped on thus desultorily. The market changed from the sample-showing hour to the idle hour before starting homewards, when tales were told. Henchard had not called on Lucetta though he had stood so near. He must have been too busy, she thought. He would come on Sunday or Monday.

The days came but not the visitor, though Lucetta repeated her dressing with scrupulous care. She was disheartened. It may at once be declared that Lucetta no longer bore towards Henchard all that warm allegiance which had characterized her in their first acquaintance; the then unfortunate issue of things had chilled pure love considerably. But there remained a conscientious wish to bring about her union with him, now that there was nothing to hinder it—to right her position—which in itself was a happiness to sigh for. With strong social reasons on her side why their marriage should take place there had ceased to be any worldly reason on his why it should be postponed, since she had succeeded to fortune.

Tuesday was the great Candlemas fair. At breakfast she said to Elizabeth-Jane quite coolly: "I imagine your father may call to see you to-day. I suppose he stands close by in the market-place with the rest of the corn-dealers?"

She shook her head. "He won't come."

"Why?"

"He has taken against me," she said in a husky voice.

"You have quarrelled more deeply than I know of."

Elizabeth, wishing to shield the man she believed to be her father from any charge of unnatural dislike, said "Yes."

"Then where you are is, of all places, the one he will avoid?"

Elizabeth nodded sadly.

Lucetta looked blank, twitched up her lovely eyebrows and lip, and burst into hysterical sobs. Here was a disaster —her ingenious scheme completely stultified.

"Oh, my dear Miss Templeman—what's the matter?" cried her companion.

"I like your company much!" said Lucetta, as soon as she could speak.

"Yes, yes—and so do I yours!" Elizabeth chimed in soothingly.

"But—but——" she could not finish the sentence, which was, naturally, that if Henchard had such a rooted dislike for the girl as now seemed to be the case, Elizabeth-Jane would have to be got rid of—a disagreeable necessity.

A provisional resource suggested itself. "Miss Henchard —will you go on an errand for me as soon as breakfast is over?—Ah, that's very good of you. Will you go and order——" Here she enumerated several commissions at sundry shops, which would occupy Elizabeth's time for the next hour or two, at least.

"And have you ever seen the Museum?"

Elizabeth-Jane had not.

"Then you should do so at once. You can finish the morning by going there. It is an old house in a back street —I forget where—but you'll find out—and there are crowds of interesting things—skeletons, teeth, old pots and pans, ancient boots and shoes, birds' eggs—all charmingly instructive. You'll be sure to stay till you get quite hungry."

Elizabeth hastily put on her things and departed. "I wonder why she wants to get rid of me to-day!" she said sorrowfully as she went. That her absence, rather than her services or instruction, was in request, had been readily apparent to Elizabeth-Jane, simple as she seemed, and difficult as it was to attribute a motive for the desire.

She had not been gone ten minutes when one of Lucetta's servants was sent to Henchard's with a note. The contents were briefly:—

DEAR MICHAEL,—You will be standing close to my house to-day for two or three hours in the course of your business, so do please call and see me. I am sadly disappointed that you have not come before, for can I help anxiety about my own equivocal relation to you?—especially now my aunt's fortune has brought me more prominently before society? Your daughter's presence here may be the cause of your neglect; and I have therefore sent her away for the morning. Say you come on business—I shall be quite alone.
                                        LUCETTA.

When the messenger returned her mistress gave directions that if a gentleman called he was to be admitted at once, and sat down to await results.

Sentimentally she did not much care to see him—his delays had wearied her; but it was necessary; and with a sigh she arranged herself picturesquely in the chair; first this way, then that; next so that the light fell over her head. Next she flung herself on the couch in the cyma-recta curve which so became her, and with her arm over her brow looked towards the door. This, she decided, was the best position after all; and thus she remained till a man's step was heard on the stairs. Whereupon Lucetta, forgetting her curve (for Nature was too strong for Art as yet), jumped up and ran and hid herself behind one of the window-curtains in a freak of timidity. In spite of the waning of passion the situation was an agitating one— she had not seen Henchard since his (supposed) temporary parting from her in Jersey.

She could hear the servant showing the visitor into the room, shutting the door upon him, and leaving as if to go and look for her mistress. Lucetta flung back the curtain with a nervous greeting. The man before her was not Henchard.

XXIII

A conjecture that her visitor might be some other person had, indeed, flashed through Lucetta's mind when she was on the point of bursting out; but it was just too late to recede.

He was years younger than the Mayor of Casterbridge; fair, fresh, and slenderly handsome. He wore genteel cloth leggings with white buttons, polished boots with infinite lace holes, light cord breeches under a black velveteen coat and waistcoat; and he had a silver-topped switch in his hand. Lucetta blushed, and said with a curious mixture of pout and laugh on her face—"Oh, I've made a mistake!"

The visitor, on the contrary, did not laugh half a wrinkle.

"But I'm very sorry!" he said, in deprecating tones. "I came and I inquired for Miss Henchard, and they showed me up here, and in no case would I have caught ye so unmannerly if I had known!"

"I was the unmannerly one," said she.

"But is it that I have come to the wrong house, madam?" said Mr. Farfrae, blinking a little in his bewilderment and nervously tapping his legging with his switch.

"Oh no, sir,—sit down. You must come and sit down now you are here," replied Lucetta kindly, to relieve his embarrassment. "Miss Henchard will be here directly."

Now this was not strictly true; but that something about the young man—that hyperborean crispness, stringency, and charm, as of a well-braced musical instrument, which had awakened the interest of Henchard, and of Elizabeth-Jane, and of the Three Mariners' jovial crew, at sight, made his unexpected presence here attractive to Lucetta. He hesitated, looked at the chair, thought there was no danger in it (though there was), and sat down.

Farfrae's sudden entry was simply the result of Henchard's permission to him to see Elizabeth if he were minded to woo her. At first he had taken no notice of Henchard's brusque letter; but an exceptionally fortunate business transaction put him on good terms with everybody, and revealed to him that he could undeniably marry if he chose. Then who so pleasing, thrifty, and satisfactory in every way as Elizabeth-Jane? Apart from her personal recommendations a reconciliation with his former friend Henchard would, in the natural course of things, flow from such a union. He therefore forgave the Mayor his curtness; and this morning on his way to the fair he had called at her house, where he learnt that she was staying at Miss Templeman's. A little stimulated at not finding her ready and waiting—so fanciful are men!—he hastened on to High-Place Hall, to encounter no Elizabeth but its mistress herself.

"The fair to-day seems a large one," she said when, by a natural deviation, their eyes sought the busy scene without. "Your numerous fairs and markets keep me interested. How many things I think of while I watch from here!"

He seemed in doubt how to answer, and the babble without reached them as they sat—voices as of wavelets on a lopping sea, one ever and anon rising above the rest. "Do you look out often?" he asked.

"Yes—very often."

"Do you look for any one you know?"

Why should she have answered as she did?

"I look as at a picture merely. But," she went on, turning pleasantly to him, "I may do so now—I may look for you. You are always there, are you not? Ah—I don't mean it seriously! But it is amusing to look for somebody one knows in a crowd, even if one does not want him. It takes off the terrible oppressiveness of being surrounded by a throng, and having no point of junction with it through a single individual."

"Ay! Maybe you'll be very lonely, ma'am?"

"Nobody knows how lonely."

"But you are rich, they say?"

"If so, I don't know how to enjoy my riches. I came to Casterbridge thinking I should like to live here. But I wonder if I shall."

"Where did ye come from, ma'am?"

"The neighborhood of Bath."

"And I from near Edinboro'," he murmured. "It's better to stay at home, and that's true; but a man must live where his money is made. It is a great pity, but it's always so! Yet I've done very well this year. Oh yes," he went on with ingenious enthusiasm. "You see that man with the drab kerseymere coat? I bought largely of him in the autumn when wheat was down, and then afterwards when it rose a little I sold off all I had! It brought only a small profit to me; while the farmers kept theirs, expecting higher figures—yes, though the rats were gnawing the ricks hollow. Just when I sold the markets went lower, and I bought up the corn of those who had been holding back at less price than my first purchases. And then," cried Farfrae impetuously, his face alight, "I sold it a few weeks after, when it happened to go up again! And so, by contenting mysel' with small profits frequently repeated, I soon made five hundred pounds—yes!"—(bringing down his hand upon the table, and quite forgetting where he was)—"while the others by keeping theirs in hand made nothing at all!"

Lucetta regarded him with a critical interest. He was quite a new type of person to her. At last his eye fell upon the lady's and their glances met.

"Ay, now, I'm wearying you!" he exclaimed.

She said, "No, indeed," coloring a shade.

"What then?"

"Quite otherwise. You are most interesting."

It was now Farfrae who showed the modest pink.

"I mean all you Scotchmen," she added in hasty correction. "So free from Southern extremes. We common people are all one way or the other—warm or cold, passionate or frigid. You have both temperatures going on in you at the same time."

"But how do you mean that? Ye were best to explain clearly, ma'am."

"You are animated—then you are thinking of getting on. You are sad the next moment—then you are thinking of Scotland and friends."

"Yes. I think of home sometimes!" he said simply.

"So do I—as far as I can. But it was an old house where I was born, and they pulled it down for improvements, so I seem hardly to have any home to think of now."

Lucetta did not add, as she might have done, that the house was in St. Helier, and not in Bath.

"But the mountains, and the mists and the rocks, they are there! And don't they seem like home?"

She shook her head.

"They do to me—they do to me," he murmured. And his mind could be seen flying away northwards. Whether its origin were national or personal, it was quite true what Lucetta had said, that the curious double strands in Farfrae's thread of life—the commercial and the romantic —were very distinct at times. Like the colors in a variegated cord those contrasts could be seen intertwisted, yet not mingling.

"You are wishing you were back again," said she.

"Ah, no, ma'am," said Farfrae, suddenly recalling himself.

The fair without the windows was now raging thick and loud. It was the chief hiring fair of the year, and differed quite from the market of a few days earlier. In substance it was a whitey-brown crowd flecked with white —this being the body of laborers waiting for places. The long bonnets of the women, like wagon-tilts, their cotton gowns and checked shawls, mixed with the carters' smock-frocks; for they, too, entered into the hiring. Among the rest, at the corner of the pavement, stood an old shepherd, who attracted the eyes of Lucetta and Farfrae by his still-ness. He was evidently a chastened man. The battle of life had been a sharp one with him, for, to begin with, he was a man of small frame. He was now so bowed by hard work and years that, approaching from behind, a person could hardly see his head. He had planted the stem of his crook in the gutter and was resting upon the bow, which was polished to silver brightness by the long friction of his hands. He had quite forgotten where he was, and what he had come for, his eyes being bent on the ground. A little way off negotiations were proceeding which had reference to him; but he did not hear them, and there seemed to be passing through his mind pleasant visions of the hiring successes of his prime, when his skill laid open to him any farm for the asking.

The negotiations were between a farmer from a distant county and the old man's son. In these there was a difficulty. The farmer would not take the crust without the crumb of the bargain, in other words, the old man without the younger; and the son had a sweetheart on his present farm, who stood by, waiting the issue with pale lips.

"I'm sorry to leave ye, Nelly," said the young man with emotion. "But, you see, I can't starve father, and he's out o' work at Lady-day. 'Tis only thirty-five mile."

The girl's lips quivered. "Thirty-five mile!" she mur-mured. "Ah! 'tis enough! I shall never see 'ee again!" It was, indeed, a hopeless length of traction for Dan Cupid's magnet; for young men were young men at Casterbridge as elsewhere.

"Oh! no, no—I never shall," she insisted, when he pressed her hand; and she turned her face to Lucetta's wall to hide her weeping. The farmer said he would give the young man half-an-hour for his answer, and went away, leaving the group sorrowing.

Lucetta's eyes, full of tears, met Farfrae's. His, too, to her surprise, were moist at the scene.

"It is very hard," she said with strong feelings. "Lovers ought not to be parted like that! Oh, if I had my wish, I'd let people live and love at their pleasure!"

"Maybe I can manage that they'll not be parted," said Farfrae. "I want a young carter; and perhaps I'll take the old man too—yes; he'll not be very expensive, and doubtless he will answer my pairrpose somehow."

"Oh, you are so good!" she cried, delighted. "Go and tell them, and let me know if you have succeeded!"

Farfrae went out, and she saw him speak to the group. The eyes of all brightened; the bargain was soon struck. Farfrae returned to her immediately it was concluded.

"It is kind-hearted of you, indeed," said Lucetta. "For my part, I have resolved that all my servants shall have lovers if they want them! Do make the same resolve!"

Farfrae looked more serious, waving his head a half turn. "I must be a little stricter than that," he said.

"Why?"

"You are a—a thriving woman; and I am a struggling hay-and-corn merchant."

"I am a very ambitious woman."

"Ah, well, I cannet explain. I don't know how to talk to ladies, ambitious or no; and that's true," said Donald with grave regret. "I try to be civil to a' folk—no more!"

"I see you are as you say," replied she, sensibly getting the upper hand in these exchanges of sentiment. Under this revelation of insight Farfrae again looked out of the window into the thick of the fair.

Two farmers met and shook hands, and being quite near the window their remarks could be heard as others' had been.

"Have you seen young Mr. Farfrae this morning?" asked one. "He promised to meet me here at the stroke of twelve; but I've gone athwart and about the fair half-a-dozen times, and never a sign of him: though he's mostly a man to his word."

"I quite forgot the engagement," murmured Farfrae.

"Now you must go," said she; "must you not?"

"Yes," he replied. But he still remained.

"You had better go," she urged. "You will lose a customer."

"Now, Miss Templeman, you will make me angry," exclaimed Farfrae.

"Then suppose you don't go; but stay a little longer?"

He looked anxiously at the farmer who was seeking him, and who just then ominously walked across to where Henchard was standing, and he looked into the room and at her. "I like staying; but I fear I must go!" he said. "Business ought not to be neglected, ought it?"

"Not for a single minute."

"It's true. I'll come another time—if I may, ma'am?"

"Certainly," she said. "What has happened to us to-day is very curious."

"Something to think over when we are alone, it's like to be?"

"Oh, I don't know that. It is commonplace after all."

"No, I'll not say that. Oh no!"

"Well, whatever it has been, it is now over; and the market calls you to be gone."

"Yes, yes. Market—business! I wish there were no business in the warrld."

Lucetta almost laughed—she would quite have laughed—but that there was a little emotion going in her at the time. "How you change!" she said. "You should not change like this."

"I have never wished such things before," said the Scotchman, with a simple, shamed, apologetic look for his weakness. "It is only since coming heere and seeing you!"

"If that's the case, you had better not look at me any longer. Dear me, I feel I have quite demoralized you!"

"But look or look not, I will see you in my thoughts. Well, I'll go—thank you for the pleasure of this visit."

"Thank you for staying."

"Maybe I'll get into my market-mind when I've been out a few minutes," he murmured. "But I don't know—I don't know!"

As he went she said eagerly, "You may hear them speak of me in Casterbridge as time goes on. If they tell you I'm a coquette, which some may, because of the incidents of my life, don't believe it, for I am not."

"I swear I will not!" he said fervidly.

Thus the two. She had enkindled the young man's enthusiasm till he was quite brimming with sentiment; while he, from merely affording her a new form of idleness had gone on to wake her serious solicitude. Why was this? They could not have told.

Lucetta as a young girl would hardly have looked at a tradesman. But her ups and downs, capped by her indiscretions with Henchard, had made her uncritical as to station. In her poverty she had met with repulse from the society to which she had belonged, and she had no great zest for renewing an attempt upon it now. Her heart longed for some ark into which it could fly and be at rest. Rough or smooth she did not care so long as it was warm.

Farfrae was shown out, it having entirely escaped him that he had called to see Elizabeth. Lucetta at the window watched him threading the maze of farmers and farmers' men. She could see by his gait that he was conscious of her eyes, and her heart went out to him for his modesty—pleaded with her sense of his unfitness that he might be allowed to come again. He entered the market-house, and she could see him no more.

Three minutes later, when she had left the window, knocks, not of multitude but of strength, sounded through the house, and the waiting-maid tripped up.

"The Mayor," she said.

Lucetta had reclined herself, and was looking dreamily through her fingers. She did not answer at once, and the maid repeated the information with the addition, "And he's afraid he hasn't much time to spare, he says."

"Oh! Then tell him that as I have a headache I won't detain him to-day."

The message was taken down, and she heard the door close.

Lucetta had come to Casterbridge to quicken Henchard's feelings with regard to her. She had quickened them, and now she was indifferent to the achievement.

Her morning view of Elizabeth-Jane as a disturbing element changed, and she no longer felt strongly the necessity of getting rid of the girl for her stepfather's sake. When the young woman came in, sweetly unconscious of the turn in the tide, Lucetta went up to her, and said quite sincerely—

"I'm so glad you've come. You'll live with me a long time, won't you?"

Elizabeth as a watch-dog to keep her father off—what a new idea. Yet it was not unpleasing. Henchard had neglected her all these days, after compromising her indescribably in the past. The least he could have done when he found himself free, and herself affluent, would have been to respond heartily and promptly to her invitation.

Her emotions rose, fell, undulated, filled her with wild surmise at their suddenness; and so passed Lucetta's experiences of that day.

XXIV

Poor Elizabeth-Jane, little thinking what her malignant star had done to blast the budding attentions she had won from Donald Farfrae, was glad to hear Lucetta's words about remaining.

For in addition to Lucetta's house being a home, that raking view of the market-place which it afforded had as much attraction for her as for Lucetta. The *carrefour* was like the regulation Open Place in spectacular dramas, where the incidents that occur always happen to bear on the lives of the adjoining residents. Farmers, merchants, dairymen, quacks, hawkers, appeared there from week to week, and disappeared as the afternoon wasted away. It was the node of all orbits.

From Saturday to Saturday was as from day to day with the two young women now. In an emotional sense they did not live at all during the intervals. Wherever they might go wandering on other days, on market-day they were sure to be at home. Both stole sly glances out of the window at Farfrae's shoulders and poll. His face they seldom saw, for, either through shyness, or not to disturb his mercantile mood, he avoided looking towards their quarters.

Thus things went on, till a certain market-morning brought a new sensation. Elizabeth and Lucetta were sitting at breakfast when a parcel containing two dresses arrived for the latter from London. She called Elizabeth from her breakfast, and entering her friend's bedroom Elizabeth saw the gowns spread out on the bed, one of a deep cherry color, the other lighter—a glove lying at the end of each sleeve, a bonnet at the top of each neck, and parasols across the gloves, Lucetta standing beside the suggested human figure in an attitude of contemplation.

"I wouldn't think so hard about it," said Elizabeth, marking the intensity with which Lucetta was alternating the question whether this or that would suit best.

"But settling upon new clothes is so trying," said Lucetta. "You are that person" (pointing to one of the arrangements), "or you are *that* totally different person" (pointing to the other), "for the whole of the coming spring: and one of the two, you don't know which, may turn out to be very objectionable."

It was finally decided by Miss Templeman that she would be the cherry-colored person at all hazards. The dress was pronounced to be a fit, and Lucetta walked with it into the front room, Elizabeth following her.

The morning was exceptionally bright for the time of year. The sun fell so flat on the houses and pavements opposite Lucetta's residence that they poured their brightness into her rooms. Suddenly, after a rumbling of wheels, there were added to this steady light a fantastic series of circling irradiations upon the ceiling, and the companions turned to the window. Immediately opposite a vehicle of strange description had come to a standstill, as if it had been placed there for exhibition.

It was the new-fashioned agricultural implement called a horse-drill, till then unknown, in its modern shape, in this part of the country, where the venerable seed-lip was still used for sowing as in the days of the Heptarchy. Its arrival created about as much sensation in the corn-market as a flying machine would create at Charing Cross. The farmers crowded round it, women drew near it, children crept under and into it. The machine was painted in bright hues of green, yellow, and red, and it resembled as a whole a compound of hornet, grasshopper, and shrimp, magnified enormously. Or it might have been likened to an upright musical instrument with the front gone. That was how it struck Lucetta. "Why, it is a sort of agricultural piano," she said.

"It has something to do with corn," said Elizabeth.

"I wonder who thought of introducing it here?"

Donald Farfrae was in the minds of both as the innovator, for though not a farmer he was closely leagued with farming operations. And as if in response to their thought he came up at that moment, looked at the machine, walked round it, and handled it as if he knew something about its make. The two watchers had inwardly started at his coming, and Elizabeth left the window, went to the back of the room, and stood as if absorbed in the panelling of the wall. She hardly knew that she had done this till Lucetta, animated by the conjunction of her new attire with the sight of Farfrae, spoke out: "Let us go and look at the instrument, whatever it is."

Elizabeth-Jane's bonnet and shawl were pitchforked on in a moment, and they went out. Among all the agriculturists gathering round the only appropriate possessor of the new machine seemed to be Lucetta, because she alone rivalled it in color.

They examined it curiously; observing the rows of

trumpet-shaped tubes one within the other, the little scoops, like revolving salt-spoons, which tossed the seed into the upper ends of the tubes that conducted it to the ground; till somebody said, "Good morning, Elizabeth-Jane." She looked up, and there was her stepfather.

His greeting had been somewhat dry and thunderous, and Elizabeth-Jane, embarrassed out of her equanimity, stammered at random, "This is the lady I live with, father—Miss Templeman."

Henchard put his hand to his hat, which he brought down with a great wave till it met his body at the knee. Miss Templeman bowed. "I am happy to become acquainted with you, Mr. Henchard," she said. "This is a curious machine."

"Yes," Henchard replied; and he proceeded to explain it, and still more forcibly to ridicule it.

"Who brought it here?" said Lucetta.

"Oh, don't ask me, ma'am!" said Henchard. "The thing—why 'tis impossible it should act. 'Twas brought here by one of our machinists on the recommendation of a jumped-up jackanapes of a fellow who thinks——" His eye caught Elizabeth-Jane's imploring face, and he stopped, probably thinking that the suit might be progressing.

He turned to go away. Then something seemed to occur which his stepdaughter fancied must really be a hallucination of hers. A murmur apparently came from Henchard's lips in which she detected the words, "You refused to see me!" reproachfully addressed to Lucetta. She could not believe that they had been uttered by her stepfather; unless, indeed, they might have been spoken to one of the yellow-gaitered farmers near them. Yet Lucetta seemed silent; and then all thought of the incident was dissipated by the humming of a song, which sounded as though from the interior of the machine. Henchard had by this time vanished into the market-house, and both the women glanced towards the corn-drill. They could see behind it the bent back of a man who was pushing his head into the internal works to master their simple secrets. The hummed song went on—

" 'Tw—s on a s—m—r aftern—n,
A wee be—re the s—n w—nt d—n,
When Kitty wi' a braw n—w g—wn
C—me ow're the h—lls to Gowrie."

Elizabeth-Jane had apprehended the singer in a moment, and looked guilty of she did know what. Lucetta next recognized him, and more mistress of herself said archly, "The 'Lass of Gowrie' from the inside of a seed-drill—what a phenomenon!"

Satisfied at last with his investigation the young man stood upright, and met their eyes across the summit.

"We are looking at the wonderful new drill," Miss Templeman said. "But practically it is a stupid thing—is it not?" she added, on the strength of Henchard's information.

"Stupid? Oh no!" said Farfrae gravely. "It will revolutionize sowing heerabout! No more sowers flinging their seed about broadcast, so that some falls by the wayside and some among thorns, and all that. Each grain will go straight to its intended place, and nowhere else whatever!"

"Then the romance of the sower is gone for good," observed Elizabeth-Jane, who felt herself at one with Farfrae in Bible-reading at least. " 'He that observeth the wind shall not sow,' so the Preacher said; but his words will not be to the point any more. How things change!"

"Ay; ay. . . . It must be so!" Donald admitted, his gaze fixing itself on a blank point far away. "But the machines are already very common in the East and North of England," he added apologetically.

Lucetta seemed to be rather outside this train of sentiment, her acquaintance with the Scriptures being somewhat limited. "Is the machine yours?" she asked of Farfrae.

"Oh no, madam," said he, becoming embarrassed and deferential at the sound of her voice, though with Elizabeth-Jane he was quite at his ease. "No, no—I merely recommended that it should be got."

In the silence which followed Farfrae appeared only conscious of her; to have passed from perception of Elizabeth into a brighter sphere of existence than she appertained to. Lucetta, discerning that he was much mixed that day, partly in his mercantile mood and partly in his romantic one, said gaily to him—

"Well, don't forsake the machine for us," and went indoors with her companion.

The latter felt that she had been in the way, though why was unaccountable to her. Lucetta explained the matter somewhat by saying when they were again in the sitting-room—

"I had occasion to speak to Mr. Farfrae the other day, and so I knew him this morning."

Lucetta was very kind towards Elizabeth that day. Together they saw the market thicken, and in course of time thin away with the slow decline of the sun towards the upper end of the town, its rays taking the street endways and enfilading the long thoroughfare from top to bottom. The gigs and vans disappeared one by one till there was not a vehicle in the street. The time of the riding world is over; the pedestrian world held sway. Field laborers and their wives and children trooped in from the villages for their weekly shopping, and instead of a rattle of wheels and a tramp of horses ruling the sound as earlier, there was nothing but the shuffle of many feet. All the implements were gone; all the farmers; all the moneyed class. The character of the town's trading had changed from bulk to multiplicity, and pence were handled now as pounds had been handled earlier in the day.

Lucetta and Elizabeth looked out upon this, for though it was night and the street lamps were lighted, they had kept their shutters unclosed. In the faint blink of the fire they spoke more freely.

"Your father was distant with you," said Lucetta.

"Yes." And having forgotten the momentary mystery of Henchard's seeming speech to Lucetta she continued, "It is because he does not think I am respectable. I have tried to be so more than you can imagine, but in vain! My mother's separation from my father was unfortunate for me. You don't know what it is to have shadows like that upon your life."

Lucetta seemed to wince. "I do not—of that kind precisely," she said, "but you may feel a—sense of disgrace—shame—in other ways."

"Have you ever had any such feeling?" said the younger innocently.

"Oh no," said Lucetta quickly. "I was thinking of—what happens sometimes when women get themselves in strange positions in the eyes of the world from no fault of their own."

"It must make them very unhappy afterwards."

"It makes them anxious; for might not other women despise them?"

"Not altogether despise them. Yet not quite like or respect them."

Lucetta winced again. Her past was by no means secure from investigation, even in Casterbridge. For one thing Henchard had never returned to her the cloud of letters she had written and sent him in her first excitement. Possibly they were destroyed; but she could have wished that they had never been written.

The rencounter with Farfrae and his bearing towards Lucetta had made the reflective Elizabeth more observant of her brilliant and amiable companion. A few days afterwards, when her eyes met Lucetta's as the latter was going out, she somehow knew that Miss Templeman was nourishing a hope of seeing the attractive Scotchman. The fact was printed large all over Lucetta's cheeks and eyes to any one who read her as Elizabeth-Jane was beginning to do. Lucetta passed on and closed the street door.

A seer's spirit took possession of Elizabeth, impelling her to sit down by the fire and divine events so surely from data already her own that they could be held as witnessed. She followed Lucetta thus mentally—saw her encounter Donald somewhere as if by chance—saw him wear his special look when meeting women, with an added intensity because this one was Lucetta. She depicted his impassioned manner; beheld the indecision of both between their lothness to separate and their desire not to be observed; depicted their shaking of hands; how they probably parted with frigidity in their general contour and movements, only in the smaller features showing the spark of passion, thus invisible to all but themselves. The discerning silent witch had not done thinking of these things when Lucetta came noiselessly behind her and made her start.

It was all true as she had pictured—she could have sworn it. Lucetta had a heightened luminousness in her eye over and above the advanced color of her cheeks.

"You've seen Mr. Farfrae," said Elizabeth demurely.

"Yes," said Lucetta. "How did you know?"

She knelt down on the hearth and took her friend's hands excitedly in her own. But after all she did not say when or how she had seen him or what he had said.

That night she became restless; in the morning she was feverish; and at breakfast-time she told her companion that she had something on her mind—something which concerned a person in whom she was interested much. Elizabeth was earnest to listen and sympathize.

"This person—a lady—once admired a man much— very much," she said tentatively.

"Ah," said Elizabeth-Jane.

"They were intimate—rather. He did not think so deeply of her as she did of him. But in an impulsive moment, purely out of reparation, he proposed to make her his wife. She agreed. But there was an unexpected hitch in the proceedings; though she had been so far compromised with him that she felt she could never belong to another man, as a pure matter of conscience, even if she should wish to. After that they were much apart, heard nothing of each other for a long time, and she felt her life quite closed up for her."

"Ah—poor girl!"

"She suffered much on account of him; though I should add that he could not altogether be blamed for what had happened. At last the obstacle which separated them was providentially removed; and he came to marry her."

"How delightful!"

"But in the interval she—my poor friend—had seen a

man she liked better than him. Now comes the point:
Could she in honor dismiss the first?"

"A new man she liked better—that's bad!"

"Yes," said Lucetta, looking pained at a boy who was
swinging the town pump-handle. "It is bad! Though you
must remember that she was forced into an equivocal
position with the first man by an accident—that he was
not so well educated or refined as the second, and that
she had discovered some qualities in the first that rendered
him less desirable as a husband than she had at first
thought him to be."

"I cannot answer," said Elizabeth-Jane thoughtfully. "It
is so difficult. It wants a Pope to settle that!"

"You prefer not to, perhaps?" Lucetta showed in her
appealing tone how much she leant on Elizabeth's judgment.

"Yes, Miss Templeman," admitted Elizabeth. "I would
rather not say."

Nevertheless, Lucetta seemed relieved by the simple
fact of having opened out the situation a little, and was
slowly convalescent of her headache. "Bring me a looking-
glass. How do I appear to people?" she said languidly.

"Well—a little worn," answered Elizabeth, eyeing her
as a critic eyes a doubtful painting; fetching the glass she
enabled Lucetta to survey herself in it, which Lucetta
anxiously did.

"I wonder if I wear well, as times go!" she observed
after a while.

"Yes—fairly."

"Where am I worst?"

"Under your eyes—I notice a little brownness there."

"Yes. That is my worst place, I know. How many years
more do you think I shall last before I get hopelessly
plain?"

There was something curious in the way in which
Elizabeth, though the younger, had come to play the
part of experienced sage in these discussions. "It may be
five years," she said judicially. "Or, with a quiet life, as
many as ten. With no love you might calculate on ten."

Lucetta seemed to reflect on this as on an unalterable, impartial verdict. She told Elizabeth-Jane no more of the past attachment she had roughly adumbrated as the experiences of a third person; and Elizabeth, who in spite of her philosophy was very tender-hearted, sighed that night in bed at the thought that her pretty, rich Lucetta did not treat her to the full confidence of names and dates in her confessions. For by the "she" of Lucetta's story Elizabeth had not been beguiled.

XXV

The next phase of the supersession of Henchard in Lucetta's heart was an experiment in calling on her performed by Farfrae with some apparent trepidation. Conventionally speaking he conversed with both Miss Templeman and her companion; but in fact it was rather that Elizabeth sat invisible in the room. Donald appeared not to see her at all, and answered her wise little remarks with curtly indifferent monosyllables, his looks and faculties hanging on the woman who could boast of a more Protean variety in her phases, moods, opinions, and also principles, than could Elizabeth. Lucetta had persisted in dragging her into the circle; but she had remained like an awkward third point which that circle would not touch.

Susan Henchard's daughter bore up against the frosty ache of the treatment, as she had borne up under worse things, and contrived as soon as possible to get out of the inharmonious room without being missed. The Scotchman seemed hardly the same Farfrae who had danced with her and walked with her in a delicate poise between love and friendship—that period in the history of a love when alone it can be said to be unalloyed with pain.

She stoically looked from her bedroom window, and contemplated her fate as if it were written on the top of the church-tower hard by. "Yes," she said at last, bringing down her palm upon the sill with a pat: "*He* is the second man of that story she told me!"

All this time Henchard's smouldering sentiments towards

Lucetta had been fanned into higher and higher inflammation by the circumstances of the case. He was discovering that the young woman for whom he once felt a pitying warmth which had been almost chilled out of him by reflection, was, when now qualified with a slight inaccessibility and a more matured beauty, the very being to make him satisfied with life. Day after day proved to him, by her silence, that it was no use to think of bringing her round by holding aloof; so he gave in, and called upon her again, Elizabeth-Jane being absent.

He crossed the room to her with a heavy tread of some awkwardness, his strong, warm gaze upon her—like the sun beside the moon in comparison with Farfrae's modest look—and with something of a hail-fellow bearing, as, indeed, was not unnatural. But she seemed so transubstantiated by her change of position, and held out her hand to him in such cool friendship, that he became deferential, and sat down with a perceptible loss of power. He understood but little of fashion in dress, yet enough to feel himself inadequate in appearance beside her whom he had hitherto been dreaming of as almost his property. She said something very polite about his being good enough to call. This caused him to recover balance. He looked her oddly in the face, losing his awe.

"Why, of course I have called, Lucetta," he said. "What does that nonsense mean? You know I couldn't have helped myself if I had wished—that is, if I had any kindness at all. I've called to say that I am ready, as soon as custom will permit, to give you my name in return for your devotion, and what you lost by it in thinking too little of yourself and too much of me; to say that you can fix the day or month, with my full consent, whenever in your opinion it would be seemly: you know more of these things than I."

"It is full early yet," she said evasively.

"Yes, yes; I suppose it is. But you know, Lucetta, I felt directly my poor ill-used Susan died, and when I could not bear the idea of marrying again, that after what had happened between us it was my duty not to let any unnecessary delay occur before putting things to rights. Still, I wouldn't call in a hurry, because—well, you can guess how this money you've come into made me feel." His voice slowly fell; he was conscious that in this room his accents and manner wore a roughness not observable in the street. He looked about the room at the novel hangings and ingenious furniture with which she had surrounded herself.

"Upon my life I didn't know such furniture as this could be bought in Casterbridge," he said.

"Nor can it be," said she. "Nor will it till fifty years more of civilization have passed over the town. It took a wagon and four horses to get it here."

"H'm. It looks as if you were living on capital."

"O no, I am not."

"So much the better. But the fact is, your setting up like this makes my bearing towards you rather awkward."

"Why?"

An answer was not really needed, and he did not furnish one. "Well," he went on, "there's nobody in the world I would have wished to see enter into this wealth before you, Lucetta, and nobody, I am sure, who will become it more." He turned to her with congratulatory admiration so fervid that she shrank somewhat, notwithstanding that she knew him so well.

"I am greatly obliged to you for all that," said she, rather with an air of speaking ritual. The stint of reciprocal feeling was perceived, and Henchard showed chagrin at once—nobody was more quick to show that than he.

"You may be obliged or not for't. Though the things I say may not have the polish of what you've lately learnt to expect for the first time in your life, they are real, my lady Lucetta."

"That's rather a rude way of speaking to me," pouted Lucetta, with stormy eyes.

"Not at all!" replied Henchard hotly. "But there, there, I don't want to quarrel with 'ee. I come with an honest proposal for silencing your Jersey enemies, and you ought to be thankful."

"How can you speak so!" she answered, firing quickly. "Knowing that my only crime was the indulging in a foolish girl's passion for you with too little regard for correctness, and that I was what *I* call innocent all the time they called me guilty, you ought not to be so cutting! I suffered enough at that worrying time, when you wrote to tell me of your wife's return and my consequent dismissal, and if I am a little independent now, surely the privilege is due to me!"

"Yes, it is," he said. "But it is not by what is, in this life, but by what appears, that you are judged; and I therefore think you ought to accept me—for your own good name's sake. What is known in your native Jersey may get known here."

"How you keep on about Jersey! I am English!"

"Yes, yes. Well, what do you say to my proposal?"

For the first time in their acquaintance Lucetta had the move; and yet she was backward. "For the present let things be," she said with some embarrassment. "Treat me as an acquaintance; and I'll treat you as one. Time will——" she stopped; and he said nothing to fill the gap for awhile, there being no pressure of half acquaintance to drive them into speech if they were not minded for it.

"That's the way the wind blows, is it?" he said at last grimly, nodding an affirmative to his own thoughts.

A yellow flood of reflected sunlight filled the room for a few instants. It was produced by the passing of a load of newly trussed hay from the country, in a wagon marked with Farfrae's name. Beside it rode Farfrae himself on horseback. Lucetta's face became—as a woman's face becomes when the man she loves rises upon her gaze like an apparition.

A turn of the eye by Henchard, a glance from the window, and the secret of her inaccessibility would have been revealed. But Henchard in estimating her tone was looking down so plumb-straight that he did not note the warm consciousness upon Lucetta's face.

"I shouldn't have thought it—I shouldn't have thought it of women!" he said emphatically by-and-by, rising and shaking himself into activity; while Lucetta was so anxious to divert him from any suspicion of the truth that she asked him to be in no hurry. Bringing him some apples she insisted upon paring one for him.

He would not take it. "No, no; such is not for me," he said drily, and moved to the door. At going out he turned his eye upon her.

"You came to live in Casterbridge entirely on my account," he said. "Yet now you are here you won't have anything to say to my offer!"

He had hardly gone down the staircase when she dropped upon the sofa and jumped up again in a fit of desperation. "*I* will love him!" she cried passionately; "as for *him*— he's hot-tempered and stern, and it would be madness to bind myself to him knowing that. I won't be a slave to the past—I'll love where I choose!"

Yet having decided to break away from Henchard one might have supposed her capable of aiming higher than Farfrae. But Lucetta reasoned nothing: she feared hard words from the people with whom she had been earlier associated; she had no relatives left; and with native lightness of heart took kindly to what fate offered.

Elizabeth-Jane, surveying the position of Lucetta between her two lovers from the crystalline sphere of a straightforward mind, did not fail to perceive that her father, as she called him, and Donald Farfrae became more desperately enamored of her friend every day. On Farfrae's side it was the unforced passion of youth. On Henchard's the artificially stimulated coveting of maturer age.

The pain she experienced from the almost absolute obliviousness to her existence that was shown by the pair of them became at times half dissipated by her sense of its humorousness. When Lucetta had pricked her finger they were as deeply concerned as if she were dying; when she herself had been seriously sick or in danger they uttered a conventional word of sympathy at the news, and forgot all about it immediately. But, as regarded

Henchard, this perception of hers also caused her some
filial grief; she could not help asking what she had done
to be neglected so, after the professions of solicitude he
had made. As regarded Farfrae, she thought, after honest
reflection, that it was quite natural. What was she beside
Lucetta?—as one of the "meaner beauties of the night,"
when the moon had risen in the skies.

She had learnt the lesson of renunciation, and was as
familiar with the wreck of each day's wishes as with the
diurnal setting of the sun. If her earthly career had taught
her few book philosophies it had at least well practised
her in this. Yet her experience had consisted less in a
series of pure disappointments than in a series of sub-
stitutions. Continually it had happened that what she
had desired had not been granted her, and that what had
been granted her she had not desired. So she viewed
with an approach to equanimity the now cancelled days
when Donald had been her undeclared lover, and wondered what unwished-for thing Heaven might send her
in place of him.

XXVI

It chanced that on a fine spring morning Henchard and
Farfrae met in the chestnut-walk which ran along the
south wall of the town. Each had just come out from his
early breakfast, and there was not another soul near.
Henchard was reading a letter from Lucetta, sent in
answer to a note from him, in which she made some excuse
for not immediately granting him a second interview that
he had desired.

Donald had no wish to enter into conversation with his
former friend on their present constrained terms; neither
would he pass him in scowling silence. He nodded, and
Henchard did the same. They had receded from each
other several paces when a voice cried "Farfrae!" It was
Henchard's, who stood regarding him.

"Do you remember," said Henchard, as if it were the
presence of the thought and not of the man which made

him speak, "do you remember my story of that second woman—who suffered for her thoughtless intimacy with me?"

"I do," said Farfrae.

"Do you remember my telling 'ee how it all began and how it ended?"

"Yes."

"Well, I have offered to marry her now that I can; but she won't marry me. Now what would you think of her—I put it to you?"

"Well, ye owe her nothing more now," said Farfrae heartily.

"It is true," said Henchard, and went on.

That he had looked up from a letter to ask his questions completely shut out from Farfrae's mind all vision of Lucetta as the culprit. Indeed, her present position was so different from that of the young woman of Henchard's story as of itself to be sufficient to blind him absolutely to her identity. As for Henchard, he was reassured by Farfrae's words and manner against a suspicion which had crossed his mind. They were not those of a conscious rival.

Yet that there was rivalry by some one he was firmly persuaded. He could feel it in the air around Lucetta, see it in the turn of her pen. There was an antagonistic force in exercise, so that when he had tried to hang near her he seemed standing in a refluent current. That it was not innate caprice he was more and more certain. Her windows gleamed as if they did not want him; her curtains seemed to hang slily, as if they screened an ousting presence. To discover whose presence that was—whether really Farfrae's after all, or another's—he exerted himself to the utmost to see her again; and at length succeeded.

At the interview, when she offered him tea, he made it a point to launch a cautious inquiry if she knew Mr. Farfrae.

Oh yes, she knew him, she declared; she could not help knowing almost everybody in Casterbridge, living in such a gazebo over the center and arena of the town.

"Pleasant young fellow," said Henchard.

"Yes," said Lucetta.

"We both know him," said kind Elizabeth-Jane, to relieve her companion's divined embarrassment.

There was a knock at the door; literally, three full knocks and a little one at the end.

"That kind of knock means half-and-half—somebody between gentle and simple," said the corn-merchant to himself. "I shouldn't wonder therefore if it is he." In a few seconds surely enough Donald walked in.

Lucetta was full of little fidgets and flutters, which increased Henchard's suspicions without affording any special proof of their correctness. He was well-nigh ferocious at the sense of the queer situation in which he stood towards this woman. One who had reproached him for deserting her when calumniated, who had urged claims upon his consideration on that account, who had lived waiting for him, who at the first decent moment had come to ask him to rectify, by making her his, the false position into which she had placed herself for his sake; such she had been. And now he sat at her tea-table eager to gain her attention, and in his amatory rage feeling the other man present to be a villain, just as any young fool of a lover might feel.

They sat stiffly side by side at the darkening table, like some Tuscan painting of the two disciples supping at Emmaus. Lucetta, forming the third and haloed figure, was opposite them; Elizabeth-Jane, being out of the game, and out of the group, could observe all from afar, like the evangelist who had to write it down: that there were long spaces of taciturnity, when all exterior circumstance was subdued to the touch of spoons and china, the click of a heel on the pavement under the window, the passing of a wheelbarrow or cart, the whistling of the carter, the gush of water into householders' buckets at the town-pump opposite; the exchange of greetings among their neighbors, and the rattle of the yokes by which they carried off their evening supply.

"More bread-and-butter?" said Lucetta to Henchard and

Farfrae equally, holding out between them a plateful of long slices. Henchard took a slice by one end and Donald by the other; each feeling certain he was the man meant; neither let go, and the slice came in two.

"Oh—I am so sorry!" cried Lucetta, with a nervous titter. Farfrae tried to laugh; but he was too much in love to see the incident in any but a tragic light.

"How ridiculous of all three of them!" said Elizabeth to herself.

Henchard left the house with a ton of conjecture, though without a grain of proof, that the counter-attraction was Farfrae; and therefore he would not make up his mind. Yet to Elizabeth-Jane it was plain as the town-pump that Donald and Lucetta were incipient lovers. More than once, in spite of her care, Lucetta had been unable to restrain her glance from flitting across into Farfrae's eyes like a bird to its nest. But Henchard was constructed upon too large a scale to discern such minutiæ as these by an evening light, which to him were as the notes of an insect that lie above the compass of the human ear.

But he was disturbed. And the sense of occult rivalry in suitorship was so much superadded to the palpable rivalry of their business lives. To the coarse materiality of that rivalry it added an inflaming soul.

The thus vitalized antagonism took the form of action by Henchard sending for Jopp, the manager originally displaced by Farfrae's arrival. Henchard had frequently met this man about the streets, observed that his clothing spoke of neediness, heard that he lived in Mixen Lane— a back slum of the town, the *pis aller* of Casterbridge domiciliation—itself almost a proof that a man had reached a stage when he would not stick at trifles.

Jopp came after dark, by the gates of the store-yard, and felt his way through the hay and straw to the office where Henchard sat in solitude awaiting him.

"I am again out of a foreman," said the corn-factor. "Are you in a place?"

"Not so much as a beggar's, sir."

"How much do you ask?"

Jopp named his price, which was very moderate.

"When can you come?"

"At this hour and moment, sir," said Jopp, who, standing hands-pocketed at the street corner till the sun had faded the shoulders of his coat to scarecrow green, had regularly watched Henchard in the market-place, measured him, and learnt him, by virtue of the power which the still man has in his stillness of knowing the busy one better than he knows himself. Jopp, too, had had a convenient experience; he was the only one in Casterbridge besides Henchard and the close-lipped Elizabeth who knew that Lucetta came truly from Jersey, and but proximately from Bath. "I know Jersey, too, sir," he said. "Was living there when you used to do business that way. Oh yes—have often seen ye there."

"Indeed! Very good. Then the thing is settled. The testimonials you showed me when you first tried for't are sufficient."

That characters deteriorate in time of need possibly did not occur to Henchard. Jopp said, "Thank you," and stood more firmly, in the consciousness that at last he officially belonged to that spot.

"Now," said Henchard, digging his strong eyes into Jopp's face, "one thing is necessary to me, as the biggest corn-and-hay-dealer in these parts. The Scotchman, who's taking the town trade so bold in his hands, must be cut out. D'ye hear? We two can't live side by side—that's clear and certain."

"I've seen it all," said Jopp.

"By fair competition I mean, of course," Henchard continued. "But as hard, keen, and unflinching as fair—rather more so. By such a desperate bid against him for the farmers' custom as will grind him into the ground—starve him out. I've capital, mind ye, and I can do it."

"I'm all that way of thinking," said the new foreman. Jopp's dislike of Farfrae as the man who had once usurped his place, while it made him a willing tool, made him, at the same time, commercially as unsafe a colleague as Henchard could have chosen.

"I sometimes think," he added, "that he must have some glass that he sees next year in. He has such a knack of making everything bring him fortune."

"He's deep beyond all honest men's discerning; but we must make him shallower. We'll under-sell him, and over-buy him, and so snuff him out."

They then entered into specific details of the process by which this would be accomplished, and parted at a late hour.

Elizabeth-Jane heard by accident that Jopp had been engaged by her stepfather. She was so fully convinced that he was not the right man for the place that, at the risk of making Henchard angry, she expressed her apprehension to him when they met. But it was done to no purpose. Henchard shut up her argument with a sharp rebuff.

The season's weather seemed to favor their scheme. The time was in the years immediately before foreign competition had revolutionized the trade in grain; when still, as from the earliest ages, the wheat quotations from month to month depended entirely upon the home harvest. A bad harvest, or the prospect of one, would double the price of corn in a few weeks; and the promise of a good yield would lower it as rapidly. Prices were like the roads of the period, steep in gradient, reflecting in their phases the local conditions, without engineering, levellings, or averages.

The farmer's income was ruled by the wheat-crop within his own horizon, and the wheat-crop by the weather. Thus, in person, he became a sort of flesh-barometer, with feelers always directed to the sky and wind around him. The local atmosphere was everything to him; the atmospheres of other countries a matter of indifference. The people, too, who were not farmers, the rural multitude, saw in the god of the weather a more important personage than they do now. Indeed, the feeling of the peasantry in this matter was so intense as to be almost unrealizable in these equable days. Their impulse was well-nigh to prostrate themselves in lamentation before untimely rains and tempests, which came as the Alastor of those households whose crime it was to be poor.

After midsummer they watched the weather-cocks as men waiting in antechambers watch the lackey. Sun elated them; quiet rain sobered them; weeks of watery tempest stupefied them. That aspect of the sky which they now regard as disagreeable they then beheld as maleficent.

It was June, and the weather was very unfavorable. Casterbridge, being as it were the bell-board on which all the adjacent hamlets and villages sounded their notes, was decidedly dull. Instead of new articles in the shop-windows those that had been rejected in the foregoing summer were brought out again; superseded reap-hooks, badly-shaped rakes, shop-worn leggings, and time-stiffened water-tights reappeared, furbished up as near to new as possible.

Henchard, backed by Jopp, read a disastrous garnering, and resolved to base his strategy against Farfrae upon that reading. But before acting he wished—what so many have wished—that he could know for certain what was at present only strong probability. He was superstitious—as such headstrong natures often are—and he nourished in his mind an idea bearing on the matter; an idea he shrank from disclosing even to Jopp.

In a lonely hamlet a few miles from the town—so lonely that what are called lonely villages were teeming by comparison—there lived a man of curious repute as a forecaster or weather-prophet. The way to his house was crooked and miry—even difficult in the present unpropitious season. One evening when it was raining so heavily that ivy and laurel resounded like distant musketry, and an out-door man could be excused for shrouding himself to his ears and eyes, such a shrouded figure on foot might have been perceived travelling in the direction of the hazel-copse which dripped over the prophet's cot. The turnpike-road became a lane, the lane a cart-track, the cart-track a bridle-path, the bridle-path a foot-way, the foot-way over-grown. The solitary walker slipped here and there, and stumbled over the natural springes formed by the brambles, till at length he reached the house, which, with its garden, was surrounded with a high, dense hedge. The cottage, comparatively a large one, had been built of mud by the occupier's own hands, and thatched also by himself. Here he had always lived, and here it was assumed he would die.

He existed on unseen supplies; for it was an anomalous thing that while there was hardly a soul in the neighborhood but affected to laugh at this man's assertions, uttering the formula, "There's nothing in 'em," with full assurance on the surface of their faces, very few of them were unbelievers in their secret hearts. Whenever they consulted him they did it "for a fancy." When they paid him they said, "Just a trifle for Christmas," or "Candlemas," as the case might be.

He would have preferred more honesty in his clients, and less sham ridicule; but fundamental belief consoled him for superficial irony. As stated, he was enabled to live; people supported him with their backs turned. He was sometimes astonished that men could profess so little and believe so much at his house, when at church they professed so much and believed so little.

Behind his back he was called "Wide-oh," on account of his reputation; to his face "Mr." Fall.

The hedge of his garden formed an arch over the entrance, and a door was inserted as in a wall. Outside the door the tall traveller stopped, bandaged his face with a handkerchief as if he were suffering from toothache, and went up the path. The window shutters were not closed, and he could see the prophet within, preparing his supper.

In answer to the knock Fall came to the door, candle in hand. The visitor stepped back a little from the light, and said, "Can I speak to 'ee?" in significant tones. The other's invitation to come in was responded to by the country formula, "This will do, thank 'ee," after which the householder has no alternative but to come out. He placed the candle on the corner of the dresser, took his hat from a nail, and joined the stranger in the porch, shutting the door behind him.

"I've long heard that you can—do things of a sort?"

began the other, repressing his individuality as much as he could.

"Maybe so, Mr. Henchard," said the weather-caster.

"Ah—why do you call me that?" asked the visitor with a start.

"Because it's your name. Feeling you'd come I've waited for 'ee; and thinking you might be leery from your walk I laid two supper plates—look ye here." He threw open the door and disclosed the supper-table, at which appeared a second chair, knife and fork, plate and mug, as he had declared.

Henchard felt like Saul at his reception by Samuel; he remained in silence for a few moments, then throwing off the disguise of frigidity which he had hitherto preserved he said, "Then I have not come in vain. . . . Now, for instance, can ye charm away warts?"

"Without trouble."

"Cure the evil?"

"That I've done—with consideration—if they will wear the toad-bag by night as well as by day."

"Forecast the weather?"

"With labor and time."

"Then take this," said Henchard. " 'Tis a crown-piece. Now, what is the harvest fortnight to be? When can I know?"

"I've worked it out already, and you can know at once." (The fact was that five farmers had already been there on the same errand from different parts of the country.) "By the sun, moon, and stars, by the clouds, the winds, the trees, and grass, the candle-flame and swallows, the smell of the herbs; likewise by the cats' eyes, the ravens, the leeches, the spiders, and the dung-mixen, the last fortnight in August will be—rain and tempest."

"You are not certain, of course?"

"As one can be in a world where all's unsure. 'Twill be more like living in Revelations this autumn than in England. Shall I sketch it out for 'ee in a scheme?"

"Oh no, no," said Henchard. "I don't altogether believe in forecasts, come to second thoughts on such. But I——"

"You don't—you don't—'tis quite understood," said Wide-oh, without a sound of scorn. "You have given me a crown because you've one too many. But won't you join me at supper, now 'tis waiting and all?"

Henchard would gladly have joined; for the savor of the stew had floated from the cottage into the porch with such appetizing distinctness that the meat, the onions, the pepper, and the herbs could be severally recognized by his nose. But as sitting down to hob-and-nob there would have seemed to mark him too implicitly as the weather-caster's apostle, he declined, and went his way.

The next Saturday Henchard bought grain to such an enormous extent that there was quite a talk about his purchases among his neighbors the lawyer, the wine-merchant, and the doctor; also on the next, and on all available days. When his granaries were full to choking, all the weathercocks of Casterbridge creaked and set their faces in another direction, as if tired of the south-west. The weather changed; the sunlight, which had been like tin for weeks, assumed the hues of topaz. The temperament of the welkin passed from the phlegmatic to the sanguine; an excellent harvest was almost a certainty; and as a consequence prices rushed down.

All these transformations, lovely to the outsider, to the wrongheaded corn-dealer were terrible. He was reminded of what he had well known before, that a man might gamble upon the square green areas of fields as readily as upon those of a card-room.

Henchard had backed bad weather, and apparently lost. He had mistaken the turn of the flood for the turn of the ebb. His dealings had been so extensive that settlement could not long be postponed, and to settle he was obliged to sell off corn that he had bought only a few weeks before at figures higher by many shillings a quarter. Much of the corn he had never seen; it had not even been moved from the ricks in which it lay stacked miles away. Thus he lost heavily.

In the blaze of an early August day he met Farfrae in the market-place. Farfrae knew of his dealings (though he did not guess their intended bearing on himself) and commiserated him; for since their exchange of words in the South Walk they had been on stiffly speaking terms. Henchard for the moment appeared to resent the sympathy; but he suddenly took a careless turn.

"Ho, no, no!—nothing serious, man!" he cried with fierce gaiety. "These things always happen, don't they? I know it has been said that figures have touched me tight lately; but is that anything rare? The case is not so bad as folk make out perhaps. And dammy, a man must be a fool to mind the common hazards of trade!"

But he had to enter the Casterbridge Bank that day for reasons which had never before sent him there—and to sit a long time in the partners' room with a constrained bearing. It was rumored soon after that much real property as well as vast stores of produce, which had stood in Henchard's name in the town and neighborhood, was actually the possession of his bankers.

Coming down the steps of the bank he encountered Jopp. The gloomy transactions just completed within had added fever to the original sting of Farfrae's sympathy that morning, which Henchard fancied might be satire disguised, so that Jopp met with anything but a bland reception. The latter was in the act of taking off his hat to wipe his forehead, and saying, "A fine hot day," to an acquaintance.

"You can wipe and wipe, and say, 'A fine hot day,' can ye!" cried Henchard in a savage undertone, imprisoning Jopp between himself and the bank wall. "If it hadn't been for your blasted advice it might have been a fine day enough! Why did ye let me go on, hey?—when a word of doubt from you or anybody would have made me think twice! For you can never be sure of weather till 'tis past."

"My advice, sir, was to do what you thought best."

"A useful fellow! And the sooner you help somebody else in that way the better!" Henchard continued his address to Jopp in similar terms till it ended in Jopp's dismissal there and then, Henchard turning upon his heel and leaving him.

"You shall be sorry for this, sir; sorry as a man can be!" said Jopp, standing pale, and looking after the corn-merchant as he disappeared in the crowd of market-men hard by.

XXVII

It was the eve of harvest. Prices being low Farfrae was buying. As was usual, after reckoning too surely on famine weather the local farmers had flown to the other extreme, and (in Farfrae's opinion) were selling off too recklessly—calculating with just a trifle too much certainty upon an abundant yield. So he went on buying old corn at its comparatively ridiculous price: for the produce of the previous year, though not large, had been of excellent quality.

When Henchard had squared his affairs in a disastrous way, and got rid of his burdensome purchases at a monstrous loss, the harvest began. There were three days of excellent weather, and then—"What if that curst conjuror should be right after all!" said Henchard.

The fact was, that no sooner had the sickles begun to play than the atmosphere suddenly felt as if cress would grow in it without other nourishment. It rubbed people's cheeks like damp flannel when they walked abroad. There was a gusty, high, warm wind; isolated raindrops starred the window-panes at remote distances: the sunlight would flap out like a quickly opened fan, throw the pattern of the window upon the floor of the room in a milky, color-less shine, and withdraw as suddenly as it had appeared.

From that day and hour it was clear that there was not to be so successful an ingathering after all. If Henchard had only waited long enough he might at least have avoided loss though he had not made a profit. But the momentum of his character knew no patience. At this turn of the scales he remained silent. The movements of his mind seemed to tend to the thought that some power was working against him.

"I wonder," he asked himself with eerie misgiving; "I

wonder if it can be that somebody has been roasting a waxen image of me, or stirring an unholy brew to confound me! I don't believe in such power; and yet—what if they should ha' been doing it!" Even he could not admit that the perpetrator, if any, might be Farfrae. These isolated hours of superstition came to Henchard in time of moody depression, when all his practical largeness of view had oozed out of him.

Meanwhile Donald Farfrae prospered. He had purchased in so depressed a market that the present moderate stiffness of prices was sufficient to pile for him a large heap of gold where a little one had been.

"Why, he'll soon be Mayor!" said Henchard. It was indeed hard that the speaker should, of all others, have to follow the triumphal chariot of this man to the Capitol.

The rivalry of the masters was taken up by the men.

September-night shades had fallen upon Casterbridge; the clocks had struck half-past eight, and the moon had risen. The streets of the town were curiously silent for such a comparatively early hour. A sound of jangling horse-bells and heavy wheels passed up the street. These were followed by angry voices outside Lucetta's house, which led her and Elizabeth-Jane to run to the windows, and pull up the blinds.

The neighboring Market House and Town Hall abutted against its next neighbor the Church except in the lower storey, where an arched thoroughfare gave admittance to a large square called Bull Stake. A stone post rose in the midst, to which the oxen had formerly been tied for baiting with dogs to make them tender before they were killed in the adjoining shambles. In a corner stood the stocks.

The thoroughfare leading to this spot was now blocked by two four-horse wagons and horses, one laden with hay-trusses, the leaders having already passed each other, and become entangled head to tail. The passage of the vehicles might have been practicable if empty; but built up with hay to the bedroom windows as one was, it was impossible.

"You must have done it a' purpose!" said Farfrae's

wagoner. "You can hear my horses' bells half-a-mile such a night as this!"

"If ye'd been minding your business instead of zwailing along in such a gawk-hammer way, you would have zeed me!" retorted the wroth representative of Henchard.

However, according to the strict rule of the road it appeared that Henchard's man was most in the wrong; he therefore attempted to back into the High Street. In doing this the near hind-wheel rose against the churchyard wall, and the whole mountainous load went over, two of the four wheels rising in the air, and the legs of the thill horse.

Instead of considering how to gather up the load the two men closed in a fight with their fists. Before the first round was quite over Henchard came upon the spot, somebody having run for him.

Henchard sent the two men staggering in contrary directions by collaring one with each hand, turned to the horse that was down, and extricated him after some trouble. He then inquired into the circumstances; and seeing the state of his wagon and its load began hotly rating Farfrae's man.

Lucetta and Elizabeth-Jane had by this time run down to the street corner, whence they watched the bright heap of new hay lying in the moon's rays, and passed and re-passed by the forms of Henchard and the wagoners. The women had witnessed what nobody else had seen— the origin of the mishap; and Lucetta spoke.

"I saw it all, Mr. Henchard," she cried; "and your man was most in the wrong!"

Henchard paused in his harangue and turned. "Oh, I didn't notice you, Miss Templeman," said he. "My man in the wrong? Ah, to be sure; to be sure! But I beg your pardon notwithstanding. The other's is the empty wagon, and he must have been most to blame for coming on."

"No; I saw it, too," said Elizabeth-Jane. "And I can assure you he couldn't help it."

"You can't trust *their* senses!" murmured Henchard's man.

"Why not?" asked Henchard sharply.

"Why, you see, sir, all the women side with Farfrae—being a damn young dand—of the sort that he is—one that creeps into a maid's heart like the giddying worm into a sheep's brain—making crooked seem straight to their eyes!"

"But do you know who that lady is you talk about in such a fashion? Do you know that I pay my attentions to her, and have for some time? Just be careful!"

"Not I. I know nothing, sir, outside eight shillings a week."

"And that Mr. Farfrae is well aware of it? He's sharp in trade, but he wouldn't do anything so under-hand as what you hint at."

Whether because Lucetta heard this low dialogue, or not, her white figure disappeared from her doorway inward, and the door was shut before Henchard could reach it to converse with her further. This disappointed him, for he had been sufficiently disturbed by what the man had said to wish to speak to her more closely. While pausing the old constable came up.

"Just see that nobody drives against that hay and wagon tonight, Stubberd," said the corn-merchant. "It must bide till the morning, for all hands are in the fields still. And if any coach or road-wagon wants to come along, tell 'em they must go round by the back street, and be hanged to 'em. . . . Any case to-morrow up in Hall?"

"Yes, sir. One in number, sir."

"Oh, what's that?"

"An old flagrant female, sir, swearing and committing a nuisance in a horrible profane manner against the church wall, sir, as if 'twere no more than a pot-house! That's all, sir."

"Oh. The Mayor's out o' town, isn't he?"

"He is, sir."

"Very well, then I'll be there. Don't forget to keep an eye on that hay. Good night t' 'ee."

During those moments Henchard had determined to follow up Lucetta, notwithstanding her elusiveness, and he knocked for admission.

The answer he received was an expression of Miss Templeman's sorrow at being unable to see him again that evening because she had an engagement to go out.

Henchard walked away from the door to the opposite side of the street, and stood by his hay in a lonely reverie, the constable having strolled elsewhere, and the horses being removed. Though the moon was not bright as yet there were no lamps lighted, and he entered the shadow of one of the projecting jambs which formed the thoroughfare to Bull Stake; here he watched Lucetta's door.

Candle-lights were flitting in and out of her bedroom, and it was obvious that she was dressing for the appointment, whatever the nature of that might be at such an hour. The lights disappeared, the clock struck nine, and almost at the moment Farfrae came round the opposite corner and knocked. That she had been waiting just inside for him was certain, for she instantly opened the door herself. They went together by the way of a back lane westward, avoiding the front street; guessing where they were going he determined to follow.

The harvest had been so delayed by the capricious weather that whenever a fine day occurred all sinews were strained to save what could be saved of the damaged crops. On account of the rapid shortening of the days the harvesters worked by moonlight. Hence to-night the wheat-fields abutting on the two sides of the square formed by Casterbridge town were animated by the gathering hands. Their shouts and laughter had reached Henchard at the Market House, while he stood there waiting, and he had little doubt from the turn which Farfrae and Lucetta had taken that they were bound for the spot.

Nearly the whole town had gone into the fields. The Casterbridge populace still retained the primitive habit of helping one another in time of need; and thus, though the corn belonged to the farming section of the little community—that inhabiting the Durnover quarter—the remainder was no less interested in the labor of getting it home.

Reaching the end of the lane Henchard crossed the

shaded avenue on the walls, slid down the green rampart, and stood amongst the stubble. The "stitches" or shocks rose like tents about the yellow expanse, those in the distance becoming lost in the moonlit hazes.

He had entered at a point removed from the scene of immediate operations; but two others had entered at that place, and he could see them winding among the shocks. They were paying no regard to the direction of their walk, whose vague serpentining soon began to bear down towards Henchard. A meeting promised to be awkward, and he therefore stepped into the hollow of the nearest shock, and sat down.

"You have my leave," Lucetta was saying gaily. "Speak what you like."

"Well, then," replied Farfrae, with the unmistakable inflection of the lover pure, which Henchard had never heard in full resonance on his lips before, "you are sure to be much sought after for your position, wealth, talents, and beauty. But will ye resist the temptation to be one of those ladies with lots of admirers—ay—and be content to have only a homely one?"

"And he the speaker?" said she, laughing. "Very well, sir, what next?"

"Ah! I'm afraid that what I feel will make me forget my manners!"

"Then I hope you'll never have any, if you lack them only for that cause." After some broken words which Henchard lost she added, "Are you sure you won't be jealous?"

Farfrae seemed to assure her that he would not, by taking her hand.

"You are convinced, Donald, that I love nobody else," she presently said. "But I should wish to have my own way in some things."

"In everything! What special thing did you mean?"

"If I wished not to live always in Casterbridge, for instance, on finding that I should not be happy here?"

Henchard did not hear the reply; he might have done so and much more, but he did not care to play the eavesdropper. They went on towards the scene of activity, where the sheaves were being handed, a dozen a minute, upon the carts and wagons which carried them away.

Lucetta insisted on parting from Farfrae when they drew near the workpeople. He had some business with them and, though he entreated her to wait a few minutes, she was inexorable, and tripped off homeward alone.

Henchard thereupon left the field and followed her. His state of mind was such that on reaching Lucetta's door he did not knock but opened it, and walked straight up to her sitting-room, expecting to find her there. But the room was empty, and he perceived that in his haste he had somehow passed her on the way hither. He had not to wait many minutes, however, for he soon heard her dress rustling in the hall, followed by a soft closing of the door. In a moment she appeared.

The light was so low that she did not notice Henchard at first. As soon as she saw him she uttered a little cry, almost of terror.

"How can you frighten me so?" she exclaimed, with a flushed face. "It is past ten o'clock, and you have no right to surprise me here at such a time."

"I don't know that I've not the right. At any rate I have the excuse. Is it so necessary that I should stop to think of manners and customs?"

"It is too late for propriety, and might injure me."

"I called an hour ago, and you would not see me, and I thought you were in when I called now. It is you, Lucetta, who are doing wrong. It is not proper in 'ee to throw me over like this. I have a little matter to remind you of, which you seem to forget."

She sank into a chair, and turned pale.

"I don't want to hear it—I don't want to hear it!" she said through her hands, as he, standing close to the edge of her gown, began to allude to the Jersey days.

"But you ought to hear it," said he.

"It came to nothing; and through you. Then why not leave me the freedom that I gained with such sorrow! Had I found that you proposed to marry me for pure love I might have felt bound now. But I soon learnt that you had planned it out of mere charity—almost as an unpleasant duty—because I had nursed you, and compromised myself, and you thought you must repay me. After that I did not care for you so deeply as before."

"Why did you come here to find me, then?"

"I thought I ought to marry you for conscience' sake, since you were free, even though I—did not like you so well."

"And why then don't you think so now?"

She was silent. It was only too obvious that conscience had ruled well enough till new love had intervened and usurped that rule. In feeling this she herself forgot for the moment her partially justifying argument—that having discovered Henchard's infirmities of temper, she had some excuse for not risking her happiness in his hands after once escaping them. The only thing she could say was, "I was a poor girl then; and now my circumstances have altered, so I am hardly the same person."

"That's true. And it makes the case awkward for me. But I don't want to touch your money. I am quite willing that every penny of your property shall remain to your personal use. Besides, that argument has nothing in it. The man you are thinking of is no better than I."

"If you were as good as he you would leave me!" she cried passionately.

This unluckily aroused Henchard. "You cannot in honor refuse me," he said. "And unless you give me your promise this very night to be my wife, before a witness, I'll reveal our intimacy—in common fairness to other men!"

A look of resignation settled upon her. Henchard saw its bitterness; and had Lucetta's heart been given to any other man in the world than Farfrae he would probably have had pity upon her at that moment. But the supplanter was the upstart (as Henchard called him) who had mounted into prominence upon his shoulders, and he could bring himself to show no mercy.

Without another word he rang the bell, and directed

that Elizabeth-Jane should be fetched from her room. The latter appeared, surprised in the midst of her lucubrations. As soon as she saw Henchard she went across to him dutifully.

"Elizabeth-Jane," he said, taking her hand, "I want you to hear this." And turning to Lucetta: "Will you, or will not you, marry me?"

"If you—wish it, I must agree!"

"You say yes?"

"I do."

No sooner had she given the promise than she fell back in a fainting state.

"What dreadful thing drives her to say this, father, when it is such a pain to her?" asked Elizabeth, kneeling down by Lucetta. "Don't compel her to do anything against her will! I have lived with her, and know that she cannot bear much."

"Don't be a no'thern simpleton!" said Henchard drily. "This promise will leave him free for you, if you want him, won't it?"

At this Lucetta seemed to wake from her swoon with a start.

"Him? Who are you talking about?" she said wildly.

"Nobody, as far as I am concerned," said Elizabeth firmly.

"Oh—well. Then it is my mistake," said Henchard. "But the business is between me and Miss Templeman. She agrees to be my wife."

"But don't dwell on it just now," entreated Elizabeth, holding Lucetta's hand.

"I don't wish to, if she promises," said Henchard.

"I have, I have," groaned Lucetta, her limbs hanging like flails, from very misery and faintness. "Michael, please don't argue it any more!"

"I will not," he said. And taking up his hat he went away.

Elizabeth-Jane continued to kneel by Lucetta. "What is this?" she said. "You called my father 'Michael' as if you knew him well? And how is it he has got this power over you, that you promise to marry him against your will? Ah—you have many, many secrets from me!"

"Perhaps you have some from me," Lucetta murmured with closed eyes, little thinking, however, so unsuspicious was she, that the secret of Elizabeth's heart concerned the young man who had caused this damage to her own.

"I would not—do anything against you at all!" stammered Elizabeth, keeping in all signs of emotion till she was ready to burst. "I cannot understand how my father can command you so; I don't sympathize with him in it at all. I'll go to him and ask him to release you."

"No, no," said Lucetta. "Let it all be."

XXVIII

The next morning Henchard went to the Town Hall below Lucetta's house, to attend Petty Sessions, being still a magistrate for the year by virtue of his late position as Mayor. In passing he looked up at her windows, but nothing of her was to be seen.

Henchard as a Justice of the Peace may at first seem to be an even greater incongruity than Shallow and Silence themselves. But his rough and ready perceptions, his sledge-hammer directness, had often served him better than nice legal knowledge in despatching such simple business as fell to his hands in this Court. To-day Dr. Chalkfield, the Mayor for the year, being absent, the cornmerchant took the big chair, his eyes still abstractedly stretching out of the window to the ashlar front of High-Place Hall.

There was one case only, and the offender stood before him. She was an old woman of mottled countenance, attired in a shawl of that nameless tertiary hue which comes, but cannot be made—a hue neither tawny, russet, hazel, nor ash; a sticky black bonnet that seemed to have been worn in the country of the Psalmist where the clouds drop fatness; and an apron that had been white in times so comparatively recent as still to contrast visibly with the rest of her clothes. The steeped aspect of the woman as a whole showed her to be no native of the country-side or even of a country-town.

She looked cursorily at Henchard and the second magistrate, and Henchard looked at her, with a momentary pause, as if she had reminded him indistinctly of somebody or something which passed from his mind as quickly as it had come. "Well, and what has she been doing?" he said, looking down at the charge-sheet.

"She is charged, sir, with the offense of disorderly female and nuisance," whispered Stubberd.

"Where did she do that?" said the other magistrate.

"By the church, sir, of all the horrible places in the world!—I caught her in the act, your worship."

"Stand back then," said Henchard, "and let's hear what you've got to say."

Stubberd was sworn, the magistrate's clerk dipped his pen, Henchard being no note-taker himself, and the constable began—

"Hearing a' illegal noise I went down the street at twenty-five minutes past eleven P.M. on the night of the fifth instinct, Hannah Dominy. When I had——"

"Don't go on so fast, Stubberd," said the clerk.

The constable waited, with his eyes on the clerk's pen, till the latter stopped scratching and said, "yes." Stubberd continued: "When I had proceeded to the spot I saw defendant at another spot, namely, the gutter." He paused, watching the point of the clerk's pen again.

"Gutter, yes, Stubberd."

"Spot measuring twelve feet nine inches or thereabouts, from where I——" Still careful not to outrun the clerk's penmanship, Stubberd pulled up again; for having got his evidence by heart it was immaterial to him whereabouts he broke off.

"I object to that," spoke up the old woman, " 'spot measuring twelve feet nine or thereabouts from where I,' is not sound testimony!"

The magistrates consulted, and the second one said that the bench was of opinion that twelve feet nine inches from a man on his oath was admissible.

Stubberd, with a suppressed gaze of victorious rectitude

at the old woman, continued: "Was standing myself. She was wambling about quite dangerous to the thoroughfare, and when I approached to draw near she committed the nuisance, and insulted me."

" 'Insulted me.' . . . Yes, what did she say?"

"She said, 'Put away that dee lantern,' she says."

"Yes."

"Says she, 'Dost hear, old turmit-head? Put away that dee lantern. I have floored fellows a dee sight finer-looking than a dee fool like thee, you son of a bee, dee me if I haint,' she says."

"I object to that conversation!" interposed the old woman. "I was not capable enough to hear what I said, and what is said out of my hearing is not evidence."

There was another stoppage for consultation, a book was referred to, and finally Stubberd was allowed to go on again. The truth was that the old woman had appeared in court so many more times than the magistrates themselves, that they were obliged to keep a sharp look-out upon their procedure. However, when Stubberd had rambled on a little further Henchard broke out impatiently, "Come—we don't want to hear any more of them cust dees and bees! Say the words out like a man, and don't be so modest, Stubberd; or else leave it alone!" Turning to the woman, "Now then, have you any questions to ask him, or anything to say?"

"Yes," she replied with a twinkle in her eye; and the clerk dipped his pen.

"Twenty years ago or thereabout I was a selling of furmity in a tent at Weydon Fair——"

" 'Twenty years ago'—well, that's beginning at the beginning; suppose you go back to the Creation!" said the clerk, not without satire.

But Henchard stared, and quite forgot what was evidence and what was not.

"A man and a woman with a little child came into my tent," the woman continued. "They sat down and had a basin apiece. Ah, Lord's my life! I was of a more respectable station in the world then than I am now, being a land smuggler in a large way of business; and I used to season my furmity with rum for them who asked for't. I did it for the man; and then he had more and more; till at last he quarrelled with his wife, and offered to sell her to the highest bidder. A sailor came in and bid five guineas, and paid the money, and led her away. And the man who sold his wife in that fashion is the man sitting there in the great big chair." The speaker concluded by nodding her head at Henchard and folding her arms.

Everybody looked at Henchard. His face seemed strange, and in tint as if it had been powdered over with ashes. "We don't want to hear your life and adventures," said the second magistrate sharply, filling the pause which followed. "You've been asked if you've anything to say bearing on the case."

"That bears on the case. It proves that he's no better than I, and has no right to sit there in judgment upon me."

" 'Tis a concocted story," said the clerk. "So hold your tongue!"

"No—'tis true." The words came from Henchard. " 'Tis as true as the light," he said slowly. "And upon my soul it does prove that I'm no better than she! And to keep out of any temptation to treat her hard for her revenge, I'll leave her to you."

The sensation in the court was indescribably great. Henchard left the chair, and came out, passing through a group of people on the steps and outside that was much larger than usual; for it seemed that the old furmity dealer had mysteriously hinted to the denizens of the lane in which she had been lodging since her arrival, that she knew a queer thing or two about their great local man Mr. Henchard, if she chose to tell it. This had brought them hither.

"Why are there so many idlers round the Town Hall to-day?" said Lucetta to her servant when the case was over. She had risen late, and had just looked out of the window.

"Oh, please, ma'am, 'tis this larry about Mr. Henchard. A woman has proved that before he became a gentleman he sold his wife for five guineas in a booth at a fair."

In all the accounts which Henchard had given her of the separation from his wife Susan for so many years, of his belief in her death, and so on, he had never clearly explained the actual and immediate cause of that separation. The story she now heard for the first time.

A gradual misery overspread Lucetta's face as she dwelt upon the promise wrung from her the night before. At bottom, then, Henchard was this. How terrible a contingency for a woman who should commit herself to his case.

During the day she went out to the Ring and to other places, not coming in till nearly dusk. As soon as she saw Elizabeth-Jane after her return indoors she told her that she had resolved to go away from home to the seaside for a few days—to Port-Bredy; Casterbridge was so gloomy.

Elizabeth, seeing that she looked wan and disturbed, encouraged her in the idea, thinking a change would afford her relief. She could not help suspecting that the gloom which seemed to have come over Casterbridge in Lucetta's eyes might be partially owing to the fact that Farfrae was away from home.

Elizabeth saw her friend depart for Port-Bredy, and took charge of High-Place Hall till her return. After two or three days of solitude and incessant rain Henchard called at the house. He seemed disappointed to hear of Lucetta's absence, and though he nodded with outward indifference he went away handling his beard with a nettled mien.

The next day he called again. "Is she come now?" he asked.

"Yes. She returned this morning," replied his step-daughter. "But she is not indoors. She has gone for a walk along the turnpike-road to Port-Bredy. She will be home by dusk."

After a few words, which only served to reveal his restless impatience, he left the house again.

XXIX

At this hour Lucetta was bounding along the road to
Port-Bredy just as Elizabeth had announced. That she
had chosen for her afternoon walk the road along which
she had returned to Casterbridge three hours earlier in
a carriage was curious—if anything should be called curious in concatenations of phenomena wherein each is known
to have its accounting cause. It was the day of the chief
market—Saturday—and Farfrae for once had been missed
from his corn-stand in the dealers' room. Nevertheless, it
was known that he would be home that night—"for Sunday," as Casterbridge expressed it.

Lucetta, in continuing her walk, had at length reached
the end of the ranked trees which bordered the highway
in this and other directions out of the town. This end
marked a mile; and here she stopped.

The spot was a vale between two gentle acclivities, and
the road, still adhering to its Roman foundation, stretched
onward straight as a surveyor's line till lost to sight on
the most distant ridge. There was neither hedge nor tree
in the prospect now, the road clinging to the stubbly
expanse of corn-land like a stripe to an undulating garment. Near her was a barn—the single building of any
kind within her horizon.

She strained her eyes up the lessening road, but nothing
appeared thereon—not so much as a speck. She sighed
one word—"Donald!" and turned her face to the town
for retreat.

Here the case was different. A single figure was approaching her—Elizabeth-Jane's.

Lucetta, in spite of her loneliness, seemed a little vexed.
Elizabeth's face, as soon as she recognized her friend,
shaped itself into affectionate lines while yet beyond speaking distance. "I suddenly thought I would come and meet
you," she said, smiling.

Lucetta's reply was taken from her lips by an unexpected diversion. A by-road on her right hand descended
from the fields into the highway at the point where she

stood, and down the track a bull was rambling uncertainly towards her and Elizabeth, who, facing the other way, did not observe him.

In the latter quarter of each year cattle were at once the mainstay and the terror of families about Casterbridge and its neighborhood, where breeding was carried on with Abrahamic success. The head of stock driven into and out of the town at this season to be sold by the local auctioneer was very large; and all these horned beasts, in travelling to and fro, sent women and children to shelter as nothing else could do. In the main the animals would have walked along quietly enough; but the Casterbridge tradition was that to drive stock it was indispensable that hideous cries, coupled with Yahoo antics and gestures, should be used, large sticks flourished, stray dogs called in, and in general everything done that was likely to infuriate the viciously disposed and terrify the mild. Nothing was commoner than for a householder on going out of his parlor to find his hall or passage full of little children, nursemaids, aged women, or a ladies' school, who apologized for their presence by saying, "A bull passing down street from the sale."

Lucetta and Elizabeth regarded the animal in doubt, he meanwhile drawing vaguely towards them. It was a large specimen of the breed, in color rich dun, though disfigured at present by spotches of mud about his seamy sides. His horns were thick and tipped with brass; his two nostrils like the Thames Tunnel as seen in the perspective toys of yore. Between them, through the gristle of his nose, was a stout copper ring, welded on, and irremovable as Gurth's collar of brass. To the ring was attached an ash staff about a yard long, which the bull with the motions of his head flung about like a flail.

It was not till they observed this dangling stick that the young women were really alarmed; for it revealed to them that the bull was an old one, too savage to be driven, which had in some way escaped, the staff being the means by which the drover controlled him and kept his horns at arms' length.

They looked round for some shelter or hiding-place, and thought of the barn hard by. As long as they had kept their eyes on the bull he had shown some deference in his manner of approach; but no sooner did they turn their backs to seek the barn than he tossed his head and decided to thoroughly terrify them. This caused the two helpless girls to run wildly, whereupon the bull advanced in a deliberate charge.

The barn stood behind a green slimy pond, and it was closed save as to one of the usual pair of doors facing them, which had been propped open by a hurdle-stake, and for this opening they made. The interior had been cleared by a recent bout of threshing except at one end, where there was a stack of dry clover. Elizabeth-Jane took in the situation. "We must climb up there," she said.

But before they had even approached it they heard the bull scampering through the pond without, and in a second he dashed into the barn, knocking down the hurdle-stake in passing; the heavy door slammed behind him; and all three were imprisoned in the barn together. The mistaken creature saw them, and stalked towards the end of the barn into which they had fled. The girls doubled so adroitly that their pursuer was against the wall when the fugitives were already half way to the other end. By the time that his length would allow him to turn and follow them thither they had crossed over; thus the pursuit went on, the hot air from his nostrils blowing over them like a sirocco, and not a moment being attainable by Elizabeth or Lucetta in which to open the door. What might have happened had their situation continued cannot be said; but in a few moments a rattling of the door distracted their adversary's attention, and a man appeared. He ran forward towards the leading-staff, seized it, and wrenched the animal's head as if he would snap it off. The wrench was in reality so violent that the thick neck seemed to have lost its stiffness and to become half paralyzed, whilst the nose dropped blood. The premeditated human contrivance of the nose-ring was too cunning for impulsive brute force, and the creature flinched.

The man was seen in the partial gloom to be large-framed and unhesitating. He led the bull to the door, and the light revealed Henchard. He made the bull fast without, and re-entered to the succor of Lucetta; for he had not perceived Elizabeth, who had climbed on to the clover-heap. Lucetta was hysterical, and Henchard took her in his arms and carried her to the door.

"You—have saved me!" she cried, as soon as she could speak.

"I have returned your kindness," he responded tenderly. "You once saved me."

"How—comes it to be you—you?" she asked, not heeding his reply.

"I came out here to look for you. I have been wanting to tell you something these two or three days; but you have been away, and I could not. Perhaps you cannot talk now?"

"Oh—no! Where is Elizabeth?"

"Here am I!" cried the missing one cheerfully; and without waiting for the ladder to be placed she slid down the face of the clover-stack to the floor.

Henchard supporting Lucetta on one side, and Elizabeth-Jane on the other, they went slowly along the rising road. They had reached the top and were descending again when Lucetta, now much recovered, recollected that she had dropped her muff in the barn.

"I'll run back," said Elizabeth-Jane. "I don't mind it at all, as I am not tired as you are." She thereupon hastened down again to the barn, the others pursuing their way.

Elizabeth soon found the muff, such an article being by no means small at that time. Coming out she paused to look for a moment at the bull, now rather to be pitied with his bleeding nose, having perhaps rather intended a practical joke than a murder. Henchard had secured him by jamming the staff into the hinge of the barn-door, and wedging it there with a stake. At length she turned to hasten onward after her contemplation, when she saw a green-and-black gig approaching from the contrary direction, the vehicle being driven by Farfrae.

His presence here seemed to explain Lucetta's walk that

way. Donald saw her, drew up, and was hastily made acquainted with what had occurred. At Elizabeth-Jane mentioning how greatly Lucetta had been jeopardized, he exhibited an agitation different in kind no less than in intensity from any she had seen in him before. He became so absorbed in the circumstances that he scarcely had sufficient knowledge of what he was doing to think of helping her up beside him.

"She has gone on with Mr. Henchard, you say?" he inquired at last.

"Yes. He is taking her home. They are almost there by this time."

"And you are sure she can get home?"

Elizabeth-Jane was quite sure.

"Your stepfather saved her?"

"Entirely."

Farfrae checked his horse's pace; she guessed why. He was thinking that it would be best not to intrude on the other two just now. Henchard had saved Lucetta, and to provoke a possible exhibition of her deeper affection for himself was as ungenerous as it was unwise.

The immediate subject of their talk being exhausted she felt more embarrassed at sitting thus beside her past lover; but soon the two figures of the others were visible at the entrance to the town. The face of the woman was frequently turned back, but Farfrae did not whip on the horse. When these reached the town walls Henchard and his companion had disappeared down the street; Farfrae set down Elizabeth-Jane on her expressing a particular wish to alight there, and drove round to the stables at the back of his lodgings.

On this account he entered the house through his garden, and going up to his apartments found them in a particularly disturbed state, his boxes being hauled out upon the landing, and his bookcase standing in three pieces. These phenomena, however, seemed to cause him not the least surprise. "When will everything be sent up?" he said to the mistress of the house, who was superintending.

"I am afraid not before eight, sir," said she. "You see we wasn't aware till this morning that you were going to move, or we could have been forwarder."

"A—well, never mind, never mind!" said Farfrae cheerily, "Eight o'clock will do well enough if it be not later. Now, don't ye be standing here talking, or it will be twelve, I doubt." Thus speaking he went out by the front door and up the street.

During this interval Henchard and Lucetta had had experiences of a different kind. After Elizabeth's departure for the muff the corn-merchant opened himself frankly, holding her hand within his arm, though she would fain have withdrawn it. "Dear Lucetta, I have been very, very anxious to see you these two or three days," he said; "ever since I saw you last! I have thought over the way I got your promise that night. You said to me, 'If I were a man I should not insist.' That cut me deep. I felt that there was some truth in it. I don't want to make you wretched; and to marry me just now would do that as nothing else could—it is but too plain. Therefore I agree to an indefinite engagement—to put off all thought of marriage for a year or two."

"But—but—can I do nothing of a different kind?" said Lucetta. "I am full of gratitude to you—you have saved my life. And your care of me is like coals of fire on my head! I am a monied person now. Surely I can do something in return for your goodness—something practical?"

Henchard remained in thought. He had evidently not expected this. "There is one thing you might do, Lucetta," he said. "But not exactly of that kind."

"Then of what kind is it?" she asked with renewed misgiving.

"I must tell you a secret to ask it. —— You have heard that I have been unlucky this year? I did what I have never done before—speculated rashly; and I lost. That's just put me in a strait."

"And you would wish me to advance some money?"

"No, no!" said Henchard, almost in anger. I'm not the man to sponge on a woman, even though she may be so nearly my own as you. No, Lucetta; what you can do is this; and it would save me. My great creditor is Grower, and it is at his hands I shall suffer if at anybody's; while a fortnight's forbearance on his part would be enough to allow me to pull through. This may be got out of him in one way—that you would let it be known to him that you are my intended—that we are to be quietly married in the next fortnight. —— Now stop, you haven't heard all! Let him have this story, without, of course, any prejudice to the fact that the actual engagement between us is to be a long one. Nobody else need know: you could go with me to Mr. Grower and just let me speak to 'ee before him as if we were on such terms. We'll ask him to keep it secret. He will willingly wait then. At the fortnight's end I shall be able to face him; and I can coolly tell him all is postponed between us for a year or two. Not a soul in the town need know how you've helped me. Since you wish to be of use, there's your way."

It being now what the people called the "pinking in" of the day, that is, the quarter-hour just before dusk, he did not at first observe the result of his own words upon her.

"If it were anything else," she began, and the dryness of her lips was represented in her voice.

"But it is such a little thing!" he said, with a deep reproach. "Less than you have offered—just the beginning of what you have so lately promised! I could have told him as much myself, but he would not have believed me."

"It is not because I won't—it is because I absolutely can't," she said, with rising distress.

"You are provoking!" he burst out. "It is enough to make me force you to carry out at once what you have promised."

"I cannot!" she insisted desperately.

"Why? When I have only within these few minutes released you from your promise to do the thing off-hand."

"Because——he was a witness!"

"Witness? Of what?"

"If I must tell you——. Don't, don't upbraid me!"

"Well! Let's hear what you mean?"

"Witness of my marriage—Mr. Grower was!"

"Marriage?"

"Yes. With Mr. Farfrae. O Michael! I am already his wife. We were married this week at Port-Bredy. There were reasons against our doing it here. Mr. Grower was witness because he happened to be at Port-Bredy at the time."

Henchard stood as if idiotized. She was so alarmed at his silence that she murmured something about lending him sufficient money to tide over the perilous fortnight.

"Married him?" said Henchard at length. "My good—what, married him whilst—bound to marry me?"

"It was like this," she explained, with tears in her eyes and quavers in her voice; "don't—don't be cruel! I loved him so much, and I thought you might tell him of the past—and that grieved me! And then, when I had promised you, I learnt of the rumor that you had—sold your first wife at a fair like a horse or cow! How could I keep my promise after hearing that? I could not risk myself in your hands; it would have been letting myself down to take your name after such a scandal. But I knew I should lose Donald if I did not secure him at once—for you would carry out your threat of telling him of our former acquaintance, as long as there was a chance of keeping me for yourself by doing so. But you will not do so now, will you, Michael? for it is too late to separate us."

The notes of St. Peter's bells in full peal had been wafted to them while he spoke; and now the genial thumping of the town band, renowned for its unstinted use of the drum-stick, throbbed down the street.

"Then this racket they are making is on account of it, I suppose?" said he.

"Yes—I think he has told them, or else Mr. Grower has. . . . May I leave you now? My—he was detained at Port-Bredy to-day, and sent me on a few hours before him."

"Then it is *his wife's* life I have saved this afternoon."

"Yes—and he will be for ever grateful to you."

"I am much obliged to him. . . . Oh, you false woman!" burst from Henchard. "You promised me!"

"Yes, yes! But it was under compulsion, and I did not know all your past——"

"And now I've a mind to punish you as you deserve! One word to this brand-new husband of how you courted me, and your precious happiness is blown to atoms!"

"Michael—pity me, and be generous!"

"You don't deserve pity! You did; but you don't now."

"I'll help you to pay off your debt."

"A pensioner of Farfrae's wife—not I! Don't stay with me longer—I shall say something worse. Go home!"

She disappeared under the trees of the south walk as the band came round the corner, awaking the echoes of every stock and stone in celebration of her happiness. Lucetta took no heed, but ran up the back street and reached her own home unperceived.

XXX

Farfrae's words to his landlady had referred to the removal of his boxes and other effects from his late lodgings to Lucetta's house. The work was not heavy, but it had been much hindered on account of the frequent pauses necessitated by exclamations of surprise at the event, of which the good woman had been briefly informed by letter a few hours earlier.

At the last moment of leaving Port-Bredy, Farfrae, like John Gilpin, had been detained by important customers, whom, even in the exceptional circumstances, he was not the man to neglect. Moreover, there was a convenience in Lucetta arriving first at her house. Nobody there as yet knew what had happened; and she was best in a position to break the news to the inmates, and give directions for her husband's accommodation. He had, therefore, sent on his two-days' bride in a hired brougham, whilst he went across the country to a certain group of wheat and barley ricks a few miles off, telling her the hour at which he might be expected the same evening. This accounted for her trotting out to meet him after their separation of four hours.

By a strenuous effort, after leaving Henchard she calmed herself in readiness to receive Donald at High-Place Hall when he came on from his lodgings. One supreme fact empowered her to this, the sense that, come what would, she had secured him. Half-an-hour after her arrival he walked in, and she met him with a relieved gladness, which a month's perilous absence could not have intensified.

"There is one thing I have not done; and yet it is important," she said earnestly, when she had finished talking about the adventure with the bull. "That is, broken the news of our marriage to my dear Elizabeth-Jane."

"Ah, and you have not?" he said thoughtfully. "I gave her a lift from the barn homewards; but I did not tell her either; for I thought she might have heard of it in the town, and was keeping back her congratulations from shyness, and all that."

"She can hardly have heard of it. But I'll find out; I'll go to her now. And, Donald, you don't mind her living on with me just the same as before? She is so quiet and unassuming."

"Oh, no, indeed I don't," Farfrae answered with, perhaps, a faint awkwardness. "But I wonder if she would care to?"

"Oh yes!" said Lucetta eagerly. "I am sure she would like to. Besides, poor thing, she has no other home."

Farfrae looked at her and saw that she did not suspect the secret of her more reserved friend. He liked her all the better for the blindness. "Arrange as you like with her by all means," he said. "It is I who have come to your house, not you to mine."

"I'll run and speak to her," said Lucetta.

When she got upstairs to Elizabeth-Jane's room the latter had taken off her out-door things, and was resting over a book. Lucetta found in a moment that she had not yet learnt the news.

"I did not come down to you, Miss Templeman," she

said simply. "I was coming to ask if you had quite recovered from your fright, but I found you had a visitor. What are the bells ringing for, I wonder? And the band, too, is playing. Somebody must be married; or else they are practicing for Christmas."

Lucetta uttered a vague "Yes," and seating herself by the other young woman looked musingly at her. "What a lonely creature you are," she presently said; "never knowing what's going on, or what people are talking about everywhere with keen interest. You should get out, and gossip about as other women do, and then you wouldn't be obliged to ask me a question of that kind. Well, now, I have something to tell you."

Elizabeth-Jane said she was so glad, and made herself receptive.

"I must go rather a long way back," said Lucetta, the difficulty of explaining herself satisfactorily to the pondering one beside her growing more apparent at each syllable. "You remember that trying case of conscience I told you of some time ago—about the first lover, and the second lover?" She let out in jerky phrases a leading word or two of the story she had told.

"Oh yes—I remember; the story of *your friend*," said Elizabeth drily, regarding the irises of Lucetta's eyes as though to catch their exact shade. "The two lovers—the old and the new: how she wanted to marry the second, but felt she ought to marry the first; so that she neglected the better course to follow the evil, like the poet Ovid I've just been construing: 'Video meliora proboque, deteriora sequor.' "

"Oh no; she didn't follow evil exactly!" said Lucetta hastily.

"But you said that she—or as I may say *you*"—answered Elizabeth, dropping the mask, "were in honor and conscience bound to marry the first?"

Lucetta's blush at being seen through came and went again before she replied anxiously, "You will never breathe this, will you, Elizabeth-Jane?"

"Certainly not, if you say not."

"Then I will tell you that the case is more complicated —worse, in fact—than it seemed in my story. I and the first man were thrown together in a strange way, and felt that we ought to be united, as the world had talked of us. He was a widower, as he supposed. He had not heard of his first wife for many years. But the wife returned, and we parted. She is now dead; and the husband comes paying me addresses again, saying, 'Now we'll complete our purpose.' But, Elizabeth-Jane, all this amounts to a new courtship of me by him; I was absolved from all vows by the return of the other woman."

"Have you not lately renewed your promise?" said the younger with quiet surmise. She had divined Man Number One.

"That was wrung from me by a threat."

"Yes, it was. But I think when any one gets coupled up with a man in the past so unfortunately as you have done, she ought to become his wife if she can, even if she were not the sinning party."

Lucetta's countenance lost its sparkle. "He turned out to be a man I should be afraid to marry," she pleaded. "Really afraid! And it was not till after my renewed promise that I knew it."

"Then there is only one course left to honesty. You must remain a single woman."

"But think again! Do consider——"

"I am certain," interrupted her companion hardily, "I have guessed very well who the man is. My father; and I say it is him or nobody for you."

Any suspicion of impropriety was to Elizabeth-Jane like a red rag to a bull. Her craving for correctness of procedure was, indeed, almost vicious. Owing to her early troubles with regard to her mother a semblance of irregularity had terrors for her which those whose names are safeguarded from suspicion know nothing of. "You ought to marry Mr. Henchard or nobody—certainly not another man!" she went on with a quivering lip in whose movement two passions shared.

"I don't admit that!" said Lucetta passionately.

"Admit it or not, it is true!"

Lucetta covered her eyes with her right hand, as if she could plead no more, holding out her left to Elizabeth-Jane.

"Why, you *have* married him!" cried the latter, jumping up with pleasure after a glance at Lucetta's fingers. "When did you do it? Why did you not tell me, instead of teasing me like this? How very honorable of you! He did treat my mother badly once, it seems, in a moment of intoxication. And it is true that he is stern sometimes. But you will rule him entirely, I am sure, with your beauty and wealth and accomplishments. You are the woman he will adore, and we shall all three be happy together now!"

"Oh, my Elizabeth-Jane!" cried Lucetta distressfully. " 'Tis somebody else that I have married! I was so desperate—so afraid of being forced to anything else—so afraid of revelations that would quench his love for me, that I resolved to do it off-hand, come what might, and purchase a week of happiness at any cost!"

"You—have—married Mr. Farfrae!" cried Elizabeth-Jane, in Nathan tones.

Lucetta bowed. She had recovered herself.

"The bells are ringing on that account," she said. "My husband is downstairs. He will live here till a more suitable house is ready for us; and I have told him that I want you to stay with me just as before."

"Let me think of it alone," the girl quickly replied, corking up the turmoil of her feeling with grand control.

"You shall. I am sure we shall be happy together."

Lucetta departed to join Donald below, a vague uneasiness floating over her joy at seeing him quite at home there. Not on account of her friend Elizabeth did she feel it: for of the bearings of Elizabeth-Jane's emotions she had not the least suspicion; but on Henchard's alone.

Now the instant decision of Susan Henchard's daughter was to dwell in that house no more. Apart from her estimate of the propriety of Lucetta's conduct, Farfrae had been so nearly her avowed lover that she felt she could not abide there.

It was still early in the evening when she hastily put on her things and went out. In a few minutes, knowing the ground, she had found a suitable lodging, and arranged to enter it that night. Returning and entering noiselessly she took off her pretty dress and arrayed herself in a plain one, packing up the other to keep as her best; for she would have to be very economical now. She wrote a note to leave for Lucetta, who was closely shut up in the drawing-room with Farfrae; and then Elizabeth-Jane called a man with a wheelbarrow; and seeing her boxes put into it she trotted off down the street to her rooms. They were in the street in which Henchard lived, and almost opposite his door.

Here she sat down and considered the means of subsistence. The little annual sum settled on her by her stepfather would keep body and soul together. A wonderful skill in netting of all sorts—acquired in childhood by making seines in Newson's home—might serve her in good stead; and her studies, which were pursued unremittingly, might serve her in still better.

By this time the marriage that had taken place was known throughout Casterbridge; had been discussed noisily on curbstones, confidentially behind counters, and jovially at the Three Mariners. Whether Farfrae would sell his business and set up for a gentleman on his wife's money, or whether he would show independence enough to stick to his trade in spite of his brilliant alliance, was a great point of interest.

XXXI

The retort of the furmity-woman before the magistrates had spread; and in four-and-twenty hours there was not a person in Casterbridge who remained unacquainted with the story of Henchard's mad freak at Weydon-Priors Fair, long years before. The amends he had made in after life were lost sight of in the dramatic glare of the original act. Had the incident been well known of old and always, it might by this time have grown to be lightly regarded as the rather tall wild oat, but well-nigh the single one, of a young man with whom the steady and mature (if somewhat headstrong) burgher of to-day had scarcely a point in common. But the act having lain as dead and buried ever since, the interspace of years was unperceived; and the black spot of his youth wore the aspect of a recent crime.

Small as the police-court incident had been in itself, it formed the edge or turn in the incline of Henchard's fortunes. On that day—almost at that minute—he passed the ridge of prosperity and honor, and began to descend rapidly on the other side. It was strange how soon he sank in esteem. Socially he had received a startling fillip downwards; and, having already lost commercial buoyancy from rash transactions, the velocity of his descent in both aspects became accelerated every hour.

He now gazed more at the pavements and less at the housefronts when he walked about; more at the feet and leggings of men, and less into the pupils of their eyes with the blazing regard which formerly had made them blink.

New events combined to undo him. It had been a bad year for others besides himself, and the heavy failure of a debtor whom he had trusted generously completed the overthrow of his tottering credit. And now, in his desperation, he failed to preserve that strict correspondence between bulk and sample which is the soul of commerce in grain. For this, one of his men was mainly to blame; that worthy, in his great unwisdom, having picked over the sample of an enormous quantity of second-rate corn which Henchard had in hand, and removed the pinched, blasted, and smutted grains in great numbers. The produce if honestly offered would have created no scandal; but the blunder of misrepresentation, coming at such a moment, dragged Henchard's name into the ditch.

The details of his failure were of the ordinary kind. One day Elizabeth-Jane was passing the King's Arms, when she saw people bustling in and out more than usual when there was no market. A bystander informed her, with some surprise at her ignorance, that it was a meeting of the Commissioners under Mr. Henchard's bankruptcy. She felt quite tearful, and when she heard that he was present in the hotel she wished to go in and see him, but was advised not to intrude that day.

The room in which debtor and creditors had assembled was a front one, and Henchard, looking out of the window, had caught sight of Elizabeth-Jane through the wire blind. His examination had closed, and the creditors were leaving. The appearance of Elizabeth threw him into a reverie; till, turning his face from the window, and towering above all the rest, he called their attention for a moment more. His countenance had somewhat changed from its flush of prosperity; the black hair and whiskers were the same as ever, but a film of ash was over the rest.

"Gentleman," he said, "over and above the assets that we've been talking about, and that appear on the balance-sheet, there be these. It all belongs to ye, as much as everything else I've got, and I don't wish to keep it from you, not I." Saying this, he took his gold watch from his pocket and laid it on the table; then his purse—the yellow canvas money-bag, such as was carried by all farmers and dealers—untying it, and shaking the money out upon the table beside the watch. The latter he drew back quickly for an instant, to remove the hair-guard made and given him by Lucetta. "There, now you have all I've got in the world," he said. "And I wish for your sakes 'twas more."

The creditors, farmers almost to a man, looked at the watch, and at the money, and into the street; when Farmer James Everdene of Weatherbury spoke.

"No, no, Henchard," he said warmly. "We don't want that. 'Tis honorable in ye; but keep it. What do you say, neighbors—do ye agree?"

"Ay, sure: we don't wish it at all," said Grower, another creditor.

"Let him keep it, of course," murmured another in the background—a silent, reserved young man named Bold-wood; and the rest responded unanimously.

"Well," said the senior Commissioner, addressing Henchard, "though the case is a desperate one, I am bound to admit that I have never met a debtor who behaved more fairly. I've proved the balance-sheet to be as honestly made out as it could possibly be; we have had no trouble; there have been no evasions and no concealments. The rashness of dealing which led to this unhappy situation is obvious enough; but as far as I can see every attempt has been made to avoid wronging anybody."

Henchard was more affected by this than he cared to let them perceive, and he turned aside to the window again. A general murmur of agreement followed the Commissioner's words; and the meeting dispersed. When they were gone Henchard regarded the watch they had returned to him. " 'Tisn't mine by rights," he said to himself. "Why the devil didn't they take it?—I don't want what don't belong to me!" Moved by a recollection he took the watch to the maker's just opposite, sold it there and then for what the tradesman offered, and went with the proceeds to one among the smaller of his creditors, a cottager of Durnover in straitened circumstances, to whom he handed the money.

When everything was ticketed that Henchard had owned, and the auctions were in progress, there was quite a sympathetic reaction in the town, which till then for some time past had done nothing but condemn him. Now that Henchard's whole career was pictured distinctly to his neighbors, and they could see how admirably he had used his one talent of energy to create a position of affluence out of absolutely nothing—which was really all he could show when he came to the town as a journeyman hay-trusser, with his wimble and knife in his basket —they wondered and regretted his fall.

Try as she might, Elizabeth could never meet with him. She believed in him still, though nobody else did; and she wanted to be allowed to forgive him for his roughness to her, and to help him in his trouble.

She wrote to him; he did not reply. She then went to his house—the great house she had lived in so happily for a time—with its front of dun brick, vitrified here and there, and its heavy sash-bars—but Henchard was to be found there no more. The ex-Mayor had left the home of his prosperity, and gone into Jopp's cottage by the Priory Mill—the sad purlieu to which he had wandered on the night of his discovery that she was not his daughter. Thither she went.

Elizabeth thought it odd that he had fixed on this spot to retire to, but assumed that necessity had no choice. Trees which seemed old enough to have been planted by the friars still stood around, and the back hatch of the original mill yet formed a cascade which had raised its terrific roar for centuries. The cottage itself was built of old stones from the long dismantled Priory, scraps of tracery, moulded window-jambs, and arch-labels, being mixed in with the rubble of the walls.

In this cottage he occupied a couple of rooms, Jopp, whom Henchard had employed, abused, cajoled, and dismissed by turns, being the household. But even here her stepfather could not be seen.

"Not by his daughter?" pleaded Elizabeth.

"By nobody—at present: that's his order," she was informed.

Afterwards she was passing by the corn-stores and hay-barns which had been the headquarters of his business. She knew that he ruled there no longer; but it was with amazement that she regarded the familiar gateway. A smear of decisive lead-colored paint had been laid on to obliterate Henchard's name, though its letters dimly loomed through like ships in a fog. Over these, in fresh white, spread the name of Farfrae.

Abel Whittle was edging his skeleton in at the wicket, and she said, "Mr. Farfrae is master here?"

"Yaas, Miss Henchet," he said, "Mr. Farfrae have bought the concern and all of we work-folk with it; and 'tis better for us than 'twas—though I shouldn't say that to you as a daughter-law. We work harder, but we bain't made afeard now. It was fear made my few poor hairs so thin! No busting out, no slamming of doors, no meddling with yer eternal soul and all that; and though 'tis a shilling a week less I'm the richer man; for what's all the world if yer mind is always in a larry, Miss Henchet?"

The intelligence was in a general sense true; and Henchard's stores, which had remained in a paralyzed condition during the settlement of his bankruptcy, were stirred into activity again when the new tenant had possession. Thenceforward the full sacks, looped with the shining chain, went scurrying up and down under the cat-head, hairy arms were thrust out from the different doorways, and the grain was hauled in; trusses of hay were tossed anew in and out of the barns, and the wimbles creaked; while the scales and steelyards began to be busy where guess-work had formerly been the rule.

XXXII

Two bridges stood near the lower part of Casterbridge town. The first, of weather-stained brick, was immediately at the end of High Street, where a diverging branch from that thoroughfare ran round to the low-lying Durnover lanes; so that the precincts of the bridge formed the merging point of respectability and indigence. The second bridge, of stone, was further out on the highway—in fact, fairly in the meadows, though still within the town boundary.

These bridges had speaking countenances. Every projection in each was worn down to obtuseness, partly by weather, more by friction from generations of loungers, whose toes and heels had from year to year made restless movements against these parapets, as they had stood there meditating on the aspect of affairs. In the case of the more friable bricks and stones even the flat faces were worn into hollows by the same mixed mechanism. The masonry of the top was clamped with iron at each joint; since it had been no uncommon thing for desperate men to wrench the coping off and throw it down the river, in reckless defiance of the magistrates.

For to this pair of bridges gravitated all the failures of the town; those who had failed in business, in love, in sobriety, in crime. Why the unhappy hereabout usually chose the bridges for their meditations in preference to a railing, a gate, or a stile, was not so clear.

There was a marked difference of quality between the personages who haunted the near bridge of brick, and the personages who haunted the far one of stone. Those of lowest character preferred the former, adjoining the town; they did not mind the glare of the public eye. They had been of comparatively no account during their successes; and, though they might feel dispirited, they had no particular sense of shame in their ruin. Their hands were mostly kept in their pockets; they wore a leather strap round their hips or knees, and boots that required a great deal of lacing, but seemed never to get any. Instead of sighing at their adversities they spat, and instead of saying the iron had entered into their souls they said they were down on their luck. Jopp in his times of distress had often stood here; so had Mother Cuxsom, Christopher Coney, and poor Abel Whittle.

The *misérables* who would pause on the remoter bridge were of a politer stamp. They included bankrupts, hypochondriacs, persons who were what is called "out of a situation" from fault or lucklessness, the inefficient of the professional class—shabby-genteel men, who did not know how to get rid of the weary time between breakfast and dinner, and the yet more weary time between dinner and dark. The eyes of this species were mostly directed over the parapet upon the running water below. A man seen there looking thus fixedly into the river was pretty sure to be one whom the world did not treat kindly for some reason or other. While one in straits on the townward bridge did not mind who saw him so, and kept his back to the parapet to survey the passers-by, one in straits on this never faced the road, never turned his head at coming footsteps, but sensitive to his own condition, watched the current whenever a stranger approached, as if some strange fish interested him, though every finned thing had been poached out of the river years before.

There and thus they would muse; if their grief were the grief of oppression they would wish themselves kings; if their grief were poverty, wish themselves millionaires; if sin, they would wish they were saints or angels; if despised love, that they were some much-courted Adonis of county fame. Some had been known to stand and think so long with this fixed gaze downward that eventually they had allowed their poor carcases to follow that gaze; and they were discovered the next morning out of reach of their troubles, either here or in the deep pool called Blackwater, a little higher up the river.

To this bridge came Henchard, as other unfortunates had come before him, his way thither being by the riverside path on the chilly edge of the town. Here he was standing one windy afternoon when Durnover church clock struck five. While the gusts were bringing the notes to his ears across the damp intervening flat a man passed behind him and greeted Henchard by name. Henchard turned slightly and saw that the comer was Jopp, his old foreman, now employed elsewhere, to whom, though he hated him, he had gone for lodgings because Jopp was the one man in Casterbridge whose observation and opinion the fallen corn-merchant despised to the point of indifference.

Henchard returned him a scarcely perceptible nod, and Jopp stopped.

"He and she are gone into their new house to-day," said Jopp.

"Oh," said Henchard absently. "Which house is that?"

"Your old one."

"Gone into my house?" And starting up Henchard added, "*My* house of all others in the town!"

"Well, as somebody was sure to live there, and you couldn't, it can do 'ee no harm that he's the man."

It was quite true: he felt that it was doing him no harm. Farfrae, who had already taken the yards and stores, had acquired possession of the house for the obvious convenience of its contiguity. And yet this act of his taking up residence within those roomy chambers while he, their former tenant, lived in a cottage, galled Henchard inde-scribably.

Jopp continued: "And you heard of that fellow who bought all the best furniture at your sale? He was bidding for no other than Farfrae all the while! It has never been moved out of the house, as he'd already got the lease."

"My furniture too! Surely he'll buy my body and soul likewise!"

"There's no saying he won't, if you be willing to sell." And having planted these wounds in the heart of his once imperious master Jopp went on his way; while Henchard stared and stared into the racing river till the bridge seemed moving backward with him.

The low land grew blacker, and the sky a deeper grey. When the landscape looked like a picture blotted in with ink, another traveller approached the great stone bridge. He was driving a gig, his direction being also townwards. On the round of the middle of the arch the gig stopped. "Mr. Henchard?" came from it in the voice of Farfrae. Henchard turned his face.

Finding that he had guessed rightly Farfrae told the man who accompanied him to drive home; while he alighted and went up to his former friend.

"I have heard that you think of emigrating, Mr. Hen-chard," he said. "Is it true? I have a real reason for asking."

Henchard withheld his answer for several instants, and then said, "Yes; it is true. I am going where you were going to a few years ago, when I prevented you and got you to bide here. 'Tis turn and turn about, isn't it! Do ye mind how we stood like this in the Chalk Walk when I persuaded 'ee to stay? You then stood without a chattel to your name, and I was the master of the house in Corn Street. But now I stand without a stick or a rag, and the master of that house is you."

"Yes, yes; that's so! "It's the way o' the warrld," said Farfrae.

"Ha, ha, true!" cried Henchard, throwing himself into a mood of jocularity. "Up and down! I'm used to it. What's the odds after all!"

"Now listen to me, if it's no taking up your time," said Farfrae, "just as I listened to you. Don't go. Stay at home."

"But I can do nothing else, man!" said Henchard scornfully. "The little money I have will just keep body and soul together for a few weeks, and no more. I have not felt inclined to go back to journey-work yet; but I can't stay doing nothing, and my best chance is elsewhere."

"No; but what I propose is this—if ye will listen. Come and live in your old house. We can spare some rooms very well—I am sure my wife would not mind it at all —until there's an opening for ye."

Henchard started. Probably the picture drawn by the unsuspecting Donald of himself under the same roof with Lucetta was too striking to be received with equanimity. "No, no," he said gruffly; "we should quarrel."

"You should hae a part to yourself," said Farfrae; "and nobody to interfere wi' you. It will be a deal healthier than down there by the river where you live now."

Still Henchard refused. "You don't know what you ask," he said. "However, I can do no less than thank 'ee."

They walked into the town together side by side, as they had done when Henchard persuaded the young Scotchman to remain. "Will you come in and have some supper?" said Farfrae when they reached the middle of the town, where their paths diverged right and left.

"No, no."

"By-the-bye, I had nearly forgot. I bought a good deal of your furniture."

"So I have heard."

"Well, it was no that I wanted it so very much for myself; but I wish ye to pick out all that you care to have—such things as may be endeared to ye by associations, or particularly suited to your use. And take them to your own house—it will not be depriving me; we can do with less very well, and I will have plenty of opportunities of getting more."

"What—give it to me for nothing?" said Henchard. "But you paid the creditors for it!"

"Ah, yes; but maybe it's worth more to you than it is to me."

Henchard was a little moved. "I—sometimes think I've wronged 'ee!" he said, in tones which showed the disquietude that the night shades hid in his face. He shook Farfrae abruptly by the hand, and hastened away as if unwilling to betray himself further. Farfrae saw him turn through the thoroughfare into Bull Stake and vanish down towards the Priory Mill.

Meanwhile Elizabeth-Jane, in an upper room no larger than the Prophet's chamber, and with the silk attire of her palmy days packed away in a box, was netting with great industry between the hours which she devoted to studying such books as she could get hold of.

Her lodgings being nearly opposite her stepfather's former residence, now Farfrae's, she could see Donald and Lucetta speeding in and out of their door with all the bounding enthusiasm of their situation. She avoided looking that way as much as possible, but it was hardly in human nature to keep the eyes averted when the door slammed.

While living on thus quietly she heard the news that Henchard had caught cold and was confined to his room —possibly a result of standing about the meads in damp weather. She went off to his house at once. This time she was determined not to be denied admittance, and made her way upstairs. He was sitting up in the bed with a greatcoat round him, and at first resented her intrusion. "Go away—go away," he said. "I don't like to see 'ee!"

"But, father——"

"I don't like to see 'ee," he repeated.

However, the ice was broken, and she remained. She made the room more comfortable, gave directions to the people below, and by the time she went away had reconciled her stepfather to her visiting him.

The effect, either of her ministrations or of her mere presence, was a rapid recovery. He soon was well enough to go out; and now things seemed to wear a new color in his eyes. He no longer thought of emigration, and thought more of Elizabeth. The having nothing to do made him more dreary than any other circumstance; and one day, with better views of Farfrae than he had held for some time, and a sense that honest work was not a thing to be ashamed of, he stoically went down to Farfrae's yard and asked to be taken on as a journeyman hay-trusser. He was engaged at once. This hiring of Henchard was done through a foreman, Farfrae feeling that it was undesirable to come personally in contact with the ex-corn-factor more than was absolutely necessary. While anxious to help him he was well aware by this time of his uncertain temper, and thought reserved relations best. For the same reason his orders to Henchard to proceed to this and that country farm trussing in the usual way were always given through a third person.

For a time these arrangements worked well, it being the custom to truss in the respective stack-yards, before bringing it away, the hay bought at the different farms about the neighborhood; so that Henchard was often absent at such places the whole week long. When this was all done, and Henchard had become in a measure broken in, he came to work daily on the home premises like the rest. And thus the once flourishing merchant and Mayor and what not stood as a day-laborer in the barns and granaries he formerly had owned.

"I have worked as a journeyman before now, ha'n't I?" he would say in his defiant way; "and why shouldn't I do it again?" But he looked a far different journeyman from the one he had been in his earlier days. Then he had worn clean, suitable clothes, light and cheerful in hue; leggings yellow as marigolds, corduroys immaculate as new flax, and a neckerchief like a flower-garden. Now he wore the remains of an old blue cloth suit of his gentlemanly times, a rusty silk hat, and a once black satin stock, soiled and shabby. Clad thus, he went to and fro, still comparatively an active man—for he was not much over forty—and saw with the other men in the yard Donald Farfrae going in and out the green door that led to the garden, and the big house, and Lucetta.

At the beginning of the winter it was rumored about Casterbridge that Mr. Farfrae, already in the Town Council, was to be proposed for Mayor in a year or two.

"Yes; she was wise, she was wise in her generation!" said Henchard to himself when he heard of this one day on his way to Farfrae's hay-barn. He thought it over as he wimbled his bonds, and the piece of news acted as a reviviscent breath to that old view of his—of Donald Farfrae as his triumphant rival who rode rough-shod over him.

"A fellow of his age going to be Mayor, indeed!" he murmured with a corner-drawn smile on his mouth. "But 'tis her money that floats en upward. Ha-ha—how cust odd it is! Here be I, his former master, working for him as man, and he the man standing as master, with my house and my furniture and my what-you-may-call wife all his own."

He repeated these things a hundred times a day. During the whole period of his acquaintance with Lucetta he had never wished to claim her as his own so desperately as he now regretted her loss. It was no mercenary hankering after her fortune that moved him; though that fortune had been the means of making her so much the more desired by giving her the air of independence and sauciness which attracts men of his composition. It had given her servants, house, and fine clothing—a setting that invested Lucetta with a startling novelty in the eyes of him who had known her in her narrow days.

He accordingly lapsed into moodiness, and at every allusion to the possibility of Farfrae's near election to the municipal chair his former hatred of the Scotchman returned. Concurrently with this he underwent a moral change. It resulted in his significantly saying every now and then, in tones of recklessness, "Only a fortnight more!" —"Only a dozen days!" and so forth, lessening his figures day by day.

"Why d'ye say only a dozen days?" asked Solomon Longways as he worked beside Henchard in the granary weighing oats.

"Because in twelve days I shall be released from my oath."

"What oath?"

"The oath to drink no spirituous liquid. In twelve days it will be twenty-one years since I swore it, and then I mean to enjoy myself, please God!"

Elizabeth-Jane sat at her window one Sunday, and while there she heard in the street below a conversation which introduced Henchard's name. She was wondering what was the matter, when a third person who was passing by asked the question in her mind.

"Michael Henchard have busted out drinking after taking nothing for twenty-one years!"

Elizabeth-Jane jumped up, put on her things, and went out.

XXXIII

At this date there prevailed in Casterbridge a convivial custom—scarcely recognized as such, yet none the less established. On the afternoon of every Sunday a large contingent of the Casterbridge journeymen—steady church-goers and sedate characters—having attended service, filed from the church doors across the way to the Three Mariners Inn. The rear was usually brought up by the choir, with their bass-viols, fiddles, and flutes under their arms.

The great point, the point of honor, on these sacred occasions was for each man to strictly limit himself to half-a-pint of liquor. This scrupulosity was so well understood by the landlord that the whole company was served in cups of that measure. They were all exactly alike—straight-sided, with two leafless lime-trees done in eel-brown on the sides—one towards the drinker's lips, the other confronting his comrade. To wonder how many of these cups the landlord possessed altogether was a favorite exercise of children in the marvellous. Forty at least might have been seen at these times in the large room, forming a ring round the margin of the great sixteen-legged oak table, like the monolithic circle at Stonehenge in its pristine days. Outside and above the forty cups came a circle of forty smoke-jets from forty clay pipes; outside the pipes the countenances of the forty church-goers, supported at the back by a circle of forty chairs.

The conversation was not the conversation of week-days, but a thing altogether finer in point and higher in tone. They invariably discussed the sermon, dissecting it, weighing it, as above or below the average—the general tendency being to regard it as a scientific feat or performance which had no relation to their own lives, except as between critics and the thing criticized. The bass-viol player and the clerk usually spoke with more authority than the rest on account of their official connection with the preacher.

Now the Three Mariners was the inn chosen by Henchard as the place for closing his long term of dramless years. He had so timed his entry as to be well established in the large room by the time the forty church-goers entered to their customary cups. The flush upon his face proclaimed at once that the vow of twenty-one years had lapsed, and the era of recklessness begun anew. He was seated on a small table, drawn up to the side of the massive oak board reserved for the churchmen, a few of whom nodded to him as they took their places, and said, "How be ye, Mr. Henchard? Quite a stranger here."

Henchard did not take the trouble to reply for a few moments, and his eyes rested on his stretched-out legs and boots. "Yes," he said at length; "that's true. I've been down in spirit for weeks; some of ye know the cause. I am better now; but not quite serene. I want you fellows of the choir to strike up a tune; and what with that and this brew of Stannidge's, I am in hopes of getting altogether out of my minor key."

"With all my heart," said the first fiddle. "We've let back our strings, that's true; but we can soon pull 'em up again. Sound A, neighbors, and give the man a stave."

"I don't care a curse what the words be," said Henchard. "Hymns, ballets, or rantipole rubbish; the Rogue's March or the cherubim's warble—'tis all the same to me if 'tis good harmony, and well put out."

"Well—heh, heh—it may be we can do that, and not

a man among us that have sat in the gallery less than twenty year," said the leader of the band. "As 'tis Sunday, neighbors, suppose we raise the Fourth Psa'am, to Samuel Wakely's tune, as improved by me?"

"Hang Samuel Wakely's tune, as improved by thee!" said Henchard. "Chuck across one of your psalters—old Wiltshire is the only tune worth singing—the psalm-tune that would make my blood ebb and flow like the sea when I was a steady chap. I'll find some words to fit en." He took one of the psalters and began turning over the leaves.

Chancing to look out of the window at that moment he saw a flock of people passing by, and perceived them to be the congregation of the upper church, now just dismissed, their sermon having been a longer one than that the lower parish was favored with. Among the rest of the leading inhabitants walked Mr. Councillor Farfrae with Lucetta upon his arm, the observed and imitated of all the smaller tradesmen's womankind. Henchard's mouth changed a little, and he continued to turn over the leaves.

"Now then," he said, "Psalm the Hundred-and-Ninth, to the tune of Wiltshire: verses ten to fifteen. I gi'e ye the words:

> "His seed shall orphans be, his wife
>   A widow plunged in grief;
> His vagrant children beg their bread
>   Where none can give relief.
>
> "His ill-got riches shall be made
>   To usurers a prey;
> The fruit of all his toil shall be
>   By strangers borne away.
>
> "None shall be found that to his wants
>   Their mercy will extend,
> Or to his helpless orphan seed
>   The least assistance lend.
>
> "A swift destruction soon shall seize
>   On his unhappy race;
> And the next age his hated name
>   Shall utterly deface."

"I know the Psa'am—I know the Psa'am!" said the leader hastily; "but I would as lief not sing it. 'Twasn't made for singing. We chose it once when the gipsy stole the pa'son's mare, thinking to please him, but pa'son were quite upset. Whatever Servant David were thinking about when he made a Psalm that nobody can sing without disgracing himself, I can't fathom! Now then, the Fourth Psalm, to Samuel Wakely's tune, as improved by me."

" 'Od seize your sauce—I tell ye to sing the Hundred-and-Ninth to Wiltshire, and sing it you shall!" roared Henchard. "Not a single one of all the droning crew of ye goes out of this room till that Psalm is sung!" He slipped off the table, seized the poker, and going to the door placed his back against it. "Now then, go ahead, if you don't wish to have your cust pates broke!"

"Don't 'ee, don't 'ee take on so! — As 'tis the Sabbath-day, and 'tis Servant David's words and not ours, perhaps we don't mind for once, hey?" said one of the terrified choir, looking round upon the rest. So the instruments were tuned and the comminatory verses sung.

"Thank ye, thank ye," said Henchard in a softened voice, his eyes growing downcast, and his manner that of a man much moved by the strains. "Don't you blame David," he went on in low tones, shaking his head without raising his eyes. "He knew what he was about when he wrote that! . . . If I could afford it, be hanged if I wouldn't keep a church choir at my own expense to play and sing to me at these low, dark times of my life. But the bitter thing is, that when I was rich I didn't need what I could have, and now I be poor I can't have what I need!"

While they paused, Lucetta and Farfrae passed again, this time homeward, it being their custom to take, like others, a short walk out on the highway and back, between church and tea-time. "There's the man we've been singing about," said Henchard.

The players and singers turned their heads, and saw his meaning. "Heaven forbid!" said the bass-player.

" 'Tis the man," repeated Henchard doggedly.

"Then if I'd known," said the performer on the clarionet solemnly, "that 'twas meant for a living man, nothing should have drawn out of my wynd-pipe the breath for that Psalm, so help me!"

"Nor from mine," said the first singer. "But, thought I, as it was made so long ago perhaps there isn't much in it, so I'll oblige a neighbor; for there's nothing to be said against the tune."

"Ah, my boys, you've sung it," cried Henchard triumphantly. "As for him, it was partly by his songs that he got over me, and heaved me out. . . . I could double him up like that—and yet I don't." He laid the poker across his knee, bent it as if it were a twig, flung it down, and came away from the door.

It was at this time that Elizabeth-Jane, having heard where her stepfather was, entered the room with a pale and agonized countenance. The choir and the rest of the company moved off, in accordance with their half-pint regulation. Elizabeth-Jane went up to Henchard, and entreated him to accompany her home.

By this hour the volcanic fires of his nature had burnt down, and having drunk no great quantity as yet he was inclined to acquiesce. She took his arm, and together they went on. Henchard walked blankly, like a blind man, repeating to himself the last words of the singers—

"And the next age his hated name
Shall utterly deface."

At length he said to her, "I am a man to my word. I have kept my oath for twenty-one years; and now I can drink with a good conscience. . . . If I don't do for him— well, I am a fearful practical joker when I choose! He has taken away everything from me, and by heavens, if I meet him I won't answer for my deeds!"

These half-uttered words alarmed Elizabeth—all the more by reason of the still determination of Henchard's mien.

"What will you do?" she asked cautiously, while trembling with disquietude, and guessing Henchard's allusion only too well.

Henchard did not answer, and they went on till they had reached his cottage. "May I come in?" she said.

"No, no; not to-day," said Henchard; and she went away; feeling that to caution Farfrae was almost her duty, as it was certainly her strong desire.

As on the Sunday, so on the week-days, Farfrae and Lucetta might have been seen flitting about the town like two butterflies—or rather like a bee and a butterfly in league for life. She seemed to take no pleasure in going anywhere except in her husband's company; and hence when business would not permit him to waste an afternoon she remained indoors waiting for the time to pass till his return, her face being visible to Elizabeth-Jane from her window aloft. The latter, however, did not say to herself that Farfrae should be thankful for such devotion, but, full of her reading, she cited Rosalind's exclamation: "Mistress, know yourself; down on your knees and thank Heaven fasting for a good man's love."

She kept her eye upon Henchard also. One day he answered her inquiry for his health by saying that he could not endure Abel Whittle's pitying eyes upon him while they worked together in the yard. "He is such a fool," said Henchard, "that he can never get out of his mind the time when I was master there."

"I'll come and wimble for you instead of him, if you will allow me," said she. Her motive on going to the yard was to get an opportunity of observing the general position of affairs on Farfrae's premises now that her stepfather was a workman there. Henchard's threats had alarmed her so much that she wished to see his behavior when the two were face to face.

For two or three days after her arrival Donald did not make any appearance. Then one afternoon the green door opened, and through came, first Farfrae, and at his heels Lucetta. Donald brought his wife forward without hesitation, it being obvious that he had no suspicion whatever of any antecedents in common between her and the now journeyman hay-trusser.

Henchard did not turn his eyes toward either of the pair, keeping them fixed on the bond he twisted, as if that alone absorbed him. A feeling of delicacy, which ever prompted Farfrae to avoid anything that might seem like triumphing over a fallen rival, led him to keep away from the hay-barn where Henchard and his daughter were working, and to go on to the corn department. Meanwhile Lucetta, never having been informed that Henchard had entered her husband's service, rambled straight on to the barn, where she came suddenly upon Henchard, and gave vent to a little "Oh!" which the happy and busy Donald was too far off to hear. Henchard, with withering humility of demeanor, touched the brim of his hat to her as Whittle and the rest had done, to which she breathed a dead-alive "Good afternoon."

"I beg your pardon, ma'am?" said Henchard, as if he had not heard.

"I said good afternoon," she faltered.

"Oh, yes, good afternoon, ma'am," he replied, touching his hat again. "I am glad to see you, ma'am." Lucetta looked embarrassed, and Henchard continued: "For we humble workmen here feel it a great honor that a lady should look in and take an interest in us."

She glanced at him entreatingly; the sarcasm was too bitter, too unendurable.

"Can you tell me the time, ma'am?" he asked.

"Yes," she said hastily; "half-past four."

"Thank 'ee. An hour and a half longer before we are released from work. Ah, ma'am, we of the lower classes know nothing of the gay leisure that such as you enjoy!"

As soon as she could do so Lucetta left him, nodded and smiled to Elizabeth-Jane, and joined her husband at the other end of the enclosure, where she could be seen leading him away by the outer gates, so as to avoid passing Henchard again. That she had been taken by surprise was obvious. The result of this casual rencounter was that the next morning a note was put into Henchard's hand by the postman.

'Will you," said Lucetta, with as much bitterness as she could put into a small communication, "will you kindly undertake not to speak to me in the biting undertones

you used to-day, if I walk through the yard at any time?
I bear you no ill-will, and I am only too glad that you
should have employment of my dear husband; but in
common fairness treat me as his wife, and do not try to
make me wretched by covert sneers. I have committed
no crime, and done you no injury."

"Poor fool!" said Henchard with fond savagery, holding out the note. "To know no better than commit herself
in writing like this! Why, if I were to show that to her
dear husband—pooh!" He threw the letter into the fire.

Lucetta took care not to come again among the hay
and corn. She would rather have died than run the risk
of encountering Henchard at such close quarters a second
time. The gulf between them was growing wider every day.
Farfrae was always considerate to his fallen acquaintance;
but it was impossible that he should not, by degrees,
cease to regard the ex-corn-merchant as more than one
of his other workmen. Henchard saw this, and concealed
his feelings under a cover of stolidity, fortifying his heart
by drinking more freely at the Three Mariners every
evening.

Often did Elizabeth-Jane, in her endeavors to prevent
his taking other liquor, carry tea to him in a little basket
at five o'clock. Arriving one day on this errand she found
her stepfather was measuring up clover-seed and rape-seed
in the corn-stores on the top floor, and she ascended to
him. Each floor had a door opening into the air under a
cat-head, from which a chain dangled for hoisting the
sacks.

When Elizabeth's head rose through the trap she perceived that the upper door was open, and that her stepfather and Farfrae stood just within it in conversation,
Farfrae being nearest the dizzy edge, and Henchard a little
way behind. Not to interrupt them she remained on the
steps without raising her head any higher. While waiting
thus she saw—or fancied she saw, for she had a terror
of feeling certain—her stepfather slowly raise his hand
to a level behind Farfrae's shoulders, a curious expression
taking possession of his face. The young man was quite

unconscious of the action, which was so indirect that, if Farfrae had observed it, he might almost have regarded it as an idle outstretching of the arm. But it would have been possible, by a comparatively light touch, to push Farfrae off his balance, and send him head over heels into the air.

Elizabeth felt quite sick at heart on thinking of what this *might* have meant. As soon as they turned she mechanically took the tea to Henchard, left it, and went away. Reflecting, she endeavored to assure herself that the movement was an idle eccentricity, and no more. Yet, on the other hand, his subordinate position in an establishment where he once had been master might be acting on him like an irritant poison; and she finally resolved to caution Donald.

XXXIV

Next morning, accordingly, she rose at five o'clock and went into the street. It was not yet light; a dense fog prevailed, and the town was as silent as it was dark, except that from the rectangular avenues which framed in the borough there came a chorus of tiny rappings, caused by the fall of water-drops condensed on the boughs; now it was wafted from the West Walk, now from the South Walk; and then from both quarters simultaneously. She moved on to the bottom of Corn Street, and, knowing his time well, waited only a few minutes before she heard the familiar bang of his door, and then his quick walk towards her. She met him at the point where the last tree of the engirding avenue flanked the last house in the street.

He could hardly discern her till, glancing inquiringly, he said, "What—Miss Henchard—and are ye up so airly?"

She asked him to pardon her for waylaying him at such an unseemly time. "But I am anxious to mention something," she said, "And I wished not to alarm Mrs. Farfrae by calling."

"Yes?" said he, with the cheeriness of a superior. "And what may it be? It's very kind of ye, I'm sure."

She now felt the difficulty of conveying to his mind the exact aspect of possibilities in her own. But she somehow began, and introduced Henchard's name. "I sometimes fear," she said with an effort, "that he may be betrayed into some attempt to—insult you, sir."

"But we are the best of friends?"

"Or to play some practical joke upon you, sir. Remember that he has been hardly used."

"But we are quite friendly?"

"Or to do something—that would injure you—hurt you—wound you." Every word cost her twice its length of pain. And she could see that Farfrae was still incredulous. Henchard, a poor man in his employ, was not to Farfrae's view the Henchard who had ruled him. Yet he was not only the same man, but that man with his sinister qualities, formerly latent, quickened into life by his buffetings.

Farfrae, happy, and thinking no evil, persisted in making light of her fears. Thus they parted, and she went homeward, journeymen now being in the street, wagoners going to the harness-makers for articles left to be repaired, farm-horses going to the shoeing-smiths, and the sons of labor showing themselves generally on the move. Elizabeth entered her lodging unhappily, thinking she had done no good, and only made herself appear foolish by her weak note of warning.

But Donald Farfrae was one of those men upon whom an incident is never absolutely lost. He revised impressions from a subsequent point of view, and the impulsive judgment of the moment was not always his permanent one. The vision of Elizabeth's earnest face in the rimy dawn came back to him several times during the day. Knowing the solidity of her character he did not treat her hints altogether as idle sounds.

But he did not desist from a kindly scheme on Henchard's account that engaged him just then; and when he met Lawyer Joyce, the town-clerk, later in the day, he spoke of it as if nothing had occurred to damp it.

"About that little seedsman's shop," he said "the shop overlooking the churchyard, which is to let. It is not for myself I want it, but for our unlucky fellow-townsman Henchard. It would be a new beginning for him, if a small one; and I have told the Council that I would head a private subscription among them to set him up in it— that I would be fifty pounds, if they would make up the other fifty among them."

"Yes, yes; so I've heard; and there's nothing to say against it for that matter," the town-clerk replied, in his plain, frank way. "But, Farfrae, others see what you don't. Henchard hates 'ee—ay, hates 'ee; and 'tis right that you should know it. To my knowledge he was at the Three Mariners last night, saying in public that about you which a man ought not to say about another."

"Is that so—ah, is that so?" said Farfrae, looking down. "Why should he do it?" added the young man bitterly; "what harm have I done him that he should try to wrong me?"

"God only knows," said Joyce, lifting his eyebrows. "It shows much long-suffering in you to put up with him, and keep him in your employ."

"But I cannot discharge a man who was once a good friend to me? How can I forget that when I came here 'twas he enabled me to make a footing for mysel'? No, no. As long as I've a day's wark to offer he shall do it if he chooses. 'Tis not I who will deny him such a little as that. But I'll drop the idea of establishing him in a shop till I can think more about it."

It grieved Farfrae much to give up this scheme. But a damp having been thrown over it by these and other voices in the air, he went and countermanded his orders. The then occupier of the shop was in it when Farfrae spoke to him, and feeling it necessary to give some explanation of his withdrawal from the negotiation Donald mentioned Henchard's name, and stated that the intentions of the Council had been changed.

The occupier was much disappointed, and straightway informed Henchard, as soon as he saw him, that a scheme of the Council for setting him up in a shop had been knocked on the head by Farfrae. And thus out of error enmity grew.

When Farfrae got indoors that evening the teakettle was singing on the high hob of the semi-egg-shaped grate. Lucetta, light as a sylph, ran forward and seized his hands, whereupon Farfrae duly kissed her.

"Oh!" she cried playfully, turning to the window. "See— the blinds are not drawn down, and the people can look in—what a scandal!"

When the candles were lighted, the curtains drawn, and the twain sat at tea, she noticed that he looked serious. Without directly inquiring why she let her eyes linger solicitously on his face.

"Who has called? he absently asked. "Any folk for me?"

"No," said Lucetta. "What's the matter, Donald?"

"Well—nothing worth talking of," he responded sadly.

"Then, never mind it. You will get through it. Scotchmen are always lucky."

"No—not always!" he said, shaking his head gloomily as he contemplated a crumb on the table. "I know many who have not been so! There was Sandy Macfarlane, who started to America to try his fortune, and he was drowned; and Archibald Leith, he was murdered! And poor Willie Dunbleeze and Maitland Macfreeze—they fell into bad courses, and went the way of all such!"

"Why—you old goosey—I was only speaking in a general sense, of course! You are always so literal. Now when we have finished tea, sing me that funny song about high-heeled shoon and siller tags, and the one-and-forty wooers."

"No, no. I couldna sing to-night! It's Henchard—he hates me; so that I may not be his friend if I would. I would understand why there should be a wee bit envy; but I cannet see a reason for the whole intensity of what he feels. Now, can you, Lucetta? It is more like old-fashioned rivalry in love than just a bit of rivalry in trade."

Lucetta had grown somewhat wan. "No," she replied.

"I give him employment—I cannet refuse it. But neither

can I blind myself to the fact that with a man of passions such as his, there is no safeguard for conduct!"

"What have you heard—O Donald, dearest?" said Lucetta in alarm. The words on her lips were "anything about me?"—but she did not utter them. She could not, however, suppress her agitation, and her eyes filled with tears.

"No, no—it is not so serious as ye fancy," declared Farfrae soothingly; though he did not know its seriousness so well as she.

"I wish you would do what we have talked of," mournfully remarked Lucetta. "Give up business, and go away from here. We have plenty of money, and why should we stay?"

Farfrae seemed seriously disposed to discuss this move, and they talked thereon till a visitor was announced. Their neighbor Alderman Vatt came in.

"You've heard, I suppose, of poor Doctor Chalkfield's death? Yes—died this afternoon at five," said Mr. Vatt. Chalkfield was the Councilman who had succeeded to the Mayoralty in the preceding November.

Farfrae was sorry at the intelligence, and Mr. Vatt continued: "Well, we know he's been going some days, and as his family is well provided for we must take it all as it is. Now I have called to ask 'ee this—quite privately. If I should nominate 'ee to succeed him, and there should be no particular opposition, will 'ee accept the chair?"

"But there are folk whose turn is before mine; and I'm over young, and may be thought pushing!" said Farfrae after a pause.

"Not at all. I don't speak for myself only, several have named it. You won't refuse?"

"We thought of going away," interposed Lucetta, looking at Farfrae anxiously.

"It was only a fancy," Farfrae murmured. "I wouldna refuse if it is the wish of a respectable majority in the Council."

"Very well, then, look upon yourself as elected. We have had older men long enough."

When he was gone Farfrae said musingly, "See now how it's ourselves that are ruled by the Powers above us! We plan this, but we do that. If they want to make me Mayor I will stay, and Henchard must rave as he will."

From this evening onward Lucetta was very uneasy. If she had not been imprudence incarnate she would not have acted as she did when she met Henchard by accident a day or two later. It was in the bustle of the market, when no one could readily notice their discourse.

"Michael," said she, "I must again ask you what I asked you months ago—to return me any letters or papers of mine that you may have—unless you have destroyed them? You must see how desirable it is that the time at Jersey should be blotted out, for the good of all parties."

"Why, bless the woman! — I packed up every scrap of your handwriting to give you in the coach—but you never appeared."

She explained how the death of her aunt had prevented her taking the journey on that day. "And what became of the parcel then?" she asked.

He could not say—he would consider. When she was gone he recollected that he had left a heap of useless papers in his former dining-room safe—built up in the wall of his old house—now occupied by Farfrae. The letters might have been amongst them.

A grotesque grin shaped itself on Henchard's face. Had that safe been opened?

On the very evening which followed this there was a great ringing of bells in Casterbridge, and the combined brass, wood, catgut, and leather bands played round the town with more prodigality of percussion-notes than ever. Farfrae was Mayor—the two-hundredth odd of a series forming an elective dynasty dating back to the days of Charles I—and the fair Lucetta was the courted of the town. . . . But, ah! that worm i' the bud—Henchard; what he could tell!

He, in the meantime, festering with indignation at some erroneous intelligence of Farfrae's opposition to the scheme for installing him in the little seed-shop, was greeted with the news of the municipal election (which,

by reason of Farfrae's comparative youth and his Scottish
nativity—a thing unprecedented in the case—had an
interest far beyond the ordinary). The bell-ringing and
the band-playing, loud as Tamerlane's trumpet, goaded
the downfallen Henchard indescribably: the ousting now
seemed to him to be complete.

The next morning he went to the corn-yard as usual,
and about eleven o'clock Donald entered through the
green door, with no trace of the worshipful about him.
The yet more emphatic change of places between him
and Henchard which this election had established renewed a slight embarrassment in the manner of the modest
younger man; but Henchard showed the front of one who
had overlooked all this; and Farfrae met his amenities
half-way at once.

"I was going to ask you," said Henchard, "about a
packet that I may possibly have left in my old safe in
the dining-room." He added particulars.

"If so, it is there now," said Farfrae. "I have never
opened the safe at all as yet; for I keep ma papers at
the bank, to sleep easy o' nights."

"It was not of much consequence—to me," said Henchard. "But I'll call for it this evening, if you don't mind?"

It was quite late when he fulfilled his promise. He had
primed himself with grog, as he did very frequently now,
and a curl of sardonic humor hung on his lip as he approached the house, as though he were contemplating some
terrible form of amusement. Whatever it was, the incident
of his entry did not diminish its force, this being his
first visit to the house since he had lived there as owner.
The ring of the bell spoke to him like the voice of a
familiar drudge who had been bribed to forsake him; the
movements of the doors were revivals of dead days.

Farfrae invited him into the dining-room, where he at
once unlocked the iron safe built into the wall, *his*, Henchard's safe, made by an ingenious locksmith under his
direction. Farfrae drew thence the parcel, and other papers,
with apologies for not having returned them.

"Never mind," said Henchard drily. "The fact is they

are letters mostly. . . . Yes," he went on, sitting down and unfolding Lucetta's passionate bundle, "here they be. That ever I should see 'em again! I hope Mrs. Farfrae is well after her exertions of yesterday?"

"She has felt a bit weary; and has gone to bed airly on that account."

Henchard returned to the letters, sorting them over with interest, Farfrae being seated at the other end of the dining-table. "You don't forget, of course," he resumed, "that curious chapter in the history of my past which I told you of, and that you gave me some assistance in? These letters are, in fact, related to that unhappy business. Though, thank God, it is all over now."

"What became of the poor woman?" asked Farfrae.

"Luckily she married, and married well," said Henchard. "So that these reproaches she poured out on me do not now cause me any twinges, as they might otherwise have done. . . . Just listen to what an angry woman will say!"

Farfrae, willing to humor Henchard, though quite uninterested, and bursting with yawns, gave well-mannered attention.

"'For me,'" Henchard read, "'there is practically no future. A creature too unconventionally devoted to you—who feels it impossible that she can be wife of any other man; and who is yet no more to you than the first woman you meet in the street—such am I. I quite acquit you of any intention to wrong me, yet you are the door through which wrong has come to me. That in the event of your present wife's death you will place me in her position is a consolation so far as it goes—but how far does it go? Thus I sit here, forsaken by my few acquaintance, and forsaken by you!'"

"That's how she went on to me," said Henchard, "acres of words like that, when what had happened was what I could not cure."

"Yes," said Farfrae absently, "it is the way wi' women." But the fact was that he knew very little of the sex; yet detecting a sort of resemblance in style between the effu-

sions of the woman he worshipped and those of the supposed stranger, he concluded that Aphrodite ever spoke
thus, whosesoever the personality she assumed.

Henchard unfolded another letter, and read it through
likewise, stopping at the subscription as before. "Her name
I don't give," he said blandly. "As I didn't marry her, and
another man did, I can scarcely do that in fairness to her."

"Tr-rue, tr-rue," said Farfrae. "But why didn't you
marry her when your wife Susan died?" Farfrae asked this
and the other questions in the comfortably indifferent tone
of one whom the matter very remotely concerned.

"Ah—well you may ask that!" said Henchard, the new-
moon-shaped grin adumbrating itself again upon his
mouth. "In spite of all her protestations, when I came
forward to do so, as in generosity bound, she was not
the woman for me."

"She had already married another—maybe?"

Henchard seemed to think it would be sailing too near
the wind to descend further into particulars, and he
answered "Yes."

"The young lady must have had a heart that bore
transplanting very readily!"

"She had, she had," said Henchard emphatically.

He opened a third and fourth letter, and read. This
time he approached the conclusion as if the signature were
indeed coming with the rest. But again he stopped short.
The truth was that, as may be divined, he had quite intended to effect a grand catastrophe at the end of this
drama by reading out the name; he had come to the house
with no other thought. But sitting here in cold blood he
could not do it. Such a wrecking of hearts appalled even
him. His quality was such that he could have annihilated
them both in the heat of action; but to accomplish the
deed by oral poison was beyond the nerve of his enmity.

XXXV

As Donald stated, Lucetta had retired early to her room
because of fatigue. She had, however, not gone to rest, but
sat in the bedside chair reading and thinking over the

events of the day. At the ringing of the door-bell by Henchard she wondered who it should be that would call at that comparatively late hour. The dining-room was almost under her bed-room; she could hear that somebody was admitted there, and presently the indistinct murmur of a person reading became audible.

The usual time for Donald's arrival upstairs came and passed, yet still the reading and conversation went on. This was very singular. She could think of nothing but that some extraordinary crime had been committed, and that the visitor, whoever he might be, was reading an account of it from a special edition of the *Casterbridge Chronicle*. At last she left the room, and descended the stairs. The dining-room door was ajar, and in the silence of the resting household the voice and the words were recognizable before she reached the lower flight. She stood transfixed. Her own words greeted her in Henchard's voice, like spirits from the grave.

Lucetta leant upon the banister with her cheek against the smooth hand-rail, as if she would make a friend of it in her misery. Rigid in this position, more and more words fell successively upon her ear. But what amazed her most was the tone of her husband. He spoke merely in the accents of a man who made a present of his time.

"One word," he was saying, as the crackling of paper denoted that Henchard was unfolding yet another sheet. "Is it quite fair to this young woman's memory to read at such length to a stranger what was intended for your eye alone?"

"Well, yes," said Henchard. "By not giving her name I make it an example of all womankind, and not a scandal to one."

"If I were you I would destroy them," said Farfrae, giving more thought to the letters than he had hitherto done. "As another man's wife it would injure the woman if it were known."

"No, I shall not destroy them," murmured Henchard, putting the letters away. Then he arose, and Lucetta heard no more.

She went back to her bedroom in a semi-paralyzed state.

For very fear she could not undress, but sat on the edge of the bed, waiting. Would Henchard let out the secret in his parting words? Her suspense was terrible. Had she confessed all to Donald in their early acquaintance he might possibly have got over it, and married her just the same—unlikely as it had once seemed; but for her or any one else to tell him now would be fatal.

The door slammed; she could hear her husband bolting it. After looking round in his customary way he came leisurely up the stairs. The spark in her eyes well-nigh went out when he appeared round the bed-room door. Her gaze hung doubtful for a moment, then to her joyous amazement she saw that he looked at her with the rallying smile of one who had just been relieved of a scene that was irksome. She could hold out no longer, and sobbed hysterically.

When he had restored her Farfrae naturally enough spoke of Henchard. "Of all men he was the least desirable as a visitor," he said; "but it is my belief that he's just a bit crazed. He has been reading to me a long lot of letters relating to his past life; and I could do no less than indulge him by listening."

This was sufficient. Henchard, then, had not told. Henchard's last words to Farfrae, in short, as he stood on the door-step, had been these: "Well—I'm much obliged to 'ee for listening. I may tell more about her some day."

Finding this, she was much perplexed as to Henchard's motives in opening the matter at all; for in such cases we attribute to an enemy a power of consistent action which we never find in ourselves or in our friends; and forget that abortive efforts from want of heart are as possible to revenge as to generosity.

Next morning Lucetta remained in bed, meditating how to parry this incipient attack. The bold stroke of telling Donald the truth, dimly conceived, was yet too bold; for she dreaded lest in doing so he, like the rest of the world, should believe that the episode was rather her fault than her misfortune. She decided to employ persuasion—not with Donald, but with the enemy himself. It seemed the only practicable weapon left her as a woman. Having laid her plan she rose, and wrote to him who kept her on these tenterhooks:—

"I overheard your interview with my husband last night, and saw the drift of your revenge. The very thought of it crushes me! Have pity on a distressed woman! If you could see you would relent. You do not know how anxiety has told upon me lately. I will be at the Ring at the time you leave work—just before the sun goes down. Please come that way. I cannot rest till I have seen you face to face, and heard from your mouth that you will carry this horse-play no further."

To herself she said, on closing up this appeal: "If ever tears and pleadings have served the weak to fight the strong, let them do so now!"

With this view she made a toilette which differed from all she had ever attempted before. To heighten her natural attractions had hitherto been the unvarying endeavor of her adult life, and one in which she was no novice. But now she neglected this, and even proceeded to impair the natural presentation. Beyond a natural reason for her slightly drawn look, she had not slept all the previous night, and this had produced upon her pretty though slightly worn features the aspect of a countenance ageing prematurely from extreme sorrow. She selected—as much from want of spirit as design—her poorest, plainest, and longest discarded attire.

To avoid the contingency of being recognized she veiled herself, and slipped out of the house quickly. The sun was resting on the hill like a drop of blood on an eyelid by the time she had got up the road opposite the amphitheater, which she speedily entered. The interior was shadowy, and emphatic of the absence of every living thing.

She was not disappointed in the fearful hope with which she awaited him. Henchard came over the top, descended, and Lucetta waited breathlessly. But having reached the arena she saw a change in his bearing: he stood still at a little distance from her; she could not think why.

Nor could any one else have known. The truth was that in appointing this spot, and this hour, for the rendezvous, Lucetta had unwittingly backed up her entreaty by the strongest argument she could have used outside words, with this man of moods, glooms, and superstitions. Her figure in the midst of the huge enclosure, the unusual plainness of her dress, her attitude of hope and appeal, so strongly revived in his soul the memory of another ill-used woman who had stood there and thus in bygone days, and had now passed away into her rest, that he was unmanned, and his heart smote him for having attempted reprisals on one of a sex so weak. When he approached her, and before she had spoken a word, her point was half gained.

His manner as he had come down had been one of cynical carelessness; but he now put away his grim half-smile, and said in a kindly subdued tone, "Good-night t'ye. Of course I'm glad to come if you want me."

"Oh, thank you," she said apprehensively.

"I am sorry to see 'ee looking so ill," he stammered with unconcealed compunction.

She shook her head. "How can you be sorry," she asked, "when you deliberately cause it?"

"What!" said Henchard uneasily. "Is it anything I have done that has pulled you down like that?"

"It is all your doing," said she. "I have no other grief. My happiness would be secure enough but for your threats. O Michael! don't wreck me like this! You might think that you have done enough! When I came here I was a young woman; now I am rapidly becoming an old one. Neither my husband nor any other man will regard me with interest long."

Henchard was disarmed. His old feeling of supercilious pity for womankind in general was intensified by this suppliant appearing here as the double of the first. Moreover, that thoughtless want of foresight which had led to all her trouble remained with poor Lucetta still; she had come to meet him here in this compromising way without perceiving the risk. Such a woman was very small deer to hunt; he felt ashamed, lost all zest and desire to humiliate Lucetta there and then, and no longer envied Farfrae his bargain. He had married money, but nothing more. Henchard was anxious to wash his hands of the game.

"Well, what do you want me to do?" he said gently. "I am sure I shall be very willing. My reading of those letters was only a sort of practical joke, and I revealed nothing."

"To give me back the letters and any papers you may have that breathe of matrimony or worse."

"So be it. Every scrap shall be yours. . . . But, between you and me, Lucetta, he is sure to find out something of the matter, sooner or later."

"Ah!" she said with eager tremulousness; "but not till I have proved myself a faithful and deserving wife to him, and then he may forgive me everything!"

Henchard silently looked at her: he almost envied Farfrae such love as that, even now. "H'm—I hope so," he said. "But you shall have the letters without fail. And your secret shall be kept. I swear it."

"How good you are!"—how shall I get them?"

He reflected, and said he would send them the next morning. "Now don't doubt me," he added. "I can keep my word."

XXXVI

Returning from her appointment Lucetta saw a man waiting by the lamp nearest to her own door. When she stopped to go in he came and spoke to her. It was Jopp.

He begged her pardon for addressing her. But he had heard that Mr. Farfrae had been applied to by a neighboring corn-merchant to recommend a working partner; if so, he wished to offer himself. He could give good security, and had stated as much to Mr. Farfrae in a letter; but he would feel much obliged if Lucetta would say a word in his favor to her husband.

"It is a thing I know nothing about," said Lucetta coldly.

"But you can testify to my trustworthiness better than anybody, ma'am," said Jopp. "I was in Jersey several years, and knew you there by sight."

"Indeed," she replied. "But I knew nothing of you."

"I think, ma'am, that a word or two from you would secure for me what I covet very much," he persisted.

She steadily refused to have anything to do with the affair, and cutting him short, because of her anxiety to get indoors before her husband should miss her, left him on the pavement.

He watched her till she had vanished, and then went home. When he got there he sat down in the fireless chimney corner looking at the iron dogs, and the wood laid across them for heating the morning kettle. A movement upstairs disturbed him, and Henchard came down from his bedroom, where he seemed to have been rummaging boxes.

"I wish," said Henchard, "you would do me a service, Jopp, now—to-night, I mean, if you can. Leave this at Mrs. Farfrae's for her. I should take it myself, of course, but I don't wish to be seen there."

He handed a package in brown paper, sealed. Henchard had been as good as his word. Immediately on coming indoors he had searched over his few belongings; and every scrap of Lucetta's writing that he possessed was here. Jopp indifferently expressed his willingness.

"Well, how have ye got on to-day?" his lodger asked. "Any prospect of an opening?"

"I am afraid not," said Jopp, who had not told the other of his application to Farfrae.

"There never will be in Casterbridge," declared Henchard decisively. "You must roam further afield." He said good-night to Jopp, and returned to his own part of the house.

Jopp sat on till his eyes were attracted by the shadow of the candle-snuff on the wall, and looking at the original he found that it had formed itself into a head like a red-hot cauliflower. Henchard's packet next met his gaze. He knew there had been something of the nature of wooing between Henchard and the now Mrs. Farfrae; and his vague ideas on the subject narrowed themselves down to these: Henchard had a parcel belonging to Mrs. Farfrae, and he had reasons for not returning that parcel to her in person. What could be inside it? So he went on and on till, animated by resentment at Lucetta's haughtiness, as he thought it, and curiosity to learn if there were any weak sides to this transaction with Henchard, he examined the package. The pen and all its relations being awkward tools in Henchard's hands he had affixed the seals without an impression, it never occurring to him that the efficacy of such a fastening depended on this. Jopp was far less of a tyro; he lifted one of the seals with his penknife, peeped in at the end thus opened, saw that the bundle consisted of letters; and, having satisfied himself thus far, sealed up the end again by simply softening the wax with the candle, and went off with the parcel as requested.

His path was by the river-side at the foot of the town. Coming into the light at the bridge which stood at the end of High Street he beheld lounging thereon Mother Cuxsom and Nance Mockridge.

"We be just going down Mixen Lane way, to look into Peter's Finger afore creeping to bed," said Mrs. Cuxsom. "There's a fiddle and tambourine going on there. Lord, what's all the world—do ye come along too, Jopp—'twon't hinder ye five minutes."

Jopp had mostly kept himself out of this company, but present circumstances made him somewhat more reckless than usual, and without many words he decided to go to his destination that way.

Though the upper part of Durnover was mainly composed of a curious congeries of barns and farmsteads, there was a less picturesque side to the parish. This was Mixen Lane, now in great part pulled down.

Mixen Lane was the Adullam of all the surrounding villages. It was the hiding-place of those who were in distress, and in debt, and trouble of every kind. Farm-laborers and other peasants, who combined a little poaching with their farming, and a little brawling and bibbing with their poaching, found themselves sooner or later in Mixen Lane. Rural mechanics too idle to mechanize, rural servants too rebellious to serve, drifted or were forced into Mixen Lane.

The lane and its surrounding thicket of thatched cottages stretched out like a spit into the moist and misty lowland. Much that was sad, much that was low, some things that were baneful, could be seen in Mixen Lane. Vice ran freely in and out certain of the doors of the neighborhood; recklessness dwelt under the roof with the crooked chimney; shame in some bow-windows; theft (in times of privation) in the thatched and mud-walled houses by the sallows. Even slaughter had not been altogether unknown here. In a block of cottages up an alley there might have been erected an altar to disease in years gone by. Such was Mixen Lane in the times when Henchard and Farfrae were Mayors.

Yet this mildewed leaf in the sturdy and flourishing Casterbridge plant lay close to the open country; not a hundred yards from a row of noble elms, and commanding a view across the moor of airy uplands and cornfields, and mansions of the great. A brook divided the moor from the tenements, and to outward view there was no way across it—no way to the houses but round about by the road. But under every householder's stairs there was kept a mysterious plank nine inches wide; which plank was a secret bridge.

If you, as one of those refugee householders, came in from business after dark—and this was the business time here—you stealthily crossed the moor, approached the border of the aforesaid brook, and whistled opposite the house to which you belonged. A shape thereupon made its appearance on the other side bearing the bridge on end against the sky; it was lowered; you crossed, and a hand helped you to land yourself, together with the pheasants and hares gathered from neighboring manors. You sold them slily the next morning, and the day after you stood before the magistrates, with the eyes of all your sympathizing neighbors concentrated on your back. You disappeared for a time; then you were again found quietly living in Mixen Lane.

Walking along the lane at dusk the stranger was struck by two or three peculiar features therein. One was an intermittent rumbling from the back premises of the inn half-way up; this meant a skittle alley. Another was the extensive prevalence of whistling in the various domiciles —a piped note of some kind coming from nearly every open door. Another was the frequency of white aprons over dingy gowns among the women around the doorways. A white apron is a suspicious vesture in situations where spotlessness is difficult; moreover, the industry and cleanliness which the white apron expressed were belied by the postures and gaits of the women who wore it—their knuckles being mostly on their hips (an attitude which lent them the aspect of two-handled mugs), and their shoulders against door-posts; while there was a curious alacrity in the turn of each honest woman's head upon her neck and in the twirl of her honest eyes, at any noise resembling a masculine footfall along the lane.

Yet amid so much that was bad needy respectability also found a home. Under some of the roofs abode pure and virtuous souls whose presence there was due to the iron hand of necessity, and to that alone. Families from decayed villages—families of that once bulky, but now nearly extinct, section of village society called "liviers," or lifeholders—copy-holders and others, whose roof-trees had fallen for some reason or other, compelling them to quit the rural spot that had been their home for generations— came here, unless they chose to lie under a hedge by the wayside.

The inn called Peter's Finger was the church of Mixen Lane.

It was centrally situate, as such places should be, and bore about the same social relation to the Three Mariners as the latter bore to the King's Arms. At first sight the inn was so respectable as to be puzzling. The front door was kept shut, and the step was so clean that evidently but few persons entered over its sanded surface. But at the corner of the public-house was an alley, a mere slit, dividing it from the next building. Half-way up the alley was a narrow door, shiny and paintless from the rub of infinite hands and shoulders. This was the actual entrance to the inn.

A pedestrian would be seen abstractedly passing along Mixen Lane; and then, in a moment, he would vanish, causing the gazer to blink like Ashton at the disappearance of Ravenswood. That abstracted pedestrian had edged into the slit by the adroit fillip of his person sideways; from the slit he edged into the tavern by a similar exercise of skill.

The company at the Three Mariners were persons of quality in comparison with the company which gathered here; though it must be admitted that the lowest fringe of the Mariner's party touched the crest of Peter's at points. Waifs and strays of all sorts loitered about here. The landlady was a virtuous woman who years ago had been unjustly sent to gaol as an accessory to something or other after the fact. She underwent her twelvemonth, and had worn a martyr's countenance ever since, except at times of meeting the constable who apprehended her, when she winked her eye.

To this house Jopp and his acquaintances had arrived. The settles on which they sat down were thin and tall, their tops being guyed by pieces of twine to hooks in the ceiling; for when the guests grew boisterous the settles would rock and overturn without some such security. The thunder of bowls echoed from the backyard; swingels hung behind the blower of the chimney; and ex-poachers and ex-gamekeepers, whom squires had persecuted without a cause, sat elbowing each other—men who in past times had met in fights under the moon, till lapse of sentences on the one part, and loss of favor and expulsion from service on the other, brought them here together to a common level, where they sat calmly discussing old times.

"Dos't mind how you could jerk a trout ashore with a bramble, and not ruffle the stream, Charl?" a deposed keeper was saying. " 'Twas at that I caught 'ee once, if you can mind?"

"That can I. But the worst larry for me was that pheasant business at Yalbury Wood. Your wife swore false that time, Joe—O, by Gad, she did—there's no denying it."

"How was that?" asked Jopp.

"Why—Joe closed wi' me, and we rolled down together, close to his garden-hedge. Hearing the noise, out ran his wife with the oven pyle, and it being dark under the trees she couldn't see which was uppermost. 'Where beest thee, Joe, under or top?' she screeched. 'Oh—under, by Gad!' says he. She then began to rap down upon my skull, back, and ribs with the pyle till we'd roll over again. 'Where beest now, dear Joe, under or top?' she'd scream again. By George, 'twas through her I was took! And then when we got up in hall she sware that the cock pheasant was one of her rearing, when 'twas not your bird at all, Joe; 'twas Squire Brown's bird—that's whose 'twas—one that we'd picked off as we passed his wood, an hour afore. It did hurt my feelings to be so wronged! . . . Ah well—'tis over now."

"I might have had 'ee days afore that," said the keeper. "I was within a few yards of 'ee dozens of times, with a sight more of birds than that poor one."

"Yes—'tis not our greatest doings that the world gets wind of," said the furmity-woman, who, lately settled in this purlieu, sat among the rest. Having travelled a great deal in her time she spoke with cosmopolitan largeness of idea. It was she who presently asked Jopp what was the parcel he kept so snugly under his arm.

"Ah, therein lies a grand secret," said Jopp. "It is the passion of love. To think that a woman should love one man so well, and hate another so unmercifully."

"Who's the object of your meditation, sir?"

"One that stands high in this town. I'd like to shame her! Upon my life, 'twould be as good as a play to read her love-letters, the proud piece of silk and wax-work! For 'tis her love-letters that I've got here."

"Love-letters? then let's hear 'em, good soul," said Mother Cuxsom. "Lord, do ye mind, Richard, what fools we used to be when we were younger? Getting a school-boy to write ours for us; and giving him a penny, do ye mind, not to tell other folks what he'd put inside, do ye mind?"

By this time Jopp had pushed his finger under the seals, and unfastened the letters, tumbling them over and picking up one here and there at random, which he read aloud. These passages soon began to uncover the secret which Lucetta had so earnestly hoped to keep buried, though the epistles, being allusive only, did not make it altogether plain.

"Mrs. Farfrae wrote that!" said Nance Mockridge. " 'Tis a humbling thing for us, as respectable women, that one of the same sex could do it. And now she's vowed herself to another man!"

"So much the better for her," said the aged furmity-woman. "Ah, I saved her from a real bad marriage, and she's never been the one to thank me."

"I say, what a good foundation for a skimmity-ride," said Nance.

"True," said Mrs. Cuxsom, reflecting. " 'Tis as good a ground for a skimmity-ride as ever I knowed; and it ought not to be wasted. The last one seen in Casterbridge must have been ten years ago, if a day."

At this moment there was a shrill whistle, and the landlady said to the man who had been called Charl, " 'Tis Jim coming in. Would ye go and let down the bridge for me?"

Without replying Charl and his comrade Joe rose, and receiving a lantern from her went out at the back door and down the garden-path, which ended abruptly at the edge of the stream already mentioned. Beyond the stream was the open moor, from which a clammy breeze smote upon their faces as they advanced. Taking up the board that had lain in readiness one of them lowered it across the water, and the instant its further end touched the ground footsteps entered upon it, and there appeared from the shade a stalwart man with straps round his knees, a double-barrelled gun under his arm and some birds slung up behind him. They asked him if he had had much luck.

"Not much," he said indifferently. "All safe inside?"

Receiving a reply in the affirmative he went on inwards, the others withdrawing the bridge and beginning to retreat in his rear. Before, however, they had entered the house a cry of "Ahoy" from the moor led them to pause.

The cry was repeated. They pushed the lantern into an outhouse, and went back to the brink of the stream.

"Ahoy—is this the way to Casterbridge?" said some one from the other side.

"Not in particular," said Charl. "There's a river afore 'ee."

"I don't care—here's for through it!" said the man in the moor. "I've had travelling enough for to-day."

"Stop a minute, then," said Charl, finding that the man was no enemy. "Joe, bring the plank and lantern; here's somebody that's lost his way. You should have kept along the turnpike road, friend, and not have strook across here."

"I should—as I see now. But I saw a light here, and says I to myself, that's an outlying house, depend on't."

The plank was now lowered; and the stranger's form shaped itself from the darkness. He was a middle-aged man, with hair and whiskers prematurely grey, and a broad and genial face. He had crossed on the plank without hesitation, and seemed to see nothing odd in the transit. He thanked them, and walked between them up the garden. "What place is this?" he asked, when they reached the door.

"A public-house."

"Ah. Perhaps it will suit me to put up at. Now then, come in and wet your whistle at my expense for the lift over you have given me."

They followed him into the inn, where the increased light exhibited him as one who would stand higher in an estimate by the eye than in one by the ear. He was dressed with a certain clumsy richness—his coat being furred, and his head covered by a cap of sealskin, which, though the nights were chilly, must have been warm for the daytime, spring being somewhat advanced. In his hand he carried a small mahogany case, strapped, and clamped with brass.

Apparently surprised at the kind of company which confronted him through the kitchen door, he at once abandoned his idea of putting up at the house; but taking the situation lightly, he called for glasses of the best, paid for them as he stood in the passage, and turned to proceed on his way by the front door. This was barred, and while the landlady was unfastening it the conversation about the skimmington was continued in the sitting-room, and reached his ears.

"What do they mean by a 'skimmity-ride'?" he asked.

"Oh, sir!" said the landlady, swinging her long earrings with deprecating modesty; "'tis a' old foolish thing they do in these parts when a man's wife is—well, not too particularly his own. But as a respectable householder I don't encourage it."

"Still, are they going to do it shortly? It is a good sight to see, I suppose?"

"Well, sir!" she simpered. And then, bursting into naturalness, and glancing from the corner of her eye, "'Tis the funniest thing under the sun! And it costs money."

"Ah! I remember hearing of some such thing. Now I shall be in Casterbridge for two or three weeks to come, and should not mind seeing the performance. Wait a moment." He turned back, entered the sitting room, and said, "Here, good folks; I should like to see the old custom you are talking of, and I don't mind being something towards it—take that." He threw a sovereign on the table and returned to the landlady at the door, of whom, having inquired the way into the town, he took his leave.

"There were more where that one came from," said Charl, when the sovereign had been taken up and handed to the landlady for safe keeping. "By George! we ought to have got a few more while we had him here."

"No, no," answered the landlady. "This is a respectable house, thank God! And I'll have nothing done but what's honorable."

"Well," said Jopp; "now we'll consider the business begun, and will soon get it in train."

"We will!" said Nance. "A good laugh warms my heart more than a cordial, and that's the truth on't."

Jopp gathered up the letters, and it being now some-what late he did not attempt to call at Farfrae's with them that night. He reached home, sealed them up as before, and delivered the parcel at its address next morning. Within an hour its contents were reduced to ashes by Lucetta, who, poor soul! was inclined to fall down on her knees in thankfulness that at last no evidence remained of the unlucky episode with Henchard in her past. For though hers had been rather the laxity of inadvertence than of intention, that episode, if known, was not the less likely to operate fatally between herself and her husband.

XXXVII

Such was the state of things when the current affairs of Casterbridge were interrupted by an event of such magni-tude that its influence reached to the lowest social stratum there, stirring the depths of its society simultaneously with the preparations for the skimmington. It was one of those excitements which, when they move a country town, leave a permanent mark upon its chronicles, as a warm sum-mer permanently marks the ring in the tree-trunk cor-responding to its date.

A Royal Personage was about to pass through the borough, on his course further west, to inaugurate an im-mense engineering work out that way. He had consented to halt half-an-hour or so in the town, and to receive an address from the corporation of Casterbridge, which, as a representative center of husbandry, wished thus to express its sense of the great services he had rendered to agricul-tural science and economics, by his zealous promotion of designs for placing the art of farming on a more scientific footing.

Royalty had not been seen in Casterbridge since the days of the third King George, and then only by candle-light for a few minutes, when that monarch, on a night-journey, had stopped to change horses at the King's Arms. The inhabitants therefore decided to make a thorough *fête carillonnée* of the unwonted occasion. Half-an-hour's pause was not long, it is true; but much might be done in it by a judicious grouping of incidents, above all, if the weather were fine.

The address was prepared on parchment by an artist who was handy at ornamental lettering, and was laid on with the best gold-leaf and colors that the sign-painter had in his shop. The Council met on the Tuesday before the appointed day, to arrange the details of procedure. While they were sitting, the door of the Council Chamber standing open, they heard a heavy footstep coming up the stairs. It advanced along the passage, and Henchard entered the room, in clothes of frayed and threadbare shabbiness, the very clothes which he had used to wear in the primal days when he had sat among them.

"I have a feeling," he said, advancing to the table and laying his hand upon the green cloth, "that I should like to join ye in this reception of our illustrious visitor. I suppose I could walk with the rest?"

Embarrassed glances were exchanged by the Council, and Grower nearly ate the end of his quill-pen off, so gnawed he it during the silence. Farfrae the young Mayor, who by virtue of his office sat in the large chair, intuitively caught the sense of the meeting, and as spokesman was obliged to utter it, glad as he would have been that the duty should have fallen to another tongue.

"I hardly see that it would be proper, Mr. Henchard," said he. "The Council are the Council, and as ye are no longer one of the body, there would be an irregularity in the proceeding. If ye were included, why not others?"

"I have a particular reason for wishing to assist at the ceremony."

Farfrae looked round. "I think I have expressed the feeling of the Council," he said.

"Yes, yes," from Dr. Bath, Lawyer Long, Alderman Tubber, and several more.

"Then I am not to be allowed to have anything to do with it officially?"

"I am afraid so; it is out of the question, indeed. But of course you can see the doings full well, such as they are to be, like the rest of the spectators."

Henchard did not reply to that very obvious suggestion, and, turning on his heel, went away.

It had been only a passing fancy of his, but opposition crystallized it into a determination. "I'll welcome his Royal Highness, or nobody shall!" he went about saying. "I am not going to be sat upon by Farfrae, or any of the rest of the paltry crew! You shall see."

The eventful morning was bright, a full-faced sun confronting early window-gazers eastward, and all perceived (for they were practised in weather-lore) that there was permanence in the glow. Visitors soon began to flock in from county houses, villages, remote copses, and lonely uplands, the latter in oiled boots and tilt bonnets, to see the reception, or if not to see it, at any rate to be near it. There was hardly a workman in the town who did not put a clean shirt on. Solomon Longways, Christopher Coney, Buzzford, and the rest of that fraternity, showed their sense of the occasion by advancing their customary eleven o'clock pint to half-past ten; from which they found a difficulty in getting back to the proper hour for several days.

Henchard had determined to do no work that day. He primed himself in the morning with a glass of rum, and walking down the street met Elizabeth-Jane, whom he had not seen for a week. "It was lucky," he said to her, "my twenty-one years had expired before this came on, or I should never have had the nerve to carry it out."

"Carry out what?" said she, alarmed.

"This welcome I am going to give our Royal visitor."

She was perplexed. "Shall we go and see it together?" she said.

"See it! I have other fish to fry. You see it. It will be worth seeing!"

She could do nothing to elucidate this, and decked herself out with a heavy heart. As the appointed time drew near she got sight again of her stepfather. She thought he was going to the Three Mariners; but no, he elbowed his way through the gay throng to the shop of Woolfrey, the draper. She waited in the crowd without.

In a few minutes he emerged, wearing, to her surprise, a brilliant rosette, while more surprising still, in his hand he carried a flag of somewhat homely construction, formed by tacking one of the small Union Jacks, which abounded in the town to-day, to the end of a deal wand—probably the roller from a piece of calico. Henchard rolled up his flag on the doorstep, put it under his arm, and went down the street.

Suddenly the taller members of the crowd turned their heads, and the shorter stood on tiptoe. It was said that the Royal *cortège* approached. The railway had stretched out an arm towards Casterbridge at this time, but had not reached it by several miles as yet; so that the intervening distance, as well as the remainder of the journey, was to be traversed by road in the old fashion. People thus waited—the county families in their carriages, the masses on foot—and watched the far-stretching London highway to the ringing of bells and chatter of tongues.

From the background Elizabeth-Jane watched the scene. Some seats had been arranged from which ladies could witness the spectacle, and the front seat was occupied by Lucetta, the Mayor's wife, just at present. In the road under her eyes stood Henchard. She appeared so bright and pretty that, as it seemed, he was experiencing the momentary weakness of wishing for her notice. But he was far from attractive to a woman's eye, ruled as that is so largely by the superficies of things. He was not only a journeyman, unable to appear as he formerly had appeared, but he disdained to appear as well as he might. Everybody else, from the Mayor to the washerwoman, shone in new vesture according to means; but Henchard had doggedly retained the fretted and weather-beaten garments of by-gone years.

Hence, alas, this occurred: Lucetta's eyes slid over him to this side and to that without anchoring on his features—as gaily dressed women's eyes will too often do on such occasions. Her manner signified quite plainly that she meant to know him in public no more.

But she was never tired of watching Donald, as he

stood in animated converse with his friends a few yards off, wearing round his young neck the official gold chain with great square links, like that round the Royal unicorn. Every trifling emotion that her husband showed as he talked had its reflex on her face and lips, which moved in little duplicates to his. She was living his part rather than her own, and cared for no one's situation but Farfrae's that day.

At length a man stationed at the furthest turn of the high road, namely, on the second bridge of which mention has been made, gave a signal; and the Corporation in their robes proceeded from the front of the Town Hall to the archway erected at the entrance to the town. The carriages containing the Royal visitor and his suite arrived at the spot in a cloud of dust, a procession was formed, and the whole came on to the Town Hall at a walking pace.

This spot was the center of interest. There were a few clear yards in front of the Royal carriage, sanded; and into this space a man stepped before any one could prevent him. It was Henchard. He had unrolled his private flag, and removing his hat he staggered to the side of the slowing vehicle, waving the Union Jack to and fro with his left hand, while he blandly held out his right to the Illustrious Personage.

All the ladies said with bated breath, "Oh, look there!" and Lucetta was ready to faint. Elizabeth-Jane peeped through the shoulders of those in front, saw what it was, and was terrified; and then her interest in the spectacle as a strange phenomenon got the better of her fear.

Farfrae, with Mayoral authority, immediately rose to the occasion. He seized Henchard by the shoulder, dragged him back, and told him roughly to be off. Henchard's eyes met his, and Farfrae observed the fierce light in them despite his excitement and irritation. For a moment Henchard stood his ground rigidly; then by an unaccountable impulse gave way and retired. Farfrae glanced to the ladies' gallery, and saw that his Calphurnia's cheek was pale.

"Why—it is your husband's old patron!" said Mrs.

Blowbody, a lady of the neighborhood who sat beside Lucetta.

"Patron!" said Donald's wife with quick indignation.

"Do you say the man is an acquaintance of Mr. Farfrae's?" observed Mrs. Bath, the physician's wife, a newcomer to the town through her recent marriage with the doctor.

"He works for my husband," said Lucetta.

"Oh—is that all? They have been saying to me that it was through him your husband first got a footing in Casterbridge. What stories people will tell!"

"They will indeed. It was not so at all. Donald's genius would have enabled him to get a footing anywhere, without anybody's help! He would have been just the same if there had been no Henchard in the world!"

It was partly Lucetta's ignorance of the circumstances of Donald's arrival which led her to speak thus; partly the sensation that everybody seemed bent on snubbing her at this triumphant time. The incident had occupied but a few moments, but it was necessarily witnessed by the Royal Personage, who, however, with practised tact, affected not to have noticed anything unusual. He alighted, the Mayor advanced, the address was read; the Illustrious Personage replied, then said a few words to Farfrae, and shook hands with Lucetta as the Mayor's wife. The ceremony occupied but a few minutes, and the carriages rattled heavily as Pharaoh's chariots down Corn Street and out upon the Budmouth Road, in continuation of the journey coastward.

In the crowd stood Coney, Buzzford, and Longways. "Some difference between him now and when he zung at the Dree Mariners," said the first. " 'Tis wonderful how he could get a lady of her quality to go snacks wi' en in such quick time."

"True. Yet how folk do worship fine clothes! Now there's a better-looking woman than she that nobody notices at all, because she's akin to that hontish fellow Henchard."

"I could worship ye, Buzz, for saying that," remarked Nance Mockridge. "I do like to see the trimming pulled off such Christmas candles. I am quite unequal to the part of villain myself, or I'd gi'e all my small silver to see that lady toppered. . . . And perhaps I shall soon," she added significantly.

"That's not a noble passiont for a 'oman to keep up," said Longways.

Nance did not reply, but every one knew what she meant. The ideas diffused by the reading of Lucetta's letters at Peter's Finger had condensed into a scandal, which was spreading like a miasmatic fog through Mixen Lane, and thence up the back streets of Casterbridge.

This mixed assemblage of idlers known to each other presently fell apart into two bands by a process of natural selection, the frequenters of Peter's Finger going off Mixen Lane-wards, where most of them lived, while Coney, Buzzford, Longways, and that connection remained in the street.

"You know what's brewing down there, I suppose?" said Buzzford mysteriously to the others.

Coney looked at him. "Not the skimmity-ride?"

Buzzford nodded.

"I have my doubts if it will be carried out," said Longways. "If they are getting it up they are keeping it mighty close."

"I heard they were thinking of it a fortnight ago, at all events."

"If I were sure o't I'd lay information," said Longways emphatically. " 'Tis too rough a joke, and apt to wake riots in towns. We know that the Scotchman is a right enough man, and that his lady has been a right enough 'oman since she came here, and if there was anything wrong about her afore, that's their business, not ours."

Coney reflected. Farfrae was still liked in the community; but it must be owned that, as the Mayor and man of money, engrossed with affairs and ambitions, he had lost in the eyes of the poorer inhabitants something of that wondrous charm which he had had for them as a light-hearted, penniless young man, who sang ditties as readily as the birds in the trees. Hence the anxiety to keep him from annoyance showed not quite the ardor that would have animated it in former days.

"Suppose we make inquiration into it, Christopher,"

continued Longways; "and if we find there's really anything in it, drop a letter to them most concerned, and advise 'em to keep out of the way?"

This course was decided on, and the group separated, Buzzford saying to Coney, "Come, my ancient friend; let's move on. There's nothing more to see here."

These well-intentioned ones would have been surprised had they known how ripe the great jocular plot really was. "Yes, to-night," Jopp had said to the Peter's party at the corner of Mixen Lane. "As a wind-up to the Royal visit the hit will be all the more pat by reason of their great elevation to-day."

To him, at least, it was not a joke, but a retaliation.

XXXVIII

The proceedings had been brief—too brief—to Lucetta, whom an intoxicating *Weltlust* had fairly mastered; but they had brought her a great triumph nevertheless. The shake of the Royal hand still lingered in her fingers; and the chit-chat she had overheard, that her husband might possibly receive the honor of knighthood, though idle to a degree, seemed not the wildest vision; stranger things had occurred to men so good and captivating as her Scotchman was.

After the collision with the Mayor, Henchard had withdrawn behind the ladies' stand; and there he stood, regarding with a stare of abstraction the spot on the lapel of his coat where Farfrae's hand had seized it. He put his own hand there, as if he could hardly realize such an outrage from one whom it had once been his wont to treat with ardent generosity. While pausing in this half-stupefied state the conversation of Lucetta with the other ladies reached his ears; and he distinctly heard her deny him—deny that he had assisted Donald, that he was anything more than a common journeyman.

He moved on homeward, and met Jopp in the archway to the Bull Stake. "So you've had a snub," said Jopp.

"And what if I have?" answered Henchard sternly.

"Why, I've had one too, so we are both under the same cold shade." He briefly related his attempt to win Lucetta's intercession.

Henchard merely heard his story, without taking it deeply in. His own relation to Farfrae and Lucetta overshadowed all kindred ones. He went on saying brokenly to himself, "She has supplicated to me in her time; and now her tongue won't own me nor her eyes see me! . . . And he—how angry he looked. He drove me back as if I were a bull breaking fence. . . . I took it like a lamb, for I saw it could not be settled there. He can rub brine on a green wound! . . . But he shall pay for it, and she shall be sorry. It must come to a tussle—face to face; and then we'll see how a coxcomb can front a man!"

Without further reflection the fallen merchant, bent on some wild purpose, ate a hasty dinner and went forth to find Farfrae. After being injured by him as a rival, and snubbed by him as a journeyman, the crowning degradation had been reserved for this day—that he should be shaken at the collar by him as a vagabond in the face of the whole town.

The crowds had dispersed. But for the green arches which still stood as they were erected Casterbridge life had resumed its ordinary shape. Henchard went down Corn Street till he came to Farfrae's house, where he knocked, and left a message that he would be glad to see his employer at the granaries as soon as he conveniently could come there. Having done this he proceeded round to the back and entered the yard.

Nobody was present, for, as he had been aware, the laborers and carters were enjoying a half-holiday on account of the events of the morning—though the carters would have to return for a short time later on, to feed and litter down the horses. He had reached the granary steps and was about to ascend, when he said to himself aloud, "I'm stronger than he."

Henchard returned to a shed, where he selected a short piece of rope from several pieces that were lying about; hitching one end of this to a nail, he took the other in his right hand and turned himself bodily round, while keeping his arm against his side; by this contrivance he pinioned the arm effectively. He now went up the ladders to the top floor of the corn-stores.

It was empty except of a few sacks, and at the further end was the door often mentioned, opening under the cat-head and chain that hoisted the sacks. He fixed the door open and looked over the sill. There was a depth of thirty or forty feet to the ground; here was the spot on which he had been standing with Farfrae when Elizabeth-Jane had seen him lift his arm, with many misgivings as to what the movement portended.

He retired a few steps into the loft and waited. From this elevated perch his eye could sweep the roofs round about, the upper parts of the luxurious chestnut trees, now delicate in leaves of a week's age, and the drooping boughs of the limes; Farfrae's garden and the green door leading therefrom. In course of time—he could not say how long—that green door opened and Farfrae came through. He was dressed as if for a journey. The low light of the nearing evening caught his head and face when he emerged from the shadow of the wall, warming them to a complexion of flame-color. Henchard watched him with his mouth firmly set, the squareness of his jaw and the verticality of his profile being unduly marked.

Farfrae came on with one hand in his pocket, and humming a tune in a way which told that the words were most in his mind. They were those of the song he had sung when he arrived years before at the Three Mariners, a poor young man, adventuring for life and fortune, and scarcely knowing whitherward:—

> "And here's a hand, my trusty fiere,
>   And gie's a hand o' thine."

Nothing moved Henchard like an old melody. He sank back. "No; I can't do it!" he gasped. "Why does the infernal fool begin that now!"

At length Farfrae was silent, and Henchard looked out of the loft door. "Will ye come up here?" he said.

"Ay, man," said Farfrae. "I couldn't see ye. What's wrang?"

A minute later Henchard heard his feet on the lowest ladder. He heard him land on the first floor, ascend and land on the second, begin the ascent to the third. And then his head rose through the trap behind.

"What are you doing up here at this time?" he asked, coming forward. "Why didn't ye take your holiday like the rest of the men?" He spoke in a tone which had just severity enough in it to show that he remembered the untoward event of the forenoon, and his conviction that Henchard had been drinking.

Henchard said nothing; but going back he closed the stair hatchway, and stamped upon it so that it went tight into its frame; he next turned to the wondering young man, who by this time observed that one of Henchard's arms was bound to his side.

"Now," said Henchard quietly, "we stand face to face —man and man. Your money and your fine wife no longer lift 'ee above me as they did but now, and my poverty does not press me down."

"What does it all mean?" asked Farfrae simply.

"Wait a bit, my lad. You should ha' thought twice before you affronted to extremes a man who had nothing to lose. I've stood your rivalry, which ruined me, and your snubbing, which humbled me; but your hustling, that disgraced me, I won't stand!"

Farfrae warmed a little at this. "Ye'd no business there," he said.

"As much as any one among ye! What, you forward stripling, tell a man of my age he'd no business there!" The anger-vein swelled in his forehead as he spoke.

"You insulted Royalty, Henchard; and 'twas my duty, as the chief magistrate, to stop you."

"Royalty be damned," said Henchard. "I am as loyal as you, come to that!"

"I am not here to argue. Wait till you cool doon, wait till you cool; and you will see things the same way as I do."

"You may be the one to cool first," said Henchard

grimly. "Now this is the case. Here be we, in this four-square loft, to finish out that little wrestle you began this morning. There's the door, forty foot above ground. One of us puts the other out by that door—the master stays inside. If he likes he may go down afterwards and give the alarm that the other has fallen out by accident—or he may tell the truth—that's his business. As the strongest man I've tied one arm to take no advantage of 'ee. D'ye understand? Then here's at 'ee!"

There was no time for Farfrae to do aught but one thing, to close with Henchard, for the latter had come on at once. It was a wrestling match, the object of each being to give his antagonist a back fall; and on Henchard's part, unquestionably, that it should be through the door.

At the outset Henchard's hold by his only free hand, the right, was on the left side of Farfrae's collar, which he firmly grappled, the latter holding Henchard by his collar with the contrary hand. With his right he endeavored to get hold of his antagonist's left arm, which, however, he could not do, so adroitly did Henchard keep it in the rear as he gazed upon the lowered eyes of his fair and slim antagonist.

Henchard planted the first toe forward, Farfrae crossing him with his; and thus far the struggle had very much the appearance of the ordinary wrestling of those parts. Several minutes were passed by them in this attitude, the pair rocking and writhing like trees in a gale, both preserving an absolute silence. By this time their breathing could be heard. Then Farfrae tried to get hold of the other side of Henchard's collar, which was resisted by the larger man exerting all his force in a wrenching move-ment, and this part of the struggle ended by his forcing Farfrae down on his knees by sheer pressure of one of his muscular arms. Hampered as he was, however, he could not keep him there, and Farfrae finding his feet again the struggle proceeded as before.

By a whirl Henchard brought Donald dangerously near the precipice; seeing his position the Scotchman for the first time locked himself to his adversary, and all the efforts of that infuriated Prince of Darkness—as he might have been called from his appearance just now—were inadequate to lift or loosen Farfrae for a time. By an extraordinary effort he succeeded at last, though not until they had got far back again from the fatal door. In doing so Henchard contrived to turn Farfrae a complete somersault. Had Henchard's other arm been free it would have been all over with Farfrae then. But again he regained his feet, wrenching Henchard's arm considerably, and causing him sharp pain, as could be seen from the twitching of his face. He instantly delivered the younger man an annihilating turn by the left fore-hip, as it used to be expressed, and following up his advantage thrust him towards the door, never loosening his hold till Farfrae's fair head was hanging over the window-sill, and his arm dangling down outside the wall.

"Now," said Henchard between his gasps, "this is the end of what you began this morning. Your life is in my hands."

"Then take it, take it!" said Farfrae. "Ye've wished to long enough!"

Henchard looked down upon him in silence, and their eyes met. "O Farfrae!—that's not true!" he said bitterly. "God is my witness that no man ever loved another as I did thee at one time. . . . And now—though I came here to kill 'ee, I cannot hurt thee! Go and give me in charge—do what you will—I care nothing for what comes of me!"

He withdrew to the back part of the loft, loosened his arm, and flung himself into a corner upon some sacks, in the abandonment of remorse. Farfrae regarded him in silence; then went to the hatch and descended through it. Henchard would fain have recalled him; but his tongue failed in its task, and the young man's steps died on his ear.

Henchard took his full measure of shame and self-reproach. These scenes of his first acquaintance with Farfrae rushed back upon him—that time when the curious mixture of romance and thrift in the young man's composition so commanded his heart that Farfrae could play upon him as on an instrument. So thoroughly subdued was he that he remained on the sacks in a crouching attitude, unusual for a man, and for such a man. Its womanliness sat tragically on the figure of so stern a piece of virility. He heard a conversation below, the opening of the coach-house door, and the putting in of a horse, but took no notice.

Here he stayed till the thin shades thickened to opaque obscurity, and the loft-door became an oblong of gray light—the only visible shape around. At length he arose, shook the dust from his clothes wearily, felt his way to the hatch, and gropingly descended the steps till he stood in the yard.

"He thought highly of me once," he murmured. "Now he'll hate me and despise me for ever!"

He became possessed by an overpowering wish to see Farfrae again that night, and by some desperate pleading to attempt the well-nigh impossible task of winning pardon for his late mad attack. But as he walked towards Farfrae's door he recalled the unheeded doings in the yard while he had lain above in a sort of stupor. Farfrae he remembered had gone to the stable and put the horse into the gig; while doing so, Whittle had brought him a letter; Farfrae had then said that he would not go towards Budmouth as he had intended—that he was unexpectedly summoned to Weatherbury, and meant to call at Mellstock on his way thither, that place lying but one or two miles out of his course.

He must have come prepared for a journey when he first arrived in the yard, unsuspecting enmity; and he must have driven off (though in a changed direction) without saying a word to any one on what had occurred between themselves.

It would therefore be useless to call at Farfrae's house till very late.

There was no help for it but to wait till his return, though waiting was almost torture to his restless and self-accusing soul. He walked about the streets and outskirts of the town, lingering here and there till he reached the stone bridge of which mention has been made, an accustomed halting-place with him now. Here he spent a long time, the purl of waters through the weirs meeting his ear, and the Casterbridge lights glimmering at no great distance off.

While leaning thus upon the parapet his listless attention was awakened by sounds of an unaccustomed kind from the town quarter. They were a confusion of rhythmical noises, to which the streets added yet more confusion by encumbering them with echoes. His first incurious thought that the clangor arose from the town band, engaged in an attempt to round off a memorable day by a burst of evening harmony, was contradicted by certain peculiarities of reverberation. But inexplicability did not rouse him to more than a cursory heed; his sense of degradation was too strong for the admission of foreign ideas; and he leant against the parapet as before.

XXXIX

When Farfrae descended out of the loft breathless from his encounter with Henchard, he paused at the bottom to recover himself. He arrived at the yard with the intention of putting the horse into the gig himself (all the men having a holiday), and driving to a village on the Budmouth Road. Despite the fearful struggle he decided still to persevere in his journey, so as to recover himself before going indoors and meeting the eyes of Lucetta. He wished to consider his course in a case so serious.

When he was just on the point of driving off Whittle arrived with a note badly addressed, and bearing the word "immediate" upon the outside. On opening it he was surprised to see that it was unsigned. It contained a brief request that he would go to Weatherbury that evening about some business which he was conducting there. Farfrae knew nothing that could make it pressing; but as he was bent upon going out he yielded to the anonymous request, particularly as he had a call to make at Mellstock which could be included in the same tour. Thereupon he told Whittle of his change of direction, in words which Henchard had overheard; and set out on his way. Farfrae had not directed his man to take the message indoors, and Whittle had not been supposed to do so on his own responsibility.

Now the anonymous letter was the well-intentioned but clumsy contrivance of Longways and other of Farfrae's men to get him out of the way for the evening, in order that the satirical mummery should fall flat, if it were attempted. By giving open information they would have brought down upon their heads the vengeance of those among their comrades who enjoyed these boisterous old games; and therefore the plan of sendling a letter recommended itself by its indirectness.

For poor Lucetta they took no protective measure, believing with the majority there was some truth in the scandal, which she would have to bear as she best might.

It was about eight o'clock, and Lucetta was sitting in the drawing-room alone. Night had set in for more than half an hour, but she had not had the candles lighted, for when Farfrae was away she preferred waiting for him by the fire light, and, if it were not too cold, keeping one of the window-sashes a little way open that the sound of his wheels might reach her ears early. She was leaning back in her chair, in a more hopeful mood than she had enjoyed since her marriage. The day had been such a success; and the temporary uneasiness which Henchard's show of effrontery had wrought in her disappeared with the quiet disappearance of Henchard himself under her husband's reproof. The floating evidences of her absurd passion for him, and its consequences, had been destroyed, and she really seemed to have no cause for fear.

The reverie in which these and other subjects mingled was disturbed by a hubbub in the distance, that increased moment by moment. It did not greatly surprise her, the afternoon having been given up to recreation by a majority of the populace since the passage of the Royal equipages. But her attention was at once riveted to the matter by the voice of a maid-servant next door, who spoke from an upper window across the street to some other maid even more elevated than she.

"Which way be they going now?" inquired the first with interest.

"I can't be sure for a moment," said the second, "because of the malter's chimbley. Oh yes—I can see 'em. Well, I declare, I declare!"

"What, what?" from the first, more enthusiastically.

"They are coming up Corn Street after all! They sit back to back!"

"What—two of 'em—are there two figures?"

"Yes. Two images on a donkey, back to back, their elbows tied to one another's! She's facing the head, and he's facing the tail."

"Is it meant for anybody particular?"

"Well—it mid be. The man has got on a blue coat and kerseymere leggings; he has black whiskers, and a reddish face. 'Tis a stuffed figure, with a falseface."

The din was increasing now—then it lessened a little.

"There—I shan't see, after all!" cried the disappointed first maid.

"They have gone into a back street—that's all," said the one who occupied the enviable position in the attic. "There—now I have got 'em all endways nicely!"

"What's the woman like? Just say, and I can tell in a moment if 'tis meant for one I've in mind."

"My—why—'tis dressed just as *she* was dressed when she sat in the front seat at the time the play-actors came to the Town Hall!"

Lucetta started to her feet; and almost at the instant the door of the room was quickly and softly opened. Elizabeth-Jane advanced into the firelight.

"I have come to see you," she said breathlessly. "I did not stop to knock—forgive me! I see you have not shut your shutters, and the window is open."

Without waiting for Lucetta's reply she crossed quickly to the window, and pulled out one of the shutters. Lucetta glided to her side. "Let it be—hush!" she said peremptorily, in a dry voice, while she seized Elizabeth-Jane by the hand,

and held up her finger. Their intercourse had been so low and hurried that not a word had been lost of the conversation without; which had thus proceeded:—

"Her neck is uncovered, and her hair in bands, and her back-comb in place; she's got on a puce silk, and white stockings, and colored shoes."

Again Elizabeth-Jane attempted to close the window, but Lucetta held her by main force.

"'Tis me," she said, with a face pale as death. "A procession—a scandal—an effigy of me, and him!"

The look of Elizabeth betrayed that the latter knew it already.

"Let us shut it out," coaxed Elizabeth-Jane, noting that the rigid wildness of Lucetta's features were growing yet more rigid and wild with the nearing of the noise and laughter. "Let us shut it out!"

"It is of no use!" she shrieked out. "He will see it, won't he? Donald will see it! He is just coming home—and it will break his heart—he will never love me any more—and O, it will kill me—kill me!"

Elizabeth-Jane was frantic now. "Oh, can't something be done to stop it?" she cried. "Is there nobody to do it —not one?"

She relinquished Lucetta's hands, and ran to the door. Lucetta herself, saying recklessly "I will see it!" turned to the window, threw up the sash, and went out upon the balcony. Elizabeth immediately followed her, and put her arm round her to pull her in. Lucetta's eyes were straight upon the spectacle of the uncanny revel, now advancing rapidly. The numerous lights around the two effigies threw them up into lurid distinctness; it was impossible to mistake the pair for other than the intended victims.

"Come in, come in," implored Elizabeth; "and let me shut the window!"

"She's me—she's me—even to the parasol—my green parasol!" cried Lucetta with a wild laugh as she stepped in. She stood motionless for one second—then fell heavily to the floor.

Almost at the instant of her fall the rude music of

the skimmington ceased. The roars of sarcastic laughter went off in ripples, and the trampling died out like the rustle of a spent wind. Elizabeth was only indirectly conscious of this; she had rung the bell, and was bending over Lucetta, who remained convulsed on the carpet in the paroxysms of an epileptic seizure. She rang again and again, in vain; the probability being that the servants had all run out of the house to see more of the Dæmonic Sabbath than they could see within.

At last Farfrae's man, who had been agape on the door-step, came up; then the cook. The shutters, hastily pushed to by Elizabeth, were quite closed, a light was obtained, Lucetta carried to her room, and the man sent off for a doctor. While Elizabeth was undressing her she recovered consciousness; but as soon as she remembered what had passed the fit returned.

The doctor arrived with unhoped-for promptitude; he had been standing at his door, like others, wondering what the uproar meant. As soon as he saw the unhappy sufferer he said, in answer to Elizabeth's mute appeal, "This is serious."

"It is a fit," Elizabeth said.

"Yes. But a fit in the present state of her health means mischief. You must send at once for Mr. Farfrae. Where is he?"

"He has driven into the country, sir," said the parlor-maid; "to some place on the Budmouth Road. He's likely to be back soon."

"Never mind; he must be sent for, in case he should not hurry." The doctor returned to the bedside again. The man was despatched, and they soon heard him clattering out of the yard at the back.

Meanwhile Mr. Benjamin Grower, that prominent burgess of whom mention has been already made, hearing the din of cleavers, tongs, tambourines, kits, crouds, humstrums, serpents, rams'-horns, and other historical kinds of music as he sat indoors in the High Street, had put on his hat and gone out to learn the cause. He came to the corner above Farfrae's, and soon guessed the nature of the proceedings; for being a native of the town he had witnessed such rough jests before. His first move was to search hither and thither for the constables; there were two in the town, shrivelled men whom he ultimately found in hiding up an alley yet more shrivelled than usual, having some not ungrounded fears that they might be roughly handled if seen.

"What can we two poor lammigers do against such a multitude!" expostulated Stubberd, in answer to Mr. Grower's chiding. " 'Tis tempting 'em to commit *felo de se* upon us, and that would be the death of the perpetrator; and we wouldn't be the cause of a fellow-creature's death on no account, not we!"

"Get some help, then! Here, I'll come with you. We'll see what a few words of authority can do. Quick now; have you got your staves?"

"We didn't want the folk to notice us as law officers, being so short-handed, sir; so we pushed our Gover'ment staves up this water-pipe."

"Out with 'em, and come along, for Heaven's sake! Ah, here's Mr. Blowbody; that's lucky." (Blowbody was the third of the three borough magistrates.)

"Well, what's the row?" said Blowbody. "Got their names—hey?"

"No. Now," said Grower to one of the constables, "you go with Mr. Blowbody round by the Old Walk and come up the street; and I'll go with Stubberd straight forward. By this plan we shall have 'em between us. Get their names only: no attack or interruption."

Thus they started. But as Stubberd with Mr. Grower advanced into Corn Street, whence the sounds had proceeded, they were surprised that no procession could be seen. They passed Farfrae's, and looked to the end of the street. The lamp flames waved, the Walk trees soughed, a few loungers stood about with their hands in their pockets. Everything was as usual.

"Have you seen a motley crowd making a disturbance?" Grower said magisterially to one of these in a fustian jacket, who smoked a short pipe and wore straps round his knees.

"Beg yer pardon, sir?" blandly said the person addressed, who was no other than Charl, of Peter's Finger. Mr. Grower repeated the words.

Charl shook his head to the zero of childlike ignorance. "No; we haven't seen anything; have we, Joe? And you was here afore I."

Joseph was quite as blank as the other in his reply.

"H'm—that's odd," said Grower. "Ah—here's a respectable man coming that I know by sight. Have you," he inquired, addressing the nearing shape of Jopp, "have you seen any gang of fellows making a devil of a noise—skimmington riding, or something of the sort?"

"Oh no—nothing, sir," Jopp replied, as if receiving the most singular news. "But I've not been far to-night, so perhaps——"

"Oh, 'twas here—just here," said the magistrate.

"Now, I've noticed, come to think o't, that the wind in the Walk trees makes a peculiar poetical-like murmur to-night, sir; more than common; so perhaps 'twas that?" Jopp suggested, as he rearranged his hand in his greatcoat pocket (where it ingeniously supported a pair of kitchen tongs and a cow's horn, thrust up under his waistcoat).

"No, no, no,—d'ye think I'm a fool? Constable, come this way. They must have gone into the back street."

Neither in back street nor in front street, however, could the disturbers be perceived; and Blowbody and the second constable, who came up at this time, brought similar intelligence. Effigies, donkey, lanterns, band, all had disappeared like the crew of *Comus*.

"Now," said Mr. Grower, "there's only one thing more we can do. Get ye half-a-dozen helpers, and go in a body to Mixen Lane, and into Peter's Finger. I'm much mistaken if you don't find a clue to the perpetrators there."

The rusty-jointed executors of the law mustered assistance as soon as they could, and the whole party marched off to the lane of notoriety. It was no rapid matter to get there at night, not a lamp or glimmer of any sort offering itself to light the way, except an occasional pale radiance through some window-curtain, or through the chink of some door which could not be closed because of the smoky chimney within. At last they entered the inn boldly, by the till then bolted front-door, after a prolonged knocking of loudness commensurate with the importance of their standing.

In the settles of the large room, guyed to the ceiling by cords as usual for stability, an ordinary group sat drinking and smoking with statuesque quiet of demeanor. The landlady looked mildly at the invaders, saying in honest accents, "Good evening, gentlemen; there's plenty of room. I hope there's nothing amiss?"

They looked round the room. "Surely," said Stubberd to one of the men, "I saw you by now in Corn Street—Mr. Grower spoke to 'ee?"

The man, who was Charl, shook his head absently. "I've been here this last hour, hain't I, Nance?" he said to the woman who mediatively sipped her ale near him.

"Faith, that you have. I came in for my quiet supper-time half-pint, and you was here then, as was all the rest."

The other constable was facing the clock-case, where he saw reflected in the glass a quick motion by the landlady. Turning sharply, he caught her closing the oven-door.

"Something curious about that oven, ma'am!" he observed advancing, opening it, and drawing out a tambourine.

"Ah," she said, apologetically, "that's what we keep here to use when there's a little quiet dancing. You see damp weather spoils it, so I put it there to keep it dry."

The constable nodded knowingly, but what he knew was nothing. Nohow could anything be elicited for this mute and inoffensive assembly. In a few minutes the investigators went out, and joining those of their auxiliaries who had been left at the door they pursued their way elsewhither.

XL

Long before this time Henchard, weary of his ruminations on the bridge, had repaired towards the town. When he stood at the bottom of the street a procession burst upon his view, in the act of turning out of an alley just above him. The lanterns, horns, and multitude startled him; he saw the mounted images, and knew what it all meant.

They crossed the way, entered another street, and disappeared. He turned back a few steps and was lost in grave reflection, finally wending his way homeward by the obscure river-side path. Unable to rest there he went to his stepdaughter's lodging, and was told that Elizabeth-Jane had gone to Mrs. Farfrae's. Like one acting in obedience to a charm, and with a nameless apprehension, he followed in the same direction in the hope of meeting her, the roysterers having vanished. Disappointed in this he gave the gentlest of pulls to the door-bell, and then learnt particulars of what had occurred, together with the doctor's imperative orders that Farfrae should be brought home, and how they had set out to meet him on the Budmouth Road.

"But he has gone to Mellstock and Weatherbury!" exclaimed Henchard, now unspeakably grieved. "Not Budmouth way at all."

But, alas! for Henchard; he had lost his good name. They would not believe him, taking his words but as the frothy utterances of recklessness. Though Lucetta's life seemed at that moment to depend upon her husband's return (she being in great mental agony lest he should never know the unexaggerated truth of her past relations with Henchard), no messenger was despatched towards Weatherbury. Henchard, in a state of bitter anxiety and contrition, determined to seek Farfrae himself.

To this end he hastened down the town, ran along the eastern road over Durnover moor, up the hill beyond, and thus onward in the moderate darkness of this spring night till he had reached a second and almost a third hill about three miles distant. In Yalbury Bottom, or Plain, at the foot of the hill, he listened. At first nothing, beyond his own heart-throbs, was to be heard but the slow wind making its moan among the masses of spruce and larch of Yalbury Wood which clothed the heights on either hand; but presently there came the sound of light wheels whetting their felloes against the newly stoned patches of road, accompanied by the distant glimmer of lights.

He knew it was Farfrae's gig descending the hill from an indescribable personality in its noise, the vehicle having been his own till bought by the Scotchman at the sale of his efforts. Henchard thereupon retraced his steps along Yalbury Plain, the gig coming up with him as its driver slackened speed between two plantations.

It was a point in the highway near which the road to Mellstock branched off from the homeward direction. By diverging to that village, as he had intended to do, Farfrae might probably delay his return by a couple of hours. It soon appeared that his intention was to do so still, the light swerving towards Cuckoo Lane, the by-road aforesaid. Farfrae's off gig-lamp flashed in Henchard's face. At the same time, Farfrae discerned his late antagonist.

"Farfrae—Mr. Farfrae!" cried the breathless Henchard, holding up his hand.

Farfrae allowed the horse to turn several steps into the branch lane before he pulled up. He then drew rein, and said "Yes?" over his shoulder, as one would towards a pronounced enemy.

"Come back to Casterbridge at once!" Henchard said. "There's something wrong at your house—requiring your return. I've run all the way here on purpose to tell ye."

Farfrae was silent, and at his silence Henchard's soul sank within him. Why had he not, before this, thought of what was only too obvious? He who, four hours earlier, had enticed Farfrae into a deadly wrestle stood now in the darkness of late night-time on a lonely road, inviting him to come a particular way, where an assailant might have confederates, instead of going his purposed way, where there might be a better opportunity of guarding himself from attack. Henchard could almost feel this view of things in course of passage through Farfrae's mind.

"I have to go to Mellstock," said Farfrae coldly, as he loosened his rein to move on.

"But," implored Henchard, "the matter is more serious than your business at Mellstock. It is—your wife! She is ill. I can tell you particulars as we go along."

The very agitation and abruptness of Henchard increased Farfrae's suspicion that this was a *ruse* to decoy him on to the next wood, where might be effectually compassed what, from policy or want of nerve, Henchard had failed to do earlier in the day. He started the horse.

"I know what you think," deprecated Henchard running after, almost bowed down with despair as he perceived the image of unscrupulous villainy that he assumed in his former friend's eyes. "But I am not what you think!" he cried hoarsely. "Believe me, Farfrae; I have come entirely on your own and your wife's account. She is in danger. I know no more; and they want you to come. Your man has gone the other way in a mistake. O Farfrae! don't mistrust me—I am a wretched man; but my heart is true to you still!"

Farfrae, however, did distrust him utterly. He knew his wife was with child, but he had left her not long ago in perfect health; and Henchard's treachery was more credible than his story. He had in his time heard bitter ironies from Henchard's lips, and there might be ironies now. He quickened the horse's pace, and had soon risen into the high country lying between there and Mellstock, Henchard's spasmodic run after him lending yet more substance to his thought of evil purposes.

The gig and its driver lessened against the sky in Henchard's eyes; his exertions for Farfrae's good had been in vain. Over this repentant sinner, at least, there was to be no joy in heaven. He cursed himself like a less scrupulous Job, as a vehement man will do when he loses self-respect, the last mental prop under poverty. To this he had come after a time of emotional darkness of which the adjoining woodland shade afforded inadequate illustration. Presently he began to walk back again along the way by which he had arrived. Farfrae should at all events have no reason for delay upon the road by seeing him there when he took his journey homeward later on.

Arriving at Casterbridge Henchard went again to Farfrae's house to make inquiries. As soon as the door opened anxious faces confronted his from the staircase, hall, and landing; and they all said in grievous disappointment. "Oh

—it is not he!" The manservant, finding his mistake, had long since returned, and all hopes had been centered upon Henchard.

"But haven't you found him?" said the doctor.

"Yes. . . . I cannot tell 'ee!" Henchard replied as he sank down on a chair within the entrance. "He can't be home for two hours."

"H'm," said the surgeon, returning upstairs.

"How is she?" asked Henchard of Elizabeth, who formed one of the group.

"In great danger, father. Her anxiety to see her husband makes her fearfully restless. Poor woman—I fear they have killed her!"

Henchard regarded the sympathetic speaker for a few instants as if she struck him in a new light; then, without further remark, went out of the door and onward to his lonely cottage. So much for man's rivalry, he thought. Death was to have the oyster, and Farfrae and himself the shells. But about Elizabeth-Jane; in the midst of his gloom she seemed to him as a pin-point of light. He had liked the look of her face as she answered him from the stairs. There had been affection in it, and above all things what he desired now was affection from anything that was good and pure. She was not his own; yet, for the first time, he had a faint dream that he might get to like her as his own,—if she would only continue to love him.

Jopp was just going to bed when Henchard got home. As the latter entered the door Jopp said, "This is rather bad about Mrs. Farfrae's illness."

"Yes," said Henchard shortly, though little dreaming of Jopp's complicity in the night's harlequinade, and raising his eyes just sufficiently to observe that Jopp's face was lined with anxiety.

"Somebody has called for you," continued Jopp, when Henchard was shutting himself into his own apartment. "A kind of traveller, or sea-captain of some sort."

"Oh!—who could he be?"

"He seemed a well-be-doing man—had grey hair and a broadish face; but he gave no name, and no message."

"Nor do I gi'e him any attention." And, saying this, Henchard closed his door.

The divergence to Mellstock delayed Farfrae's return very nearly the two hours of Henchard's estimate. Among the other urgent reasons for his presence had been the need of his authority to send to Budmouth for a second physician; and when at length Farfrae did come back he was in a state bordering on distraction at his misconception of Henchard's motives.

A messenger was despatched to Budmouth, late as it had grown; the night wore on, and the other doctor came in the small hours. Lucetta had been much soothed by Donald's arrival; he seldom or never left her side; and when, immediately after his entry, she had tried to lisp out to him the secret which so oppressed her, he checked her feeble words, lest talking should be dangerous, assuring her there was plenty of time to tell him everything.

Up to this time he knew nothing of the skimmington-ride. The dangerous illness and miscarriage of Mrs. Farfrae was soon rumored through the town, and an apprehensive guess having been given as to its cause by the leaders in the exploit, compunction and fear threw a dead silence over all particulars of their orgie; while those immediately around Lucetta would not venture to add to her husband's distress by alluding to the subject.

What, and how much, Farfrae's wife ultimately explained to him of her past entanglement with Henchard, when they were alone in the solitude of that sad night, cannot be told. That she informed him of the bare facts of her peculiar intimacy with the corn-merchant became plain from Farfrae's own statements. But in respect of her subsequent conduct—her motive in coming to Casterbridge to unite herself with Henchard—her assumed justification in abandoning him when she discovered reasons for fearing him (though in truth her inconsequent passion for another man at first sight had most to do with that abandonment) —her method of reconciling to her conscience a marriage with the second when she was in a measure committed to the first: to what extent she spoke of these things remained Farfrae's secret alone.

Besides the watchman who called the hours and weather in Casterbridge that night there walked a figure up and down Corn Street hardly less frequently. It was Henchard's whose retiring to rest had proved itself a futility as soon as attempted; and he gave it up to go hither and thither, and make inquiries about the patient every now and then. He called as much on Farfrae's account as on Lucetta's, and on Elizabeth-Jane's even more than on either's. Shorn one by one of all other interests, his life seemed centering on the personality of the stepdaughter whose presence but recently he could not endure. To see her on each occasion of his inquiry at Lucetta's was a comfort to him.

The last of his calls was made about four o'clock in the morning, in the steely light of dawn. Lucifer was fading into day across Durnover Moor, the sparrows were just alighting into the street, and the hens had begun to cackle from the outhouses. When within a few yards of Farfrae's he saw the door gently opened, and a servant raise her hand to the knocker, to untie the piece of cloth which had muffled it. He went across, the sparrows in his way scarcely flying up from the road-litter, so little did they believe in human aggression at so early a time.

"Why do you take off that?" said Henchard.

She turned in some surprise at his presence, and did not answer for an instant or two. Recognizing him, she said, "Because they may knock as loud they will; she will never hear it any more."

XLI

Henchard went home. The morning having now fully broke he lit his fire, and sat abstractedly beside it. He had not sat there long when a gentle footstep approached the house and entered the passage, a finger tapping lightly at the door. Henchard's face brightened, for he knew the motions to be Elizabeth's. She came into his room, looking wan and sad.

"Have you heard?" she asked. "Mrs. Farfrae! She is—dead! Yes, indeed—about an hour ago!"

"I know it," said Henchard. "I have but lately come in from there. It is so very good of 'ee, Elizabeth, to come and tell me. You must be so tired out, too, with sitting up. Now do you bide here with me this morning. You can go and rest in the other room; and I will call 'ee when breakfast is ready."

To please him, and herself—for his recent kindliness was winning a surprised gratitude from the lonely girl—she did as he bade her, and lay down on a sort of couch which Henchard had rigged up out of a settle in the adjoining room. She could hear him moving about in his preparations; but her mind ran most strongly on Lucetta, whose death in such fulness of life and amid such cheerful hopes of maternity was appallingly unexpected. Presently she fell asleep.

Meanwhile her stepfather in the outer room had set the breakfast in readiness; but finding that she dozed he would not call her; he waited on, looking into the fire and keeping the kettle boiling with housewifely care, as if it were an honor to have her in his house. In truth, a great change had come over him with regard to her, and he was developing the dream of a future lit by her filial presence, as though that way alone could happiness lie.

He was disturbed by another knock at the door, and rose to open it, rather deprecating a call from anybody just then. A stoutly built man stood on the doorstep, with an alien, unfamiliar air about his figure and bearing—an air which might have been called colonial by people of cosmopolitan experience. It was the man who had asked the way at Peter's Finger. Henchard nodded, and looked inquiry.

"Good morning, good morning," said the stranger with profuse heartiness. "Is it Mr. Henchard I am talking to?"

"My name is Henchard."

"Then I caught 'ee at home—that's right. Morning's the time for business, says I. Can I have a few words with you?"

"By all means," Henchard answered, showing the way in.

"You may remember me?" said his visitor, seating himself.

Henchard observed him indifferently, and shook his head.

"Well—perhaps you may not. My name is Newson."

Henchard's face and eyes seemed to die. The other did not notice it. "I know the name well," Henchard said at last, looking on the floor.

"I make no doubt of that. Well, the fact is, I've been looking for 'ee this fortnight past. I landed at Havenpool and went through Casterbridge on my way to Falmouth, and when I got there, they told me you had some years before been living at Casterbridge. Back came I again, and by long and by late I got here by coach, ten minutes ago. 'He lives down by the mill,' says they. So here I am. Now—that transaction between us some twenty years agone—'tis that I've called about. 'Twas a curious business. I was younger then than I am now, and perhaps the less said about it, in one sense, the better."

"Curious business! 'Twas worse than curious. I cannot even allow that I'm the man you met then. I was not in my senses, and a man's senses are himself."

"We were young and thoughtless," said Newson. "However, I've come to mend matters rather than open arguments. Poor Susan—hers was a strange experience."

"It was."

"She was a warm-hearted, home-spun woman. She was not what they call shrewd or sharp at all—better she had been."

"She was not."

"As you in all likelihood know, she was simple-minded enough to think that the sale was in a way binding. She was as guiltless o' wrong-doing in that particular as a saint in the clouds."

"I know it, I know it. I found it out directly," said Henchard, still with averted eyes. "There lay the sting o't to me. If she had seen it as what it was she would never have left me. Never! But how should she be expected to know? What advantages had she? None. She could write her own name, and no more."

"Well, it was not in my heart to undeceive her when the deed was done," said the sailor of former days. "I thought, and there was not much vanity in thinking it, that she would be happier with me. She was fairly happy, and I never would have undeceived her till the day of her death. Your child died; she had another, and all went well. But a time came—mind me, a time always does come. A time came—it was some while after she and I and the child returned from America—when somebody she had confided her history to, told her my claim to her was a mockery, and made a jest of her belief in my right. After that she was never happy with me. She pined and pined, and socked and sighed. She said she must leave me, and then came the question of our child. Then a man advised me how to act, and I did it, for I thought it was best. I left her at Falmouth, and went off to sea. When I got to the other side of the Atlantic there was a storm, and it was supposed that a lot of us, including myself, had been washed overboard. I got ashore at Newfoundland, and then I asked myself what I should do. 'Since I'm here, here I'll bide,' I thought to myself; ' 'twill be most kindness to her, now she's taken against me, to let her believe me lost; for,' I thought, 'while she supposes us both alive she'll be miserable; but if she thinks me dead she'll go back to him, and the child will have a home.' I've never returned to this country till a month ago, and I found that, as I had supposed, she went to you, and my daughter with her. They told me in Falmouth that Susan was dead. But my Elizabeth-Jane—where is she?"

"Dead likewise," said Henchard doggedly. "Surely you learnt that too?"

The sailor started up, and took an enervated pace or two down the room. "Dead!" he said, in a low voice. "Then what's the use of my money to me?"

Henchard, without answering, shook his head as if that were rather a question for Newson himself than for him.

"Where is she buried?" the traveller inquired.

"Beside her mother," said Henchard, in the same stolid tones.

"When did she die?"

"A year ago and more," replied the other without hesitation.

The sailor continued standing. Henchard never looked up from the floor. At last Newson said: "My journey hither has been for nothing! I may as well go as I came! It has served me right. I'll trouble you no longer!"

Henchard heard the retreating footsteps of Newson upon the sanded floor, the mechanical lifting of the latch, the slow opening and closing of the door that was natural to a baulked or dejected man; but he did not turn his head. Newson's shadow passed the window. He was gone.

Then Henchard, scarcely believing the evidence of his senses, rose from his seat amazed at what he had done. It had been the impulse of a moment. The regard he had lately acquired for Elizabeth, the new-sprung hope of his loneliness that she would be to him a daughter of whom he could feel as proud as of the actual daughter she still believed herself to be, had been stimulated by the unexpected coming of Newson to a greedy exclusiveness in relation to her; so that the sudden prospect of her loss had caused him to speak mad lies like a child, in pure mockery of consequences. He had expected questions to close in round him, and unmask his fabrication in five minutes; yet such questioning had not come. But surely they would come; Newson's departure could be but momentary; he would learn all by inquiries in the town; and return to curse him, and carry his last treasure away!

He hastily put on his hat, and went out in the direction that Newson had taken. Newson's back was soon visible up the road, crossing Bull-stake. Henchard followed; and saw his visitor stop at the Kings Arms, where the morning coach which had brought him waited half-an-hour for another coach which crossed there. The coach Newson had come by was now about to move again. Newson mounted; his luggage was put in, and in a few minutes the vehicle disappeared with him.

He had not so much as turned his head. It was an act of simple faith in Henchard's words—faith so simple as to be almost sublime. The young sailor who had taken Susan Henchard on the spur of the moment and on the faith of a glance at her face, more than twenty years before, was still living and acting under the form of the grizzled traveller who had taken Henchard's words on trust so absolute as to shame him as he stood.

Was Elizabeth-Jane to remain his by virtue of this hardy invention of a moment? "Perhaps not for long," said he. Newson might converse with his fellow-travellers, some of whom might be Casterbridge people; and the trick would be discovered.

This probability threw Henchard into a defensive attitude, and instead of considering how best to right the wrong, and acquaint Elizabeth's father with the truth at once, he bethought himself of ways to keep the position he had accidentally won. Towards the young woman herself his affection grew more jealously strong with each new hazard to which his claim to her was exposed.

He watched the distant highway expecting to see Newson return on foot, enlightened and indignant, to claim his child. But no figure appeared. Possibly he had spoken to nobody on the coach, but buried his grief in his own heart.

His grief!—what was it, after all, to that which he, Henchard, would feel at the loss of her? Newson's affection, cooled by years, could not equal his who had been constantly in her presence. And thus his jealous soul speciously argued to excuse the separation of father and child.

He returned to the house half expecting that she would have vanished. No; there she was—just coming out from the inner room, the marks of sleep upon her eyelids, and exhibiting a generally refreshed air.

"O father!" she said, smiling. "I had no sooner lain down than I napped, though I did not mean to. I wonder I did not dream about poor Mrs. Farfrae, after thinking of her so; but I did not. How strange it is that we do not often dream of latest events, absorbing as they may be."

"I am glad you have been able to sleep," he said, taking

her hand with anxious proprietorship—an act which gave her a pleasant surprise.

They sat down to breakfast, and Elizabeth-Jane's thoughts reverted to Lucetta. Their sadness added charm to a countenance whose beauty had ever lain in its meditative soberness.

"Father," she said, as soon as she recalled herself to the outspread meal, "it is so kind of you to get this nice breakfast with your own hands, and I idly asleep the while."

"I do it every day," he replied. "You have left me; everybody has left me; how should I live but by my own hands."

"You are very lonely, are you not?"

"Ay, child—to a degree that you know nothing of! It is my own fault. You are the only one who has been near me for weeks. And you will come no more."

"Why do you say that? Indeed I will, if you would like to see me."

Henchard signified dubiousness. Though he had so lately hoped that Elizabeth-Jane might again live in his house as daughter, he would not ask her to do so now. Newson might return at any moment, and what Elizabeth would think of him for his deception it were best to bear apart from her.

When they had breakfasted his stepdaughter still lingered, till the moment arrived at which Henchard was accustomed to go to his daily work. Then she arose, and with assurances of coming again soon went up the hill in the morning sunlight.

"At this moment her heart is as warm towards me as mine is towards her; she would live with me here in this humble cottage for the asking! Yet before the evening probably he will have come; and then she will scorn me!"

This reflection, constantly repeated by Henchard to himself, accompanied him everywhere through the day. His mood was no longer that of the rebellious, ironical, reckless misadventurer; but the leaden gloom of one who has lost all that can make life interesting, or even tolerable. There would remain nobody for him to be proud of, nobody to fortify him; for Elizabeth-Jane would soon be but as a stranger, and worse. Susan, Farfrae, Lucetta, Elizabeth—all had gone from him, one after one, either by his fault or by his misfortune.

In place of them he had no interest, hobby, or desire. If he could have summoned music to his aid, his existence might even now have been borne; for with Henchard music was of regal power. The merest trumpet or organ tone was enough to move him, and high harmonies transubstantiated him. But hard fate had ordained that he should be unable to call up this Divine spirit in his need.

The whole land ahead of him was as darkness itself; there was nothing to come, nothing to wait for. Yet in the natural course of life he might possibly have to linger on earth another thirty or forty years—scoffed at; at best pitied.

The thought of it was unendurable.

To the east of Casterbridge lay moors and meadows, through which much water flowed. The wanderer in this direction who should stand still for a few moments on a quiet night, might hear singular symphonies from these waters, as from a lampless orchestra, all playing in their sundry tones from near and far parts of the moor. At a hole in a rotten weir they executed a recitative; where a tributary brook fell over a stone breastwork they trilled cheerily; under an arch they performed a metallic cymbal-ling; and at Durnover Hole they hissed. The spot at which their instrumentation rose loudest was a place called Ten Hatches, whence during high springs there proceeded a very fugue of sounds.

The river here was deep and strong at all times, and the hatches on this account were raised and lowered by cogs and a winch. A path led from the second bridge over the highway (so often mentioned) to these Hatches, crossing the stream at their head by a narrow plank-bridge. But after night-fall human beings were seldom found going that way, the path leading only to a deep reach of the stream called Blackwater, and the passage being dangerous.

Henchard, however, leaving the town by the east road, proceeded to the second, or stone bridge, and thence struck into this path of solitude, following its course beside the stream till the dark shapes of the Ten Hatches cut the sheen thrown upon the river by the weak luster that still lingered in the west. In a second or two he stood beside the weir-hole where the water was at its deepest. He looked backwards and forwards, and no creature appeared in view. He then took off his coat and hat, and stood on the brink of the stream with his hands clasped in front of him.

While his eyes were bent on the water beneath there slowly became visible a something floating in the circular pool formed by the wash of centuries; the pool he was intending to make his death-bed. At first it was indistinct by reason of the shadow from the bank; but it emerged thence and took shape, which was that of a human body, lying stiff and stark upon the surface of the stream.

In the circular current imparted by the central flow the form was brought forward, till it passed under his eyes; and then he perceived with a sense of horror that it was *himself*. Not a man somewhat resembling him, but one in all respects his counterpart, his actual double, was floating as if dead in Ten Hatches Hole.

The sense of the supernatural was strong in this unhappy man, and he turned away as one might have done in the actual presence of an appalling miracle. He covered his eyes and bowed his head. Without looking again into the stream he took his coat and hat, and went slowly away.

Presently he found himself by the door of his own dwelling. To his surprise Elizabeth-Jane was standing there. She came forward, spoke, called him "father" just as before. Newson, then, had not even yet returned.

"I thought you seemed very sad this morning," she said, "so I have come again to see you. Not that I am anything but sad myself. But everybody and everything seem against you so; and I know you must be suffering."

How this woman divined things! Yet she had not divined their whole extremity.

He said to her, "Are miracles still worked, do ye think, Elizabeth? I am not a read man. I don't know so much as

I could wish. I have tried to peruse and learn all my life; but the more I try to know the more ignorant I seem."

"I don't quite think there are any miracles nowadays," she said.

"No interference in the case of desperate intentions, for instance? Well, perhaps not, in a direct way. Perhaps not. But will you come and walk with me, and I will show 'ee what I mean."

She agreed willingly, and he took her over the highway, and by the lonely path to Ten Hatches. He walked restlessly, as if some haunting shade, unseen of her, hovered round him and troubled his glance. She would gladly have talked of Lucetta, but feared to disturb him. When they got near the weir he stood still, and asked her to go forward and look into the pool, and tell him what he saw.

She went, and soon returned to him ."Nothing," she said.

"Go again," said Henchard, "and look narrowly."

She proceeded to the river brink a second time. On her return, after some delay, she told him that she saw something floating round and round there; but what it was she could not discern. It seemed to be a bundle of old clothes.

"Are they like mine?" asked Henchard.

"Well—they are. Dear me—I wonder if—— Father, let us go away!"

"Go and look once more; and then we will get home."

She went back, and he could see her stoop till her head was close to the margin of the pool. She started up, and hastened back to his side.

"Well," said Henchard; "what do you say now?"

"Let us go home."

"But tell me—do—what is it floating there?"

"The effigy," she answered hastily. "They must have thrown it into the river, higher up amongst the willows at Blackwater, to get rid of it in their alarm at discovery by the magistrates; and it must have floated down here."

"Ah—to be sure—the image o' me! But where is the other? Why that one only? . . . That performance of theirs killed her, but kept me alive!"

Elizabeth-Jane thought and thought of these words "kept

me alive," as they slowly retraced their way to the town,
and at length guessed their meaning. "Father!—I will not
leave you alone like this!" she cried. "May I live with you,
and tend upon you as I used to do? I do not mind your
being poor. I would have agreed to come this morning,
but you did not ask me."

"May you come to me;" he cried bitterly. "Elizabeth,
don't mock me! If you only would come!"

"I will," said she.

"How will you forgive all my roughness in former
days? You cannot!"

"I have forgotten it. Talk of that no more."

Thus she assured him, and arranged their plans for
reunion; and at length each went home. Then Henchard
shaved for the first time during many days, and put on
clean linen, and combed his hair; and was as a man re-
suscitated thenceforward.

The next morning the fact turned out to be as Elizabeth-
Jane had stated; the effigy was discovered by a cowherd,
and that of Lucetta a little higher up in the same stream.
But as little as possible was said of the matter, and the
figures were privately destroyed.

Despite this natural solution of the mystery Henchard
no less regarded it as an intervention that the figure should
have been floating there. Elizabeth-Jane heard him say,
"Who is such a reprobate as I! And yet it seems that even
I be in Somebody's hand!"

XLII

But the emotional conviction that he was in Somebody's
hand began to die out of Henchard's breast as time slowly
removed into distance the event which had given that feeling birth. The apparition of Newson haunted him. He
would surely return.

Yet Newson did not arrive. Lucetta had been borne
along the churchyard path; Casterbridge had for the last
time turned its regard upon her, before proceeding to its
work as if she had never lived. But Elizabeth remained

undisturbed in the belief of her relationship to Henchard, and now shared his home. Perhaps, after all, Newson was gone for ever.

In due time the bereaved Farfrae had learnt the, at least, proximate cause of Lucetta's illness and death; and his first impulse was naturally enough to wreak vengeance in the name of the law upon the perpetrators of the mischief. He resolved to wait till the funeral was over ere he moved in the matter. The time having come he reflected. Disastrous as the result had been, it was obviously in no way foreseen or intended by the thoughtless crew who arranged the motley procession. The tempting prospect of putting to the blush people who stand at the head of affairs—that supreme and piquant enjoyment of those who writhe under the heel of the same—had alone animated them, so far as he could see; for he knew nothing of Jopp's incitements. Other considerations were also involved. Lucetta had confessed everything to him before her death, and it was not altogether desirable to make much ado about her history, alike for her sake, for Henchard's, and for his own. To regard the event as an untoward accident seemed, to Farfrae, truest consideration for the dead one's memory, as well as best philosophy.

Henchard and himself mutually forbore to meet. For Elizabeth's sake the former had fettered his pride sufficiently to accept the small seed and root business which some of the Town Council, headed by Farfrae, had purchased to afford him a new opening. Had he been only personally concerned Henchard, without doubt, would have declined assistance even remotely brought about by the man whom he had so fiercely assailed. But the sympathy of the girl seemed necessary to his very existence; and on her account pride itself wore the garments of humility.

Here they settled themselves; and on each day of their lives Henchard anticipated her every wish with a watchfulness in which paternal regard was heightened by a burning jealous dread of rivalry. Yet that Newson would ever now return to Casterbridge to claim her as a daughter there was little reason to suppose. He was a wanderer and a stranger, almost an alien; he had not seen his daughter for several years; his affection for her could not in the nature of things be keen; other interests would probably soon obscure his recollections of her, and prevent any such renewal of inquiry into the past as would lead to a discovery that she was still a creature of the present. To satisfy his conscience somewhat Henchard repeated to himself that the lie which had retained for him the coveted treasure had not been deliberately told to that end, but had come from him as the last defiant word of a despair which took no thought of consequences. Furthermore he pleaded within himself that no Newson could love her as he loved her, or would tend her to his life's extremity as he was prepared to do cheerfully.

Thus they lived on in the shop overlooking the church-yard, and nothing occurred to mark their days during the remainder of the year. Going out but seldom, and never on a market-day, they saw Donald Farfrae only at rarest intervals, and then mostly as a transitory object in the distance of the street. Yet he was pursuing his ordinary avocations, smiling mechanically to fellow-tradesmen, and arguing with bargainers—as bereaved men do after a while.

Time, "in his own grey style," taught Farfrae how to estimate his experience of Lucetta—all that it was, and all that it was not. There are men whose hearts insist upon a dogged fidelity to some image or cause thrown by chance into their keeping, long after their judgment has pronounced it no rarity—even the reverse, indeed; and without them the band of the worthy is incomplete. But Farfrae was not of those. It was inevitable that the insight, briskness, and rapidity of his nature should take him out of the dead blank which his loss threw about him. He could not but perceive that by the death of Lucetta he had exchanged a looming misery for a simple sorrow. After that revelation of her history, which must have come sooner or later in any circumstances, it was hard to believe that life with her would have been productive of further happiness.

But as a memory, notwithstanding such conditions,

Lucetta's image still lived on with him, her weaknesses provoking only the gentlest criticism, and her sufferings attenuating wrath at her concealments to a momentary spark now and then.

By the end of a year Henchard's little retail seed and grain shop, not much larger than a cupboard, had developed its trade considerably, and the stepfather and daughter enjoyed much serenity in the pleasant, sunny corner in which it stood. The quiet bearing of one who brimmed with an inner activity characterized Elizabeth-Jane at this period. She took long walks into the country two or three times a week, mostly in the direction of Budmouth. Sometimes it occurred to him that when she sat with him in the evening after these invigorating walks she was civil rather than affectionate; and he was troubled; one more bitter regret being added to those he had already experienced at having, by his severe censorship, frozen up her precious affection when originally offered.

She had her own way in everything now. In going and coming, in buying and selling, her word was law.

"You have got a new muff, Elizabeth," he said to her one day quite humbly.

"Yes; I bought it," she said.

He looked at it again as it lay on an adjoining table. The fur was of a glossy brown, and though he was no judge of such articles, he thought it seemed an unusually good one for her to possess.

"Rather costly, I suppose, my dear, was it not?" he hazarded.

"It was rather above my figure," she said quietly. "But it is not showy."

"Oh no," said the netted lion, anxious not to pique her in the least.

Some little time after, when the year had advanced into another spring, he paused opposite her empty bedroom in passing it. He thought of the time when she had cleared out of his then large and handsome house in Corn Street, in consequence of his dislike and harshness, and he had looked into her chamber in just the same way. The present room was much humbler, but what struck him about it was the abundance of books lying everywhere. Their number and quality made the meager furniture that supported them seem absurdly disproportionate. Some, indeed many, must have been recently purchased; and though he encouraged her to buy in reason, he had no notion that she indulged her innate passion so extensively in proportion to the narrowness of their income. For the first time he felt a little hurt by what he thought her extravagance, and resolved to say a word to her about it. But, before he had found the courage to speak an event happened which set his thoughts flying in quite another direction.

The busy time of the seed trade was over; and the quiet weeks that preceded the hay-season had come—setting their special stamp upon Casterbridge by thronging the market with wood rakes, new wagons in yellow, green, and red, formidable scythes, and pitchforks of prong sufficient to skewer up a small family. Henchard, contrary to his wont, went out one Saturday afternoon towards the market-place, from a curious feeling that he would like to pass a few minutes on the spot of his former triumphs. Farfrae, to whom he was still a comparative stranger, stood a few steps below the Corn Exchange door—a usual position with him at this hour—and he appeared lost in thought about something he was looking at a little way off.

Henchard's eyes followed Farfrae's, and he saw that the object of his gaze was no sample-showing farmer, but his own stepdaughter, who had just come out of a shop over the way. She, on her part, was quite unconscious of his attention, and in this was less fortunate than those young women whose very plumes, like those of Juno's birds, are set with Argus eyes whenever possible admirers are within ken.

Henchard went away, thinking that perhaps there was nothing significant after all in Farfrae's look at Elizabeth-Jane at that juncture. Yet he could not forget that the Scotchman had once shown a tender interest in her, of a fleeting kind. Thereupon promptly came to the surface that idiosyncrasy of Henchard's which had ruled his courses

from the beginning and had mainly made him what he was.
Instead of thinking that a union between his cherished
stepdaughter and the energetic thriving Donald was a thing
to be desired for her good and his own, he hated the very
possibility.

Time had been when such instinctive opposition would
have taken shape in action. But he was not now the
Henchard of former days. He schooled himself to accept
her will, in this as in other matters, as absolute and unquestionable. He dreaded lest an antagonistic word should
lose for him such regard as he had regained from her by
his devotion, feeling that to retain this under separation
was better than to incur her dislike by keeping her near.

But the mere thought of such separation fevered his
spirit much, and in the evening he said, with the stillness
of suspense: "Have you seen Mr. Farfrae to-day, Elizabeth?"

Elizabeth-Jane started at the question; and it was with
some confusion that she replied "No."

"Oh—that's right—that's right. . . . It was only that
I saw him in the street when we both were there." He was
wondering if her embarrassment justified him in a new
suspicion—that the long walks which she had latterly been
taking, that the new books which had so surprised him,
had anything to do with the young man. She did not
enlighten him, and lest silence should allow her to shape
thoughts unfavorable to their present friendly relations, he
diverted the discourse into another channel.

Henchard was, by original make, the last man to act
stealthily, for good or for evil. But the *solicitus timor* of his
love—the dependence upon Elizabeth's regard into which
he had declined (or, in another sense, to which he had
advanced)—denaturalized him. He would often weigh and
consider for hours together the meaning of such and such
a deed or phrase of hers, when a blunt settling question
would formerly have been his first instinct. And now,
uneasy at the thought of a passion for Farfrae which should
entirely displace her mild filial sympathy with himself, he
observed her going and coming more narrowly.

There was nothing secret in Elizabeth-Jane's movements beyond what habitual reserve induced; and it may at once be owned on her account that she was guilty of occasional conversations with Donald when they chanced to meet. Whatever the origin of her walks on the Budmouth Road, her return from those walks was often coincident with Farfrae's emergence from Corn Street for a twenty minutes' blow on that rather windy highway—just to winnow the seeds and chaff out of him before sitting down to tea, as he said. Henchard became aware of this by going to the Ring, and, screened by its enclosure, keeping his eye upon the road till he saw them meet. His face assumed an expression of extreme anguish.

"Of her, too, he means to rob me!" he whispered. "But he has the right. I do not wish to interfere."

The meeting, in truth, was of a very innocent kind, and matters were by no means so far advanced between the young people as Henchard's jealous grief inferred. Could he have heard such conversation as passed he would have been enlightened thus much:—

He.—"You like walking this way, Miss Henchard—and is it not so?" (uttered in his undulatory accents, and with an appraising, pondering gaze at her).

She.—"Oh yes. I have chosen this road latterly. I have no great reason for it."

He.—"But that may make a reason for others."

She (reddening).—"I don't know that. My reason, however, such as it is, is that I wish to get a glimpse of the sea every day."

He.—"Is it a secret why?"

She (reluctantly).—"Yes."

He (with the pathos of one of his native ballards).—"Ah, I doubt there will be any good in secrets! A secret cast a deep shadow over my life. And well you know what it was."

Elizabeth admitted that she did, but she refrained from confessing why the sea attracted her. She could not herself account for it fully, not knowing the secret possibly to be that, in addition to early marine associations, her blood was a sailor's.

"Thank you for those new books, Mr. Farfrae," she added shyly. "I wonder if I ought to accept so many!"

"Ay! why not? It gives me more pleasure to get them for you, than you to have them!"

"It cannot!"

They proceeded along the road together till they reached the town, and their paths diverged.

Henchard vowed that he would leave them to their own devices, put nothing in the way of their courses, whatever they might mean. If he were doomed to be bereft of her, so it must be. In the situation which their marriage would create he could see no *locus standi* for himself at all. Farfrae would never recognize him more than superciliously; his poverty ensured that, no less than his past conduct. And So Elizabeth would grow to be a stranger to him, and the end of his life would be friendless solitude.

With such a possibility impending he could not help watchfulness. Indeed, within certain lines, had the right to keep an eye upon her as his charge. The meetings seemed to become matters of course with them on special days of the week.

At last full proof was given him. He was standing behind a wall close to the place at which Farfrae encountered her. He heard the young man address her as "Dearest Elizabeth-Jane," and then kiss her, the girl looking quickly round to assure herself that nobody was near.

When they were gone their way Henchard came out from the wall, and mournfully followed them to Casterbridge. The chief looming trouble in this engagement had not decreased. Both Farfrae and Elizabeth-Jane, unlike the rest of the people, must suppose Elizabeth to be his actual daughter, from his own assertion while he himself had the same belief; and though Farfrae must have so far forgiven him as to have no objection to own him as a father-in-law, intimate they could never be. Thus would the girl, who was his only friend, be withdrawn from him by degrees through her husband's influence, and learn to despise him.

Had she lost her heart to any other man in the world than the one he had rivalled, cursed, wrestled with for life in days before his spirit was broken, Henchard would have said, "I am content." But content with the prospect as now depicted was hard to acquire.

There is an outer chamber of the brain in which thoughts unowned, unsolicited, and of noxious kind, are sometimes allowed to wander for a moment prior to being sent off whence they came. One of these thoughts sailed into Henchard's ken now.

Suppose he were to communicate to Farfrae the fact that his betrothed was not the child of Michael Henchard at all—legally, nobody's child; how would that correct and leading townsman receive the information? He might possibly forsake Elizabeth-Jane, and then she would be her stepsire's own again.

Henchard shuddered, and exclaimed, "God forbid such a thing! Why should I still be subject to these visitations of the devil, when I try so hard to keep him away?"

XLIII

What Henchard saw thus early was, naturally enough, seen at a little later date by other people. That Mr. Farfrae "walked with that bankrupt Henchard's stepdaughter, of all women," became a common topic in the town, the simple perambulating term being used hereabouts to signify a wooing; and the nineteen superior young ladies of Casterbridge, who had each looked upon herself as the only woman capable of making the merchant Councilman happy, indignantly left off going to the church Farfrae attended, left off conscious mannerisms, left off putting him in their prayers at night amongst their blood relations; in short, reverted to their natural courses.

Perhaps the only inhabitants of the town to whom this looming choice of the Scotchman's gave unmixed satisfaction were the members of the philosophic party, which included Longways, Christopher Coney, Billy Wills, Mr. Buzzford, and the like. The Three Mariners having been, years before, the house in which they had witnessed the young man and woman's first and humble appearance on the Casterbridge stage, they took a kindly interest in their career, not unconnected, perhaps, with visions of festive treatment at their hands hereafter. Mrs. Stannidge, having rolled into the large parlor one evening and said that it was a wonder such a man as Mr. Farfrae, "a pillow of the town," who might have chosen one of the daughters of the professional men or private residents, should stoop so low, Coney ventured to disagree with her.

"No, ma'am, no wonder at all. 'Tis she that's a stooping to he—that's my opinion. A widow man—whose first wife was no credit to him—what is it for a young perusing woman that's her own mistress and well liked? But as a neat patching up of things I see much good in it. When a man have put up a tomb of best marble-stone to the other one, as he've done, and weeped his fill, and thought it all over, and said to hisself, 'T'other took me in; I knowed this one first; she's a sensible piece for a partner, and there's no faithful woman in high life now';—well, he may do worse than not to take her, if she's tender-inclined."

Thus they talked at the Mariners. But we must guard against a too liberal use of the conventional declaration that a great sensation was caused by the prospective event, that all the gossips' tongues were set wagging thereby, and so on, even though such a declaration might lend some eclat to the career of our poor only heroine. When all has been said about busy rumorers, a superficial and temporary thing is the interest of anybody in affairs which do not directly touch them. It would be a truer representation to say that Casterbridge (ever excepting the nineteen young ladies) looked up for a moment at the news, and withdrawing its attention, went on laboring and victualling, bringing up its children, and burying its dead, without caring a tittle for Farfrae's domestic plans.

Not a hint of the matter was thrown out to her stepfather by Elizabeth herself or by Farfrae either. Reasoning on the cause of their reticence he concluded that, estimating him by his past, the throbbing pair were afraid to broach the subject, and looked upon him as an irksome obstacle whom they would be heartily glad to get out of the way. Embittered as he was against society, this moody view of himself took deeper and deeper hold of Henchard, till the daily necessity of facing mankind, and of them particularly Elizabeth-Jane, became well-nigh more than he could endure. His health declined; he became morbidly sensitive. He wished he could escape those who did not want him, and hide his head for ever.

But what if he were mistaken in his views, and there were no necessity that his own absolute separation from her should be involved in the incident of her marriage?

He proceeded to draw a picture of the alternative—himself living like a fangless lion about the back rooms of a house in which his stepdaughter was mistress; an inoffensive old man, tenderly smiled on by Elizabeth, and good-naturedly tolerated by her husband. It was terrible to his pride to think of descending so low; and yet, for the girl's sake he might put up with anything, even from Farfrae; even snubbings and masterful tongue-scourgings. The privilege of being in the house she occupied would almost outweigh the personal humiliation.

Whether this were a dim possibility or the reverse, the courtship—which it evidently now was—had an absorbing interest for him.

Elizabeth, as has been said, often took her walks on the Budmouth Road, and Farfrae as often made it convenient to create an accidental meeting with her there. Two miles out, a quarter of a mile from the highway, was the prehistoric fort called Mai Dun, of huge dimensions and many ramparts, within or upon whose enclosures a human being, as seen from the road, was but an insignificant speck. Hitherward Henchard often resorted, glass in hand, and scanned the hedgeless *Via*—for it was the original track laid out by the legions of the Empire—to a distance of two or three miles, his object being to read the progress of affairs between Farfrae and his charmer.

One day Henchard was at this spot when a masculine figure came along the road from Budmouth, and lingered. Applying his telescope to his eye Henchard expected that

Farfrae's features would be disclosed as usual. But the lenses revealed that to-day the man was not Elizabeth-Jane's lover.

It was one clothed as a merchant captain; and as he turned in his scrutiny of the road he revealed his face. Henchard lived a lifetime the moment he saw it. The face was Newson's.

Henchard dropped the glass, and for some seconds made no other movement. Newson waited, and Henchard waited —if that could be called a waiting which was a transfixture. But Elizabeth-Jane did not come. Something or other had caused her to neglect her customary walk that day. Perhaps Farfrae and she had chosen another road for variety's sake. But what did that amount to? She might be here to-morrow, and in any case Newson, if bent on a private meeting and a revelation of the truth to her, would soon make his opportunity.

Then he would tell her not only of his paternity, but of the ruse by which he had been once sent away. Elizabeth's strict nature would cause her for the first time to despise her stepfather, would root out his image as that of an arch-deceiver, and Newson would reign in her heart in his stead.

But Newson did not see anything of her that morning. Having stood still awhile he at last retraced his steps, and Henchard felt like a condemned man who has a few hours' respite. When he reached his own house he found her there.

"O father!" she innocently, "I have had a letter—a strange one—not signed. Somebody has asked me to meet him, either on the Budmouth Road at noon to-day, or in the evening at Mr. Farfrae's. He says he came to see me some time ago, but a trick was played him, so that he did not see me. I don't understand it; but between you and me I think Donald is at the bottom of the mystery, and that it is a relation of his who wants to pass an opinion on his choice. But I did not like to go till I had seen you. Shall I go?"

The question of his remaining in Casterbridge was for

ever disposed of by this closing in of Newson on the scene. Henchard was not the man to stand the certainty of condemnation on a matter so near his heart. And being an old hand at bearing anguish in silence, and haughty withal, he resolved to make as light as he could of his intention, while immediately taking his measures.

He surprised the young woman whom he had looked upon as his all in this world by saying to her, as if he did not care about her more: "I am going to leave Caster-bridge, Elizabeth-Jane."

"Leave Casterbridge!" she cried, "and leave—me?"

"Yes, this little shop can be managed by you alone as well as by us both; I don't care about shops and streets and folk—I would rather get into the country by myself, out of sight, and follow my own ways, and leave you to yours."

She looked down and her tears fell silently. It seemed to her that this resolve of his had come on account of her attachment and its probable result. She showed her devotion to Farfrae, however, by mastering her emotion and speaking out.

"I am sorry you have decided on this," she said with difficult firmness. "For I thought it probable—possible—that I might marry Mr. Farfrae some little time hence, and I did not know that you disapproved of the step!"

"I approve of anything you desire to do, Izzy," said Henchard huskily. "If I did not approve, it would be no matter! I wish to go away. My presence might make things awkward in the future; and, in short, it is best that I go."

Nothing that her affection could urge would induce him to reconsider his determination; for she could not urge what she did not know—that when she should learn he was not related to her other than as a step-parent she would refrain from despising him, and that when she knew what he had done to keep her in ignorance she would refrain from hating him. It was his conviction that she would not so refrain; and there existed as yet neither word nor event which could argue it away.

"Then," she said at last, "you will not be able to come to my wedding; and that is not as it ought to be."

"I don't want to see it—I don't want to see it!" he exclaimed; adding more softly, "but think of me sometimes in your future life—you'll do that, Izzy?—think of me when you are living as the wife of the richest, the foremost man in the town, and don't let my sins, *when you know them all*, cause 'ee to quite forget that though I loved 'ee late I loved 'ee well."

"It is because of Donald!" she sobbed.

"I don't forbid you to marry him," said Henchard. "Promise not to quite forget me when——" He meant when Newson should come.

She promised mechanically, in her agitation; and the same evening at dusk Henchard left the town, to whose development he had been one of the chief stimulants for many years. During the day he had bought a new tool-basket, cleaned up his old hay-knife and wimble, set himself up in fresh leggings, knee-naps and corduroys, and in other ways gone back to the working clothes of his young manhood, discarding for ever the shabby-genteel suit of cloth and rusty silk hat that since his decline had characterized him in the Casterbridge street as a man who had seen better days.

He went secretly and alone, not a soul of the many who had known him being aware of his departure. Elizabeth-Jane accompanied him as far as the second bridge on the highway—for the hour of her appointment with the unguessed visitor at Farfrae's had not yet arrived—and parted from him with unfeigned wonder and sorrow—keeping him back a minute or two before finally letting him go. She watched his form diminish across the moor, the yellow rush-basket at his back moving up and down with each tread, and the creases behind his knees coming and going alternately till she could no longer see them. Though she did not know it Henchard formed at this moment much the same picture as he had presented when entering Casterbridge for the first time nearly a quarter of a century before; except, to be sure, that the serious addition to his years had considerably lessened the spring of his stride, that his state of hopelessness had weakened him, and imparted to his shoulders, as weighted by the basket, a perceptible bend.

He went on till he came to the first milestone, which stood in the bank, half way up a steep hill. He rested his basket on the top of the stone, placed his elbows on it, and gave way to a convulsive twitch, which was worse than a sob, because it was so hard and so dry.

"If I had only got her with me—if I only had!" he said. "Hard work would be nothing to me then! But that was not to be. I—Cain—go alone as I deserve—an outcast and a vagabond. But my punishment is *not* greater than I can bear!"

He sternly subdued his anguish, shouldered his basket, and went on.

Elizabeth, in the meantime, had breathed him a sigh, recovered her equanimity, and turned her face to Casterbridge. Before she had reached the first house she was met in her walk by Donald Farfrae. This was evidently not their first meeting that day; they joined hands without ceremony, and Farfrae anxiously asked, "And is he gone—and did you tell him?—I mean of the other matter—not of ours."

"He is gone; and I told him all I knew of your friend. Donald, who is he?"

"Well, well, dearie; you will know soon about that. And Mr. Henchard will hear of it if he does not go far."

"He will go far—he's bent upon getting out of sight and sound!"

She walked beside her lover, and when they reached the Crossways, or Bow, turned with him into Corn Street instead of going straight on to her own door. At Farfrae's house they stopped and went in.

Farfrae flung open the door of the ground-floor sitting-room, saying, "There he is waiting for you," and Elizabeth entered. In the arm-chair sat the broad-faced genial man who had called on Henchard on a memorable morning between one and two years before this time, and whom

the latter had seen mount the coach and depart within half-
an-hour of his arrival. It was Richard Newson. The meeting
with the light-hearted father from whom she had been
separated half-a-dozen years, as if by death, need hardly
be detailed. It was an affecting one, apart from the question of paternity. Henchard's departure was in a moment
explained. When the true facts came to be handled the
difficulty of restoring her to her old belief in Newson was
not so great as might have seemed likely, for Henchard's
conduct itself was a proof that those facts were true.
Moreover, she had grown up under Newson's paternal care;
and even had Henchard been her father in nature, this
father in early domiciliation might almost have carried the
point against him, when the incidents of her parting with
Henchard had a little worn off.

Newson's pride in what she had grown up to be was
more than he could express. He kissed her again and again.

"I've saved you the trouble to come and meet me—
ha-ha!" said Newson. "The fact is that Mr. Farfrae here,
he said, 'Come up and stop with me for a day or two,
Captain Newson, and I'll bring her round.' 'Faith,' says I,
'so I will'; and here I am."

"Well, Henchard is gone," said Farfrae, shutting the
door. "He has done it all voluntarily, and, as I gather
from Elizabeth, he has been very nice with her. I was
got rather uneasy; but all is as it should be, and we will
have no more deefficulties at all."

"Now, that's very much as I thought," said Newson,
looking into the face of each by turns. "I said to myself,
ay, a hundred times, when I tried to get a peep at her
unknown to herself—'Depend upon it, 'tis best that I
should live on quiet for a few days like this till something
turns up for the better.' I now know you are all right,
and what can I wish for more?"

"Well, Captain Newson, I will be glad to see ye here
every day now, since it can do no harm," said Farfrae.
"And what I've been thinking is that the wedding may as
well be kept under my own roof, the house being large,
and you being in lodgings by yourself—so that a great

deal of trouble and expense would be saved ye?—and 'tis
a convenience when a couple's married not to hae far
to go to get home!"

"With all my heart," said Captain Newson; since, as
ye say, it can do no harm, now poor Henchard's gone;
though I wouldn't have done it otherwise, or put myself
in his way at all; for I've already in my lifetime been an
intruder into his family quite as far as politeness can be
expected to put up with. But what do the young woman
say herself about it? Elizabeth, my child, come and hearken
to what we be talking about, and not bide staring out o'
the window as if ye didn't hear."

"Donald and you must settle it," murmured Elizabeth,
still keeping up a scrutinizing gaze at some small object
in the street.

"Well, then," continued Newson, turning anew to Farfrae with a face expressing thorough entry into the subject,
"that's how we'll have it. And, Mr. Farfrae, as you provide
so much, and houseroom, and all that, I'll do my part in
the drinkables, and see to the rum and schiedam—maybe a
dozen jars will be sufficient—as many of the folk will be
ladies, and perhaps they won't drink hard enough to make
a high average in the reckoning? But you know best. I've
provided for men and shipmates times enough, but I'm
as ignorant as a child how many glasses of grog a woman,
that's not a drinking woman, is expected to consume at
these ceremonies?"

"Oh, none—we'll no want much of that—O no!" said
Farfrae, shaking his head with appalled gravity. "Do you
leave all to me."

When they had gone a little further in these particulars
Newson, leaning back in his chair and smiling reflectively
at the ceiling, said, "I've never told ye, or have I, Mr.
Farfrae, how Henchard put me off the scent that time?"

He expressed ignorance of what the Captain alluded to.

"Ah, I thought I hadn't. I resolved that I would not, I
remember, not to hurt the man's name. But now he's gone
I can tell ye. Why, I came to Casterbridge nine or ten
months before that day last week that I found ye out.

I had been here twice before then. The first time I passed through the town on my way westward, not knowing Elizabeth lived here. Then hearing at some place—I forget where—that a man of the name of Henchard had been mayor here, I came back, and called at his house one morning. The old rascal!—he said Elizabeth-Jane had died years ago."

Elizabeth now gave earnest heed to his story.

"Now, it never crossed my mind that the man was selling me a packet," continued Newson. "And, if you'll believe me, I was that upset, that I went back to the coach that had brought me, and took passage onward without lying in the town half-an-hour. Ha-ha!—'twas a good joke, and well carried out, and I give the man credit for't!"

Elizabeth-Jane was amazed at the intelligence. "A joke? —O no!" she cried. "Then he kept you from me, father, all those months, when you might have been here?"

The father admitted that such was the case.

"He ought not to have done it!" said Farfrae.

Elizabeth sighed. "I said I would never forget him. But O! I think I ought to forget him now!"

Newson, like a good many rovers and sojourners among strange men and strange moralities, failed to perceive the enormity of Henchard's crime, notwithstanding that he himself had been the chief sufferer therefrom. Indeed, the attack upon the absent culprit waxing serious, he began to take Henchard's part.

"Well, 'twas not ten words that he said, after all," Newson pleaded. "And how could he know that I should be such a simpleton as to believe him? 'Twas as much my fault as his, poor fellow!"

"No," said Elizabeth-Jane firmly, in her revulsion of feeling. "He knew your disposition—you always were so trusting, father; I've heard my mother say so hundreds of times—and he did it to wrong you. After weaning me from you these five years by saying he was my father, he should not have done this."

Thus they conversed; and there was nobody to set before Elizabeth any extenuation of the absent one's deceit.

Even had he been present Henchard might scarce have pleaded it, so little did he value himself or his good name.

"Well, well—never mind—it is all over and past," said Newson good-naturedly. "Now, about this wedding again."

XLIV

Meanwhile, the man of their talk had pursued his solitary way eastward till weariness overtook him, and he looked about for a place of rest. His heart was so exacerbated at parting from the girl that he could not face an inn, or even a household of the most humble kind; and entering a field he lay down under a wheat-rick, feeling no want of food. The very heaviness of his soul caused him to sleep profoundly.

The bright autumn sun shining into his eyes across the stubble awoke him the next morning early. He opened his basket and ate for his breakfast what he had packed for his supper; and in doing so overhauled the remainder of his kit. Although everything he brought necessitated carriage at his own back, he had secreted among his tools a few of Elizabeth-Jane's cast-off belongings, in the shape of gloves, shoes, a scrap of her handwriting, and the like; and in his pocket he carried a curl of her hair. Having looked at these things he closed them up again, and went onward.

During five consecutive days Henchard's rush basket rode along upon his shoulder between the highway hedges, the new yellow of the rushes catching the eye of an occasional field-laborer as he glanced through the quickset, together with the wayfarer's hat and head, and down-turned face, over which the twig shadows moved in endless procession. It now became apparent that the direction of his journey was Weydon Priors, which he reached on the afternoon of the sixth day.

The renowned hill whereon the annual fair had been held for so many generations was now bare of human beings, and almost of aught besides. A few sheep grazed thereabout, but these ran off when Henchard halted upon the summit. He deposited his basket upon the turf, and looked about with sad curiosity; till he discovered the road by which his wife and himself had entered on the upland so memorable to both five-and-twenty years before.

"Yes, we came up that way," he said, after ascertaining his bearings. "She was carrying the baby, and I was reading a ballet-sheet. Then we crossed about here—she so sad and weary, and I speaking to her hardly at all, because of my cursed pride and mortification at being poor. Then we saw the tent—that must have stood more this way." He walked to another spot; it was not really where the tent had stood but it seemed so to him. "Here we went in, and here we sat down. I faced this way. Then I drank, and committed my crime. It must have been just on that very pixy-ring that she was standing when she said her last words to me before going off with him; I can hear their sound now, and the sound of her sobs: 'O Mike! I've lived with thee all this while, and had nothing but temper. Now I'm no more to 'ee—I'll try my luck elsewhere.' "

He experienced not only the bitterness of a man who finds, in looking back upon an ambitious course, that what he has sacrificed in sentiment was worth as much as what he has gained in substance; but the superadded bitterness of seeing his very recantation nullified. He had been sorry for all this long ago; but his attempts to replace ambition by love had been as fully foiled as his ambition itself. His wronged wife had foiled them by a fraud so grandly simple as to be almost a virtue. It was an odd sequence that out of all this tampering with social law came that flower of Nature, Elizabeth. Part of his wish to wash his hands of life arose from his perception of its contrarious inconsistencies—of Nature's jaunty readiness to support unorthodox social principles.

He intended to go on from this place—visited as an act of penance—into another part of the country altogether. But he could not help thinking of Elizabeth, and the quarter of the horizon in which she lived. Out of this it happened that the centrifugal tendency imparted by weariness of the world was counteracted by the centripetal influence of his love for his stepdaughter. As a consequence, instead of following a straight course yet further away from Casterbridge, Henchard gradually, almost unconsciously, deflected from that right line of his first intention; till, by degrees, his wandering, like that of the Canadian woodsman, became part of a circle of which Casterbridge formed the center. In ascending any particular hill he ascertained the bearings as nearly as he could by means of the sun, moon, or stars, and settled in his mind the exact direction in which Casterbridge and Elizabeth-Jane lay. Sneering at himself for his weakness he yet every hour—nay, every few minutes—conjectured her actions for the time being—her sitting down and rising up, her goings and comings, till thought of Newson's and Farfrae's counter-influence would pass like a cold blast over a pool, and efface her image. And then he would say of himself, "O you fool! All this about a daughter who is no daughter of thine!"

At length he obtained employment at his own occupation of hay-trusser, work of that sort being in demand at this autumn time. The scene of his hiring was a pastoral farm near the old western highway, whose course was the channel of all such communications as passed between the busy centers of novelty and the remote Wessex boroughs. He had chosen the neighborhood of this artery from a sense that, situated here, though at a distance of fifty miles, he was virtually nearer to her whose welfare was so dear than he would be at a roadless spot only half as remote.

And thus Henchard found himself again on the precise standing which he had occupied a quarter of a century before. Externally there was nothing to hinder his making another start on the upward slope, and by his new lights achieving higher things than his soul in its half-formed state had been able to accomplish. But the ingenious machinery contrived by the Gods for reducing human possibilities of amelioration to a minimum—which arranges that wisdom to do shall come *pari passu* with the departure of zest for doing—stood in the way of all that. He had no wish to make an arena a second time of a world that had become a mere painted scene to him.

Very often, as his hay-knife crunched down among the sweet-smelling grassy stems, he would survey mankind and say to himself: "Here and everywhere be folk dying before their time like frosted leaves, though wanted by their families, the country, and the world; while I, an outcast, an encumberer of the ground, wanted by nobody, and despised by all, live on against my will!"

He often kept an eager ear upon the conversation of those who passed along the road—not from a general curiosity by any means—but in the hope that among these travellers between Casterbridge and London some would, sooner or later, speak of the former place. The distance, however, was too great to lend much probability to his desire; and the highest result of his attention to wayside words was that he did indeed hear the name "Casterbridge" uttered one day by the driver of a road-wagon. Henchard ran to the gate of the field he worked in, and hailed the speaker, who was a stranger.

"Yes—I've come from there, maister," he said, in answer to Henchard's inquiry. "I trade up and down, ye know; though, what with this travelling without horses that's getting so common, my work will soon be done."

"Anything moving in the old place, mid I ask?"

"All the same as usual."

"I've heard that Mr. Farfrae, the late mayor, is thinking of getting married. Now is that true or not?"

"I couldn't say for the life o' me. Oh no, I should think not."

"But yes, John—you forget," said a woman inside the wagon-tilt. "What were them packages we carr'd there at the beginning o' the week? Surely they said a wedding was coming off soon—on Martin's Day?"

The man declared he remembered nothing about it; and the wagon went on jangling over the hill.

Henchard was convinced that the woman's memory served her well. The date was an extremely probable one, there being no reason for delay on either side. He might, for that matter, write and inquire of Elizabeth; but his instinct for sequestration had made the course difficult. Yet before he left her she had said that for him to be absent from her wedding was not as she wished it to be.

The remembrance would continually revive in him now that it was not Elizabeth and Farfrae who had driven him away from them, but his own haughty sense that his presence was no longer desired. He had assumed the return of Newson without absolute proof that the Captain meant to return; still less that Elizabeth-Jane would welcome him; and with no proof whatever that if he did return he would stay. What if he had been mistaken in his views; if there had been no necessity that his own absolute separation from her he loved should be involved in these untoward incidents? To make one more attempt to be near her: to go back; to see her, to plead his cause before her, to ask forgiveness for his fraud, to endeavor strenuously to hold his own in her love; it was worth the risk of repulse, ay, of life itself.

But how to initiate this reversal of all his former resolves without causing husband and wife to despise him for his inconsistency was a question which made him tremble and brood.

He cut and cut his trusses two days more, and then he concluded his hesitancies by a sudden reckless determination to go to the wedding festivity. Neither writing nor message would be expected of him. She had regretted his decision to be absent—his unanticipated presence would fill the little unsatisfied corner that would probably have place in her just heart without him.

To intrude as little of his personality as possible upon a gay event with which that personality could show nothing in keeping, he decided not to make his appearance till evening—when stiffness would have worn off, and a gentle wish to let bygones be bygones would exercise its sway in all hearts.

He started on foot, two mornings before St. Martin's-tide, allowing himself about sixteen miles to perform for each of the three days' journey, reckoning the wedding-day as one. There were only two towns, Melchester and Shottsford, of any importance along his course, and at the latter he stopped on the second night, not only to rest, but to prepare himself for the next evening.

Possessing no clothes but the working suit he stood in—now stained and distorted by their two months of hard usage, he entered a shop to make some purchases which should put him, externally at any rate, a little in harmony with the prevailing tone of the morrow. A rough yet respectable coat and hat, a new shirt and neck-cloth, were the chief of these; and having satisfied himself that in appearance at least he would not now offend her, he proceeded to the more interesting particular of buying her some present.

What should that present be? He walked up and down the street. regarding dubiously the display in the shop windows, from a gloomy sense that what he might most like to give her would be beyond his miserable pocket. At length a caged goldfinch met his eye. The cage was a plain and small one, the shop humble, and on inquiry he concluded he could afford the modest sum asked. A sheet of newspaper was tied round the little creature's wire prison, and with the wrapped up cage in his hand Henchard sought a lodging for the night.

Next day he set out upon the last stage, and was soon within the district which had been his dealing ground in bygone years. Part of the distance he travelled by carrier, seating himself in the darkest corner at the back of that trader's van; and as the other passengers, mainly women going short journeys, mounted and alighted in front of Henchard, they talked over much local news, not the least portion of this being the wedding then in course of celebration at the town they were nearing. It appeared from their accounts that the town band had been hired for the evening party, and, lest the convivial instincts of that body should get the better of their skill, the further step had been taken of engaging the string band from Budmouth, so that there would be a reserve of harmony to fall back upon in case of need.

He heard, however, but few particulars beyond those known to him already, the incident of the deepest interest on the journey being the soft pealing of the Casterbridge bells, which reached the travellers' ears while the van paused on the top of Yalbury Hill to have the drag lowered. The time was just after twelve o'clock.

Those notes were a signal that all had gone well; that there had been no slip 'twist cup and lip in this case; that Elizabeth-Jane and Donald Farfrae were man and wife.

Henchard did not care to ride any further with his chattering companions after hearing this sound. Indeed, it quite unmanned him; and in pursuance of his plan of not showing himself in Casterbridge street till evening, lest he should mortify Farfrae and his bride, he alighted here, with his bundle and bird-cage, and was soon left as a lonely figure on the broad white highway.

It was the hill near which he had waited to meet Farfrae, almost two years earlier, to tell him of the serious illness of his wife Lucetta. The place was unchanged, the same larches sighed the same notes; but Farfrae had another wife —and, as Henchard knew, a better one. He only hoped that Elizabeth-Jane had obtained a better home than had been hers at the former time.

He passed the remainder of the afternoon in a curious highstrung condition, unable to do much but to think of the approaching meeting with her, and sadly satirize himself for his emotions thereon, as a Samson shorn. Such an innovation on Casterbridge customs as a flitting of bridegroom and bride from the town immediately after the ceremony, was not likely, but if it should have taken place he would wait till their return. To assure himself on this point he asked a market-man when near the borough if the newly-married couple had gone away, and was promptly informed that they had not; they were at that hour, according to all accounts, entertaining a houseful of guests at their home in Corn Street.

Henchard dusted his boots, washed his hands at the riverside, and proceeded up the town under the feeble lamps. He need have made no inquiries beforehand, for on drawing near Farfrae's residence it was plain to the least observant that festivity prevailed within, and that Donald himself shared it, his voice being distinctly audible in the street, giving strong expression to a song of his dear native country that he loved so well as never to have revisited it. Idlers were standing on the pavement in front; and wishing to escape the notice of these Henchard passed quickly on to the door.

It was wide open; the hall was lighted extravagantly, and people were going up and down the stairs. His courage failed him; to enter footsore, laden, and poorly dressed into the midst of such resplendency was to bring needless humiliation upon her he loved, if not to court repulse from her husband. Accordingly he went round into the street at the back that he knew so well, entered the garden, and came quietly into the house through the kitchen, temporarily depositing the bird and cage under a bush outside, to lessen the awkwardness of his arrival.

Solitude and sadness had so emolliated Henchard that he now feared circumstances he would formerly have scorned, and he began to wish that he had not taken upon himself to arrive at such a juncture. However, his progress was made unexpectedly easy by his discovering alone in the kitchen an elderly woman who seemed to be acting as provisional housekeeper during the convulsions from which Farfrae's establishment was just then suffering. She was one of those people whom nothing surprises, and though to her, a total stranger, his request must have seemed odd, she willingly volunteered to go up and inform the master and mistress of the house that "a humble old friend" had come.

On second thoughts she said that he had better not wait in the kitchen, but come up into the little back-parlor, which was empty. He thereupon followed her thither, and she left him. Just as she had got across the landing to the door of the best parlor a dance was struck up, and she returned to say that she would wait till that was over before announcing him—Mr. and Mrs. Farfrae having both joined in the figure.

The door of the front room had been taken off its

hinges to give more space, and that of the room Henchard sat in being ajar, he could see fractional parts of the dancers whenever their gyrations brought them near the doorway, chiefly in the shape of the skirts of dresses and streaming curls of hair; together with about three-fifths of the band in profile, including the restless shadow of a fiddler's elbow, and the tip of the bass-viol bow.

The gaiety jarred upon Henchard's spirits; and he could not quite understand why Farfrae, a much-sobered man, and a widower, who had had his trials, should have cared for it all, notwithstanding the fact that he was quite a young man still, and quickly kindled to enthusiasm by dance and song. That the quiet Elizabeth, who had long ago appraised life at a moderate value, and who knew in spite of her maidenhood that marriage was as a rule no dancing matter, should have had zest for this revelry surprised him still more. However, young people could not be quite old people, he concluded, and custom was omnipotent.

With the progress of the dance the performers spread out somewhat, and then for the first time he caught a glimpse of the once despised daughter who had mastered him, and made his heart ache. She was in a dress of white silk or satin, he was not near enough to say which—snowy white, without a tinge of milk or cream; and the expression of her face was one of nervous pleasure rather than of gaiety. Presently Farfrae came round, his exuberant Scotch movement making him conspicuous in a moment. The pair were not dancing together, but Henchard could discern that whenever the changes of the figure made them the partners of a moment their emotions breathed a much subtler essence than at other times.

By degrees Henchard became aware that the measure was trod by some one who out-Farfraed Farfrae in saltatory intenseness. This was strange, and it was stranger to find that the eclipsing personage was Elizabeth-Jane's partner. The first time that Henchard saw him he was sweeping grandly round, his head quivering and low down, his legs in the form of an X and his back towards the door. The next time he came round in the other direction, his white waistcoat preceding his face, and his toes preceding his white waistcoat. That happy face—Henchard's complete discomfiture lay in it. It was Newson's, who had indeed come and supplanted him.

Henchard pushed to the door, and for some seconds made no other movement. He rose to his feet, and stood like a dark ruin, obscured by "the shade from his own soul upthrown."

But he was no longer the man to stand these reverses unmoved. His agitation was great, and he would fain have been gone, but before he could leave the dance had ended, the housekeeper had informed Elizabeth-Jane of the stranger who awaited her, and she entered the room immediately.

"Oh—it is—Mr. Henchard!" she said, starting back.

"What; Elizabeth?" he cried, as he seized her hand. "What do you say?—*Mr.* Henchard? Don't. don't scourge me like that! Call me worthless old Henchard—anything— but don't 'ee be so cold as this! O, my maid—I see you have another—a real father in my place. Then you know all; but don't give all your thought to him! Do ye save a little room for me!"

She flushed up, and gently drew her hand away. "I could have loved you always—I would have, gladly," said she. "But how can I when I know you have deceived me so— so bitterly deceived me! You persuaded me that my father was not my father—allowed me to live on in ignorance of the truth for years; and then when he, my warm-hearted real father, came to find me, cruelly sent him away with a wicked invention of my death, which nearly broke his heart. Oh how can I love as I once did a man who has served us like this!"

Henchard's lips half parted to begin an explanation. But he shut them up like a vice, and uttered not a sound. How should he, there and then, set before her with any effect the palliatives of his great faults—that he had himself been deceived in her identity at first, till informed by her mother's letter that his own child had died; that, in the second accusation, his lie had been the last desperate throw of a gamester who loved her affection better than his own honor? Among the many hindrances to such a pleading not the least was this, that he did not sufficiently value himself to lessen his sufferings by strenuous appeal or elaborate argument.

Waiving, therefore, his privilege of self-defence, he regarded only her discomposure. "Don't ye distress yourself on my account," he said, with proud superiority. "I would not wish it—at such a time, too, as this. I have done wrong in coming to 'ee—I see my error. But it is only for once, so forgive it. I'll never trouble 'ee again, Elizabeth-Jane—no, not to my dying day! Good-night. Good-bye!"

Then, before she could collect her thoughts, Henchard went out from her rooms, and departed from the house by the back way as he had come; and she saw him no more.

XLV

It was about a month after the day which closed as in the last chapter. Elizabeth-Jane had grown accustomed to the novelty of her situation, and the only difference between Donald's movements now and formerly was that he hastened indoors rather more quickly after business hours than he had been in the habit of doing for some time.

Newson had stayed in Casterbridge three days after the wedding party (whose gaiety, as might have been surmised, was of his making rather than of the married couple's), and was stared at and honored as became the returned Crusoe of the hour. But whether or not because Casterbridge was difficult to excite by dramatic returns and disappearances, through having been for centuries an assize town, in which sensational exits from the world, antipodean absences, and such like, were half-yearly occurrences, the inhabitants did not altogether lose their equanimity on his account. On the fourth morning he was discovered disconsolately climbing a hill, in his craving to get a glimpse of the sea from somewhere or other. The contiguity of salt water proved to be such a necessity of his existence that he preferred Budmouth as a place of residence, notwithstanding the society of his daughter in the other town. Thither he went, and settled in lodgings in a green-shuttered cottage which had a bow-window, jutting out sufficiently to afford glimpses of a vertical strip of blue sea to any one opening the sash, and leaning forward far enough to look through a narrow lane of tall intervening houses.

Elizabeth-Jane was standing in the middle of her upstairs parlor, critically surveying some re-arrangement of articles with her head to one side, when the housemaid came in with the announcement, "Oh, please ma'am, we know now how that bird-cage came there."

In exploring her new domain during the first week of residence, gazing with critical satisfaction on this cheerful room and that, penetrating cautiously into dark cellars, sallying forth with gingerly tread to the garden, now leaf-strewn by autumn winds, and thus, like a wise field-marshal, estimating the capabilities of the site whereon she was about to open her housekeeping campaign—Mrs. Donald Farfrae had discovered in a screened corner a new bird-cage, shrouded in newspaper, and at the bottom of the cage a little ball of feathers—the dead body of a goldfinch. Nobody could tell her how the bird and cage had come there; though that the poor little songster had been starved to death was evident. The sadness of the incident had made an impression on her. She had not been able to forget it for days, despite Farfrae's tender banter; and now when the matter had been nearly forgotten it was again revived.

"Oh, please ma'am, we know how that bird-cage came there. That farmer's man who called on the evening of the wedding—he was seen wi' it in his hand as he came up the street; and 'tis thoughted that he put it down while he came in with his message, and then went away forgetting where he had left it."

This was enough to set Elizabeth thinking, and in thinking she seized hold of the idea, at one feminine bound, that the caged bird had been brought by Henchard for her as a wedding gift and token of repentance. He had not expressed to her any regrets or excuses for what he had done in the past; but it was a part of his nature to extenuate nothing, and live on as one of his own worst accusers. She went out, looked at the cage, buried the starved little singer, and from that hour her heart softened towards the self-alienated man.

When her husband came in she told him her solution of the bird-cage mystery; and begged Donald to help her in finding out, as soon as possible, whither Henchard had banished himself, that she might make her peace with him; try to do something to render his life less that of an outcast, and more tolerable to him. Although Farfrae had never so passionately liked Henchard as Henchard had liked him, he had, on the other hand, never so passionately hated in the same direction as his former friend had done; and he was therefore not the least indisposed to assist Elizabeth-Jane in her laudable plan.

But it was by no means easy to set about discovering Henchard. He had apparently sunk into the earth on leaving Mr. and Mrs. Farfrae's door. Elizabeth-Jane remembered what he had once attempted; and trembled.

But though she did not know it Henchard had become a changed man since then—as far, that is, as change of emotional basis can justify such a radical phrase; and she needed not to fear. In a few days Farfrae's inquiries elicited that Henchard had been seen by one who knew him walking steadily along the Melchester highway eastward, at twelve o'clock at night—in other words, retracing his steps on the road by which he had come.

This was enough; and the next morning Farfrae might have been discovered driving his gig out of Casterbridge. in that direction, Elizabeth-Jane sitting beside him, wrapped in a thick flat fur—the victorine of the period—her complexion somewhat richer than formerly, and an incipient matronly dignity, which the serene Minerva-eyes of one "whose gestures beamed with mind" made becoming, settling on her face. Having herself arrived at a promising haven from at least the grosser troubles of her life, her object was to place Henchard in some similar quietude before he should sink into that lower stage of existence which was only too possible to him now.

After driving along the highway for a few miles they made further inquiries, and learnt of a road-mender, who had been working thereabouts for weeks, that he had observed such a man at the time mentioned; he had left the Melchester coach-road at Weatherbury by a forking highway which skirted the north of Egdon Heath. Into this road they directed the horse's head, and soon were bowling across that ancient country whose surface never had been stirred to a finger's depth, save by the scratchings of rabbits, since brushed by the feet of the earliest tribes. The tumuli these had left behind, dun and shagged with heather, jutted roundly into the sky from the uplands, as though they were the full breasts of Diana Multimammia supinely extended there.

They searched Egdon, but found no Henchard. Farfrae drove onward, and by the afternoon reached the neighborhood of some extension of the heath to the north of Anglebury, a prominent feature of which, in the form of a blasted slump of firs on the summit of a hill, they soon passed under. That the road they were following had, up to this point, been Henchard's track on foot they were pretty certain; but the ramifications which now began to reveal themselves in the route made further progress in the right direction a matter of pure guess-work, and Donald strongly advised his wife to give up the search in person, and trust to other means for obtaining news of her stepfather. They were now a score of miles at least from home, but, by resting the horse for a couple of hours at a village they had just traversed, it would be possible to get back to Casterbridge that same day; while to go much further afield would reduce them to the necessity of camping out for the night; "and that will make a hole in a sovereign," said Farfrae. She pondered the position, and agreed with him.

He accordingly drew rein, but before reversing their direction paused a moment and looked vaguely round upon the wide country which the elevated position disclosed. While they looked a solitary human form came from under the clump of trees, and crossed ahead of them. The person was some laborer; his gait was shambling, his regard fixed in front of him as absolutely as if he wore blinkers; and in his hand he carried a few sticks. Having crossed the road he descended into a ravine, where a cottage revealed itself, which he entered.

"If it were not so far away Casterbridge I should say that must be poor Whittle. 'Tis just like him," observed Elizabeth-Jane."

"And it may be Whittle, for he's never been to the yard these three weeks, going away without saying any word at all; and I owing him for two days' work, without knowing who to pay it to."

The possibility led them to alight, and at least make an inquiry at the cottage. Farfrae hitched the reins to the gate-post, and they approached what was of humble dwellings surely the humblest. The walls, built of kneaded clay originally faced with a trowel, had been worn by years of rain-washings to a lumpy crumbling surface, channelled and sunken from its plane, its grey rents held together here and there by a leafy strap of ivy which could scarcely find substance enough for the purpose. The rafters were sunken, and the thatch of the roof in ragged holes. Leaves from the fence had been blown into the corners of the doorway, and lay there undisturbed. The door was ajar; Farfrae knocked; and he who stood before them was Whittle, as they had conjectured.

His face showed marks of deep sadness, his eyes lighting on them with an unfocused gaze; and he still held in his hand the few sticks he had been out to gather. As soon as he recognized them he started.

"What, Abel Whittle; is it that ye are heere?" said Farfrae.

"Ay, yes, sir! You see he was kind-like to mother when she wer here below, though 'a was rough to me."

"Who are you talking of?"

"O sir—Mr. Henchet! Didn't ye know it? He's just gone—about half-an-hour ago, by the sun; for I've got no watch to my name."

"Not—dead?" faltered Elizabeth-Jane.

"Yes, ma'am, he's gone! He was kind-like to mother when she wer here below, sending her the best ship-coal, and hardly any ashes from it at all; and taties, and such-like that were very needful to her. I seed en go down street on the night of your worshipful's wedding to the lady at yer side, and I thought he looked low and faltering. And I followed en over Grey's Bridge, and he turned and zeed me, and said, 'You go back!' But I followed, and he turned again, and said, 'Do you hear, sir? Go back!' But I zeed that he was low, and I followed on still. Then 'a said, 'Whittle, what do ye follow me for when I've told ye to go back all these times?' And I said, 'Because, sir, I see things be bad with 'ee, and ye wer kind-like to mother if ye were rough to me, and I would fain be kind-like to you.' Then he walked on, and I followed; and he never complained at me no more. We walked on like that all night; and in the blue o' the morning, when 'twas hardly day, I looked ahead o' me, and I zeed that he wambled, and could hardly drag along. By that time we had got past here, but I had seen that this house was empty as I went by, and I got him to come back; and I took down the boards from the windows, and helped him inside. 'What, Whittle,' he said, 'and can ye really be such a poor fond fool as to care for such a wretch as I!' Then I went on further, and some neighborly woodmen lent me a bed, and a chair, and a few other traps, and we brought 'em here, and made him as comfortable as we could. But he didn't gain strength, for you see, ma'am, he couldn't eat—no, no appetite at all —and he got weaker; and to-day he died. One of the neighbors have gone to get a man to measure him."

"Dear me—is that so!" said Farfrae.

As for Elizabeth, she said nothing.

"Upon the head of his bed he pinned a piece of paper, with some writing upon it," continued Abel Whittle. "But not being a man o' letters, I can't read writing; so I don't know what it is. I can get it and show ye."

They stood in silence while he ran into the cottage; returning in a moment with a crumpled scrap of paper. On it there was pencilled as follows:—

"MICHAEL HENCHARD'S WILL

"That Elizabeth-Jane Farfrae be not told of my death, or made to grieve on account of me.

"& that I be not bury'd in consecrated ground.

"& that no sexton be asked to toll the bell.

"& that nobody is wished to see my dead body.

"& that no murners walk behind me at my funeral.

"& that no flours be planted on my grave.

"& that no man remember me.

"To this I put my name.   MICHAEL HENCHARD."

"What are we to do?" said Donald, when he had handed the paper to her.

She could not answer distinctly. "O Donald!" she said at last through her tears, "what bitterness lies there! Oh I would not have minded so much if it had not been for my unkindness at that last parting! . . . But there's no altering—so it must be."

What Henchard had written in the anguish of his dying was respected as far as practicable by Elizabeth-Jane, though less from a sense of the sacredness of last words, as such, than from her independent knowledge that the man who wrote them meant what he said. She knew the directions to be a piece of the same stuff that his whole life was made of, and hence were not to be tampered with to give herself a mournful pleasure, or her husband credit for large-heartedness.

All was over at last, even her regrets for having mis-understood him on his last visit, for not having searched him out sooner, though these were deep and sharp for a good while. From this time forward Elizabeth-Jane found herself in a latitude of calm weather, kindly and grateful in itself, and doubly so after the Capharnaum in which some of her preceding years had been spent. As the lively and sparkling emotions of her early married life cohered into an equable serenity, the finer movements of her nature found scope in discovering to the narrow-lived ones around her the secret (as she had once learnt it) of making limited opportunities endurable; which she deemed to consist in the cunning enlargement, by a species of microscopic treat-ment, of those minute forms of satisfaction that offer them-selves to everybody not in positive pain; which, thus handled, have much of the same inspiriting effect upon life as wider interests cursorily embraced.

Her teaching had a reflex action upon herself, insomuch that she thought she could perceive no great personal difference between being respected in the nether parts of Casterbridge and glorified at the uppermost end of the social world. Her position was, indeed, to a marked degree one that, in the common phrase, afforded much to be thankful for. That she was not demonstratively thankful was no fault of hers. Her experience had been of a kind to teach her, rightly or wrongly, that the doubtful honor of a brief transit through a sorry world hardly called for effusiveness, even when the path was suddenly irradiated at some half-way point by daybeams rich as hers. But her strong sense that neither she nor any human being deserved less than was given, did not blind her to the fact that there were others receiving less who had deserved much more. And in being forced to class herself among the fortunate she did not cease to wonder at the persistence of the unforeseen, when the one to whom such unbroken tranquillity had been accorded in the adult stage was she whose youth had seemed to teach that happiness was but the occasional episode in a general drama of pain.

3

POEMS
1866–1928

Editor's Note

Hardy began writing verse in the 1860s while working in London as an assistant architect. His early enthusiasms were for Shelley and Swinburne, but the strongest influence was from William Barnes of Dorset, a Dorchester schoolmaster whose exquisitely metered poems in Dorset dialect on rural themes exhibited in Hardy's words an "aim at closeness of phrase to his vision" which Hardy pursued as his own aim throughout his poetic career.

Once begun, Hardy wrote verse during all the years of his novel-writing but published none of it in book form until 1898 when he had ceased to write fiction. At the time of his death in his eighty-ninth year, he was revising

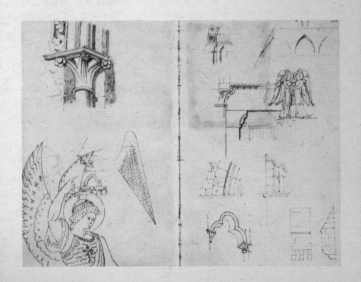

proof for the volume entitled *Winter Words*. The *Collected Poems* (1932), comprising nearly a thousand poems in eight substantial volumes, established Hardy, not instantly but in the long run, as the last great poet of the nineteenth century and as one of the greatest, if not the greatest of poets, writing in English during the twentieth century.

Hardy's rank as a major English poet has been recognized by nearly all his fellow poets, including Ezra Pound, John Crowe Ransom, Dylan Thomas, and Philip Larkin. Here there is space for just a few remarks the truth of which is perhaps certified by their obviousness. His poetry neither sets nor follows a period style nor does it undergo any drastic changes of manner or theme from early to late. His occasional ruggedness of metrical accent and oddness of diction are a deliberate technique employed by a master craftsman for the conveyance of sincere emotion and authentic drama. Some of his best verse is deeply personal, even confessional: it is about loving and losing; about mistakings and perplexities lived through once, then hauntingly recalled; about the sadness and strangeness of outliving so many of his contemporaries; about the sober joy he took in registering the world of Wessex in all its weathers and moods, and in all the variety of its human and natural occupants. Finally, the many poems he wrote of a meditative and philosophical cast are probings and questionings of reality, including cosmic reality, as he constantly maintained they were, and not the exercises in an amateurish ironical determinism which a few critics have made them out to be.

FROM *WESSEX POEMS* (1898)
POEMS, 1866–67

Hap

If but some vengeful god would call to me
From up the sky, and laugh: "Thou suffering thing,
Know that thy sorrow is my ecstasy,
That thy love's loss is my hate's profiting!"

Then would I bear it, clench myself, and die,
Steeled by the sense of ire unmerited;
Half-eased in that a Powerfuller than I
Had willed and meted me the tears I shed.

But not so.   How arrives it joy lies slain,
And why unblooms the best hope ever sown?
—Crass Casualty obstructs the sun and rain,
And dicing Time for gladness casts a moan. . . .
These purblind Doomsters had as readily strown
Blisses about my pilgrimage as pain.

    1866.

A Confession to a Friend in Trouble

Your troubles shrink not, though I feel them less
Here, far away, than when I tarried near;
I even smile old smiles—with listlessness—
Yet smiles they are, not ghastly mockeries mere.

A thought too strange to house within my brain
Haunting its outer precincts I discern:
—*That I will not show zeal again to learn
Your griefs, and, sharing them, renew my pain. . . .*

It goes, like murky bird or buccaneer
That shapes its lawless figure on the main,
And staunchness tends to banish utterly
The unseemly instinct that had lodgment here;
Yet, comrade old, can bitterer knowledge be
Than that, though banned, such instinct was in me!

    1866.

Neutral Tones

We stood by a pond that winter day,
And the sun was white, as though chidden of God,
And a few leaves lay on the starving sod;
      —They had fallen from an ash, and were
      grey.

Your eyes on me were as eyes that rove
Over tedious riddles of years ago;
And some words played between us to and fro
      On which lost the more by our love.

The smile on your mouth was the deadest thing
Alive enough to have strength to die:
And a grin of bitterness swept thereby
      Like an ominous bird a-wing. . . .

Since then, keen lessons that love deceives,
And wrings with wrong, have shaped to me
Your face, and the God-curst sun, and a tree,
      And a pond edged with greyish leaves.

    1867.

Her Dilemma

(IN —— CHURCH)

The two were silent in a sunless church,
Whose mildewed walls, uneven paving-stones,
And wasted carvings passed antique research;
And nothing broke the clock's dull monotones.

Leaning against a wormy poppy-head,
So wan and worn that he could scarcely stand,
—For he was soon to die,—he softly said,
"Tell me you love me!"—holding long her hand.

She would have given a world to breathe "yes" truly,
So much his life seemed hanging on her mind,
And hence she lied, her heart persuaded throughly
'Twas worth her soul to be a moment kind.

But the sad need thereof, his nearing death,
So mocked humanity that she shamed to prize
A world conditioned thus, or care for breath
Where Nature such dilemmas could devise.

1866.

She, to Him

I will be faithful to thee; aye, I will!
And Death shall choose me with a wondering eye
That he did not discern and domicile
One his by right ever since that last Good-bye!

I have no care for friends, or kin, or prime
Of manhood who deal gently with me here;
Amid the happy people of my time
Who work their love's fulfilment, I appear

Numb as a vane that cankers on its point,
True to the wind that kissed ere canker came:
Despised by souls of Now, who would disjoint
The mind from memory, making Life all aim,

My old dexterities in witchery gone,
And nothing left for Love to look upon.

    1866.

The Ruined Maid

"O 'Melia, my dear, this does everything crown!
Who could have supposed I should meet you in Town?
And whence such fair garments, such prosperi-ty?"—
"O didn't you know I'd been ruined?" said she.

—"You left us in tatters, without shoes or socks,
Tired of digging potatoes, and spudding up docks;
And now you've gay bracelets and bright feathers three!"—
"Yes: that's how we dress when we're ruined," said she.

—"At home in the barton you said 'thee' and 'thou,'
And 'thik oon,' and 'theäs oon,' and 't'other'; but now
Your talking quite fits 'ee for high compa-ny!"—
"Some polish is gained with one's ruin," said she.

—"Your hands were like paws then, your face blue and
  bleak
But now I'm bewitched by your delicate cheek,
And your little gloves fit as on any la-dy!"—
"We never do work when we're ruined," said she.

—"You used to call home-life a hag-ridden dream,
And you'd sigh, and you'd sock; but at present you seem
To know not of megrims or melancho-ly!"—
"True.   One's pretty lively when ruined," said she.

—"I wish I had feathers, a fine sweeping gown,
And a delicate face, and could strut about Town!"—
"My dear—a raw country girl, such as you be,
Cannot quite expect that.   You ain't ruined," said she.

WESTBOURNE PARK VILLAS, 1866.

1967

In five-score summers!   All new eyes,
New minds, new modes, new fools, new wise;
New woes to weep, new joys to prize;

With nothing left of me and you
In that live century's vivid view
Beyond a pinch of dust or two;

A century which, if not sublime,
Will show, I doubt not, at its prime,
A scope above this blinkered time.

—Yet what to me how far above?
For I would only ask thereof
That thy worm should be my worm, Love!

16 WESTBOURNE PARK VILLAS, 1867.

Heiress and Architect

FOR A. W. BLOMFIELD

She sought the Studios, beckoning to her side
An arch-designer, for she planned to build.
He was of wise contrivance, deeply skilled
In every intervolve of high and wide—
       Well fit to be her guide.

       "Whatever it be,"
       Responded he,
With cold, clear voice, and cold, clear view,
"In true accord with prudent fashionings
For such vicissitudes as living brings,
And thwarting not the law of stable things,
       That will I do."

"Shape me," she said, "high halls with tracery
And open ogive-work, that scent and hue
Of buds, and travelling bees, may come in through,
The note of birds, and singings of the sea,
       For these are much to me."

       "An idle whim!"
       Broke forth from him
Whom nought could warm to gallantries:
"Cede all these buds and birds, the zephyr's call,
And scents, and hues, and things that falter all,
And choose as best the close and surly wall,
       For winters freeze."

"Then frame," she cried, "wide fronts of crystal glass,
That I may show my laughter and my light—
Light like the sun's by day, the stars' by night—
Till rival heart-queens, envying, wail, 'Alas,
       Her glory!' as they pass."

"O maid misled!"
He sternly said

Whose facile foresight pierced her dire;
"Where shall abide the soul when, sick of glee,
It shrinks, and hides, and prays no eye may see?
Those house them best who house for secrecy,
        For you will tire."

"A little chamber, then, with swan and dove
Ranged thickly, and engrailed with rare device
Of reds and purples, for a Paradise
Wherein my Love may greet me, I my Love,
        When he shall know thereof?"

        "This, too, is ill,"
        He answered still,
The man who swayed her like a shade.
"An hour will come when sight of such sweet nook
Would bring a bitterness too sharp to brook,
When brighter eyes have won away his look;
        For you will fade."

Then said she faintly: "O, contrive some way—
Some narrow winding turret, quite mine own,
To reach a loft where I may grieve alone!
It is a slight thing; hence do not, I pray,
        This last dear fancy slay!"

        "Such winding ways
        Fit not your days,"
Said he, the man of measuring eye;
"I must even fashion as the rule declares,
To wit: Give space (since life ends unawares)
To hale a coffined corpse adown the stairs;
        For you will die."

8 ADELPHI TERRACE, 1867.

The Stranger's Song

(As sung by Mr. Charles Charrington *in the play of
"The Three Wayfarers")*

O my trade it is the rarest one,
                    Simple shepherds all—
          My trade is a sight to see;
For my customers I tie, and take 'em up on high,
          And waft 'em to a far countree!

My tools are but common ones,
                    Simple shepherds all—
          My tools are no sight to see:
A little hempen string, and a post whereon to swing.
          Are implements enough for me!

To-morrow is my working day,
                    Simple shepherds all—
          To-morrow is a working day for me:
For the farmer's sheep is slain, and the lad who did it ta'en,
          And on his soul may God ha' mer-cy!

In a Wood

From "The Woodlanders"

Pale beech and pine so blue,
          Set in one clay,
Bough to bough cannot you
          Live out your day?
When the rains skim and skip,
Why mar sweet comradeship,
Blighting with poison-drip
          Neighbourly spray?

Heart-halt and spirit-lame,
          City-opprest,
Unto this wood I came
          As to a nest;

Dreaming that sylvan peace
Offered the harrowed ease—
Nature a soft release
    From men's unrest.

But, having entered in,
    Great growths and small
Show them to men akin—
    Combatants all!
Sycamore shoulders oak,
Bines the slim sapling yoke,
Ivy-spun halters choke
    Elms stout and tall.

Touches from ash, O wych,
    Sting you like scorn!
You, too, brave hollies, twitch
    Sidelong from thorn.
Even the rank poplars bear
Lothly a rival's air,
Cankering in black despair
    If overborne.

Since, then, no grace I find
    Taught me of trees,
Turn I back to my kind,
    Worthy as these.
There at least smiles abound,
There discourse trills around,
There, now and then, are found
    Life-loyalties.

    1887: 1896.

Her Immortality

Upon a noon I pilgrimed through
    A pasture, mile by mile,
Unto the place where last I saw
    My dead Love's living smile.

And sorrowing I lay me down
    Upon the heated sod:
It seemed as if my body pressed
    The very ground she trod.

I lay, and thought; and in a trance
    She came and stood thereby—
The same, even to the marvellous ray
    That used to light her eye.

"You draw me, and I come to you,
    My faithful one," she said,
In voice that had the moving tone
    It bore ere she was wed.

"Seven years have circled since I died:
    Few now remember me;
My husband clasps another bride,
    My children's love has she.

"My brethren, sisters and my friends
    Care not to meet my sprite:
Who prized me most I did not know
    Till I passed down from sight."

I said: "My days are lonely here;
    I need thy smile alway:
I'll use this night my ball or blade,
    And join thee ere the day."

A tremor stirred her tender lips,
    Which parted to dissuade:
"That cannot be, O friend," she cried;
    "Think, I am but a Shade!

"A Shade but in its mindful ones
    Has immortality;
By living, me you keep alive,
    By dying you slay me.

"In you resides my single power
    Of sweet continuance here;

On your fidelity I count
    Through many a coming year."

—I started through me at her plight,
    So suddenly confessed:
Dismissing late distaste for life,
    I craved its bleak unrest.

"I will not die, my One of all!—
    To lengthen out thy days
I'll guard me from minutest harms
    That may invest my ways!"

She smiled and went.   Since then she comes
    Oft when her birth-moon climbs,
Or at the seasons' ingresses,
    Or anniversary times;

But grows my grief.   When I surcease,
    Through whom alone lives she,
Her spirit ends its living lease,
    Never again to be!

The Ivy-Wife

I longed to love a full-boughed beech
    And be as high as he:
I stretched an arm within his reach,
    And signalled unity.
But with his drip he forced a breach,
    And tried to poison me.

I gave the grasp of partnership
    To one of other race—
A plane: he barked him strip by strip
    From upper bough to base;
And me therewith; for gone my grip,
    My arms could not enlace.

In new affection next I strove
    To coll an ash I saw,
And he in trust received my love;
    Till with my soft green claw
I cramped and bound him as I wove . . .
    Such was my love: ha-ha!

By this I gained his strength and height
    Without his rivalry.
But in my triumph I lost sight
    Of afterhaps.   Soon he,
Being bark-bound, flagged, snapped, fell outright,
    And in his fall felled me!

Friends Beyond

William Dewy, Tranter Reuben, Farmer Ledlow
    late at plough,
    Robert's kin, and John's, and Ned's,
And the Squire, and Lady Susan, lie in Mellstock
    churchyard now!

"Gone," I call them, gone for good, that group of
    local hearts and heads;
    Yet at mothy curfew-tide,
And at midnight when the noon-heat breathes it back
    from walls and leads,

They've a way of whispering to me—fellow-wight who
    yet abide—
    In the muted, measured note
Of a ripple under archways, or a lone cave's stillicide:

"We have triumphed: this achievement turns the
    bane to antidote,
    Unsuccesses to success,
Many thought-worn eves and morrows to a morrow
    free of thought.

"No more need we corn and clothing, feel of old
          terrestial stress;
     Chill detraction stirs no sigh;
Fear of death has even bygone us: death gave all
          that we possess."

W. D.—"Ye mid burn the old bass-viol that I set
          such value by."
Squire.—"You may hold the manse in fee,
          You may wed my spouse, may let my children's
          memory of me die."

Lady S.—"You may have my rich brocades, my laces;
          take each household key;
     Ransack coffer, desk, bureau;
     Quiz the few poor treasures hid there, con the
          letters kept by me."

Far.—"Ye mid zell my favourite heifer, ye mid let
          the charlock grow,
     Foul the grinterns, give up thrifts."
Far. Wife.—"If ye break my best blue china, children,
          I shan't care or ho."

All.—"We've no wish to hear the tidings, how the
          people's fortunes shift;
     What your daily doings are;
     Who are wedded, born, divided; if your lives
          beat slow or swift.

"Curious not the least are we if our intents you make
          or mar,
     If you quire to our old tune,
If the City stage still passes, if the weirs still roar afar."

—Thus, with very gods' composure, freed those
          crosses late and soon
     Which in life, the Trine allow
(Why, none witteth), and ignoring all that haps beneath
          the moon,

William Dewy, Tranter Reuben, Farmer Ledlow
  late at plough,
    Robert's kin, and John's, and Ned's,
And the Squire, and Lady Susan, murmur mildly
    to me now.

Thoughts of Phena

AT NEWS OF HER DEATH

Not a line of her writing have I,
    Not a thread of her hair,
No mark of her late time as dame in her dwelling, whereby
    I may picture her there;
  And in vain do I urge my unsight
    To conceive my lost prize
At her close, whom I knew when her dreams were
    upbrimming with light,
    And with laughter her eyes.

What scenes spread around her last days,
    Sad, shining, or dim?
Did her gifts and compassions enray and enarch her
    sweet ways
    With an aureate nimb?
  Or did life-light decline from her years,

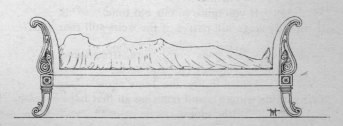

                And mischances control
Her full day-star; unease, or regret, or forebodings,
                    or fears
            Disennoble her soul?

        Thus I do but the phantom retain
            Of the maiden of yore
As my relic; yet haply the best of her—fined in my brain
            It may be the more
        That no line of her writing have I,
            Nor a thread of her hair,
No mark of her late time as dame in her dwelling, whereby
            I may picture her there.

    March 1890.

Nature's Questioning

    When I look forth at dawning, pool,
            Field, flock, and lonely tree,
            All seem to gaze at me
Like chastened children sitting silent in a school;

        Their faces dulled, constrained, and worn,
            As though the master's ways
            Through the long teaching days
Had cowed them till their early zest was overborne.

        Upon them stirs in lippings mere
            (As if once clear in call,
            But now scarce breathed at all)—
"We wonder, ever wonder, why we find us here!

        "Has some Vast Imbecility,
            Mighty to build and blend,
            But impotent to tend,
Framed us in jest, and left us now to hazardry?

        "Or come we of an Automaton
            Unconscious of our pains? . . .

Or are we live remains
Of Godhead dying downwards, brain and eye now gone?

"Or is it that some high Plan betides,
          As yet not understood,
          Of Evil stormed by Good,
We the Forlorn Hope over which Achievement strides?"

Thus things around.   No answer I. . . .
          Meanwhile the winds, and rains,
          And Earth's old glooms and pains
Are still the same, and Life and Death are neighbours nigh.

The Impercipient

(AT A CATHEDRAL SERVICE)

That with this bright believing band
          I have no claim to be,
That faiths by which my comrades stand
          Seem fantasies to me,
And mirage-mists their Shining Land,
          Is a strange destiny.

Why thus my soul should be consigned
          To infelicity,
Why always I must feel as blind
          To sights my brethren see,
Why joys they've found I cannot find,
          Abides a mystery.

Since heart of mine knows not that ease
          Which they know; since it be
That He who breathes All's Well to these
          Breathes no All's Well to me,
My lack might move their sympathies
          And Christian charity!

I am like a gazer who should mark
          An inland company

Standing upfingered, with, "Hark! hark!
    The glorious distant sea!"
And feel, "Alas, 'tis but yon dark
    And wind-swept pine to me!"

Yet I would bear my shortcomings
    With meet tranquillity,
But for the charge that blessed things
    I'd liefer not have be.
O, doth a bird deprived of wings
    Go earth-bound wilfully!

  .   .   .   .   .

Enough.   As yet disquiet clings
    About us. Rest shall we.

At an Inn

When we as strangers sought
    Their catering care,
Veiled smiles bespoke their thought
    Of what we were.
They warmed as they opined
    Us more than friends—
That we had all resigned
    For love's dear ends.

And that swift sympathy
    With living love
Which quicks the world—maybe
    The spheres above,
Made them our ministers,
    Moved them to say,
"Ah, God, that bliss like theirs
    Would flush our day!"

And we were left alone
    As Love's own pair;

Yet never the love-light shone
    Between us there!
But that which chilled the breath
    Of afternoon,
And palsied unto death
    The pane-fly's tune.

The kiss their zeal foretold,
    And now deemed come,
Came not: within his hold
    Love lingered numb.
Why cast he on our port
    A bloom not ours?
Why shaped us for his sport
    In after-hours?

As we seemed we were not
    That day afar,
And now we seem not what
    We aching are.
O severing sea and land,
    O laws of men,
Ere death, once let us stand
    As we stood then!

In a Eweleaze near Weatherbury

The years have gathered greyly
  Since I danced upon this leaze
With one who kindled gaily
  Love's fitful ecstasies!
But despite the term as teacher,
  I remain what I was then
In each essential feature
  Of the fantasies of men.

Yet I note the little chisel
  Of never-napping Time
Defacing wan and grizzel
  The blazon of my prime.
When at night he thinks me sleeping
  I feel him boring sly
Within my bones, and heaping
  Quaintest pains for by-and-by.

Still, I'd go the world with Beauty,
  I would laugh with her and sing,
I would shun divinest duty
  To resume her worshipping.
But she'd scorn my brave endeavour,
  She would not balm the breeze
By murmuring "Thine for ever!"
  As she did upon this leaze.
1890.

FROM *POEMS OF THE PAST AND PRESENT* (1901)

Drummer Hodge

I

They throw in Drummer Hodge, to rest
Uncoffined—just as found:

His landmark is a kopje-crest
    That breaks the veldt around;
And foreign constellations west
    Each night above his mound.

II

Young Hodge the Drummer never knew—
    Fresh from his Wessex home—
The meaning of the broad Karoo,
    The Bush, the dusty loam,
And why uprose to nightly view
    Strange stars amid the gloam.

III

Yet portion of that unknown plain
    Will Hodge for ever be;
His homely Northern breast and brain
    Grow to some Southern tree,
And strange-eyed constellations reign
    His stars eternally.

The Souls of the Slain

I

The thick lids of Night closed upon me
    Alone at the Bill
    Of the Isle by the Race*—
Many-caverned, bald, wrinkled of face—
And with darkness and silence the spirit was on me
    To brood and be still.

II

No wind fanned the flats of the ocean,
    Or promontory sides,
    Or the ooze by the strand,

* The "Race" is the turbulent sea-area off the Bill of Portland, where contrary tides meet.

Or the bent-bearded slope of the land,
Whose base took its rest amid everlong motion
            Of criss-crossing tides.

III

Soon from out of the Southward seemed nearing
            A whirr, as of wings
            Waved by mighty-vanned flies,
Or by night-moths of measureless size,
And in softness and smoothness well-nigh beyond hearing
            Of corporal things.

IV

And they bore to the bluff, and alighted—
            A dim-discerned train
            Of sprites without mould,
Frameless souls none might touch or might hold—
On the ledge by the turreted lantern, far-sighted
            By men of the main.

V

And I heard them say "Home!" and I knew them
            For souls of the felled
            On the earth's nether bord
Under Capricorn, whither they'd warred,
And I neared in my awe, and gave heedfulness to them
            With breathings inheld.

VI

Then, it seemed, there approached from the
                northward
            A senior soul-flame
            Of the like filmy hue:
And he met them and spake: "Is it you,
O my men?" Said they, "Aye! We bear homeward
                and hearthward
            To feast on our fame!"

VII

"I've flown there before you," he said then:
"Your households are well;
But—your kin linger less
On your glory and war-mightiness
Than on dearer things."—"Dearer?" cried these
from the dead then,
"Of what do they tell?"

VIII

"Some mothers muse sadly, and murmur
Your doings as boys—
Recall the quaint ways
Of your babyhood's innocent days.
Some pray that, ere dying, your faith had grown firmer,
And higher your joys.

IX

"A father broods: 'Would I had set him
To some humble trade,
And so slacked his high fire,
And his passionate martial desire;
And told him no stories to woo him and whet him
To this dire crusade!' "

X

"And, General, how hold out our sweethearts,
Sworn loyal as doves?"
—"Many mourn; many think
It is not unattractive to prink
Them in sables for heroes.   Some fickle and fleet hearts
Have found them new loves."

XI

"And our wives?" quoth another resignedly,
"Dwell they on our deeds?"
—"Deeds of home; that live yet
Fresh as new—deeds of fondness or fret;

Ancient words that were kindly expressed or unkindly,
       These, these have their heeds."

XII

  —"Alas! then it seems that our glory
      Weighs less in their thought
      Than our old homely acts,
  And the long-ago commonplace facts
Of our lives—held by us as scarce part of our story,
      And rated as nought!"

XIII

Then bitterly some: "Was it wise now
      To raise the tomb-door
      For such knowledge? Away!"
But the rest: "Fame we prized till to-day;
Yet that hearts keep us green for old kindness we prize now
      A thousand times more!"

XIV

Thus speaking, the trooped apparitions
      Began to disband
      And resolve them in two:
Those whose record was lovely and true
Bore to northward for home: those of bitter traditions
      Again left the land,

XV

And, towering to seaward in legions,
      They paused at a spot
      Overbending the Race—
That engulphing, ghast, sinister place—
Whither headlong they plunged, to the fathomless regions
      Of myriads forgot.

XVI

And the spirits of those who were homing
      Passed on, rushingly,
      Like the Pentecost Wind;

And the whirr of their wayfaring thinned
And surceased on the sky, and but left in the gloaming
Sea-mutterings and me.

December 1899.

Rome: On the Palatine

(*April* 1887)

We walked where Victor Jove was shrined awhile,
And passed to Livia's rich red mural show,
Whence, thridding cave and Criptoportico,
We gained Caligula's dissolving pile.

And each ranked ruin tended to beguile
The outer sense, and shape itself as though
It wore its marble gleams, its pristine glow
Of scenic frieze and pompous peristyle.

When lo, swift hands, on strings nigh overhead,
Began to melodize a waltz by Strauss:
It stirred me as I stood, in Cæsar's house,
Raised the old routs Imperial lyres had led,

And blended pulsing life with lives long done,
Till Time seemed fiction, Past and Present one.

A Commonplace Day

The day is turning ghost,
And scuttles from the kalendar in fits and furtively,
To join the anonymous host
Of those that throng oblivion; ceding his place, maybe,
To one of like degree.

                        I part the fire-gnawed logs,
Rake forth the embers, spoil the busy flames, and lay
                        the ends
                Upon the shining dogs;
Further and further from the nooks the twilight's
                stride extends,
                        And beamless black impends.

                Nothing of tiniest worth
Have I wrought, pondered, planned; no one thing asking
                blame or praise,
                        Since the pale corpse-like birth
Of this diurnal unit, bearing blanks in all its rays—
                        Dullest of dull-hued Days!

                Wanly upon the panes
The rain slides, as have slid since morn my colourless
                thoughts; and yet
                        Here, while Day's presence wanes,
And over him the sepulchre-lid is slowly lowered and set,
                        He wakens my regret.

                Regret—though nothing dear
That I wot of, was toward in the wide world at his prime,
                Or bloomed elsewhere than here,
To die with his decrease, and leave a memory sweet,
                sublime,
                        Or mark him out in Time. . . .

                —Yet, maybe, in some soul,
In some spot undiscerned on sea or land, some impulse rose,
                Or some intent upstole
Of that enkindling ardency from whose maturer glows
                        The world's amendment flows;

                But which, benumbed at birth
By momentary chance or wile, has missed its hope to be
                        Embodied on the earth;
And undervoicings of this loss to man's futurity
                        May wake regret in me.

The Subalterns

I

"Poor wanderer," said the leaden sky,
    "I fain would lighten thee,
But there are laws in force on high
    Which say it must not be."

II

—"I would not freeze thee, shorn one," cried
    The North, "knew I but how
To warm my breath, to slack my stride;
    But I am ruled as thou."

III

—"To-morrow I attack thee, wight,"
    Said Sickness.   "Yet I swear
I bear thy little ark no spite,
    But am bid enter there."

IV

—"Come hither, Son," I heard Death say;
    "I did not will a grave
Should end thy pilgrimage to-day,
    But I, too, am a slave!"

V

We smiled upon each other then,
    And life to me had less
Of that fell look it wore ere when
    They owned their passiveness.

To an Unborn Pauper Child

I

Breathe not, hid Heart: cease silently,
And though thy birth-hour beckons thee,

Sleep the long sleep:
The Doomsters heap
Travails and teens around us here,
And Time-wraiths turn our songsingings to fear.

II

Hark, how the peoples surge and sigh,
And laughters fail, and greetings die:
Hopes dwindle; yea,
Faiths waste away,
Affections and enthusiasms numb;
Thou canst not mend these things if thou dost come.

III

Had I the ear of wombèd souls
Ere their terrestrial chart unrolls,
And thou wert free
To cease, or be,
Then would I tell thee all I know,
And put it to thee: Wilt thou take Life so?

IV

Vain vow! No hint of mine may hence
To theeward fly: to thy locked sense
Explain none can
Life's pending plan:
Thou wilt thy ignorant entry make
Though skies spout fire and blood and nations quake.

V

Fain would I, dear, find some shut plot
Of earth's wide wold for thee, where not
One tear, one qualm,
Should break the calm.
But I am weak as thou and bare;
No man can change the common lot to rare.

VI

Must come and bide.   And such are we—
Unreasoning, sanguine, visionary—
    That I can hope
    Health, love, friends, scope
In full for thee; can dream thou'lt find
Joys seldom yet attained by humankind!

To Lizbie Browne

I

Dear Lizbie Browne,
Where are you now?
In sun, in rain?—
Or is your brow
Past joy, past pain,
Dear Lizbie Browne?

II

Sweet Lizbie Browne,
How you could smile,
How you could sing!—
How archly wile
In glance-giving,
Sweet Lizbie Browne!

III

And, Lizbie Browne,
Who else had hair
Bay-red as yours,
Or flesh so fair
Bred out of doors,
Sweet Lizbie Browne?

IV

When, Lizbie Browne,
You had just begun
To be endeared
By stealth to one,
You disappeared
My Lizbie Browne!

v

Ay, Lizbie Browne,
So swift your life
And mine so slow,
You were a wife
Ere I could show
Love, Lizbie Browne.

VI

Still, Lizbie Browne,
You won, they said,
The best of men
When you were wed. . . .
Where went you then,
O Lizbie Browne?

VII

Dear Lizbie Browne,
I should have thought,
"Girls ripen fast,"
And coaxed and caught
You ere you passed,
Dear Lizbie Browne!

VIII

But, Lizbie Browne,
I let you slip;
Shaped not a sign;

Touched never your lip
With lip of mine,
Lost Lizbie Browne!

IX

So, Lizbie Browne,
When on a day
Men speak of me
As not, you'll say,
"And who was he?"—
Yes, Lizbie Browne!

A Broken Appointment

You did not come,
And marching Time drew on, and wore me numb.—
Yet less for loss of your dear presence there
Than that I thus found lacking in your make
That high compassion which can overbear
Reluctance for pure lovingkindness' sake
Grieved I, when, as the hope-hour stroked its sum,
You did not come.

You love not me,
And love alone can lend you loyalty;
—I know and knew it.   But, unto the store
Of human deeds divine in all but name,
Was it not worth a little hour or more
To add yet this: Once you, a woman, came
To soothe a time-torn man; even though it be
You love not me?

At a Hasty Wedding

(TRIOLET)

If hours be years the twain are blest,
For now they solace swift desire

By bonds of every bond the best,
If hours be years.   The twain are blest
Do eastern stars slope never west,
Nor pallid ashes follow fire:
If hours be years the twain are blest,
For now they solace swift desire.

His Immortality

I

I saw a dead man's finer part
Shining within each faithful heart
Of those bereft.   Then said I: "This must be
            His immortality."

II

I looked there as the seasons wore,
And still his soul continuously bore
A life in theirs.   But less its shine excelled
Than when I first beheld.

III

His fellow-yearsmen passed, and then
In later hearts I looked for him again;
And found him—shrunk, alas! into a thin
And spectral mannikin.

IV

Lastly I ask—now old and chill—
If aught of him remain unperished still;
And find, in me alone, a feeble spark,
Dying amid the dark.

February 1899.

Wives in the Sere

I

Never a careworn wife but shows,
If a joy suffuse her,
Something beautiful to those
Patient to peruse her,
Some one charm the world unknows
Precious to a muser,
Haply what, ere years were foes,
Moved her mate to choose her.

II

But, be it a hint of rose
That an instant hues her,
Or some early light or pose

Wherewith thought renews her—
Seen by him at full, ere woes
Practised to abuse her—
Sparely comes it, swiftly goes,
Time again subdues her.

Winter in Durnover Field

SCENE.—*A wide stretch of fallow ground recently sown with wheat, and frozen to iron hardness. Three large birds walking about thereon, and wistfully eyeing the surface. Wind keen from north-east: sky a dull grey.*

(TRIOLET)

Rook.—Throughout the field I find no grain;
           The cruel frost encrusts the cornland!
Starling.—Aye: patient pecking now is vain
           Throughout the field, I find . . .
Rook.—   No grain!
Pigeon.—Nor will be, comrade, till it rain,
           Or genial thawings loose the lorn land
           Throughout the field.
Rook.—   I find no grain:
           The cruel frost encrusts the cornland!

The Last Chrysanthemum

Why should this flower delay so long
        To show its tremulous plumes?
Now is the time of plaintive robin-song,
           When flowers are in their tombs.

Through the slow summer, when the sun
           Called to each frond and whorl

That all he could for flowers was being done,
       Why did it not uncurl?

  It must have felt that fervid call
       Although it took no heed,
Waking but now, when leaves like corpses fall,
       And saps all retrocede.

Too late its beauty, lonely thing,
       The season's shine is spent,
Nothing remains for it but shivering
       In tempests turbulent.

Had it a reason for delay,
       Dreaming in witlessness
That for a bloom so delicately gay
       Winter would stay its stress?

—I talk as if the thing were born
       With sense to work its mind;
Yet it is but one mask of many worn
       By the Great Face behind.

The Darkling Thrush

I leant upon a coppice gate
       When Frost was spectre-grey,
And Winter's dregs made desolate
       The weakening eye of day.
The tangled bine-stems scored the sky
       Like strings of broken lyres,
And all mankind that haunted nigh
       Had sought their household fires.

The land's sharp features seemed to be
       The Century's corpse outleant,
His crypt the cloudy canopy,
       The wind his death-lament.
The ancient pulse of germ and birth
       Was shrunken hard and dry,

And every spirit upon earth
     Seemed fervourless as I.

At once a voice arose among
     The bleak twigs overhead
In a full-hearted evensong
     Of joy illimited;
An aged thrush, frail, gaunt, and small,
     In blast-beruffled plume,
Had chosen thus to fling his soul
     Upon the growing gloom.

So little cause for carolings
     Of such ecstatic sound
Was written on terrestrial things
     Afar or nigh around,
That I could think there trembled through
     His happy good-night air
Some blessed Hope, whereof he knew
     And I was unaware.

    31st December 1900.

The Self-Unseeing

Here is the ancient floor,
Footworn and hollowed and thin,
Here was the former door
Where the dead feet walked in.

She sat here in her chair,
Smiling into the fire;
He who played stood there,
Bowing it higher and higher.

Childlike, I danced in a dream;
Blessings emblazoned that day;
Everything glowed with a gleam;
Yet we were looking away!

In Tenebris

I

"Percussus sum sicut foenum, et aruit cor meum."—*Ps.* ci.

Wintertime nighs;
But my bereavement-pain
It cannot bring again:
Twice no one dies.

Flower-petals flee;
But, since it once hath been,
No more that severing scene
Can harrow me.

Birds faint in dread:
I shall not lose old strength
In the lone frost's black length:
Strength long since fled!

Leaves freeze to dun;
But friends can not turn cold
This season as of old
For him with none.

Tempests may scath;
But love can not make smart
Again this year his heart
Who no heart hath.

Black is night's cope;
But death will not appal
One who, past doubtings all,
Waits in unhope.

FROM *TIME'S LAUGHINGSTOCK* (1909)

A Trampwoman's Tragedy

(182–)

I

From Wynyard's Gap the livelong day.
   The livelong day,
We beat afoot the northward way
   We had travelled times before.
The sun-blaze burning on our backs,
Our shoulders sticking to our packs,
By fosseway, fields, and turnpike tracks
   We skirted sad Sedge-Moor.

II

Full twenty miles we jaunted on,
   We jaunted on,—
My fancy-man, and jeering John,
   And Mother Lee, and I.
And, as the sun drew down to west,
We climbed the toilsome Poldon crest,
And saw, of landskip sights the best,
   The inn that beamed thereby.

III

For months we had padded side by side,
   Ay, side by side
Through the Great Forest, Blackmoor wide,
   And where the Parret ran.
We'd faced the gusts on Mendip ridge,
Had crossed the Yeo unhelped by bridge,
Been stung by every Marshwood midge,
   I and my fancy-man.

IV

Lone inns we loved, my man and I,
            My man and I;
"King's Stag," "Windwhistle" high and dry,
            "The Horse" on Hintock Green,
The cosy house at Wynyard's Gap,
"The Hut" renowned on Bredy Knap,
And many another wayside tap
            Where folk might sit unseen.

V

Now as we trudged—O deadly day,
            O deadly day!—
I teased my fancy-man in play
            And wanton idleness.
I walked alongside jeering John,
I laid his hand my waist upon;
I would not bend my glances on
            My lover's dark distress.

VI

Thus Poldon top at last we won,
            At last we won,
And gained the inn at sink of sun
            Far-famed as "Marshal's Elm."
Beneath us figured tor and lea,
From Mendip to the western sea—
I doubt if finer sight there be
            Within this royal realm.

VII

Inside the settle all a-row—
            All four a-row
We sat, I next to John, to show
            That he had wooed and won.
And then he took me on his knee,
And swore it was his turn to be
My favoured mate, and Mother Lee
            Passed to my former one.

VIII

Then in a voice I had never heard,
      I had never heard,
My only Love to me: "One word,
      My lady, if you please!
Whose is the child you are like to bear?—
His?   After all my months o' care?"
God knows 'twas not!   But, O despair!
      I nodded—still to tease.

IX

Then up he sprung, and with his knife—
      And with his knife
He let out jeering Johnny's life,
      Yes; there, at set of sun.
The slant ray through the window nigh
Gilded John's blood and glazing eye,
Ere scarcely Mother Lee and I
      Knew that the deed was done.

X

The taverns tell the gloomy tale,
      The gloomy tale,
How that at Ivel-chester jail
      My Love, my sweetheart swung;
Though stained till now by no misdeed
Save one horse ta'en in time o' need;
(Blue Jimmy stole right many a steed
      Ere his last fling he flung).

XI

Thereaft I walked the world alone,
      Alone, alone!
On his death-day I gave my groan
      And dropt his dead-born child
'Twas nigh the jail, beneath a tree,
None tending me; for Mother Lee
Had died at Glaston, leaving me
      Unfriended on the wild.

XII

And in the night as I lay weak,
  As I lay weak,
The leaves a-falling on my cheek,
  The red moon low declined—
The ghost of him I'd die to kiss
Rose up and said: "Ah, tell me this!
Was the child mine, or was it his?
  Speak, that I rest may find!"

XIII

O doubt not but I told him then,
  I told him then,
That I had kept me from all men
  Since we joined lips and swore.
Whereat he smiled, and thinned away
As the wind stirred to call up day . . .
—'Tis past! And here alone I stray
  Haunting the Western Moor.

 April 1902.

A Sunday Morning Tragedy

(*circa* 186–)

I bore a daughter flower-fair,
In Pydel Vale, alas for me;
I joyed to mother one so rare,
But dead and gone I now would be.

Men looked and loved her as she grew,
And she was won, alas for me;
She told me nothing, but I knew,
And saw that sorrow was to be.

I knew that one had made her thrall,
A thrall to him, alas for me;

And then, at last, she told me all,
And wondered what her end would be.

She owned that she had loved too well,
Had loved too well, unhappy she,
And bore a secret time would tell,
Though in her shroud she'd sooner be.

I plodded to her sweetheart's door
In Pydel Vale, alas for me:
I pleaded with him, pleaded sore,
To save her from her misery.

He frowned, and swore he could not wed.
Seven times he swore it could not be:
"Poverty's worse than shame," he said,
Till all my hope went out of me.

"I've packed my traps to sail the main—
Roughly he spake, alas did he—
"Wessex beholds me not again,
'Tis worse than any jail would be!"

—There was a shepherd whom I knew,
A subtle man, alas for me:
I sought him all the pastures through,
Though better I had ceased to be.

I traced him by his lantern light,
And gave him hint, alas for me,
Of how she found her in the plight
That is so scorned in Christendie.

"Is there an herb . . . ?" I asked.   "Or none?"
Yes, thus I asked him desperately.
"—There is," he said; "a certain one. . . ."
Would he had sworn that none knew he!

"To-morrow I will walk your way,"
He hinted low, alas for me.—
Fieldwards I gazed throughout next day;
Now fields I never more would see!

The sunset-shine, as curfew strook,
As curfew strook beyond the lea,
Lit his white smock and gleaming crook.
While slowly he drew near to me.

He pulled from underneath his smock
The herb I sought, my curse to be—
"At times I use it in my flock,"
He said, and hope waxed strong in me.

" 'Tis meant to balk ill-motherings"—
(Ill-motherings!   Why should they be?)—
"If not, would God have sent such things?"
So spoke the shepherd unto me.

That night I watched the poppling brew,
With bended back and hand on knee:
I stirred it till the dawnlight grew,
And the wind whiffled wailfully.

"This scandal shall be slain," said I,
"That lours upon her innocency:
I'll give all whispering tongues the lie;"—
But worse than whispers was to be.

"Here's physic for untimely fruit,"
I said to her, alas for me,
Early that morn in fond salute;
And in my grave I now would be.

—Next Sunday came, with sweet church chimes
In Pydel Vale, alas for me:
I went into her room betimes;
No more may such a Sunday be!

"Mother, instead of rescue nigh,"
She faintly breathed, alas for me,
"I feel as I were like to die,
And underground soon, soon should be."

From church that noon the people walked
In twos and threes, alas for me,

Showed their new raiment—smiled and talked,
Though sackcloth-clad I longed to be.

Came to my door her lover's friends,
And cheerly cried, alas for me,
"Right glad are we he makes amends,
For never a sweeter bride can be."

My mouth dried, as 'twere scorched within,
Dried at their words, alas for me:
More and more neighbours crowded in,
(O why should mothers ever be!)

"Ha-ha! Such well-kept news!" laughed they,
Yes—so they laughed, alas for me.
"Whose banns were called in church to-day?"—
Christ, how I wished my soul could flee!

"Where is she?   O the stealthy miss,"
Still bantered they, alas for me,
"To keep a wedding close as this. . . ."
Ay, Fortune worked thus wantonly!

"But you are pale—you did not know?"
They archly asked, alas for me,
I stammered, "Yes—some days—ago,"
While coffined clay I wished to be.

" 'Twas done to please her, we surmise?"
(They spoke quite lightly in their glee)
"Done by him as a fond surprise?"
I thought their words would madden me.

Her lover entered.   "Where's my bird?—
My bird—my flower—my picotee?
First time of asking, soon the third!"
Ah, in my grave I well may be.

To me he whispered: "Since your call—"
So spoke he then, alas for me—
"I've felt for her, and righted all."
—I think of it to agony.

"She's faint to-day—tired—nothing more—"
Thus did I lie, alas for me. . . .
I called her at her chamber door
As one who scarce had strength to be.

No voice replied.   I went within—
O women! scourged the worst are we. . . .
I shrieked.   The others hastened in
And saw the stroke there dealt on me.

There she lay—silent, breathless, dead,
Stone dead she lay—wronged, sinless she!—
Ghost-white the cheeks once rosy-red:
Death had took her.   Death took not me.

I kissed her colding face and hair,
I kissed her corpse—the bride to be!—
My punishment I cannot bear,
But pray God *not* to pity me.

January 1904.

Shut Out That Moon

Close up the casement, draw the blind,
    Shut out that stealing moon,
She wears too much the guise she wore
    Before our lutes were strewn
With years-deep dust, and names we read
    On a white stone were hewn.

Step not forth on the dew-dashed lawn
    To view the Lady's Chair,
Immense Orion's glittering form,
    The Less and Greater Bear:
Stay in; to such sights we were drawn
    When faded ones were fair.

Brush not the bough for midnight scents
    That come forth lingeringly,

And wake the same sweet sentiments
　　　They breathed to you and me
When living seemed a laugh, and love
　　　All it was said to be.

Within the common lamp-lit room
　　　Prison my eyes and thought;
Let dingy details crudely loom,
　　　Mechanic speech be wrought:
Too fragrant was Life's early bloom,
　　　Too tart the fruit it brought!

　　1904.

The End of the Episode

Indulge no more may we
In this sweet-bitter pastime:
The love-light shines the last time
　　Between you, Dear, and me.

There shall remain no trace
Of what so closely tied us,
And blank as ere love eyed us
　　Will be our meeting-place.

The flowers and thymy air,
Will they now miss our coming?
The dumbles thin their humming
　　To find we haunt not there?

Though fervent was our vow,
Though ruddily ran our pleasure,
Bliss has fulfilled its measure,
　　And sees its sentence now.

Ache deep; but make no moans:
Smile out; but stilly suffer:
The paths of love are rougher
　　Than thoroughfares of stones.

FROM At Casterbridge Fair

II

FORMER BEAUTIES

These market-dames, mid-aged, with lips thin-drawn,
    And tissues sere,
Are they the ones we loved in years agone,
    And courted here?

Are these the muslined pink young things to whom
    We vowed and swore
In nooks on summer Sundays by the Froom,
    Or Budmouth shore?

Do they remember those gay tunes we trod
    Clasped on the green;
Aye; trod till moonlight set on the beaten sod
    A satin sheen?

They must forget, forget! They cannot know
    What once they were,
Or memory would transfigure them, and show
    Them always fair.

VII

AFTER THE FAIR

The singers are gone from the Cornmarket-place
    With their broadsheets of rhymes,
The street rings no longer in treble and bass
    With their skits on the times,
And the Cross, lately thronged, is a dim naked space
    That but echoes the stammering chimes.

From Clock-corner steps, as each quarter ding-dongs,
    Away the folk roam
By the "Hart" and Grey's Bridge into byways and "drongs,"
    Or across the ridged loam;

The younger ones shrilling the lately heard songs,
    The old saying, "Would we were home."

The shy-seeming maiden so mute in the fair
    Now rattles and talks,
And that one who looked the most swaggering there
    Grows sad as she walks,
And she who seemed eaten by cankering care
    In statuesque sturdiness stalks.

And midnight clears High Street of all but the ghosts
    Of its buried burghees,
From the latest far back to those old Roman hosts
    Whose remains one yet sees,
Who loved, laughed, and fought, hailed their
        friends, drank their toasts
    At their meeting-times here, just as these!

    1902.

Julie-Jane

Sing; how 'a would sing!
    How 'a would raise the tune
When we rode in the waggon from harvesting
        By the light o' the moon!

Dance; how 'a would dance!
    If a fiddlestring did but sound
She would hold out her coats, give a slanting glance,
        And go round and round.

Laugh; how 'a would laugh!
    Her peony lips would part
As if none such a place for a lover to quaff
        At the deeps of a heart.

Julie, O girl of joy,
    Soon, soon that lover he came.

Ah, yes; and gave thee a baby-boy,
      But never his name. . . .

—Tolling for her, as you guess;
      And the baby too. . . . 'Tis well.
You knew her in maidhood likewise?—Yes,
      That's her burial bell.

"I suppose," with a laugh, she said,
      "I should blush that I'm not a wife;
But how can it matter, so soon to be dead,
      What one does in life!"

When we sat making the mourning
      By her death-bed side, said she,
"Dears, how can you keep from your lovers, adorning
      In honour of me!"

Bubbling and brightsome eyed!
      But now—O never again.
She chose her bearers before she died
      From her fancy-men.

NOTE.—It is, or was, a common custom in Wessex, and probably other country places, to prepare the mourning beside the death-bed, the dying person sometimes assisting, who also selects his or her bearers on such occasions.

"Coats" (line 7), old name for petticoats.

News for Her Mother

I

One mile more is
    Where your door is,
        Mother mine!—
Harvest's coming,
    Mills are strumming,
        Apples fine,
And the cider made to-year will be as wine.

II

Yet, not viewing
What's a-doing
            Here around
Is it thrills me,
And so fills me
            That I bound
Like a ball or leaf or lamb along the ground

III

Tremble not now
At your lot now,
            Silly soul!
Hosts have sped them
Quick to wed them,
            Great and small,
Since the first two sighing half-hearts made a whole.

IV

Yet I wonder,
Will it sunder
            Her from me?
Will she guess that
I said "Yes,"—that
            His I'd be,
Ere I thought she might not see him as I see!

V

Old brown gable,
Granary, stable,
            Here you are!
O my mother,
Can another
            Ever bar
Mine from thy heart, make thy nearness seem afar?

The Homecoming

*Gruffly growled the wind on Toller downland broad
    and bare,*
*And lonesome was the house, and dark; and few came
    there.*

"Now don't ye rub your eyes so red; we're home and
    have no cares;
Here's a skimmer-cake for supper, peckled onions,
    and some pears;
I've got a little keg o' summat strong, too, under stairs:
—What, slight your husband's victuals? Other brides
    can tackle theirs!"

*The wind of winter mooed and mouthed their chimney
    like a horn,*
*And round the house and past the house 'twas leafless
    and lorn.*

"But my dear and tender poppet, then, how came ye
    to agree
In Ivel church this morning? Sure, there-right you
    married me!"
—"Hoo-hoo!—I don't know—I forgot how strange
    and far 'twould be,
An' I wish I was at home again with dear daddee!"

*Gruffly growled the wind on Toller downland broad
    and bare,*
*And lonesome was the house and dark; and few came
    there.*

"I didn't think such furniture as this was all you'd own,
And great black beams for ceiling, and a floor o' wretched
    stone,
And nasty pewter platters, horrid forks of steel and bone,
And a monstrous crock in chimney. 'Twas to me quite
    unbeknown!"

Rattle rattle went the door; down flapped a cloud of smoke,
As shifting north the wicked wind assayed a smarter stroke.

"Now sit ye by the fire, poppet; put yourself at ease:
And keep your little thumb out of your mouth, dear, please!
And I'll sing to 'ee a pretty song of lovely flowers and bees,
And happy lovers taking walks within a grove o' trees."

Gruffly growled the wind on Toller Down, so bleak and
*   bare,*
And lonesome was the house, and dark; and few came
*   there.*

"Now, don't ye gnaw your handkercher; 'twill hurt
      your little tongue,
And if you do feel spitish, 'tis because ye are over young;
But you'll be getting older, like us all, ere very long,
And you'll see me as I am—a man who never did 'ee
      wrong."

Straight from Whit'sheet Hill to Benvill Lane the
*   blusters pass,*
Hitting hedges, milestones, handposts, trees, and tufts
*   of grass.*

"Well, had I only known, my dear, that this was how
      you'd be,
I'd have married her of riper years that was so fond of me.
But since I can't, I've half a mind to run away to sea,
And leave 'ee to go barefoot to your d—d daddee!"

Up one wall and down the other—past each window-
*   pane—*
Prance the gusts, and then away down Crimmercrock's
*   long lane.*

"I—I—don't know what to say to't, since your wife I've
      vowed to be;
And as 'tis done, I s'pose here I must bide—poor me!
Aye—as you are ki-ki-kind, I'll try to live along with 'ee,
Although I'd fain have stayed at home with dear daddee!"

Gruffly growled the wind on Toller Down, so bleak and
  bare,
And lonesome was the house and dark; and few came there.

"That's right, my Heart! And though on haunted
   Toller Down we be,
And the wind swears things in chimley, we'll to supper
   merrily!
So don't ye tap your shoe so pettish-like; but smile at me,
And ye'll soon forget to sock and sigh for dear daddee!"

  December 1901.

Night in the Old Home

When the wasting embers redden the chimney-breast,
And Life's bare pathway looms like a desert track to me,
And from hall and parlour the living have gone to their
   rest,
My perished people who housed them here come back
   to me.

They come and seat them around in their mouldy places,
Now and then bending towards me a glance of wistfulness,
A strange upbraiding smile upon all their faces,
And in the bearing of each a passive tristfulness.

"Do you uphold me, lingering and languishing here,
A pale late plant of your once strong stock?" I say
   to them;
"A thinker of crooked thoughts upon Life in the sere,
And on That which consigns men to night after showing
   the day to them?"

"—O let be the Wherefore! We fevered our years
   not thus:
Take of Life what it grants, without question!" they
   answer me seemingly.

"Enjoy, suffer, wait: spread the table here freely like us,
And, satisfied, placid, unfretting, watch Time away
    beamingly!"

She Hears the Storm

There was a time in former years—
    While my roof-tree was his—
When I should have been distressed by fears
    At such a night as this!

I should have murmured anxiously,
    "The pricking rain strikes cold;
His road is bare of hedge or tree,
    And he is getting old."

But now the fitful chimney-roar,
    The drone of Thorncombe trees,
The Froom in flood upon the moor,
    The mud of Mellstock Leaze,

The candle slanting sooty-wick'd,
    The thuds upon the thatch,
The eaves-drops on the window flicked,
    The clacking garden-hatch,

And what they mean to wayfarers,
    I scarcely heed or mind;
He has won that storm-tight roof of hers
    Which Earth grants all her kind.

The Man He Killed

"Had he and I but met
    By some old ancient inn,
We should have sat us down to wet
    Right many a nipperkin!

"But ranged as infantry,
And staring face to face,
I shot at him as he at me,
And killed him in his place.

"I shot him dead because—
Because he was my foe,
Just so: my foe of course he was:
That's clear enough; although

"He thought he'd 'list, perhaps,
Off-hand like—just as I—
Was out of work—had sold his traps—
No other reason why.

"Yes; quaint and curious war is!
You shoot a fellow down
You'd treat if met where any bar is,
Or help to half-a-crown."

1902.

FROM *SATIRES OF CIRCUMSTANCE AND LYRICS AND REVERIES* (1914)

Channel Firing

That night your great guns, unawares,
Shook all our coffins as we lay,
And broke the chancel window-squares,
We thought it was the Judgment-day

And sat upright.   While drearisome
Arose the howl of wakened hounds:
The mouse let fall the altar-crumb,
The worms drew back into the mounds,

The glebe cow drooled.   Till God called, "No;
It's gunnery practice out at sea
Just as before you went below;
The world is as it used to be:

"All nations striving strong to make
Red war yet redder.   Mad as hatters
They do no more for Christés sake
Than you who are helpless in such matters.

"That this is not the judgment-hour
For some of them's a blessed thing,
For if it were they'd have to scour
Hell's floor for so much threatening. . . .

"Ha-ha.   It will be warmer when
I blow the trumpet (if indeed
I ever do; for you are men,
And rest eternal sorely need)."

So down we lay again.   "I wonder,
Will the world ever saner be,"
Said one, "than when He sent us under
In our indifferent century!"

And many a skeleton shook his head.
"Instead of preaching forty year,"
My neighbour Parson Thirdly said,
"I wish I had stuck to pipes and beer."

Again the guns disturbed the hour,
Roaring their readiness to avenge,
As far inland as Stourton Tower,
And Camelot, and starlit Stonehenge.

April 1914.

The Convergence of the Twain

(*Lines on the loss of the "Titanic"*)

I

In a solitude of the sea
Deep from human vanity,
And the Pride of Life that planned her, stilly couches she.

II

Steel chambers, late the pyres
Of her salamandrine fires,
Cold currents thrid, and turn to rhythmic tidal lyres.

III

Over the mirrors meant
To glass the opulent
The sea-worm crawls—grotesque, slimed, dumb, indifferent.

IV

Jewels in joy designed
To ravish the sensuous mind
Lie lightless, all their sparkles bleared and black and blind.

V

Dim moon-eyed fishes near
Gaze at the gilded gear
And query: "What does this vaingloriousness down here?"

VI

Well: while was fashioning
This creature of cleaving wing,
The Immanent Will that stirs and urges everything

VII

Prepared a sinister mate
For her—so gaily great—
A Shape of Ice, for the time far and dissociate.

VIII

And as the smart ship grew
In stature, grace, and hue,
In shadowy silent distance grew the Iceberg too.

IX

Alien they seemed to be:
No mortal eye could see
The intimate welding of their later history,

X

Or sign that they were bent
By paths coincident
On being anon twin halves of one august event.

XI

Till the Spinner of the Years
Said "Now!"   And each one hears,
And consummation comes, and jars two hemispheres.

"When I Set Out for Lyonnesse"

(1870)

When I set out for Lyonnesse,
A hundred miles away,
The rime was on the spray,
And starlight lit my lonesomeness
When I set out for Lyonnesse
A hundred miles away.

What would bechance at Lyonnesse
While I should sojourn there
No prophet durst declare,
Nor did the wisest wizard guess
What would bechance at Lyonnesse
While I should sojourn there.

When I came back from Lyonnesse
With magic in my eyes,
All marked with mute surmise
My radiance rare and fathomless,
When I came back from Lyonnesse
With magic in my eyes!

Wessex Heights

(1896)

There are some heights in Wessex, shaped as if by a
kindly hand
For thinking, dreaming, dying on, and at crises when
I stand,
Say, on Ingpen Beacon eastward, or on Wylls-Neck
westwardly,
I seem where I was before my birth, and after death
may be.

In the lowlands I have no comrade, not even the
lone man's friend—
Her who suffereth long and is kind; accepts what he is
too weak to mend:
Down there they are dubious and askance; there
nobody thinks as I,
But mind-chains do not clank where one's next neighbour is the sky.

In the towns I am tracked by phantoms having weird
detective ways—
Shadows of beings who fellowed with myself of earlier
days:
They hang about at places, and they say harsh heavy
things—
Men with a wintry sneer, and women with tart disparagings.

Down there I seem to be false to myself, my simple
self that was,

And is not now, and I see him watching, wondering
    what crass cause
Can have merged him into such a strange continuator
    as this,
Who yet has something in common with himself, my
    chrysalis.

I cannot go to the great grey Plain; there's a figure
    against the moon,
Nobody sees it but I, and it makes my breast beat
    out of tune;
I cannot go to the tall-spired town, being barred by
    the forms now passed
For everybody but me, in whose long vision they
    stand there fast.

There's a ghost at Yell'ham Bottom chiding loud at the
    fall of the night,
There's a ghost in Froom-side Vale, thin-lipped and
    vague, in a shroud of white,
There is one in the railway train whenever I do not want
    it near,
I see its profile against the pane, saying what I would
    not hear.

As for one rare fair woman, I am now but a thought
    of hers,
I enter her mind and another thought succeeds me
    that she prefers:
Yet my love for her in its fulness she herself even did
    not know;
Well, time cures hearts of tenderness, and now I can
    let her go.

So I am found on Ingpen Beacon, or on Wylls-Neck to
    the west,
Or else on homely Bulbarrow, or little Pilsdon Crest,
Where men have never cared to haunt, nor women
    have walked with me,
And ghosts then keep their distance; and I know some
    liberty.

Aquae Sulis

The chimes called midnight, just at interlune,
And the daytime parle on the Roman investigations
Was shut to silence, save for the husky tune
The bubbling waters played near the excavations.

And a warm air came up from underground
And the flutter of a filmy shape unsepulchred,
That collected itself, and waited, and looked around:
Nothing was seen, but utterances could be heard:

Those of the Goddess whose shrine was beneath the pile
Of the God with the baldachined altar overhead:
"And what did you win by raising this nave and aisle
Close on the site of the temple I tenanted?

"The notes of your organ have thrilled down out of view
To the earth-clogged wrecks of my edifice many a year,
Though stately and shining once—ay, long ere you
Had set up crucifix and candle here.

"Your priests have trampled the dust of mine without
        rueing.
Despising the joys of man whom I so much loved,
Though my springs boil on by your Gothic arcades
        and pewing,
And sculptures crude. . . . Would Jove they could be
        removed!"

"Repress, O lady proud, your traditional ires;
You know not by what a frail thread we equally hang;
It is said we are images both—twitched by people's desires;
And that I, as you, fail like a song men yesterday sang!"

"What—a Jumping-jack you, and myself but a poor
        Jumping-jill,
Now worm-eaten, times agone twitched at Humanity's bid?
O I cannot endure it!—But, chance to us whatso there will,
Let us kiss and be friends!   Come, agree you?"—None
        heard if he did. . . .

And the olden dark hid the cavities late laid bare,
And all was suspended and soundless as before,
Except for a gossamery noise fading off in the air,
And the boiling voice of the waters' medicinal pour.

BATH.

"Ah, Are You Digging on My Grave?"

"Ah, are you digging on my grave,
      My loved one?—planting rue?"
—"No: yesterday he went to wed
One of the brightest wealth has bred.
'It cannot hurt her now,' he said,
      'That I should not be true.' "

"Then who is digging on my grave?
      My nearest dearest kin?"
—"Ah, no: they sit and think, 'What use!
What good will planting flowers produce?
No tendance of her mound can loose
      Her spirit from Death's gin.' "

"But some one digs upon my grave?
      My enemy?—prodding sly?"
—"Nay: when she heard you had passed the Gate
That shuts on all flesh soon or late,
She thought you no more worth her hate,
      And cares not where you lie."

"Then, who is digging on my grave?
      Say—since I have not guessed!"
—"O it is I, my mistress dear,
Your little dog, who still lives near,
And much I hope my movements here
      Have not disturbed your rest?"

"Ah, yes!   *You* dig upon my grave. . .
      Why flashed it not on me

That one true heart was left behind!
What feeling do we ever find
To equal among human kind
    A dog's fidelity!"

"Mistress, I dug upon your grave
    To bury a bone, in case
I should be hungry near this spot
When passing on my daily trot.
I am sorry, but I quite forgot
    It was your resting-place."

The Discovery

I wandered to a crude coast
    Like a ghost;
Upon the hills I saw fires—
    Funeral pyres
Seemingly—and heard breaking
Waves like distant cannonades that set the land shaking.

And so I never once guessed
    A Love-nest,
Bowered and candle-lit, lay
    In my way,
Till I found a hid hollow,
Where I burst on her my heart could not but follow.

At Day-Close in November

The ten hours' light is abating,
    And a late bird wings across,
Where the pines, like waltzers waiting,
    Give their black heads a toss.

Beech leaves, that yellow the noon-time,
    Float past like specks in the eye;
I set every tree in my June time,
    And now they obscure the sky.

And the children who ramble through here
    Conceive that there never has been
A time when no tall trees grew here,
    That none will in time be seen.

Under the Waterfall

"Whenever I plunge my arm, like this,
In a basin of water, I never miss
The sweet sharp sense of a fugitive day
Fetched back from its thickening shroud of grey.
        Hence the only prime
        And real love-rhyme
        That I know by heart,
        And that leaves no smart,
Is the purl of a little valley fall
About three spans wide and two spans tall
Over a table of solid rock,
And into a scoop of the self-same block;
The purl of a runlet that never ceases
In stir of kingdoms, in wars, in peaces;
With a hollow boiling voice it speaks
And has spoken since hills were turfless peaks."

"And why gives this the only prime
Idea to you of a real love-rhyme?
And why does plunging your arm in a bowl
Full of spring water, bring throbs to your soul?"

"Well, under the fall, in a crease of the stone,
Though where precisely none ever has known,
Jammed darkly, nothing to show how prized,
And by now with its smoothness opalized,

Is a drinking-glass:
For, down that pass
My lover and I
Walked under a sky
Of blue with a leaf-wove awning of green,
In the burn of August, to paint the scene,
And we placed our basket of fruit and wine
By the runlet's rim, where we sat to dine;
And when we had drunk from the glass together,
Arched by the oak-copse from the weather,
I held the vessel to rinse in the fall,
Where it slipped, and sank, and was past recall,
Though we stooped and plumbed the little abyss
With long bared arms.   There the glass still is.
And, as said, if I thrust my arm below
Cold water in basin or bowl, a throe
From the past awakens a sense of that time,
And the glass we used, and the cascade's rhyme.
The basin seems the pool, and its edge
The hard smooth face of the brook-side ledge,
And the leafy pattern of china-ware
The hanging plants that were bathing there.

"By night, by day, when it shines or lours,
There lies intact that chalice of ours,
And its presence adds to the rhyme of love
Persistently sung by the fall above.
No lip has touched it since his and mine
In turns therefrom sipped lovers' wine."

POEMS OF 1912–13

Veteris vestigia flammae

The Going

Why did you give no hint that night
That quickly after the morrow's dawn,
And calmly, as if indifferent quite,
You would close your term here, up and be gone
      Where I could not follow
      With wing of swallow
To gain one glimpse of you ever anon!

      Never to bid good-bye,
      Or lip me the softest call,
Or utter a wish for a word, while I
Saw morning harden upon the wall,
      Unmoved, unknowing
      That your great going
Had place that moment, and altered all.

Why do you make me leave the house
And think for a breath it is you I see
At the end of the alley of bending boughs
Where so often at dusk you used to be;
      Till in darkening dankness
      The yawning blankness
Of the perspective sickens me!

      You were she who abode
      By those red-veined rocks far West,
You were the swan-necked one who rode
Along the beetling Beeny Crest,
      And, reining nigh me,
      Would muse and eye me,
While Life unrolled us its very best.

Why, then, latterly did we not speak,
Did we not think of those days long dead,
And ere your vanishing strive to seek
That time's renewal?   We might have said,
          "In this bright spring weather
          We'll visit together
Those places that once we visited."

          Well, well!   All's past amend,
          Unchangeable.   It must go.
I seem but a dead man held on end
To sink down soon. . . . O you could not know
          That such swift fleeing
          No soul foreseeing—
Not even I—would undo me so!

   December 1912.

Your Last Drive

Here by the moorway you returned,
And saw the borough lights ahead
That lit your face—all undiscerned
To be in a week the face of the dead,
And you told of the charm of that haloed view
That never again would beam on you.

And on your left you passed the spot
Where eight days later you were to lie,
And be spoken of as one who was not;
Beholding it with a heedless eye
As alien from you, though under its tree
You soon would halt everlastingly.

I drove not with you. . . . Yet had I sat
At your side that eve I should not have seen
That the countenance I was glancing at
Had a last-time look in the flickering sheen,

Nor have read the writing upon your face,
"I go hence soon to my resting-place;

"You may miss me then.   But I shall not know
How many times you visit me there,
Or what your thoughts are, or if you go
There never at all.   And I shall not care.
Should you censure me I shall take no heed,
And even your praises no more shall need."

True: never you'll know.   And you will not mind
But shall I then slight you because of such?
Dear ghost, in the past did you ever find
The thought "What profit," move me much?
Yet abides the fact, indeed, the same,—
You are past love, praise, indifference, blame.

December 1912.

The Walk

You did not walk with me
Of late to the hill-top tree
By the gated ways,
As in earlier days;
You were weak and lame,
So you never came,
And I went alone, and I did not mind
Not thinking of you as left behind.

I walked up there to-day
Just in the former way;
Surveyed around
The familiar ground
By myself again:
What difference, then?
Only that underlying sense
Of the look of a room on returning thence.

Rain on a Grave

Clouds spout upon her
  Their water amain
  In ruthless disdain,—
Her who but lately
  Had shivered with pain
As at touch of dishonour
If there had lit on her
So coldly, so straightly
  Such arrows of rain:

One who to shelter
  Her delicate head
Would quicken and quicken
  Each tentative tread
If drops chanced to pelt her
  That summertime spills
  In dust-paven rills
When thunder-clouds thicken
  And birds close their bills.

Would that I lay there
  And she were housed here!
Or better, together
Were folded away there
Exposed to one weather
We both,—who would stray there
When sunny the day there
  Or evening was clear
  At the prime of the year.

Soon will be growing
  Green blades from her mound,
And daisies be showing
  Like stars on the ground,
Till she form part of them—
Ay—the sweet heart of them,
Loved beyond measure
With a child's pleasure
  All her life's round.

January 31, 1913.

"I Found Her Out There"

I found her out there
On a slope few see,
That falls westwardly
To the salt-edged air,
Where the ocean breaks
On the purple strand,
And the hurricane shakes
The solid land.

I brought her here,
And have laid her to rest
In a noiseless nest
No sea beats near.
She will never be stirred
In her loamy cell
By the waves long heard
And loved so well.

So she does not sleep
By those haunted heights
The Atlantic smites
And the blind gales sweep,
Whence she often would gaze
At Dundagel's famed head,
While the dipping blaze
Dyed her face fire-red;

And would sigh at the tale
Of sunk Lyonnesse,
As a wind-tugged tress
Flapped her cheek like a flail;
Or listen at whiles
With a thought-bound brow
To the murmuring miles
She is far from now.

Yet her shade, maybe,
Will creep underground

Till it catch the sound
    Of that western sea
As it swells and sobs
    Where she once domiciled,
And joy in its throbs
    With the heart of a child.

The Haunter

He does not think that I haunt here nightly:
    How shall I let him know
That whither his fancy sets him wandering
    I, too, alertly go?—

Hover and hover a few feet from him
    Just as I used to do,
But cannot answer the words he lifts me—
    Only listen thereto!

When I could answer he did not say them:
    When I could let him know
How I would like to join in his journeys
    Seldom he wished to go.
Now that he goes and wants me with him
    More than he used to do,
Never he sees my faithful phantom
    Though he speaks thereto.

Yes, I companion him to places
    Only dreamers know,
Where the shy hares print long paces,
    Where the night rooks go;
Into old aisles where the past is all to him
    Close as his shade can do,
Always lacking the power to call to him,
    Near as I reach thereto!

What a good haunter I am, O tell him!
      Quickly make him know
If he but sigh since my loss befell him
      Straight to his side I go.
Tell him a faithful one is doing
      All that love can do
Still that his path may be worth pursuing,
      And to bring peace thereto.

The Voice

Woman much missed, how you call to me, call to me,
Saying that now you are not as you were
When you had changed from the one who was all to me,
But as at first, when our day was fair.

Can it be you that I hear?   Let me view you, then,
Standing as when I drew near to the town
Where you would wait for me: yes, as I knew you then,
Even to the original air-blue gown!

Or is it only the breeze, in its listlessness
Travelling across the wet mead to me here,
You being ever dissolved to wan wistlessness,
Heard no more again far or near?

      Thus I; faltering forward,
      Leaves around me falling,
Wind oozing thin through the thorn from norward,
      And the woman calling.

December 1912.

After a Journey

Hereto I come to view a voiceless ghost;
   Whither, O whither will its whim now draw me?
Up the cliff, down, till I'm lonely, lost,
   And the unseen waters' ejaculations awe me.
Where you will next be there's no knowing,
   Facing round about me everywhere,
       With your nut-coloured hair,
And grey eyes, and rose-flush coming and going.

Yes: I have re-entered your olden haunts at last;
   Through the years, through the dead scenes I
       have tracked you;
What have you now found to say of our past—
   Scanned across the dark space wherein I have
       lacked you?
Summer gave us sweets, but autumn wrought division?
   Things were not lastly as firstly well
       With us twain, you tell?
But all's closed now, despite Time's derision.

I see what you are doing: you are leading me on
   To the spots we knew when we haunted here together,
The waterfall, above which the mist-bow shone
   At the then fair hour in the then fair weather,
And the cave just under, with a voice still so hollow
   That it seems to call out to me from forty years ago,
       When you were all aglow,
And not the thin ghost that I now frailly follow!

Ignorant of what there is flitting here to see,
   The waked birds preen and the seals flop lazily;
Soon you will have, Dear, to vanish from me,
   For the stars close their shutters and the dawn whitens
       hazily.
Trust me, I mind not, though Life lours,
   The bringing me here; nay, bring me here again!
       I am just the same as when
Our days were a joy, and our paths through flowers.

PENTARGAN BAY.

Seen by the Waits

Through snowy woods and shady
   We went to play a tune
To the lonely manor-lady
   By the light of the Christmas moon.

We violed till, upward glancing
   To where a mirror leaned,
It showed her airily dancing,
   Deeming her movements screened;

Dancing alone in the room there,
   Thin-draped in her robe of night;
Her postures, glassed in the gloom there,
   Were a strange phantasmal sight.

She had learnt (we heard when homing)
   That her roving spouse was dead:
Why she had danced in the gloaming
   We thought, but never said.

In the Moonlight

"O lonely workman, standing there
In a dream, why do you stare and stare
At her grave, as no other grave there were?

"If your great gaunt eyes so importune
Her soul by the shine of this corpse-cold moon
Maybe you'll raise her phantom soon!"

"Why, fool, it is what I would rather see
Than all the living folk there be;
But alas, there is no such joy for me!"

"Ah—she was one you loved, no doubt,
Through good and evil, through rain and drought,
And when she passed, all your sun went out?"

"Nay: she was the woman I did not love,
Whom all the others were ranked above,
Whom during her life I thought nothing of."

In Church

"And now to God the Father," he ends,
And his voice thrills up to the topmost tiles:
Each listener chokes as he bows and bends,
And emotion pervades the crowded aisles.
Then the preacher glides to the vestry-door,
And shuts it, and thinks he is seen no more.

The door swings softly ajar meanwhile,
And a pupil of his in the Bible class,
Who adores him as one without gloss or guile,
Sees her idol stand with a satisfied smile
And re-enact at the vestry-glass
Each pulpit gesture in deft dumb-show
That had moved the congregation so.

MOMENTS OF VISION AND MISCELLANEOUS VERSES

In a Museum

I

Here's the mould of a musical bird long passed from light,
Which over the earth before man came was winging;
There's a contralto voice I heard last night,
That lodges in me still with its sweet singing.

II

Such a dream is Time that the coo of this ancient bird
Has perished not, but is blent, or will be blending
Mid visionless wilds of space with the voice that I heard,
In the full-fugued song of the universe unending.

EXETER.

Heredity

I am the family face;
Flesh perishes, I live on,
Projecting trait and trace
Through time to times anon,
And leaping from place to place
Over oblivion.

The years-heired feature that can
In curve and voice and eye
Despise the human span
Of durance—that is I;
The eternal thing in man,
That heeds no call to die.

Lines

TO A MOVEMENT IN MOZART'S E-FLAT SYMPHONY

Show me again the time
When in the Junetide's prime
We flew by meads and mountains northerly!—
Yea, to such freshness, fairness, fulness, fineness, freeness,
Love lures life on.

Show me again the day
When from the sandy bay
We looked together upon the pestered sea!—
Yea, to such surging, swaying, sighing, swelling, shrinking,
Love lures life on.

Show me again the hour
When by the pinnacled tower
We eyed each other and feared futurity!—
Yea, to such bodings, broodings, beatings, blanchings,
        blessings
Love lures life on.

Show me again just this:
The moment of that kiss
Away from the prancing folk, by the strawberry-tree!—
Yea, to such rashness, rathcness, rareness, ripeness,
        richness,
Love lures life on.

Begun November 1898.

The Oxen

Christmas Eve, and twelve of the clock.
    "Now they are all on their knees,"
An elder said as we sat in a flock
    By the embers in hearthside ease.

We pictured the meek mild creatures where
    They dwelt in their strawy pen,
Nor did it occur to one of us there
    To doubt they were kneeling then.

So fair a fancy few would weave
    In these years!   Yet, I feel,
If someone said on Christmas Eve,
    "Come; see the oxen kneel

"In the lonely barton by yonder coomb
    Our childhood used to know,"
I should go with him in the gloom,
    Hoping it might be so.

    1915.

The Tresses

"When the air was damp
It made my curls hang slack
As they kissed my neck and back
While I footed the salt-aired track
    I loved to tramp.

"When it was dry
They would roll up crisp and tight
As I went on in the light
Of the sun, which my own sprite
    Seemed to outvie.

"Now I am old;
And have not one gay curl
As I had when a girl
For dampness to unfurl
    Or sun uphold!"

Transformations

Portion of this yew
Is a man my grandsire knew,
Bosomed here at its foot:
This branch may be his wife,
A ruddy human life
Now turned to a green shoot.

These grasses must be made
Of her who often prayed,
Last century, for repose;
And the fair girl long ago
Whom I often tried to know
May be entering this rose.

So, they are not underground,
But as nerves and veins abound

In the growths of upper air,
And they feel the sun and rain,
And the energy again
That made them what they were!

The Last Signal

(*October* 11, 1886)

A MEMORY OF WILLIAM BARNES

Silently I footed by an uphill road
That led from my abode to a spot yew-boughed;
Yellowly the sun sloped low down to westward,
    And dark was the east with cloud.

Then, amid the shadow of that livid sad east,
Where the light was least, and a gate stood wide,
Something flashed the fire of the sun that was facing it,
    Like a brief blaze on that side.

Looking hard and harder I knew what it meant—
The sudden shine sent from the livid east scene;
It meant the west mirrored by the coffin of my friend there,
    Turning to the road from his green,

To take his last journey forth—he who in his prime
Trudged so many a time from that gate athwart the land!
Thus a farewell to me he signalled on his grave-way,
    As with a wave of his hand.

WINTERBOURNE-CAME PATH.

Great Things

Sweet cyder is a great thing,
    A great thing to me,
Spinning down to Weymouth town
    By Ridgway thirstily,

And maid and mistress summoning
  Who tend the hostelry:
O cyder is a great thing,
  A great thing to me!

The dance it is a great thing,
  A great thing to me,
With candles lit and partners fit
  For night-long revelry;
And going home when day-dawning
  Peeps pale upon the lea:
O dancing is a great thing,
  A great thing to me!

Love is, yea, a great thing,
  A great thing to me,
When, having drawn across the lawn
  In darkness silently,
A figure flits like one a-wing
  Out from the nearest tree:
O love is, yes, a great thing,
  A great thing to me!

Will these be always great things,
  Great things to me? . . .
Let it befall that One will call,
  "Soul, I have need of thee:"
What then?   Joy-jaunts, impassioned flings,
  Love, and its ecstasy,
Will always have been great things,
  Great things to me!

The Figure in the Scene

It pleased her to step in front and sit
  Where the cragged slope was green,
While I stood back that I might pencil it
  With her amid the scene;
Till it gloomed and rained;

But I kept on, despite the drifting wet
      That fell and stained
My draught, leaving for curious quizzings yet
      The blots engrained.

And thus I drew her there alone,
      Seated amid the gauze
Of moisture, hooded, only her outline shown,
      With rainfall marked across.
      —Soon passed our stay;
Yet her rainy form is the Genius still of the spot,
      Immutable, yea,
Though the place now knows her no more, and has known
      her not
      Ever since that day.

From an olde note.

The Blow

That no man schemed it is my hope—
Yea, that it fell by will and scope
      Of That Which some enthrone,
And for whose meaning myriads grope.

For I would not that of my kind
There should, of his unbiassed mind,
      Have been one known
Who such a stroke could have designed.

Since it would augur works and ways
Below the lowest that man assays
      To have hurled that stone
Into the sunshine of our days!

And if it prove that no man did,
And that the Inscrutable, the Hid,
      Was cause alone
Of this foul crash our lives amid,

I'll go in due time, and forget
In some deep graveyard's oubliette
    The thing whereof I groan,
And cease from troubling; thankful yet

Time's finger should have stretched to show
No aimful author's was the blow
    That swept us prone,
But the Immanent Doer's That doth not know,

Which in some age unguessed of us
May lift Its blinding incubus,
    And see, and own:
"It grieves me I did thus and thus!"

The Five Students

The sparrow dips in his wheel-rut bath,
    The sun grows passionate-eyed,
And boils the dew to smoke by the paddock-path;
    As strenuously we stride,—
Five of us; dark He, fair He, dark She, fair She, I,
    All beating by.

The air is shaken, the high-road hot,
    Shadowless swoons the day,
The greens are sobered and cattle at rest; but not
    We on our urgent way,—
Four of us; fair She, dark She, fair He, I, are there,
    But one—elsewhere.

Autumn moulds the hard fruit mellow,
    And forward still we press
Through moors, briar-meshed plantations, clay-pits
    yellow,
    As in the spring hours—yes,
Three of us; fair He, fair She, I, as heretofore,
    But—fallen one more.

The leaf drops: earthworms draw it in
      At night-time noiselessly,
The fingers of birch and beech are skeleton-thin
      And yet on the beat are we,—
Two of us; fair She, I.   But no more left to go
      The track we know.

Icicles tag the church-aisle leads,
      The flag-rope gibbers hoarse,
The home-bound foot-folk wrap their snow-flaked heads,
      Yet I still stalk the course—
One of us. . . . Dark and fair He, dark and fair She,
            gone:
      The rest—anon.

During Wind and Rain

      They sing their dearest songs—
      He, she, all of them—yea,
      Treble and tenor and bass,
            And one to play;
      With the candles mooning each face. . . .
            Ah, no; the years O!
How the sick leaves reel down in throngs!

      They clear the creeping moss—
      Elders and juniors—aye,
      Making the pathways neat
            And the garden gay;
      And they build a shady seat. . . .
            Ah, no; the years, the years;
See, the white storm-birds wing across!

      They are blithely breakfasting all—
      Men and maidens—yea,
      Under the summer tree,
            With a glimpse of the bay,

While pet fowl come to the knee. . . .
        Ah, no; the years O!
And the rotten rose is ript from the wall.

They change to a high new house,
He, she, all of them—aye,
Clocks and carpets and chairs
        On the lawn all day,
And brightest things that are theirs. . . .
        Ah, no; the years, the years;
Down their carved names the rain-drop ploughs.

Molly Gone

No more summer for Molly and me;
        There is snow on the tree,
And the blackbirds plump large as the rooks are,
                almost,
        And the water is hard
Where they used to dip bills at the dawn ere her figure
                was lost
        To these coasts, now my prison close-barred.

No more planting by Molly and me
        Where the beds used to be
Of sweet-william; no training the clambering rose
        By the framework of fir
Now bowering the pathway, whereon it swings gaily
                and blows
        As if calling commendment from her.

No more jauntings by Molly and me
        To the town by the sea,
Or along over Whitesheet to Wynyard's green Gap,
        Catching Montacute Crest
To the right against Sedgmoor, and Corton-Hill's far-
                distant cap,
        And Pilsdon and Lewsdon to west.

No more singing by Molly to me
    In the evenings when she
Was in mood and in voice, and the candles were lit,
    And past the porch-quoin
The rays would spring out on the laurels; and dumble-
       dores hit
    On the pane, as if wishing to join.

Where, then, is Molly, who's no more with me?
    —As I stand on this lea,
Thinking thus, there's a many-flamed star in the air,
    That tosses a sign
That her glance is regarding its face from her home, so
      that there
    Her eyes may have meetings with mine.

An Upbraiding

Now I am dead you sing to me
    The songs we used to know,
But while I lived you had no wish
    Or care for doing so.

Now I am dead you come to me
    In the moonlight, comfortless;
Ah, what would I have given alive
    To win such tenderness!

When you are dead, and stand to me
    Not differenced, as now,
But like again, will you be cold
    As when we lived, or how?

The Young Glass-Stainer

"These Gothic windows, how they wear me out
    With cusp and foil, and nothing straight or square,

Crude colours, leaden borders roundabout,
And fitting in Peter here, and Matthew there!

"What a vocation!   Here do I draw now
The abnormal, loving the Hellenic norm;
Martha I paint, and dream of Hera's brow,
Mary, and think of Aphrodite's form."

November 1893.

"For Life I Had Never Cared Greatly"

For Life I had never cared greatly,
 As worth a man's while;
 Peradventures unsought,
Peradventures that finished in nought,
Had kept me from youth and through manhood till lately
 Unwon by its style.

In earliest years—why I know not—
 I viewed it askance;
 Conditions of doubt,
Conditions that leaked slowly out,
May haply have bent me to stand and to show not
 Much zest for its dance.

With symphonies soft and sweet colour
 It courted me then,
 Till evasions seemed wrong,
Till evasions gave in to its song,
And I warmed, until living aloofly loomed duller
 Than life among men.

Anew I found nought to set eyes on,
 When, lifting its hand,
 it uncloaked a star,
Uncloaked it from fog-damps afar,
And showed its beams burning from pole to horizon
 As bright as a brand.

And so, the rough highway forgetting,
   I pace hill and dale
   Regarding the sky,
  Regarding the vision on high,
And thus re-illumed have no humour for letting
    My pilgrimage fail.

In Time of "The Breaking of Nations"

I

Only a man harrowing clods
   In a slow silent walk
With an old horse that stumbles and nods
   Half asleep as they stalk.

II

Only thin smoke without flame
   From the heaps of couch-grass:
Yet this will go onward the same
   Though Dynasties pass.

III

Yonder a maid and her wight
   Come whispering by:
War's annals will cloud into night
   Ere their story die.

   1915.

Afterwards

When the Present has latched its postern behind my
    tremulous stay,
  And the May month flaps its glad green leaves like wings,
Delicate-filmed as new-spun silk, will the neighbours say,
  "He was a man who used to notice such things"?

If it be in the dusk when, like an eyelid's soundless blink,
  The dewfall-hawk comes crossing the shades to alight
Upon the wind-warped upland thorn, a gazer may think,
  "To him this must have been a familiar sight."

If I pass during some nocturnal blackness, mothy and
        warm,
  When the hedgehog travels furtively over the lawn,
One may say, "He strove that such innocent creatures
        should come to no harm,
  But he could do little for them; and now he is gone."

If, when hearing that I have been stilled at last, they
        stand at the door,
  Watching the full-starred heavens that winter sees,
Will this thought rise on those who will meet my face
        no more,
  "He was one who had an eye for such mysteries"?

And will any say when my bell of quittance is heard in
        the gloom,
  And a crossing breeze cuts a pause in its outrollings,
Till they rise again, as they were a new bell's boom,
  "He hears it not now, but used to notice such things"?

᙭᙭᙭᙭᙭᙭᙭᙭᙭᙭᙭᙭᙭᙭᙭᙭᙭᙭᙭᙭᙭᙭

FROM LATE LYRICS AND EARLIER

The Garden Seat

Its former green is blue and thin,
And its once firm legs sink in and in;
Soon it will break down unaware,
Soon it will break down unaware.

At night when reddest flowers are black
Those who once sat thereon come back;

Quite a row of them sitting there,
Quite a row of them sitting there.

With them the seat does not break down,
Nor winter freeze them, nor floods drown,
For they are as light as upper air,
They are as light as upper air!

"The Curtains Now Are Drawn"

(SONG)

I

The curtains now are drawn,
And the spindrift strikes the glass,
Blown up the jaggèd pass
By the surly salt sou'-west,
And the sneering glare is gone
Behind the yonder crest,
　　While she sings to me:
"O the dream that thou art my Love, be it thine,
And the dream that I am thy Love, be it mine,
And death may come, but loving is divine."

II

I stand here in the rain,
With its smite upon her stone,
And the grasses that have grown
Over women, children, men,
And their texts that "Life is vain;"
But I hear the notes as when
　　Once she sang to me:
"O the dream that thou art my Love, be it thine,
And the dream that I am thy Love, be it mine,
And death may come, but loving is divine."

1913.

"According to the Mighty Working"

I

When moiling seems at cease
    In the vague void of night-time,
    And heaven's wide roomage stormless
    Between the dusk and light-time,
    And fear at last is formless,
We call the allurement Peace.

II

Peace, this hid riot, Change,
    This revel of quick-cued mumming,
    This never truly being,
    This evermore becoming,
    This spinner's wheel onfleeing
Outside perception's range.

    1917.

Going and Staying

I

The moving sun-shapes on the spray,
The sparkles where the brook was flowing,
Pink faces, plightings, moonlit May,
These were the things we wished would stay:
    But they were going.

II

Seasons of blankness as of snow,
The silent bleed of a world decaying,
The moan of multitudes in woe,
These were the things we wished would go;
    But they were staying.

III

Then we looked closelier at Time,
And saw his ghostly arms revolving
To sweep off woeful things with prime,
Things sinister with things sublime
    Alike dissolving.

The Two Houses

In the heart of night,
  When farers were not near,
The left house said to the house on the right,
"I have marked your rise, O smart newcomer here."

Said the right, cold-eyed:
  "Newcomer here I am,
Hence haler than you with your cracked old hide,
Loose casements, wormy beams, and doors that jam.

"Modern my wood,
  My hangings fair of hue:
While my windows open as they should,
And water-pipes thread all my chambers through.

"Your gear is grey,
  Your face wears furrows untold."
"—Yours might," mourned the other, "if you held,
    brother,
The Presences from aforetime that I hold.

"You have not known
  Men's lives, deaths, toils, and teens;
You are but a heap of stick and stone:
A new house has no sense of the have-beens.

"Void as a drum
  You stand: I am packed with these,
Though, strangely, living dwellers who come
See not the phantoms all my substance sees!

"Visible in the morning
Stand they, when dawn drags in;
Visible at night; yet hint or warning
Of these thin elbowers few of the inmates win.

"Babes new-brought-forth
Obsess my rooms; straight-stretched
Lank corpses, ere outborne to earth:
Yea, throng they as when first from the Byss upfetched.

"Dancers and singers
Throb in me now as once;
Rich-noted throats and gossamered flingers
Of heels; the learned in love-lore and the dunce.

"Note here within
The bridegroom and the bride,
Who smile and greet their friends and kin,
And down my stairs depart for tracks untried.

"Where such inbe,
A dwelling's character
Takes theirs, and a vague semblancy
To them in all its limbs, and light, and atmosphere.

"Yet the blind folk
My tenants, who come and go
In the flesh mid these, with souls unwoke,
Of such sylph-like surrounders do not know."

"—Will the day come,"
Said the new one, awestruck, faint,
"When I shall lodge shades dim and dumb—
And with such spectral guests become acquaint?"

"—That will it, boy;
Such shades will people thee,
Each in his misery, irk, or joy,
And print on thee their presences as on me."

At a House in Hampstead

SOMETIME THE DWELLING OF JOHN KEATS

O poet, come you haunting here
Where streets have stolen up all around,
And never a nightingale pours one
      Full-throated sound?

Drawn from your drowse by the Seven famed Hills
Thought you to find all just the same
Here shining, as in hours of old,
      If you but came?

What will you do in your surprise
At seeing that changes wrought in Rome
Are wrought yet more on the misty slope
      One time your home?

Will you wake wind-wafts on these stairs?
Swing the doors open noisily?
Show as an umbraged ghost beside
      Your ancient tree?

Or will you, softening, the while
You further and yet further look,
Learn that a laggard few would fain
      Preserve your nook? . . .

—Where the Piazza steps incline,
And catch late light at eventide,
I once stood, in that Rome, and thought
      " 'Twas here he died."

I drew to a violet-sprinkled spot,
Where day and night a pyramid keeps
Uplifted its white hand, and said,
      " 'Tis there he sleeps."

Pleasanter now it is to hold
That here, where sang he, more of him
Remains than where he, tuneless, cold,
      Passed to the dim.

July 1920.

"And There Was a Great Calm"

(ON THE SIGNING OF THE ARMISTICE, NOV. 11, 1918)

I

There had been years of Passion—scorching, cold,
And much Despair, and Anger heaving high,
Care whitely watching, Sorrows manifold,
Among the young, among the weak and old,
And the pensive Spirit of Pity whispered, "Why?"

II

Men had not paused to answer.   Foes distraught
Pierced the thinned peoples in a brute-like blindness,
Philosophies that sages long had taught,
And Selflessness, were as an unknown thought,
And "Hell!" and "Shell!" were yapped at Lovingkindness.

III

The feeble folk at home had grown full-used
To "dug-outs," "snipers," "Huns," from the war-adept
In the mornings heard, and at evetides perused;
To day-dreamt men in millions, when they mused—
To nightmare-men in millions when they slept.

IV

Waking to wish existence timeless, null,
Sirius they watched above where armies fell;
He seemed to check his flapping when, in the lull
Of night a boom came thencewise, like the dull
Plunge of a stone dropped into some deep well.

V

So, when old hopes that earth was bettering slowly
Were dead and damned, there sounded "War is done!"
One morrow.   Said the bereft, and meek, and lowly,
"Will men some day be given to grace? yea, wholly,
And in good sooth, as our dreams used to run?"

VI

Breathless they paused. Out there men raised their glance
To where had stood those poplars lank and lopped,
As they had raised it through the four years' dance
Of Death in the now familiar flats of France;
And murmured, "Strange, this!   How?   All firing
   stopped?"

VII

Aye; all was hushed.   The about-to-fire fired not,
The aimed-at moved away in trance-lipped song.
One checkless regiment slung a clinching shot
And turned.   The Spirit of Irony smirked out, "What?
Spoil peradventures woven of Rage and Wrong?"

VIII

Thenceforth no flying fires inflamed the grey,
No hurtlings shook the dewdrop from the thorn,
No moan perplexed the mute bird on the spray;
Worn horses mused: "We are not whipped to-day";
No weft-winged engines blurred the moon's thin horn.

IX

Calm fell.   From Heaven distilled a clemency;
There was peace on earth, and silence in the sky;
Some could, some could not, shake off misery:
The Sinister Spirit sneered: "It had to be!"
And again the Spirit of Pity whispered, "Why?"

Voices From Things Growing in a Churchyard

These flowers are I, poor Fanny Hurd,
                  Sir or Madam,
A little girl here sepultured.
Once I flit-fluttered like a bird

Above the grass, as now I wave
In daisy shapes above my grave,
       All day cheerily,
       All night eerily!

—I am one Bachelor Bowring, "Gent,"
       Sir or Madam;
In shingled oak my bones were pent;
Hence more than a hundred years I spent
In my feat of change from a coffin-thrall
To a dancer in green as leaves on a wall,
       All day cheerily,
       All night eerily!

—I, these berries of juice and gloss,
       Sir or Madam,
Am clean forgotten as Thomas Voss;
Thin-urned, I have burrowed away from the moss
That covers my sod, and have entered this yew,
And turned to clusters ruddy of view,
       All day cheerily,
       All night eerily!

—The Lady Gertrude, proud, high-bred,
       Sir or Madam,
Am I—this laurel that shades your head;
Into its veins I have stilly sped,
And made them of me; and my leaves now shine,
As did my satins superfine,
       All day cheerily,
       All night eerily!

—I, who as innocent withwind climb,
       Sir or Madam,
Am one Eve Greensleeves, in olden time
Kissed by men from many a clime,
Beneath sun, stars, in blaze, in breeze,
As now by glowworms and by bees,
       All day cheerily,
       All night eerily!

—I'm old Squire Audeley Grey, who grew
                    Sir or Madam,
Aweary of life, and in scorn withdrew;
Till anon I clambered up anew
As ivy-green, when my ache was stayed,
And in that attire I have longtime gayed
                    All day cheerily,
                    All night eerily!

—And so these maskers breathe to each
                    Sir or Madam
Who lingers there, and their lively speech
Affords an interpreter much to teach,
As their murmurous accents seem to come
Thence hitheraround in a radiant hum,
                    All day cheerily,
                    All night eerily!

The Singing Woman

There was a singing woman
        Came riding across the mead
At the time of the mild May weather,
        Tameless, tireless;
This song she sung: "I am fair, I am young!"
        And many turned to heed.

And the same singing woman
        Sat crooning in her need
At the time of the winter weather:
        Friendless, fireless,
She sang this song: "Life, thou'rt too long!"
        And there was none to heed.

In the Small Hours

I lay in my bed and fiddled
  With a dreamland viol and bow,
And the tunes flew back to my fingers
  I had melodied years ago.
It was two or three in the morning
  When I fancy-fiddled so
Long reels and country-dances,
  And hornpipes swift and slow.

And soon anon came crossing
  The chamber in the gray
Figures of jigging fieldfolk—
  Saviours of corn and hay—
To the air of "Haste to the Wedding,"
  As after a wedding-day;
Yea, up and down the middle
  In windless whirls went they!

There danced the bride and bridegroom,
  And couples in a train,
Gay partners time and travail
  Had longwhiles stilled amain! . . .
It seemed a thing for weeping
  To find, at slumber's wane
And morning's sly increeping,
  That Now, not Then, held reign.

The Dream Is—Which?

I am laughing by the brook with her,
  Splashed in its tumbling stir;
And then it is a blankness looms
  As if I walked not there,
Nor she, but found me in haggard rooms,
  And treading a lonely stair.

With radiant cheeks and rapid eyes
  We sit where none espies;
Till a harsh change comes edging in
  As no such scene were there,
But winter, and I were bent and thin,
  And cinder & grey my hair.

We dance in heys around the hall,
  Weightless as thistleball;
And then a curtain drops between,
  As if I danced not there,
But wandered through a mounded green
  To find her, I knew where.

March 1913.

A Drizzling Easter Morning

And he is risen?   Well, be it so. . . .
And still the pensive lands complain,
And dead men wait as long ago,
As if, much doubting, they would know
What they are ransomed from, before
They pass again their sheltering door.

I stand amid them in the rain,
While blusters vex the yew and vane;
And on the road the weary wain
Plods forward, laden heavily;
And toilers with their aches are fain
For endless rest—though risen is he.

"I Was the Midmost"

I was the midmost of my world
  When first I frisked me free,
For though within its circuit gleamed
  But a small company,

And I was immature, they seemed
To bend their looks on me.

She was the midmost of my world
    When I went further forth,
And hence it was that, whether I turned
    To south, east, west, or north,
Beams of an all-day Polestar burned
    From that new axe of earth.

Where now is midmost in my world?
    I trace it not at all:
No midmost shows it here, or there,
    When wistful voices call
"We are fain!   We are fain!" from everywhere
    On Earth's bewildering ball!

Surview

"Cogitavi vias meas"

A cry from the green-grained sticks of the fire
        Made me gaze where it seemed to be:
'Twas my own voice talking therefrom to me
On how I had walked when my sun was higher—
        My heart in its arrogancy.

"You held not to whatsoever was true,"
        Said my own voice talking to me:
*"Whatsoever was just you were slack to see;
Kept not things lovely and pure in view,"*
        Said my own voice talking to me.

"You slighted her that endureth all,"
        Said my own voice talking to me;
*"Vaunteth not, trusteth hopefully;
That suffereth long and is kind withal,"*
        Said my own voice talking to me.

"*You taught not that which you set about,*"
    Said my own voice talking to me;
"*That the greatest of things is Charity. . . .*"
—And the sticks burnt low, and the fire went out,
And my voice ceased talking to me.

FROM *HUMAN SHOWS, FAR PHANTASIES, SONGS, AND TALES*

Waiting Both

Λ star looks down at me,
And says: "Here I and you
Stand, each in our degree:
What do you mean to do,—
    Mean to do?"

I say: "For all I know,
Wait, and let Time go by,
Till my change come."—"Just so,"
The star says: "So mean I:—
    So mean I."

The Later Autumn

Gone are the lovers, under the bush
    Stretched at their ease;
    Gone the bees,
Tangling themselves in your hair as they rush
    On the line of your track,
    Leg-laden, back
    With a dip to their hive
    In a prepossessed dive.

Toadsmeat is mangy, frosted, and sere;
       Apples in grass
       Crunch as we pass,
And rot ere the men who make cyder appear.
       Couch-fires abound
       On fallows around,
       And shades far extend
       Like lives soon to end.

Spinning leaves join the remains shrunk and brown
       Of last year's display
       That lie wasting away,
On whose corpses they earlier as scorners gazed down
       From their aery green height:
       Now in the same plight
       They huddle; while yon
       A robin looks on.

An East-End Curate

A small blind street off East Commercial Road;
       Window, door; window door;
       Every house like the one before,
Is where the curate, Mr. Dowle, has found a pinched
       abode.
Spectacled, pale, moustache straw-coloured, and with a
       long thin face,
Day or dark his lodgings' narrow doorstep does he pace.

A bleached pianoforte, with its drawn silk plaitings faded,
Stands in his room, its keys much yellowed, cyphering,
       and abraded,
"Novello's Anthems" lie at hand, and also a few glees,
And "Laws of Heaven for Earth" in a frame upon the wall
       one sees.

He goes through his neighbours' houses as his own, and
       none regards,

And opens their back-doors off-hand, to look for them in
their yards:
A man is threatening his wife on the other side of the wall,
But the curate lets it pass as knowing the history of it all.

Freely within his hearing the children skip and laugh
and say:
"There's Mister Dow-well!   There's Mister
Dow-well!" in their play;
And the long, pallid, devoted face notes not,
But stoops along abstractedly, for good, or in vain,
God wot!

Coming Up Oxford Street: Evening

The sun from the west glares back,
And the sun from the watered track,
And the sun from the sheets of glass,
And the sun from each window-brass;
Sun-mirrorings, too, brighten
From show-cases beneath
The laughing eyes and teeth
Of ladies who rouge and whiten.
And the same warm god explores
Panels and chinks of doors;
Problems with chymists' bottles
Profound as Aristotle's
He solves, and with good cause,
Having been ere man was.

Also he dazzles the pupils of one who walks west,
A city-clerk, with eyesight not of the best,
Who sees no escape to the verge of his days
From the rut of Oxford Street into open ways;
And he goes along with head and eyes flagging forlorn,
Empty of interest in things, and wondering why he was
born.

As seen July 4, 1872.

Snow in the Suburbs

Every branch big with it,
Bent every twig with it;
Every fork like a white web-foot;
Every street and pavement mute:
Some flakes have lost their way, and grope back upward,
when
Meeting those meandering down they turn and descend
again.
The palings are glued together like a wall,
And there is no waft of wind with the fleecy fall.

A sparrow enters the tree,
Whereon immediately
A snow-lump thrice his own slight size
Descends on him and showers his head and eyes,
And overturns him,
And near inurns him,
And lights on a nether twig, when its brush
Starts off a volley of other lodging lumps with a rush.

The steps are a blanched slope,
Up which, with feeble hope,
A black cat comes, wide-eyed and thin;
And we take him in.

Winter Night in Woodland

(OLD TIME)

The bark of a fox rings, sonorous and long:—
Three barks, and then silentness; "wong, wong,
wong!"
In quality horn-like, yet melancholy,
As from teachings of years; for an old one is he.
The hand of all men is against him, he knows; and
yet, why?

That he knows not,—will never know, down to his death-
    halloo cry.

    With clap-nets and lanterns off start the bird-
        baiters,
    In trim to make raids on the roosts in the copse,
    Where they beat the boughs artfully, while their
        awaiters
    Grow heavy at home over divers warm drops.
The poachers, with swingels, and matches of brimstone,
    outcreep
To steal upon pheasants and drowse them a-perch and
    asleep.

    Out there, on the verge, where a path wavers
        through,
    Dark figures, filed singly, thrid quickly the view,
    Yet heavily laden: land-carriers are they
    In the hire of the smugglers from some nearest bay.
Each bears his two "tubs," slung across, one in front, one
    behind,
To a further snug hiding, which none but themselves are
    to find.

    And then, when the night has turned twelve the
        air brings
    From dim distance, a rhythm of voices and strings:
    'Tis the quire, just afoot on their long yearly rounds,
    To rouse by worn carols each house in their bounds;
Robert Penny, the Dewys, Mail, Voss, and the rest;
    till anon
Tired and thirsty, but cheerful, they home to their beds in
    the dawn.

"She Opened the Door"

She opened the door of the West to me,
    With its loud sea-lashings,

                And cliff-side clashings
        Of waters rife with revelry.

        She opened the door of Romance to me,
                The door from a cell
                I had known too well,
        Too long, till then, and was fain to flee.

        She opened the door of a Love to me,
                That passed the wry
                World-welters by
        As far as the arching blue the lea.

        She opens the door of the Past to me,
                Its magic lights,
                Its heavenly heights,
        When forward little is to see!

            1913.

The Harbour Bridge

From here, the quay, one looks above to mark
The bridge across the harbour, hanging dark
Against the day's-end sky, fair-green in glow
Over and under the middle archway's bow:
It draws its skeleton where the sun has set,
Yea, clear from cutwater to parapet;
On which mild glow, too, lines of rope and spar
        Trace themselves black as char.

Down here in shade we hear the painters shift
Against the bollards with a drowsy lift,
As moved by the incoming stealthy tide.
High up across the bridge the burghers glide
As cut black-paper portraits hastening on
In conversation none knows what upon:
Their sharp-edged lips move quickly word by word
        To speech that is not heard.

There trails the dreamful girl, who leans and stops,
There presses the practical woman to the shops,
There is a sailor, meeting his wife with a start,
And we, drawn nearer, judge they are keeping apart.
Both pause. She says: "I've looked for you.   I thought
We'd make it up."   Then no words can be caught.
At last: "Won't you come home?"   She moves still
          nigher:
     " 'Tis comfortable, with a fire."

"No," he says gloomily.   "And, anyhow,
I can't give up the other woman now:
You should have talked like that in former days,
When I was last home."   They go different ways.
And the west dims, and yellow lamplights shine:
And soon above, like lamps more opaline,
White stars ghost forth, that care not for men's wives,
     Or any other lives.

WEYMOUTH.

The Missed Train

          How I was caught
Hieing home, after days of allure,
And forced to an inn—small, obscure—
          At the junction, gloom-fraught.

          How civil my face
To get them to chamber me there—
A roof I had scorned, scarce aware
          That it stood at the place.

          And how all the night
I had dreams of the unwitting cause
Of my lodgment.   How lonely I was;
          How consoled by her sprite!

Thus onetime to me . . .
Dim wastes of dead years bar away
Then from now.   But such happenings to-day
Fall to lovers, may be!

Years, years as shoaled seas,
Truly, stretch now between! Less and less
Shrink the visions then vast in me.—Yes,
Then in me: Now in these.

Retty's Phases

I

Retty used to shake her head,
Look with wicked eye;
Say, "I'd tease you, simple Ned,
If I cared to try!"
Then she'd hot-up scarlet red,
Stilly step away,
Much afraid that what she'd said
Sounded bold to say.

II

Retty used to think she loved
(Just a little) me.
Not untruly, as it proved
Afterwards to be.
For, when weakness forced her rest
If we walked a mile,
She would whisper she was blest
By my clasp awhile.

III

Retty used at last to say
When she neared the Vale,
"Mind that you, Dear, on that day
Ring my wedding peal!"

And we all, with pulsing pride,
   Vigorous sounding gave
Those six bells, the while outside
   John filled in her grave.

IV

Retty used to draw me down
   To the turfy heaps,
Where, with yeoman, squire, and clown
   Noticeless she sleeps.
Now her silent slumber-place
   Seldom do I know,
For when last I saw her face
   Was so long ago!

From an old draft of 1868.

NOTE.—In many villages it was customary after the funeral
of an unmarried young woman to ring a peal as for her wedding
while the grave was being filled in, as if Death were not to be
allowed to balk her of bridal honours. Young unmarried men
were always her bearers.—T.H.

Cynic's Epitaph

A race with the sun as he downed
   I ran at evetide,
Intent who should first gain the ground
   And there hide.

He beat me by some minutes then,
   But I triumphed anon,
For when he'd to rise up again
   I stayed on.

A Popular Personage at Home

"I lived here: 'Wessex' is my name:
I am a dog known rather well:
I guard the house; but how that came
To be my whim I cannot tell.

"With a leap and a heart elate I go
At the end of an hour's expectancy
To take a walk of a mile or so
With the folk I let live here with me.

"Along the path, amid the grass
I sniff, and find out rarest smells
For rolling over as I pass
The open fields towards the dells.

"No doubt I shall always cross this sill,
And turn the corner, and stand steady,
Gazing back for my mistress till
She reaches where I have run already,

"And that this meadow with its brook,
And bulrush, even as it appears
As I plunge by with hasty look,
Will stay the same a thousand years."

Thus "Wessex."   But a dubious ray
At times informs his steadfast eye,
Just for a trice, as though to say,
"Yet, will this pass, and pass shall I?"

    1924.

The Six Boards

Six boards belong to me:
I do not know where they may be;
If growing green, or lying dry
        In a cockloft nigh.

Some morning I shall claim them,
And who may then possess will aim them
To bring to me those boards I need
    With thoughtful speed.

But though they hurry so
To yield me mine, I shall not know
How well my want they'll have supplied
    When notified.

Those boards and I—how much
In common we, of feel and touch
Shall share thence on,—earth's far core-quakings,
    Hill-shocks, tide-shakings—

Yea, hid where none will note,
The once live tree and man, remote
From mundane hurt as if on Venus, Mars,
    Or furthest stars.

FROM *WINTER WORDS IN VARIOUS MOODS AND METRES*

We Field-Women

How it rained
When we worked at Flintcomb-Ash,
And could not stand upon the hill
Trimming swedes for the slicing-mill.
The wet washed through us—plash, plash, plash:
    How it rained!

How it snowed
When we crossed from Flintcomb-Ash
To the Great Barn for drawing reed,

Since we could nowise chop a swede.—
Flakes in each doorway and casement-sash:
How it snowed!

How it shone
When we went from Flintcomb-Ash
To start at dairywork once more
In the laughing meads, with cows three-score,
And pails, and songs, and love—too rash:
How it shone!

He Never Expected Much

[or]

A CONSIDERATION

[*A reflection*] ON MY EIGHTY-SIXTH BIRTHDAY

Well, World, you have kept faith with me,
Kept faith with me;
Upon the whole you have proved to be
Much as you said you were.
Since as a child I used to lie
Upon the leaze and watch the sky,
Never, I own, expected I
That life would all be fair.

'Twas then you said, and since have said,
Times since have said,
In that mysterious voice you shed
From clouds and hills around:
"Many have loved me desperately,
Many with smooth serenity,
While some have shown contempt of me
Till they dropped underground.

"I do not promise overmuch,
Child; overmuch;

Just neutral-tinted haps and such,"
　　　　You said to minds like mine.
Wise warning for your credit's sake!
Which I for one failed not to take,
And hence could stem such strain and ache
　　　　As each year might assign.

Christmas: 1924

"Peace upon earth!" was said.　　We sing it,
And pay a million priests to bring it.
After two thousand years of mass
We've got as far as poison-gas.

　　1924.

How She Went to Ireland

　　Dora's gone to Ireland
　　　　Through the sleet and snow;
　　Promptly she has gone there
　　　　In a ship, although
　　Why she's gone to Ireland
　　　　Dora does not know.

　　That was where, yea, Ireland,
　　　　Dora wished to be:
　　When she felt, in lone times,
　　　　Shoots of misery,
　　Often there, in Ireland,
　　　　Dora wished to be.

　　Hence she's gone to Ireland,
　　　　Since she meant to go,

Through the drift and darkness
Onward labouring, though
That she's gone to Ireland
Dora does not know.

He Resolves to Say No More

O my soul, keep the rest unknown!
It is too like a sound of moan
        When the charnel-eyed
        Pale Horse has nighed:
Yea, none shall gather what I hide!

Why load men's minds with more to bear
That bear already ails to spare?
        From now alway
        Till my last day
What I discern I will not say.

Let Time roll backward if it will;
(Magians who drive the midnight quill
        With brain aglow
        Can see it so,)
What I have learnt no man shall know.

And if my vision range beyond
The blinkered sight of souls in bond,
        —By truth made free—
        I'll let all be,
And show to no man what I see.

4

>C>C>C>C>C>C>C>C>C>C>C>C>C>C>C>C>C>C>C>C>C>C>C

THE EPIC OF
NAPOLEON

Editor's Note

The seed of *The Dynasts*, a vast historical and philosophic drama in Three Parts, Nineteen Acts, and One Hundred and Thirty Scenes, was planted in local Dorset traditions about a threatened French invasion of the Dorset coast in 1804 that never came off, and burgeoned into Hardy's most ambitious literary work. Beginning in 1875, when he projected "an Iliad of Europe from 1789 to 1815," and went so far as to interview all those veterans of Waterloo still living at Chelsea Hospital in London, the subject solicited Hardy's imagination for decades during which he regularly researched the era's history at the British Museum. In 1896, after a visit to Brussels and to Waterloo field, he wrote in his notebook: "Europe in Throes. Three Parts. Five Acts Each. Characters: Burke, Pitt, Napoleon, George III, Wellington . . ." This scheme developed into *The Dynasts*, Parts One and Two (1904–6) and Part Three (1908).

In its historical aspect *The Dynasts* is intensely patriotic and tends to show that it was English true grit and English military and naval prowess which finally banished the spectre of Napoleon's imperial power from Europe. On the other hand, the drama's philosophic bias is toward predestinarianism and automatism. All men, including Napoleon and the other dynasts of the period, are mannikins, mere puppets whose destiny is at the disposal of the Immanent Will. The Fore Scene introduces a panoply of Spirits—Hardy called them "abstract realisms"–who overlook the human scene from an immense height and with varying degrees of detachment. These figments return at the end to luxuriate in hindsight and to hint that man's condition may improve in the future when Will becomes more conscious of what it is about. In between, the drama ranges over the entire historical scene–in our excerpts from the beleaguered Dorset coast in 1804, through Russia in 1812, to Napoleon's last pathetic rendezvous with destiny near Waterloo in 1814.

The Dynasts, which was never intended to be performed, is much more than a historical curiosity, although it is not "the greatest of Hardy's writings" as it was widely believed to be during the 1920s and 1930s. It is a work of genuine if fitful dramatic power, still worth reading as a whole and even worth sampling through the excerpts here reprinted. I have also reprinted Hardy's two letters to *The Times* about *The Dynasts* for the light they shed on his intentions.

"The Alarm," a humorous chapter from Hardy's historical romance, *The Trumpet-Major*, is about the false alarm of the French amphibious assault on Dorset, with cowardly Festus playing Sancho Panza to a quixotic, no-show Napoleon who perhaps slept peacefully at his headquarters near Boulogne throughout that "historic and memorable" night.

FROM *THE TRUMPET MAJOR* (1880)

THE ALARM

XXVI

The night which followed was historic and memorable. Mrs. Loveday was awakened by the boom of a distant gun: she told the miller, and they listened awhile. The sound was not repeated, but such was the state of their feelings that Mr. Loveday went to Bob's room and asked if he had heard it. Bob was wide awake, looking out of the window; he had heard the ominous sound, and was inclined to investigate the matter. While the father and son were dressing they fancied that a glare seemed to be rising in the sky in the direction of the beacon hill. Not wishing to alarm Anne and her mother, the miller assured them that Bob and himself were merely going out of doors to inquire into the cause of the report, after which they plunged into the gloom together. A few steps' progress opened up more of the sky, which, as they had thought, was indeed irradiated by a lurid light; but whether it came from the beacon or from a more distant point they were unable to clearly tell. They pushed on rapidly towards higher ground.

Their excitement was merely of a piece with that of all men at this critical juncture. Everywhere expectation was at fever heat. For the last year or two only five-and-twenty miles of shallow water had divided quiet English homesteads from an enemy's army of a hundred and fifty thousand men. We had taken the matter lightly enough, eating and drinking as in the days of Noe, and singing satires without end. We punned on Buonaparte and his gunboats, chalked his effigy on stage coaches, and published the same in prints. Still, between these bursts of hilarity, it was sometimes recollected that England was the only European country which had not succumbed to the mighty little man who was less than human in feeling, and more than human in will; that our spirit for resistance was greater than our strength; and that the Channel was often calm. Boats built of wood which was greenly growing in its native forest three days before it was bent as wales to their sides, were ridiculous enough; but they might be, after all, sufficient for a single trip between two visible shores.

The English watched Buonaparte in these preparations, and Buonaparte watched the English. At the distance of Boulogne details were lost, but we were impressed on fine days by the novel sight of a huge army moving and twinkling like a school of mackerel under the rays of the sun. The regular way of passing an afternoon in the coast towns was to stroll up to the signal posts and chat with the lieutenant on duty there about the latest inimical object seen at sea. About once a week there appeared in the newspapers either a paragraph concerning some adventurous English gentleman who had sailed out in a pleasure-boat till he lay near enough to Boulogne to see Buonaparte standing on the heights among his marshals; or else some lines about a mysterious stranger with a foreign accent, who, after collecting a vast deal of information on our resources, had hired a boat at a southern port, and vanished with it towards France before his intention could be divined.

In forecasting his grand venture, Buonaparte postulated the help of Providence to a remarkable degree. Just at the hour when his troops were on board the flat-bottomed boats and ready to sail, there was to be a great fog, that should spread a vast obscurity over the length and breadth of the Channel, and keep the English blind to events on the other side. The fog was to last twenty-four hours, after which it might clear away. A dead calm was to prevail simultaneously with the fog, with the twofold object of affording the boats easy transit and dooming our ships to lie motionless. Thirdly, there was to be a spring tide, which should combine its manœuvres with those of the fog and calm.

Among the many thousands of minor Englishmen whose
lives were affected by these tremendous designs may be
numbered our old acquaintance Corporal Tullidge, who
sported the crushed arm, and poor old Simon Burden,
the dazed veteran who had fought at Minden. Instead of
sitting snugly in the settle of the Old Ship, in the village
adjoining Overcombe, they were obliged to keep watch on
the hill. They made themselves as comfortable as was possible in the circumstances, dwelling in a hut of clods and
turf, with a brick chimney for cooking. Here they observed
the nightly progress of the moon and stars, grew familiar
with the heaving of moles, the dancing of rabbits on the
hillocks, the distant hoot of owls, the bark of foxes from
woods further inland; but saw not a sign of the enemy.
As, night after night, they walked round the two ricks
which it was their duty to fire at a signal—one being of
furze for a quick flame, the other of turf, for a long,
slow radiance—they thought and talked of old times, and
drank patriotically from a large wood flagon that was
filled every day.

Bob and his father soon became aware that the light
was from the beacon. By the time that they reached the
top it was one mass of towering flame, from which the
sparks fell on the green herbage like a fiery dew; the forms
of the two old men being seen passing and repassing in
the midst of it. The Lovedays, who came up on the smoky
side, regarded the scene for a moment, and then emerged
into the light.

"Who goes there?" said Corporal Tullidge, shouldering
a pike with his sound arm. "O, 'tis neighbour Loveday!"

"Did you get your signal to fire it from the east?" said
the miller hastily.

"No; from Abbotsea Beach."

"But you are not to go by a coast signal!"

"Chok' it all, wasn't the Lord-Lieutenant's direction,
whenever you see Rainbarrow's Beacon burn to the
nor'east'ard, or Haggardon to the nor'west'ard, or the
actual presence of the enemy on the shore?"

"But is he here?"

"No doubt o't! The beach light is only just gone down, and Simon heard the guns even better than I."

"Hark, hark! I hear 'em!" said Bob.

They listened with parted lips, the night wind blowing through Simon Burden's few teeth as through the ruins of Stonehenge. From far down on the lower levels came the noise of wheels and the tramp of horses upon the turnpike road.

"Well, there must be something in it," said Miller Loveday gravely. "Bob, we'll go home and make the women-folk safe, and then I'll don my soldier's clothes and be off. God knows where our company will assemble!"

They hastened down the hill, and on getting into the road waited and listened again. Travellers began to come up and pass them in vehicles of all descriptions. It was difficult to attract their attention in the dim light, but by standing on the top of a wall which fenced the road Bob was at last seen.

"What's the matter?" he cried to a butcher who was flying past in his cart, his wife sitting behind him without a bonnet.

"The French have landed!" said the man, without drawing rein.

"Where?" shouted Bob.

"In West Bay; and all Budmouth is in uproar!" replied the voice, now faint in the distance.

Bob and his father hastened on till they reached their own house. As they had expected, Anne and her mother, in common with most of the people, were both dressed, and stood at the door bonneted and shawled, listening to the traffic on the neighbouring highway, Mrs. Loveday having secured what money and small valuables they possessed in a huge pocket which extended all round her waist, and added considerably to her weight and diameter.

" 'Tis true enough," said the miller: "he's come! You and Anne and the maid must be off to Cousin Jim's at King's-Bere, and when you get there you must do as they do. I must assemble with the company."

"And I?" said Bob.

"Thou'st better run to the church, and take a pike before they be all gone."

The horse was put into the gig, and Mrs. Loveday, Anne, and the servant-maid were hastily packed into the vehicle, the latter taking the reins; David's duties as a fighting-man forbidding all thought of his domestic offices now. Then the silver tankard, teapot, pair of candlesticks like Ionic columns, and other articles too large to be pocketed were thrown into a basket and put up behind. Then came the leave-taking, which was as sad as it was hurried. Bob kissed Anne, and there was no affectation in her receiving that mark of affection as she said through her tears, "God bless you!" At last they moved off in the dim light of dawn, neither of the three women knowing which road they were to take, but trusting to chance to find it.

As soon as they were out of sight Bob went off for a pike, and his father, first new-flinting his firelock, proceeded to don his uniform, pipe-claying his breeches with such cursory haste as to bespatter his black gaiters with the same ornamental compound. Finding when he was ready that no bugle had as yet sounded, he went with David to the cart-house, dragged out the waggon, and put therein some of the most useful and easily-handled goods, in case there might be an opportunity for conveying them away. By the time this was done and the waggon pushed back and locked in, Bob had returned with his weapon, somewhat mortified at being doomed to this low form of defense. The miller gave his son a parting grasp of the hand, and arranged to meet him at King's-Bere at the first opportunity if the news were true; if happily false, here at their own house.

"Bother it all!" he exclaimed, looking at his stock of flints.

"What?" said Bob.

"I've got no ammunition: not a blessed round!"

"Then what's the use of going?" asked his son.

The miller paused. "O, I'll go," he said. "Perhaps somebody will lend me a little if I get into a hot corner."

"Lend ye a little! Father, you was always so simple!" said Bob reproachfully.

"Well—I can bagnet a few, anyhow," said the miller.

The bugle had been blown ere this, and Loveday the father disappeared towards the place of assembly, his empty cartridge-box behind him. Bob seized a brace of loaded pistols which he had brought home from the ship, and, armed with these and a pike, he locked the door and sallied out again towards the turnpike road.

By this time the yeomanry of the district were also on the move, and among them Festus Derriman, who was sleeping at his uncle's, and had been awakened by Cripplestraw. About the time when Bob and his father were descending from the beacon the stalwart yeoman was standing in the stable-yard adjusting his straps, while Cripplestraw saddled the horse. Festus clanked up and down, looked gloomily at the beacon, heard the retreating carts and carriages, and called Cripplestraw to him, who came from the stable leading the horse at the same moment that Uncle Benjy peeped unobserved from a mullioned window above their heads, the distant light of the beacon fire touching up his features to the complexion of an old brass clock-face.

"I think that before I start, Cripplestraw," said Festus, whose lurid visage was undergoing a bleaching process curious to look upon, "you shall go on to Budmouth, and make a bold inquiry whether the cowardly enemy is on shore as yet, or only looming in the bay."

"I'd go in a moment, sir," said the other, "if I hadn't my bad leg again. I should have joined my company afore this; but they said at last drill that I was too old. So I shall wait up in the hay-loft for tidings as soon as I have packed you off, poor gentleman!"

"Do such alarms as these, Cripplestraw, ever happen without foundation? Buonaparte is a wretch, a miserable wretch, and this may be only a false alarm to disappoint such as me?"

"O no, sir; O no!"

"But sometimes there are false alarms?"

"Well, sir, yes. There was a pretended sally o' gunboats last year."

"And was there nothing else pretended—something more like this, for instance?"

Cripplestraw shook his head. "I notice yer modesty, Mr. Festus, in making light of things. But there never was, sir. You may depend upon it he's come. Thank God, my duty as a Local don't require me to go to the front, but only the valiant men like my master. Ah, if Boney could only see 'ee now, sir, he'd know too well there is nothing to be got from such a determined skilful officer but blows and musketballs!"

"Yes, yes. Cripplestraw, if I ride off to Budmouth and meet 'em, all my training will be lost. No skill is required as a forlorn hope."

"True; that's a point, sir. You would outshine 'em all, and be picked off at the very beginning as a too-dangerous brave man."

"But if I stay here and urge on the faint-hearted ones, or get up into the turret-stair by that gateway, and pop at the invaders through the loophole, I shouldn't be so completely wasted, should I?"

"You would not, Mr. Derriman. But, as you was going to say next, the fire in yer veins won't let 'ee do that. You be valiant; very good: you don't want to husband yer valiance at home. The arg'ment is plain."

"If my birth had been more obscure," murmured the yeoman, "and I had only been in the militia, for instance, or among the humble pikemen, so much wouldn't have been expected of me—of my fiery nature. Cripplestraw, is there a drop of brandy to be got at in the house? I don't feel very well."

"Dear nephew," said the old gentleman from above, whom neither of the others had as yet noticed, "I haven't any spirits opened—so unfortunate! But there's a beautiful barrel of crab-apple cider in draught; and there's some cold tea from last night."

"What, is he listening?" said Festus, staring up. "Now I warrant how glad he is to see me forced to go—called out of bed without breakfast, and he quite safe, and sure to escape because he's an old man!—Cripplestraw, I like being in the yeomanry cavalry; but I wish I hadn't been in the ranks; I wish I had been only the surgeon, to stay in the rear while the bodies are brought back to him— I mean, I should have thrown my heart at such a time as this more into the labour of restoring wounded men and joining their shattered limbs together—u-u-ugh!—more than I can into causing the wounds—I am too humane, Cripplestraw, for the ranks!"

"Yes, yes," said his companion, depressing his spirits to a kindred level. "And yet, such is fate, that, instead of joining men's limbs together, you'll have to get your own joined—poor young sojer!—all through having such a warlike soul."

"Yes," murmured Festus, and paused. "You can't think how strange I feel here, Cripplestraw," he continued, laying his hand upon the centre buttons of his waistcoat. "How I do wish I was only the surgeon!"

He slowly mounted, and Uncle Benjy, in the meantime, sang to himself as he looked on, *"Twen-ty-three and half from N.W. Six-teen and three-quar-ters from N.E."*

"What's that old mummy singing?" said Festus savagely.

"Only a hymn for preservation from our enemies, dear nephew," meekly replied the farmer, who had heard the remark. *"Twen-ty-three and half from N.W."*

Festus allowed his horse to move on a few paces, and then turned again, as if struck by a happy invention. "Cripplestraw," he began, with an artificial laugh, "I am obliged to confess, after all—I must see her! 'Tisn't nature that makes me draw back—'tis love. I must go and look for her."

"A woman, sir?"

"I didn't want to confess it; but 'tis a woman. Strange that I should be drawn so entirely against my natural wish to rush at 'em!"

Cripplestraw, seeing which way the wind blew, found it advisable to blow in harmony. "Ah, now at last I see, sir! Spite that few men live that be worthy to command ye; spite that you could rush on, marshal the troops to victory,

as I may say; but then—what of it?—there's the unhappy
fate of being smit with the eyes of a woman, and you
are unmanned! Maister Derriman, who is himself when
he's got a woman round his neck like a millstone?"

"It is something like that."

"I feel the case. Be you valiant?—I know, of course,
the words being a matter of form—be you valiant, I ask?
Yes, of course. Then don't you waste it in the open field.
Hoard it up, I say, sir, for a higher class of war—the
defence of yer adorable lady. Think what you owe her
at this terrible time! Now, Maister Derriman, once more
I ask 'ee to cast off that first haughty wish to rush to
Budmouth, and to go where your mis'ess is defenceless
and alone."

"I will. Cripplestraw, now you put it like that!"

"Thank 'ee, thank 'ee heartily, Maister Derriman. Go
now and hide with her."

"But can I? Now, hang flattery!—can a man hide without a stain? Of course I would not hide in any mean
sense; no, not I!"

"If you be in love, 'tis plain you may, since it is not
your own life, but another's, that you are concerned for,
and you only save your own because it can't be helped."

" 'Tis true, Cripplestraw, in a sense. But will it be understood that way? Will they see it as a brave hiding?"

"Now, sir, if you had not been in love I own to 'ee
that hiding would look queer, but being to save the tears,
groans, fits, swowndings, and perhaps death of a comely
young woman, yer principle is good; you honourably retreat
because you be too gallant to advance. This sounds
strange, ye may say, sir; but it is plain enough to less fiery
minds."

Festus did for a moment try to uncover his teeth in
a natural smile, but it died away. "Cripplestraw, you flatter
me; or do you mean it? Well, there's truth in it. I am more
gallant in going to her than in marching to the shore.
But we cannot be too careful about our good names, we
soldiers. I must not be seen. I'm off."

Cripplestraw opened the hurdle which closed the arch
under the portico gateway, and Festus passed through,

Uncle Benjamin singing *Twen-ty-three and a half from N.W.* with a sort of sublime ecstasy, feeling, as Festus had observed, that his money was safe, and that the French would not personally molest an old man in such a ragged, mildewed coat as that he wore, which he had taken the precaution to borrow from a scarecrow in one of his fields for the purpose.

Festus rode on full of his intention to seek out Anne, and under cover of protecting her retreat accompany her to King's-Bere, where he knew the Lovedays had relatives. In the lane he met Granny Seamore, who, having packed up all her possessions in a small basket, was placidly retreating to the mountains till all should be over.

"Well, granny, have ye seen the French?" asked Festus.

"No," she said, looking up at him through her brazen spectacles. "If I had I shouldn't ha' seed thee!"

"Faugh!" replied the yeoman, and rode on. Just as he reached the old road, which he had intended merely to cross and avoid, his countenance fell. Some troops of regulars, who appeared to be dragoons, were rattling along the road. Festus hastened towards an opposite gate, so as to get within the field before they should see him; but, as ill-luck would have it, as soon as he got inside, a party of six or seven of his own yeomanry troop were straggling across the same field and making for the spot where he was. The dragoons passed without seeing him; but when he turned out into the road again it was impossible to retreat towards Overcombe village because of the yeomen. So he rode straight on, and heard them coming at his heels. There was no other gate, and the highway soon became as straight as a bowstring. Unable thus to turn without meeting them, and caught like an eel in a water-pipe, Festus drew nearer and nearer to the fateful shore. But he did not relinquish hope. Just ahead there were crossroads, and he might have a chance of slipping down one of them without being seen. On reaching the spot he found that he was not alone. A horseman had come up the right-hand lane and drawn rein. It was an officer of the German legion, and seeing Festus he held up his hand. Festus rode up to him and saluted.

"It ist false report!" said the officer.

Festus was a man again. He felt that nothing was too much for him. The officer, after some explanation of the cause of alarm, said that he was going across to the road which led by the moor, to stop the troops and volunteers converging from that direction, upon which Festus offered to give information along the Casterbridge road. The German crossed over, and was soon out of sight in the lane, while Festus turned back upon the way by which he had come. The party of yeomanry cavalry was rapidly drawing near, and he soon recognized among them the excited voices of Stubb of Duddle Hole, Noakes of Nether Moynton, and other comrades of his orgies at the hall. It was a magnificent opportunity, and Festus drew his sword. When they were within speaking distance he reined round his charger's head to Budmouth and shouted, "On, comrades, on! I am waiting for you. You have been a long time getting up with me, seeing the glorious nature of our deeds to-day!"

"Well said, Derriman, well said!" replied the foremost of the riders. "Have you heard anything new?"

"Only that he's here with his tens of thousands, and that we are to ride to meet him sword in hand as soon as we have assembled in the town ahead here."

"O Lord!" said Noakes, with a slight falling of the lower jaw.

"The man who quails now is unworthy of the name of yeoman," said Festus, still keeping ahead of the other troopers and holding up his sword to the sun. "O Noakes, fie, fie! You begin to look pale, man."

"Faith, perhaps you'd look pale," said Noakes, with an envious glance upon Festus's daring manner, "if you had a wife and family depending upon ye!"

"I'll take three frog-eating Frenchmen single-handed!" rejoined Derriman, still flourishing his sword.

"They have as good swords as you; as you will soon find," said another of the yeomen.

"If they were three times armed," said Festus—"ay, thrice three times—I would attempt 'em three to one. How do you feel now, my old friend Stubb?" (turning to another of the warriors). "O, friend Stubb! no bouncing health to our lady-loves in Oxwell Hall this summer as last. Eh, Brownjohn?"

"I am afraid not," said Brownjohn gloomily.

"No rattling dinners at Stacie's Hotel, and the King below with his staff. No wrenching off door-knockers and sending 'em to the bakehouse in a pie that nobody calls for. Weeks of cut-and-thrust work rather!"

"I suppose so."

"Fight how we may we shan't get rid of the cursed tyrant before autumn, and many thousand brave men will lie low before it's done," remarked a young yeoman with a calm face, who meant to do his duty without much talking.

"No grinning matches at Mai-dun Castle this summer," Festus resumed; "no thread-the-needle at Greenhill Fair, and going into shows and driving the showman crazy with cock-a-doodle-doo."

"I suppose not."

"Does it make you seem just a trifle uncomfortable, Noakes? Keep up your spirits, old comrade. Come, forward! we are only ambling on like so many donkey-women. We have to get into Budmouth, join the rest of the troop, and then march along the coast west'ard, as I imagine. At this rate we shan't be well into the thick of battle before twelve o'clock. Spur on, comrades. No dancing on the green, Lockham, this year in the moonlight! You was tender upon that girl; gad, what will become o' her in the struggle?"

"Come, come, Derriman," expostulated Lockham—"this is all very well, but I don't care for 't. I am as ready to fight as any man, but——"

"Perhaps when you get into battle, Derriman, and see what it's like, your courage will cool down a little," added Noakes on the same side, but with secret admiration of Festus's reckless bravery.

"I shall be bayoneted first," said Festus. "Now let's rally, and on!"

Since Festus was determined to spur on wildly, the rest

of the yeomen did not like to seem behindhand, and they rapidly approached the town. Had they been calm enough to reflect, they might have observed that for the last half-hour no carts or carriages had met them on the way, as they had done further back. It was not till the troopers reached the turnpike that they learnt what Festus had known a quarter of an hour before. At the intelligence Derriman sheathed his sword with a sigh; and the party soon fell in with comrades who had arrived there before them, whereupon the source and details of the alarm were boisterously discussed.

"What, didn't you know of the mistake till now?" asked one of these of the new-comers. "Why, when I was dropping over the hill by the cross-roads I looked back and saw that man talking to the messenger, and he must have told him the truth." The speaker pointed to Festus. They turned their indignant eyes full upon him. That he had sported with their deepest feelings, while knowing the rumour to be baseless, was soon apparent to all.

"Beat him black and blue with the flat of our blades!" shouted two or three, turning their horses' heads to drop back upon Derriman, in which move they were followed by most of the party.

But Festus, foreseeing danger from the unexpected revelation, had already judiciously placed a few intervening yards between himself and his fellow-yeomen, and now, clapping spurs to his horse, rattled like thunder and lightning up the road homeward. His ready flight added hotness to their pursuit, and as he rode and looked fearfully over his shoulder he could see them following with enraged faces and drawn swords, a position which they kept up for a distance of more than a mile. Then he had the satisfaction of seeing them drop off one by one, and soon he and his panting charger remained alone on the highway.

FROM *THE DYNASTS*

[First and Second Parts 1904;
Part Third, 1908]

Part First

FORE SCENE
THE OVERWORLD

Enter the Ancient Spirit and Chorus of the Years, the Spirit and Chorus of the Pities, the Shade of the Earth, the Spirits Sinister and Ironic with their Choruses, Rumours, Spirit-Messengers, and Recording Angels.

SHADE OF THE EARTH
What of the Immanent Will and Its designs?

SPIRIT OF THE YEARS
It works unconsciously, as heretofore,
Eternal artistries in Circumstance,
Whose patterns, wrought by rapt aesthetic rote,
Seem in themselves It's single listless aim,
And not their consequence.

CHORUS OF THE PITIES (aerial music)
Still thus? Still thus?
Ever unconscious!
An automatic sense
Unweeting why or whence?
Be, then, the inevitable, as of old,
Although that so it be we dare not hold!

SPIRIT OF THE YEARS
Hold what yet list, fond unbelieving Sprites,
You cannot swerve the pulsion of the Byss,
Which thinking on, yet weighing not Its thought,
Unchecks Its clock-like laws.

SPIRIT SINISTER (aside)

                 Good, as before.
My little engines, then, will still have play.

SPIRIT OF THE PITIES

Why doth It so and so, and ever so,
This viewless, voiceless Turner of the Wheel?

SPIRIT OF THE YEARS

As one sad story runs, It lends Its heed
To other worlds, being wearied out with this;
Wherefore Its mindlessness of earthly woes.
Some, too, have told at whiles that rightfully
Its warefulness, Its care, this planet lost
When in her early growth and crudity
By bad mad acts of severance men contrived,
Working such nescience by their own device.—
Yea, so it stands in certain chronicles,
Though not in mine.

SPIRIT OF THE PITIES

              Meet is it, none the less,
To bear in thought that though Its consciousness
May be estranged, engrossed afar, or sealed,
Sublunar shocks may wake Its watch anon?

SPIRIT OF THE YEARS

Nay. In the Foretime, even to the germ of Being,
Nothing appears of shape to indicate
That cognizance has marshalled things terrene,
Or will (such is my thinking) in my span.
Rather than show that, like a knitter drowsed,
Whose fingers play in skilled unmindfulness,
The Will has woven with an absent heed
Since life first was; and ever will so weave.

SPIRIT SINISTER

Hence we've rare dramas going—more so since
It wove Its web in that Ajaccian womb!

SPIRIT OF THE YEARS

Well, no more thus on what no mind can mete.
Our scope is but to register and watch
By means of this great gift accorded us—
The free trajection of our entities.

SPIRIT OF THE PITIES

On things terrene, then, I would say that though
The human news wherewith the Rumours stirred us
May please thy temper, Years, 'twere better far
Such deeds were nulled, and this strange man's career
Wound up, as making inharmonious jars
In her creation whose meek wraith we know.
The more that he, turned man of mere traditions,
Now profits naught. For the large potencies
Instilled into his idiosyncrasy—
To throne fair Liberty in Privilege' room—
Are taking taint, and sink to common plots
For his own gain.

SHADE OF THE EARTH

And who, then, Cordial One,
Wouldst substitute for this Intractable?

CHORUS OF THE PITIES (aerial music)

We would establish those of kindlier build,
In fair Compassions skilled,
Men of deep art in life-development;
Watchers and warders of thy varied lands,
Men surfeited of laying heavy hands
Upon the innocent,
The mild, the fragile, the obscure content
Among the myriads of thy family.
Those, too, who love the true, the excellent,
And make their daily moves a melody.

SHADE OF THE EARTH

They may come, will they. I am not averse.
Yet know I am but the ineffectual Shade
Of her the Travailler, herself a thrall
To It; in all her labourings curbed and kinged!

SPIRIT OF THE YEARS

Shall such be mooted now? Already change
Hath played strange pranks since first I brooded here.
But old Laws operate yet; and phase and phase
Of men's dynastic and imperial moils
Shape on accustomed lines. Though, as for me,
I care not how they shape, or what they be.

SPIRIT OF THE PITIES

You seem to have small sense of mercy, Sire?

SPIRIT OF THE YEARS

Mercy I view, not urge;—nor more than mark
What designate your titles Good and Ill.
'Tis not in me to feel with, or against,
These flesh-hinged mannikins Its hand upwinds
To click-clack off Its preadjusted laws;
But only through my centuries to behold
Their aspects, and their movements, and their mould.

SPIRIT OF THE PITIES

They are shapes that bleed, mere mannikins or no,
And each has parcel in the total Will.

SPIRIT OF THE YEARS

Which overrides them as a whole its parts
In other entities.

SPIRIT SINISTER (aside)
                Limbs of Itself:
Each one a jot of It in quaint disguise?
I'll fear all men henceforward!

SPIRIT OF THE PITIES

Go to. Let this terrestrial tragedy—

SPIRIT IRONIC

Nay, comedy—

SPIRIT OF THE PITIES
                Let this earth-tragedy
Whereof ye spake, afford a spectacle
Forthwith conned closelier than your custom is.—

SPIRIT OF THE YEARS

How does it stand?   (To a Recording Angel)

          Open and chant the page
Thou'st lately writ, that sums these happenings,
In brief reminder of their instant points
Slighted by us amid our converse here.

RECORDING ANGEL (from a book, in recitative)

Now mellow-eyed Peace is made captive,
    And Vengeance is chartered
To deal forth its dooms on the Peoples
    With sword and with spear.

Men's musings are busy with forecasts
    Of musters and battle,
And visions of shock and disaster
    Rise red on the year.

The easternmost ruler sits wistful,
    And tense he to midward;
The King to the west mans his borders
    In front and in rear.

While one they eye, flushed from his crowning,
    Ranks legions around him
To shake the enisled neighbour nation
    And close her career!

SEMICHORUS I OF RUMOURS (aerial music)

O woven-winged squadrons of Toulon
    And fellows of Rochefort,
Wait, wait for a wind, and draw westward
    Ere Nelson be near!

For he reads not your force, or your freightage
    Of warriors fell-handed,
Or when they will join for the onset,
    Or whither they steer!

SEMICHORUS II

O Nelson, so zealous a watcher
    Through months-long of cruizing,

Thy foes may elude thee a moment,
Put forth, and get clear;

And rendezvous westerly straightway
With Spain's aiding navies,
And hasten to head violation
Of Albion's frontier!

SPIRIT OF THE YEARS

Methinks too much assurance thrills your note
On secrets in my locker, gentle sprites;
But it may serve.—Our thought being now reflexed
To forces operant on this English isle,
Behoves it us to enter scene by scene,
And watch the spectacle of Europe's moves
In her embroil, as they were self-ordained
According to the naïve and liberal creed
Of our great-hearted young Compassionates,
Forgetting the Prime Mover of the gear,
As puppet-watchers him who pulls the strings.—
You'll mark the twitchings of this Bonaparte
As he with other figures foots his reel,
Until he twitch him into his lonely grave:
Also regard the frail ones that his flings
Have made gyrate like animalcula
In tepid pools.—Hence to the precinct, then,
And count as framework to the strategy
You architraves of sunbeam-smitten cloud.—
So may ye judge Earth's jackaclocks to be
Not fugled by one Will, but function-free.

The nether sky opens, and Europe is disclosed as a prone and emaciated figure, the Alps shaping like a backbone, and the branching mountain-chains like ribs, the peninsular plateau of Spain forming a head. Broad and lengthy lowlands stretch from the north of France across Russia like a grey-green garment hemmed by the Ural mountains and the glistening Arctic Ocean.

The point of view then sinks downwards through space, and draws near to the surface of the perturbed countries, where the peoples, distressed by events which they did not cause, are seen writhing, crawling, heaving, and vibrating in their various cities and nationalities.

SPIRIT OF THE YEARS (to the Spirit of the Pities)
As key-scene to the whole, I first lay bare
The Will-webs of thy fearful questioning;
For know that of my antique privileges
This gift to visualize the Mode is one
(Though by exhaustive strain and effort only).
See, then, and learn, ere my power pass again.

A new and penetrating light descends on the spectacle, enduing
men and things with a seeming transparency, and exhibiting as one
organism the anatomy of life and movement in all humanity and
vitalized matter included in the display.

SPIRIT OF THE PITIES (after a pause)
Amid this scene of bodies substantive
Strange waves I sight like winds grown visible,
Which bear men's forms on their innumerous coils,
Twining and serpentining round and through.
Also retracting threads like gossamers—
Except in being irresistible—
Which complicate with some, and balance all.

SPIRIT OF THE YEARS
These are the Prime Volitions,—fibrils, veins,
Will-tissues, nerves, and pulses of the Cause,
That heave throughout the Earth's compositure.
Their sum is like the lobule of a Brain
Evolving always that it wots not of;
A Brain whose whole connotes the Everywhere,
And whose procedure may but be discerned
By phantom eyes like ours; the while unguessed
Of those it stirs, who (even as ye do) dream
Their motions free, their orderings supreme;
Each life apart from each, with power to mete
Its own day's measures; balanced, self-complete;
Though they subsist but atoms of the One
Labouring through all, divisible from none;
But this no further now. Deem yet man's deeds self-done.

The anatomy of the Immanent Will disappears.

GENERAL CHORUS OF INTELLIGENCES (aerial music)
> *We'll close up Time, as a bird its van,*
> *We'll traverse Space, as spirits can,*
> *Link pulses severed by leagues and years,*
> *Bring cradles into touch with biers;*
> *So that the far-off Consequence appears*
> *Prompt at the heel of foregone Cause.—*
> *The Prime, that willed ere wareness was,*
> *Whose Brain perchance is Space, whose Thought its laws,*
> *Which we as threads and streams discern,*
> *We may but muse on, never learn.*

END OF THE FORE SCENE

ACT II

SCENE V

THE SAME: RAINBARROWS BEACON, EGDON HEATH

Night in mid-August of the same summer. A lofty ridge of heathland reveals itself dimly, terminating in an abrupt slope, at the summit of which are three tumuli. On the sheltered side of the most prominent of these stands a hut of turves with a brick chimney. In front are two ricks of fuel, one of heather and furze for quick ignition, the other of wood, for slow burning. Something in the feel of the darkness and in the personality of the spot imparts a sense of uninterrupted space around, the view by day extending from the cliffs of the Isle of Wight eastward to Blackdon Hill by Deadman's Bay westward, and south across the Valley of the Froom to the ridge that screens the Channel.

Two men with pikes loom up, on duty as beacon-keepers beside the ricks.

OLD MAN

Now, Jems Purchess, once more mark my words. Black'on is the point we've to watch, and not Kingsbere; and I'll tell 'ee for why. If he do land anywhere hereabout 'twill be inside Deadman's Bay, and the signal will straightway come from Black'on. But there thou'st stand, glowering and staring with all thy eyes at Kingsbere! I tell 'ee what 'tis, Jem Purchess, your brain is softening; and you be getting too old for business of state like ours!

YOUNG MAN

You've let your tongue wrack your few rames of good breeding, John.

OLD MAN

The words of my Lord-Lieutenant was, whenever you see Kingsbere-Hill Beacon fired to the eastward, or Black'on to the westward, light up; and keep your second fire burning for two hours. Was that our documents or was it not?

YOUNG MAN

I don't gainsay it. And so I keep my eye on Kingsbere, because that's most likely o' the two, says I.

OLD MAN

That shows the curious depths of your ignorance. However, I'll have patience, and say on. Didst ever larn geography?

YOUNG MAN

No. Nor no other corrupt practices.

OLD MAN

Tcht-tcht!—Well, I'll have patience, and put it to him in another form. Dost know the world is round—eh! I warrant doesn't!

YOUNG MAN

I warrant I do!

OLD MAN

How d'ye make that out, when th'st never been to school?

YOUNG MAN

I larned it at church, thank God.

OLD MAN

Church? What have God A'mighty got to do with profane knowledge? Beware that you baint blaspheming, Jems Purchess!

YOUNG MAN

I say I did, whether or no! 'Twas the zingers up in gallery that I had it from. They busted out that strong with "the round world and they that dwell therein," that we common fokes down under could do no less than believe 'em.

OLD MAN

Canst be sharp enough in the wrong place as usual—I warrant canst! However, I'll have patience with 'en, and say on!—Suppose, now, my hat is the world; and there, as might be, stands the Camp of Belong, where Boney is. The world goes round, so, and Belong goes round too. Twelve hours pass; round goes the world still—so. Where's Belong now?

A pause. Two other figures, a man's and a woman's, rise against the sky out of the gloom.

OLD MAN (shouldering his pike)

Who goes there? Friend or foe, in the King's name!

WOMAN

Piece o' trumpery! "Who goes" yourself! What d'ye talk o', John Whiting! Can't your eyes earn their living any longer, then, that you don't know your own neighbors? 'Tis Private Cantle of the Locals and his wife Keziar, down at Bloom's-End—who else should it be!

OLD MAN (lowering his pike)

A form o' words, Mis'ess Cantle, no more; ordained by his Majesty's Gover'ment to be spoke by all we on sworn duty for the defence o' the country. Strict rank-and-file rules is our only horn of salvation in these times.—But, my dear woman, why ever have ye come lumpering up to Rainbarrows at this time o' night?

WOMAN

We've been troubled with bad dreams, owing to the firing out at sea yesterday; and at last I could sleep no more, feeling sure that sommat boded of His coming. And I said to Cantle, I'll ray myself, and go up to Beacon, and ask if anything have been heard or seen to-night. And here we be.

OLD MAN

Not a sign or sound—all's as still as a churchyard. And how is your good man?

PRIVATE (advancing)

Clk! I be all right! I was in the ranks, helping to keep the ground at the review by the King this week. We was a wonderful sight—wonderful! The King said so again and again.—Yes, there was he, and there was I, though not daring to move a' eyebrow in the presence of Majesty. I have come home on a night's leave—off there again to-morrow. Boney's expected every day, the Lord be praised! Yes, our hopes are to be fulfilled soon, as we say in the army.

OLD MAN

There, there, Cantle; don't ye speak quite so large, and stand so over-upright. Your back is as holler as a fire-dog's. Do ye suppose that we on active service here don't know war news? Mind you don't go taking to your heels when the next alarm comes, as you did at last year's.

PRIVATE

That had nothing to do with fighting, for I'm as bold as a lion when I'm up, and "Shoulder Fawlocks!" sounds as common as my own name to me. 'Twas—— (Lowering his voice.) Have ye heard?

OLD MAN

To be sure we have.

PRIVATE

Ghastly, isn't it!

OLD MAN

Ghastly! Frightful!

YOUNG MAN (to Private)

He don't know what it is! That's his pride and puffery. What is it that's so ghastly—hey?

PRIVATE

Well, there, I can't tell it. 'Twas that that made the whole eighty of our company run away—though we be the bravest of the brave in natural jeopardies, or the little boys wouldn't run after us and call us the "Bang-up-Locals."

WOMAN (in undertones)

I can tell you a word or two on't. It is about His victuals. They say that He lives upon human flesh, and has rashers o' baby every morning for breakfast—for all the world like the Cernel Gant in old ancient times!

YOUNG MAN

Ye can't believe all ye hear.

PRIVATE

I only believe half. And I only own—such is my challengeful character—that perhaps He do eat pagan infants when He's in the desert. But not Christian ones at home. Oh no—'tis too much.

WOMAN

Whether or no, I sometimes—God forgive me!—laugh wi' horror at the queerness o't, till I am that weak I can hardly go round house. He should have the washing of 'em a few times; I warrant 'a wouldn't want to eat babies any more!

A silence, during which they gaze around at the dark dome of starless sky.

YOUNG MAN

There'll be a change in the weather soon, by the look o't. I can hear the cows moo in Froom Valley as if I were close to 'em, and the lantern at Max Turnpike is shining quite plain.

OLD MAN

Well, come in and taste a drop o' sommat we've got here, that will warm the cockles of your heart as ye wamble homealong. We housed eighty tubs last night for them that shan't be named—landed at Lullwind Cove the night afore, though they had a narrow shave with the riding-officers this run.

They make towards the hut, when a light on the west horizon becomes visible, and quickly enlarges.

YOUNG MAN

He's come!

OLD MAN

Come he is, though you do say it! This, then, is the beginning of what England's waited for!

They stand and watch the light awhile.

YOUNG MAN

Just what you was praising the Lord for by-now, Private Cantle.

PRIVATE

My meaning was——

WOMAN (simpering)

Oh that I hadn't married a fiery sojer, to make me bring fatherless children into the world, all through his dreadful calling! Why didn't a man of no sprawl content me!

OLD MAN (shouldering his pike)

We can't heed your innocent pratings any longer, good neighbours, being in the King's service, and a hot invasion on. Fall in, fall in, mate. Straight to the tinder-box. Quick march!

The two men hasten to the hut, and are heard striking a flint and steel. Returning with a lit lantern they ignite a wisp of furze, and with this set the first stack of fuel in a blaze. The private of the Locals and his wife hastily retreat by the light of the flaming beacon, under which the purple rotundities of the heath show like bronze, and the pits like the eye-sockets of a skull.

Part Second

ACT IV

SCENE VIII

WALCHEREN

A marshy island at the mouth of the Scheldt, lit by the low sunshine of an evening in late summer. The horizontal rays from the west lie in yellow sheaves across the vapours that the day's heat has drawn from the sweating soil. Sour grasses grow in places, and strange fishy smells, now warm, now cold, pass along. Brass-hued and opalescent bubbles, compounded of many gases, rise where passing feet have trodden the damper spots. At night the place is the haunt of the Jack-lantern.

DUMB SHOW

A vast army is encamped here, and in the open spaces are infantry on parade—skeletoned men, some flushed, some shivering, who are kept moving because it is dangerous to stay still. Every now and then one falls down, and is carried away to a hospital with no roof, where he is laid, bedless, on the ground.

In the distance soldiers are digging graves for the funerals which are to take place after dark, delayed till then that the sight of so many may not drive the living melancholy-mad. Faint noises are heard in the air.

SHADE OF THE EARTH

What storm is this of souls dissolved in sighs,
And what the dingy doom it signifies?

SPIRIT OF THE PITIES

We catch a lamentation shaped thuswise:

CHORUS OF PITIES (aerial music)

"We who withstood the blasting blaze of war
When marshalled by the gallant Moore awhile,
Beheld the grazing death-bolt with a smile,
Closed combat edge to edge and bore to bore,
          Now rot upon this Isle!

"The ever wan morass, the dune, the blear
Sandweed, and tepid pool, and putrid smell,
Emaciate purpose to a fractious fear,

Beckon the body to its last low cell—
   A chink no chart will tell.

"O ancient Delta, where the fen-lights flit!
Ignoble sediment of loftier lands,
Thy humour clings about our hearts and hands
And solves us to its softness, till we sit
   As we were part of it.

"Such force as fever leaves is maddened now,
With tidings trickling in from day to day
Of others' differing fortunes, wording how
They yield their lives to baulk a tyrant's sway—
   Yield them not vainly, they!

"In champaigns green and purple, far and near,
In town and thorpe where quiet spire-cocks turn,
Through vales, by rocks, beside the brooding burn
Echoes the aggressor's arrogant career;
   And we pent pithless here!

"Here, where each creeping day the creeping file
Draws past with shouldered comrades score on score,
Bearing them to their lightless last asile,
Where weary wave-wails from the clammy shore
   Will reach their ears no more.

"We might have fought, and had we died, died well,
Even if in dynasts' discords not our own;
Our death-spot some sad haunter might have shown,
Some tongue have asked our sires or sons to tell
   The tale of how we fell;

"But such bechanced not. Like the mist we fade,
No lustrous lines engrave in story we,
Our country's chiefs, for their own fames afraid,
Will leave our names and fates by this pale sea
   To perish silently!"

SPIRIT OF THE YEARS

Why must ye echo as mechanic mimes
These mortal minions' bootless cadences,

Played on the stops of their anatomy
As is the newling music on the strings
Of yonder ship-masts by the unweeting wind,
Or the frail tune upon this withering sedge
That holds its papery blades against the gale?
—Men pass to dark corruption, at the best,
Ere I can count five score: these why not now?—
The Immanent Shaper builds Its being so
Whether ye sigh their sighs with them or no!

The night fog enwraps the isle and the dying English army.

ACT V

SCENE II

PARIS. THE TUILERIES

The evening of the next day. A saloon of the Palace, with folding-doors communicating with a dining-room. The doors are flung open, revealing on the dining-table an untouched dinner, NAPOLÉON and JOSÉPHINE rising from it, and DE BAUSSET, chamberlain-in-waiting, pacing up and down. The EMPEROR and EMPRESS come forward into the saloon, the latter pale and distressed, and patting her eyes with her handkerchief.

The doors are closed behind them; a page brings in coffee; NAPOLÉON signals to him to leave. JOSÉPHINE goes to pour out the coffee, but NAPOLÉON pushes her aside and pours it out himself, looking at her in a way which causes her to sink cowering into a chair like a frightened animal.

JOSÉPHINE
I see my doom, my friend, upon your face!

NAPOLÉON
You see me bored by Cambacérès' ball.

JOSÉPHINE
It means divorce!—a thing more terrible
Than carrying elsewhere the dalliances
That formerly were mine. I kicked at that;
But now agree, as I for long have done,
To any infidelities of act
May I be yours in name!

NAPOLÉON

                    My mind must bend
To other things than our domestic pettings:
The Empire orbs above our happiness,
And 'tis the Empire dictates this divorce.
I reckon on your courage and calm sense
To breast with me the law's formalities,
And get it through before the year has flown.

JOSÉPHINE

But are you *really* going to part from me?
O no, no, my dear husband; no, in truth,
It cannot be my Love will serve me so!

NAPOLÉON

I mean but mere divorcement, as I said,
On simple grounds of sapient sovereignty.

JOSÉPHINE

But nothing have I done save good to you:—
Since the fond day we wedded into one
I never even have *thought* you jot of harm!
Many the happy junctures when you have said
I stood as guardian-angel over you,
As your Dame Fortune, too, and endless things
Of such-like pretty tenor—yes, you have!
Then how can you so gird against me now?
You had not pricked me with it much of late,
And so I hoped and hoped the ugly spectre
Had been laid dead and still.

NAPOLÉON (impatiently)

                    I tell you, dear,
The thing's decreed, and even the princess chosen.

JOSÉPHINE

Ah—so—the princess chosen! . . . I surmise
It is none else than the Grand-Duchess Anne:
Gossip was right—though I would not believe.
She's young; but no great beauty!—Yes, I see

Her silly, soulless eyes and horrid hair;
In which new gauderies you'll forget sad me!

NAPOLÉON

Upon my soul you are childish, Joséphine:
A woman of your years to pout it so!—
I say it's not the Tsar's Grand-Duchess Anne.

JOSÉPHINE

Some other Fair, then. You whose name can nod
The flower of all the world's virginity
Into your bed, will well take care of that!
(Spitefully.)   She may not have a child, friend, after all.

NAPOLÉON (drily)

You hope she won't, I know!—But don't forget
Madame Walewska did, and had she shown
Such cleverness as yours, poor little fool,
Her withered husband might have been displaced,
And her boy made my heir.—Well, let that be.
The severing parchments will be signed by us
Upon the fifteenth, prompt.

JOSÉPHINE

                              What—I have to sign
My putting away upon the fifteenth next?

NAPOLÉON

Ay—both of us.

JOSÉPHINE (falling on her knees)
                    So far advanced—so far!
Fixed?—for the fifteenth? O I do implore you,
My very dear one, by our old, old love,
By my devotion, don't, don't cast me off
Now, after these long years!

NAPOLÉON

                    Heavens, how you jade me!
Must I repeat that I don't cast you off;
We merely formally arrange divorce—
We live and love, but call ourselves divided.

A silence.

JOSÉPHINE (with sudden calm)

Very well. Let it be. I must submit!   (Rises.)

NAPOLÉON

And this much likewise you must promise me,
To act in the formalities thereof
As if you shaped them of your own free will.

JOSÉPHINE

How can I—when no free will's left in me?

NAPOLÉON

You are a willing party—do you hear?

JOSÉPHINE (quivering)

I hardly—can—bear this!—It is—too much
For a poor weak and broken woman's strength!
But—but I yield!—I am so helpless now;
I give up all—ay, kill me if you will,
I won't cry out!

NAPOLÉON

And one thing further still,
You'll help me in my marriage overtures
To win the Duchess—Austrian Marie she,—
Concentring all your force to forward them.

JOSÉPHINE

It is the—last humiliating blow!—
I cannot—O, I will not!

NAPOLÉON (fiercely)
But you *shall!*
And from your past experience you may know
That what I say I mean!

JOSÉPHINE (breaking into sobs)

O my dear husband—do not make me—don't!
If you but cared for me—the hundredth part
Of how—I care for you, you could not be
So cruel as to lay this torture on me.

It hurts me so!—it cuts me like a sword.
Don't make me, dear! Don't, will you! O, O, O!

(She sinks down in a hysterical fit.)

NAPOLÉON (calling)

Bausset!

Enter DE BAUSSET, Chamberlain-in-waiting.

Bausset, come in and shut the door.
Assist me here. The Empress has fallen ill.
Don't call for help. We two can carry her
By the small private staircase to her rooms.
Here—I will take her feet.

They lift JOSÉPHINE between them and carry her out. Her moans
die away as they recede towards the stairs.

Enter two servants, who remove coffee-service, readjust chairs, etc.

FIRST SERVANT

So, poor old girl, she's wailed her *Miserere Mei*, as
Mother Church says. I knew she was to get the sack ever
since he came back.

SECOND SERVANT

Well, there will be a little civil huzzaing, a little crowing
and cackling among the Bonapartes at the downfall of the
Beauharnais family at last, mark me there will! They've
had their little hour, as the poets say, and now 'twill be
somebody else's turn. O it is droll! Well, Father Time is a
great philosopher, if you take him right. Who is to be the
new woman?

Part Third

ACT I

SCENE X

THE BRIDGE OF THE BERESINA

The bridge is over the Beresina at Studzianka. On each side of the river are swampy meadows, now hard with frost, while further back are dense forests. Ice floats down the deep black stream in large cakes.

DUMB SHOW

The French sappers are working up to their shoulders in the water at the building of the bridge. Those so immersed work till, stiffened with ice to immobility, they die from the chill, when others succeed them.

Cavalry meanwhile attempt to swim their horses across, and some infantry try to wade through the stream.

Another bridge is begun hard by, the construction of which advances with greater speed; and it becomes fit for the passage of carriages and artillery.

NAPOLÉON is seen to come across to the homeward bank, which is the foreground of the scene. A good portion of the army also, under DAVOUT, NEY, and OUDINOT, lands by degrees on this side. But VICTOR'S corps is yet on the left or Moscow side of the stream, moving towards the bridge, and PARTONNEAUX with the rear-guard, who has not yet crossed, is at Borissow, some way below, where there is an old permanent bridge partly broken.

Enter with speed from the distance the Russians under TCHAPLITZ. More under TCHICHAGOFF enter the scene down the river on the left or further bank, and cross by the old bridge of Borissow. But they are too far from the new crossing to intercept the French as yet.

PLATOFF with his Cossacks next appears on the stage which is to be such a tragic one. He comes from the forest and approaches the left bank likewise. So also does WITTGENSTEIN, who strikes in between the uncrossed VICTOR and PARTONNEAUX. PLATOFF thereupon descends on the latter, who surrenders with the rear-guard; and thus seven thousand more are cut off from the already emaciated Grand Army.

TCHAPLITZ, of TCHICHAGOFF'S division, has meanwhile got round by the old bridge at Borissow to the French side of the new one, and attacks OUDINOT; but he is repulsed with the strength of despair. The French lose a further five thousand in this.

We now look across the river at VICTOR and his division, not yet over, and still defending the new bridges. WITTGENSTEIN descends upon him; but he holds his ground.

The determined Russians set up a battery of twelve cannon, so as to command the two new bridges, with the confused crowd of soldiers, carriages, and baggage, pressing to cross. The battery discharges into the surging multitude. More Russians come up, and, forming a semicircle round the bridges and the mass of French, fire yet more hotly on them with round shot and canister. As it gets dark the flashes light up the strained faces of the fugitives. Under the discharge and the weight of traffic, the bridge for the artillery gives way, and the throngs upon it roll shrieking into the stream and are drowned.

SEMICHORUS I OF THE PITIES (aerial music).

So loudly swell their shrieks as to be heard above
the roar of guns and the wailful wind,
Giving in one brief cry their last wild word on
the mock life through which they have harlequined!

SEMICHORUS II

To the other bridge the living heap betakes itself,
the weak pushed over by the strong;
They loop together by their clutch like snakes;
in knots they are submerged and borne along.

CHORUS

Then women are seen in the waterflow—limply
bearing their infants between wizened white arms
stretching above;
Yet, motherhood, sheerly sublime in her last
despairing, and lighting her darkest declension with
limitless love.

Meanwhile TCHICHAGOFF has come up with his twenty-seven thousand men, and falls on OUDINOT, NEY, and "the Sacred Squadron." Altogether we see forty or fifty thousand assailing eighteen thousand half-naked, badly armed wretches, emaciated with hunger and encumbered with several thousands of sick, wounded, and stragglers.

VICTOR and his rear-guard, who have protected the bridges all day, come over themselves at last. No sooner have they done so than the final bridge is set on fire. Those who are upon it burn or drown; those who are on the further side have lost their last chance, and perish either in attempting to wade the stream or at the hands of the Russians.

SEMICHORUS I OF THE PITIES (aerial music).

What will be seen in the morning light?
What will be learnt when the spring breaks bright,
And the frost unlocks to the sun's soft sight?

SEMICHORUS II

Death in a thousand motley forms;
Charred corpses hooking each other's arms
In the sleep that defies all war's alarms!

CHORUS

Pale cysts of souls in every stage,
Still bent to embraces of love or rage,—
Souls passed to where History pens no page.

The flames of the burning bridge go out as it consumes to the water's edge, and darkness mantles all, nothing continuing but the purl of the river and the clickings of floating ice.

SCENE XI

THE OPEN COUNTRY BETWEEN SMORGONI AND WILNA

The winter is more merciless, and snow continues to fall upon a deserted expanse of unenclosed land in Lithuania. Some scattered birch bushes merge in a forest in the background.

It is growing dark, though nothing distinguishes where the sun sets. There is no sound except that of a shuffling of feet in the direction of a bivouac. Here are gathered tattered men like skeletons. Their noses and ears are frost-bitten, and pus is oozing from their eyes.

These stricken shades in a limbo of gloom are among the last survivors of the French army. Few of them carry arms. One squad, ploughing through snow above their knees, and with icicles dangling from their hair that clink like glass-lustres as they walk, go into the birch wood, and are heard chopping. They bring back boughs, with which they make a screen on the windward side, and contrive to light a fire. With their swords they cut rashers from a dead horse, and grill them in the flames, using gunpowder for salt to eat them with. Two others return from a search, with a dead rat and some candle-ends. Their meal shared, some try to repair their gaping shoes and to tie up their feet, that are chilblained to the bone.

A straggler enters, who whispers to one or two soldiers of the group. A shudder runs through them at his words.

FIRST SOLDIER (dazed)

What—gone, do you say? Gone?

STRAGGLER

Yes, I say gone!
He left us at Smorgoni hours ago.
The Sacred Squadron even he has left behind.
By this time he's at Warsaw or beyond,
Full pace for Paris.

SECOND SOLDIER (jumping up wildly)
                Gone? How did he go?
No, surely! He could not desert us so!

STRAGGLER

He started in a carriage, with Roustan
The Mameluke on the box: Caulaincourt, too,
Was inside with him. Mouton and Duroc
Rode on a sledge behind.—the order bade
That we should not be told it for a while.

Other soldiers spring up as they realize the news, and stamp
hither and thither, impotent with rage, grief, and despair, many in
their physical weakness sobbing like children.

SPIRIT SINISTER

*Good. It is the selfish and unconscionable characters
who are so much regretted.*

STRAGGLER

He felt, or feigned, he ought to leave no longer
A land like Prussia 'twixt himself and home.
There was great need for him to go, he said,
To quiet France, and raise another army
That shall replace our bones.

SEVERAL (distractedly)
                Deserted us!
Deserted us!—O, after all our pangs
We shall see France no more!

Some become insane, and go dancing round. One of them sings.

MAD SOLDIER'S SONG

I

Ha, for the snow and hoar!
Ho, for our fortune's made!
We can shape our bed without sheets to spread,
    And our graves without a spade.
So foolish Life adieu,
And ingrate Leader too.
—Ah, but we loved you true!

Yet—he-he-he! and ho-ho-ho!—
　　We'll never return to you.

II

　　What can we wish for more?
　　Thanks to the frost and flood
We are grinning crones—thin bags of bones
　　Who once were flesh and blood.
　　So foolish Life adieu,
　　And ingrate Leader too.
　　—Ah, but we loved you true!
Yet—he-he-he! and ho-ho-ho!—
　　We'll never return to you.

Exhausted, they again crouch round the fire. Officers and privates press together for warmth. Other stragglers arrive, and sit at the backs of the first. With the progress of the night the stars come out in unusual brilliancy, Sirius and those in Orion flashing like stilettos; and the frost stiffens.

The fire sinks and goes out; but the Frenchmen do not move. The day dawns, and still they sit on.

In the background enter some light horse of the Russian army, followed by KUTÚZOF himself and a few of his staff. He presents a terrible appearance now—bravely serving though slowly dying, his face puffed with the intense cold, his one eye staring out as he sits in a heap in the saddle, his head sunk into his shoulders. The whole detachment pauses at the sight of the French asleep. They shout; but the bivouackers give no sign.

KUTÚZOF

Go, stir them up! We slay not sleeping men.

The Russians advance and prod the French with their lances.

RUSSIAN OFFICER

Prince, here's a curious picture. They are dead.

KUTÚZOF (with indifference)

Oh, naturally. After the snow was down
I marked a sharpening of the air last night.
We shall be stumbling on such frost-baked meats
Most of the way to Wilna.

OFFICER (examining the bodies)

　　　　　　　　　They all sit
As they were living still, but stiff as horns;
And even the colour has not left their cheeks;

Whereon the tears remain in strings of ice.——
It was a marvel they were not consumed:
Their clothes are cindered by the fire in front,
While at their back the frost has caked them hard.

KUTÚZOF

'Tis well. So perish Russia's enemies!

Exeunt KUTÚZOF, *his staff, and the detachment of horse in the direction of Wilna; and with the advance of day the snow resumes its fall, slowly burying the dead bivouackers.*

ACT VII

SCENE IX

THE WOOD OF BOSSU

It is midnight. NAPOLÉON *enters a glade of the wood, a solitary figure on a jaded horse, The shadows of the boughs travel over his listless form as he moves along. The horse chooses its own path, comes to a standstill, and feeds. The tramp of* BERTRAND, SOULT, DROUOT, *and* LOUBAU's *horses, gone forward in hope to find a way of retreat, is heard receding over the hill.*

NAPOLÉON (to himself, languidly)

Here should have been some troops of Gérard's corps,
Left to protect the passage of the convoys,
Yet they, too, fail. . . . I have nothing more to lose,
But life!

Flocks of fugitive soldiers pass along the adjoining road without seeing him. NAPOLÉON's *head droops lower and lower as he sits listless in the saddle, and he falls into a fitful sleep. The moon shines upon his face, which is drawn and waxen.*

SPIRIT OF THE YEARS

"Sic diis immortalibus placet,"——
"Thus is it pleasing to the immortal gods,"
As earthlings used to say. Thus, to this last,
The Will in thee has moved thee, Bonaparte,
As we say now.

NAPOLÉON (starting)

Whose frigid tones are those,
Breaking upon my lurid loneliness

So brusquely? . . . Yet, 'tis true, I have ever known
That such a Will I passively obeyed!

[He drowses again.

SPIRIT IRONIC

Nothing care I for these high-doctrined dreams,
And shape the case in quite a common way,
So I would ask, Ajaccian Bonaparte,
Has all this been worth while?

NAPOLÉON

O hideous hour,
Why am I stung by spectral questionings?
Did not my clouded soul incline to match
Those of the corpses yonder, thou should'st rue
Thy saying, Fiend, whoever thou may'st be! . . .
    Why did the death-drops fail to bite me close
I took at Fontainebleau? Had I then ceased,
This deep had been unplumbed; had they but worked,
I had thrown threefold the glow of Hannibal
Down History's dusky lanes!—Is it too late? . . .
Yes. Self-sought death would smoke but damply here!
    If but a Kremlin cannon-shot had met me
My greatness would have stood: I should have scored
A vast repute, scarce paralleled in time.
As it did not, the fates had served me best
If in the thick and thunder of to-day,
Like Nelson, Harold, Hector, Cyrus, Saul,
I had been shifted from this jail of flesh,
To wander as a greatened ghost elsewhere.
—Yes, a good death, to have died on yonder field;
But never a ball came passing down my way!
    So, as it is, a miss-mark they will dub me;
And yet—I found the crown of France in the mire,
And with the point of my prevailing sword
I picked it up! But for all this and this
I shall be nothing. . . .
To shoulder Christ from out the topmost niche
In human fame, as once I fondly felt,

Was not for me. I came too late in time
To assume the prophet or the demi-god,
A part past playing now. My only course
To make good showance to posterity
Was to implant my line upon the throne.
And how shape that, if now extinction nears?
Great men are meteors that consume themselves
To light the earth. This is my burnt-out hour.

SPIRIT OF THE YEARS
Thou sayest well. Thy full meridian-shine
Was in the glory of the Dresden days,
When well-nigh every monarch throned in Europe
Bent at thy footstool.

NAPOLÉON
                    Saving always England's—
Rightly dost say "well-nigh."—Not England's,—she
Whose tough, enisled, self-centered, kindless craft
Has tracked me, springed me, thumbed me by the throat,
And made herself the means of mangling me!

SPIRIT IRONIC
Yea, the dull peoples and the Dynasts both,
Those counter-castes not oft adjustable,
Interests antagonistic, proud and poor,
Have for the nonce been bonded by a wish
To overthrow thee.

SPIRIT OF THE PITIES
                    Peace. His loaded heart
Bears weight enough for one bruised, blistered while!

SPIRIT OF THE YEARS
Worthless these kneadings of thy narrow thought,
Napoléon; gone they opportunity!
Such men as thou, who wade across the world
To make an epoch, bless, confuse, appal,
Are in the elemental ages' chart
Like meanest insects on obscurest leaves
But incidents and grooves of Earth's unfolding;

Or as the brazen rod that stirs the fire
Because it must.

The moon sinks, and darkness blots out NAPOLÉON and the scene.

AFTER SCENE

THE OVERWORLD

Enter the Spirit and Chorus of the Years, the Spirit and Chorus of the Pities, the Shade of the Earth, the Spirits Sinister and Ironic with their Choruses, Rumours, Spirit-messengers and Recording Angels.

Europe has now sunk netherward to its far-off position as in the Fore Scene, and it is beheld again as a prone and emaciated figure of which the Alps form the vertebræ, and the branching mountain-chains the ribs, the Spanish Peninsula shaping the head of the écorché. The lowlands look like a grey-green garment half-thrown off, and the sea around like a disturbed bed on which the figure lies.

SPIRIT OF THE YEARS

Thus doth the Great Foresightless mechanize
In blank entrancement now as evermore
Its ceaseless artistries in Circumstance
Of curious stuff and braid, as just forthshown.

Yet but one flimsy riband of Its web
Have we here watched in weaving—web Enorm,
Whose furthest hem and selvage may extend
To where the roars and plashings of the flames
Of earth-invisible suns swell noisily,
And onwards into ghastly gulfs of sky,
Where hideous presences churn through the dark—
Monsters of magnitude without a shape,
Hanging amid deep wells of nothingness.
Yet seems this vast and singular confection
Wherein our scenery glints of scantest size,
Inutile all—so far as reasonings tell.

SPIRIT OF THE PITIES

Thou arguest still the Inadvertent Mind.—
But, even so, shall blankness be for aye?
Men gained cognition with the flux of time,
And wherefore not the Force informing them,

When far-range aions past all fathoming
Shall have swung by, and stand as backward years?

SPIRIT OF THE YEARS
What wouldst have hoped and had the Will to be?—
How wouldst have pæaned It, if what hadst dreamed
Thereof were truth, and all my showings dream?

SPIRIT OF THE PITIES
The Will that fed my hope was far from thine,
One I would thus have hymned eternally:—

SEMICHORUS I OF THE PITIES (aerial music)
To Thee whose eye all Nature owns,
Who hurlest Dynasts from their thrones,
And liftest those of low estate
We sing, with Her men consecrate!

SEMICHORUS II
Yea, Great and Good, Thee, Thee we hail,
Who shak'st the strong, Who shield'st the frail,
Who hadst not shaped such souls as we
If tendermercy lacked in Thee!

SEMICHORUS I
Though times be when the mortal moan
Seems unascending to Thy throne,
Though seers do not as yet explain
Why Suffering sobs to Thee in vain;

SEMICHORUS II
We hold that Thy unscanted scope
Affords a food for final Hope,
That mild-eyed Prescience ponders nigh
Life's loom, to lull it by-and-by.

SEMICHORUS I
Therefore we quire to highest height
The Wellwiller, the kindly Might
That balances the Vast for weal,
That purges as by wounds to heal.

SEMICHORUS II

The systemed suns the skies enscoll
Obey Thee in their rhythmic roll,
Ride radiantly at Thy command,
Are darkened by Thy Masterhand!

SEMICHORUS I

And these pale panting multitudes
Seen surging here, their moils, their moods,
All shall "fulfil their joy" in Thee
In Thee abide eternally!

SEMICHORUS II

Exultant adoration give
The Alone, through Whom all living live,
The Alone, in Whom all dying die,
Whose means the End shall justify! Amen.

SPIRIT OF THE PITIES

So did we evermore sublimely sing;
So would we now, despise they forthshowing!

SPIRIT OF THE YEARS

Something of difference animates your quiring,
O half-convinced Compassionates and fond,
From chords consistent with our spectacle!
You almost charm my long philosophy
Out of my strong-built thought, and bear me back
To when I thanksgave thus. . . . Ay, start not, Shades;
In the Foregone I knew what dreaming was,
And could let raptures rule! But not so now.
Yea. I psalmed thus and thus. . . . But not so now.

SEMICHORUS I OF THE YEARS (aerial music)

O Immanence, That reasonest not
In putting forth all things begot,
Thou build'st Thy house in space—for what?

SEMICHORUS II

O Loveless, Hateless!—past the sense
Of kindly eyed benevolence,
To what tune danceth this Immense?

SPIRIT IRONIC

For one I cannot answer. But I know
'Tis handsome of our Pities so to sing
The praises of the dreaming, dark, dumb Thing
That turns the handle of this idle Show!
As once a Greek asked I would fain ask too,
Who knows if all the Spectacle be true,
Or an illusion of the gods (the Will,
To wit) some hocus-pocus to fulfil?

SEMICHORUS I OF THE YEARS (aerial music)

Last as first the question rings
Of the Will's long travailings;
Why the All-mover,
Why the All-prover
Ever urgest on and measures out the chordless chime of
Things.

SEMICHORUS II

Heaving dumbly
As we deem,
Moulding numbly
As in dream,
Apprehending not how fare the sentient subjects of
Its scheme.

SEMICHORUS I OF THE PITIES

Nay;—shall not Its blindness break?
Yea, must not Its heart awake,
Promptly tending
· To Its mending
In a genial germing purpose, and for loving
kindness' sake?

SEMICHORUS II

Should It never
Curb or cure
Aught whatever
Those endure
Whom It quickens, let them darkle to extinction swift
and sure.

CHORUS
But—a stirring thrills the air
Like to sounds of joyance there
That the rages
Of the ages
Shall be cancelled, and deliverance offered from the
darts that were,
Consciousness the Will informing, till it fashion
all things fair!

THE END OF "THE DYNASTS"

September 25, 1907.

ᕦᕤᕦᕤᕦᕤᕦᕤᕦᕤᕦᕤᕦᕤᕦᕤᕦᕤᕦᕤᕦᕤᕦᕤ

TWO LETTERS TO *THE TIMES* ABOUT *THE DYNASTS*

The Dynasts: A Rejoinder [1]

[*The Times Literary Supplement*,
February 5, 1904, pp. 36–37]

TO THE EDITOR OF *The Times:*

SIR, The objections raised by your dramatic critic to the stage-form adopted in *The Dynasts* for presenting a rapid mental vision of the Napoleonic wars—objections which I had in some degree anticipated in the preface to the book —seem to demand a reply, inasmuch as they involve a question of literary art that is of far wider importance than as it affects a single volume. I regret that in the space of a letter I shall only be able to touch upon it briefly.

Your critic is as absolute as the gravedigger in *Hamlet*. I understand his contention to be that to give a panoramic poem (which *The Dynasts* may perhaps be called) the form of a stage-drama—even a conventionalized form—or to give such a form to anything whatever that is intended for the study only, is false in principle. Whether the aim of *The Dynasts* was to dumbfound the worthy burgher (as your critic surmises in the French tongue) or not, his theory certainly does dumbfound, or, as he would say, *épate*, the present writer. According to it one must conclude that such productions as Shelley's *Prometheus Unbound*, Byron's *Cain*, and many other unactable play-like poems are a waste of means, and, in his own words, "may be read just as, *faute de mieux*, shoe-leather may be used as an article of diet."

His view would seem to be based on an assumption that in no circumstances must an art borrow the methods of a neighbour art. Yet if there is one thing needful to the vitality of any art it is the freedom of the worker therein from the restraint of such scientific reasoning as would lay down this law, freedom from the *rationale* of every development that he adopts. The artistic spirit is at bottom a spirit of caprice, and in some of its finest productions in the past it could have given no clear reason why they were run in this or that particular mould, and not in some more obvious one. And if it could be proved that in *The Dynasts* nothing is gained, but much lost, by its form, that attempt would still have been legitimate.

Nevertheless, if your reviewer's statement that the stage-form is inherently an unnatural one for reading, a waste of available means, were strictly accurate, I would concede to him the expediency, though not the obligation, of avoiding it in a book. But why, one asks, is it bad for reading? Because, I understand him to answer, it was invented for the stage. He might as well assert that bitter ale is bad drinking for England because it was invented for India. His critical hand is, indeed, subdued to what it works in when he pens such a theory. It surely ought to have occurred to him that this play-shape is essentially, if not quite literally, at one with the instinctive, primitive, narrative shape. In legends and old ballads, in the telling of "an owre true tale" by country-folks on winter nights over a dying fire, the place and time are briefly indicated at the beginning in almost all cases; and then the body of the story follows as what he said and what she said, the action being often suggested by the speeches alone. This likeness between the order of natural recital and the order of theatrical utility may be accidental; but there it is; and to write Scene so-and-so, Time so-and-so, instead of Once upon a time, At such a place, is a trifling variation that makes no difference to the mental images raised. Of half-a-dozen people I have spoken to about reading plays, four say that they can imagine the enactment in a read play better than in a read novel or epic poem. It is a matter of idiosyncrasy.

The methods of a book and the methods of a play, which he says are so different, are fundamentally similar. It must be remembered that the printed story is not a representation, but, like the printed play, a means of producing a representation, which is done in the one case by sheer imaginativeness, in the other by imaginativeness pieced out with material helps. Why, then, should not a somewhat idealized semblance of the latter means be used in the former case?

For a rather digressive reason your reviewer drags in the art of architecture. In mercy to his own argument he should have left architecture alone. Like those of a play for reading, its features are continually determined by no mechanical, material, or methodic necessities (which are confused together by your critic). As for mechanical necessities, that purest relic of Greek architecture, the Parthenon, is a conventionalized representation of the necessities of a timber house, many of which are not necessities in stone, such as the imitations of wood rafter-ends, beam-ends, and ceiling-joists. As for necessities of purpose, medieval architects constructed church-parapets with the embrasures of those of a fortress, and on the Continent planned the eastern ends of their Cathedrals in resemblance of a Roman Hall of Justice. In respect of necessities of method, that art, throughout its history, has capriciously subdued to its service, in sheer waywardness, the necessities of other arts, so that one can find in it a very magazine of examples of my own procedure in *The Dynasts*. Capitals, cornices, bosses, and scores of other details, instead of confining their shapes to those strictly demanded by their office, borrow from the art of sculpture without scruple and without reason. Sculptured human figures are boldly taken, and, by the name of caryatids, are used as columns. In sculpture itself we find the painter's "necessity" borrowed—a superficies—and used for bas-reliefs, even though shapes are misrepresented by so doing. And if we turn to poetry we find that rhythm and rhyme are a non-necessitous presentation of language under conditions that in strictness appertain only to music.

But analogies between the arts are apt to be misleading, and having said thus much in defence of the form chosen, even supposing another to have been available, I have no room left for more than a bare assertion that there was available no such other form that would readily allow of the necessary compression of space and time. I believe that any one who should sit down and consider at leisure how to present so wide a subject within reasonable compass would decide that this was, broadly speaking, the only way.

Before concluding I should like to correct a misapprehension of your critic's, and of others, that I have "hankerings after actual performance" of *The Dynasts*. My hankerings, if any, do not lie that way. But I fancy his do. His laborious search in cyclopaedias for some means of performing it plainly betray that he is dying to see the show; which is flattering. But if he will look again at the last paragraph of the preface he will perceive that my remarks on performance refer to old English dramas only.

Your obedient servant,

Max Gate, Dorset, Feb. 2.   THOMAS HARDY.

The Dynasts: A Postscript [2]

[*The Times Literary Supplement,*
February 19, 1904, p. 53]

To the Editor of *The Times:*

Sir,—Your critic has humorously conducted his discourse
away from his original charge against *The Dynasts* into
the quaint and unexpected channel of real performance by
means of fantoccini, Chinese shadows, and other startling
apparatus. This is highly creditable to his ingenious mind;
yet we must remember that the whole fabric of his vision
arose only out of his altruistic desire to provide me with a
means of escape from what he holds to be an untenable
position. But I still absolutely deny it to be such, though
I may seem ungrateful. I think I have shown that an
attempt to write a spectacular poem (if he will allow me
to use the expression for want of a better), more or less
resembling a stage-play, though not one, has full artistic
justification and is not "false in principle," as he stated.
He naturally continues to think the other way; and there
I fear the matter must remain.

But the truth seems to be—if I may say a final word
here on a point outside the immediate discussion—that the
real offence of *The Dynasts* lies, not in its form as such,
but in the philosophy which gave rise to the form. This is
revealed by symptoms in various quarters, even (if I am
not mistaken) by your critic's own faint tendency to harden
his heart against the "Immanent Will." Worthy British
Philistia, unlike that ancient Athens it professes to admire,
not only does not ask for a new thing, but even shies at
that which merely appears at first sight to be a new thing.
As with a certain King, the reverse of worthy, in the case
of another play, some people ask, "Have you read the
argument? Is there no offence in't? There can hardly be,
assuredly, on a fair examination. The philosophy of *The*

Dynasts, under various titles and phases, is almost as old as civilization. Its fundamental principle, under the name of Predestination, was preached by St. Paul. "Being predestinated"—says the author of the Epistle to the Ephesians, "Being predestinated according to the purpose of Him who worketh all things after the counsel of His own Will"; and much more to the same effect, the only difference being that externality is assumed by the Apostle rather than immanence. It has run through the history of the Christian Church ever since. St. Augustine held it vaguely, Calvin held it fiercely, and, if our English Church and its Nonconformist contemporaries have now almost abandoned it to our men of science (among whom determinism is a commonplace), it was formerly taught by Evangelical divines of the finest character and conduct. I should own in fairness that I think this has been shrewdly recognized in some quarters whose orthodoxy is unimpeachable, where the philosophy of *The Dynasts* has been handled as sanely and as calmly as I could wish.

Nevertheless, as was said in the Preface, I have used the philosophy as a plausible theory only. Though, for that matter, I am convinced that, whether we uphold this or any other conjecture on the cause of things, men's lives and actions will be little affected thereby, these being less dependent on abstract reasonings than on the involuntary inter-social emotions, which would more probably be strengthened than weakened by a sense that humanity and other animal life (roughly, though not accurately, definable as puppetry) forms the conscious extremity of a pervading urgence, or will.

Your obedient servant,

Max Gate, Dorset, Feb. 16.   THOMAS HARDY.

5

FROM THE NON-FICTIONAL PROSE

Editor's Note

Included in the first part of this section are the essays and prefaces which seem most essential for a full understanding of Hardy's creative undertakings in fiction and poetry. He was a resourceful defender of his own work—his apologies are not usually very apologetic—and we should recognize that the defensive posture was natural and appropriate for a man who emerged from nowhere to make his own career unaided, and whose candour in writing about sexual feelings, blighted marriages, and the hard lives of the poor and obscure frequently outraged the presuppositions and prejudices of his mainly middle-class public.

Presented at the end of this section is a miscellany of Hardy's personal comments on life and the arts set down year by year in his notebooks and journals. These were first printed in Florence Emily Hardy's two-volume biography of her husband, *The Early Years* (1928) and *The Later Years* (1930) and remain acutely interesting as the spontaneous, unguarded reflections of a great literary personality who yet remained a deeply private and reserved man to the end of his days.

❉❉❉❉❉❉❉❉❉❉❉❉❉❉❉❉❉❉❉❉❉

PREFACES, ESSAYS, AND APOLOGIES

Preface to the Fifth and Later Editions of *Tess of the d'Urbervilles* (1891)

This novel being one wherein the great campaign of the heroine begins after an event in her experience which has usually been treated as fatal to her part of protagonist, or at least as the virtual ending of her enterprises and hopes, it was quite contrary to avowed conventions that the public should welcome the book and agree with me in holding that there was something more to be said in fiction than had been said about the shaded side of a well-known catastrophe. But the responsive spirit in which *Tess of the d'Urbervilles* has been received by the readers of England and America would seem to prove that the plan of laying down a story on the lines of tacit opinion, instead of making it to square with the merely vocal formulæ of society, is not altogether a wrong one, even when exemplified in so unequal and partial an achievement as the present. For this responsiveness I cannot refrain from expressing my thanks; and my regret is that, in a world where one so often hungers in vain for friendship, where even not to be wilfully misunderstood is felt as a kindness, I shall never meet in person these appreciative readers, male and female, and shake them by the hand.

I include amongst them the reviewers—by far the majority—who have so generously welcomed the tale. Their words show that they, like the others, have only too largely repaired my defects of narration by their own imaginative intuition.

Nevertheless, though the novel was intended to be neither didactic nor aggressive, but in the scenic parts to be representative simply, and in the contemplative to be oftener charged with impressions than with convictions, there have been objectors both to the matter and to the rendering.

The more austere of these maintain a conscientious difference of opinion concerning, among other things, subjects fit for art, and reveal an inability to associate the idea of the sub-title adjective* with any but the artificial and derivative meaning which has resulted to it from the ordinances of civilization. They ignore the meaning of the word in Nature, together with all æsthetic claims upon

*Hardy's subtitle was *A Pure Woman Faithfully Presented.*—Ed.

it, not to mention the spiritual interpretation afforded by the finest side of their own Christianity. Others dissent on grounds which are intrinsically no more than an assertion that the novel embodies the views of life prevalent at the end of the nineteenth century, and not those of an earlier and simpler generation—an assertion which I can only hope may be well founded. Let me repeat that a novel is an impression, not an argument; and there the matter must rest; as one is reminded by a passage which occurs in the letters of Schiller to Goethe on judges of this class: "They are those who seek only their own ideas in a representation, and prize that which should be as higher than what is. The cause of the dispute, therefore, lies in the very first principles, and it would be utterly impossible to come to an understanding with them." And again: "As soon as I observe that any one, when judging of poetical representations, considers anything more important than the inner Necessity and Truth, I have done with him."

In the introductory words to the first edition I suggested the possible advent of the genteel person who would not be able to endure something or other in these pages. That person duly appeared among the aforesaid objectors. In one case he felt upset that it was not possible for him to read the book through three times, owing to my not having made that critical effort which "alone can prove the salvation of such an one." In another, he objected to such vulgar articles as the Devil's pitchfork, a lodging-house carving-knife, and a shame-bought parasol, appearing in a respectable story. In another place he was a gentleman who turned Christian for half-an-hour the better to express his grief that a disrespectful phrase about the Immortals should have been used; though the same innate gentility compelled him to excuse the author in words of pity that one cannot be too thankful for: "He does but give us of his best." I can assure this great critic that to exclaim illogically against the gods, singular or plural, is not such an original sin of mine as he seems to imagine. True, it may have some local originality; though if Shakespeare were an authority on history, which perhaps he is not, I could show that the sin was introduced into Wessex as early as the Heptarchy itself. Says Glo'ster in *Lear*, otherwise Ina, king of that country:

> As flies to wanton boys are we to the gods;
> They kill us for their sport.

The remaining two or three manipulators of *Tess* were of the predetermined sort whom most writers and readers would gladly forget; professed literary boxers, who put on their convictions for the occasion; modern "Hammers of Heretics"; sworn Discouragers, ever on the watch to prevent the tentative half-success from becoming the whole success later on; who pervert plain meanings, and grow personal under the name of practising the great historical method. However, they may have causes to advance, privileges to guard, traditions to keep going; some of which a mere tale-teller, who writes down how the things of the world strike him, without any ulterior intentions whatever, has overlooked, and may by pure inadvertence have run foul of when in the least aggressive mood. Perhaps some passing perception, the outcome of a dream hour, would, if generally acted on, cause such an assailant considerable inconvenience with respect to position, interests, family, servant, ox, ass, neighbour, or neighbour's wife. He therefore valiantly hides his personality behind a publisher's shutters, and cries "Shame!" So densely is the world thronged with any shifting of positions, even the best warranted advance, galls somebody's kibe. Such shiftings often begin in sentiment, and such sentiment sometimes begins in a novel.

July 1892.

The foregoing remarks were written during the early career of this story, when a spirited public and private criticism of its points was still fresh to the feelings. The pages are allowed to stand for what they are worth, as something once said; but probably they would not have been written now. Even in the first short time which has elapsed since the book was first published, some of the critics who provoked the reply have "gone down into silence," as if to remind one of the infinite unimportance of both their say and mine.

January 1895.

_____

The present edition of this novel contains a few pages that have never appeared in any previous edition. When the detached episodes were collected as stated in the preface of 1891, these pages were overlooked, though they were in the original manuscript. They occur in Chapter X.

Respecting the sub-title, to which allusion was made above, I may add that it was appended at the last moment, after reading the final proofs, as being the estimate left in a candid mind of the heroine's character—an estimate that nobody would be likely to dispute. It was disputed more than anything else in the book. *Melius fuerat non scribere.* But there it stands.

The novel was first published complete, in three volumes, in November, 1891.

March 1912.

Preface to *Jude the Obscure* (1896)

The history of this novel (whose birth in its present shape has been much retarded by the necessities of periodical publication) is briefly as follows. The scheme was jotted down in 1890, from notes made in 1887 and onwards, some of the circumstances being suggested by the death of a woman in the former year. The scenes were revisited in October, 1892; the narrative was written in outline in 1892 and the spring of 1893, and at full length, as it now appears, from August, 1893, onwards into the next year; the whole, with the exception of a few chapters, being in the hands of the publisher by the end of 1894. It was begun as a serial story in *Harper's Magazine* at the end of November, 1894, and was continued in monthly parts.

But, as in the case of *Tess of the d'Urbervilles,* the maga-

zine version was for various reasons an abridged and modified one, the present edition being the first in which the whole
appears as originally written. And in the difficulty of coming
to an early decision in the matter of a title, the tale was
issued under a provisional name, two such titles having,
in fact, been successively adopted. The present and final
title, deemed on the whole the best, was one of the earliest
thought of.

For a novel addressed by a man to men and women of
full age; which attempts to deal unaffectedly with the fret
and fever, derision and disaster, that may press in the wake
of the strongest passion known to humanity; to tell, without a mincing of words, a deadly war waged between flesh
and spirit; and to point the tragedy of unfulfilled aims, I
am not aware that there is anything in the handling to
which exception can be taken.

Like former productions of this pen, *Jude the Obscure*
is simply an endeavour to give shape and coherence to a
series of seemings, or personal impressions, the question
of their consistency or their discordance, of their permanence or their transitoriness, being regarded as not of the
first moment.

August 1895.

POSTSCRIPT

The issue of this book sixteen years ago, with the explanatory Preface given above, was followed by unexpected incidents, and one can now look back for a
moment at what happened. Within a day or two of its
publication the reviewers pronounced upon it in tones to
which the reception of *Tess of the d'Urbervilles* bore no
comparison, though there were two or three dissentients
from the chorus. This salutation of the story in England
was instantly cabled to America, and the music was reinforced on that side of the Atlantic in a shrill crescendo.

In my own eyes the sad feature of the attack was that
the greater part of the story—that which presented the
shattered ideals of the two chief characters, and had been

more especially, and indeed almost exclusively, the part of interest to myself—was practically ignored by the adverse press of the two countries; the while that some twenty or thirty pages of sorry detail deemed necessary to complete the narrative, and show the antitheses in Jude's life, were almost the sole portions read and regarded. And curiously enough, a reprint the next year of a fantastic tale* that had been published in a family paper some time before, drew down upon my head a continuation of the same sort of invective from several quarters.

So much for the unhappy beginning of *Jude*'s career as a book. After these verdicts from the press its next misfortune was to be burnt by a bishop—probably in his despair at not being able to burn me.

Then somebody discovered that *Jude* was a moral work —austere in its treatment of a difficult subject—as if the writer had not all the time said that it was in the Preface. Thereupon many uncursed me, and the matter ended, the only effect of it on human conduct that I could discover being its effect on myself—the experience completely curing me of further interest in novel-writing.

One incident among many arising from the storm of words was that an American man of letters, who did not whitewash his own morals, informed me that, having bought a copy of the book on the strength of the shocked criticisms, he read on and on, wondering when the harmfulness was going to begin, and at last flung it across the room with execrations at having been induced by the rascally reviewers to waste a dollar-and-half on what he was pleased to call "a religious and ethical treatise."

I sympathized with him, and assured him honestly that the misrepresentations had been no collusive trick of mine to increase my circulation among the subscribers to the papers in question.

Then there was the case of the lady who having shuddered at the book in an influential article bearing intermediate headlines of horror, and printed in a world-read

* *The Well-Beloved* (1897)—Ed.

journal, wrote to me shortly afterwards that it was her desire to make my acquaintance.

To return, however, to the book itself. The marriage laws being used in great part as the tragic machinery of the tale, and its general drift on the domestic side tending to show that, in Diderot's words, the civil law should be only the enunciation of the law of nature (a statement that requires some qualifications, by the way), I have been charged since 1895 with a large responsibility in this country for the present "shop-soiled" condition of the marriage theme (as a learned writer characterized it the other day). I do not know. My opinion at that time, if I remember rightly, was what it is now, that a marriage should be dissolvable as soon as it becomes a cruelty to either of the parties—being then essentially and morally no marriage—and it seemed a good foundation for the fable of a tragedy, told for its own sake as a presentation of particulars containing a good deal that was universal, and not without a hope that certain cathartic, Aristotelian qualities might be found therein.

The difficulties down to twenty or thirty years back of acquiring knowledge in letters without pecuniary means were used in the same way; though I was informed that some readers thought these episodes an attack on venerable institutions, and that when Ruskin College was subsequently founded it should have been called the College of Jude the Obscure.

Artistic effort always pays heavily for finding its tragedies in the forced adaptation of human instincts to rusty and irksome moulds that do not fit them. To do Bludyer and the conflagratory bishop justice, what they meant seems to have been only this: "We Britons hate ideas, and we are going to live up to that privilege of our native country. Your pictures may not show the untrue, or the uncommon, or even be contrary to the canons of art; but it is not the view of life that we who thrive on conventions can permit to be painted."

But what did it matter. As for the matrimonial scenes, in spite of their "touching the spot," and the screaming of a poor lady in *Blackwood* that there was an unholy anti-marriage league afoot, the famous contract—sacrament I mean—is doing fairly well still, and people marry and give in what may or may not be true marriage as light-heartedly as ever. The author has even been reproached by some earnest correspondents that he has left the question where he found it, and has not pointed the way to a much-needed reform.

After the issue of *Jude the Obscure* as a serial story in Germany, an experienced reviewer of that country informed the writer that Sue Bridehead, the heroine, was the first delineation in fiction of the woman who was coming into notice in her thousands every year—the woman of the feminist movement—the slight, pale "bachelor" girl—the intellectualized, emancipated bundle of nerves that modern conditions were producing, mainly in cities as yet; who do not recognize the necessity for most of her sex to follow marriage as a profession, and boast themselves as superior people because they are licensed to be loved on the premises. The regret of this critic was that the portrait of the newcomer had been left to be drawn by a man, and was not done by one of her own sex, who would never have allowed her to break down at the end.

Whether this assurance is borne out by dates I cannot say. Nor am I able, across the gap of years since the production of the novel, to exercise more criticism upon it of a general kind than extends to a few verbal corrections, whatever, good or bad, it may contain. And no doubt there can be more in a book than the author consciously puts there, which will help either to its profit or to its disadvantage as the case may be.

April 1912.

Three Letters on *Jude the Obscure*

I

MAX GATE,
DORCHESTER,
November 10th, 1895.

. . . Your review (of *Jude the Obscure*) is the most discriminating that has yet appeared. It required an artist to see that the plot is almost geometrically constructed—I ought not to say *constructed*, for, beyond a certain point, the characters necessitated it, and I simply let it come. As for the story itself, it is really sent out to those into whose souls the iron has entered, and has entered deeply at some time of their lives. But one cannot choose one's readers.

It is curious that some of the papers should look upon the novel as a manifesto on "the marriage question" (although, of course, it involves it), seeing that it is concerned first with the labours of a poor student to get a University degree, and secondly with the tragic issues of two bad marriages, owing in the main to a doom or curse of hereditary temperament peculiar to the family of the parties. The only remarks which can be said to bear on the *general* marriage question occur in dialogue, and comprise no more than half a dozen pages in a book of five hundred. And of these remarks I state (p. 362) that my own views are not expressed therein. I suppose the attitude of these critics is to be accounted for by the accident that, during the serial publication of my story, a sheaf of "purpose" novels on the matter appeared.

You have hardly an idea how poor and feeble the book seems to me, as executed, beside the idea of it that I had formed in prospect.

I have received some interesting letters about it already

—yours not the least so. Swinburne writes, too enthusiastically for me to quote with modesty.

Believe me, with sincere thanks for your review,

Ever yours,

Thomas Hardy."

P.S. One thing I did not answer. The "grimy" features of the story go to show the contrast between the ideal life a man wished to lead, and the squalid real life he was fated to lead. The throwing of the pizzle, at the supreme moment of his young dream, is to sharply initiate this contrast. But I must have lamentably failed, as I feel I have, if this requires explanation and is not self-evident. The idea was meant to run all through the novel. It is, in fact, to be discovered in *everybody's* life, though it lies less on the surface perhaps than it does in my poor puppet's.

II

Max Gate,

Dorchester,

November 20th, 1895

I am keen about the new magazine. How interesting that you should be writing this review for it! I wish the book were more worthy of such notice and place.

You are quite right; there is nothing perverted or depraved in Sue's nature. The abnormalism consists in disproportion, not in inversion, her sexual instinct being healthy as far as it goes, but unusually weak and fastidious. Her sensibilities remain painfully alert notwithstanding, as they do in nature with such women. One point illustrating this I could not dwell upon: that, though she has children, her intimacies with Jude have never been more than occasional, even when they were living together (I mention that they occupy separate rooms, except towards the end), and one of her reasons for fearing the marriage ceremony is that she fears it would be breaking faith with Jude to withhold herself at pleasure, or altogether, after it; though while uncontracted she feels at liberty to yield herself as seldom as she chooses. This has tended to keep his passion as hot at the end as at the beginning, and helps to break his heart. He has never really possessed her as freely as he desired.

Sue is a type of woman which has always had an attraction for me, but the difficulty of drawing the type has kept me from attempting it till now.

Of course the book is all contrasts—or was meant to be in its original conception. Alas, what a miserable accomplishment it is, when I compare it with what I meant to make it!—*e.g.* Sue and her heathen gods set against Jude's reading the Greek testament; Christminster academical, Christminster in the slums; Jude the saint, Jude the sinner; Sue the Pagan, Sue the saint; marriage, no marriage; &c., &c.

As to the "coarse" scenes with Arabella, the battle in the schoolroom, etc., the newspaper critics might, I thought, have sneered at them for their Fieldingism rather than for their Zolaism. But your everyday critic knows nothing of Fielding. I am read in Zola very little, but have felt akin locally to Fielding, so many of his scenes having been laid down this way, and his home near.

Did I tell you I feared I should seem too High-Churchy at the end of the book where Sue recants? You can imagine my surprise at some of the reviews.

What a self-occupied letter!

Ever sincerely,
T. H.

III

Max Gate,
Dorchester,

January 4, 1896.

For the last three days I have been tantalized by a difficulty in getting *Cosmopolis*, and had only just read your review when I received your note. My sincere thanks for the generous view you take of the book, which to me is a mass of imperfections. We have both been amused—

or rather delighted—by the sub-humour (is there such a word?) of your writing. I think it a rare quality in living essayists, and that you ought to make more of it—I mean write more in that vein than you do.

But this is apart from the review itself, of which I will talk to you when we meet. The rectangular lines of the story were not premeditated, but came by chance: except, of course, that the involutions of four lives must necessarily be a sort of quadrille. The only point in the novel on which I feel sure is that it makes for morality; and that delicacy or indelicacy in a writer is according to his object. If I say to a lady "I met a naked woman," it is indelicate. But if I go on to say "I found she was mad with sorrow," it ceases to be indelicate. And in writing Jude my mind was fixed on the ending.

Sincerely yours,

T. H.

General Preface to the Novels and Poems

[Wessex Edition, I, 1912]

In accepting a proposal for a definite edition of these productions in prose and verse I have found an opportunity of classifying the novels under heads that show approximately the author's aim, if not his achievement, in each book of the series at the date of its composition. Sometimes the aim was lower than at other times; sometimes, where the intention was primarily high, force of circumstances (among which the chief were the necessities of magazine publication) compelled a modification, great or slight, of the original plan. Of a few, however, of the longer novels, and of many of the shorter tales, it may be assumed that they stand to-day much as they would have stood if no accidents had obstructed the channel between the writer and the public. That many of them, if any, stand as they would stand if written *now* is not to be supposed.

In the classification of these fictitious chronicles—for which the name of "The Wessex Novels" was adopted, and is still retained—the first group is called "Novels of Character and Environment," and contains those which approach most nearly to uninfluenced works; also one or two which, whatever their quality in some few of their episodes, may claim a verisimilitude in general treatment and detail.

The second group is distinguished as "Romances and Fantasies," a sufficiently descriptive definition. The third class—"Novels of Ingenuity"—show a not infrequent disregard of the probable in the chain of events, and depend for their interest mainly on the incidents themselves. They might also be characterized as "Experiments," and were written for the nonce simply; though despite the artificiality of their fable some of their scenes are not without fidelity to life.

It will not be supposed that these differences are distinctly perceptible in every page of every volume. It was inevitable that blendings and alternations should occur at all. Moreover, as it was not thought desirable in every instance to change the arrangement of the shorter stories to which readers have grown accustomed, certain of these may be found under headings to which an acute judgment might deny appropriateness.

It has sometimes been conceived of novels that evolve their action on a circumscribed scene—as do many (though not all) of these—that they cannot be so inclusive in their exhibition of human nature as novels wherein the scenes cover large extents of country, in which events figure amid towns and cities, even wander over the four quarters of the globe. I am not concerned to argue this point further than to suggest that the conception is an untrue one in respect of the elementary passions. But I would state that the geographical limits of the stage here trodden were not absolutely forced upon the writer by circumstances; he forced them upon himself from judgment. I considered that our magnificent heritage from the Greeks in dramatic literature found sufficient room for a large proportion of its action in an extent of their country not much larger than the half-dozen counties here reunited under the old name of Wessex, that the domestic emotions have throbbed in Wessex nooks with as much intensity as in the palaces of Europe, and that, anyhow, there was quite enough human nature in Wessex for one man's literary purpose. So far was I possessed by this idea that I kept within the frontiers when it would have been easier to overleap them and give more cosmopolitan features to the narrative.

Thus, though the people in most of the novels (and in much of the shorter verse) are dwellers in a province bounded on the north by the Thames, on the south by the English Channel, on the east by a line running from Hayling Island to Windsor Forest, and on the west by the Cornish coast, they were meant to be typically and essentially those of any and every place where

Thought's the slave of life, and life time's fool,

—beings in whose hearts and minds that which is apparently local should be really universal.

But whatever the success of this intention, and the value of these novels as delineations of humanity, they have at least a humble supplementary quality of which I may be justified in reminding the reader, though it is one that was quite unintentional and unforeseen. At the dates represented in the various narrations things were like that in Wessex: the inhabitants lived in certain ways, engaged in certain occupations, kept alive certain customs, just as they are shown doing in these pages. And in particularizing such I have often been reminded of Boswell's remarks on the trouble to which he was put and the pilgrimages he was obliged to make to authenticate some detail, though the labour was one which would bring him no praise. Unlike his achievement, however, on which an error would as he says have brought discredit, if these country customs and vocations, obsolete and obsolescent, had been detailed wrongly, nobody would have discovered such errors to the end of Time. Yet I have instituted inquiries to correct tricks of memory, and striven against temptations to exaggerate, in order to preserve for my own satisfaction a fairly true record of a vanishing life.

It is advisable also to state here, in response to inquiries from readers interested in landscape, prehistoric antiquities, and especially old English architecture, that the description of these backgrounds has been done from the real—that is to say, has something real for its basis, however illusively treated. Many features of the first two kinds have been given under their existing names; for instance, the Vael of Blackmoor or Blakemore, Hambledon Hill, Bulbarrow, Nettlecombe Tout, Dogbury Hill, High-Stoy, Bubb-Down Hill, The Devil's Kitchen, Cross-in-Hand, Long-Ash Lane, Benvill Lane, Giant's Hill, Crimmercrock Lane, and Stonehenge. The rivers Froom, or Frome, and Stour, are, of course, well known as such. And the further idea was that large towns and points tending to mark the outline of Wessex—such as Bath, Plymouth, The Start, Portland Bill, Southampton, etc.—should be named clearly. The scheme was not greatly elaborated, but, whatever its value, the names remain still.

In respect of places described under fictitious or ancient names in the novels—for reasons that seemed good at the time of writing them—and kept up in the poems—discerning people have affirmed in print that they clearly recognize the originals: such as Shaftesbury in "Shaston," Sturminster Newton in "Stourcastle," Dorchester in "Casterbridge," Salisbury Plain in "The Great Plain," Cranborne Chase in "The Chase," Beaminster in "Emminster," Bere Regis in "Kingsbere," Woodbury Hill in "Greenhill," Wool Bridge in "Wellbridge," Harfoot or Harput Lane in "Stagfoot Lane," Hazlebury in "Nuttlebury," Bridport in "Port Bredy," Maiden Newton in "Chalk Newton," a farm near Nettlecombe Tout in "Flintcomb Ash," Sherborne in "Sherton Abbas," Milton Abbey in "Middleton Abbey," Cerne Abbas in "Abbot's Cernel," Evershot in "Evershed," Taunton in "Toneborough," Bournemouth in "Sandbourne," Winchester in "Wintoncester," Oxford in "Christminster," Reading in "Aldbrickham," Newbury in "Kennetbridge," Wantage in "Alfredston," Basingstoke in "Stoke Barehills," and so on. Subject to the qualifications above given, that no detail is guaranteed—that the portraiture of fictitiously named towns and villages was only suggested by certain real places, and wantonly wanders from inventorial descriptions of them—I do not contradict these keen hunters for the real; I am satisfied with their statements as as least an indication of their interest in the scenes.

Thus much for the novels. Turning now to the verse— to myself the more individual part of my literary fruitage —I would say that, unlike some of the fiction, nothing interfered with the writer's freedom in respect of its form or content. Several of the poems—indeed many—were produced before novel-writing had been thought of as a pursuit; but few saw the light till all the novels had been published. The limited stage to which the majority of the latter confine their exhibitions has not been adhered to here in the same proportion, the dramatic part especially having a very broad theatre of action. It may thus relieve the circumscribed areas treated in the prose, if such relief be needed. To be sure, one might argue that by surveying Europe from a celestial point of vision—as in *The Dynasts* —that continent becomes virtually a province—a Wessex, an Attica, even a mere garden—and hence is made to conform to the principle of the novels, however far it outmeasures their region. But that may be as it will.

The few volumes filled by the verse cover a producing period of some eighteen years first and last, while the seventeen or more volumes of novels represent correspondingly about four-and-twenty years. One is reminded by this disproportion in time and result how much more concise and quintessential expression becomes when given in rhythmic form than when shaped in the language of prose.

One word on what has been called the present writer's philosophy of life, as exhibited more particularly in this metrical section of his compositions. Positive views on the Whence and the Wherefore of things have never been advanced by this pen as a consistent philosophy. Nor is it likely, indeed, that imaginative writings extending over more than forty years would exhibit a coherent scientific theory of the universe even if it had been attempted—of that universe concerning which Spencer* owns to the "paralyzing thought" that possibly there exists no comprehension of it anywhere. But such objectless consistency never has been attempted, and the sentiments in the following pages have been stated truly to be mere impressions of the moment, and not convictions or arguments.

That these impressions have been condemned as "pessimistic"—as if that were a very wicked adjective—shows a curious muddle-mindedness. It must be obvious that there is a higher characteristic of philosophy than pessimism, or than meliorism, or even than the optimism of these critics—which is truth. Existence is either ordered in a certain way, or it is not so ordered, and conjectures which harmonize best with experience are removed above all comparison with other conjectures which do not so harmonize. So that to say one view is worse than other views without proving it erroneous implies the possibility of a false view being better or more expedient than a true view; and no pragmatic proppings can make that *idolum specus* stand on its feet, for it postulates a prescience denied to humanity.

And there is another consideration. Differing natures find their tongue in the presence of differing spectacles. Some natures become vocal at tragedy, some are made vocal by comedy, and it seems to me that to whichever of these aspects of life a writer's instinct for expression the more readily responds, to that he should allow it to respond. That before a contrasting side of things he remains undemonstrative need not be assumed to mean that he remains unperceiving.

It was my hope to add to these volumes of verse as many more as would make a fairly comprehensive cycle of the whole. I had wished that those in dramatic, ballad, and narrative form should include most of the cardinal situations which occur in social and public life, and those

* The British philosopher, Herbert Spencer (1820–1903)—Ed.

in lyric form a round of emotional experiences of some completeness. But

> The petty done, the undone vast!

The more written the more seems to remain to be written; and the night cometh. I realize that these hopes and plans, except possibly to the extent of a volume or two, must remain unfulfilled.

T.H.

October 1911.

From the Preface to *Select Poems of William Barnes* (1908)

. . . In the exceptional instance of a poet like Barnes who writes in a dialect only, a new condition arises to influence considerations of assortment. Lovers of poetry who are but imperfectly acquainted with his vocabulary and idiom may yet be desirous of learning something of his message; and the most elementary guidance is of help to such students, for they are liable to mistake their author on the very threshold. For some reason or none, many persons suppose that when anything is penned in the tongue of the countryside, the primary intent is burlesque or ridicule, and this especially if the speech be one in which the sibilant has the rough sound, and is expressed by Z. Indeed, scores of thriving storytellers and dramatists seem to believe that by transmuting the flattest conversation into a dialect that never existed, and making the talkers say "be" where they would really say "is," a Falstaffian richness is at once imparted to its qualities.

But to a person to whom a dialect is native its sounds are as consonant with moods of sorrow as with moods of mirth: there is no grotesqueness in it as such. Nor was there to Barnes. To provide an alien reader with a rough clue to the taste of the kernel that may be expected under the shell of the spelling has seemed to be worth while, and to justify a division into heads that may in some cases appear arbitrary.

In respect of the other helps—the glosses and paraphrases given on each page—it may be assumed that they are but a sorry substitute for the full significance the original words bear to those who read them without translation, and know their delicate ability to express the doings, joys and jests, troubles, sorrows, needs and sicknesses of life in the rural world as elsewhere. The Dorset dialect being— or having been—a tongue, and not a corruption, it is the old question over again, that of the translation of poetry; which, to the full, is admittedly impossible. And further; gesture and facial expression figure so largely in the speech of the husbandmen as to be speech itself; hence in the mind's eye of those who know it in its original setting each word of theirs is accompanied by the qualifying face-play which no construing can express.

It may appear strange to some, as it did to friends in his lifetime, that a man of insight who had the spirit of poesy in him should have persisted year after year in writing in a fast-perishing language, and on themes which in some not remote time would be familiar to nobody, leaving him pathetically like

A ghostly cricket, creaking where a house was burned;

—a language with the added disadvantage by comparison with other dead tongues that no master or books would be readily available for the acquisition of its finer meanings. He himself simply said that he could not help it, no doubt feeling his idylls to be an extemporization, or impulse, without prevision or power of appraisement on his own part.

Yet it seems to the present writer that Barnes, despite this, really belonged to the literary school of such poets as Tennyson, Gray, and Collins, rather than to that of the old unpremeditating singers in dialect. Primarily spontaneous, he was academic closely after; and we find him warbling

his native wood-notes with a watchful eye on the predetermined score, a far remove from the popular impression of him as the naif and rude bard who sings only because he must, and who submits the uncouth lines of his
page to us without knowing how they come there. Goethe
never knew better of his; nor Milton; nor, in their rhymes,
Poe; nor, in their whimsical alliterations here and there,
Langland and the versifiers of the fourteenth and fifteen
centuries.

In his aim at closeness of phrase to his vision he strained
at times the capacities of dialect, and went willfully outside the dramatization of peasant talk. Such a lover of the
art of expression was this penman of a dialect that had no
literature, that on some occasions he would allow art to
overpower spontaneity and to cripple inspiration; though,
be it remembered, he never tampered with the dialect
itself. His ingenious internal rhymes, his subtle juxtaposition
of kindred lippings and vowel-sounds, show a fastidious-
ness in word-selection that is surprising in verse which
professes to represent the habitual modes of language
among the western peasantry. We do not find in the dialect
balladists of the seventeenth century, or in Burns (with
whom he has sometimes been measured), such careful
finish, such verbal dexterities, such searchings for the most
cunning syllables, such satisfaction with the best phrase.
Had he not begun with dialect, and seen himself recognized as an adept in it before he had quite found himself
as a poet, who knows that he might not have brought
upon his muse the disaster that has befallen so many earnest versifiers of recent time, have become a slave to the
passion for form, and have wasted all his substance in
whittling at its shape.

From such, however, he was saved by the conditions of
his scene, characters, and vocabulary. It may have been,
indeed, that he saw this tendency in himself, and retained
the dialect as a corrective to the tendency. Whether or no,
by a felicitous instinct he does at times break into sudden
irregularities in the midst of his subtle rhythms and meas-

ures, as if feeling rebelled against further drill. Then his self-consciousness ends, and his naturalness is saved.

But criticism is so easy, and art so hard: criticism so flimsy, and the life-seer's voice so lasting. When we consider what such appreciativeness as Arnold's could allow his prejudices to say about the highest-soaring among all our lyricists; what strange criticism Shelley himself could indulge in now and then; that the history of criticism is mainly the history of error, which has not even, as many errors have, quaintness enough to make it interesting, we may well doubt the utility of such writing on the sand. What is the use of saying, as has been said of Barnes, that compound epithets like "the blue-hill'd worold," "the wide-horn'd cow," "the grey-topp'd heights of Paladore," are a high-handed enlargement of the ordinary ideas of the field-folk into whose mouths they are put? These things are justified by the art of every age when they can claim to be, as here, singularly precise and beautiful definitions of what is signified; which in these instances, too, apply with double force to the deeply tinged horizon, to the breed of kine, to the aspect of Shaftesbury Hill, characteristic of the Vale within which most of his revelations are enshrined.

Dialect, it may be added, offered another advantage to him as the writer, whatever difficulties it may have for strangers who try to follow it. Even if he often used the dramatic form of peasant speakers as a pretext for the expression of his own mind and experiences—which cannot be doubted—yet he did not always do this, and the assumed character of husbandman or hamleteer enabled him to elude in his verse those dreams and speculations that cannot leave alone the mystery of things,—possibly an unworthy mystery and disappointing if solved, though one that has a harrowing fascination for many poets,—and helped him to fall back on dramatic truth, by making his personages express the notions of life prevalent in their sphere.

As by the screen of dialect, so by the intense localization aforesaid, much is lost to the outsider who by looking into

Barnes' pages only revives general recollections of country life. Yet many passages may shine into that reader's mind through the veil which partly hides them; and it is hoped and believed that, even in a superficial reading, something more of this poet's charm will be gathered from the present selection by persons to whom the Wessex R and Z are uncouth misfortunes, and the dying words those of an unlamented language that need leave behind it no grammar of its secrets and no key to its tomb.

"Candour in English Fiction" (1890)

Even imagination is the slave of stolid circumstance; and the unending flow of inventiveness which finds expression in the literature of Fiction is no exception to the general law. It is conditioned by its surroundings like a river-stream. The varying character and strength of literary creation at different times may, indeed, at first sight seem to be the symptoms of some inherent, arbitrary, and mysterious variation; but if it were possible to compute, as in mechanics, the units of power or faculty, revealed and unrevealed, that exist in the world at stated intervals, an approximately even supply would probably be disclosed. At least there is no valid reason for a contrary supposition. Yet of the inequality in its realisations there can be no question; and the discrepancy would seem to lie in contingencies which, at one period, doom high expression to dumbness and encourage the lower forms, and at another call forth the best in expression and silence triviality.

That something of this is true has indeed been pretty generally admitted in relation to art-products of various other kinds. But when observers and critics remark, as they often do remark, that the great bulk of English fiction of the present day is characterised by its lack of sincerity, they usually omit to trace this serious defect to external, or even eccentric causes. They connect it with an assumption that the attributes of insight, conceptive power, imaginative emotion, are distinctly weaker nowadays than at particular epochs of earlier date. This may or may not be the case to some degree; but, on considering the conditions under which our popular fiction is produced, imaginative deterioration can hardly be deemed the sole or even chief explanation why such an undue proportion of this sort of literature is in England a literature of quackery.

By a sincere school of Fiction we may understand a Fiction that expresses the views of life prevalent in its time, by means of a selected chain of action best suited for their exhibition. What are the prevalent views of life just now is a question upon which it is not necessary to enter further than to suggest that the most natural method of presenting them, the method most in accordance with the views themselves, seems to be by a procedure mainly impassive in its tone and tragic in its developments.

Things move in cycles; dormant principles renew themselves, and exhausted principles are thrust by. There is a revival of the artistic instincts towards great dramatic motives—setting forth that "collision between the individual and the general"—formerly worked out with such force by the Periclean and Elizabethan dramatists, to name no other. More than this, the periodicity which marks the course of taste in civilised countries does not take the form of a true cycle of repetition, but what Comte, in speaking of general progress, happily characterises as "a looped orbit": not a movement of revolution but—to use the current word—evolution. Hence, in perceiving that taste is arriving anew at the point of high tragedy, writers are conscious that its revived presentation demands enrichment by further truths—in other words, original treatment: treatment which seeks to show Nature's unconsciousness not of essential laws, but of those laws framed merely as social expedients by humanity, without a basis in the heart of things; treatment which expresses the triumph of the crowd over the hero, of the commonplace majority over the exceptional few.

But originality makes scores of failures for one final success, precisely because its essence is to acknowledge no immediate precursor or guide. It is probably to these inevitable conditions of further acquisition that may be attributed some developments of naturalism in French novelists of the present day, and certain crude results from meritorious attempts in the same direction by intellectual adventurers here and there among our own authors.

Anyhow, conscientious fiction alone it is which can excite a reflective and abiding interest in the minds of thoughtful readers of mature age, who are weary of puerile inventions and famishing for accuracy; who consider that, in representations of the world, the passions ought to be proportioned as in the world itself. This is the interest which was excited in the minds of the Athenians by their immortal tragedies, and in the minds of Londoners at the first performance of the finer plays of three hundred years ago. They reflected life, revealed life, criticised life. Life being a physiological fact, its honest portrayal must be largely concerned with, for one thing, the relations of the sexes, and the substitution for such catastrophes as favour the false colouring best expressed by the regulation finish that "they married and were happy ever after," of catastrophes based upon sexual relations as it is. To this expansion English society opposes a well-nigh insuperable bar.

The popular vehicles for the introduction of a novel to the public have grown to be, from one cause and another, the magazine and the circulating library; and the object of the magazine and circulating library is not upward advance but lateral advance; to suit themselves to what is called household reading, which means, or is made to mean, the reading either of the majority in a household or of the household collectively. The number of adults, even in a large household, being normally two, and these being the members which, as a rule, have least time on their hands to bestow on current literature, the taste of the majority can hardly be, and seldom is, tempered by the ripe judgment which desires fidelity. However, the immature members of a household often keep an open

mind, and they might, and no doubt would, take sincere
fiction with the rest but for another condition, almost
generally co-existent: which is that adults who would desire true views for their own reading insist, for a plausible
but questionable reason, upon false views for the reading
of their young people.

As a consequence, the magazine in particular and the
circulating library in general do not foster the growth of
the novel which reflects and reveals life. They directly tend
to exterminate it by monopolising all literary space. Cause
and effect were never more clearly conjoined, though com-
mentators upon the result, both French and English, seem
seldom if ever to trace their connection. A sincere and
comprehensive sequence of the ruling passions, however
moral in its ultimate bearings, must not be put on paper
as the foundation of imaginative works, which have to
claim notice through the above-named channels, though
it is extensively welcomed in the form of newspaper reports. That the magazine and library have arrogated to
themselves the dispensation of fiction is not the fault of
the authors, but of circumstances over which they, as
representatives of Grub Street, have no control.

What this practically amounts to is that the patrons of
literature—no longer Peers with a taste—acting under
the censorship of prudery, rigorously exclude from the
pages they regulate subjects that have been made, by general approval of the best judges, the bases of the finest
imaginative compositions since literature rose to the dignity
of an art. The crash of broken commandments is as necessary an accompaniment to the catastrophe of a tragedy as
the noise of drum and cymbals to a triumphal march. But
the crash of broken commandments shall not be heard; or,
if at all, but gently, like the roaring of Bottom—gently as any
sucking dove, or as 'twere any nightingale, lest we should
fright the ladies out of their wits. More precisely, an arbitrary proclamation has gone forth that certain picked commandments of the ten shall be preserved intact—to wit, the
first, third, and seventh; that the ninth shall be infringed
but gingerly; the sixth only as much as necessary; and the

remainder alone as much as you please, in a genteel manner.

It is in the self-consciousness engendered by interference with spontaneity, and in aims at a compromise to square with circumstances, that the real secret lies of the charlatanry pervading so much of English fiction. It may be urged that abundance of great and profound novels might be written which should require no compromising, contain not an episode deemed questionable by prudes. This I venture to doubt. In a ramification of the profounder passions the treatment of which makes the great style, something "unsuitable" is sure to arise; and then comes the struggle with the literary conscience. The opening scenes of the would-be great story may, in a rash moment, have been printed in some popular magazine before the remainder is written; as it advances month by month the situations develop, and the writer asks himself, what will his characters do next? What would probably happen to them, given such beginnings? On his life and conscience, though he had not foreseen the thing, only one event could possibly happen, and that therefore he should narrate, as he calls himself a faithful artist. But, though pointing a fine moral, it is just one of those issues which are not to be mentioned in respectable magazines and select libraries. The dilemma then confronts him, he must either whip and scourge those characters into doing something contrary to their natures, to produce the spurious effect of their being in harmony with social forms and ordinances, or, by leaving them alone to act as they will, he must bring down the thunders of respectability upon his head, not to say ruin his editor, his publisher, and himself.

What he often does, indeed can scarcely help doing in such a strait, is, belie his literary conscience, do despite to his best imaginative instincts by arranging a *dénouement* which he knows to be indescribably unreal and meretricious, but dear to the Grundyist and subscriber. If the true artist ever weeps it probably is then, when he first discovers the fearful price that he has to pay for the privilege of writing

in the English language—no less a price than the complete
extinction, in the mind of every mature and penetrating
reader, of sympathetic belief in his personages.

To say that few of the old dramatic masterpieces, if
newly published as a novel (the form which, experts tell
us, they would have taken in modern conditions), would
be tolerated in English magazines and libraries is a ludicrous understatement. Fancy a brazen young Shakespeare
of our time—*Othello, Hamlet*, or *Antony and Cleopatra*
never having yet appeared—sending up one of those creations in narrative form to the editor of a London magazine,
with the author's compliments, and his hope that the
story will be found acceptable to the editor's pages; suppose him, further, to have the temerity to ask for the
candid remarks of the accomplished editor upon his manuscript. One can imagine the answer that young William
would get for his mad supposition of such fitness from any
one of the gentlemen who so correctly conduct that branch
of the periodical Press.

Were the objections of the scrupulous limited to a
prurient treatment of the relations of the sexes, or to any
view of vice calculated to undermine the essential principles
of social order, all honest lovers of literature would be in
accord with them. All really true literature directly or
indirectly sounds as its refrain the words in the *Agamem-
non:* "Chant Ælinon, Ælinon! but may the good prevail."
But the writer may print the *not* of his broken command-
ment in capitals of flame; it makes no difference. A question which should be wholly a question of treatment is
confusedly regarded as a question of subject.

Why the ancient classic and old English tragedy can be
regarded thus deeply, both by young people in their teens
and by old people in their moralities, and the modern
novel cannot be so regarded; why the honest and uncom-
promising delineation which makes the old stories and
dramas lessons in life must make of the modern novel,
following humbly on the same lines, a lesson in iniquity,
is to some thinkers a mystery inadequately accounted for
by the difference between old and new.

Whether minors should read unvarnished fiction based on the deeper passions, should listen to the eternal verities in the form of narrative, is somewhat a different question from whether the novel ought to be exclusively addressed to those minors. The first consideration is one which must be passed over here; but it will be conceded by most friends of literature that all fiction should not be shackled by conventions concerning budding womanhood, which may be altogether false. It behoves us then to inquire how best to circumvent the present lording of nonage over maturity, and permit the explicit novel to be more generally written.

That the existing magazine and book-lending system will admit of any great modification is scarcely likely. As far as the magazine is concerned it has long been obvious that as a vehicle for fiction dealing with human feeling on a comprehensive scale it is tottering to its fall; and it will probably in the course of time take up openly the position that it already covertly occupies, that of a purveyor of tales for the youth of both sexes, as it assumes that tales for those rather numerous members of society ought to be written.

There remain three courses by which the adult may find deliverance. The first would be a system of publication under which books could be bought and not borrowed, when they would naturally resolve themselves into classes instead of being, as now, made to wear a common livery in style and subject, enforced by their supposed necessities in addressing indiscriminately a general audience.

But it is scarcely likely to be convenient to either authors or publishers that the periodical form of publication for the candid story should be entirely forbidden, and in retaining the old system thus far, yet ensuring that the emancipated serial novel should meet the eyes of those for whom it is intended, the plan of publication as a *feuilleton* in newspapers read mainly by adults might be more generally followed, as in France. In default of this, or coexistent with it, there might be adopted what, upon the whole, would perhaps find more favour than any with those who have artistic interests at heart, and that is, maga-

zines for adults; exclusively for adults, if necessary. As
an offshoot there might be at least one magazine for the
middle-aged and old.

There is no foretelling; but this (since the magazine
form of publication is so firmly rooted) is at least a promising remedy, if English prudery be really, as we hope,
only a parental anxiety. There should be no mistaking
the matter, no half measures. *La dignité de la pensée*, in
the words of Pascal, might then grow to be recognised in
the treatment of fiction as in other things, and untram-
melled adult opinion on conduct and theology might be
axiomatically assumed and dramatically appealed to.
Nothing in such literature should for a moment exhibit
lax views of that purity of life upon which the well-being
of society depends; but the position of man and woman
in nature, and the position of belief in the minds of man
and woman—things which everybody is thinking but nobody is saying—might be taken up and treated frankly.

The Science of Fiction (1891)

Since Art is science with an addition, since some science
underlies all Art, there is seemingly no paradox in the use
of such a phrase as "the Science of Fiction." One concludes
it to mean that comprehensive and accurate knowledge of
realities which must be sought for, or intuitively possessed,
to some extent, before anything deserving the name of an
artistic performance in narrative can be produced.

The particulars of this science are the generals of almost
all others. The materials of Fiction being human nature
and circumstances, the science thereof may be dignified by
calling it the codified law of things as they really are. No
single pen can treat exhaustively of this. The Science of
Fiction is contained in that large work, the cyclopædia of
life.

In no proper sense can the term "science" be applied to

other than this fundamental matter. It can have no part or share in the construction of a story, however recent speculations may have favoured such an application. We may assume with certainty that directly the constructive stage is entered upon, Art—high or low—begins to exist.

The most devoted apostle of realism, the sheerest naturalist, cannot escape, any more than the withered old gossip over her fire, the exercise of Art in his labour or pleasure of telling a tale. Not until he becomes an automatic reproducer of all impressions whatsoever can he be called purely scientific, or even a manufacturer on scientific principles. If in the exercise of his reason he select or omit, with an eye to being more truthful than truth (the just aim of Art), he transforms himself into a technicist at a move.

As this theory of the need for the exercise of the Dædalian faculty for selection and cunning manipulation has been disputed, it may be worth while to examine the contrary proposition. That it should ever have been maintained by such a romancer as M. Zola, in his work on the *Roman Expérimental*, seems to reveal an obtuseness to the disproof conveyed in his own novels which, in a French writer, is singular indeed. To be sure that author—whose powers in story-telling, rightfully and wrongfully exercised, may be partly owing to the fact that he is not a critic— does in a measure concede something in the qualified counsel that the novel should keep as close to reality *as it can;* a remark which may be interpreted with infinite latitude, and would no doubt have been cheerfully accepted by Dumas *père* or Mrs. Radcliffe. It implies discriminative choice; and if we grant that we grant all. But to maintain in theory what he abandons in practice, to subscribe to rules and to work by instinct, is a proceeding not confined to the author of *Germinal* and *La Faute de l'Abbé Mouret.*

The reasons that make against such conformation of storywriting to scientific processes have been set forth so many times in examining the theories of the realist, that it is not necessary to recapitulate them here. Admitting the desirability, the impossibility of reproducing in its entirety the phantasmagoria of experience with infinite and atomic truth, without shadow, relevancy, or subordination, is not the least of them. The fallacy appears to owe its origin to the just perception that with our widened knowledge of the universe and its forces, and man's position therein, narrative, to be artistically convincing, must adjust itself to the new alignment, as would also artistic works in form and colour, if further spectacles in their sphere could be presented. Nothing but the illusion of truth can permanently please, and when the old illusions begin to be penetrated, a more natural magic has to be supplied.

Creativeness in its full and ancient sense—the making a thing or situation out of nothing that ever was before—is apparently ceasing to satisfy a world which no longer believes in the abnormal—ceasing at least to satisfy the van-couriers of taste; and creative fancy has accordingly to give more and more place to realism, that is, to an artificiality distilled from the fruits of closest observation.

This is the meaning deducible from the work of the realists, however stringently they themselves may define realism in terms. Realism is an unfortunate, an ambiguous word, which has been taken up by literary society like a view-halloo, and has been assumed in some places to mean copyism, and in others pruriency, and has led to two classes of delineators being included in one condemnation.

Just as bad a word is one used to express a consequence of this development, namely "brutality," a term which, first applied by French critics, has since spread over the English school like the other. It aptly hits off the immediate impression of the thing meant; but it has the disadvantage of defining impartiality as a passion, and a plan as a caprice. It certainly is very far from truly expressing the aims and methods of conscientious and well-intentioned authors who, notwithstanding their excesses, errors, and rickety theories, attempt to narrate the *vérité vraie*.

To return for a moment to the theories of the scientific realists. Every friend to the novel should and must be in sympathy with their error, even while distinctly perceiving it. Though not true, it is well founded. To advance realism as complete copyism, to call the idle trade of storytelling a science, is the hyperbolic flight of an admirable enthusiasm, the exaggerated cry of an honest reaction from the false, in which the truth has been impetuously approached and overleapt in fault of lighted on.

Possibly, if we only wait, the third something, akin to perfection, will exhibit itself on its due pedestal. How that third something may be induced to hasten its presence, who shall say? Hardly the English critic.

But this appertains to the Art of novel-writing, and is outside the immediate subject. To return to the "science." . . . Yet what is the use? Its very comprehensiveness renders the attempt to dwell upon it a futility. Being an observative responsiveness to everything within the cycle of the suns that has to do with actual life, it is easier to say what it is not than to categorise its *summa genera*. It is not, for example, the paying of a great regard to adventitious externals to the neglect of vital qualities, not a precision about the outside of the platter and an obtuseness to the contents. An accomplished lady once confessed to the writer that she could never be in a room two minutes without knowing every article of furniture it contained and every detail in the attire of the inmates, and, when she left, remembering every remark. Here was a person, one might feel for the moment, who could prime herself to an unlimited extent and at the briefest notice in the scientific data of fiction; one who, assuming her to have some slight artistic power, was a born novelist. To explain why such a keen eye to the superficial does not imply a sensitiveness to the intrinsic is a psychological matter beyond the scope of these notes; but that a blindness to material particulars often accompanies a quick perception of the more etheral characteristics of humanity, experience continually shows.

A sight for the finer qualities of existence, an ear for the "still sad music of humanity," are not to be acquired by the outer senses alone, close as their powers in photography may be. What cannot be discerned by eye and ear, what may be apprehended only by the mental tactility that comes from a sympathetic appreciativeness of life in all of its manifestations, this is the gift which renders its possessor a more accurate delineator of human nature than many another with twice his powers and means of external observation, but without that sympathy. To see in half and quarter views the whole picture, to catch from a few bars the whole tune, is the intuitive power that supplies the would-be storywriter with the scientific bases for his pursuit. He may not count the dishes at a feast, or accurately estimate the value of the jewels in a lady's diadem; but through the smoke of those dishes, and the rays from these jewels, he sees written on the wall:—

> We are such stuff
> As dreams are made of, and our little life
> Is rounded with a sleep.

Thus, as aforesaid, an attempt to set forth the Science of Fiction in calculable pages is futility; it is to write a whole library of human philosophy, with instructions how to feel.

Once in a crowd a listener heard a needy and illiterate woman saying of another poor and haggard woman who had lost her little son years before: "You can see the ghost of that child in her face even now."

That speaker was one who, though she could probably neither read nor write, had the true means towards the "Science" of Fiction innate within her; a power of observation informed by a living heart. Had she been trained in the technicalities, she might have fashioned her view of mortality with good effect; a reflection which leads to a conjecture that, perhaps, true novelists, like poets, are born, not made.

The Dorsetshire Labourer (1883)

It seldom happens that a nickname which affects to portray a class is honestly indicative of the individuals composing that class. The few features distinguishing them from other bodies of men have been seized on and exaggerated, while the incomparably more numerous features common to all humanity have been ignored. In the great world this wild colouring of so-called typical portraits is clearly enough recognized. Nationalities, the aristocracy, the plutocracy, the citizen class, and many others have their allegorical representatives, which are received with due allowance for flights of imagination in the direction of burlesque.

But when the class lies somewhat out of the ken of ordinary society the caricature begins to be taken as truth. Moreover, the original is held to be an actual unit of the multitude signified. He ceases to be an abstract figure and becomes a sample. Thus when we arrive at the farm-labouring community we find it to be seriously personified by the pitiable picture known as Hodge; not only so, but the community is assumed to be a uniform collection of concrete Hodges.

This supposed real but highly conventional Hodge is a degraded being of uncouth manner and aspect, stolid understanding, and snail-like movement. His speech is such a chaotic corruption of regular language that few persons of progressive aims consider it worth while to enquire what views, if any, of life, of nature, or of society are conveyed in these utterances. Hodge hangs his head or looks sheepish when spoken to, and thinks Lunnon a place paved with gold. Misery and fever lurk in his cottage, while, to paraphrase the words of a recent writer on the labouring classes, in his future there are only the workhouse and the grave. He hardly dares to think at all. He has few thoughts of joy, and little hope of rest. His life slopes into a darkness not "quieted by hope."

If one of the many thoughtful persons who hold this view were to go by rail to Dorset, where Hodge in his most unmitigated form is supposed to reside, and seek out a retired district, he might by and by certainly meet a man who, at first contact with an intelligence fresh from the contrasting world of London, would seem to exhibit some of the above-mentioned qualities. The latter items in the list, the mental miseries, the visitor might hardly look for in their fulness, since it would have become perceptible to him as an explorer, and to any but the chamber theorist, that no uneducated community, rich or poor, bond or free, possessing average health and personal liberty, could exist in an unchangeable slough of despond, or that it would for many months if it could. Its members, like the accursed swine, would rush down a steep place and be choked in the waters. He would have learnt that wherever a mode of supporting life is neither noxious nor absolutely inadequate, there springs up happiness, and will spring up happiness, of some sort or other. Indeed, it is among such communities as these that happiness will find her last refuge on earth, since it is among them that a perfect insight into the conditions of existence will be longest postponed.

That in their future there are only the workhouse and the grave is no more and no less true than that in the future of the average well-to-do householder there are only the invalid chair and the brick vault.

Waiving these points, however, the investigator would insist that the man he had encountered exhibited a suspicious blankness of gaze, a great uncouthness and inactivity; and he might truly approach the unintelligible if addressed by a stranger on any but the commonest subject. But suppose that, by some accident, the visitor were obliged to go home with this man, take pot-luck with him and his, as one of the family. For the nonce the very sitting down would seem an undignified performance, and at first, the ideas, the modes, and the surroundings generally, would be puzzling—even impenetrable; or if in a measurable penetrable, would seem to have but little meaning. But living on there for a few days the sojourner would become conscious of a new aspect in the life around him. He would find that, without any objective change whatever, variety had taken the place of monotony; that the man who had brought him home—the typical Hodge, as he conjectured—was somehow not typical of anyone but himself. His host's brothers, uncles, and neighbours, as they became personally known, would appear as different from his host himself as one member of a club, or inhabitant of a city street, from another. As, to the eye of a diver, contrasting colours shine out by degrees from what has originally painted itself of an unrelieved earthy hue, so would shine out the characters, capacities, and interests of these people to him. He would, for one thing, find that the language, instead of being a vile corruption of cultivated speech, was a tongue with grammatical inflection rarely disregarded by his entertainer, though his entertainer's children would occasionally make a sad hash of their talk. Having attended the National School they would mix the printed tongue as taught therein with the unwritten, dying, Wessex English that they had learnt of their parents, the result of this transitional state of their being a composite language without rule or harmony.

Six months pass, and our gentleman leaves the cottage, bidding his friends good-bye with genuine regret. The great change in his perception is that Hodge, the dull, unvarying, joyless one, has ceased to exist for him. He has become disintegrated into a number of dissimilar fellow-creatures, men of many minds, infinite in difference; some happy, many serene, a few depressed; some clever, even to genius, some stupid, some wanton, some austere; some mutely Miltonic, some Cromwellian; into men who have private views of each other, as he has of his friends; who applaud or condemn each other; amuse or sadden themselves by the contemplation of each other's foibles or vices; and each of whom walks in his own way the road to dusty death. Dick the carter, Bob the shepherd, and Sam the ploughman, are, it is true, alike in the narrowness of their means and their general open-air life; but they cannot be rolled together again into such a Hodge as he dreamt of, by any possible enchantment. And should time and distance render an abstract being, representing the field labourer, possible again to the mind of the inquirer (a questionable possibility) he will find that the Hodge of current conception no longer sums up the capacities of the class so defined.

The pleasures enjoyed by the Dorset labourer may be far from pleasures of the highest kind desirable for him. They may be pleasures of the wrong shade. And the in-

evitable glooms of a straitened hard-working life occasionally enwrap him from such pleasures as he has; and in times
of special storm and stress the "Complaint of Piers the
Ploughman" is still echoed in his heart. But even Piers had
his flights of merriment and humour; and ploughmen as a
rule do not give sufficient thought to the morrow to be
miserable when not in physical pain. Drudgery in the slums
and alleys of a city, too long pursued, and accompanied as
it too often is by indifferent health, may induce a mood of
despondency which is well-nigh permanent; but the same
degree of drudgery in the fields results at worst in a mood
of painless passivity. A pure atmosphere and a pastoral
environment are a very appreciable portion of the sustenance which tends to produce the sound mind and body,
and thus much sustenance is, at least, the labourer's birth-
right.

If it were possible to gauge the average sufferings of
classes, the probability is that in Dorsetshire the figure
would be lower with the regular farmer's labourers—"work-
folk" as they call themselves—than with the adjoining class,
the unattached labourers, approximating to the free labourers of the middle ages, who are to be found in the larger
villages and small towns of the county—many of them,
no doubt, descendants of the old copyholders* who were
ousted from their little plots when the system of leasing
large farms grew general. They are, what the regular
labourer is not, out of sight of patronage; and to be out
of sight is to be out of mind when misfortune arises, and
pride or sensitiveness leads them to conceal their privations.

The happiness of a class can rarely be estimated aright
by philosophers who look down upon that class from the
Olympian heights of society. Nothing, for instance, is more
common than for some philanthropic lady to burst in upon
a family, be struck by the apparent squalor of the scene,
and to straightway mark down that household in her notebook as a frightful example of the misery of the labouring

---

* Tenants who retain occupancy of their holdings at the pleasure
of the manor landlord.—Ed.

classes. There are two distinct probabilities of error in forming any such estimate. The first is that the apparent squalor is no squalor at all. I am credibly informed that the conclusion is nearly always based on *colour*. A cottage in which the walls, the furniture, and the dress of the inmates reflect the brighter rays of the solar spectrum is read by these amiable visitors as a cleanly, happy home while one whose prevailing hue happens to be dingy russet, or a quaint old leather tint, or any of the numerous varieties of mud colour, is thought necessarily the abode of filth and Giant Despair. "I always kip a white apron behind the door to slip on when the gentlefolk knock, for if so be they see a white apron they think ye be clane," said an honest woman one day, whose bedroom floors could have been scraped with as much advantage as a pigeon-loft; but who, by a judicious use of high lights, shone as a pattern of neatness in her patrons' eyes.

There was another woman who had long nourished an unreasoning passion for burnt umber, and at last acquired a pot of the same from a friendly young carpenter. With this pigment she covered every surface in her residence to which paint is usually applied, and having more left, and feeling that to waste it would be a pity as times go, she went on to cover other surfaces till the whole was consumed. Her dress and that of the children were mostly of faded snuff-colour, her natural thrift inducing her to cut up and re-make a quantity of old stuffs that had been her mother's; and to add to the misery the floor of her cottage was of Mayne brick—a material which has the complexion of gravy mottled with cinders. Notwithstanding that the bed-linen and underclothes of this unfortunate woman's family were like the driven snow, and that the insides of her cooking utensils were concave mirrors, she was used with great effect as the frightful example of slovenliness for many years in that neighbourhood.

The second probability arises from the error of supposing that actual slovenliness is always accompanied by unhappiness. If it were so, a windfall of any kind would be utilised in most cases in improving the surroundings. But the money always goes in the acquisition of something new, and not in the removal of what there is already too much of, dirt. And most frequently the grimiest families are not the poorest; nay, paradoxical as it may seem, external neglect in a household implies something above the lowest level of poverty. Copyholders, cottage freeholders, and the like, are as a rule less trim and neat, more muddling in their ways, than the dependent labourer; and yet there is no more comfortable or serene being than the cottager who is sure of his roof. An instance of probable error through inability to see below the surface of things occurred the other day in an article by a lady on the peasant proprietors of Auvergne. She states that she discovered these persons living on an earth floor, mixed up with onions, dirty clothes, and the "indescribable remnants of never stirred rubbish"; while one of the houses had no staircase, the owners of the premises reaching their bedrooms by climbing up a bank, and stepping in at the higher level. This was an inconvenient way of getting upstairs; but we must guard against the inference that because these peasant proprietors are in a slovenly condition, and certain English peasants who are not proprietors live in model cottages copied out of a book by the squire, the latter are so much happier than the former as the dignity of their architecture is greater. It were idle to deny that, other things being equal, the family which dwells in a cleanly and spacious cottage has the probability of a more cheerful existence than a family narrowly housed and draggletailed. It has guarantees for health which the other has not. But it must be remembered that melancholy among the rural poor arises primarily from a sense of incertitude and precariousness of their position. Like Burns's field mouse, they are overawed and timorous lest those who can wrong them should be inclined to exercise their power. When we know that the Damocles' sword of the poor is the fear of being turned out of their houses by the farmer or squire, we may wonder how many scrupulously clean English labourers would not be glad with half-an-acre of the complaint that afflicts these unhappy freeholders of Auvergne.

It is not at all uncommon to find among the workfolk philosophers who recognise, as clearly as Lord Palmerston did, that dirt is only matter in the wrong place. A worthy man holding these wide views had put his clean shirt on a gooseberry bush one Sunday morning, to be aired in the sun, whence it blew off into the mud, and was much soiled. His wife would have got him another, but "No," he said, "the shirt shall wear his week. 'Tis fresh dirt, anyhow, and starch is no more."

On the other hand, true poverty—that is, the actual want of necessaries—is constantly trying to be decent, and one of the clearest signs of deserving poverty is the effort it makes to appear otherwise by scrupulous neatness.

To see the Dorset labourer at his worst and saddest time, he should be viewed when attending a wet hiring-fair at Candlemas, in search of a new master. His natural cheerfulness bravely struggles against the weather and the incertitude; but as the day passes on, and his clothes get wet through, and he is still unhired, there does appear a factitiousness in the smile which, with a self-repressing mannerliness hardly to be found among any other class, he yet has ready when he encounters and talks with friends who have been more fortunate. In youth and manhood, this disappointment occurs but seldom; but at threescore and over, it is frequently the lot of those who have no sons and daughters to fall back upon, or whose children are ingrates, or far away.

Here, at the corner of the street, in this aforesaid wet hiring-fair, stands an old shepherd. He is evidently a lonely man. The battle of life has always been a sharp one with him, for, to begin with, he is a man of small frame. He is now so bowed by hard work and years that, approaching from behind, you can scarcely see his head. He has planted the stem of his crook in the gutter, and rests upon the bow, which is polished to silver brightness by the long friction of his hands. He has quite forgotten where he is and what he has come for, his eyes being bent on the ground. "There's work in en," says one farmer to another, as they look dubiously across; "there's work left in en still; but not so much as I want for my acreage." "You'd get en cheap," says the other. The shepherd does not hear them, and there seem to be passing through his mind pleasant visions of the hiring successes of his prime—when his skill in ovine surgery laid open any farm to him for the asking, and his employer would say uneasily in the early days of February, "You don't mean to leave us this year?"

But the hale and strong have not to wait thus, and having secured places in the morning, the day passes merrily enough with them.

The hiring-fair of recent years presents an appearance unlike that of former times. A glance up the high street of the town on a Candlemas-fair day twenty or thirty years ago revealed a crowd whose general colour was whity-brown flecked with white. Black was almost absent, the few farmers who wore that shade hardly discernible. Now the crowd is as dark as a London crowd. This change is owing to the rage for cloth clothes which possesses the labourers of to-day. Formerly they came in smock-frocks and gaiters, the shepherds with their crooks, the carters with a zone of whipcord round their hats, thatchers with a straw tucked into the brim, and so on. Now, with the exception of the crook in the hands of an occasional old shepherd, there is no mark of speciality in the groups, who might be tailors or undertakers' men, for what they exhibit externally. Out of a group of eight, for example, who talk together in the middle of the road, only one wears corduroy trousers. Two wear cloth pilot-coats and black trousers, two patterned tweed suits with black canvas overalls, the remaining four suits being of faded broadcloth. To a great extent these are their Sunday suits; but the genuine white smock-frock of Russia duck and the whity-brown one of drabbet, are rarely seen now afield, except on the shoulders of old men. Where smocks are worn by the young and middle-aged, they are of blue material. The mechanic's "slop" has also been adopted; but a mangy old cloth coat is preferred; so that often a group of these honest fellows on the arable has the aspect of a body of tramps up to some mischief in the field, rather than its natural tillers at work there.

That peculiarity of the English urban poor (which M.

Taine ridicules, and unfavourably contrasts with the taste of the Continental working-people)—their preference for the cast-off clothes of a richer class to a special attire of their own—has, in fact, reached the Dorset farm folk. Like the men, the women are, pictorially, less interesting than they used to be. Instead of the wing bonnet like the tilt of a waggon, cotton gown, bright-hued neckerchief, and strong flat boots and shoes, they (the younger ones at least) wear shabby millinery bonnets and hats with beads and feathers, "material" dresses, and boot-heels almost as foolishly shaped as those of ladies of highest education.

Having "agreed for a place," as it is called, either at the fair, or (occasionally) by private intelligence, or (with growing frequency) by advertisement in the penny local papers, the terms are usually reduced to writing: though formerly a written agreement was unknown, and is now, as a rule, avoided by the farmer if the labourer does not insist upon one. It is signed by both, and a shilling is passed to bind the bargain. The business is then settled, and the man returns to his place of work, to do no more in the matter till Lady Day, Old Style—April 6.

Of all the days in the year, people who love the rural poor of the south-west should pray for a fine day then. Dwellers near the highways of the country are reminded of the anniversary surely enough. They are conscious of a disturbance of their night's rest by noises beginning in the small hours of darkness, and intermittently continuing till daylight—noises as certain to recur on that particular night of the month as the voice of the cuckoo on the third or fourth week of the same. The day of fulfillment has come, and the labourers are on the point of being fetched from the old farm by the carters of the new. For it is always by the waggon and horses of the farmer who requires his services that the hired man is conveyed to his destination; and that this may be accomplished within the day is the reason that the noises begin so soon after midnight. Suppose the distance to be an ordinary one of a dozen or fifteen miles. The carter at the prospective place rises "when Charles's Wain is over the new chimney," harnesses his team of three horses by lantern light, and proceeds to the present home of his coming comrade. It is the passing of these empty waggons in all directions that is heard breaking the stillness of the hours before dawn. The aim is usually to be at the door of the removing household by six o'clock, when the loading of goods at once begins; and at nine or ten the start to the new home is made. From this hour till one or two in the day, when the other family arrives at the old house, the cottage is empty, and it is only in that short interval that the interior can be in any way cleaned and lime-whitened for the new comers, however dirty it may have become, or whatever sickness may have prevailed among members of the departed family.

Should the migrant himself be a carter there is a slight modification in the arrangement, for carters do not fetch carters, as they fetch shepherds and general hands. In this case the man has to transfer himself. He relinquishes charge of the horses of the old farm in the afternoon of April 5, and starts on foot the same afternoon for the new place. There he makes the acquaintance of the horses which are to be under his care for the ensuing year, and passes the night sometimes on a bundle of clean straw in the stable, for he is as yet a stranger here, and too indifferent to the comforts of a bed on this particular evening to take much trouble to secure one. From this couch he uncurls himself about two o'clock, a.m. (for the distance we have assumed), and, harnessing his new charges, moves off with them to his old home, where, on his arrival, the packing is already advanced by the wife, and loading goes on as before mentioned.

The goods are built up on the waggon to a well-nigh unvarying pattern, which is probably as peculiar to the country labourer as the hexagon to the bee. The dresser, with its finger-marks and domestic evidences thick upon it, stands importantly in front, over the backs of the shaft horses, in its erect and natural position, like some Ark of the Covenant, which must not be handled slightingly or overturned. The hive of bees is slung up to the axle of the waggon, and alongside it the cooking pot or crock, within which are stowed the roots of garden flowers. Barrels are largely used for crockery, and budding gooseberry bushes are suspended by the roots; while on the top of the furniture a circular nest is made of the bed and bedding for the matron and children, who sit there through the journey. If there is no infant in arms, the woman holds the head of the clock, which at any exceptional lurch of the waggon strikes one, in thin tones. The other object of solicitude is the looking-glass, usually held in the lap of the eldest girl. It is emphatically spoken of as *the* looking-glass, there being but one in the house, except possibly a small shaving-glass for the husband. But labouring men are not much dependent upon mirrors for a clean chin. I have seen many men shaving in the chimney corner, looking into the fire; or, in summer, in the garden, with their eyes fixed upon a gooseberry-bush, gazing as steadfastly as if there were a perfect reflection of their image—from which it would seem that the concentrated look of shavers in general was originally demanded rather by the mind than by the eye. On the other hand, I knew a man who used to walk about the room all the time he was engaged in the operation, and how he escaped cutting himself was a marvel. Certain luxurious dandies of the furrow, who could not do without a reflected image of themselves when using the razor, obtained it till quite recently by placing the crown of an old hat outside the window-pane, then confronting it inside the room and falling to—a contrivance which formed a very clear reflection of a face in high light.

The day of removal, if fine, wears an aspect of jollity, and the whole proceeding is a blithe one. A bundle of provisions for the journey is usually hung up at the side of the vehicle, together with a three-pint stone jar of extra strong ale; for it is as impossible to move house without beer as without horses. Roadside inns, too, are patronized, where, during the halt, a mug is seen ascending and descending through the air to and from the feminine portion of the household at the top of the waggon. The drinking at these times is, however, moderate, the beer supplied to travelling labourers being of a preternaturally small brew;

as was illustrated by a dialogue which took place on such an occasion quite recently. The liquor was not quite to the taste of the male travellers, and they complained. But the landlady upheld its merits. " 'Tis our own brewing, and there is nothing in it but malt and hops," she said, with rectitude. "Yes, there is," said the traveller. "There's water." "Oh! I forgot the water," the landlady replied. "I'm d——d if you did, mis'ess," replied the man; "for there's hardly anything else in the cup."

Ten or a dozen of these families, with their goods, may be seen halting simultaneously at an out-of-the-way inn, and it is not possible to walk a mile on any of the high roads this day without meeting several. This annual migration from farm to farm is much in excess of what it was formerly. For example, on a particular farm where, a generation ago, not more than one cottage on an average changed occupants yearly, and where the majority remained all their lifetime, the whole number of tenants were changed at Lady Day just past, and this though nearly all of them had been new arrivals on the previous Lady Day. Dorset labourers now look upon an annual removal as the most natural thing in the world, and it becomes with the younger families a pleasant excitement. Change is also a certain sort of education. Many advantages accrue to the labourers from the varied experience it brings, apart from the discovery of the best market for their abilities. They have become shrewder and sharper men of the world, and have learnt how to hold their own with firmness and judgment. Whenever the habitually-removing man comes into contact with one of the old-fashioned stationary sort, who are still to be found, it is impossible not to perceive that the former is much more wide awake than his fellow-worker, astonishing him with stories of the wide world comprised in a twenty-mile radius from their homes.

They are also losing their peculiarities as a class; hence the humorous simplicity which formerly characterised the men and the unsophisticated modesty of the women are rapidly disappearing or lessening, under the constant attrition of lives mildly approximating to those of workers in a manufacturing town. It is the common remark of villagers above the labouring class, who know the latter well as personal acquaintances, that "there are no nice homely workfolk now as there used to be." There may be, and is, some exaggeration in this, but it is only natural that, now different districts of them are shaken together once a year and redistributed, like a shuffled pack of cards, they have ceased to be so local in feeling or manner as formerly, and have entered on the condition of inter-social citizens, "whose city stretches the whole county over." Their brains are less frequently than they once were "as dry as the remainder biscuit after a voyage," and they vent less often the result of their own observations than what they have heard to be the current ideas of smart chaps in towns. The women have, in many districts, acquired the rollicking air of factory hands. That seclusion and immutability, which was so bad for their pockets, was an unrivalled fosterer of their personal charm in the eyes of those whose experiences had been less limited. But the artistic merit of their old condition is scarcely a reason why they should have continued in it when other communities were marching on so vigorously towards uniformity and mental equality. It is only the old story that progress and picturesqueness do not harmonise. They are losing their individuality, but they are widening the range of their ideas, and gaining in freedom. It is too much to expect them to remain stagnant and old-fashioned for the pleasure of romantic spectators.

But, picturesqueness apart, a result of this increasing nomadic habit of the labourer is naturally a less intimate and kindly relation with the land he tills than existed before enlightenment enabled him to rise above the condition of a serf who lived and died on a particular plot, like a tree. During the centuries of serfdom, of copyholding tenants, and down to twenty or thirty years ago, before the power of unlimited migration had been clearly realised, the husbandman of either class had the interest of long personal association with his farm. The fields were those he had ploughed and sown from boyhood, and it was impossible for him, in such circumstances, to sink altogether the

character of natural guardian in that of hireling. Not so
very many years ago, the landowner, if he were good for
anything, stood as a court of final appeal in cases of the
harsh dismissal of a man by the farmer. "I'll go to my
lord" was a threat which overbearing farmers respected,
for "my lord" had often personally known the labourer
long before he knew the labourer's master. But such arbit-
rament is rarely practicable now. The landlord does not
know by sight, if even by name, half the men who preserve
his acres from the curse of Eden. They come and go yearly,
like birds of passage, nobody thinks whence or whither.
This disociation is favoured by the customary system of
letting the cottages with the land, so that, far from having
a guarantee of a holding to keep him fixed, the labourer
has not even the stability of a landlord's tenant; he is only
tenant of a tenant, the latter possibly a new comer, who
takes strictly commercial views of his man and cannot
afford to waste a penny on sentimental considerations.

Thus, while their pecuniary condition in the prime of
life is bettered, and their freedom enlarged, they have lost
touch with their environment, and that sense of long local
participancy which is one of the pleasures of age. The old
casus conscientiae of those in power—whether the weak
tillage of an enfeebled hand ought not to be put up with
in fields which have had the benefit of that hand's strength
—arises less frequently now that the strength has often
been expended elsewhere. The sojourning existence of the
town masses is more and more the existence of the rural
masses, with its corresponding benefits and disadvantages.
With uncertainty of residence often comes a laxer morality,
and more cynical views of the duties of life. Domestic
stability is a factor in conduct which nothing else can
equal. On the other hand, new varieties of happiness evolve
themselves like new varieties of plants, and new charms
may have arisen among the classes who have been driven
to adopt the remedy of locomotion for the evils of oppression and poverty—charms which compensate in some
measure for the lost sense of home.

A practical injury which this wandering entails on the

children of the labourers should be mentioned here. In
shifting from school to school, their education cannot possibly progress with that regularity which is essential to
their getting the best knowledge in the short time available to them. It is the remark of village school-teachers of
experience, that the children of the vagrant workfolk form
the mass of those who fail to reach the ordinary standard
of knowledge expected of their age. The rural schoolmaster
or mistress enters the schoolroom on the morning of the
sixth of April, and finds that a whole flock of the brightest
young people has suddenly flown away. In a village school
which may be taken as a fair average specimen, containing
seventy-five scholars, thirty-three vanished thus on the
Lady Day of the present year. Some weeks elapse before
the new comers drop in, and a longer time passes before they
take root in the school, their dazed, unaccustomed mood
rendering immediate progress impossible; while the original
bright ones have by this time themselves degenerated into
the dazed strangers of other districts.

That the labourers of the country are more independent
since their awakening to the sense of an outer world cannot
be disputed. It was once common enough on inferior farms
to hear a farmer, as he sat on horseback amid a field of
workers, address them with a contemptuousness which
could not have been greatly exceeded in the days when
the thralls of Cedric wore their collars of brass. Usually
no answer was returned to these tirades; they were received
as an accident of the land on which the listeners had happened to be born, calling for no more resentment than the
blows of the wind and rain. But now, no longer fearing to
avail himself of his privilege of flitting, these acts of con-
tumely have ceased to be regarded as inevitable by the
peasant. And while men do not of their own accord leave
a farm without a grievance, very little fault-finding is often
deemed a sufficient one among the younger and stronger.
Such ticklish relations are the natural result of generations
of unfairness on one side, and on the other an increase of
knowledge, which has been kindled into activity by the
exertions of Mr. Joseph Arch.

Nobody who saw and heard Mr. Arch in his early tours through Dorsetshire will ever forget him and the influence his presence exercised over the crowds he drew. He hailed from Shakespeare's county, where the humours of the peasantry have a marked family relationship with those of Dorset men; and it was this touch of nature, as much as his logic, which afforded him such ready access to the minds and hearts of the labourers here. It was impossible to hear and observe the speaker for more than a few minutes without perceiving that he was a humourist—moreover, a man by no means carried away by an idea beyond the bounds of common sense. Like his renowned fellow-dalesman Corin, he virtually confessed that he was never in court, and might, with that eminent shepherd, have truly described himself as a "natural philosopher," who had discovered that "he that wants money, means, and content, is without three good friends."

"Content" may for a moment seem a word not exactly explanatory of Mr. Arch's views; but on the single occasion, several years ago, on which the present writer numbered himself among those who assembled to listen to that agitator, there was a remarkable moderation in his tone, and an exhortation to contentment with a reasonable amelioration, which, to an impartial auditor, went a long way in the argument. His views showed him to be rather the social evolutionist—what M. Émile de Laveleye would call a "Possibilist"—than the anarchic irreconcilable. The picture he drew of a comfortable cottage life as it should be, was so cosy, so well within the grasp of his listeners' imagination, that an old labourer in the crowd held up a coin between his finger and thumb exclaiming, "Here's zixpence towards that, please God!" "Towards what?" said a bystander. "Faith, I don't know that I can spak the name o't, but I know 'tis a good thing," he replied.

The result of the agitation, so far, upon the income of the labourers, has been testified by independent witnesses with a unanimity which leaves no reasonable doubt of its accuracy. It amounts to an average rise of three shillings a week in wages nearly all over the county. The absolute

number of added shillings seems small; but the increase is
considerable when we remember that it is three shillings on
eight or nine— *i.e.*, between thirty and forty per cent. And
the reflection is forced upon everyone who thinks of the
matter, that if a farmer can afford to pay thirty per cent
more wages in times of agricultural depression than he paid
in times of agricultural prosperity, and yet live, and keep
a carriage, while the landlord still thrives on the reduced
rent which has resulted, the labourer must have been greatly
wronged in those prosperous times. That the maximum of
wage has been reached for the present is, however, pretty
clear; and indeed it should be added that on several farms
the labourers have submitted to a slight reduction during
the past year, under stress of representations which have
appeared reasonable.

It is hardly necessary to observe that the quoted wages
never represent the labourer's actual income. Beyond the
weekly payment—now standing at eleven or twelve shillings—he invariably receives a lump sum of 2*l.* or 3*l.* for
harvest work. A cottage and garden is almost as invariably
provided, free of rent, with, sometimes, an extra piece of
ground for potatoes in some field near at hand. Fuel, too,
is frequently furnished, in the form of wood faggots. At
springtime, on good farms, the shepherd receives a shilling
for every twin reared, while a carter gets what is called
journey-money, that is, a small sum, mostly a shilling, for
every journey taken beyond the bounds of the farm. Where
all these supplementary trifles are enjoyed together, the
weekly wage in no case exceeds eleven shillings at the
present time.

The question of enough or not enough often depends
less upon the difference of two or three shillings a week
in the earnings of the head of a family than upon the
nature of his household. With a family of half a dozen
children, the eldest of them delicate girls, nothing that he
can hope to receive for the labour of his one pair of hands
can save him from many hardships during a few years. But
with a family of strong boys, of ages from twelve to seventeen or eighteen, he enjoys a season of prosperity. The very

manner of the farmer towards him is deferential; for home-living boys, who in many cases can do men's work at half the wages, and without requiring the perquisites of house, garden-land, and so on, are treasures to the employer of agricultural labour. These precious lads are, according to the testimony of several respectable labourers, a more frequent cause of contention between employer and man than any other item in their reckonings. As the boys grow, the father asks for a like growth in their earnings; and disputes arise which frequently end in the proprietor of the valuables taking himself off to a farm where he and his will be better appreciated. The mother of the same goodly row of sons can afford to despise the farmer's request for female labour; she stays genteelly at home, and looks with some superciliousness upon wives who, having no useful children, are obliged to work in the fields like their hus-bands. A triumphant family of the former class, which recently came under notice, may be instanced. The father and eldest son were paid eleven shillings a week each, the younger son ten shillings, three nearly grown-up daughters four shillings a week each, the mother the same when she chose to go out, and all the women two shillings a week additional at harvest; the men, of course, receiving their additional harvest-money as previously stated, with house, garden, and allotment free of charge. And since "*sine prole*"* would not frequently be written of the Dorset labourer if his pedigree were recorded in the local history like that of the other country families, such cases as the above are not uncommon.

Women's labour, too, is highly in request, for a woman who, like a boy, fills the place of a man at half the wages, can be better depended on for steadiness. Thus where a boy is useful in driving a cart or a plough, a woman is invaluable in work which, though somewhat lighter, de-mands thought. In winter and spring a farmwoman's occu-pation is often "turnip-hacking"—that is, picking out from the land the stumps of turnips which have been eaten off

* without offspring—Ed.

by the sheep—or feeding the threshing-machine, clearing away straw from the same, and standing on the rick to hand forward the sheaves. In mid-spring and early summer her services are required for weeding wheat and barley (cutting up thistles and other noxious plants with a spud), and clearing weeds from pasture-land in like manner. In later summer her time is entirely engrossed by haymaking —quite a science, though it appears the easiest thing in the world to toss hay about in the sun. The length to which a skilful raker will work and retain command over her rake without moving her feet is dependent largely upon practice, and quite astonishing to the uninitiated.

Haymaking is no sooner over than the women are hurried off to the harvest-field. This is a lively time. The bonus in wages during these few weeks, the cleanliness of the occupation, the heat, the cider and ale, influence to facetiousness and vocal strains. Quite the reverse do these lively women feel in the occupation which may be said to stand, emotionally, at the opposite pole to gathering in corn: that is, threshing it. Not a woman in the county but hates the threshing machine. The dust, the din, the sustained exertion demanded to keep up with the steam tyrant, are distasteful to all women but the coarsest. I am not sure whether, at the present time, women are employed to feed the machine, but some years ago a woman had frequently to stand just above the whizzing wire drum, and feed from morning to night—a performance for which she was quite unfitted, and many were the manœuvres to escape that responsible position. A thin saucer-eyed woman of fifty-five, who had been feeding the machine all day, declared on one occasion that in crossing a field on her way home in the fog after dusk, she was so dizzy from the work as to be unable to find the opposite gate, and there she walked round and round the field, bewildered and terrified, till three o'clock in the morning, before she could get out. The farmer said that the ale had got into her head, but she maintained that it was the spinning of the machine. The point was never clearly settled between them; and the poor woman is now dead and buried.

To be just, however, to the farmers, they do not enforce the letter of the Candlemas agreement in relation to the woman, if she makes any reasonable excuse for breaking it; and indeed, many a nervous farmer is put to flight by a matron who has a tongue with a tang, and who chooses to assert, without giving any reason whatever, that, though she had made fifty agreements, "be cust if she will come out unless she is minded"—possibly terrifying him with accusations of brutality at asking her, when he knows "how she is just now." A farmer of the present essayist's acquaintance, who has a tendency to blush in the presence of beauty, and is in other respects a bashful man for his years, says that when the ladies of his farm are all together in the field, and he is the single one of the male sex present, he would as soon put his head into a hornet's nest as utter a word of complaint, or even a request beyond the commonest.

The changes which are so increasingly discernible in village life by no means originate entirely with the agricultural unrest. A depopulation is going on which in some quarters is truly alarming. Villages used to contain, in addition to the agricultural inhabitatnts, an interesting and better-informed class, ranking distinctly above those— the blacksmith, the carpenter, the shoemaker, the small higgler, the shopkeeper (whose stock-in-trade consisted of a couple of loaves, a pound of candles, a bottle of brandy-balls and lumps of delight, three or four scrubbing-brushes, and a frying-pan), together with nondescript-workers other than farm-labourers, who had remained in the houses where they were born for no especial reason beyond an instinct of association with the spot. Many of these families had been life-holders, who built at their own expense the cottages they occupied, and as the lives dropped, and the property fell in they would have been glad to remain as weekly or monthly tenants of the owner. But the policy of all but some few philanthropic landowners is to disapprove of these petty tenants who are not in the estate's employ, and to pull down each cottage as it falls in, leaving standing a sufficient number for the use of the farmer's

men and no more. The occupants who formed the backbone of the village life have to seek refuge in the boroughs.
This process, which is designated by statisticians as "the
tendency of the rural population towards the large towns,"
is really the tendency of water to flow uphill when forced.
The poignant regret of those who are thus obliged to forsake the old nest can only be realised by people who have
witnessed it—concealed as it often is under a mask of
indifference. It is anomalous that landowners who are showing unprecedented activity in the erection of comfortable
cottages for their farm labourers, should see no reason for
benefiting in the same way these unattached natives of the
village who are nobody's care. They might often expostu-
late in the words addressed to King Henry the Fourth by
his fallen subject:—

> Our house, my sovereign liege, little deserves
> The scourge of greatness to be used on it;
> And that same greatness, too, which our own hands
> Have holp to make so portly.

The system is much to be deplored, for every one of these
banished people imbibes a sworn enmity to the existing
order of things, and not a few of them, far from becoming
merely honest Radicals, degenerate into Anarchists, waiters
on chance, to whom danger to the State, the town—nay,
the street they live in, is a welcomed opportunity.

A reason frequently advanced for dismissing these families from the villages where they have lived for centuries
is that it is done in the interests of morality; and it is
quite true that some of the "liviers" (as these half-independ-
ent villagers used to be called) were not always shining
examples of churchgoing, temperance, and quiet walking.
But a natural tendency to evil, which develops to unlaw-
ful action when excited by contact with others like-minded,
would often have remained latent amid the simple isolated
experiences of a village life. The cause of morality cannot
be served by compelling a population hitherto evenly distributed over the country to concentrate in a few towns,
with the inevitable results of overcrowding and want of

regular employment. But the question of the Dorset cottager here emerges in that of all the houseless and landless poor, and the vast topic of the Rights of Man, to consider which is beyond the scope of a merely descriptive article.

Maumbury Ring (1908)

The present month sees the last shovelful filled in, the last sod replaced, of the excavations in the well-known amphitheatre at Dorchester, which have been undertaken at the instance of the Dorset Field and Antiquarian Club and others, for the purpose of ascertaining the history and date of the ruins. The experts have scraped their spades and gone home to meditate on the results of their exploration, pending the resumption of the work next spring. Mr. St. George Gray, of Taunton, has superintended the labour, assisted by Mr. Charles Prideaux, an enthusiastic antiquary of the town, who, with disinterested devotion to discovery, has preferred to spend his annual holiday from his professional duties at the bottom of chalk trenches groping for *fibulae* or arrow-heads in a drizzling rain, to idling it away on any other spot in Europe.

As usual, revelations have been made of an unexpected kind. There was a moment when the blood of us onlookers ran cold, and we shivered a shiver that was not occasioned by our wet feet and dripping clothes. For centuries the town, the county, and England generally, novelists, poets, historians, guide-book writers, and what not, had been freely indulging their imaginations in picturing scenes that, they assumed, must have been enacted within those oval slopes; the feats, the contests, animal exhibitions, even gladiatorial combats, before throngs of people

> Who loved the games men played with death,
>   Where death must win

—briefly, the Colosseum programme on a smaller scale. But up were thrown from one corner prehistoric implements, chipped flints, horns, and other remains, and a voice announced that the earthworks were of the palæolithic or neolithic age, and not Roman at all!

This, however, was but a temporary and, it is believed, unnecessary alarm. At other points in the structure, as has been already stated in *The Times*, the level floor of an arena, trodden smooth, and coated with traces of gravel, was discovered with Roman relics and coins on its surface; and at the entrance and in front of the podium, a row of post-holes, apparently for barriers, as square as when they were dug, together with other significant marks, which made it fairly probable that, whatever the place had been before Julius Caesar's landing, it had been used as an amphitheatre at some time during the Roman occupation. The obvious explanation, to those who are not specialists, seems to be that here, as elsewhere, the colonists, to save labour, shaped and adapted to their own use some earthworks already on the spot. This was antecedently likely from the fact that the amphitheatre stands on an elevated site—or, in the enigmatic words of Hutchins, is "artfully set on the top of a plain,"—and that every similar spot in the neighbourhood has a tumulus or tumuli upon it; or had till some were carted away within living memory.

But this is a matter on which the professional investigators will have their conclusive say when funds are forthcoming to enable them to dig further. For some reason they have hitherto left undisturbed the ground about the southern end of the arena, underneath which the *cavea* or vault for animals is traditionally said to be situated, though it is doubtful if any such vault, supposing it ever to have existed, would have been suffered to remain there, stones being valuable in a chalk district. And if it had been built of chalk blocks the frost and rains of centuries would have pulverized them by this time.

While the antiquaries are musing on the puzzling problems that arise from the confusion of dates in the remains, the mere observer who possesses a smattering of local history, and remembers local traditions that have been recounted by people now dead and gone, may walk round the familiar arena, and consider. And he is not, like the archaists, compelled to restrict his thoughts to the early centuries of our era. The sun has gone down behind the avenue on the Roman Via and modern road that adjoins, and the October moon is rising on the south-east behind the parapet, the two terminations of which by the north entrance jut against the sky like knuckles. The place is now in its normal state of repose and silence, save for the occasional bray of a motorist passing along outside in sublime ignorance of amphitheatrical lore, or the clang of shunting at the nearest railway station. The breeze is not strong enough to stir even the grass-bents with which the slopes are covered, and over which the loiterer's footsteps are quite noiseless.

Like all such taciturn presences, Maumbury is less taciturn by night than by day, which simply means that the episodes and incidents associated therewith come back more readily to the mind in nocturnal hours. First, it recalls to us that, if probably Roman, it is a good deal more. Its history under the rule of the Romans would not extend to a longer period than 200 or 300 years, while it has had a history of 1,600 years since they abandoned this island, through which ages it may have been regarded as a handy place for early English council-gatherings, may have been the scene of many an exciting episode in the life of the Western kingdom. But for century after century it keeps itself closely curtained, except at some moments to be mentioned.

The civil wars of Charles I unscreen it a little, and we vaguely learn that it was used by the artillery when the struggle was in this district, and that certain irregularities in its summit were caused then. The next incident that flashes a light over the contours is Sir Christopher Wren's visit a quarter of a century later. Nobody knows what the inhabitants thought to be the origin of its elliptic banks— differing from others in the vicinity by having no trench around them—until the day came when, according to

legend, Wren passed up the adjoining highway on his
journey to Portland to select stone for St. Paul's Cathedral,
and was struck with the sight of the mounds. Possibly he
asked some rustic at plough there for information. That all
tradition of their use as an amphitheatre had been lost is
to be inferred from their popular name, and one can quite
understand how readily, as he entered and stood on the
summit, a man whose studies had lain so largely in the
direction of Roman architecture should have ascribed a
Roman origin to the erection. That the offhand guess of a
passing architect should have turned out to be true—and
it does not at present seem possible to prove the whole
construction to be prehistoric—is a remarkable tribute to
his insight.

The curtain drops for another forty years, and then
Maumbury was the scene of as sinister an event as any
associated with it, because it was a definite event. It is
one which darkens its concave to this day. This was the
death suffered there on March 21, 1705–06, of a girl who
had not yet reached her nineteenth year. Here, at any rate,
we touch real flesh and blood, and no longer uncertain
visions of possible Romans at their games or barbarians
at their sacrifices. The story is a ghastly one, but nevertheless very distinctly a chapter of Maumbury's experiences.
This girl was the wife of a grocer in the town, a handsome
young woman "of good natural parts," and educated "to
a proficiency suitable enough to one of her sex, to which
likewise was added dancing." She was tried and condemned
for poisoning her husband, a Mr. Thomas Channing, to
whom she had been married against her wish by the compulsion of her parents. The present writer has examined
more than once a report of her trial, and can find no distinct evidence that the thoughtless, pleasure-loving creature
committed the crime, while it contains much to suggest that
she did not. Nor is any motive discoverable for such an
act. She was allowed to have her former lover or lovers
about her by her indulgent and weak-minded husband,
who permitted her to go her own ways, give parties, and
supplied her with plenty of money. However, at the assizes

at the end of July, she was found guilty, after a trial in which the testimony chiefly went to show her careless character before and after marriage. During the three sultry days of its continuance, she, who was soon to become a mother, stood at the bar—then, as may be known, an actual bar of iron—"by reason of which (runs the account) and her much talking, being quite spent, she moved the Court for the liberty of a glass of water." She conducted her own defence with the greatest ability, and was complimented thereupon by Judge Price, who tried her, but did not extend his compliment to a merciful summing-up. Maybe that he, like Pontius Pilate, was influenced by the desire of the townsfolk to wreak vengeance on somebody, right or wrong. When sentence was about to be passed, she pleaded her condition; and execution was postponed. Whilst awaiting the birth of her child in the old damp gaol by the river at the bottom of the town, near the White Hart inn, which stands there still, she was placed in the common room for women prisoners and no bed provided for her, no special payment having been made to her gaoler, Mr. Knapton, for a separate cell. Someone obtained for her the old tilt of a wagon to screen her from surrounding eyes, and under this she was delivered of a son, in December. After her lying-in, she was attacked with an intermittent fever of a violent and lasting kind, which preyed upon her until she was nearly wasted away. In this state, at the next assizes, on the 8th of March following, the unhappy woman, who now said that she longed for death, but still persisted in her innocence, was again brought to the bar, and her execution fixed for the 21st.

On that day two men were hanged before her turn came, and then, "the under-sheriff having taken some refreshment," he proceeded to his biggest and last job with this girl not yet 19, now reduced to a skeleton by the long fever, and already more dead than alive. She was conveyed from the gaol in a cart "by her father's and husband's house," so that the course of the procession must have been up High-East-street as far as the Bow, thence down South-street and up the straight old Roman road to the Ring beside it. "When fixed to the stake she justified her innocence to the very last, and left the world with a courage seldom found in her sex. She being first strangled, the fire was kindled about five in the afternoon, and in the sight of many thousands she was consumed to ashes." There is nothing to show that she was dead before the burning began, and from the use of the word "strangled" and not "hanged," it would seem that she was merely rendered insensible before the fire was lit. An ancestor of the present writer, who witnessed the scene, has handed down the information that "her heart leapt out" during the burning, and other curious details that cannot be printed here. Was man ever "slaughtered by his fellow man" during the Roman or barbarian use of this place of games or of sacrifice in circumstances of greater atrocity?

A melodramatic, though less gruesome, exhibition within the arena was that which occurred at the time of the "No Popery" riots, and was witnessed by this writer when a small child. Highly realistic effigies of the Pope and Cardinal Wiseman were borne in procession from Fordington Hill round the town, followed by a long train of mock priests, monks, and nuns, and preceded by a young man discharging Roman candles, till the same wicked old place was reached, in the centre of which there stood a huge rick of furze, with a gallows above. The figures were slung up, and the fire blazed till they were blown to pieces by fireworks contained within them.

Like its more famous prototype, the Colosseum, this spot of sombre records has also been the scene of Christian worship, but only on one occasion, so far as the writer of these columns is aware, that being the Thanksgiving service for Peace a few years ago. The surplices of the clergy and choristers, as seen against the green grass, the shining brass musical instruments, the enormous chorus of singing voices, formed not the least impressive of the congregated masses that Maumbury Ring has drawn into its midst during its existence of a probable eighteen hundred years in its present shape, and of some possible thousands of years in an earlier form.

So large was the quantity of material thrown up in the course of the excavations at Maumbury Ring, Dorchester, especially from the prehistoric pit which was unexpectedly struck, that the work of filling in, which has been in progress eight days, is likely to last nearly a week longer. The pit, situated at the base of the bank on the north-west side, between the bank and the arena, was found at the conclusion of the excavations to be thirty feet deep, and Mr. St. George Gray thinks it is the deepest archæological excavation on record in Britain. Of irregular shape, and apparently excavated in the solid chalk subsoil, it diminished in size from a diameter of about six feet at the mouth to about eighteen inches by fifteen inches at the bottom. One of three red-deer antler picks recovered from the deposit in the pit was found resting on the solid chalk floor of the bottom, and worked flint was found within a few feet of the bottom. The picks exactly resemble those which Mr. St. George Gray found in the great fosse at Avebury last May. Roman deposits and specimens were found in the upper part of the pit down to the level of the chalk floor of the arena, but not below it.

From the Apology to *Late Lyrics and Earlier* (1922)

The launching of a volume of this kind in neo-Georgian days by one who began writing in mid-Victorian, and has published nothing to speak of for some years, may seem to call for a few words of excuse or explanation. Whether or no, readers may feel assured that a new book is submitted to them with great hesitation at so belated a date. Insistent practical reasons, however, among which were requests from some illustrious men of letters who are in sympathy with my productions, the accident that several of the poems have already seen the light, and that dozens of them have been lying about for years, compelled the course adopted, in spite of the natural disinclination of a writer whose works have been so frequently regarded askance by a pragmatic section here and there, to draw attention to them once more.

I do not know that it is necessary to say much on the contents of the book, even in deference to suggestions that will be mentioned presently. I believe that those readers who care for my poems at all—readers to whom no passport is required—will care for this new instalment of them, perhaps the last, as much as for any that have preceded them. Moreover, in the eyes of a less friendly class the pieces, though a very mixed collection indeed, contain, so far as I am able to see, little or nothing in technic or teaching that can be considered a Star-Chamber matter, or so much as agitating to a ladies' school; even though, to use Wordsworth's observation in his Preface to *Lyrical Ballads*, such readers may suppose "that by the act of writing in verse an author makes a formal engagement that he will gratify certain known habits of association: that he not only thus apprises the reader that certain classes of ideas and expressions will be found in his book, but that others will be carefully excluded."

It is true, nevertheless, that some grave, positive, stark delineations are interspersed among those of the passive, lighter, and traditional sort presumably nearer to stereotyped tastes. For—while I am quite aware that a thinker is not expected, and, indeed, is scarcely allowed, now more than heretofore, to state all that crosses his mind concerning existence in this universe, in his attempts to explain or excuse the presence of evil and the incongruity of penalizing the irresponsible—it must be obvious to open intelligences that, without denying the beauty and faithful service of certain venerable cults, such disallowance of "obstinate questionings" and "blank misgivings" tends to a paralysed intellectual stalemate. Heine observed nearly a hundred years ago that the soul has her eternal rights; that she will not be darkened by statutes, nor lullabied by the music of bells. And what is to-day, in allusions to the present author's pages, alleged to be "pessimism" is, in truth, only such "questionings" in the exploration of reality, and is the first step towards the soul's betterment, and the body's also.

If I may be forgiven for quoting my own old words, let me repeat what I printed in this relation more than twenty years ago, and wrote much earlier, in a poem entitled "In Tenebris":

> If way to the Better there be, it exacts a full look
>   at the Worst:

that is to say, by the exploration of reality, and its frank recognition stage by stage along the survey, with an eye to the best consummation possible: briefly, evolutionary meliorism. But it is called pessimism nevertheless; under which word, expressed with condemnatory emphasis, it is regarded by many as some pernicious new thing (though so old as to underlie the Gospel scheme, and even to permeate the Greek drama); and the subject is charitably left to decent silence, as if further comment were needless.

Happily there are some who feel such Levitical passing-by to be, alas, by no means a permanent dismissal of the matter; that comment on where the world stands is very much the reverse of needless in these disordered years of our prematurely afflicted century: that amendment and not madness lies that way. And looking down the future these few hold fast to the same: that whether the human and kindred animal races survive till the exhaustion or destruction of the globe, or whether these races perish and are succeeded by others before that conclusion comes, pain to all upon it, tongued or dumb, shall be kept down to a minimum by loving-kindness, operating through scientific knowledge, and actuated by the modicum of free will conjecturally possessed by organic life when the mighty necessitating forces—unconscious or other—that have "the balancings of the clouds," happen to be in equilibrium, which may or may not be often.

To conclude this question I may add that the argument of the so-called optimists is neatly summarized in a stern pronouncement against me by my friend Mr. Frederic

Harrison in a late essay of his, in the words: "This view of life is not mine." The solemn declaration does not seem to me to be so annihilating to the said "view" (really a series of fugitive impressions which I have never tried to co-ordinate) as is complacently assumed. Surely it embodies a too human fallacy quite familiar in logic. Next, a knowing reviewer, apparently a Roman Catholic young man, speaks, with some rather gross instances of the *suggestio falsi* in his whole article, of "Mr. Hardy refusing consolation," the "dark gravity of his ideas," and so on. When a Positivist and a Romanist agree there must be something wonderful in it, which should make a poet sit up. But . . . O that 'twere possible!

I would not have alluded in this place or anywhere else to such casual personal criticisms—for casual and unreflecting they must be—but for the satisfaction of two or three friends in whose opinion a short answer was deemed desirable, on account of the continual repetition of these criticisms, or more precisely, quizzings. After all, the serious and truly literary inquiry in this connection is: Should a shaper of such stuff as dreams are made on disregard considerations of what is customary and expected, and apply himself to the real function of poetry, the application of ideas to life (in Matthew Arnold's familiar phrase)? This bears more particularly on what has been called the "philosophy" of these poems—usually reproved as "queer." Whoever the author may be that undertakes such application of ideas in this "philosophic" direction—where it is specially required—glacial judgments must inevitably fall upon him amid opinion whose arbiters largely decry individuality, to whom *ideas* are oddities to smile at, who are moved by a yearning the reverse of that of the Athenian inquirers on Mars Hill; and stiffen their features not only at sound of a new thing, but at a restatement of old things in new terms. Hence should anything of this sort in the following adumbrations seem "queer" —should any of them seem to good Panglossians to embody strange and disrespectful conceptions of this best of all possible worlds, I apologize; but cannot help it.

Such divergences, which, though piquant for the nonce,
it would be affectation to say are not saddening and dis-
couraging likewise, may, to be sure, arise sometimes from
superficial aspect only, writer and reader seeing the same
thing at different angles. But in palpable cases of divergence they arise, as already said, whenever a serious effort
is made towards that which the authority I have cited—
who would now be called old-fashioned, possibly even
parochial—affirmed to be what no good critic could deny
as the poet's province, the application of ideas to life. One
might shrewdly guess, by the by, that in such recommendation the famous writer may have overlooked the cold-
shouldering results upon an enthusiastic disciple that would
be pretty certain to follow his putting the high aim in
practice, and have forgotten the disconcerting experience
of Gil Blas with the Archbishop.

To add a few more words to what has already taken
up too many, there is a contingency liable to miscellanies
of verse that I have never seen mentioned, so far as I can
remember; I mean the chance little shocks that may be
caused over a book of various character like the present
and its predecessors by the juxtaposition of unrelated, even
discordant, effusions; poems perhaps years apart in the
making, yet facing each other. An odd result of this has
been that dramatic anecdotes of a satirical and humorous
intention following verse in graver voice, have been read
as misfires because they raise the smile that they were intended to raise, the journalist, deaf to the sudden change
of key, being unconscious that he is laughing with the
author and not at him. I admit that I did not foresee such
contingencies as I ought to have done, and that people
might not perceive when the tone altered. But the difficulties of arranging the themes in a graduated kinship of
moods would have been so great that irrelation was almost
unavoidable with efforts so diverse. I must trust for right
note-catching to those finely-touched spirits who can divine
without half a whisper, whose intuitiveness is proof against

all the accidents of inconsequence. In respect of the less alert, however, should any one's train of thought be thrown out of gear by a consecutive piping of vocal reeds in jarring tonics, without a semiquaver's rest between, and be led thereby to miss the writer's aim and meaning in one out of two contiguous compositions, I shall deeply regret it.

Having at last, I think, finished with the personal points that I was recommended to notice, I will forsake the immediate object of this Preface; and, leaving *Late Lyrics* to whatever fate it deserves, digress for a few moments to more general considerations. The thoughts of any man of letters concerned to keep poetry alive cannot but run uncomfortably on the precarious prospects of English verse at the present day. Verily the hazards and casualties surrounding the birth and setting forth of almost every modern creation in numbers are ominously like those of one of Shelley's paper-boats on a windy lake. And a forward conjecture scarcely permits the hope of a better time, unless men's tendencies should change. So indeed of all art, literature, and "high thinking" nowadays. Whether owing to the barbarizing of taste in the younger minds by the dark madness of the late war, the unabashed cultivation of selfishness in all classes, the plethoric growth of knowledge simultaneously with the stunting of wisdom, "a degrading thirst after outrageous stimulation" (to quote Wordsworth again), or from any other cause, we seem threatened with a new Dark Age.

I formerly thought, like other much exercised writers, that so far as literature was concerned a partial cause might be impotent or mischievous criticism; the satirizing of individuality, the lack of whole-seeing in contemporary estimates of poetry and kindred work, the knowingness affected by junior reviewers, the over growth of meticulousness in their peerings for an opinion, as if it were a cultivated habit in them to scrutinize the toolmarks and be blind to the building, to hearken for the key-creaks and be deaf to the diapason, to judge the landscape by a noc-

turnal exploration with a flash-lantern. In other words, to
carry on the old game of sampling the poem or drama
by quoting the worst line or worst passage only, in ignorance or not of Coleridge's proof that a versification of any
length neither can be nor ought to be all poetry; of reading meanings into a book that its author never dreamt of
writing there. I might go on interminably.

But I do not now think any such temporary obstructions
to be the cause of the hazard, for these negligences and
ignorances, though they may have stifled a few true poets
in the run of generations, disperse like stricken leaves before the wind of next week, and are no more heard of
again in the region of letters than their writers themselves.
No: we may be convinced that something of the deeper
sort mentioned must be the cause.

In any event poetry, pure literature in general, religion—
I include religion, in its essential and undogmatic sense,
because poetry and religion touch each other, or rather
modulate into each other; are, indeed, often but different
names for the same thing—these, I say, the visible signs
of mental and emotional life, must like all other things
keep moving, becoming; even though at present, when belief in witches of Endor is displacing the Darwinian
theory and "the truth that shall make you free," men's
minds appear, as above noted, to be moving backwards
rather than on. I speak somewhat sweepingly, and should
except many thoughtful writers in verse and prose; also
men in certain worthy but small bodies of various denomi-
nations, and perhaps in the homely quarter where advance
might have been the very least expected a few years back—
the English Church—if one reads it rightly as showing
evidence of "removing those things that are shaken," in
accordance with the wise Epistolary recommendation to
the Hebrews. For since the historic and once august hier-
archy of Rome some generation ago lost its chance of
being the religion of the future by doing otherwise, and
throwing over the little band of New Catholics who were
making a struggle for continuity by applying the principle
of evolution to their own faith, joining hands with mod-

ern science, and outflanking the hesitating English instinct towards liturgical restatement (a flank march which I at the time quite expected to witness, with the gathering of many millions of waiting agnostics into its fold); since then, one may ask, what other purely English establishment than the Church, of sufficient dignity and footing, with such strength of old association, such scope for transmutability, such architectural spell, is left in this country to keep the shreds of morality together?*

It may indeed be a forlorn hope, a mere dream, that of an alliance between religion, which must be retained unless the world is to perish, and complete rationality, which must come, unless also the world is to perish, by means of the interfusing effect of poetry—"the breath and finer spirit of all knowledge; the impassioned expression of science,"† as it was defined by an English poet who was quite orthodox in his ideas. But if it be true, as Comte argued, that advance is never in a straight line, but in a looped orbit, we may, in the aforesaid ominous moving backward, be doing it *pour mieux sauter*, drawing back for a spring. I repeat that I forlornly hope so, notwithstanding the supercilious regard of hope by Schopenhauer, von Hartmann, and other philosophers down to Einstein who have my respect. But one dares not prophesy. Physical, chronological, and other contingencies keep me in these days from critical studies and literary circles

> Where once we held debate, a band
> Of youthful friends, on mind and art

(if one may quote Tennyson in this century). Hence I cannot know how things are going so well as I used to know them, and the aforesaid limitations must quite prevent my knowing henceforward.

* However, one must not be too sanguine in reading signs, and since the above was written evidence that the Church will go far in the removal of "things that are shaken" has not been encouraging.—T.H.
† From William Wordsworth's *Preface, Second Edition of Lyrical Ballads*—Ed.

ᚖᚖᚖᚖᚖᚖᚖᚖᚖᚖᚖᚖᚖᚖᚖᚖᚖᚖᚖᚖ

HARDY TALKS TO HIMSELF
1873–1888

1873

July 1. A day's trip with Miss G. To Chepstow, the Wye, the Wynd Cliff, which we climbed, and Tintern, where we repeated some of Wordsworth's lines thereon.

At Tintern, silence is part of the pile. Destroy that, and you take a limb from an organism. . . . A wooded slope visible from every unmullioned window. But compare the age of the building with that of the marble hills from which it was drawn! . . .

1874

Read again Addison, Macaulay, Newman, Sterne, Defoe, Lamb, Gibbon, Burke, *Times* leaders, etc., in a study of style. Am more and more confirmed in an idea I have long held, as a matter of common sense, long before I thought of any old aphorism bearing on the subject: "Ars est celare artem." The whole secret of a living style and the difference between it and a dead style, lies in not having too much style—being, in fact, a little careless, or rather seeming to be, here and there. It brings wonderful life into the writing . . .

Otherwise your style is like worn half-pence—all the fresh images rounded off by rubbing, and no crispness or movement at all.

It is, of course, simply a carrying into prose the knowledge I have acquired in poetry—that inexact rhymes and rhythms now and then are far more pleasing than correct ones.

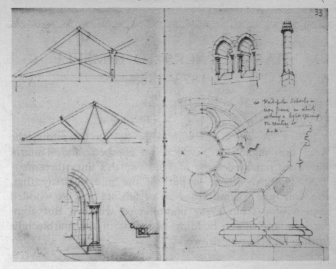

1877

I sometimes look upon all things in inanimate Nature as pensive mutes.

August 13. We hear that Jane, our late servant, is soon to have a baby. Yet never a sign of one is there for us.

September 28. An object or mark raised or made by man on a scene is worth ten times any such formed by unconscious Nature. Hence clouds, mists, and mountains are unimportant beside the wear on a threshold, or the print of a hand.

1878

April—Note. A Plot,, or Tragedy, should arise from the gradual closing in of a situation that comes of ordinary human passions, prejudices, and ambitions, by reason of the characters taking no trouble to ward off the disastrous events produced by the said passions, prejudices, and ambitions.

April 22. The method of Boldini, the painter of "The Morning Walk" in the French Gallery two or three years ago (a young lady beside an ugly blank wall on an ugly highway)—of Hobbema, in his view of a road with formal lopped trees and flat tame scenery—is that of infusing emotion into the baldest external objects either by the presence of a human figure among them, or by mark of some human connection with them.

This accords with my feeling about, say, Heidelberg and Baden *versus* Scheveningen—as I wrote at the beginning of *The Return of the Native*—that the beauty of association is entirely superior to the beauty of aspect, and a beloved relative's old battered tankard to the finest Greek vase. Paradoxically put, it is to see the beauty in ugliness.

1880

Arnold is wrong about provincialism, if he means anything more than a provincialism of style and manner in exposition. A certain provincialism of feeling is invaluable. It is of the essence of individuality, and is largely made up of that crude enthusiasm without which no great thoughts are thought, no great deeds done.

1881

The writer's problem is, how to strike the balance between the uncommon and the ordinary so as on the one hand to give interest, on the other to give reality.

In working out this problem, human nature must never be made abnormal, which is introducing incredibility. The uncommonness must be in the events, not in the characters; and the writer's art lies in shaping that uncommonness while disguising its unlikelihood, if it be unlikely.

1882

June 3. . . . As, in looking at a carpet, by following
one colour a certain pattern is suggested, by following
another colour, another; so in life the seer should watch
that pattern among general things which his idiosyncrasy
moves him to observe, and describe that alone. This is,
quite accurately, a going to Nature; yet the result is no
mere photograph, but purely the product of the writer's
own mind.

Since I discovered, several years ago, that I was living
in a world where nothing bears out in practice what it
promises incipiently, I have troubled myself very little
about theories. . . . Where development according to perfect reason is limited to the narrow region of pure mathe-
matics, I am content with tentativeness from day to day.

1884

October 20. Query: Is not the present quasi-scientific
system of writing history mere charlatanism? Events and
tendencies are traced as if they were rivers of voluntary
activity, and courses reasoned out from the circumstances
in which natures, religions, or what-not, have found themselves. But are they not in the main the outcome of
passivity—acted upon by unconscious propensity?

Easter Sunday. Evidences of art in Bible narratives.
They are written with a watchful attention (though disguised) as to their effect on their reader. Their so-called
simplicity is, in fact, the simplicity of the highest cunning.
And one is led to inquire, when even in these latter days
artistic development and arrangement are the qualities
least appreciated by readers, who was there likely to appreciate the art in these chronicles at that day?

Looking round on a well-selected shelf of fiction or
history, how few stories of any length does one recognize

as well told from beginning to end! The first half of this story, the last half of that, the middle of another. . . . The modern art of narration is yet in its infancy.

But in these Bible lives and adventures there is the spherical completeness of perfect art. And our first, and second, feeling that they must be true because they are so impressive, becomes, as a third feeling, modified to "Are they so very true, after all? Is not the fact of their being so convincing an argument, not for their actuality, but for the actuality of a consummate artist who was no more content with what Nature offered than Sophocles and Pheidias were content?"

1885

November 21–22. Tragedy. It may be put thus in brief: a tragedy exhibits a state of things in the life of an individual which unavoidably causes some natural aim or desire of his to end in a catastrophe when carried out.

1886

January 3. My art is to intensify the expression of things, as is done by Crivelli, Bellini, etc., so that the heart and inner meaning is made vividly visible.

1887

January. After looking at the landscape ascribed to Bonington in our drawing-room I feel that Nature is played out as a Beauty, but not as a Mystery. I don't want to see landscapes, *i.e.*, scenic paintings of them, because I don't want to see the original realities—as optical effects, that is. I want to see the deeper reality underlying the scenic, the expression of what are sometimes called abstract imaginings.

The "simply natural" is interesting no longer. The much decried, mad, late-Turner rendering is now necessary to create my interest. The exact truth as to material fact

ceases to be of importance in art—it is a student's style
—the style of a period when the mind is serene and un-
awakened to the tragical mysteries of life; when it does
not bring anything to the object that coalesces with and
translates the qualities that are already there,—half hidden,
it may be—and the two united are depicted as the All.

1888

June. I have attempted many modes [of finding the value
of life]. For my part, if there is any way of getting a melancholy satisfaction out of life it lies in dying, so to speak,
before one is out of the flesh; by which I mean putting on
the manners of ghosts, wandering in their haunts, and
taking their views of surrounding things. To think of life
as passing away is a sadness; to think of it as past is at
least tolerable. Hence even when I enter into a room to
pay a simple morning call I have unconsciously the habit
of regarding the scene as if I were a spectre not solid
enough to influence my environment; only fit to behold
and say, as another spectre said: "Peace be unto you!"

STUDIES OF THOMAS HARDY:
A SELECTED BIBLIOGRAPHY

Douglas Brown. *Thomas Hardy*. London: Longmans, 1961.

Mary Ellen Chase. *Thomas Hardy From Serial to Novel*. New York: Russell and Russell, 1964.

R. G. Cox, ed. *Thomas Hardy: The Critical Heritage*. London: Routledge and Paul; New York: Barnes and Noble, 1970.

Donald Davie. *Thomas Hardy and British Poetry*. New York: Oxford University Press, 1972.

Ruth Firor. *Folkways in Thomas Hardy*. Philadelphia: University of Pennsylvania Press, 1951.

Robert Gittings. *Young Thomas Hardy*. Boston: Atlantic–Little, Brown, 1975.

Albert G. Guerard. *Thomas Hardy*. New York: New Directions, 1964.

————. *Hardy: A Collection of Critical Essays*. Englewood Cliffs, N.J.: Prentice-Hall, 1963.

Evelyn Hardy. *Thomas Hardy: A Critical Biography*. London: Hogarth Press, 1954.

Florence Emily Hardy. *The Life of Thomas Hardy, 1840–1928*. London and New York: Macmillan, 1962.

John Holloway. *The Victorian Sage: Studies in Argument*. Hamden, Conn.: Archon Books, 1952.

Irving Howe. *Thomas Hardy*. New York: Macmillan, 1967.

Samuel Hynes. *The Pattern of Hardy's Poetry*. Chapel Hill: University of North Carolina Press, 1961.

Lionel Johnson. *The Art of Thomas Hardy*. London: Lane, 1928.

D. H. Lawrence. "Study of Thomas Hardy," *Phoenix: The Posthumous Writings of D. H. Lawrence*, ed. Edward D. McDonald. New York: Viking, 1936.

Kenneth Marsden. *The Poems of Thomas Hardy: A Critical Introduction*. New York: Oxford University Press, 1969.

J. Hillis Miller. *Thomas Hardy: Distance and Desire*. Cambridge: Harvard University Press, 1970.

Michael Millgate. *Thomas Hardy: His Career as a Novelist*. New York: Random House, 1971.

Julian Moynahan. "*The Mayor of Casterbridge* and the First Book of Samuel: A Study of Some Literary Relationships," *Biblical Images in Literature*, ed. R. Bartel, J. S. Ackerman, T. S. Warshaw. New York: Abingdon Press, 1975, pp. 71–88.

F. B. Pinion. *A Hardy Companion*. London: Macmillan, 1968.

W. R. Rutland. *Thomas Hardy: A Study of His Writings and Their Background*. Oxford: Oxford University Press, 1938.

Thomas Hardy Centennial Issue of the Southern Review. VI (Summer 1940).

J. I. M. Stewart. *Thomas Hardy: A Critical Biography*. London: Longmans, 1971.

Carl J. Weber. *Hardy of Wessex: His Life and Literary Career*. Rev. ed. New York: Columbia University Press, 1965.

Merryn Williams. *Thomas Hardy and Rural England*. New York: Columbia University Press, 1972.

Raymond Williams. *The English Novel from Dickens to Lawrence*. London: Chatto and Windus, 1970.

————. *The Country and the City*. New York: Oxford University Press, 1973.

Bibliographical Studies

Helmut E. Gerber. *Thomas Hardy: An Annotated Bibliography of Writings About Him*. De Kalb: Northern Illinois University Press, 1973.

R. L. Purdy. *Thomas Hardy: A Bibliographical Study*. London: Oxford University Press, 1954.